WHEN COMES THE SPRING

JANETTE OKE

BETHANY HOUSE PUBLISHERS

MINNEAPOLIS, MINNESOTA 55438

Published by Bethany House Publishers
A Ministry of Bethany Fellowship, Inc.
6820 Auto Club Road, Minneapolis, MN 55438

Printed in the United States of America

ISBN 1-56865-549-5

Dedicated with love to
my patient and peace-loving
fourth sister,
Margie L. Wiens,
and to her equally easygoing
husband, Wilf.
I love you both.

JANETTE OKE was born in Champion, Alberta, during the depression years, to a Canadian prairie farmer and his wife. She is a graduate of Mountain View Bible College in Didsbury, Alberta, where she met her husband, Edward. They were married in May of 1957, and went on to pastor churches in Indiana as well as Calgary and Edmonton, Canada.

The Okes have three sons and one daughter and are enjoying the addition to the family of grandchildren. Edward and Janette have both been active in their local church, serving in various capacities as Sunday-school teachers and board members. They make their home in Didsbury, Alberta.

Contents

Synopsis—When Calls the Heart

When well-bred, sophisticated Elizabeth Thatcher, a city girl from Toronto, agreed to a term of teaching in the newly formed province of Alberta, it was more to please her mother and to become reacquainted with her half-brother Jonathan than from a sense of adventure on her own part. Elizabeth was more than a bit hesitant to leave the comfort and security of her father's house to mix with the rough and uncultured people of the new frontier.

But upon arrival in the West, Elizabeth soon learned to love her big brother and his wife Mary and their four small children. She also was captivated by families and students of the small, one-room school and by the West itself.

Then into Elizabeth's life came Wynn, the tall, handsome and dedicated member to the Royal North West Mounted Police. Elizabeth, previously determined never to marry a Westerner, began to have second thoughts. Wynn was the one who now resisted. He was adamant in his belief that the rigors of the Mountie's life were too demanding to be shared by a wife, particularly a woman as lovely and cultured as Elizabeth.

Elizabeth, feeling rejected and hurt by Wynn's apparent lack of feeling for her, decided to return to Toronto where she belonged. But Wynn knew he could not let her go—at least not without expressing to her his deep feelings of love and giving her the opportunity to respond. A proposal at the train depot brought Elizabeth into Wynn's arms with her assurance that she was more than willing to face whatever the future held—for them together.

Characters

ELIZABETH THATCHER—young, Eastern schoolteacher who loved her God, her family and her pupils. Pretty, sheltered, yet with a mind of her own, Elizabeth was quick to respond to the promptings of her God and the needs of others.

JONATHAN, MARY, WILLIAM, SARAH, KATHLEEN, BABY ELIZABETH—Elizabeth's Western family. Jonathan was a half-brother from her mother's first marriage. The West had drawn him from Toronto as a young man. There he met and married the red-haired Mary, and their home was blessed with one son and three daughters. Little Kathleen was especially fond of her Aunt Beth.

JULIE—the attractive, rather flighty, but much-loved younger sister of Elizabeth.

MATTHEW—Elizabeth's younger brother. Matthew was the youngest, rather pampered member of the Thatcher family.

Elizabeth's Toronto family also included two older married sisters, Margaret and Ruthie.

WYNN DELANEY—nicknamed "Dee" by Jon's children. Wynn was a dedicated, competent member of the Royal North West Mounted Police. He had already spent some time at a northern Post and knew the difficulties and loneliness that such a Post presented.

Chapter One

Days of Preparation

"Is it done yet?"

It must have been at least the tenth time that my young niece, Kathleen, had asked the question in the last few days.

"No," I answered patiently, "not yet."

She stood silently beside me, her favorite doll dangling lopsidedly from her arms.

"How come it takes so many times to make a wedding dress?" she asked again.

Much time, the schoolteacher in me silently corrected her. Aloud I said without lifting my eyes from the needle moving smoothly in and out of the creamy white satin, "Because a wedding dress must be perfect."

"Per-fect?" queried Kathleen.

"Um-hum. That means 'just right'—for the man I'm going to marry."

"Dee's not gonna wear it." Her voice boded no argument.

I lifted my head and chuckled softly at Kathleen's perplexed look. It sounded as if Wynn's nickname was still firmly in place.

"No, *he* won't wear it. But he is going to see *me* wear it, and I want it to be just right."

Kathleen stood there stubbornly, now a look of frustration on her pixie face.

"He won't care," she said with feeling. "Daddy said that Mama would'a looked beau'ful in an old 'tata sack."

I laughed and drew Kathleen to me. "Maybe you're right," I said, pushing back a soft curl from her forehead. Her eyes told me that something else was troubling her. I decided the dress could wait for a few minutes. Checking to see that I had left the sewing machine foot in proper position and the precious folds of satin material carefully placed on the tissue paper spread beneath them, I rose from the chair. My back ached and my shoulders felt cramped. I needed a break. Perhaps I should have done as Mother had suggested and arranged for Madam Tanier to sew my dress after all. I had wanted to sew my wedding gown myself, but I had had no idea what a big job it was going to be. I took Kathleen's tiny, somewhat sticky, hand in mine and led her to the door.

"Why don't we take a little walk around the garden?" I asked her.

The shine in her eyes was her answer. She wedged her flopping doll under one arm and skipped along beside me.

We walked through the garden together. The early flowers were already in bloom. As I looked at them, I found my mind rushing ahead to the wedding planned for the first part of September, and I wondered what flowers would be available. That was another decision that had to be made. Oh, my! Was there no end to them? It seemed that ever since Wynn had asked me to become his wife, I had been making one decision after the other—some big and some not-so-big. As my thoughts turned to Wynn, I smiled to myself. How fortunate I was to be engaged to marry such a man. He was everything a girl could ever desire—his height, his bearing, his smile, his quiet self-assurance, his caring. And he loved *me*! I would have gone on and on daydreaming but Kathleen interrupted me.

"Mama's gonna make my dress."

I nodded.

"Have you seen the color?"

I nodded again, remembering the hours Mary and I had spent poring over materials and styles, debating and deciding. Both Kathleen and Sarah were to be in my wedding party.

"*It's* gonna be perfect, too," insisted Kathleen.

"Yes," I agreed. "With your mama doing the sewing, it's going to be perfect, too."

"Mama is already done Sarah's dress."

There was silence while I studied the soft shades of a garden rose. *These colors would be just right,* I was thinking, *but will they still be blooming in September? I must ask Mary.* But again Kathleen interrupted my thoughts.

"How come I'm last?"

"Pardon?" My busy mind had not followed Kathleen's line of wondering.

"How come I'm last? Sarah's dress is already made, but Mama has just started mine."

I looked at her anxious face. It was an honest question but, for such a small girl, a troubling one.

"Well," I stammered, reaching for some satisfactory explanation. "Well . . . your dress will be ready in no time. Your mama is a very good seamstress and a very efficient one. It doesn't take her long at all to sew a dress—even a fancy dress like she will be making for you. Your dress will be ready long, long before September gets here. In fact, your dress will be ready long before mine will, I'm sure. So yours won't be last . . . mine will."

Kathleen's eyes had not left my face as I spoke. She seemed to relax with my final words. Her breath escaped in a soft little sigh.

"You're slow, all right," she agreed solemnly. "I'm glad Mama's fast."

Then her thoughts turned in another direction.

"Why is Mama making the dresses so quick?"

"So soon? Because your mama has so many things that she wants to do, and the dresses are one thing that she can do now."

"What things?"

"Well, she is planning the reception dinner. And she wants lots of time to get ready for Grandma and Grandpa. And she has some redecorating she wants to do. And she plans to give the house a thorough cleaning . . ."

I continued thinking of poor Mary and all of the work that my coming wedding was causing her. How I loved her! It wasn't one bit necessary for her to fuss so, but she insisted. After all, it would be the first time her in-laws would be in her home and she, too, wanted everything to be perfect.

"Is Grandma fuzzy?" asked Kathleen seriously.

"Fussy?" I smiled but did not let Kathleen know her word had come out wrong. "Well, yes and no. Grandma likes nice things, and when she is in charge she tries very hard to see that everything is just right. But she does not judge other people by the same rules she uses on herself."

"What's that mean?"

"It means that Grandma loves people as they are. She doesn't ask for everyone to be perfect or to live in perfect houses."

"It's gonna be fun to see Grandma," Kathleen enthused.

My eyes misted and I swallowed the lump in my throat. "Yes, it will," I said softly. "It will be just wonderful."

But it still seemed such a long way off. The folks would not be arriving in Calgary until just before our September tenth wedding, and this was only the middle of July.

"Would you like to swing for a minute?" I asked the now quiet Kathleen, to get my thoughts back to safer ground.

She grinned at me, and I took that for her answer. Kathleen loved the swing.

"The tree swing or the porch swing?" I asked her.

"The porch swing," she quickly decided. "Then you can sit by me."

We settled on the porch swing and set it in motion with the rhythm of our bodies. Kathleen cuddled up closely against me and rearranged the dangling doll into a more baby-like position. I realized then that she had been missing personal attention. With my thoughts all concentrated on the upcoming wedding, and even Mary wildly involved in the preparations, we had both subconsciously pushed the youngsters aside. I determined that in the days ahead I would be more sensitive and considerate. I pulled Kathleen closer to me and held her—such a precious little thing. We swung in silence for many minutes. My mind went to the other children. Were they feeling the strain of the busy household as well?

"Where is Sarah?" I asked Kathleen.

"She went to Molly's house. Molly's mama is letting them make doll dresses out of the scraps from Sarah's new dress."

Good for Molly's mama, I thought, *but no wonder Kathleen has been wandering around feeling left out.*

"And where's William?"

"Daddy took him down to the store. He's gonna help pile things. He even gets money for it." Kathleen squirmed to look at me, her envy showing on her face. "William thinks he's *big*," she said with some disgust. "He's gonna save the money and buy a gun that shoots little roun' things."

Kathleen curled up her short fingers to demonstrate the little round things. Then she ventured some more information. "An' Baby 'Lisbeth is sleepin'. She sleeps most all the time. An' Mama is sewing. Not for me—for Baby 'Lisbeth. An' Stacy said that the cookie jar is already full, so we can't bake any more cookies."

My arm tightened about her. *Poor little dear,* I thought, but I didn't say it. Instead I said, "How would you like to take the streetcar uptown and stop at the ice cream parlor?"

The shine was back. "Could we?" she cried. "Could we, Aunt Beth?"

"I'll ask your mama."

Kathleen clapped her hands in her excitement and then threw her arms around my neck. I felt the combs holding my hair in place being pushed all askew.

"Let's go check," I said. Kathleen jumped down and quickly ran ahead of me to find Mary.

By the time I had entered Mary's sewing room, Kathleen was already there and had excitedly posed the question. Could she go with Aunt Beth uptown for ice cream? Mary looked at me with a question in her eyes.

"Have you finished your dress?" she asked pointedly.

"No. I have quite a ways to go yet," I answered honestly, "but a rest will do me good." I didn't add that I thought Kathleen needed some special attention, too.

Mary nodded. "A little break would do me good, too," she said, pushing back from the machine. "Come, Kathleen, I will clean you up." Mary rubbed her tired neck and led Kathleen from the room.

I went back to my own room to change my dress and repair my hair. My eyes wandered to the pile of lustrous satin. Part of me ached to be there at the machine. I was so anxious to see the final product of all my labors. But I pushed the dress from my mind. Kathleen was more important. Besides, I had been so busy with details of the wedding that I had felt myself becoming tense and edgy. I had not even been able to relax and enjoy Wynn's company, and he would be coming to call in the evening. An afternoon in the pleasant company of Kathleen might be just the thing to put me in a more relaxed frame of mind. I picked up my small brocaded purse and left the room, shutting my door on all the satin and lace. I took a deep breath and smiled as I went to meet my excited niece.

Chapter Two

Good News and Bad News

Wynn arrived a little earlier than I had expected. I was still in my room making last-minute preparations, so it was Sarah who let him in. All afternoon she had been looking for people who would admire her doll all dressed up in the finery of her new hand-stitched dress, a shimmery pale blue. Wynn gave it a proper inspection and complimented the young seamstress on her fine work. Sarah beamed and deserted Wynn to wait on the steps for the return home of her father. She was most anxious to show him the new dress as well.

Kathleen took over entertaining Wynn, regaling him with all our afternoon adventures. I'm sure Wynn must have been surprised that I had found *time* in my rushed schedule to spend a rather leisurely afternoon with my niece. All he had heard from me recently was about the plans and work and preparation and diligence I was giving to every detail of the coming wedding. Kathleen had succeeded in bringing me up short. *People are more important than fussing over preparations. Why, I haven't even been good company for Wynn,* I realized, looking back in humiliation over some of our last evenings spent together. Well, I would change that. After all, a *marriage* was of far more importance than a *wedding*.

I hummed to myself as I walked slowly to the parlor. I had intended to be in the parlor waiting for Wynn when he arrived, instead of entering rushed and harried after he had already come . . . like I had done on so many previous evenings.

Wynn was listening attentively to the chattering Kathleen, and I couldn't help but smile at the homey picture they made.

"An' after that, we went an' looked in the store windows—just for fun," explained Kathleen. "An' then we took a ride on the streetcar just as far as it would go—just to see where it went—an' then we took it back *all the way home again!*" Kathleen waved her small hand to show Wynn just how far all the way home really was.

Wynn smiled at the little girl. Clearly he was enjoying their conversation.

"Was it fun?" he asked, not because he needed the answer but because he sensed Kathleen needed to be able to express it.

"It was *lots* of fun!" exclaimed Kathleen. "We ate *two* kinds of ice cream. Even Aunt Beth ate two kinds. An' we brought home lemon drops for Sarah and William.—Baby 'Lisbeth might choke on lemon drops," she explained seriously, so Wynn would understand why Baby 'Lisbeth had been left out. "Then we walked all the way up the hill, right from the bottom, 'stead of ridin' the streetcar—'cause Aunt Beth said she needed the ex'cise." She giggled. "To work off the ice cream," she added. "And we sang songs when we walked."

It *had* been a fun day. I realized it even more as I listened to Kathleen share it with Wynn.

"Next time will you take me, too?" Wynn asked seriously and Kathleen nodded, suddenly feeling sorry that Wynn had missed out on so much.

"Maybe we can go again tamora," she said thoughtfully. "I'll go ask Aunt Beth."

Kathleen bounded from the couch to run to my room and then noticed me standing by the door. Wynn's eyes looked up, too. Surprise, then pleasure, showed on his face as he stood to his feet and held out a hand to me. Neither of us spoke, but I could read questions coming my way.

"We had a wonderful day," I confirmed Kathleen's story.

"You *look* like you've had a wonderful day," Wynn said, taking my hand and drawing me closer to him. "Your cheeks are glowing and your eyes are shining—even more beautifully than usual."

I pulled back a little as Wynn tried to draw me close, thinking of the curious eyes of young Kathleen. Wynn must have read my thoughts.

"Kathleen," he said, turning to the wee girl, "why don't you go out on the step and wait with Sarah for your daddy and William to come home. They'll want to hear all about your big day, too."

Kathleen ran from the room, and Wynn smiled at me and pulled me close. I did not resist him. The strength of his arms about me and his gentle kiss reminded me again of how much I had missed really spending time with him during the previous distracting days. I would be so glad when the long weeks ahead had finally passed by and I would be *Mrs. Wynn Delaney*. Right now it seemed forever. I forgot about all I had to do in the next few weeks and thought instead of this man I loved.

When he stopped kissing me, he whispered against my hair, "I love you, Elizabeth. Have I told you that?"

I looked up at his face. His eyes were teasing, but his voice was serious.

"Not often enough, or recently enough," I teased back.

"I must remedy that," he said. "How about a walk in the moonlight tonight?"

I laughed, thinking of how late the Alberta night would be before the moon was shining.

"Well," I said, "I'd kind of like to hear it before that. You know it doesn't even start to get dark until after ten o'clock. That's an awful long time to wait."

Wynn laughed too. "Let's not wait for the moon then," he agreed. "I'd still like to go for a walk."

"We'll walk," I promised, "and just talk. We have so much to talk about, Wynn."

"More wedding decisions?" He sounded almost apprehensive.

"Not tonight. That can wait. Tonight we will talk—just about us. There is still much I want to know about the man I'm going to marry, you know."

Wynn kissed me again.

The sound of the front door told us that Jonathan had arrived home. He entered the house to encounter his two young daughters talking excitedly. Jonathan tried to listen to them both, attempting to share in the excitement and the enthusiasm they felt. And William had tales of his own he was bursting to tell. He had worked just like a man at his father's business and was making great plans for all the money he was sure to make over the summer.

Mary joined the happy commotion in the hall and was greeted by her husband with a warm hug and a kiss. Jonathan did not agree with the tradition of parents hiding their affection from their children's seeing eyes.

"Who needs to know more than they, that I love you?" he often told Mary; and the children grew up in a household where loving was an accepted and expected part of life.

At the sound of the family moving our way, I drew back reluctantly from Wynn. Perhaps now wasn't quite the time for me to openly show my feeling for Wynn in front of Jonathan's children, though I knew it was not in the least hidden. How could I hide it, feeling as I did?

The pleasant supper hour seemed to pass very quickly. All around the table was shared laughter and chatter. The children were allowed and even encouraged to be a part of it. Baby Elizabeth, who now insisted on feeding herself, was the reason for much of the merriment. Her intentions were good, but not all of the food got to its intended location. She ended up adorned with almost as much as she devoured. The children laughed, and Elizabeth put on even more of a show.

Wynn enthusiastically entered into the gaiety of the evening. Now and then he reached beneath the damask white tablecloth to give my hand a gentle squeeze. From all outward appearances, he was his usual amenable self; but, for some reason, the meal had not progressed very far until I sensed that something about him was different. There seemed to be an underlying tension about him. I looked around the table to see if any of the others had noticed it. Jonathan and Wynn were talking about some of the new businesses that had recently been established in our very young city. They were pleased for the growth and what it meant to the residents of the town. Jonathan seemed to sense no difference in Wynn. My eyes passed on to Mary. Though busy with the struggling Elizabeth who was refusing her proffered help,

Mary seemed to be her usual relaxed self. I decided that maybe I had imagined the undercurrent and concentrated on what was being said.

But, no. I was sure it was there. The way Wynn looked at me, the way he pressed my hand at every given opportunity, the way he leaned slightly my way so his arm brushed against my shoulder—all sent unspoken little messages to me. I found myself anxious for the meal to end so I might be alone with this man I was to marry.

I had no appetite for dessert. I begged off with the excuse that I had already eaten two cones of town ice cream with Kathleen. I sat there, impatiently twisting my coffee cup back and forth in my hands as I waited for the rest of the family to finish the meal. I had determined to be completely relaxed tonight—completely relaxed and a pleasant companion for Wynn. I had determined to push aside all of the plans and decisions concerning the coming wedding so I might concentrate only on him—and here I was, tensing up inside again. And for no reason I could explain.

"Why don't we take that walk?" I asked Wynn when the meal was finally over. I was rewarded with a broad smile.

"Why, there is nothing I would rather do, Miss Thatcher," he teased. But I saw a certain seriousness in his eyes, and a funny little chill of fear went tingling through my body.

We left the house and strolled up the familiar street. We had not gone far when I turned impulsively to him and asked, "Would you mind very much if, instead of walking, we went for a drive? I'd love to drive up to where we could see the mountains."

He smiled. "That's a wonderful idea," he agreed. "Perhaps we can stay and watch the sunset."

The sun would not be setting for several hours. I smiled back at Wynn. It sounded good to me—all of that time to sit and talk.

We walked back to the house and were about to enter Wynn's car, when he suggested, "Perhaps you should have a shawl or coat, Elizabeth. It may be cool before we get back. Can I get you one?"

"I left a light coat in the back hall. It will do."

Wynn helped me into the car and went for the coat. I

imagined that while inside he also told Jon and Mary of our change of plans. When we were on our way, Wynn chatted easily. We left the city and drove up the familiar hill to the place we could look out at the mountains to the west. Still I could sense something, though I did not question him.

When we reached the summit, we left the car and walked to a fallen log. It was a perfect spot from which to look out at the mountain grandeur before us. I sighed as I settled myself. In just about seven weeks' time, I would be visiting those mountains—visiting them as Mrs. Wynn Delaney. I wished instead that our wedding would be next week—no, I wished that it were tomorrow!

Wynn sat down beside me and his arm pulled me close. He kissed me and then we fell into silence, both of us gazing out toward the mountains. His arm tightened. He must have been thinking of the coming honeymoon, too, for he broke into my thoughts with a question.

"You aren't going to change your mind, are you, Elizabeth?"

"Me?" I said, astonished.

"Well, I wondered with all the work and preparations if you might decide that it wasn't worth it after all."

I sighed again, but this time for a different reason. "I've been a bore, haven't I? All the talk and all the fretting and all the frustrations showing. I'm afraid I haven't been much fun to be with recently, but I—"

Wynn stopped me with a gentle kiss. "I haven't been very supportive, have I?" he confessed. "The truth is, I would like to be, but I just don't know how. I had no idea that along with a wedding came so much planning and . . . and . . . frustration," he ended weakly. "I'm sometimes afraid it will all be too much for you and for Mary. You both look tired and pale."

"Oh, Wynn," I almost wailed. "It's awfully silly. Today I saw just how silly. I'm going to talk to Mary tomorrow. We can do things much more simply. There is no need to wear oneself out before beginning life together. Why, if I put half as much effort into making a marriage work as I have put into trying to prepare for a wedding—"

I left the sentence dangling. Wynn's arm tightened about me again.

"Is that what is bothering you?" I finally asked.

I felt the tension in Wynn's arm.

"Did I say something was bothering me?" he asked.

"No. You didn't say it," I said slowly, "but I could sense it somehow. I'm not sure just how, but—"

Wynn stood up, drawing me with him. He looked deeply into my eyes.

"I love you, Elizabeth," he said quietly. "I love you so very much. How foolish I was to ever think I could live without you."

He pressed my head against his chest, and I could hear the low, steady beating of his heart.

"There is something, isn't there?" I asked, without looking up, afraid of what I might find in Wynn's eyes.

Wynn took a deep breath and lifted my chin so he might look into my eyes.

"My posting came today."

His posting! My mind raced. It must be a terrible place to make Wynn look so serious. Well, it didn't matter. I could take it. I could take anything as long as we were together.

"It doesn't matter," I said evenly, willing him to believe me. "It doesn't matter, Wynn. Really. I don't mind where we go. I've told you that, and I really mean it. I can do it—really I can."

He pulled me against him again and pressed his lips against my hair.

"Oh, Elizabeth," he said, and his words were a soft moan. "It's not *where*, it's *when*," he continued.

"When?" I pulled back and searched his face. "When? What do you mean?"

"I'm to be at my new post by the first of August."

My head refused to put everything into focus. I tried hard to get it all to make sense, but for some reason nothing seemed to fit.

"But you can't," I stammered. "Our wedding isn't until September the tenth."

"But I must. When one is sent, one goes."

"But did you tell them?"

"Certainly."

"Can't they change it? I mean—"

"No, Elizabeth, they expect *me* to do the changing."

"But where are you posted? Is it up north as you had hoped?"

"Yes, it's up north."

"But that's such a long way to travel to come back for the wedding. It really doesn't make sense to . . . It would be such a long trip back and forth and would waste so much of your time—"

"Elizabeth," said Wynn gently. "The Police Force does not allow men to come out of the North until their tour of duty is finished."

"What do you mean?"

"I mean that once I go to my posting, I will be there— probably for three or four years without returning. It depends on—"

But I cut in, my eyes wide and questioning. "What are you saying?"

"I'm saying that there can't be a September wedding."

I felt the strength leave my body. I was glad Wynn was holding me—I'm afraid I could not have stood on my own. For a moment I was dazed, and then my foggy brain began to work again. No September wedding. The Police Force would not let Wynn travel back from the north country once he had set up residence there. Wynn was to be at his posting in only two short weeks. That didn't leave much time.

I willed the strength back into my legs and lifted my head to look at Wynn again. I had never seen his face so full of anguish.

"How long does it take to get there?"

He looked confused at my question, but he answered, "They said to allow six days for travel."

"Six days," I mused. "That leaves us only nine."

Wynn looked puzzled. "Nine?"

"My folks can be here in three or four days," I hurried on. "By then I should have my dress ready. That will make it about right for a Saturday wedding. That leaves us four days in the mountains and one day to pack to get ready to go. Can we do it, Wynn?"

Wynn was dumbstruck.

"Can we do it?" I repeated. "Can we pack in a day?"

"Oh, Elizabeth," Wynn said, crushing me against him. "Would you—would you—?"

I moved back and looked deeply into Wynn's eyes. The tears were burning my own.

"I couldn't let you go without me, Wynn. I couldn't," I stammered. "The wedding might not be just as we planned, but it's the marriage that counts. And we will have our family and friends there. It will still be beautiful."

There were tears in Wynn's eyes as he kissed me. I finally pulled away and looked out at the mountains. So it wouldn't be seven weeks before I would be visiting there as Mrs. Wynn Delaney. It would be less than a week. It seemed unreal, almost heady. Wynn must have thought so, too. "Bless the Police Force," he murmured in almost a whisper.

"Bless the Police Force?" I repeated, wondering at his sudden change of emotion.

He grinned at me.

"September always seemed such a long, long ways off."

I gave him a playful push, though the color rose in my cheeks. I could feel the glow. "Well, September might have been an awful long ways off," I agreed, "but this Saturday is awfully close. We have so much to do, Wynn, that it's absolutely frightening."

I suddenly realized the full impact of the statement I had just made.

"We'd better get back to Mary. My, she will be just frantic."

"Hold it," said Wynn, not letting me go. "Didn't you promise me this whole evening?"

"But that was before I knew that—"

Wynn stopped me. "Okay," he said, "I won't hold you to your original promise. I will admit that things have changed somewhat in the last five minutes. However, I am going to insist on at least half an hour of your undivided attention. Then we will go to the house and Mary."

I smiled at him and settled back into his arms.

"I think I'd like that," I answered shyly.

Chapter Three

Stepped-Up Plans

The house was full of commotion in the next few days. Mary seemed to be running in every direction at once. Surprisingly, it was I, Elizabeth, who took things rather calmly— I who had always dreamed of the perfect wedding. I who had pictured myself many times coming down the aisle of a large stained-glass cathedral on the arms of my father, the altar banded with delicate bouquets of orange blossoms or gardenias, my exquisite arrangement of orchids trailing from my satin-covered arm. I had envisioned masses of attendants with shimmering gowns designed by the best seamstress in England or Paris. I had listened wistfully to strains from the magnificent pipes of the organ, as the wedding march was played.

And now I was to be married in a very simple, tiny, rough-constructed church. There would be no stained-glass windows to let in the summer light. There would be no magnificent sounds from the throat of a pipe organ. There would be few attendants, and their gowns would be unnoteworthy by the fashion world's standards. And yet it would be sheer heaven, for I would be standing at the altar with the man I loved. That was all that mattered, I suddenly realized. And so it was I who slowed Mary down and calmed her with words of assurance that everything would be just lovely. Everything would be just right.

The telegram was sent home, and Mother and Father and Julie and Matthew would be arriving on Friday's train. My one regret was that I wouldn't have more time to see them before the Saturday wedding. Well, it was far more important that I be ready to go north with Wynn.

I hurriedly finished my wedding dress, and it was ready on time—in fact, I had a whole day to spare; so I turned my attention to other things. I went quickly through my wardrobe, selecting the few things that would be suitable for life in the North. I packed all the clothing I had used in the classroom and then took the streetcar uptown to make some more purchases. Wynn had assumed all the responsibility for purchasing and arranging the household items we would need. I felt a bit of misgiving but realized that Wynn—having lived in the North—would have a much better understanding of what would be needed than I would. Still, I found it difficult not to be involved. My womanly instincts told me that Wynn might be a little short on home comforts and concentrate instead on survival. I tried to push the anxious thoughts from me whenever they invaded my mind and told myself that I could trust Wynn completely.

Thursday fled all too quickly. I lengthened the day by staying up half the night. I continued to sort and pack and try to think ahead of what a woman would need to survive the rigors of the north country for three or four years without a return to civilization. My mind seemed to go blank. How would I know? I had never been farther than a few short miles from the city shops.

Wynn had been every bit as busy as I—sorting, crating, and labeling the items and supplies we would need for our household. It would not be fancy, he kept reminding me; and I kept assuring him that I did not care. I gave him the few items I had purchased last year for my housekeeping chores in the teacherage, hoping they would help curtail our expenses. He seemed pleased with them and told me that with all I had, plus the few essential items which would already be in stock in our northern cabin, there were few things further he would need to add.

I thought much about our home in the wilderness. I did want to make it a home, not just a bare and functional place that Wynn came to at the end of a long, hard day. But how did one go about converting log walls and wooden floors into a cozy homelike place? Curtains and cushions and rugs seemed to be the answer. I had no time for such things now. I had all I could do just to get packed and ready. I decided to purchase some materials for these things to take with me. So, early Friday morning, I boarded the streetcar for uptown. I did not buy thin, flimsy muslins. Instead, I spent my time poring over heavier, more masculine materials. They seemed far more suited to a northern cabin than the lighter, frillier furnishings would be. In the heavier materials I chose bolder, brighter prints than I normally would have purchased and then added a few finer fabrics just in case I should be sewing for a new member of the family before we got back from the North. My cheeks flushed slightly at that thought, and I hoped no one I knew was observing my shopping for pastel flannels. I had almost neglected to even think of such a possibility in my lastest rush, but three or four years was a long time.

With all my purchases weighing me down, I took the streetcar back to Jon's and tried to rearrange my trunks to crowd in the additional items. I had to leave behind a few dresses, but I decided I would do very well without them. The sewing material was much more important. After pushing and straining and shoving things as tightly into place as I could, I did manage to get the lid of the trunk down and latched.

I sat back on the floor, perspiration dampening my forehead. *I must look a mess,* I mused. I could feel my coppery curls beginning to slip from their combs. My face felt flushed and warm, my dress was crumpled, and my hands . . . I looked at my hands. They were trembling—trembling as though I had had an awful fright or just plain overexerted myself. Well, it mattered not. I had done it. I was packed and ready. Ready to go with Wynn to his north country. All that remained to be done were the final preparations for our wedding; then we would be off for a very brief honeymoon. And then, after a hurried day of final preparations, we would be on our way to the little cabin we would call home.

I pushed the hair off my forehead with my shaky hand and, with the help of my nearby bed, pulled myself to a standing position. It was twenty minutes until the noon meal would be served. I still had time for a quick bath and a hair repair job. I mustn't stand around brooding. I must hurry. Friday morning was gone and there was still much to be done for my wedding. And my family would be arriving on the four o'clock train.

"Beth!"

Julie's cry made many heads turn in time to see the pretty, well-dressed Easterner drop whatever was in her arms and rush headlong for me.

I wanted to cry her name and run just as headlong to her, but I checked myself. I did run to meet her though, and the two of us fell into each other's arms. I had not known until that very minute just how intensely I had missed her. We both wept as we held one another. It was several minutes before we could speak.

"Let me look at you," Julie said, pushing herself back from me.

I just wanted to cling to her. I knew how short our time together would be.

She had changed. She was still just as attractive. She was still just as bubbly. But there was a certain maturity about her. How I loved her! I had missed her more than I could describe.

She threw her arms wildly about me again, dislodging my hat. "Oh, I've missed you so!" she cried. "How could you, Beth? How could you come out here and decide to marry some man who will take you off from me forever?" But there was teasing in Julie's voice.

"You just wait until you *see* the man," I teased back.

"Ah," said Julie, pushing back again and reaching up one hand to help my wayward hat. It didn't seem any more secure after Julie was done with it. "Ah," she said again. "Beth, the practical one, has met her match."

We laughed together, and then I was claimed by other arms. Mother arrived not in a whirlwind as had Julie but in her usual, quiet, dignified way.

"Elizabeth," she said very softly. "How are you, dear?"

My tears came again, rushing down my cheeks and threatening to soak everyone near me. Mother was weeping, too, but softly—like gently falling rain, not in wild torrents.

We held each other close for a long time. "You look beautiful, dear," she whispered in my ear. "Methinks that love becomes you."

"Oh, Mother!" I exclaimed, "just wait until you meet him. I can hardly wait—"

"Nor can I, dear." Wynn, on duty till 5:30, could not be with us to meet the train.

Jon claimed Mother then. It was touching to see mother and son greet one another after the many years they had been separated. After Jon had held her and allowed her to again regain her composure, he proudly introduced his Mary. The two of them seemed to fall in love immediately. The children crowded around. I could hear them as they took their turns being hugged by their grandma and Aunt Julie. But I was busy getting some hugs of my own. Father held me. I had often been held in my father's arms, but this time it was different. I think we both sensed it. For this time, I was no longer his little girl. I was now about to leave his care and be turned over to the arms of another man. He brushed a kiss against my hair just above my ear and whispered to me. "I'm happy for you, Elizabeth. Happy—and sad— all at one time. Can you understand that?"

I nodded my head against his shoulder. Yes, I understood, for that was the way I felt. I hated to leave my family. It would be so wonderful if I could have just packed them all up too—like I had done my simple dresses and the yards of material—and taken them along with me into the northland. But, no. I honestly wouldn't have wanted that. I didn't even need that. Not really. Wynn was all I really needed now. Things had changed. And, though I still loved my family, I was not dependent on them anymore. I was cutting the ties. I was binding myself to another. The solemn words would be spoken on the morrow, but my heart knew it had already made its commitment. Already, in thinking and feeling, I was Wynn's—his alone for all time and eternity. He would be my family, my protector, my spiritual head, my lover, my friend.

"I love you, Daddy," I said softly. "Thank you for everything. Thank you for raising me to be ready for a home of my own. I didn't realize it until—until—now. But you did.

You prepared me for this—for Wynn—and I thank you."

Suddenly I felt calm. Very calm and sure of myself. I had been too busy to even think of just what a difference the morrow would make in my life. I had been too in love to even consider that there might be problems to face and adjustments to be made, but I saw it now. The arms of the man who held me made me think clearly of all that was ahead, and I suddenly realized that I was indeed ready for it. This was not just a whim, not just a schoolgirl romance. This was a love. A love deep and lasting, and I would be a wife and a helpmeet for the man I loved. My father had showed me how. Unconsciously, in all of those years of my growing up, he had been showing me the way to a good marriage relationship— with his kindness, consideration, and strong loyalty to those he loved. I held him more tightly. I loved him very much.

When Father released me, I was facing a tall young man with gangly arms and a lopsided grin. At first I just stared at him, unable to believe my eyes. But it was, it really was, my dear Matthew. He wasn't quite sure of himself, nor of just how he should handle all this emotional greeting of his family members; so he stood back a pace somewhat as an onlooker. I blinked away tears and looked at him again. How he had grown in the short year I had been away. I wasn't quite sure how to greet him either.

"Matthew," I said, barely above a whisper. "Matthew, my— you've—you've grown up—so tall."

He took one step toward me as I moved to him, and then I was hugging him just as I had done so often when he was a little boy. His arms tightened around me, holding me tightly.

"Oh, Matt, I can't believe it! You're taller than Father." I tried not to weep, but it was impossible to stop all the tears from falling.

Matthew swallowed hard. He was almost a man, and weeping was not to be considered. Instead, he rather awkwardly patted my back, much as one would greet an old school chum. Jonathan was there then. It was the first time my younger brother had met my older brother, and they sized each other up man to man. They must have liked what they saw; for, moving almost as one, they changed from the handshake to a warm embrace. I could see Matthew's eyes, for he was facing me. They shone with admiration. I knew then that this trip west was going to have a lifelong effect on young Matt.

We finally collected ourselves and all of our belongings, piling into the two cars waiting for us. Jonathan had engaged the services of a friend to help transport us all back to the house. Wynn was invited to join the family for supper. I could hardly wait to show him off to my family and to introduce my family to him. I was so proud of them all. I loved them all so very much!

It was a noisy group that arrived at Jonathan's. We had so much catching up to do. And then there were the children. Each one of them was in a terrible hurry to make up for lost time and get to know their grandma and grandfather and this new aunt and uncle as quickly as possible. As usual, we all seemed to talk at once.

Jon and Mary showed each of the family members to their respective rooms, Mary apologizing that the intended cleaning and redecorating had not been done because of the earlier wedding date. Mother declared that everything was just lovely as it was; and I think Mary felt that Mother meant every word of it.

Julie, as exuberant as ever, exclaimed over everything. She and Baby Elizabeth, who was now taking a few shaky steps on her own, seemed to be kindred spirits. The other children all loved Julie immediately, too, but I noticed that Kathleen still clung to me.

Matthew soon found an admirer in the young William. He looked up to Matthew with the same devotion showing in his eyes that Matthew had for Jonathan.

Julie was going to share my room with me, so with both of us loaded down with her suitcases and hat boxes, we climbed the stairs.

"Oh, that old train," lamented Julie. "It was so stuffy and so warm! And there was this fat little man with foul cigars who sat right in front of me. And there was this party of four who sat down the aisle and kept talking and laughing in such a crude manner that—"

Julie would have gone on, but I stopped her with a laugh. She looked at me, bewildered, but I reached over and gave her another hug.

"You've changed," I told her. "A few years ago, you would have been seeing each one of those men as a possible suitor."

Julie's eyes twinkled. "Oh, I did that too," she admitted. "The only difference is that I'm a bit more selective now. There were some very fine-looking specimens on that train. I just haven't gotten to that yet."

"Oh, Julie. You little goose," I teased. "I still can't believe it. My big, cautious sister marrying a frontiersman!"

"He's not a frontiersman. He's a Royal North West Mounted Policeman," I corrected her.

She shrugged and threw her hat on my bed. A few years back, I would have reminded her that was not where it was to go. Instead, I picked it up myself and laid it carefully on the closet shelf.

"You wait until you see him," I reminded Julie. "You'll be jealous of me."

Julie laughed. "Well, I sort of figured that where there is one good catch, there should be more of the same. Right, Beth? How about introducing me to a few of Wynn's friends on the Police Force? There are other unmarried ones, I expect."

"Certainly. A number of them. But don't expect to find another one like Wynn."

"He's that special, is he?" Julie's eyes shone. "Perhaps, Elizabeth Marie Thatcher, you're a wee bit prejudiced."

"We'll see," I told her, willing away the minutes until Wynn would arrive and Julie could see for herself.

"I must go help Mary," I finally told Julie, reluctant to leave her even for a minute. "You make yourself at home. The bath is just down the hall and the laundry room is down the steps to the right if you need to press anything."

It is so good to have them all here, my heart sang as I went down the stairs. *I just wish I had more time to visit with them.* But tomorrow was our wedding day, and after that Wynn and I would be leaving. And yet I did not wish, for one moment, that I could push my wedding into the future—not even for the chance to visit with my family. I started to hum as I entered the kitchen. The tune sounded something like "Here Comes the Bride."

Chapter Four

Preparing

"Is everything ready?" Wynn asked as we took a little walk alone later that night. We needed this solitude. Inside, the house was still buzzing. My family had taken an immediate liking to the man I was to marry, and it seemed to me that each one of them enjoyed monopolizing his time. Julie especially was awestruck. I could see it in her eyes. It was difficult for her to believe that her big sister, who had so many times expressed her disgust with the male side of the species, was so fortunate to be blessed with a union to one as marvelous as this.

How did you do it, Beth? her expression seemed to ask across the room. *Where did you ever find him?*

To which my eyes silently answered, *I told you so.*

But now Wynn and I were finally alone, and things were quiet enough so we could actually have a decent conversation.

I was momentarily checked by Wynn's question. Not sure that it had registered properly, I repeated it. "Is everything ready? I—I honestly don't know. My thoughts are all in a whirl. But does it matter? I mean, does it *really* matter? You have the license and the ring; I have my dress; the family is here. We're ready enough to go ahead with the wedding. So what if some of the details—"

Wynn laughed and reached for me. "You are unbelievable, Elizabeth," he said. "Who would ever have expected my stylish Eastern miss to be making such statements!"

He kissed me. It was still light and we were walking on

a Calgary sidewalk with many homes nearby. Someone was bound to see us. His "stylish Eastern miss" pushed back from him without really wanting to.

Wynn laughed again. "I'm sorry, Elizabeth," he said. "I just couldn't resist. But I'll be good, I promise. Until tomorrow." His eyes twinkled.

I flushed slightly and resumed walking.

"Your family is wonderful," Wynn said, suddenly changing the subject and our moods.

"And they all love you!" I exclaimed. "I knew they would. Oh, Wynn, I'm so happy."

Wynn reached for my hand and squeezed it. I did not try to withdraw it. Let the neighbors watch and frown if they cared. This was the eve of my wedding day, to the man I loved.

"Are *you* all ready?" I asked.

"Everything's all set and crated. I had an awful time finding enough of the medical supplies I need. Had to have some sent down from Edmonton, but I finally got it all together."

"Medical supplies?" I queried, surprised.

"We need to take everything, Elizabeth," he reminded me. "Not just for ourselves but for the whole settlement."

I had forgotten Wynn had such a big task. "They have a Hudson's Bay Post there," he went on, "and shipments of supplies coming in. But one never counts on them for such important things as medicine. Blankets, flour, salt, traps—now, those things we will be able to get there with no problem."

Traps. I thought of this strange world to which I was going. It fascinated me. There was so much to learn. I was eager to get there, to get involved in Wynn's life.

"I'm all packed, too," I proudly informed him. "I got everything shoved into the one trunk. Mind you, it took some doing! I had to leave behind those books I had wanted, and that one hat I was going to take, and two pairs of shoes and two dresses, but I got all the rest in. I won't really need all those things anyway."

"You should have some of your books, Elizabeth. They might be a—"

But I cut in, "Oh, I did take a few of my favorites. The ones I left were mostly those I thought I might use if the

Indian children would like to have a school."

"You still haven't given up on that idea, have you?"

"Well—" I hesitated. "No."

He pressed my hand again. "I'm glad," he said. "It would be wonderful if you could teach some of them to read." I smiled, appreciative of Wynn's understanding and encouragement.

"I think I might be able to find some little corner to stick more of your books in if you'd like, Elizabeth."

I wanted to throw my arms about his neck and hug him, but we were still on the Calgary streets and it was still daylight; instead, I squeezed his hand and gave him another smile. "Oh, thank you. I would so much like to take them. There really aren't very many and they don't make a very big stack, but I just couldn't get one more thing into my trunk."

We walked on, talking of our new life together and many other things. There was something very special about this night before we would become husband and wife. We hated to see it end.

When we did return to the house, the western sun had just dipped behind the distant hills. A soft light glowed from each of the windows along the lazy sidewalk. The air was becoming cooler but was still pleasant. Wynn slowed his steps as we went up the walk.

"I don't think I will come in, Elizabeth. You need this last evening with your family. I'm going to have you for the rest of our lives."

Wynn stepped from the walk to the warm shadows of the big elm tree. I knew I would not protest this time when he took me in his arms.

"I won't see you until tomorrow at the church," he whispered. "Now don't you go and change your mind."

"There's not a chance," I assured him, my arms locked tightly about his neck.

"I still can't believe it—tomorrow! And tomorrow is finally almost here. You'll never know what a fright it gave me when I got that early posting."

"Fright?"

"I thought I would have to leave you behind. I knew it

would be unfair to ask you to wait for three or four or even
five years. I was almost beside myself. I thought of quitting
the Force, but I didn't have the money to start out some place
else."

"Oh, Wynn."

"I never dreamed you would ever be able, and willing, to
rush into a wedding like this. I hope you never feel that
you've been 'cheated,' Elizabeth."

"Cheated?"

"Cheated out of the kind of wedding you've always
dreamed of."

I laughed. "The fact is, Wynn," I said, "I spent very little
time dreaming about weddings until I met you. *Then* I
dreamed—I dreamed a lot. But the wedding wouldn't be much
without you there by my side, now would it? So, if there's a
choice between the trimmings or you—then it's easy to leave
out the trimmings."

Wynn kissed me again.

"I must go," he said after several moments. "My bride
must be fresh and glowing on her wedding day; and if I don't
let you get your beauty sleep, it will be my fault if you aren't."

He saw me to the door and left. I went in to join the family.
Father and Mother were ready to retire for the night. It had
been a long, hard day for them. At Father's suggestion, we
gathered in the living room for a time of Scripture reading
and prayer. Tears squeezed out from under our eyelids as we
prayed together. Even Matthew, somewhat shyly, prayed
aloud. I was touched at his earnest petition that God would
bless his big sister Beth and her Wynn as they started out
life together. It was a time I shall always remember. Never
had I felt closer to my family than when we sat, hands intertwined, praying together as our tears flowed unheeded.

I did not really get the rest Wynn had suggested, for Julie
and I could not refrain from catching up on a whole year in
the next few short hours. We talked on and on. Each time
the downstairs cuckoo sounded out the hour, I would determine that I must stop talking and get some sleep; but each
time one or the other of us would think of something we just
had to share or had to ask the other.

Julie insisted on knowing all about Wynn—where I had

met him, how I had won him. She would have loved to hear
each detail of our romance; and, if I had been like Julie, I
might have wished to share it all. I was not like Julie and
therefore kept many of the details to myself. They were trea-
sured things and not to be shared with any other than Wynn
himself.

"When did he first tell you he loved you?" asked nosey
Julie.

"Hey," I said sleepily, "isn't that a bit personal?"

"Oh, come on, Beth. It must have taken your breath away.
Tell me about it."

"Not a chance," I countered. "It took my breath away,
yes. But it is for me alone."

I thought back to the scene at the railway station when
I was all set to head back east. That was the first time Wynn
had confessed that he loved me. I still tingled as I thought
of it.

"How long did it take before he proposed?" Julie persisted.

"Forever," I said with meaning, and Julie laughed.

"Oh, Beth. Get serious."

"I'm serious."

"Did you love him first?"

"I thought I did. I thought so for a long time. Wynn has
told me since that he did love me. He was just so sure it
wouldn't work that he wouldn't admit he loved me."

" 'Wouldn't work'?"

"Because of his job. He didn't think I was the kind of
woman who could endure the North."

"Oh, pshaw!" exploded Julie, then covered her mouth
guiltily in case she had disturbed the sleeping household.

"My feelings exactly," I returned in a loud whisper; and
we both giggled, bringing the blankets up to our faces to
muffle the sound like we used to when we were kids and had
been told to go to sleep but talked instead.

"How did you finally convince him?" Julie asked.

"Well, I—I—I'm not sure," I stammered. "I left."

"Left?"

"On the train—for home."

"But you're still here."

"Well, yes. I never really went. But I was going to leave. I was all set to go. I had even shipped my trunks. I was all ready to board the train."

Julie, sensing an exciting romantic adventure, squealed and then jerked up the cover to smother it.

"Look, Julie," I said firmly. "That's all that I'm going to tell you. I was leaving; Wynn came to get me. He asked me to stay; he asked me to marry him. I stayed. Now, let's talk about something else."

"We really should go to sleep." Julie tried to hide the disappointment in her voice.

"Well, we have only tonight to talk. Or do you want to go to sleep? You must be tired after all that time on the train."

"Oh, no. I'm not tired. Not at all. I want to talk. I haven't even told you yet—"

For several hours, I lay and listened to Julie recount her romances of the last several months. There were thrills and there were heartbreaks. There were fantastic fellows and there were bores. There were ups and there were downs. I wondered whom Julie would have to share all her secrets with once I was gone.

"Is there anyone special?" I finally asked.

Julie thought deeply. "You know, that's a funny thing, Bethie. Even as I lie here and think of them all, not a one of them is really what I want. Isn't that silly?"

"I don't think so."

"Then why do I pay any attention to them?"

"You just haven't found the right one yet," I assured her. I could have also added, *and you just haven't matured enough to know what it is that you do want,* but I didn't.

"You know what I think?" said Julie slowly, deliberately, as though a new and astonishing truth had suddenly been revealed to her. "I think I've been going at this whole thing all wrong. I've been out looking for the fellow—oh, not particularly the right one, just anyone—and I should have been like you and let him come looking for me."

"But Wynn wasn't looking for me, either," I confessed.

"Well, it happened, didn't it? You did get together. Somebody *must* have been looking for *someone!*"

We lay quietly for a few minutes.

"Beth," Julie whispered. "Did you ever pray about the man you were to marry?"

"Sometimes. I prayed that God would keep me from making a wrong decision."

"And Mother prayed. I know that. She prays all the time. She doesn't say much about it, but I'm always finding her praying. And Father prays. In our family prayer time, he always prays that God will guide each of his children in every decision of life."

"What are you getting at?" I had to ask her.

"Maybe it wasn't you—and maybe it wasn't Wynn. Maybe it was God who saw to it that you got together."

"I've always felt that," I answered simply.

"Well, I've never seen it that way before. Guess I sort of thought if I left it to God, He would pick out some sour-faced, serious older man with a kind, fatherly attitude—and poor looks. I'm not sure I was willing to trust Him to choose my future husband."

I laughed in spite of myself, but Julie was very serious.

"No, Beth, I mean it," she continued. "God didn't pick that kind of man for you. Wynn is just—is just—"

She hesitated. I wasn't sure if she couldn't come up with the right word or was afraid I would object to her "swooning" over my husband-to-be.

"Perfect." I finished for her.

"Perfect," she repeated. "Tall, muscular, strong—yet gentle, understanding, and so very *good-looking!*" she finished with an exaggerated sigh.

I laughed again.

"Do you think God could really find me one like that?"

"Oh, Julie. There is only one just like Wynn."

"I s'pose," Julie sighed again. "Well, what about second best?"

"Look, Julie, when God finds you the right one, you won't think he is second best—not to anyone in the world."

"Really? Do you truly think God could direct in *this,* too, Beth?" Julie was serious again.

"Why don't you leave it with Him and see?" I prompted her.

"Why is it so much easier to trust God for some things

than for others?" she wondered.

"I really don't know. We should be wise enough to know we can trust Him with everything, but it seems as if He is forever needing to remind us—one thing at a time. Maybe it's because we just hang onto some things too tightly, wanting our own way too much."

"It's hard to let go of some things."

"I know."

"I wasn't going to tell you this, Beth; but, after you left home, I cried. I cried every night for two weeks, and then I finally realized I had to let go. I prayed about it—and really meant what I prayed—and God took away the sorrow from my heart and gave me a new love and respect for my older sister. I can be happy with you now, Beth, even though it means I really am going to lose you."

I reached out a hand in the darkness and placed it on Julie's cheek. It was damp with tears, but her voice did not break.

"I missed you, too," I said honestly. "I missed you, too; and, Julie, my deepest desire for you is that someday God truly might bring someone into your life—oh, not another Wynn, but someone you can love just as much, be just as proud of. I'm sure that somewhere there is someone—just for you. Be ready for him, Julie. Be ready to be the kind of wife he needs, the kind of woman he can love deeply, can be proud of—not just of her outer beauty but of her inner beauty as well. I love you, Julie."

Chapter Five

The Wedding Day

In spite of the fact I had not slept much the night before, I awoke the next morning with excitement bringing me quickly and easily from my bed. Julie still slept, one hand tucked beneath her pretty face. She looked more like a beautiful child than an attractive young woman, still oblivious to the world and all the duties of this important day.

I tiptoed about as I dressed and left the room. The wedding ceremony had been set for eleven o'clock. Following that would be the reception dinner with family and close friends. Mary, bless her heart, had insisted she would be responsible for that and had engaged some caterers to help her with the preparations and serving.

After the reception, we would open the wedding gifts and spend some time with family and friends before boarding the four o'clock train for Banff.

Our honeymoon would not be nearly as long as we had once planned it. Four days in the beautiful mountains did not seem nearly enough. We would not travel leisurely. We would not be taking a cabin in some remote area where we could hike and climb and just rest and relax in the grandeur of those magnificent mountains. Instead, we would take the train; Wynn had booked a room at the hotel, and from there we would make our little excursions into privacy.

The day we would be returning from Banff would be the day before we headed north, so all of our time then would be taken with last-minute preparations and final packing.

My friends from Pine Springs had been so disappointed

we would not have time to visit them before leaving. They had planned a community shower to follow our wedding, if it had occurred in September as originally planned.

"Ve can't let you yust go off—like dat," wailed Anna. "Ve need to gif you our vishes, too!"

"Can't you come to the wedding?" I pleaded over the sputtering lines of the telephone system.

"Ve'll try. Ve'll try so hard. Da little ones vould hurt so to miss," said Anna. "Dey haf talked 'bout not'ing else for veeks."

"Perhaps Phillip would have room to bring you," I suggested. But I was afraid Phillip's car might be full.

"Ve'll see," promised Anna. "Ve'll see."

But I shoved all of that from my mind and tried to concentrate instead on what needed to be done in the few brief hours before my wedding.

Mary, already in the kitchen, motioned me to a chair beside her and nodded her head toward the coffeepot on the back of the stove.

"Pour yourself a cup, Beth, and join me. Always best to organize one's thoughts before plowing on ahead. Saves time that way."

I agreed and went for a cup. The next several minutes were spent "organizing."

Mary held a pencil in her slim fingers and jotted down as we discussed.

"The flowers!" she squealed suddenly. "Beth, did you order the flowers?"

My hand shot to my forehead. I had not. I had thought of it a number of times but never did get it done.

Mary looked nervous. "What ever will we do?" she asked me, not nearly as composed as when we began.

For a moment I was stunned; then suddenly I remembered those beautiful roses growing in Mary's backyard.

"Do you mind sharing your roses?"

"My roses?"

"The ones out back. They are beautiful. I noticed them a few days ago. They would work—"

"But we have no one to arrange them," Mary interrupted me.

"You can arrange them. You do a beautiful job. I'd like two bouquets—one on each side of the altar."

"But your bridal bouquet—"

"I'll carry roses, too."

"But—" Mary was going to protest again.

"I'll just carry a loose bouquet. Just a few long-stemmed flowers. They'll be beautiful."

"They are all thorns," Mary argued.

"We'll cut the thorns off. Matthew or William will be glad to do that."

Mary smiled. Then she nodded her head and took another swallow of coffee.

"So we have the flowers settled. Where do we go from here?"

We went over everything again. My dress was ready. Julie was to stand beside me. Her dress would need pressing after its long train ride, but Julie would take care of that. The dresses were all ready for Sarah and Kathleen. The cake had been done by a lady friend of Mary's. It was simpler than it would have been had she been given more time; but I was finding more and more beauty in simplicity. Phillip, Wynn's brother, was to stand up with Wynn; and Phillip, Jr., was to bear the rings.

"We have no pillow for the rings!" I cried suddenly when we came to that item.

"That's no problem," a soft voice said behind me. "I've been feeling bad that I have had nothing to do with getting ready for my daughter's wedding. Just give me some pretty scraps and I'll have a pillow in no time."

It was Mother. I jumped from my chair to hug her. She held me for a moment.

"Do you have any suitable pieces?" she asked at last.

"I have some nice bits left from my wedding dress."

"That will do just fine. And lace?"

"I've some of that, too, though I'm not sure it's enough."

Mary had been pouring another cup of coffee. She set it on the table and pulled up another chair for Mother.

"I've lots of ribbon and lace," she assured us. "I sew most of the girls' things, and they always insist upon 'fancies' on all of their dresses."

We drank our coffee and continued to cover all the details of the coming wedding. Here and there we had to improvise and make other arrangements. For some reason, it did not panic me. The "organized Elizabeth" of old would have been horrified to do up a wedding so—so *haphazardly*. Instead, I went through the activities of the morning in a comfortable daze. In just a few short hours, all the fussing would be behind me; and I would be Mrs. Wynn Delaney.

Chapter Six

Marriage

Our wedding day was gloriously sunshiny. I had not even thought to check the weather until I was actually in Jonathan's car and on my way to the church. It could have been pouring and I would never have noticed in my state of excitement. I stopped long enough to breathe a very short prayer of thanks to God for arranging such a beautiful day and then turned my thoughts back to my wedding again.

There had been some moments when I thought I would never make the eleven o'clock date with Wynn. In spite of our "organizing," there was much last-minute commotion, and the whole house seemed to be in a frenzy. Even Jonathan and Father were enlisted for tying little girls' bows and putting on slippers.

After I had slipped into the soft, creamy folds of my satin gown, I began to work on my hair. The locks that normally fell into place with little coaxing refused to go right. I tried again with similar results. I noticed then that my hands were shaking in my excitement. Julie came to my rescue and, with a few deft turns and skillful motions, she had my hair smartly and firmly in place, ready for the veil. I thanked her and went to slip into my wedding shoes.

By the time Julie and I came downstairs, one carload had already left for the church. Mother and Father waited in the hall looking serene and composed in spite of the last-minute flurries of the household. Mother's eyes misted slightly as she looked at me.

"You look beautiful, my dear," she whispered. "Your dress is lovely."

Father remarked, "It's a shame to spend so much time on something that will scarcely be noticed."

I looked at him, puzzled.

"With your cheeks glowing and your eyes shining so, Elizabeth, no one will be able to take their eyes from your face."

Understanding, I smiled at Father as he stepped closer, and I reached up to kiss him on the cheek.

We formed a close circle, the four of us—Father, Mother, Julie and I—our arms intertwined as we stood together for one last time in the hallway of brother Jon's lovely Calgary home. Father led in prayer, asking that the Lord would make my home, wherever it might be, a place of love. "Might there always be harmony and commitment, love and happiness. Might there be strength for the hard times, humor to ease the tense times, and shoulders always available for the times of tears," he prayed. I found it difficult to keep the tears from falling now, but I did not want to reach the church with swollen eyes and a smudged face, so I refused to allow myself to cry. Mother blew her nose softly and wiped at her eyes, and then we hastened to the car.

As I stood waiting at the entrance of the church, my eyes on the back of the man whom I would soon be joining at the altar, my heart pounded wildly. Father must have sensed it, for he reached a reassuring hand out to me and held my hand tightly. I watched Julie slowly make her way down the aisle with proper and graceful steps, her soft skirts swirling out gently as she went. For a moment it had a dizzying effect on me, and I closed my eyes. It was my turn next, and I must be ready.

I was still standing with my eyes tightly closed when Father took his first step. Startled, my eyes quickly opened and Father hesitated, to let me get in step with him. It was time—time for me to walk down the aisle to meet Wynn.

I was completely oblivious to all the people in the pews. I don't even remember seeing the preacher who stood directly at the end of the aisle. All I remember is Wynn's face as he turned to watch me make that long, long, short walk to him.

In a few minutes, I would be his wife! *My husband, Wynn,* was the refrain in my thoughts as I moved toward him. *Lord, make me a worthy wife to this man.*

With a gentle pressure on my arm, my father stopped me. Had he not checked me, I'm sure, I would have kept right on walking until I could take Wynn's hand. My thoughts began to sort themselves out, and I hurriedly went over the ceremony in my mind. I was to wait here with my father until he responded to "Who giveth this woman to be married to this man?" Then I could step forward to be at Wynn's side.

From then on, I concentrated very hard on the ceremony and was able to make the right responses at the right times. I was very, very conscious of Wynn by my side, of the significance of the words we were saying. As the soloist sang "The Wedding Prayer," we looked deeply into one another's eyes, secret messages passing between us. Wynn was saying, *Are you absolutely sure?* And I answered without a moment's hesitation, *I've never been so sure of anything in my life.* We had time for each to add, *I love you so very, very much,* and Wynn gently squeezed my hand.

The ceremony was over, and we walked back down the aisle together. Husband and wife. From now on, I would be with Wynn always. There would be no separation. Nothing would ever come between us.

The entry of the church was packed with well-wishers. Anna and her entire family were there. I did not even have opportunity to ask them how they had come. We hugged one another and she kissed my cheek, telling me how beautiful I looked. I greeted the children. Lars had grown noticeably, even since I had last seen him. Olga grinned and whispered a few well-rehearsed phrases about my future happiness, but Else stopped and cautiously reached out a small hand to caress my dress.

"It's beautiful. Did you make it?"

"Yes, I did," I answered her.

"It's beautiful," she said again. "So soft and smooth. You're a good sewer, Miss Thatcher."

I did not notice the familiar title, but Wynn did. "Whoa now, Else," he laughed. "It's not 'Miss Thatcher' anymore."

Else flushed slightly but laughed with Wynn. She put a

small hand to her mouth and giggled, "I mean 'Mrs. Wynn,' " she corrected herself.

We let that go. Mrs. Wynn. It sounded rather homey. I wouldn't mind being called Mrs. Wynn at all.

After we had been greeted by those who had shared our day, we returned to Jon and Mary's house for the reception. I don't remember much about the reception. I guess I was just too excited. I'm sure the lunch was delicious, but only because I heard other people say so.

The meal was cleared away and we opened our gifts. We received so many lovely things, it kept me busy imagining how much they would add to our little wilderness home. There would be no problem in making it cozy and homelike. I also reminded myself of the last busy day we would have when we returned from our honeymoon—all of these additional things would have to be carefully packed. I was too excited to give it further thought now. I must take one thing at a time.

It was finally time for us to change for our train trip to Banff. I went to the room I had shared the night before with Julie and eased the satin gown carefully over my head to keep from disarranging my hair. I stepped out of the brand-new shoes that pinched slightly and kicked them from me. It would be nice to wear something more comfortable.

I decided to take a quick bath before dressing for the train. It would take only a few minutes and would help me to be relaxed and fresh.

Afterward I donned a summery-looking suit of teal blue that Mother had brought with her from Madame Tanier's shop. I loved being so stylish way out here in the West! Father had chosen the hat, they said; I carefully put it in place, pleased at how well it suited me. I then picked up my bag and, with one last glance in the mirror, went to join Wynn.

Jon was driving us to the station, so it would mean saying goodbye to my family before we left. I would have hated leaving them had not the future held so much promise. To enter the new life meant to say goodbye to the old. There was no way to hang onto both. Even I knew that.

But it was hard to leave all those I loved. Our goodbyes were rather long and tearful, and repeated a number of times.

Yet I was eager to be off, and finally we were able to pull
ourselves away. Jon's car left the drive at a bit faster pace
than normal. It would never do for the Banff train to leave
without us.

We reached the station just in time and, with a flurry of
bags, managed to board the train.

At first I was still in a whirl. Though my body had ceased
to rush about, my mind still raced back and forth. Part of it
was back with my family; part of it was reliving the wonderful, the harried, the tense, the busy moments of the wedding. Part of it was busy imagining my new life with Wynn.
I tried to ease myself into the cushiony seat of the Pullman;
but neither my body nor my mind would cooperate.

Wynn seemed perfectly relaxed. He stretched out his long
legs and smiled contentedly. He looked at me, and his eyes
told me he would like to sweep me into his arms. Respecting
my reserve in front of an "audience," he refrained because of
the many other passengers on the train. Instead, he gave me
a wink that made my heart leap. He reached for my hand
and I clung to him. He must have felt the tenseness in me,
for he began to stroke my fingers, talking softly as he did so.

"It was a lovely wedding, Elizabeth. I don't see how it
could have been nicer even if you had had all the time in the
world."

My whirling thoughts went over a few things I had overlooked or mixed up or that were not as I would have planned
them.

"Your gown was beautiful; did I tell you that?"

I managed a little smile. "Father said no one would notice," I murmured.

"I almost didn't," Wynn admitted. "Then I remembered
a note of advice from brother Phillip. 'Be sure to take a good
look at the dress,' he told me. 'She will expect you to know
every detail, each row of lace, and the number of buttons.'
Well, I will admit, Elizabeth, I didn't count the buttons, nor
even the rows of lace, but I did take a good look at the lovely
silk dress."

"Satin," I corrected.

"Satin," Wynn repeated, still rubbing a big finger softly
up and down the back of my hand. "How would I know silk

from satin? All I know for sure is that it wasn't serge or denim."

In spite of my preoccupation, I laughed. It eased my tenseness some. I thought of Father's prayer about humor for the tense times! I hadn't realized before how important a bit of laughter could be. Wynn's pressure on my hand increased.

"What will you remember about today, Elizabeth?" I knew he was trying to help me relax, and I appreciated it. I tried again to let my body snuggle against the back of the seat, but it was still stiff and resistant. I turned slightly to Wynn, making my voice even and light.

"The rush. The last-minute flurry. The fear that I would never make it on time and that you would be waiting at the church, furious with me for being so late—and maybe even change your mind about getting married," I teased.

Wynn smiled. "Oh, I wouldn't have changed my mind. There were at least three other single ladies there—I checked, just in case."

I pulled my hand away in a mock pout. Wynn retrieved it.

"What else?" he prompted.

I became more serious then. "Father's prayer. He always prays with us before any big event in our lives. I remember when Margaret was married. I was her bridesmaid, so I was there for Father's prayer. It was so beautiful. I remember thinking, 'If I don't ever get married, I'll miss that.' Still, I wasn't convinced that the prayer was sufficient reason to risk a marriage."

"You're serious?"

"At the time I was. Honest! I didn't really think I would ever feel inclined to marry."

"Here I was taught to believe that every young girl is just waiting for the chance to lead some man—any man—to the altar."

"I guess some are."

"Then why not you?"

"I don't know, really. I guess it wasn't because I was so against marriage. I just didn't like the insinuation that it was all a sensible girl thought about—that women were just for the marrying, that if I didn't marry, I was nothing. I didn't like that—that *bigotry*."

I wasn't exactly calming down as Wynn had intended. The thoughts from my past and the ridiculous beliefs of some of the people I had known were stirring me up instead. I pulled slightly away from Wynn and was about to expound further on the subject.

"Women are quite capable—" I began but was interrupted.

"Hey, take it easy, Mrs. Delaney. You don't need to convince me. I believe you. I watched you in the teacherage, remember; and I'm sure that you, as a single woman, could handle anything. But I'm glad you didn't decide you must prove your point for an entire lifetime. *You* might not need a man—but I need you. That's why women marry, Elizabeth—to give their inner strength to some weak man."

His face was serious, but I knew there was a certain amount of teasing there, too. I slumped back against him and let the intensity die quickly from my eyes.

Wynn reached over and lifted my chin, tipping my face slightly so he could look into my eyes.

"Your inner strength—and your outer beauty, Elizabeth—I need both."

I wanted to lean over and kiss him, but my upbringing forbade it. Instead, I looked back at him with my love in my eyes and then leaned against him, my body finally relaxed enough to comfortably fit the seat. After a few moments of silence, I took up Wynn's little game.

"What will *you* remember about today, Wynn?"

There was no hesitation. "The look on your face when we said our vows. The way your eyes said that you meant every word of them."

"I did," I whispered. "I do."

"The dimple in your cheek when you smiled at me."

Self-consciously, I put a hand up to my cheek.

"The way your hair glistened when the sun came through the window."

I waited for more.

"The softness of your hand when I held it." He caressed the hand now, looking down at it as he did so.

"The beautiful color of your eyes, so deep and glowing."

I looked at him teasingly and added one for him. "And my 'silk' dress."

He laughed. We were both completely relaxed now. The long, beautiful, tiring, tense day was over. Our wedding had been lovely, but it now was in the past. Our whole future lay before us. Our marriage. I think that at that moment, as never before, I determined in my heart to make my marriage a thing even more beautiful than my wedding had been.

Perhaps Wynn felt it too, for he whispered softly against my hair, "This is just the beginning, Elizabeth. We have today as a memory, but we have all of the tomorrows as exciting possibilities. We can shape them with hands of love to fulfill our fondest dreams. I wasn't much for marrying either, Elizabeth, but I am so glad you came into my life to change my mind. I've never been happier—and with God's help, I plan to make you happy, too."

Chapter Seven

Banff

Banff was beautiful. There are no words to adequately describe the beauty of those mountains. I wanted to look and look at them—to carry them always in my heart.

The next morning we arose to another glorious day of sunshine. We enjoyed a leisurely breakfast in the hotel's terraced dining room and watched the sun turn the valley rose and gold as its fingers reached into the depths. After some inquiring, Wynn discovered a church, and we took hotel transportation into the sleepy little town of Banff to attend the morning services. Afterward, we found an inconspicuous little cafe where we enjoyed our lunch of mountain trout and then spent a lazy afternoon walking through the town, enjoying the sights and feel of the mountains and the enjoyable companionship of one another.

"Tell me about Banff," I said rather dreamily as we walked along in the sunshine.

"As far as the white man is concerned, this is a very young town," responded Wynn. "Of course, the Indian people have known the area for many years. Explorers came through the area first. They came and went and didn't pay too much attention, except to admire the beauty, until in the 1880s when the railroad arrived and the small town of Banff was born."

"And people loved it and just couldn't stay away," I ventured.

"Well, what really brought the visitors was the discovery of the mineral hot springs in 1883. And then, those who knew people and knew investment built and opened the Banff

Springs Hotel to care for the trade. The hotel was billed as 'The Finest on the North American Continent' and was visited by tourists from all over the world."

"And here I get to spend my honeymoon in this famous hotel," I interrupted, excited by the thought.

"People have always been fascinated with mountains; and all the unclimbed, unconquered, and uncharted mountains have brought many climbers to see if they could be the first ones to the summits. They brought in experienced Swiss guides to help attract mountaineers, and the area was soon famous."

"I think it's still rather—" I paused for the right word. "Rustic," I finally decided.

Wynn smiled at my choice. "Yes," he agreed. "I guess that's part of its charm. The ruggedness, the trail guides, the fur traders—they all mingle on the streets with the wealthy from around the world. While we've walked, have you noticed all the different languages around us?"

I had noticed. It was rather exhilarating, like being in a foreign country.

I sighed deeply. "There are so many things I would like to see that I don't know where to begin," I told Wynn. "We have such a short time."

"We'll plan carefully," he assured me. "Right now, let's start with some place to eat."

As we ate our evening meal in the luxurious hotel restaurant, I heard the people at the table next to ours discussing a hike they had taken that day and the sights they had seen.

"Could we?—" I asked Wynn. "Could we go? Please? I would so love to really see the mountains, not just the town."

"Why not?" Wynn smiled. "It's a bit of a climb, but I'm sure we could do it. It will be very exhausting, especially at these heights, but worth it."

"When?"

"Let's do it tomorrow."

I clapped like an eager child, then quickly checked myself; it was too undignified for a married woman.

For the rest of the meal, we discussed our plans for the next morning. I planned to be up bright and early so we would get a good start.

When we went back to our room, Wynn said he had a few arrangements to make. He had mentioned having the kitchen prepare us a lunch to be taken along on the trail, so I nodded and set about looking over my long skirts to decide what I would be able to wear the next day. In spite of the rigors of the trail, I did want to look good for Wynn. No man wants a plain or shabby bride. I found a skirt I thought would do. It was stylish enough to be becoming but not too full to inhibit my walking. Then I selected my shoes. None of them were really made for a long hike, but I did have one pair with me that wasn't too uncomfortable or flimsy.

After I had made my selections, I ran a nice warm bath, humming to myself. I would take a leisurely bath while Wynn was gone. My thoughts were filled with anticipation for the coming day and the glorious climb we would have together. I prayed for good weather. I wanted to look out from some lofty peak at the beautiful, tree-covered valleys beneath me.

I soon heard Wynn return and stir about our room. I hurried then. I remembered I had left my clothes for the hike spread out on the room's most comfortable chair, the one Wynn might be wishing to use. Wrapped snuggly in my new white robe, I hurried out, intending to move the skirt and other articles of clothing. They were gone. Wynn now occupied the chair. One glance told me that Wynn had hung the clothing carefully back in the closet.

"Oh, thank you," I managed, but I was a bit embarrassed that he might think I was messy and careless. "I wasn't planning to leave it there," I hastened to explain. "I was just trying to smooth out some of the wrinkles for tomorrow."

"Tomorrow?" He looked questioningly at me. "I'm afraid by the time we have our hike tomorrow, there won't be time for anything else."

"That's what I mean. For the hike."

Wynn looked surprised.

"*That* outfit—for the *hike*?"

I was a bit taken aback, but stammered, "It's all I brought that was suitable, really. I thought the other dresses too fancy to be walking in."

"You're right. So is that one," he said, with a nod toward the skirt still visible through the open closet door.

"But it's all I've got," I argued.

"I got you something." Wynn sounded quite confident.

"You got me a dress?"

"Not a dress."

"Well—skirt, then?"

"No skirt. You can't climb a mountain with a skirt swishing about your legs, Elizabeth."

"Then—" I was puzzled and a bit apprehensive by this time.

"Pants."

"Pants?"

"That's right."

"I've never worn *pants* in my life," I blurted out, emphasizing the word with some disfavor.

"Then this will be a first," said Wynn, completely unflustered, nodding his head toward the bed.

I followed his gaze. There, tossed on our bed in a rather awkward and haphazard fashion, was a pair of men's pants. They were an ugly color and very wrinkled, and I almost collapsed in shock as I looked at them.

"Those?" I gasped.

Wynn was now catching on. He stood to his feet. His eyes sought my face. He must have read my honest horror, for his voice became soft.

"I'm sorry, Elizabeth," he apologized sincerely. "I guess I didn't think how they would look to you. They are rather a mess, aren't they?" I caught a glimpse of disappointment in his eyes as he crossed to the bed and picked up the pants he had just purchased. He awkwardly began to smooth out the wrinkles with his man-sized hands. I felt repentant. I reached to take them from him. "It's all right," I said, not wanting to hurt Wynn. "I could press the wrinkles out. It's not that. It's just that—that I couldn't go out—I couldn't be seen wearing something like that—in public and all—I—" I stammered to a stop.

Wynn said nothing but continued to stroke his hands across the coarse fabric of the pants. The wrinkles refused to give up possession.

"My skirt will be fine, Wynn; but thank you for thinking about—"

Wynn looked at me evenly and didn't allow me to go on. "You cannot climb a mountain in a skirt, Elizabeth. Those are not just hiking trails. They are steep. They are dangerous. You cannot possibly go without proper clothing."

Sudden anger flared within me. "And you call *that* 'proper clothing'?" I responded, jerking a thumb at the disgusting pants.

"For what we intend to do, yes."

"Well, I won't wear them," I said, a bit too quickly.

Wynn tossed them into a chair. "Very well," he said, and his voice was calm.

I had won. I wasn't sure if I should be happy or sad. It was our first little tiff and I had won. Now, as a wife, how was I to win graciously? I sought for words, for ways to show Wynn that I would not expect to win *every* battle. I didn't know what to say, so I crossed the room and began to take down my hair and brush it with long, easy strokes. The tension remained within me, even though Wynn seemed untroubled.

I stole a glance at him. He was reading a paper. He must have bought it, too, when he had gone out for the pants. I noticed a pair of brown boots sitting on the floor by the bed. I started to ask Wynn about them and then realized how small they were. They would never fit Wynn. What were they doing in our room? Then it dawned on me: Wynn had purchased them, not for himself but for me—*for me* to wear on my hike up the mountain! Not just the unsightly pants, but the mannish boots as well. How could he even have considered being seen with a woman in such outlandish attire?

I was stroking so hard with the hairbrush that I winced with the pain of it. I couldn't imagine a man even thinking such a ridiculous thing. Well, my skirt and shoes would be just fine. I wouldn't be caught traipsing around on my honeymoon looking so utterly unkempt and ridiculous.

Someone had to break the silence of the room.

"What time do we leave?" I asked innocently. We had already established a time, but I had to say something.

"Where?" said Wynn, lowering his paper.

"Up the mountain," I replied with some impatience.

Wynn was slow in answering. "Elizabeth, I'm afraid I'm

guilty of not fully explaining our trip up the mountain." He laid the paper aside and rose to his full height. I felt dwarfed beside him.

"Parts of the trail are very steep. It's tough climbing. One doesn't need ropes, but one does need to be very careful. A fall could mean serious injury."

"You told me that. I'll be careful. I promise."

"Coming back down, there are parts of the trail where it is wise to sit down and ease yourself down over some of the steeper spots."

He looked at me to be sure I was understanding what he was saying. I nodded that I understood.

"There are places so steep that you need to use the branches of the nearby trees and the handgrips of the rocks to help boost yourself up."

I remembered that Wynn had told me that before, as well. I nodded again.

"It's a long way up to the mountain lake. It's a long, hard climb."

"Just what are you trying to say, Wynn?" I demanded. "Do you think I don't have the endurance to make the climb?"

"No," he said evenly. "I think you could make it. We wouldn't need to hurry. I could help you whenever you needed it—if you needed it. It would be my pleasure."

I thought of our much-talked-about trip up the mountainside. I thought of Wynn's description of the beautiful mountain lake. I thought of sharing the sack lunch way up there in the isolation of the mountains. The thoughts stirred my emotions. I was more anxious than ever to go.

"So when should we leave?" I asked again.

Wynn took a deep breath and looked squarely at me. "I'm afraid we won't be going, Elizabeth."

My hand stopped midstroke. I stared at him incredulously. What was he doing? Punishing me for winning? But Wynn didn't seem the type to retaliate. Yet Mother had always said you don't know a person until you live with him. So this was Wynn? I couldn't believe it.

"Not going?" I finally choked out. "Why?"

"You can't climb a mountain in a dress, Elizabeth; and you have refused to wear the pants," he stated calmly and finally.

So I hadn't won. Wynn had agreed to the "no pants," but he hadn't agreed to the "no pants" *and* the mountain hike.

"That's silly," I almost hissed. "I've been in a dress all my life, and I've never been a casualty yet."

"You've never climbed a mountain yet," was his matter-of-fact response.

"And I guess I'm not about to now," I threw back at him. Even I was surprised at the intensity of my words.

"I'm sorry," was all he said. He turned and went back to his paper. I continued to briskly brush my hair. It didn't need it. I had brushed it quite enough already, but I didn't know what else to do with myself.

My thoughts whirled in a confused state. I had heard of first quarrels. I knew that Wynn was not one to be pushed around. But this was such a silly little thing to be fighting over. *Surely he doesn't expect me to give in and wear those ridiculous and unsightly pants!* No man who loved his wife would ask such a thing. I bristled even more. *Why, Mother would be ashamed to own me were she to see me in such an outfit!* Wynn understood nothing about women's dress and propriety.

Finally Wynn laid aside the paper. I knew he really hadn't been concentrating on it—just hiding behind it.

"You're angry with me, aren't you, Elizabeth?" His voice sounded so contrite that I prepared myself for his change of mind. I did not answer. I didn't yet trust my voice.

"Do you realize that we have been married for one whole day and we have already had a disagreement?" asked Wynn softly.

I still did not answer.

"I really wasn't prepared for this," stated Wynn. "Not yet, at any rate. I'm sorry, Elizabeth. I do love you—you know that. I love you very much and I do wish this hadn't happened." He spoke so sincerely that I laid aside the brush. Maybe he wasn't so stubborn after all. I was quite ready to make up and forgive and forget. Men didn't understand about women's concern for how they looked, that was all. Now that Wynn knew, there wouldn't be any future fusses on that score.

I crossed to him and put my arms around his neck. He pulled me down on his lap and held me close. I returned his kiss and ran my fingers through his thick, dark hair. I loved him. He was my husband and I loved him.

"I'm sorry," I whispered. "Truly I am. I acted like a spoiled child and I'm—I don't usually act so silly. I guess I was just terribly disappointed."

He kissed me again, holding me very close. I could scarcely breathe, but I didn't mind.

I traced the outline of his firm jaw with a finger. "What time would you like me to be ready?" I whispered.

"You won't be too embarrassed at being seen in men's pants?"

I started, then stood up, pushing away his arms.

"Wynn," I said firmly. "I am *not* wearing those pants!"

He stood up, too, and said just as firmly, "Elizabeth, if you are not wearing the pants, then we are not going up that mountain. Do I make myself clear? I will not take you over those dangerous trails, sweeping along a skirt behind you. You could fall and kill yourself. It's the pants, or not at all, Elizabeth. You decide."

I whirled from him. *How can he be so stubborn?* I couldn't believe the man.

"Then I guess we will have to find something else to do," I said defiantly. "I will not wear those pants. *Do I make myself clear?*" I stressed every one of the words. "I wouldn't be caught dead wearing those ugly men's pants or—those—those equally ugly heavy boots. Not even to climb a mountain on my honeymoon with the man I love."

I whirled again to leave him, but Wynn caught my arm.

"Don't fight dirty, Elizabeth," he said softly, but there was steel in his voice and a soft sadness, too.

The words jarred some sense into me. I couldn't believe how I was acting. This was not the way I had been raised. In our household, the man was always the one in charge; Mother had carefully schooled each one of her daughters to believe that was the right way for a Christian household to be run, and here I was—one day married—and fighting back like a bantam hen.

I bit my lip to stop its trembling and turned away from Wynn. He did not release me.

"We need to talk, Elizabeth," he said gently. "I don't think that either of us is quite ready for it now. I'm going to take a walk—get some air. I won't be long—and when I get back—if you are ready—" He left the sentence unfinished and let go of my arm. I heard the door close quietly behind him.

I really don't know how long Wynn was gone. I only know that I spent the time in tears and, finally, in prayer. Wynn was the head of the home—my home. Even though I did not agree with him, I still needed to submit to his authority if ours was to be a truly Christian home—a happy home. He had not been wrong. I had been wrong. Deep within myself I knew I would have been disappointed in Wynn if he had allowed me to be the victor when he felt so strongly about my safety. I needed to be able to lean on him, to know for sure that he was in charge. So then, why had I tried to take over? Why was mere fashion so important to me? I didn't know. I only know that by the time Wynn's footsteps sounded in the hall, I had worked it all out with prayer and tears of repentance.

I met him at the door. Considering my concern for how I looked, I must have looked a mess, but Wynn made no mention of it. He took me in his arms and began to kiss my tear-washed face. "I'm sorry," I sobbed. "I'm truly sorry. Not for hating pants—I don't expect that I'll ever like them, Wynn; but I'm sorry for getting angry with you for doing what you thought was right for me."

Wynn smoothed back my hair. "And I'm sorry, Elizabeth. Sorry to hurt you when I love you so. Sorry there isn't some other way I could show you that mountain lake. Sorry I had to insist on the pants if—"

"*Have* to insist," I corrected him.

He frowned slightly.

"Have to insist on the pants," I repeated. "I still want to see that lake, Wynn; and, if you will still take me, I'll wear the pants. Just pray that we won't meet anyone on the trail," I added quickly. "I wouldn't even want to meet a bear wearing those things."

Wynn looked surprised, then pleased, then amused. He hugged me closer and laughed. "Believe me, Elizabeth, if there was any other way—"

"It's all right," I assured him.

"I love you, Elizabeth. I love you. Trust me?"

I nodded my head up against his broad chest.

"There will be times, Elizabeth, when we won't agree about things. Times when I will need to make decisions in our future."

I knew that Wynn was thinking ahead to our life in the North.

"I might have to ask you to do things you will find difficult, things you can't understand or don't agree with. Do you understand that?"

I nodded again. I had just been through all that in my talk with my God.

"I love you, Elizabeth. I will try to never make decisions to satisfy my ego or to show my manly authority, but I must do what I think is right for you—to care for you and protect you. Can you understand that?"

I searched his face and nodded again.

"This time—the pants—it would be too dangerous on the trail in a skirt. I know the trail, Elizabeth. I would never expose you to the possibilities of a bad fall. I—"

I stopped him then by laying a finger gently on his lips. "It's all right. I understand now. I'm glad you love me enough to fight my foolish pride. I mean it, Wynn. Thanks for standing firm—for being strong. I needed that. I'm ready to let you be the head of the home. And I want you to remind me of that as often as necessary—until I really learn it well."

I had tears in my eyes. But then, so did Wynn. I reached up to brush one of them from his cheek. "I love you, Mrs. Delaney," he whispered.

"And I love you, Mr. Delaney," I countered.

His arms tightened about me. "I'm truly sorry this happened," he said.

I looked at him, deep into his eyes. "I'm not," I said slowly, sincerely. "I'm ready now—ready to be your real wife. Ready to go with you to the North—to the ends of the earth if need be. I need you, Wynn. I need you and love you."

Chapter Eight

Mountain Lake

We were up early the next morning. We had a quick breakfast and then went to prepare ourselves for the trip up the mountain. Wynn had gone to the kitchen to pick up our lunch, which he put in a backpack along with a good supply of water. I dressed while he was gone, not wanting even my husband to see me in the ugly pants.

I wasn't going to look at myself in the mirror. I didn't want to know what I looked like. I walked to the dresser to pick up a scarf and accidentally got a full look at myself. Later I was glad I did. The sight stopped me short and resulted in my doubling over with laughter. Wynn found me like this. He wasn't sure at first if I was really amused or just hysterical.

"Look at me!" I howled. "I look like an unsightly bag of lumpy potatoes." When Wynn discovered that I really was amused at how I looked, he laughed with me. The bulky pants bagged out at unlikely points, hiding my waist and any hint of a feminine shape. I had looped a belt around my waist and gathered the pants as tightly about myself as I could. This only made them bulge more.

"They are a bit big," Wynn confessed. "I guess I should have asked you about the size."

"I wouldn't have been able to tell you anyway, never having worn pants before. Oh, well, they'll do."

I stopped to roll up the legs and exposed the awkward boots on my feet.

"Are you about ready?" asked Wynn when we both stopped

laughing at the spectacle I made.

"Ready," I answered, standing to my full height and saluting. We laughed again and headed for the door.

Wynn was kind enough to take me out the back way to avoid meeting other hotel guests. We circled around and followed the path to the mountain trail and began our long climb upward. We hadn't gone far when I realized what Wynn had meant. I had to grab for branches and roots in order to pull myself upward. Time after time, Wynn reached to assist me. We climbed slowly with frequent rests. I knew Wynn was setting an easy pace for me and I appreciated it. Every now and then, I would stop to gaze back over the trail we had just climbed. It was incredibly steep. I could catch a glimpse of one valley or another through the thickness of the trees. I could hardly wait to be above the timberline to view the lonely world beneath us.

By noon we had reached our goal. Sheer rock stretched up and up beyond us. Below us lay the valley with the little town of Banff nestled safely within its arms. It truly took my breath away. Here and there I could see the winding path we had just climbed, as it twisted in and out of the undergrowth beneath us.

"It's breathtaking," I whispered, still panting slightly from the climb. "Oh, Wynn, I'm so glad we came."

Wynn stepped over to wrap an arm securely about me. "Me, too," was all he said.

We found a place to have our lunch. By then I was ravenous. Wynn tossed his coat onto a slice of rock and motioned for me to be seated. I did, drinking in the sight before me.

"Where's the lake?" I asked him.

"See that ragged outcropping of rock there?" he pointed. I nodded.

"It's just on the other side of that."

"Does it take long to get there?"

"Only about half an hour."

"Let's hurry," I prompted.

Wynn laughed at my impatience. "We have lots of time," he assured me. "It's faster going down than coming up."

He took my hand and we bowed together to thank God for the food provided. Wynn's prayer also included thanks for the sight that stretched out before us and our opportunity to share it together. I tightened my grip on his hand, thinking back on how close we had come to not making the climb. I looked down at the funny pants I was wearing. They no longer shocked me. They only brought a bubble of laughter.

We were almost finished with our lunch when we heard voices. Another group had also made the climb. They were getting very close, and I was looking about for a place to hide. I recognized one of the voices. It belonged to a very fashionable lady I had seen in the hotel lobby the day before. Oh, my goodness! Whatever would she think of me when she spied me in the insufferable pants? I could see no place to shield myself, and then I braced myself and began to chuckle. So what! I'd likely never see the woman again in my life. The pants had provided me with a very pleasant day with my new husband. They were nothing that I needed to be ashamed of. I took another bite of sandwich and flashed Wynn a grin. He had been watching me to see which way I would choose to run.

A man appeared. He was tall and dark, with very thin shoulders and a sallow face. He looked like he was more used to trolley cars and taxis than his own legs, and I wondered how he had managed to make the climb. He did seem to be enjoying it and turned to give his hand to the person who followed him. I was right. It was the attractive young woman. I wondered how she had managed to climb a mountain with her hair so perfectly in place. Her body came slowly up over the sharp rise and into view. I gasped. She, too, was dressed in ugly men's pants. Wynn and I looked at one another, trying hard to smother our laughter.

At that moment, she spotted us and called out from where she was hoisting herself up, "Isn't it absolutely glorious?" She had an accent of some kind. I couldn't place it at the moment. Around my bit of sandwich, I called back, "Yes, isn't it?"

They came over to where we were seated and flopped down on the rock perch beside us, both breathing heavily.

"I've never done anything like this before in my life," said the young man.

"I had a hard time talking him into it at first," informed the woman to my surprise.

"You've done it before?" I asked her.

"With my father—many times. He loved to climb." She looked perfectly at home in her pants and stretched out her legs to rest them from the climb.

"This your first time?" she asked me, sensing that it must be.

"For me it is," I answered. "My husband has been here before."

She gave Wynn a fleeting smile. "Once you've been," she stated simply, "you want to come back and back and back. Me, I never tire of it."

"It's a sight all right," Wynn agreed.

I suddenly remembered my manners. I looked at our packed lunch. There were still some sandwiches left. "Here," I said, passing the package to them. "Won't you join us?"

"We brought our own," she quickly responded, and he lifted the pack from his back. "We just needed to catch our breath a bit."

We sat together enjoying the view and our lunch. We learned that they, too, were honeymooners. From Boston. She had pleaded for a mountain honeymoon and he had consented, rather reluctantly, he admitted; but he was so thankful now that he had. He was an accountant with a business firm, and she was the pampered daughter of a wealthy lawyer. Her father was now deceased and she was anxious to have another climbing mate. Her new husband hardly looked hardy enough to fill the bill, but he seemed to have more pluck than one would imagine. They were planning to take on another mountain or two before returning to Boston.

After chatting for some time, Wynn stated that we'd best be going if we wanted to see the lake before returning, and the young woman agreed. It was a steep climb back down the mountain, she stated, one that must be taken in good light.

We went on, bidding them farewell and wishing them the best in their new marriage, which they returned. I got to my feet, unembarrassed by my men's pants. If a wealthy girl from Boston could appear so clad, then I supposed that a fashion-conscious gal from Toronto could do likewise.

The trail around the mountain to the little lake was actually perilous in spots. I wondered how in the world any woman would ever have been able to make it in a skirt. She wouldn't. It was just that simple. I was glad for my unattractive pants that gave me easy movement. I was also glad for Wynn's hand which often supported me.

The lake was truly worth the trip. The blue was as deep as the cloudless sky above us, and the surface of the lake was as smooth as glass. It looked as though one should surely be able to step out and walk on it, so unrippled it was. Yet, when we got close and I leaned over carefully to get a good look into its depths, I was astonished to discover just how deep it was. Because of the clearness of the water, one could see every rock and every shadow. I stood up and carefully stepped back, feeling a bit dizzy with it all.

We did not linger long. The climb back down the mountain was a long one, so we knew we had to get on the trail. We met the other young couple. They still talked excitedly as they walked carefully over the sharp rocks and slippery places. I expected that their future would hold many such climbs. In a way, I envied them. The North held no such mountains—at least not in the place where Wynn had been presently stationed. Wynn had said the mountains did stretch way up to the north country as well; but they were for the most part uninhabited, so very few men were assigned to serve there. I was sorry for that. I would have liked to live in the mountains.

We felt our way slowly back down the trail. In a way, I found the climb down more difficult than the climb up had been. It seemed that one was forever having to put on the brakes, and it wasn't always easy to be sure just where one's brakes were. On more than one occasion, I started sliding forward much faster than I intended to. Wynn was right. One did need to sit down and attempt to ease down the steepest parts in a most undecorous fashion. *What if Mother could see me now?* I thought unruefully. I grasped for roots, branches, rocks—anything I could get my hands on to slow my descent. By the end of the day, my hands were scratched in spite of borrowing Wynn's leather gloves for the worst places; my men's pants were a sorry mess of mountain earth and forest clutter; and my hair was completely disheveled.

However, I still wore a happy smile. It had been some day, a memory I would always treasure.

We stopped at a gushing mountain stream. I knelt down and bent forward for a drink of the cold, clear water. It had come directly from an avalanche above, Wynn informed me; and I was willing to believe him. The water was so cold it made my fingers tingle and hurt my teeth as I drank it. We didn't really need the drink. Our backpack still held water we had carried with us, but Wynn felt that to make the day complete I must taste the mountain water. I agreed. I wiped the drips from my face and shook my hands free of the coldness and told Wynn how good it tasted. Wynn drank, too, as a reminder to himself that he had been right. No other water on earth tastes quite like that of a mountain stream.

Chapter Nine

Back to Calgary

The next day I ached all over. I wouldn't have believed that one had so many body parts to hurt. Wynn suggested a soak in a hot tub. It helped some, as long as I stayed there and sat very still. The minute I moved, I hurt again.

"I had no idea I had so many muscles," I complained.

Wynn offered to give me a rubdown, and I accepted it.

"I wonder how *he* feels," I mumbled into my pillow, as Wynn worked at sore muscles in my back.

"He? He who?"

"Her husband. That young couple yesterday. He didn't look exactly like he was built for climbing mountains."

Wynn chuckled at my comment. "Guess he didn't," he agreed.

"Come to think of it," I went on, "I wouldn't have picked her out as a climber either."

"Well," Wynn said seriously, "when I first saw a certain, beautiful young schoolteacher I know, I wouldn't have picked her out as a climber either."

I laughed in spite of my aches, and then I made a decision. "That's enough," I said to Wynn. "We have only one more day here in the mountains and I want to see as much as I can. Maybe my muscles will ease up some as I walk. Where can we go today?"

"You're sure?" Wynn asked, a bit doubtful.

"Positive," I answered.

"Climbing or walking?" asked Wynn.

"Just walking. Those old pants aren't fit to be worn anywhere till they are washed."

"Do you have proper shoes?" inquired my practical husband.

I pointed to the pair I had chosen for the day before. Wynn shook his head.

"Not good enough," he stated, and this time I didn't even argue.

"Okay," I said, "I'll wear the boots." I went for them, hoping with all my heart that my long skirt would hide them.

It almost did. I smiled to myself and announced to Wynn that I was ready to go.

We wasted no time. In the morning we went to Bow Falls. They were not high falls but were nevertheless lovely to watch. The water ran wildly between two uprisings of mountain rock which confined it on either side. As it pounded and boiled down the drop of several feet, the water turned from clear, bright translucent to a foaming milky white. One could hear the roar long before rounding the turn where one could look upstream and view the spectacle. It nearly took my breath away. I would have sat and watched the falls, mesmerized for the rest of the morning, had not Wynn roused me. "I hate to prod, but if we are going to fit in the Cave and Basin, we must be going. It's rather a long walk."

It *was* a long walk, and already my feet were tired from lifting the heavy boots step by step; so, as soon as we reached the area where public transportation was available, I agreed it would be wise to ride rather than try to hike all the way.

The guide at the Cave and Basin was a jolly Scot who seemed to be having the time of his life escorting visitors through what he treated as his private domain. When he saw Wynn, his face spread with a grin.

"Aye, an' how be ya, Delaney?" he cried, wringing Wynn's hand vigorously.

He didn't allow Wynn a chance for an answer. "An' shur now," he went on, "an' don't be a-tellin' me thet ye've found yerself a lass—an' a bonnie one she's bein'."

Wynn proudly introduced me. I hoped with all my heart that the jovial man would not look down and see my mannish boots peeking out from under my sweeping skirt. He didn't look down. Instead, he grabbed a lantern and hurried us off on our tour of *his* Cave and Basin.

"A sight like this ye'll never be seein', not anywhere in this world," he informed me, rolling his r's delightfully.

I shivered some as we followed the man into the cave and along rocky uneven steps to deep within the earth. It got cooler and more mysterious as we advanced; and the old man talked in a spooky, confiding tone, pointing out strange shapes and shadows as he whispered eerie suspicions about what they might have been in some long ago yesteryear. I shivered more noticeably now, and Wynn reached to place a protective arm around me. "Don't pay any attention to his stories," he whispered in my ear. "He makes them up as he goes along."

"An' look there now," went on the Scot, leaning close and lowering his voice as though someone from the dead past might hear him and take offense. "See there by yonder wall— that there mysterious shape." His finger pointed it out, and the lantern swung back and forth, making the strange shadows dance.

"Right there," the man leaned even closer to me to make sure that my eyes were following his pointing finger. "Thet there is a skeleton. Thet of an Indian warrior caught here in the cave. He must have been wounded in battle—or else waitin' out a thunderstorm—and somehow he got caught and held here an' never did leave." He paused. " 'Course, I just tell thet to the young lasses thet I don't want to spook none," he added confidentially. "What really happened, I'm a-wagerin', is thet he was murdered right here." The r's rolled round and round on his tongue.

I shivered again and we moved on, the lantern bobbing and shivering, too. Again and again, we had things pointed out to us and then we descended a ladder to an underground pool steaming with heat.

"Kneel down careful like and put yer hand in."

I wasn't very brave and clung to Wynn's hand as I knelt to feel the water. It was, indeed, nice and warm.

"What heats it?" I asked in surprise.

"Aye," laughed the Scotsman. "Only the good Lord knows. He keeps a few secrets of His own. I'm a-guessin' we'll never know unless He decides to be tellin'."

We retraced our steps. I was looking forward to being back out in the warm sun again, though I wouldn't have missed the experience for anything. I was unprepared for the brightness as I stepped out from the cave. My eyes protested and I closed them tightly and turned away in the opposite direction so I might open them at my own choosing.

My eyes soon adjusted and I was able to turn back to the cheery guide with a smile of approval for his Cave and Basin. He seemed to feel it was very important that we had enjoyed our venture. I put out my hand.

"Thank you so much," I said, meaning every word of it. "I enjoyed that ever so much."

His eyes twinkled. He took the proffered hand and shook it heartily and then turned to Wynn.

"I always wondered why ye kept on a-waitin' and a-waitin' instead of takin' ye a wife, an' now I know. Ye were just a-waitin' fer the finest thet there be."

Wynn grinned.

"Well, the best to ye both now," said the Scot, and he gave Wynn a hearty slap on the back and turned to care for more of his tourists.

We were almost back to Calgary when my honeymoon reverie was broken and my thoughts went instead to all that needed to be done in one short day. I stirred rather uncomfortably and Wynn sensed my restlessness.

"Something wrong?" he asked, very sensitive to my changing moods.

"I was just thinking of all that needs to be done tomorrow," I admitted.

"It shouldn't be too bad," he tried to assure me. "Your trunk is all ready to go and most of the other things are all packed and waiting. There will just be a few last-minute things to be gathered together."

"But all those wedding gifts?"

"Julie and Mary volunteered, didn't I tell you?"

"I don't recall—"

"I'm sorry. I meant to tell you, so your mind would be at ease."

"That's fine," I said, feeling better about it. "I do hope they are careful and use lots of packing. Some of those porcelain things are very delicate."

"Packing?" echoed Wynn. "They won't need much packing. Mary has volunteered to store them in her attic. They will be careful, I'm sure."

"Store them?"

Now it was Wynn's turn to show surprise. "Elizabeth, you weren't thinking we would be taking all these things with us, were you?"

"Well—yes—I—"

"We couldn't possibly. The Police Force allows so many pounds of baggage per person. We have already stretched our limit. Besides, such things would serve no purpose—have no function—in the North."

For a moment I wanted to argue. Their function would be to make a home—to make me feel more like a homemaker. Wasn't that function enough? I didn't argue though. I remembered well my prayer of three days before and my promise to my God to let Wynn be the head of the household. I waited for a moment until I was sure I had complete control and then I looked at Wynn and gave him one of my nicest smiles.

"I guess that is all taken care of then."

Wynn put an arm around me and drew me close, even though we were on a crowded train.

"Thank you, Elizabeth," he whispered against my hair, and I knew I had gained far more than I had lost in the exchange.

As expected, the next day was a busy one. My family was still with Jon and Mary. They would be staying for a few more days before heading back east. I was glad I still had this one brief day with them before I would be heading north.

However, there would be no more late-night chats with my sister Julie. Her things had been moved from the room I had used for so long at Jon's, and the room was now set up for Wynn's and my use. It seemed rather strange at first, but I quickly got used to the idea. Already, I didn't know how I had ever managed without Wynn, and I had been a married woman only four short days.

Wynn was gone a good share of the day, running here and there making final preparations. He had an appointment at the Royal North West Police Headquarters for last-minute instructions and took our last trunks and crates down to be weighed and checked in. We would be starting our journey by train, then switching to boat, and ending by ox cart or wagon. Had it been the winter months, we would have also used dog teams.

We did not retire early. There was no need to conserve our energy. We had all the next day to sleep on the train if we wished. It seemed far more important now to sit and chat with the family. Reluctantly, we finally went to bed.

I climbed the stairs to my room for one last time. Who knew when I might sleep here again? I had grown to love this room. I had always felt welcomed and loved in Jon's home. I would miss it. I would miss them. I would miss each one of the children. They might be nearly grown before I saw them again. And what of my dear mother and father? Would they still be in their Toronto home when I returned from the north country? What about Julie? Would she marry while I was gone? And Matthew? He would be a man.

I did not dread my future with Wynn in his North. The only thing that bothered me was that I would miss so much of what went on here. If only I could freeze everything in place until I came back again so I wouldn't need to miss so much. But that was impossible. One could only be at one place at one time. The world in Toronto and here in Calgary would continue to go on without Elizabeth Delaney, and I must accept the fact.

I felt a bit teary inside as I turned my face into my pillow. For a moment, I was afraid I was going to cry; and then Wynn reached for me and rubbed his cheek against mine.

"Are you ready for adventure, Elizabeth?" he whispered to me, and I could detect excitement in his voice.

"Um-hum," I murmured, reaching up my hand to feel the strength of his jawline. I smiled into the darkness, and Wynn could feel the pull of my facial muscles as they formed the smile. He kissed me on the temple.

"I've never been so excited about heading north, Elizabeth," he confided. "Always before, I've known how much I was really leaving behind. This time I can only think of what I am taking with me."

I stirred in his arms.

"I hope I never disappoint you, Wynn."

"I'm not worried about that." His voice was very serious now. "I only hope and pray that you are never disappointed. The North can be cruel, Elizabeth. It's beautiful, but it can be cruel, too. The people—they are simple, needy people—like children in many ways. I guess it's the people who draw me there. I love them in some mysterious way. They trust you, lean on you, so simply, so completely. You sort of feel you have to be worthy of their trust."

"And I'm sure you are."

"I don't know. It seems as if I've never been able to do enough. What they really need are doctors, schools, and most of all missions. Missions where they can really learn the truth about God and His plan for man. They have it all so mixed up in their thinking."

A new desire stirred within me, a desire not just to teach Wynn's people how to read and write, but how to find and worship God as well. Funny. I had never met them—not any of them—yet I felt as if I already loved them.

Chapter Ten

The Journey Begins

After a teary last farewell, we were on our way. I felt sad and excited all at the same time. I couldn't really understand or sort out what was going on inside of me. Wynn sensed my feeling and allowed me some quiet thoughts. On occasion he did point out things of interest, but he didn't push me for enthusiasm. The first several miles of the trip I had seen many times, as it took us through Red Deer and Lacombe. As the train stopped in Lacombe, I looked closely for someone on the street whom I might know; I was about to conclude that there was no one when Phillip, Lydia, and young Phillip—Wynn's brother, sister-in-law, and nephew—came aboard, ushering Wynn's mother down the aisle.

"The conductor says they will be here for a few minutes, so he will give us warning when they are about to leave," Phillip informed us.

We soon became busily engaged in conversation, catching up on all of the area news. It was no time until the conductor came to tell us that the train would be ready to leave again in about five minutes. We hated to see them go but were so glad for the time we were able to spend together. It was the first I had been able to call Mrs. Delaney, Sr., *Mother,* and I took pleasure in doing so.

"God bless you, Elizabeth," she said. "It isn't as hard for me to let Wynn go this time, knowing he will be well looked after. You take care, though. From what Wynn has said in the past, the North can be a lonely place for a woman."

I tried to assure Mother Delaney that I would be fine and

was quite prepared for all that lay ahead. I wasn't quite as sure of myself as I tried to sound. With every mile of the whirling train wheels, my stomach tied into a little tighter knot. Had it not been for Wynn beside me, I'm sure I would have panicked and bolted long before we had reached even Lacombe.

I tried to concentrate on the small settlements through which we passed. It was not easy. My mind was on other things. Even when Wynn spoke cheerily, pointing out this or that, I still couldn't get enthused—though I did try.

I finally decided I must be tired and what I needed was sleep, so I curled up beside Wynn with my head against his shoulder and tried to do just that. It didn't work. My mind was far too busy. Sleep would not come. I heard soft breathing coming from my husband and realized he had been success-ful. I was glad for him. He was even more tired than I, I was sure. I hoped he would rest well. I tried to sit very still so as not to disturb him. *I* might have been still, but the train was not. We made another jerky stop and then, with a hiss and a chug, we began shifting this way and that in an effort to disengage some of the cars.

Wynn quickly awoke and stirred slightly. I knew by the way he moved that he was afraid of waking me, so I sat up and smiled at him.

"It's all right," I assured him. "I'm already awake."

"Did you get any rest?" he inquired, concern in his voice.

"Rest, yes. Sleep, no," I answered.

"I'm sorry. Guess I dozed off there for a while."

"Not for long," I informed him. "You might have if the train didn't keep stopping at every little house and teepee."

Wynn chuckled. "That's the way it seems, doesn't it? Well, it isn't too much farther to Edmonton now."

"What happens at Edmonton?"

"We spend the night. I have a short meeting in the morn-ing with some officials before we move on. You can sleep late if you like."

"When do we leave?"

"Not until about eleven."

"When do I need to be up?"

"I wouldn't think until about nine—unless you want to see a bit of the city."

"I think I'll pass," I said, smiling tiredly. "Even nine sounds way too early."

When I awoke the next morning, Wynn, as promised, had left me sleeping. I looked at the clock on the wall. It was already after nine, so I climbed quickly from my bed. I would need to hurry if I was to be ready when Wynn came back for me.

I had just finished doing my hair when Wynn's key turned in the lock.

"You're up," he greeted me. "I was afraid you might oversleep."

"I did. A little," I admitted. "I really had to hurry to make up for lost time."

"I don't think your sleeping time was lost time," he assured me. "You needed that."

He crossed to kiss me. "You look more rested," he stated. "How do you feel?"

I smiled. "Fine," I returned, trying to hide any anxiety I might feel. "Ready to start the trip to your wilderness."

He gave me a big bear hug. "Then let's get going," he said. "You still need some breakfast before we start out."

We continued our trip by river barge, a new experience for me. At first I was rather apprehensive. The day was cloudy and overcast and I didn't feel too safe on the free-floating contraption. It was guided along the river with only the help of long poles held in the hands of the men in our crew.

Wynn said that in the earlier days we would have been able to make the same trip on the North Saskatchewan in the comfort of a sternwheeler cabin, but with the advent of the railroads the boats had lost business and had been retired. There was no railroad to take us where we wanted to go, and so now we traveled on the flat barge, allowing the river to carry us along as it flowed northeast. The men who owned and operated the boat did not believe in wasting fuel on the downriver trip. Coming back up-river, they would put a simple motor to work.

The sky looked like it might pour down rain. I wasn't sure how this odd boat would function if the waters started coming down from above. Would it still stay afloat?

The seats provided weren't all that comfortable, and I

soon was aching for a chance to stand up and walk around a bit. There didn't seem to be any opportunity, as nearly every square foot of the barge was piled high with something. I couldn't believe the amount of cargo it had heaped within its bulging sides. I looked around for our trunks and crates and almost panicked when I didn't see them. Wynn must have read my thoughts.

"They're over there under the canvas," he stated simply, putting my mind at ease.

"Want to stretch?" he asked after many minutes had passed by.

"I'd love to," I responded quickly, "but where?"

"Come," he said, holding out a hand to me. "I think we can manage a few minutes of it."

It was difficult. We had to step over things, around things, duck under things, and hang on for dear life. The wind was up, and at times the river was rough. I tied my scarf more tightly under my chin and told Wynn that I would be fine for the time being. We returned to our uncomfortable seats.

In the early afternoon the rains came. There wasn't any place to go to avoid them. Wynn found some kind of slicker and wrapped it tightly around me. The wind kept whipping and tearing at it, making it difficult to keep all sides of me under it at any given moment. I could feel patches of wet spots grow bigger and bigger. I tried not to think about them, but it wasn't easy. The rainwater was cold and the increasing wind made it even colder. In a few hours' time, I was really miserable but I tried hard not to show it.

Wynn kept fussing over me—shifting the makeshift shelter this way and that, tightening it here, and tucking it in there. In the meantime, he, too, was getting wet. Those operating the barge seemed to take the storm for granted. They had likely been wet many times before while making this run.

As the day passed, the sky was getting darker and the rains heavier. I wondered if we would travel all night long. How far would we go on this river anyway? I had heard the word *Athabasca*, but I didn't think that was our destination.

Wynn came to tell me, "We're going to pull in early tonight. We'll try to dry out a bit. There's a little trading post ahead where we can take shelter. We should have gone farther tonight, but we'll wait for morning."

I shivered and nodded my head thankfully. It was good news to me.

It wasn't long until the shouting and straining of the barge crew told me that we were going ashore. There was a jolt and a thump as we hit some kind of dock in the darkness. Then Wynn was there to help me to solid ground. The wind and rain loosened my scarf, and soon my hair was tumbling crazily about my face. I tried to tuck it back again but I really didn't have a free hand. I gave up and decided to just let it blow.

We headed for a dark shape in the gathering gloom. Then I spotted a light in a misty window. Though faint, the light did signal humanity; and I breathed a prayer of thankfulness as I tried, with Wynn's help, to hurry toward it.

The smell of wood smoke reached my nose, and I thought of the wonderful warmth that would go with it. I hurried faster. In my eagerness to get to the house, I did not see the tree stump in my pathway.

"Watch out!" Wynn cried when he saw what was about to happen, but it was too late. I banged my shin hard against the tough wood, and let out a sharp little cry at the stinging pain.

Wynn kept me from falling, but from there to the house I stumbled along, limping painfully. Wynn asked to carry me but I stubbornly shook my head.

When we reached what I had thought to be a house and stumbled through the door, I was disappointed to see that it was no house at all. It was a shed—a shed for trade. Boxes and crates and heaps and piles were stacked all around the single room in a haphazard fashion. One dim lamp sat upon a makeshift counter, throwing out an anemic light. The single window was so stained and dirty I wondered how I had been able to see the light from outside at all.

In the corner of the room was what looked like a stack of furs. Upon closer observation, I discovered that it was, instead, a bed—of sorts. I shuddered to think of sleeping there.

"Howdy," a voice said, and I whirled to see an ill-kempt man sitting beside the potbellied stove in the middle of the crowded room. He let fly with a line of dark spit that missed an open can, spattering against the side of the stove, causing a sizzling sound. He had not risen to meet us and he did not move now.

Wynn jerked his head at the man. "Howdy, Charlie," he said. "Mind if we borrow your chair for a minute? My wife just gave her leg an awful whack on that tree stump you've got out front."

It was the room's only chair, and Charlie rose reluctantly with a grunt of disgust.

Wynn sat me down and lifted my skirt to get a good look at my injury.

"Bring your lamp, would you, Charlie?"

From the tone of Wynn's voice, I knew that, though it was Charlie's lodging, Wynn was in charge here. Everyone knew it.

Charlie brought the lamp. My leg was bleeding, seeping through my torn stocking, making a sticky dark patch.

"You've got to get out of those stockings," Wynn said to me.

I looked helplessly about the room. There was no place to go.

"But I can't," I insisted, casting a nervous glance at Charlie.

"Turn your back, Charlie," Wynn ordered, and the grumbling Charlie obeyed. The light of the lamp turned with him. I felt a bit more comfortable in the semi-darkness and hastened to raise my skirt and unfasten the garters that held up my ruined stocking. I slipped it down as quickly as I could and let my skirt drop back in place. Charlie shifted from one foot to the other and spit again. I don't know where that one landed. Weakly I sat back down.

"Okay," said Wynn, "let's have the lamp, Charlie."

Charlie turned around. For one awful moment, I feared he might spit in my direction. He didn't. He stood holding the lamp nervously, trying not to look at the leg that Wynn was studying.

"I don't think it's too deep," Wynn was saying. "Nothing broken that—"

"Except my stocking," I interrupted. Wynn's eyebrows went up.

"Legs heal," I said, to inform him. "Stockings don't—and I was able to bring only a limited number with me."

In spite of himself, Wynn smiled but made no reply.

"Charlie, do you have any first-aid supplies around here?" he asked.

Charlie grumbled and then muttered, "A few things."

"Set the lamp down and get them, please," said Wynn. "I don't want to have to unload the barge to get at my supply."

Wynn stood up to check the kettle sitting on the stove. It held water and that seemed to please him.

While Wynn cleansed and bandaged my swelling leg, the other men entered. Apparently they were satisfied that they had secured the barge against the storm, and now wanted to be in where it was warm and dry.

They greeted Charlie boisterously. In return, he greeted them with an oath, a spit, and a slap on the back.

I felt very much out of place. It was apparent that these men didn't spend much time in the presence of a lady. They joked and swore and jabbed at one another with harmless fists. One man soon produced a rum bottle, which they seemed to think was just the thing needed to take the chill out of their bones.

Wynn took charge because no one else seemed to have any mind to do so. He put on the coffeepot and asked Charlie for some tins of food for an evening meal. Charlie seemed reluctant to share until Wynn reminded him that he would be paid for anything that the Police Force used. Charlie then produced a couple of tins, and Wynn set about making some supper.

I offered to help him but he declined my offer. "I think you should rest that leg all you can. Here, let me help you."

Before I knew what had happened, Wynn lifted me from my spot on the chair by the stove to the pile of foul-smelling skins in the corner. I wanted to protest but the words caught in my throat.

"I'm sorry, Elizabeth," whispered Wynn, "but I guess this will be your bed for tonight."

I closed my mouth against the protest and the odor that came from the pile of furs as Wynn settled me gently on the bed.

"You mean this is all there is here?" I asked incredulously.

"This is it," answered Wynn.

"But what about you—and them?"

"We'll stay here, too. At least it's dry, and the fire will have our clothes dried out by morning."

I looked quickly at the tiny, crowded, overstocked room. Suddenly it seemed terribly stuffy and suffocating. I wished for the out-of-doors so I could breathe freely again. But when I heard the howl of the wind and the lashing of the rain, I closed my eyes and tried to be thankful for the warmth of the smelly little cabin. Wynn patted my shoulder in sympathy.

When supper was ready, a makeshift arrangement of a table was dragged up close to the stove. Wynn came to help me to it. I told him I really wasn't hungry and would gladly settle for just a hot cup of tea or coffee. He realized then that I was still in my wet clothes and shivering with the cold.

"I'm sorry, Elizabeth," he said. "I was so anxious to get some hot food in you that I forgot about your wet things. I didn't realize you got as wet as you did. I guess the slicker didn't keep out much of the rain, eh?"

"Oh, it did," I insisted bravely, comparing his soaked appearance to mine. "I only have a spot here and there, that's all."

Wynn reached out to feel my clothing. "You're wet," he argued, "through and through. We'll get you out of them as soon as you get some hot soup down you."

I wanted to protest further, but Wynn would have none of it. I allowed myself to be helped to the chair, and Wynn poured me a cup of the soup he had made. I sipped it slowly. It wasn't the best meal I had ever eaten, but it was hot, even tasty in a "canned" sort of way. My clothing on the side closest to the stove began to steam. I shifted around some to direct the heat on another section. I didn't really warm up, although a few spots of me were actually hot. It was a strange sensation to feel so hot in places and yet chilled at the same time. I finished my cup of soup and motioned to Wynn that I was ready to return to the heap called a bed.

"Got a couple of blankets, Charlie?"

Charlie lumbered up from the barrel on which he was sitting and spit at the stove as he reached up to a shelf.

"Hudson's Bay," he grumbled. "Hardly used."

"They'll still be hardly used come morning," Wynn answered, not to be intimidated by Charlie's growling. Wynn moved to where he could screen me from view with the blanket. "Now," he said, "get out of those wet things."

I looked at him, wondering if he really meant what he said. The room was full of men.

He meant it. I shrugged, unfastened my wet skirt and let it fall. I then removed my shirt and my petticoats, casting apprehensive glances at the blanket Wynn held for me.

I could tell by the noises on the other side of the makeshift wall that the four men were now enjoying Wynn's supper soup. There were slurps and smacking, and I was glad I wouldn't need to see as well as hear them eat. I wondered if Charlie could eat and chew tobacco at the same time, or if he actually disposed of his wad while he was dining.

"Now climb up there and lie down," Wynn spoke softly, "and I'll tuck you in."

He did as promised, using both of the blankets Charlie had provided. I lay there shivering. Wynn went back to the stove, took the cup I had used, and poured soup for himself. He then got a cup of coffee and came back to my bed. "Are you warming any?" I thought I was, though my teeth hadn't really stopped chattering.

Now that Wynn no longer claimed the stove for his meal preparation and I no longer occupied the one chair in the room, the men moved in closer to the heat. Their clothing began to steam and smell, not improving the odor in the room. I was glad I had already eaten. I couldn't have swallowed with that strong, offensive smell in the room.

I tried to move over to give Wynn room to sit down on the bed beside me, but this was truly a one-man bed. Wynn crouched beside me and sipped his coffee. I could see the clothes hugging tightly to him.

"You're still wet," I stated. "You'll get sick."

"I'll dry soon. I'll be okay. Why don't you try to get some sleep?"

I wanted to retort, "Here?" But I knew that "here" was

the best he could offer, so I simply nodded.

Wynn moved back to the stove where the men were busy eating and joking.

"Hey, Sarge," quipped one of the boatmen. "Not bad soup for a lawman."

The other men joined in his guffaw at his tremendously funny joke. Wynn just nodded his head.

"Much obliged for your home and your bed tonight, Charlie," said Wynn sincerely.

Charlie looked over to the corner where I huddled. He had finished eating, so he was free to chew and spit again, which he now did. It landed on one of the boatmen's boots. The fellow did not even glance down.

"No problem," Charlie assured Wynn. "Me, I ain't aimin' on usin' the bed tonight nohow."

The other men laughed and I wondered why. I didn't need to wonder for long. The makeshift table was quickly cleared of the few cups and a pack of cards was produced.

"Ain't got nothin' 'gainst cards, have ya, Sarge?" asked the chubby boatman.

"Not as long as they're fair and don't cause any fights," answered Wynn.

"Then I guess thet this here's gotta be a fair game, gents," the man said to his comrades; and they all laughed uproariously again, slapping their thighs and one another's backs.

Crates or barrels served as seats, and a couple of bottles soon joined the cards on the table.

"You wantin' to join us, Sarge?" invited the little dark man with the French accent and long mustache.

Wynn shook his head.

The four men hunched over the table, and the long night began. There wasn't much place for Wynn to go. Attempting to dry out his wet clothes, he pulled a block of wood close to the stove and sat down, leaning against a pile of crates.

The lamp flickered now and then, and an unwashed hand would reach out to turn the wick up a bit. The jesting got louder and more coarse. Wynn reminded them a lady was present, and then for a few minutes it was quieter in the cabin. As the night progressed and the bottles were emptied, the commotion grew. Wynn eventually watched it without comment, seeming to pay little attention to the whole thing; but I knew he was well aware of every movement in the room.

From my bed in the corner, I watched too. I was no longer shivering—the scratchy Hudson's Bay blankets were doing their job well. I nearly dozed once or twice, and then laughter or a stream of obscenity would jerk me awake again.

Wynn rose from his place by the fire to check on me. When I saw him coming, I closed my eyes lightly. I knew it might be considered deceitful, but I did not want Wynn to worry about me. He already had enough on his mind. I did not fool him, however.

"Are you all right?" he asked softly.

I didn't answer immediately. The truth was, I felt very strange, very out of place, in the room with the cursing, gambling men. I had never been in such a situation before. It was the kind of thing I had avoided all my life. If it hadn't been for the presence of my husband, I would have been stiff with fright. I glanced quickly at the four men in the room. The big one was taking another long drink from the bottle; and the dark, little one was impatiently waiting his turn, hand outstretched. I looked quickly back to Wynn. Concern showed in his face.

"I'm fine," I managed weakly; but then I repeated it more firmly, willing myself to realize I spoke the truth. "I'm fine."

"Your leg?"

"It doesn't hurt too badly at all."

"Are you warm?"

I merely nodded my head for this one.

He knelt beside me and shifted my blankets some, tucking them in tightly around me. "I'm sorry, Elizabeth. I planned the trip so you would have better accommodations than this. If this storm—"

"It's all right," I hurried to assure him. "You're here—that's what matters."

He leaned over and kissed me, the love showing in his eyes, but the worried look did not leave his face. "Try to get some sleep," he whispered.

I smiled at him and he kissed me again, and then went back to his place by the stove.

It was getting very late and the men were still playing

cards, drinking, and cursing. Charlie rose from his crate and went to bring another bottle. When he placed it on the table, Wynn, hardly moving, stood slowly, leaned over and removed it. Four pairs of eyes turned to look at him.

"We've got a long trip ahead of us tomorrow. I want some sober barge-men. Charlie, you can drink if you want to. It's your liquor, but don't pass your bottle around."

There was authority in Wynn's voice; and, though there were some grumbles around the table, no one challenged him.

The card game went on, but it was clear that much of the "fun" had gone out of it.

At length, the men decided they'd had enough. They pushed back their makeshift seats, cleared a little space a few moments, it was blessedly silent. Then, one by one, they filled the room with a chorus of snores.

The snoring seemed even louder and more vulgar than the conversation had been. Resigned, I turned my face to the wall and tried to get some sleep in the little time that was left.

Once or twice I heard stirring as the fire in the stove was replenished. I knew without even looking that it was Wynn.

When morning came, I was still bone-weary. But at least the effort of trying to sleep was over. The rain was still falling, but the wind seemed to have died down. I was thankful for small mercies.

At my first stirring, Wynn was beside me.

"How do you feel, Elizabeth?" he whispered.

I ached all over, and my sore leg throbbed with each beat of my heart. I managed a faltering smile. "Okay," I answered. "Can you help me up?"

Wynn's strong arms helped me to my feet and shielded me with the blanket while I fumblingly got into my clothes. They were thoroughly dry now and felt much softer than the blankets had.

The men were still scattered around on the floor, sleeping off their binge of the night before.

"I need to go out, Wynn," I whispered. "Where do I go?"

Wynn nodded toward the one door.

"Anyplace in the woods," he answered me.

At my troubled look, he glanced back to the men. "Don't worry about any of them. They wouldn't wake up until next week if they were left alone. I'll watch them."

I was relieved but still apprehensive about the whole outdoors as a facility.

"Do you need help walking?" Wynn asked.

I tried my weight on my poor leg to be sure before I answered, "I'll be all right."

"Are you sure?"

I took an unsteady step. "I'll hang onto the cabin if I need support," I told him.

He helped me over to the door and opened it for me. Then he reached for his jacket. "Here," he said, "you'd better use this. It's still raining."

I wrapped the jacket tightly about me and stepped out into the misty morning. The nearby river was almost hidden by the fog that clung to it. Water from the trees dripped on the soggy ground beneath. Every step I took was in water. I was glad the wind was not blowing.

I took no longer out-of-doors than was necessary. Even then, by the time I hobbled back into the little, smelly, overcrowded cabin, my shoes were soaked through and the hem of my dress wet for several inches. I longed for the stove's warmth, but I hesitated to step over the sleeping men. Wynn helped me around them, and I took my place in the one chair and stretched my feet out toward the glow.

"Not very nice out there, is it?" Wynn commented.

"It's wet and cool, but the wind isn't blowing like yesterday."

Wynn seemed to approve of my healthy attitude. He gave me a smile and placed a hand on my shoulder as he handed me a cup of hot coffee.

"Now that you've seen the day, what do you think? Would you like to get back on the journey or wait out the storm here in the cabin?"

I looked at the four sodden men on the floor. The liquor from the night before mingled with the other smells. Snores still came forth from half-open mouths, sometimes catching in their throats in a rugged growl which snorted to a finish.

I glanced back at the makeshift bed in the corner. It was

so narrow one could scarcely turn over and so lumpy I wondered how Charlie ever managed to get any sleep at all.

"Where will we be tonight?"

"There's a small post downriver."

"Are there—are there—?" I hesitated to say "houses," for I wasn't sure if there were any *houses* as such in the North. "Are there accommodations there?" I finally managed.

"Quite comfortable," Wynn replied.

"Then I vote to move on," I said without hesitation.

Wynn smiled and moved forward to stir the sleeping barge captain.

The man didn't even open an eye, just shifted his position and started to snore again in a different key.

"Blackjack," Wynn called loudly. "Time to hit the trail!"

The man just stirred again. Wynn knelt beside him and shook his shoulder. "Time to get up. Get this crew of yours off the floor," Wynn commanded the man.

Blackjack scowled up at him as if about to argue the point, but Wynn would take no argument.

"You're being paid to get us to River's Bend, remember? If you want the pay, then deliver the goods."

The man cursed and propped himself on an elbow.

"Coffee's hot," Wynn prodded him. "Get some in you and let's get going."

It was rather amusing to watch the revelers of the night before. They didn't look so lively now. Grumbling, holding their heads and muttering oaths, they tried to get their bodies to obey.

Wynn had little sympathy. "Let's get moving," he ordered again. "The fog's about to lift, and we have some time to make up."

They were finally on their feet and stirring. Wynn poured each a cup of coffee, except for Charlie. In spite of the commotion all about him, Charlie had slept on, only stirring now and then to reposition himself.

"Finished with the bed, Elizabeth?" Wynn inquired. When I gladly nodded that I was, Wynn unceremoniously lifted Charlie up and carried him to his bed. Wynn straightened out the unconscious body to what looked like a comfortable position and threw a blanket over him. Charlie slept on.

Two of the men went out to prepare the barge for departure while the other fellow mumbled and complained about the lousy day for traveling.

Wynn looked at his pocketwatch.

"Gotta be out of here in ten minutes, Wally," he stated flatly. "Ten minutes, no more."

Wally, still grumbling, went to join the others.

Wynn left money on the shelf by the coffeepot to cover our expenses for the night's lodging and the food. Charlie was still snoring as we closed the door behind us.

Back in the boat with the slicker arranged around me, I discovered it was not raining hard. Without the wind, I was sure I would fare just fine.

In spite of the constant peppering with fine raindrops, I found myself enjoying the scenery on the riverbanks moving swiftly from view on either side. There was very little habitation, but occasionally I did spy the smoke of a woodstove and a cabin, half-hidden by the trees.

By midmorning the rain had stopped, the wind had died down to a light breeze, and early in the afternoon the sun actually came out. The slicker laid aside, I let the warm sun fall on my shoulders. We had not stopped except to eat a hurried noon meal consisting of a few tins of canned food heated over an open fire.

The country through which we passed was fresh and clean. No factory smells tainted the air with civilization. I appreciated the crispness of the air even more after having spent the night at Charlie's.

We passed through a marshy area, and Wynn moved close to me to point out two large moose. They put their heads completely under water for what seemed ever so long. When they finally lifted their heads, their mouths dripping with long marsh grass, they looked toward us almost with disdain, seeming to indicate that this was their territory and we were trespassers.

"Look at them," I said to Wynn in astonishment. "You'd think they didn't even have to breathe, they are under so long!"

"Oh, they breathe all right," Wynn assured me, "though they are unusual. They can even dive to get their food—some say as deep as thirty feet if need be. They scoop up the grasses on the bottom and then come back up again."

"Do they need to go back to land to eat it?"

"Oh, no. They just tread water. Moose are wonderful swimmers. Don't suppose there are many animals any better."

"Aren't they ugly, though? They look like—like leftover pieces of this and that."

Wynn laughed. "Well, there's a saying," he mused, "that a moose is a horse made by a committee."

We chuckled together at Wynn's joke.

Since the barge hands had started the day in bad spirits, I tried to stay as far away from them as I could. Now and then one of them would hold his head and weave back and forth. I wondered if they were in any condition to steer the barge, especially when we hit some white water; but they seemed to be alert enough when they had to be. Wynn did not seem worried, so I relaxed, too. Eventually their dispositions improved. In the later afternoon, I even heard Blackjack singing.

With the passing of the day, I guess my disposition improved as well. Wynn had often been by my side to point out interesting items in the water or on the riverbanks. The sun was swinging to the west, the men were no longer cursing with every breath, and the country all around me seemed mysterious and exciting. Yes, things were definitely improved over yesterday.

Lying in that little cabin, I had wondered if I'd ever make it as a Mountie's wife. How could anyone endure such conditions? Today I was confident I could. My leg wasn't even bothering me anymore. We would soon be at the post, and Wynn had said we would have good accommodations there. I wasn't sure how many nights it would take us to make the trip, but I was now certain I could endure. I had gotten through the first night, and it surely couldn't be any worse. From here on I would have no problem.

Chapter Eleven

Onward

The cabin was simple but seemed very adequate, and the best thing was that I didn't need to share it with four drinking men. Another nice thing was that I could share it in privacy with Wynn.

After we had gone to bed I heard a strange sound. It seemed to grow louder and louder until it was humming steadily in my ears. I was puzzled and wished I could ask Wynn about it, but I could tell by his breathing that he was already asleep.

In the darkness something stung me. I jumped and slapped at it. Another sting. I swatted again.

"Put your head under the covers if they are bothering you," said Wynn softly.

"What is it?"

"Mosquitoes."

Now I had seen mosquitoes before. I had even been bitten by a few; but this—this *din* was something new to me.

"Are you sure?" I asked Wynn.

"I'm sure," he answered. "This cabin doesn't have any screens on the windows."

"How do you ever sleep?"

"You get used to it."

Wynn turned over to pull me close and shelter my face with the blankets.

"Try to sleep, Elizabeth," he encouraged me. "You didn't get much last night."

I lay quietly in Wynn's arms, not stirring for fear I would

keep him awake. The hum was a rising and falling crescendo. I wondered how many million mosquitoes it took to make such a sound.

In spite of the protection of Wynn's arms and the blanket, the mosquitoes still found me. I could hear their hum get closer and then I would feel the sharp sting as they sucked out my blood.

One thing is sure, I promised myself. *Our cabin in the North will have coverings over the windows even if I have to tear up my petticoats!*

In the morning I rose tired and grumpy. I would be so glad to get back on the barge and away from the mosquitoes.

My triumph was short lived; though we were soon back on the river, the dreaded mosquitoes swarmed around us, following us down the stream.

"Wynn," I said crossly, "they are coming with us."

"There are lots of mosquitoes in the North," Wynn informed me. "They are one of the area's worst pests."

"What are the others?" I muttered sarcastically, but Wynn didn't catch the tone of my question.

"Blackflies," he replied. "Blackflies are another real plague to man and beast alike."

Wynn was right. The mosquitoes were joined that day by the blackflies. I thought I would be bitten and chewed to pieces. Right before my eyes, new welts would rise on my arms. I hated to think what my face must look like. I was almost frantic with the intensity of the itching.

Wynn was sympathetic. "I might have something that will help," he offered and went to dig around in his medical supplies.

He came back with an ointment. It had a vile smell and looked awful, but I allowed him to rub it on anyway. It did help some, though it didn't seem to discourage the dreadful insects from taking further bites out of me.

"Why didn't they bother us yesterday?" I asked Wynn.

"The wind and the rain kept them away."

"Really?"

"They can't fly well in strong wind. They are too light, and they don't care for the rain either." I was ready to pray for more wind and rain. Anything to be rid of the miserable pests.

I guess I eventually got used to them. I was able to think about other things after a while and even to again enjoy, in a sense, my trip.

In the late afternoon, Wynn pointed out a mother bear and her two cubs. She was foraging at a bend in the river. Perhaps she was fishing, because she was staring intently at the water, seeming to ignore the barge completely as we went by.

The cute cubs took my mind off the mosquitoes and flies for a few minutes while I considered having a cub for a pet.

It was already getting dusk before we pulled into River's Bend, the place where we were to spend the night. Wynn lifted me ashore as there was no dock. This didn't make sense to me.

"Why is it," I asked, "that there's no dock and yet this is the place where all our things need to be unloaded? Isn't it going to be an awful job carrying all those heavy trunks and crates ashore?"

Wynn rewarded me with a broad smile. Apparently he liked a wife who was observant.

"The dock is around the bend in the river. Our things will be unloaded there. There are also a couple of temporary buildings and a Hudson's Bay Post, but I thought you might prefer to use this trapper's cabin. It is more private, though I'm afraid not luxurious. I've made arrangements with Pierre to use it for the night."

"Who's Pierre?"

"He runs the post."

"Is he married?"

"Nope. He batches. And his quarters are even worse than Charlie's."

I couldn't even imagine what that would be like.

"I don't want you to have to stay in those kinds of conditions again," Wynn stated firmly. "I know it must have been extremely offensive to you."

I thought back to Charlie's. The smelly, crowded cabin. The cursing, drinking, card-playing men. No, I wasn't particularly interested in that again either. I was pleased Wynn had made other arrangements.

Wynn opened the creaky, complaining cabin door; there

was some quick scampering as some former resident took immediate cover. I stepped closer to Wynn. He put a reassuring arm around me. "Nothing that small could harm you," he smiled.

Wynn found and lit the lamp, and I placed my small case on the newspaper-covered table.

"Is this Pierre's cabin?" I asked, looking around me at the bare little room.

"No, it belongs to some trapper."

"Then why did Pierre—?"

"It's customary. Trappers always leave their cabins available for others to use. Pierre likely asked the trapper about using his lodgings for travelers like us; but even if he didn't, we still won't be considered trespassers."

Wynn moved about, swishing the heavy dust from the few pieces of furniture and checking what was available for making a fire. There was a good supply of dry wood in one corner, and Wynn soon had a fire going. "Remember your first experience with a wood stove at Pine River?" His eyes twinkled at me, and I had the grace to blush. It's a wonder I hadn't burned down the building! I wrinkled my nose at him and we laughed together at the memory.

Wynn went outside to the river, dipped the kettle full of water and placed it on to boil. Then he checked the bed. It was a very narrow one, and I secretly wondered how it would sleep two. Wynn flung back the Hudson's Bay blankets; they had seen a good deal of wear and very few washings. A heavy piece of denim material was spread across a mattress of spruce branches crisscrossing one another topped with moss. I winced and hoped Wynn hadn't noticed.

Our meal was a simple one of dried biscuits and canned police rations. Tasty it was not, but I was very hungry and ate heartily.

I insisted on washing the dishes. Wynn had been our wilderness cook all along our journey, and I was glad I could finally do something helpful.

It didn't take me long to wash the few things and place them back on the unknown trapper's shelf.

Wynn spread one of the worn blankets on the wooden floor in front of the fire and we settled down before it to talk.

I looked about the simple, quaint little cabin and wondered if my own would look like this. I decided to ask.

"Do you know what our cabin will be like?"

"Not really. I haven't been to Beaver River before."

"But you have a pretty good idea?"

"Pretty good."

"Will it have just one room?"

"Not likely. A Mountie's home usually serves a double function—office as well as home. So it likely has at least two rooms."

I was pleased to hear that. I did want the privacy of a bedroom.

"It will be log?"

"I'm sure it will."

"With wooden floors?"

"With wooden floors."

We were silent for a few moments. Wynn broke the silence, his arm tightening about me as he spoke, "That must seem awfully crude to you, Elizabeth."

I turned so I could look into his eyes.

"In a way, yes—but really—I don't mind the thought of it at all. Look at this cabin now. True, it isn't much—but with a little fixing here and there—" I hesitated, wondering even as I spoke just what "fixing" one could do to make this very bare cabin look homey.

Wynn brushed a kiss against my cheek.

A strange, mournful, bloodcurdling sound interrupted us. I felt the hair on my scalp rise and my spine tingle. I had gotten used to the coyote's cry, but this—this was something entirely different. I pressed closer to Wynn.

"A timber wolf," he commented. I shivered as the cry came again and was answered from the other direction.

I had heard of timber wolves. Most of the tales had come from imaginative Julie. Wolves traveled in murderous packs, had menacing red eyes, and crept up stealthily on those whom they would devour.

"Are they all around us?" I whispered nervously, my eyes big with fright.

Wynn hugged me, sheltering me in the circle of his two strong arms.

"I doubt it," he said, without any trace of concern whatever. "But if they are, there is nothing whatever to be worried about. I suggest you just lie here in front of the fire and listen carefully, Elizabeth. You can almost count how many there are in the pack by the difference in their cries. They are a part of our world here in the North—a part that needs to be respected but not feared. Accept them—maybe even enjoy them if you can."

I doubted I would ever live to enjoy the cry of a timber wolf, but I did try to be calm. Another cry tore through the night air.

"Hear that?" noted Wynn close to my ear. "I'm guessing that was the leader of the pack. Did you hear the authority in his voice?"

I tried to shake my head, but Wynn was holding me too close. Authority? Not particularly.

Another cry reached us. This one was shorter and farther away.

"That one now, he's answering the boss. Checking in. Could you hear the difference?"

This time I could. It was unbelievable.

There was another cry. It came from very near our cabin, yet it wasn't as spooky and bloodcurdling for some reason.

"A female," commented Wynn. "Probably the leader's mate."

"Are the females tamer than the males?" I asked, thinking that this one sounded so much gentler than others.

"Oh, no," laughed Wynn. "In fact, the female can be even more aggressive and more deadly than the males—especially if she has pups. The hunting pack always consists of some females. I'm not sure how the males would fare without them. The pack depends on their skill and aggressiveness for the kill. The female must have food not just for herself but to feed her young—and she will do anything to get what she's after."

The wolves were a part of Wynn's wilderness. I wasn't sure I would ever be able to listen to their howl without shivering, but Wynn's calm and easy acceptance of these wild creatures had certainly helped me to see them in another light.

Another howl. Another shiver. Another explanation from Wynn. He seemed to paint a picture of the pack around us, locating and identifying each member. He did not describe them with sparkling red eyes and drooling tongues. I was seeing them as needy, hungry creatures, depending on nature and their skills to feed themselves and their families.

"Contrary to what you may have heard," Wynn told me, "the wolves only hunt to survive. In the wilderness, survival is not always easy."

I listened to the echoing calls of the wolves as they moved on, away from the cabin. My heart quit thumping. I found myself even wishing them good hunting.

Chapter Twelve

By Wagon

We took the trail the next morning to the small, hastily constructed buildings that formed the small outpost. Before we had left the little cabin, I had remade the bed and washed the dishes. Wynn had brought in a fresh wood supply, making sure he left more stacked against the wall than we had found the night before.

The trail through the woods crossed a stream on steppingstones, and Wynn pointed east to where the beavers had dammed the water and made themselves a small lake. The morning sun was already promising a fair day, and the birds sang and winged overhead among the trees. The walk would have been perfect had it not been for the miserable insects. Even Wynn walked with a screen of cloth draped from his hat at the back.

When we reached the fort, I looked about at the sorry arrangement of small buildings. Even from the outside, I was sure I wouldn't have wanted to stay overnight in any of them. I was so glad Wynn had arranged for the cabin.

"I think you should wait out here," Wynn said to me. I wondered why, but did not question him. I found a nearby tree stump and sat down. No one seemed to be around, so I lifted my skirt to inspect my leg. It was no longer covered with a bandage; Wynn had decided the air would do it good.

Ugly scabs of various density and color covered the shin. I moved my foot back and forth. Almost all the pain was gone. Wynn had said that it was most important to have bodies capable of healing themselves when one was miles away from medical help. He seemed very pleased he had picked a woman with this quality.

Wynn was not in the cabin for long. He returned with a look of frustration on his face.

"What's wrong? Are they drunk?"

"Drunk isn't the word for it. They are *out*! Every last one of them. I couldn't even raise them."

"You're angry with them for drinking, aren't you? I don't blame—"

But Wynn didn't let me finish my intended consolation.

"Yes, I'm angry. With their drinking? I don't like it, but I can't stop it. That's their business, I guess—their way of life. That's the way they ease through the difficulties of life in the North. When men don't have God, they need substitutes. To my way of thinking, whiskey is a poor substitute— but many men depend upon it. But what I am angry about is that they didn't obey my orders."

I looked up in surprise.

"They were supposed to unload the barge last night before they started their drinking. I knew very well they wouldn't be any good for anything this morning. There sits the wagon, nothing on it; and in there, sprawled out on the floor, are the men who were to load it and the man who was supposed to drive it."

"What do we do now?" I finally asked in a small voice.

Wynn roused and reached over to cup my chin. He smiled then for the first time since emerging from the house.

"We do it ourselves, my love," he answered, strength and confidence back in his voice.

It was a long, hard job. The morning sun was high in the sky before we finished. I really wasn't much help. The crates and trunks were all too heavy for a woman's shoulders, and Wynn would not even let me try. Wynn had driven the wagon down as close to the dock as possible in order to save unnecessary steps. I volunteered to hold the team, as there was no hitching post. Wynn seemed pleased that I was willing to help, but the job I had did not go well.

The horses were skitterish. The mosquitoes and flies were plaguing them, and they kept tossing their heads and stamping around. Wynn watched my efforts warily for a while and them decided to unhitch the horses, take them up the bank and tie them securely to a tree. Now I had nothing to do.

I tried to give a hand now and then but soon found I was more in the way than anything else. At length I gave up and found a tree stump in the shade.

As I sat there, I angrily thought about the men in the nearby cabin. There they slept in a drunken stupor while my husband labored to do the work they had been hired to do!

Finally the loading was completed and the horses re-hitched to the wagon.

Wynn made one more visit to the cabin to check on our hired driver.

"Any luck?" I asked when he returned, his lips set in a thin line.

"None." It was a crisp, blunt reply.

"What do we do now?" I asked. "Do we have to wait here until he wakes up?"

"No, we don't wait. We are late enough getting away now. We'll never make it as far as we should today. We *drive*. When he wakes up he *walks*."

The horses were not made for speed and the wagon was clumsy and heavy. It had been much faster traveling on the river. The sun grew hot on my back and the insects buzzed persistently.

We didn't talk much. Wynn concentrated on his driving, and I tried to keep my mind busy with things other than my discomfort. The river barge seemed like a pleasure boat compared to this lumbering wagon.

We stopped at noon for a quick meal. Wynn ate with one eye on the sky, for clouds were gathering. I knew he feared a storm before we reached our destination. Neither of us voiced the concern, but I noticed that Wynn pushed the horses a little faster.

The track could, at best, be referred to as a trail. It wound up and down, around and through, following the path of least resistance, much like a river would do. At times there was no way but to challenge the terrain head-on. The horses strained up steep hills, then slid their way to the bottom again, the wagon jolting behind. Fortunately, Wynn was an expert teamster, and I breathed a prayer of thanks whenever we reached fairly level ground again.

At one point, even Wynn feared for the safety of the horses and wagon. He asked me to climb out and walk down the incline. It seemed to be almost straight down. On further thought, Wynn crawled down from the wagon, rustled through some of his belongings, and came up with the horrid men's pants. They had been washed since I had seen them last, which I assumed Wynn had done himself.

"You'd best put these on," he said. "You might spend part of the descent in a sitting position."

Without question I quickly obeyed and stuffed my simple skirt and petticoat into the overnight bag lying on top of the load.

Wynn went first. I didn't really want to watch, but I couldn't tear my eyes away. A good brake system on the wagon kept the wheels skidding downhill, always on the heels of the sliding horses.

I stood there with bated breath, now and then gasping and covering my eyes, then quickly uncovering them again to make sure Wynn was still all right.

I forgot to follow. When Wynn finally rolled the wagon to a halt on comparatively even ground, I still stood, with my mouth open, at the top of the hill.

I blushed and hurried down to join him. His call, "Slow down," came too late. Already I had picked up more speed than I could control on the steep slope. I tried to brace myself against the momentum, but soon my body was moving far too fast for my clumsy feet, and I felt myself falling and rolling end over end. The next thing I was aware of was Wynn's white face bending over me.

"Elizabeth," he pleaded, panting for air, "Elizabeth, are you all right?"

I moaned and tried to roll over into a more dignified position. I wasn't sure if I was all right or half dead. I did have enough presence of mind to be glad for the horrible pants.

Wynn began to feel my bones. I roused somewhat, my dizzy head beginning to clear.

"I think I'm okay," I told him, struggling to sit up.

"Lie still." he ordered. "Don't move until we are sure."

He continued to check. By now my head was clear.

"I'm okay," I insisted, feeling only a few places on my body smarting. "Just embarrassed to death, that's all."

Wynn satisfied himself that nothing was broken and sighed with relief. He then turned his attention to the scratches and bruises.

"Let me up," I implored him and he carefully assisted me to my feet.

He brushed the dirt from my clothing and the leaves from my hair, showing both relief and concern on his face.

"I wanted you to walk down to keep you from injury," he said softly, shaking his head in dismay.

I began to laugh. Wynn looked at me with more concern in his eyes and then he smiled slowly.

"That's some record for coming down that hill," I said between gasps of laughter.

"I think," he remarked, "I might have set a record for coming back up—Hey!" His shout made me turn to follow his gaze. The deserted team had decided to plod on without us. They were not far ahead, but they were still traveling; and if we didn't hurry or if something spooked them, we might be walking for a long way. Wynn ran down the remainder of the hill, chasing after them. I followed, but at a much slower pace. I didn't want a repeat performance. I was already smarting and aching quite enough.

Wynn caught the team about a quarter of a mile down the road. They had not exactly followed the trail though, and Wynn was hard put to back them out of the dead end they had led themselves into among the trees.

Finally back on the trail again, we noticed the clouds had gathered more darkly overhead. It had cooled off noticeably and the wind was picking up.

"Is there anyone living nearby?" I asked him, sensing his uneasiness.

"Not that I'm aware of," he answered.

Even the horses seemed to sense the coming storm and tossed their heads and complained at the load.

They balked when we came to a stretch of marshy land where they were required to cross on corduroy (wooden logs placed side by side). Wynn coaxed and then forced them to take the first steps. The logs rolled and sucked, squeezing up oozy marsh soil as we passed over. I felt as reluctant as the horses. I wished I could walk but then rethought the matter. In places the logs lay beneath the surface of the water.

The horses clomped and slipped, snorting and plunging their way ahead. One horse would balk and refuse to take another step while its teammate was still traveling on. Then the horse would give a nervous jump and scramble on, slipping on the logs as he did so. By then, his teammate would have decided to balk. We jerked our way across the precarious floating bridge, and I breathed a sigh of relief when the wagon wheels finally touched solid ground again.

The horses, sweating more from nerves than from exerted energy, were even more skittery now, so when the first loud crack of thunder greeted us, they jumped and would have bolted had Wynn not been prepared and held tightly to the reins.

I moved uneasily on the seat, my eyes on the clouds overhead. It would pour any minute and there was no place to go for shelter.

Wynn urged the team on. It was impossible to expect them to run. The wagon was much too heavy and the track too poor, but he did ask of them a brisker walk. They obliged, seeming as reluctant as we were to be caught in the storm.

Just as the rain began to spatter about us, we rounded a corner and there before us was a shed! It was not in good repair and we weren't sure what its use had been in the past; but it was shelter, and Wynn turned off the rutted track, heading the team quickly for it.

"Run in before you get soaked, Elizabeth," he urged, helping me down from the wagon seat. I did not stop to argue.

Wynn hastened to unhitch the team and then he was there, bringing the horses right in with him. He moved them to the far end of the shed and tied them to a peg in the wall. A loud crack of thunder made me jump and the horses whinney in fright. Now the rain came in sheets. I had never seen it rain so hard.

The shelter we had found was in no way waterproof. We had to watch where we stood in order to prevent the rain from running down our necks.

There was one spot along the south wall where it seemed to be quite dry. Wynn pointed to it and suggested we sit there to wait out the storm. The building had a dirt floor and again I was glad that I still wore the pants. We sat on the floor and leaned against the wall of the building. Outside the angry storm continued to sweep about us, flashing and booming as it passed over our heads.

It did not last long. In less than a half hour or so it was over. The dark clouds moved on, the thunder continuing to rumble in the distance.

The storm had not improved our road any. Where we had, a few minutes before, been traveling in dust, we now were in muck. Wynn said we were lucky—such a hard rain had a tendency to run off rather than to soak like gentler rain would have done. But I wondered how the trail could possibly have gotten any muddier.

I felt sorry for the horses as they labored through the mud which made the already heavy load even heavier. We both walked whenever we could find halfway decent footing to save them the extra weight. Wynn stopped frequently to let them catch their breath. Their sides heaved and their backs began to steam; but they seemed impatient to get on with it and were soon chomping at the bit at every stop.

The storm brought one blessing. For a few merciful minutes, the mosquitoes stayed away. I was just about to share my joy with Wynn when the pests began to buzz around us again.

"I've been told that there are some trappers who live along this route," Wynn informed me as we trudged on. "I had hoped to make it to their cabin tonight."

I was glad to hear there were people living along the trail. Then I remembered Charlie.

"Just men?" I asked.

"No, they have womenfolk—and children, I believe."

That was even better news.

"How far?"

"I'm not sure. I've never been up this way before."

"Do you think we'll make it by dark?"

"I'm hoping so—but, if not, we'll be fine camping out if we need to. Remember, you had wanted the experience of sleeping under the stars on our Banff honeymoon."

I nodded. I remembered well. And then our honeymoon had been cut so short there wasn't time.

"It might be fun," I answered Wynn. "Do you think it will rain some more?"

Wynn checked the sky. "I don't think so. Not tonight. Maybe a little tomorrow."

"Oh, dear," I fairly groaned at the news. "Will we get held up again tomorrow?"

"I hope it won't be stormy enough to stop us—but it might be rather miserable traveling for a spell."

The long summer day of sunlight allowed us to continue traveling till after ten o'clock. We had not even stopped to eat, munching instead on hard, dry sandwiches and sipping water from the flask Wynn had filled that morning.

"Well," Wynn said, just as I was beginning to realize how very weary I was, "I'm afraid we are going to have to give up on that cabin. We need to stop. You must be exhausted, Elizabeth, and the horses need a chance to rest and feed."

I looked around at the scraggly evergreens. We had passed through much prettier spots earlier in the day.

"It looks like there might be a clearing just up ahead. The grass should be better there. Let's have a look."

Wynn was right. Much to our surprise, at the opposite side of the clearing stood a small log cabin.

"Well, look at that," said Wynn, relieved. "The trappers. And right when we need them."

The cabin appeared to be very small. I looked around for another one. Wynn had mentioned more than one family. I couldn't see another cabin. It must be hidden in the trees.

"Do you think one of the families might have room for us?" I asked Wynn.

Wynn smiled. "Oh, they'll have room all right. Even if we all have to stand still to manage it, there'll be room."

I looked perplexed and Wynn explained. "Hospitality in the North is as much a part of life as eating and sleeping. They might not have much, but whatever they have is yours."

As we approached the cabin, I looked down at myself in embarrassment. Wynn had said there were women here, and I would be turning up at their door in my male attire looking like a pincushion—bites and scratches and bruises indicating a much-used pincushion at that. I didn't have the time or the opportunity to make any repairs on my appearance. We had already been spotted.

We were met in the yard by four small children—three boys and a girl. I had never seen such chewed-up hands and faces in my life. I was a mess, but they were even more so. They seemed to take it all for granted, chatting with us and swatting insects as though it was the most natural thing in the world.

The children ushered us into the house and, to my surprise, we found that it was home to two families. The men saw no reason to furnish and supply wood for more than one cabin. It was one long, open room shared by four adults and four children. Another baby was on the way, probably due any day.

The woman who met us at the door and welcomed us in was just as mosquito-bitten as the children, as was the one who turned from the stove and smiled a shy welcome. I relaxed about how I looked, but at the same time I winced. Would I look like this the entire time I lived in the north country? *Surely not, God*, I whispered in dismay.

With great ceremony we were immediately seated at a crude table, while the woman at the stove brought huge bowls of steaming stew and set them before us. They had been about to have their evening meal; and upon our arrival, the women had given us their places at the table. I wanted to protest, but Wynn nudged me forward and I understood that to decline their invitation as welcomed guests might offend them. With mixed feelings I sat down and smiled at them appreciatively. I was hungry and the food smelled delicious.

I recognized none of the vegetables I saw in my dish. Wynn informed me that the women were experts at combing the forest for edible plants. I smiled at them again, thanking them for sharing their supper.

"We be so glad to see ya, yer doin' *us* the favor," declared the older one with simple courtesy.

No grace was said before we began, so I offered, unobtrusively, my own short prayer of thanks. I blessed Wynn's food as well, as the men did not give him any time for such an observance. Immediately they began plying him with questions about the outside world.

The children ate noisily. It was plain that manners were not considered necessary around this table. A common cup passed from person to person with the hot drink that went with the meal. I smiled and passed it on. To my chagrin, Wynn lifted it without hesitation and drank deeply. I fervently prayed again—that God would keep him from getting some dreadful disease.

"That was very good," I said to the cook when we had finished. "I wish we had time to let you show me how to make it."

She dipped her head shyly.

"Wasn't nothin'," she stated. "It's the bear that gives it the flavor."

"Bear?" I echoed, feeling my stomach contract.

"Bear meat's 'bout the best there is," observed her cabin-sister.

For a moment, I thought I would bolt from the table; but then I saw Wynn's amused eyes on my face and I swallowed hard and smiled.

"Well, it certainly is," I answered her evenly. "That was very tasty."

I saw the look of unbelief cross Wynn's face, and I smiled again—directly into his eyes. "Maybe when we get settled, you can shoot a bear," I challenged him, "and *I* can make *you* some stew like this."

He laughed outright. I'm sure no one else at the table understood our little joke.

We did spend the night with the trappers and their families. There were two beds in the room. We were given one of them. The two women took the other; and the two men, without comment or protest, took robes and blankets from a stack in the corner and spread out on the floor with the children, everyone sleeping fully clothed.

Chapter Thirteen

The Last Day on the Trail

After Wynn had dressed my injured leg the next morning and expressed again his pleasure at how nicely it was healing, we were on our way. With luck, this would be our last day on the trail.

I followed Wynn's advice and draped a scarf over my head and down around my neck, but the pesky little mosquitoes and flies still got at me. The hairline at the back of my neck seemed to be their special delight.

"How do the people stand it?" I asked Wynn as I scratched at the swelling lumps.

"It's one of the things they learn to live with," he shrugged.

I didn't like the answer. Mostly because I knew that it implied I must learn to live with it as well.

It was a beautiful July day; and, though clouds passed by overhead, it did not rain. The warm sun soon had dried the rain of the day before from the track. Only in spots did we still plow through messy, gooey, wet places, the horses throwing themselves against their collars and straining to pull the heavy wagon. Wynn would always stop them for a breather and soon they were chomping and straining to be on the way again.

Occasionally, we traveled along the banks of a stream or beside a still lake. The fish would jump to feed on the swarming insects that got too near the water's surface. I wished them good hunting—each fish's dinner was one less to bother me!

We stopped around noon in an area covered with tall fir trees. I recognized several different varieties, but I didn't know enough to be able to separate them by name. Wynn was much too busy unhitching the horses and getting the fire going to answer questions, so I walked off alone, observing as I walked and storing questions for later. I kept Wynn in sight so I wouldn't get lost.

By the time the fire was burning briskly, I was back to help with our meal.

We did not stop for long.

In a swampy area I spotted a mother moose and her young one, even without Wynn pointing them out to me. I was pleased with myself.

"Look!" I cried. "A moose—two mooses."

Wynn smiled and nodded his head as he followed my pointing finger. He turned to me and said simply, "I must correct you, Elizabeth, so you won't be laughed at.—Moose is both singular and plural."

I guess I had known that; but, in my excitement, I had forgotten. I nodded in appreciation of Wynn's concern for me. I also appreciated the fact that he had not laughed.

I watched the moose until they were lost from sight and then I turned to Wynn. "What else?" I asked.

"What else, what?" he puzzled.

"What other animal names are both singular and plural?"

"Deer. Elk. Caribou." Wynn stopped.

"Bear?" I asked him.

"Bear? No, it's quite all right to refer to 'The Three Bears.' "

"Any other?"

"Likely."

"Likely? You mean you don't know?"

"They don't come to mind right now."

"How will I know what to say if—?"

He smiled at me and reached to push back a lock of unruly hair that insisted upon curling around my cheek. "You'll learn. You're very quick."

I flushed slightly under his smile and the compliment. It was good to know Wynn was not afraid that he might be embarrassed by his city-bred wife.

"Are we almost there?" I asked Wynn like a child for the tenth time. We had stopped for our evening meal.

He smiled at me and spread out his map. He carefully studied our surroundings, looking for some identifying signs. I couldn't make head nor tail of Wynn's map. After a moment of study, he pointed to a spot on the map. "We are about here," he said. "That should leave us about nine or ten miles to go. No, not quite," he corrected himself. "More like seven to eight."

"Will we make it tonight?"

"I certainly hope so—but it won't be early. It's a good thing we have lots of daylight for traveling. I'm afraid we're going to need it."

I loaded our supper things back in the wagon while Wynn hitched the horses, and we were on our way again. Perhaps we had made our last stop—I certainly hoped so. Excitement took hold of me as I thought of how close I was getting to my *new home*.

The horses seemed to sense they were getting close to home, too; and Wynn had to hold them back in spite of their tiredness and the heavy wagon they pulled.

I felt too excited and tense to even talk, so the last leg of our journey was a quiet one. But my mind was full of questions—some that even Wynn would not have been able to answer, not having lived at Beaver River himself. *What will our little cabin be like? What will our neighbors be like? Will there be any white women at the Post? Will the Indians like me and accept me? Will I ever be able to converse with them?* The thoughts whirled about in my head, making me almost dizzy.

The sun dropped into the west, closer and closer to the horizon. Still we had not reached Beaver River, and I was beginning to wonder if Wynn had made an error in his estimation—easily forgiven considering the little information he had been given. I was about to wonder aloud when Wynn spoke.

"Would you spread out that map on your lap, please? I want to take another look at it while it's still light enough to see well."

I spread out the map and, without comment, Wynn began to refigure.

"If I've got it worked out right, the settlement should be right over this next hill."

I wanted to shout for joy. In my excitement I reached over and gave Wynn a quick and unexpected hug which sent his stetson tumbling into the dust of the roadway. By the time Wynn got my arms untangled and the team stopped, his Royal North West Mounted Police hat had been run over by the steel rim of the heavy wagon wheel. Horrified, I watched Wynn walk back to retrieve the poor thing from the dirt. It was now quite flat where it should have been nicely arched. I covered my remorseful face with my hands but Wynn returned to the wagon smiling; and, after a bit of pummeling and a punch here and there, he settled the hat back on his head—a few unsightly lumps, but it was in better shape than I had dared to hope.

Wynn was right. As we rounded the brow of the hill before us, there lay the little settlement at our feet. I refrained myself from hugging Wynn again. Instead, it was Wynn who hugged me.

"There it is, Elizabeth," he whispered against my cheek. "There's home."

"Home," I repeated. It was a magic word and brought tears to my eyes. I tucked my arm within Wynn's, even though he did need both hands on the reins. To think of it! We were almost home.

In the gathering dusk, it looked like a friendly little village to me. We could see the flag flying high over the Hudson's Bay Company Store. Scattered all around that central building were others of various sizes. At our approach, dogs began to set up a howl. People appeared in doorways and looked our way. A few of them even waved an arm to the approaching team. I suppose everyone in the settlement knew well who was in the coming wagon. They would be waiting to size up the new lawman and his wife. I held Wynn's arm more tightly.

"Tell me again," I asked, "what did you say the name of the Hudson's Bay man was?"

"McLain," said Wynn. "Ian McLain."

"And he's not married?"

"I couldn't find anyone who knew. I asked, but no one had heard of a Mrs. McLain."

"I suppose that means there isn't one," I said in resignation.

"Not necessarily. There really isn't much reason for the records to show if there is a wife or not. The agent is listed, not his family."

I took this as a spark of hope, but I wasn't going to count too strongly on another white woman in the village.

Darkness was closing in quickly now that we had passed down the hill. Windows were beginning to light up with lamps. The noise of the dogs increased as more people gathered around. I looked over the crowd of white men and several Indians. My eyes searched on. Who was Mr. McLain? Was he alone?

Wynn pulled the team to a halt before the large Hudson's Bay building and called out a friendly greeting to the men gathered there. A tall, square man with a heavy beard stepped forward. "Welcome to Beaver River, Sarge," he said. "Name here is Ian McLain."

He was alone.

Chapter Fourteen

Home

Wynn shook hands with many of the men who had gathered around and nodded his head to others as he moved about. For a moment I felt forgotten. I didn't know whether to climb down from the wagon or to stay where I was until someone noticed me. Eventually I could feel eyes turning my way. Wynn invited the Hudson's Bay Post employee closer to the wagon and smiled up at me. "My wife, Elizabeth. Elizabeth, Mr. McLain."

McLain reached up and gave my hand a hearty shake.

"Come in. Come in," boomed Mr. McLain, but Wynn cut in rather quickly.

"We've had a long six days, and Elizabeth is anxious to get settled. If you could just point out the cabin for our use, we'd be grateful."

Mr. McLain nodded in understanding. He pointed west toward a stand of trees. The outline of a cabin showed faintly against the last glimmer of daylight.

"Right on over there," he informed us.

"Is there a place there to keep the horses?"

Mr. McLain took a look at the team and suddenly remembered something.

"Where's Canoue?" he asked.

"Sleeping when I last saw him. He got to sharing whiskey with the boys and I wasn't able to rouse him. I couldn't wait, so we left him behind."

The Hudson's Bay man shook his head. "He has his problems with the bottle. I warned him. 'Canoue,' I said, 'don't you go messin' this one up. I can't keep findin' you work if ya ain't able to stay with it.' Needed that money." McLain shrugged his shoulders. "There ain't no place for horses over to 'the law'; you can bring 'em back on over here. I got a corral out back," the man continued.

All the time this conversation was taking place, I could feel eyes studying me. Mostly we were surrounded by men, but now I saw a few Indian women and some young people and children. I smiled at them, though I must admit I felt as out of place and uncomfortable as I ever had in my life. I was anxious for Wynn to end his conversation and get us out of there and home.

At last he climbed back up into the wagon, turned the team around and headed for the little cabin which was to be our first home.

I felt tingles go all through me. What would it be like? Would it be in good repair? Would it have that private bedroom I wanted so badly? I fought the temptation to close my eyes until I actually got there. I was anxious and afraid—all at one time.

When Wynn said "whoa" to the team, I knew the moment was at hand. He turned to me and drew me close. "Well," he murmured softly, "are you ready?"

I couldn't get my lips to move, so I just nodded my head against him.

"What will you need tonight?"

I really didn't know. I had no idea what I might find in the cabin.

Then we heard voices behind us and turned to see a group approaching. It was McLain's voice that called out to us.

"Thought we might as well unload that there wagon tonight and save ya the trouble in the mornin'. Then ya won't need to fuss with the team ag'in."

It was a thoughtful offer, and I was sure Wynn appreciated it. I should have appreciated it, too, but I had wanted to enter our new home in privacy—just the two of us. Now we were to be ushered in by the Hudson's Bay trader and a host of local trappers. I felt disappointment wash over me. If only Wynn would quickly send them all away and tell them the load could wait until morning. He didn't. He withdrew his arm, climbed down from the wagon, and turned to help me down. "Appreciate that," he responded. "Shouldn't take long at all with the good help you've brought along." I blinked away tears in the semidarkness and knew instinctively that Wynn would not understand how I, as a woman, felt about the intrusion. He would consider the practical fact that the wagon loaded with heavy trunks and crates needed unloading. I sentimentally thought that a man and his wife deserved to walk into their first home alone and together. Perhaps foolishly, I realized now, I had had visions of being carried over the threshold.

By the time my feet were firmly planted on the ground, the men were already bustling about the wagon.

"Perhaps you'd like to go in and show them where you would like things put," Wynn suggested.

I wanted to sputter that *I* would prefer things left right where they were, but I knew that was foolish and would be misunderstood; so I walked numbly to the door as Mr. McLain, who had taken the first crate forward, stood aside to let me get the door for him. How romantic!

The door was stuck, and I had to put both hands on the knob and pull hard. It finally gave and, in the process, skinned my knuckles. The injured hand stung smartly, and the tears in my eyes multiplied and spilled down my cheeks before I could stop them.

The house was dark. I had no idea where to find light. It was quite dark outside by now and the few small windows let in very little light. I hesitated. McLain shuffled his feet. He was waiting for me to make up my mind so he could rid himself of the heavy load he carried.

"Just set it down against that wall," I told him.

I guess he realized I was a little at a loss, for he volunteered, "I'll see if I can find the lamp." He soon had it lit and placed where it could bring the most benefit to the men who were unloading our belongings.

In and out they went. Men I had never seen before were clumping in and out of my new home, never stopping to wipe their feet. One of them even spit on *my* floor. Wynn did not enter himself. He was far too busy overseeing the unloading. I stood dumbly in the middle of the room, wondering what I should do; and then I remembered I did indeed have a responsibility: I was to tell the men where to put things. How did I know where to put things? I still didn't even know what rooms we had to furnish. So I just pointed a finger, which they probably couldn't see anyway from behind their big loads, and said, "Over there," until one wall was stacked high with our belongings.

Finally the stream of groaning, heaving men stopped. There was only the sound of their voices from the yard. Wynn was talking to the men before they returned to their own homes. I tapped my foot impatiently. Why did he take so long? Why didn't he just thank them and send them away?

I noticed a soft hum, which was soon a whine. Then another and another, and I realized we had given the mosquitoes a wonderful welcome. The open door, with the lamp burning in the room to light their way in, had not been ignored. Already our cabin must be filled with hundreds of them. With an angry little cry, I rushed over and slammed the door shut.

Wynn was still talking to the men. I turned dejectedly to the stack of our belongings and wondered just where I might find some blankets to make a bed. Picking up the lamp, I went over and began to check the pile. Labels of contents didn't help me much. All the crates on the top seemed to be things for Wynn's use as northern-law-enforcer and area-medical-supplier.

How would I ever make a bed? The past few nights on the trail I had promised myself that I would need to endure sleeping in such makeshift ways only for a few nights, and then I would be in my own home and sleeping in my own clean and fresh-smelling bed. And now I couldn't find my bedding. As a matter of fact, I didn't even know if there was a bed. Just as I was leaving the room, lamp held high, to find out if there was a bed in the cabin, Wynn poked his head in the door. I sighed with relief until I heard his words, "I'm going to take the team over, Elizabeth. I shouldn't be long. You make yourself at home."

I don't suppose he could have chosen any words that would have upset me more. *Make yourself at home*. This was home? Piled boxes. No husband. No blankets for my bed. And me, bone-weary. All I wanted was a warm bath to remove the messy trail dirt and a clean bed to crawl into. *Then* I might have been able to make myself at home. And Wynn. I wanted Wynn—my husband. After all, it was because of him that I had come to this strange, faraway land.

I let the tears flow freely then. Wiping my eyes and sniffing dejectedly, I stumbled into another room with the lamp held before me. There was a table, a stove, some rough shelves, and a cot—but no bed, at least not one that would hold two people.

I did not stop to look further but went on through another door. This room had pegs along one wall, a dilapidated stand with drawers and, yes, a double bed. It even had a mattress rather than spruce boughs—at least it was a mattress of sorts. It wasn't very clean, and it was rather lumpy; but it was a mattress. There was no bedding. I looked around for a shelf and found one, but there was no bedding on it either.

Going back to the other room again, I looked all around but still found nothing that would provide bedding for the night. There were three chairs I had missed before. Two of them were wooden and the third an overstuffed chair sitting in front of a fireplace. I was pleased with the fireplace, and then I realized it was probably more functional than anything else. It was likely the only source of heat in the cabin. I flashed the lamp around the room once more. It was quite bare—and not too clean. And then I spotted something I had missed in my first perusal. Over the fireplace hung a large fur that had been tanned and used as decoration or heat-retainer—I wasn't sure which. I put my lamp down and walked over to it. I gave it a pull. The fur was firmly attached. I pulled again. It still stayed in place. I grasped it in both my hands and put all my strength into the pull. With a tearing sound and a billow of dust, it came tumbling down from the wall and I went tumbling down to the floor.

I pushed the heavy fur off and got to my feet. It felt rather unyielding and bristly, not soft like the furs I was used to seeing. I pulled it to the bedroom and worked it through the door. I then went back for the lamp. I did finally manage to get the fur up on the bed and spread out in some way.

I looked around me. This was my new home! It was bare

and dirty and had a lumpy bed, with no sheets, no blankets, and a smelly fur hide. There were no curtains, no soft rugs, no shiny windows—nothing. Even the chimney of the sputtering lamp was dirty with soot. But, worst of all, I was alone! That thought brought the tears streaming down my face again. I carried the lamp back out to the other room and set it on the table—I'm afraid it was more to coax the mosquitoes out of the bedroom than to provide a safe and welcome light for Wynn. Then I walked back to the bedroom, kicked off my shoes, crawled under the awkward animal skin, and began to cry in earnest. I didn't even have my evening talk with God. I was so miserable I thought He'd rather not hear from me. And in my present state, I really didn't want to hear from Him. I was very weary, so I did not cry for long. Sleep mercifully claimed me.

Chapter Fifteen

Making a Home

When I awoke the next morning, it took me several minutes to sort out where I was. With the knowledge came some of the hurt of the night before, but it wasn't as painful as it had been then. I looked down at myself. I was now covered with blankets. The fur I had struggled with was spread out on the floor by the bed, looking soft and even inviting. I was still in my clothes, my skirt and blouse now wrinkled as well as travel-stained. I knew my hair must be a sight—I had not even removed the pins the night before. They had worked loose in the night, so now part of my hair hung wildly about my face while part of it was still caught up with one pin or another. I removed the last pins and let my hair all tumble about my shoulders, combing my fingers through it to make some order out of the mess.

At my faintest stirring, Wynn was there, concern and pain in his face.

"Are you—?" But he didn't finish. Instead, he pulled me into his arms and held me so tightly I had to fight for air. "I'm so sorry, Elizabeth," he whispered, and there was a tremble in his voice.

I looked up at him then and saw his eyes were misted with unshed tears. It brought my tears again. I clung to Wynn and cried away all the feelings I had bottled up the night before. He let me cry.

When the tears finally stopped, Wynn tipped my head and looked deeply into my eyes. Perhaps he was looking for answers to some unspoken questions. I wasn't quite ready to smile yet, but I was ready to carry on. I avoided his eyes by shutting mine. He kissed me softly and then let me go.

"Are you hungry?" he asked. It wasn't until then that I smelled coffee. Surprisingly, I realized I *was* hungry. I looked again at my clothes and my hands.

"I'm not sure what I need the most," I said, "food or a bath."

"How about the food first? Then we'll look after that bath."

I slipped into my shoes and futiley smoothed my skirt. Then I looked at Wynn. "Where do I go here?" I asked him.

He understood my question. "Out," he answered.

"Just—out?"

He nodded.

"You mean they don't even have any—any—outbuilding here in the village?"

"We're a quarter of a mile from the village."

"Still—"

"I'll make arrangements as soon as possible," Wynn stated and turned away to return to whatever he had been doing before I awakened. The pain was in his eyes again. I thought he might be thinking that he had been right—a girl like me didn't belong in the north country. I blinked back some new tears that stung my eyes and went *out*.

The day was filled with sunshine. A large flock of birds chattered in the nearby trees where they were already gathering, making their plans to return to lands where winter snow would not blow. In the village, a quarter of a mile away, I heard distant voices and barking dogs. I breathed deeply of the morning air. The hillsides were covered with evergreens and scattered with poplar and birch trees.

It was beautiful country. I would make it. I would! I would fix the house and—and—clean myself up, and I'd prove to Wynn that I could be happy here—as long as he was with me. A nagging fear gripped me then. What about all the times Wynn's duties would take him elsewhere? Like last night? He had to care for the borrowed team. He couldn't just turn them over to the Hudson's Bay trader. That man had his own responsibilities. Wynn had done only what needed to be done, and yet . . . It was going to take a lot of resolve on my part to create a home, a happy home, in Wynn's wilderness. I couldn't crumble like I had last night every time I faced difficulties, every time modern conveniences were not at my disposal. I wanted to be happy here. Most of all, I wanted to make Wynn happy. I was going to need help. I knew of only one true source readily available to me. I stopped for a few moments of prayer.

By the time I returned to the cabin, I had myself in hand again. Wynn was busy with the crates. He had carried my trunk to the bedroom and placed it beside the wall under the one lone window. I opened the lid, hoping to find a more suitable skirt and blouse in which to be seen at breakfast; but the ones I lifted from the trunk were just as wrinkled as those I wore. I gave up and went to see if I could find a basin to wash my hands. Wynn had already set one out, and a towel was hanging on a peg beside it.

I washed and moved on to the stove. The coffeepot was sending out a delightful aroma and Wynn had made a batch of pancakes that needed only to be poured on the griddle. It was hot and ready, so I began to spoon out the batter. The sizzle and the good smell made my stomach beg for a taste.

Wynn was soon in the kitchen beside me. "Smells good," he said, his hands on my shoulder behind me. "I had a tough time waiting."

"Why didn't you go ahead—or waken me?"

"I thought you needed the rest. And I didn't want to start my first day without you."

I swallowed hard and willed away the tears. That was all over now. I needed to put it firmly behind me.

"So what do you think?" I said, in order to initiate conversation.

"Think?" asked Wynn.

"About the cabin," I went on.

"It's bigger than I had dared to hope." Wynn sounded pleased, and I realized for the first time that he was right. I had seen three rooms in the darkness. I had been hoping for at least two. I had not even thought till now to be thankful.

I smiled at Wynn now. "That's right. I had hoped for a private bedroom, and it has a private living area as well." I looked around me. It wasn't much, this living area, but it had possibilities. There was the fireplace, with one small chunk of the fur I had yanked down the night before still dangling over it. There was a window looking out to the east and the village. There was the cot with the hard-looking covering, the, well—the *easy* chair. Nearer at hand were the stove, some makeshift cupboards, the table and two chairs, and a stand where the basin and two large pails of water rested.

"Where'd they come from?" I asked Wynn. I had not noticed the pails the night before, and they weren't the ones from the teacherage that I had given Wynn to pack for our use.

"I borrowed them," he answered simply. "I thought you'd be aching for a bath last night so I asked McLain for them. It took us awhile to heat that much water—I guess I would have been wiser to have hurried back instead of waiting on it."

I looked at the heavy pails. They were filled almost to the brim. Wynn had carried them full of hot water the night before—for a quarter of a mile—hurrying and stumbling through the dark so I might have a bath. And what had he found? A childish woman who had cried herself to sleep under a musty old hide.

I crossed to Wynn, the pancake turner still in my hand. I reached my arms up and tightened them around his neck. "I'm sorry," I whispered.

He held me and kissed me. We didn't speak. I guess we were both busy sorting out thoughts. The smell of burning pancakes pulled me back to reality. Fortunately, they weren't so burned we couldn't eat them. In fact, after the dried and canned trail fare, they tasted good.

Wynn helped unpack our crates and trunks. It took us all morning to sort through our things and get them into the rooms where they would be used. After a light lunch, Wynn had some things to attend to at the store. I assured him I would be just fine. I was going to be very busy with a scrub brush and hot, soapy water.

I was scrubbing out the shelves which would be our kitchen cupboards when I heard men's voices. I expected a knock on our door, but after several minutes when none came

I went to the window and cautiously looked out. Two men, with a team of horses and a dilapidated old wagon piled with rough lumber, were busily studying a large sheet of paper and arguing over the right way to go about their assigned task. They must have figured something out, for soon shovels, hammers and saws were industriously put to work. I was puzzled at first; and then as the small building began to take shape in the late afternoon, I realized Wynn had lost no time in keeping his promise. There was to be a private outbuilding—and soon. I felt a pang at having caused Wynn this additional problem, but at the same time I was greatly relieved. I couldn't imagine living for very long without some kind of accommodation.

I kept scrubbing and cleaning, and the men outside continued pounding. My back began to ache and my arms cramp. Still I kept on. I was determined to have a clean house by nightfall.

I did the cupboards, the windows, the floors. I wiped off the mattress of the bed and managed to drag it outside for a bit of air and sunshine. I pulled the hard seat covering of the cot out into the sun, too. Then I washed all our dishes and pots and pans and put them on the newly scrubbed shelves. I arranged tins and cans of food on the remainder of the shelves, stacking some things on the floor. There just wasn't room for everything to be put away. Certain items, like the dishpan, the frying pan, and some of the utensils, I hung on the pegs on the wall.

It didn't make a particularly tidy-looking kitchen, but it was clean, and I was pleased. I put away the thought of asking Wynn for doors on my cupboards to conceal all the clutter. It was enough that I was getting the little outbuilding and, as I considered it the far more important of the two, I would just do without the cupboard doors—or I would think of some way to conceal the shelves myself.

It was getting late in the afternoon when I went out to retrieve the mattress from the stumps where I had propped it in the sun. It was even harder to drag back in than it had been to get it out; but after much tugging and yanking, I finally managed to get it back in on the bed. I made up the bed then with clean sheets and blankets. How good it would be to have our own clean bed to sleep in again. I took my clothes from the trunk and hung them on the pegs in the wall. They were still wrinkled, but I would have to wait to get to that. I couldn't do everything in one day.

By the time Wynn arrived home, the house was in quite good order—that is, the two rooms which we considered our house. The large room that was to be Wynn's office still needed to be arranged, but Wynn had told me to leave that to him. We had been delighted and surprised at the discovery of a storage room off the bedroom. Our crates, boxes, and supplies could all be kept there, out of our living accommodations. Wynn had placed the crates in the little room as we had emptied them that morning.

Our supper that night came from tins of North West Mounted Police rations. I had no other meat and no vegetables of any kind. It was a simple meal, but we ate with a deep feeling of satisfaction. We were where we belonged, doing what we felt called to do. We had a home, and we had one another. True, there was much more that needed to be done before we were *settled,* but we had made a good start. I forgot my tired arms and back and chatted with Wynn about all the possibilities the little cabin held. I looked out of my window to the rough little shanty with its crooked door and crude shingles and felt more thankful for it than for the fanciest bathroom. "Thanks, Wynn," I said, "for having that little building built so soon. I appreciate your thoughtfulness."

"I want to make you happy and as comfortable as possible," he said with a smile.

This was our start in our new life. After a good, hot soak in the tub I had found hanging on the outside wall, I was sure that I would feel content with my world.

Chapter Sixteen

Neighbors

Wynn was very busy taking on his Mountie responsibilities in the next few days, and I managed to keep just as busy. I was trying so hard to turn our little cabin into a real home. The material I had purchased in Calgary came out of the trunk, and I set to work in earnest with needle and thread. It was not an easy task. The material was heavy and, as I had no access to a sewing machine, I had to do all the sewing by hand. There were no frills. I made things as simple as I could. Soon the windows had curtains and the cot resembled a couch with its new spread over the hard foundation. I hand-stitched some cushions to toss on the cot, and it took on a homey look. Wynn surprised me with some fur rugs he purchased from an old trapper who tanned his own. They were much nicer than the old one I had pulled from the wall. Wynn moved that one onto his office floor. I placed the two new ones on the floor in front of the fireplace and beside our bed. They added a nice touch to the rooms, though I still couldn't get used to the odd smell lingering around them.

I had found the irons Wynn had packed for us and constructed a makeshift ironing board on which I was able to remove some of the wrinkles from our clothing. I wasn't satisfied with the job, however, but I shrugged it off as the best that could be done under the circumstances. We came to our first Sunday in the North. It was strange not having a church to attend. I asked Wynn what we would do in the place of a Sunday service. I suggested we might have our own and invite the people from the village to join us, but he felt it would be wise to take our time with any such plans. Then he proposed that, if I liked, we could take our lunch and go for a hike along the river. I was pleased with his idea and at once went to see what would be suitable for a picnic.

The countryside was beautiful. A few of the trees were already beginning to show their fall colors. It seemed awfully early to me, but I was reminded that we were now much farther north than I had been used to.

We didn't walk far. Everything was so new to me that I kept stopping for a good look and questions. Wynn answered them patiently. We saw a couple of cabins back in the bush, not far from the stream, and I asked Wynn if he knew who lived there.

"Not yet," he answered. "This next week I expect to find out more about our neighbors. I'll be gone a good deal of the weekdays, Elizabeth. Some nights I won't get home until quite late."

I nodded my head but said nothing.

"Does that bother you?"

I was slow to answer. I wouldn't look forward to long days without Wynn. But I had spent some time in prayer my first morning in the settlement, and some of my praying had been about that very issue.

I was able to say honestly now, "I'll miss you, certainly. But I'll be all right. I had a—a long talk with God about it and—I understand. I know that you can't stay in your office all the time. Or even around the settlement. I'll be fine. I still have so many things to do that I'll keep busy."

I managed a smile.

Wynn reached for my hand. "I know you've been very busy. Our little house looks much different since you've fixed it up, and I'm proud of you." His smile of appreciation filled me with a warm glow. "I've been wondering, though, if you might find some time now to get acquainted with some of our neighbors," he went on. "We will be living among them; it would be nice if you could soon find some friends."

"I've been meaning to," I told him. "Every day I've been telling myself, 'Today I will walk over to the store and meet some of the people.' But each time I find something more that needs to be done, so I put it off again."

Wynn nodded in understanding.

"I'll take some time this week. Tomorrow I need to do the washing, but maybe Tuesday I can go to the store."

"I'd like that. I'd like you to get to know some of the women so you might have company on the days I'm away."

I was quiet for a few moments. Wynn noticed.

"Something's bothering you," he commented, more as a statement than a question.

"Not 'bothering' really. It's just—well, I worry some about how I'll ever—" I didn't know just how to express that strange little fear twisting inside of me. Finally I just blurted out, "How do you get to know people when you can't talk to them?"

"You'll be able to talk to them. Oh, I know it will be hard and there will be times when you'll have problems expressing yourself. But you will pick up a few of their words quickly—many of the Indians already know a number of English words. Then there are always signs. The Indians are very good at making one understand them by using their limited English and their hands. They point out all kinds of messages. You'll catch on quickly—but you can't learn about them if you are not with them."

I knew Wynn was right, and I determined I would no longer hide behind my work but would venture forth and meet my new neighbors. It would be so much easier for me if Wynn could be along, but I knew his duties did not allow time for him to escort me around.

The sky was beginning to cloud over, so I picked up our picnic remains and we hurried to our cabin. The day suddenly went from sunshine to overcast to a thunderstorm. Wynn made a fire in the fireplace and we stretched out before it on the bear rug and talked about the people we had left behind and the folks who were our new neighbors here.

Thus far, my contact with the villagers was only on the night we had arrived. I had seen and been seen by a circle of friendly looking faces. Thinking back on it, though, I would have called them more curious than friendly. I could not remember even one smile except from the big man, Ian McLain. From my window I had watched as the two workmen had constructed our little shanty out back, and I had seen a few Indian women and children at a distance as they walked one or another of the paths that passed by our place. They always looked toward our cabin with a great deal of interest. But none of them had stopped and, as I hadn't known what to say to them, I had not called a greeting or invited them in.

Well, all of that must change. Even if it did mean learning a difficult new language, I must somehow break down the barriers and get to know my northern neighbors. *If only,* I mourned to myself, *one of them were a white woman.* There would be a common ground, a common bond, with her.

"You haven't even been in the Hudson's Bay Store, have you?" Wynn was asking.

"Not yet."

"I think you'll be surprised at the number of things available there. Of course, they are quite expensive. The shipping charges added to the cost make it far wiser to bring all you can with you rather than pay the extra price."

I remembered the heavy wagon loaded with all the crates, barrels, and boxes that brought our belongings to the settlement.

"Did that driver ever turn up?" I asked suddenly, my thoughts going back to our experience on the trail.

"Driver?"

"The one who should have driven us here but who was sleeping—?"

"Oh, him. Yes, he came walking in a couple of days ago—with all kinds of excuses and stories. Ian gave him a good scolding—like one would scold a child. Then Mrs. McLain filled the fellow up with roast duck and baking powder biscuits."

"Mrs. McLain?"

"Didn't I tell you? There is a Mrs. McLain after all."

My face must have beamed. I could hardly wait now for the opportunity to go into the settlement for my first visit. It would be so nice to have a chat with another woman. Perhaps I would even be able to invite her for tea on one of the afternoons when Wynn was away. It would help to fill in a long day.

"What is she like?"

"I haven't met her. I just overheard McLain telling about

the wayward team driver and the lecture and then her feeding him."

Attempting to picture Mrs. McLain, I began by imagining a woman my age, then quickly amended that. If she were married to McLain, she must be a good deal older than I.

"Do they have a family?" I queried.

"I haven't heard."

"Well, I'll find out all about them when I go to the store," I said, quite satisfied with the thought of my new venture.

Over our breakfast the next morning, I shared with Wynn my revised plans of going to the store that afternoon. He seemed pleased that I was making the venture to get acquainted.

"What can I say?" I asked him.

He looked puzzled. "What do you mean, what can you say?"

"Well, I can't just march in there and announce that I came to meet his wife."

Wynn smiled. "I'm not sure that would be so bad. People would be pleased to think that you are anxious to meet them. But—if you are hesitant to do that, do your purchasing first; and then, if you have a chance for a little chat with McLain, you shouldn't feel enbarrassed to mention the fact that you are most anxious to meet his wife."

"Purchases? I hadn't thought of purchasing anything."

"There must be something there you could use. Look around a bit."

I hesitated. Wynn looked at me questioningly.

I went on, slowly, picking out the words to voice my concern.

"You said it's a trading post, right? Well, I've never been—I've never bought anything at a trading post. I don't know how to . . . I've never *traded* for things before. What do I trade? I don't have any furs or—"

Wynn began to laugh. He reached out and lifted my chin and kissed me on the nose, but the laughter was still in his eyes. I knew I had just showed my city breeding. I either could get angry with Wynn for laughing at me or choose to laugh with him. For a moment I was very tempted to be angry. Then I remembered my father's prayer—the part about humor for the difficult times—and I began to laugh with Wynn. Well, not laugh really, but at least I smiled. "I take it I'm off-track?"

He smiled and kissed my nose again. "A little. It's true that it's a trading post and that the trappers bring their furs there. But Mr. McLain is very happy to accept good hard cash as well. However, for you that won't even be necessary. We have a charge account there with Mr. McLain. You pick what you need and he will enter it in his little book under my name. I also would like you to keep an account of what you spend, so I can enter it in my little book. That way, when Mr. McLain and I settle up each month, hopefully our accounts will agree."

I nodded. It all seemed simple enough.

After Wynn was gone, I hurried with the laundry. Wynn had already filled every available pail and the boiler that sat heating on our woodburning stove.

The clothes were all hand-scrubbed on a galvanized board we had brought with us from Calgary. On any other laundry day I would have taken my time, but today I was so excited about the prospects of meeting Mrs. McLain that I rushed through everything. I was hoping to finish the wash around noon. Then I would have time to walk down to the store while the clothes dried on the outside lines.

Wynn did not come home for the noon meal, so I had a simple lunch and then hurried to tidy myself for my trip to the store. I was still a bit concerned as to exactly how to approach the subject of meeting Mr. McLain's wife. Maybe if I was really lucky, she would be in the store as well.

The afternoon was a bit breezy and my carefully groomed hair threatened to be undone from its pinning. I had chosen one of the best dresses I had brought along. It swished in the loose dirt of the trail into the settlement. I held my hat with one hand and my skirt up with the other.

Many small, sometimes shabby, shacks lined the sides of the clearing as I neared the store. They were not placed in any regular pattern but rather built wherever a man had a mind to build. Some had smoke streaming forth through small chimney pipes. Some of them had no chimney pipe, and the smoke billowed instead out of unglassed windows. Children of various sizes and states of dress played in the dusty areas surrounding them, stopping to stare at me out of dark eyes in round brown faces. Dogs seemed to be everywhere. Some of them looked ferocious, and I was glad a few of the meaner looking ones were tied up. I dared not imagine what might happen if they were given their freedom. Once or twice I took a brief detour in order to stay a little farther away from a dog that didn't seem to be friendly.

The little children weren't too friendly either. I smiled at many of them, but the expression on the small faces did not change. I could not blame them. To them I must have looked strange indeed with my piled-up, reddish-gold hair and my long, full skirt swishing at the ground as I walked. I decided that the next time I ventured forth I would wear something less conspicuous, but this time I had so wanted to make a favorable impression on the settlement's only other white woman.

When I reached the Hudson's Bay Store, Mr. McLain was busy with another customer. The man did not look totally white nor did he look totally Indian. I assumed this was one of the mixed race people who Wynn had said were common in the North. He spoke English, even though rather brokenly, and there were some words mixed in with it that I did not understand. Mr. McLain seemed to have no difficulty. The two got along just fine. In fact, Mr. McLain himself also interchanged his English with words I had never heard before.

Mr. McLain spoke to the man and then moved my way. "Good-day to ya, ma'am," he said with a big smile, "an' may I be helpin' ya with something?"

"I'll need a while to look," I assured him. "You go right ahead with your customer. I'm in no hurry."

He nodded to me and went back to the other man.

I looked around the store. Wynn had been right. I was surprised at the amount and variety of merchandise carried. I was also shocked at the prices. Three times I selected something from the shelf, and three times my frugal nature made me put it back. I was about ready to give up and leave the place in embarrassment when I spotted some tacks. Now I did need some tacks. They, too, were expensive; but as I truly did need them and as I couldn't possibly get them from anywhere else, I decided to buy them.

I had just made my selection when the other customer left the store and Mr. McLain came my way.

"Have ya found what you're needin'?" he boomed.

"Yes. Yes, I think these will be just fine," I fairly stammered.

Mr. McLain led the way to the counter. I laid the box of tacks on the wooden square by the cash box. They looked very small and insignificant.

"And will this be all?" asked Mr. McLain.

I guessed he was used to his customers coming in and buying supplies to last them for many weeks. Here I was buying only a box of tacks. It must seem to him very much like a wasted trip. I flushed.

"I'm still not settled enough to know my needs," I tried to explain, "and we brought most of our supplies with us." Then I wondered if that was good news to a man who ran the only local store. I flushed more deeply. "I—I mean—we'll certainly be needing many things as the winter sets in and all—"

Mr. McLain seemed not to notice my discomfiture.

"Everything in good shape at the cabin?" he asked.

"Fine," I answered, not too sure just what he meant. "Just fine."

"The man before you wasn't much of a housekeeper," he commented. "I had to send one of the trappers' wives over to sorta sweep out the place after he left. The fella before him— now, he was some fussy. Made the men take their boots off when they went to his office—finally got so many complaints, the department said he had to stop it." Mr. McLain shook his head. "He was some fussy all right, that one."

I appreciated his consideration in sending over a woman to clean our cabin. I had thought it dirty when I arrived—I couldn't imagine what it might have been before.

As Mr. McLain talked, he got out a big black book and flipped to a page marked "Delaney, R.N.W.P." and began to make an entry. There were already several items listed on the page. In my brief glance I noticed some of them were to do with lumber—probably the building the two men constructed for us.

I took one more glance around the room and then let my mind go back to Mrs. McLain. How did I broach the subject of meeting the trader's wife? Mr. McLain solved the problem for me.

"My wife's out back in the garden. She's right anxious to meet ya. Got a minute to step around with me and say howdy?"

A smile flashed across my face. "I'd love to," I stated as I tucked the small box of tacks in my handbag and prepared to follow Mr. McLain.

The garden was weed-free and very productive. I wished with all my heart that I had one just like it. Next year I must try. It would be so nice to have some fresh vegetables. Some of them here were unfamiliar to me, though there wasn't much variety. I knew the frosts came much earlier this far north. I had also been told that, because of the long summer days, some vegetables did very well, with the added hours of sunshine to make them grow rapidly.

I took my eyes from the plants and looked about for a woman. She was at the far end of the garden patch, her dark head bent over a row of beets to which she was giving her total attention.

"Nimmie!" Mr. McLain hollered. "Got Mrs. Delaney here."

The dark head lifted; then, in one graceful movement, the woman was standing and facing me. A quiet smile spread over her face. She moved to meet me, extending a hand as she came.

"I am so pleased to meet you," she said softly.

She was Indian.

Chapter Seventeen

Adjustments

I walked home slowly, paying little attention to the staring children or the barking dogs. I had not stayed long to chat with Mrs. McLain. After my initial shock, there really didn't seem to be much to say. I hoped with all my heart that my shock hadn't shown on my face. Why hadn't Wynn warned me? Or had he known? And why hadn't I expected it? Wynn had told me that often the men in the North married Indian women. They were used to the lifestyle, the hardships, the work and weather, and weren't always fussing for their husbands to take them back to civilization. So why hadn't I prepared myself for that possibility?

I guess it was simply because I had so much wanted to have one white woman in the area, and it seemed that the Hudson's Bay man was the only candidate. In spite of telling myself that I was being foolish, I felt an intense disappointment. There wouldn't be a woman in the area after all with whom I could share intimacies. No one for little tête-à-têtes over an afternoon cup of tea. No one to understand women's fashions and women's fears. It was going to be a lonely time, the years ahead. They would be sure to get me down if I didn't take some serious steps to avoid allowing myself to be caught in the trap of self-pity.

I wasn't quite prepared at the moment to take those steps or to make future plans. For now it was enough just to sort out my thoughts and to spend some time in prayer concerning my feelings.

I did pray as soon as I got home, and I was feeling much

better by the time I went to bring in the clothes and apply the irons to the garments.

As I ironed, I thought, *What might I have to offer these Indian people? What things do we as wives have in common?* What could I do to improve their living conditions? I knew Wynn didn't want me rushing in trying to change their way of life, but weren't there little things we might enjoy doing together?

Perhaps a sewing class? I was a good seamstress, though I did admit difficulty in adjusting from machine to hand work. It seemed so clumsy and slow to me, and my poor fingers always seemed to be pricked full of holes in spite of a thimble.

Sewing might be a good idea. Then we could have tea. Maybe Indian ladies enjoyed tea every bit as much as white ladies did. I began to feel excited about the prospects. By the time the ironing was completed, my plans had begun to take shape.

The first thing to do was to make friends with them. At the first opportunity, no matter how difficult it seemed, I was going to speak to the Indian women. Even if I made blunders, it would be a start. I would never learn unless I tried.

But first I had another little project. The open cupboard shelves bothered me. I had lots of material I had brought along; and now, with the help of the tacks obtained from Mr. McLain, I would do something about covering them.

As soon as my ironing was done, I put away the laundry and the makeshift board and went to Wynn's office in search of a hammer. I found one hanging on a nail with the rest of his few tools and went to work. With material, scissors, hammer and tacks, I soon had the open-cupboard area nicely draped with curtains. They hung in attractive folds and I was quite pleased. They certainly were an improvement on the exposed dishes, pots and pans, and food stuffs. I cut matching place mats for the table, hemming them up as I hummed to myself.

I was finished just in time to get busy with the supper preparations. I could hardly wait for Wynn to get home and see how much nicer the kitchen looked. Again I wished for a white woman to share with. She would have understood my satisfaction and pleasure with the accomplishments of the day. Wynn, being a man and troubled with the duties of a law officer, might not be able to fully appreciate just how important this little addition was to me. A woman would, I was sure.

Wynn did notice my kitchen, complimenting me on how nice it looked. I beamed with pleasure.

As we had our evening meal together, he asked me if I had met Mrs. McLain as planned. I did not want Wynn to know about my great disappointment in not finding a white woman, so I tried to make no comments that would give away my true feelings.

"She seems to be somewhat younger than Mr. McLain," I began.

"I understand that he was married before," commented Wynn.

"She has a garden," I said with some enthusiasm. "I would love to have one like it next year. It would be so nice to have fresh things."

Wynn agreed. "You shall have your garden next year," he smiled. "I'll even see that the ground is broken for you. I think fresh vegetables would be a treat, too. That's one thing, I must confess, I miss about Calgary."

"I didn't recognize all her vegetables," I confided, "but she had lots of carrots, beets, potatoes, and onions."

"What's she look like?" Wynn asked, remembering that looks might be considered important to a woman.

I hesitated. I hadn't really looked at Mrs. McLain too closely. I drew from my memory in the brief glances I had afforded her.

"She's dark, not too tall, rather slim."

It wasn't much of a picture; but I couldn't really remember much more.

"Was she pleasant?"

"Oh, yes. Most pleasant," I hurried with my reply.

"That's nice," said Wynn. "I'm glad you have a white woman to—"

So he hadn't known. "Oh," I interrupted him, hoping my remark sounded very offhand and matter of fact, "she isn't white. She's Indian."

I turned from Wynn to get the teapot, so I didn't see if his surprise equaled mine or not. When I turned back to him, his face told me nothing.

"I'm sure she'll be good company," he encouraged. "I hope you'll be good friends."

The next morning I heard some women's voices approaching our cabin on the trail to the west; and, true to my resolve, I went outside so I could greet them. Three Indian women approached me, talking rapidly as they came.

They were dressed in a combination of Indian buckskin and calico purchased at the trading post. Lovely beadwork made a splash of color against the natural tan of the soft deerskins.

At my appearance, things were suddenly very quiet.

I knew no Indian words. I had to take the chance that they might know a few English ones.

"Good morning," I said with a smile.

There was no response.

I tried again. "Hello."

They understood this. "Hello," they all responded in unison.

"I'm Elizabeth," I said, pointing a finger at myself. That seemed like such a long name to expect anyone to learn. I changed it. "Beth," I said, jerking my finger at my chest.

The youngest woman smiled and nodded to the others.

"Beth," I said again.

She giggled, hiding her face behind her hand.

I didn't know what to try next. I wanted to invite them in but didn't know what words to use. Well, since I only had English, I would use English.

"Would you like to come in?" I asked, waving my hand toward the cabin.

They looked puzzled.

"Come in?" I repeated.

The middle one seemed to get my meaning. She held up a basket she was carrying and said distinctly, "Berries."

I understood then that they were on their way to pick berries and didn't feel they had time to stop. At least, my logic came up with this information.

I nodded, to assure them I understood. The other two women lifted their containers to show me that they were berry-pickers as well.

I nodded again. How did one tell them that she wished them great success in their picking. I scrambled around in my mind for some words; but before I could come up with something, the young woman surprised me by pointing a finger at me, lifting her basket in the air, waving a hand at the trail ahead, and saying, "Come?"

It caught me off-guard, but I was quick to respond.

"Yes," I smiled. "Yes, I'd love to come. Just wait until I get a pail."

I ran into the house, hoping they wouldn't misunderstand and go off without me. I quickly scribbled a note for Wynn in case he should come in while I was out, grabbed a small pail, my big floppy hat and a scarf to ward off mosquitoes, and dashed back out the door.

They were still waiting for me.

They took one look at my hat, pointed at it, and began to laugh loudly. There was no embarrassment, no discourtesy. They thought it looked funny and enjoyed the joke.

I laughed with them, even making the hat bounce up and down more than was necessary to give them a good show. They laughed harder, and then we moved on together down the path to the berry patch.

I had no idea where we were going. I decided to watch closely for landmarks in case I had to find my own way home. I wasn't much of a woodsman, and I would have hated to require Wynn's leaving his other duties to come looking for me.

We followed the path to the stream and the stream to the river and then followed the trail that paralleled the twists and turns of the river. I was sure I could find my way home so far.

We had gone maybe a mile and a half when the women cut away from the river and headed through the bush. There was no path now and I began to get worried. I could never find my way home without the aid of a path. I sincerely hoped the other women could. We might all be lost!

We walked for about another mile before we came to the

berry patch. The bushes were thick with them, and they were delicious-looking. The women talked excitedly as they pointed here and there. Then they set right to work.

I couldn't begin to keep up with them. Their hands seemed to flash as they whipped berries into their containers. I tried to follow their examples but ended up spilling more berries than I got to my pail, so I decided it was wiser for me to take my own time and get the berries safely where they belonged.

While the women chatted, I listened intently. I tried so hard to formulate some pattern in their speaking, to pick out a word that was repeated and sort out its meaning; but it was hopeless. As they chatted, they often stopped to double over in joyful, childlike laughter. It was clear they were a people who knew how to enjoy themselves. I wished I could share in their jokes. Then I wondered if I might indeed be the butt of their jokes; but, no, they didn't seem to be laughing at me.

It was almost noon when the youngest one came over to where I was picking. She looked in my pail and seemed to be showing approval on my good job. Then she showed me her basket. She had picked twice as many. She knelt beside me and quickly picked a few handfuls which she threw in my pail. The others came with their full containers. They gathered around me and they, too, began to pick berries and deposit them in my pail. I was the only one who still had room in my container. With four of us picking, the pail was full in no time. I thanked them with a smile, and we all got up and stretched to ease the ache in our backs.

"Ouch," said the oldest lady, and everyone laughed.

We started home then, full containers of berries carefully guarded. It was well after noon when we arrived at my house, and none of us had had anything to eat. I was starving. I wondered if they were, too.

"Would you like to come in?" I asked them, motioning toward the door.

They shook their heads and nodded toward their baskets, informing me that they had to go home to care for the berries. I lifted my pail then. "Some of these are yours," I reminded them, pointing to the berries and then at their baskets.

I began to scoop out berries to add to their already full

containers, but they shook their heads and pulled the baskets away.

"Keep," one of them said, the others echoing, "Keep."

I thanked them then and they went on their way, while I went to find something to eat and then to care for my own bountiful supply of berries. Such a delightful surprise! The berries were sweet and juicy and would be such a welcome addition to our simple meals. And the contact with the Indian women had been just as pleasant a surprise.

I wondered where they lived and if I would see them again.

I told Wynn I had a surprise for supper that night.

"Where did you get these?" he asked in astonishment when I brought out the pie.

"I picked them myself—well, at least most of them."

"How did you find them?"

"You'll never believe this," I began enthusiastically. "Some Indian women came by today; and when I greeted them, they said they were going berry picking and they invited me to go along . . . so I did. I didn't quite fill my pail on my own. They helped me."

"So you found some women who could speak English?"

"No. Not really."

"Then how—?"

"Oh, they said 'hello' and 'berries' and 'come.' "

Wynn smiled.

"We sort of filled in the rest with gestures. Oh, Wynn, I wish I could understand them! They had so much fun."

"Give yourself a little time. You'll soon be joining in. Who were they?"

"That's part of the problem. I don't even know their names. I couldn't ask them where they live or anything."

Wynn reached out and gently stroked my hair. "It's hard, isn't it?" he said.

"I might have found some friends—and lost them—in the very same day," I mourned.

I was working about my kitchen the next morning, wondering how I was going to fill my long day, when a loud call—

almost in my ear—spun me around. There stood the young-est member of the trio who had shared the berry patch the day before. After my initial fright, I was able to smile at her and indicate a chair for her. She shook her head and held up her basket. She was going to pick berries again.

"Yes, I'll go," I nodded to her. "Thank you for stopping for me. It will take me just a minute to get my things."

I thought as I bustled about finding my hat and my pail that she probably hadn't understood one word of what I had just said.

We went out into the sunshiny day and there, waiting at the end of our path, were four more women. Two of them had been with us the day before and the other two were new to me. I smiled at all of them, pointed to myself and said, "Beth," which they repeated with many giggles and varying degrees of success, and we started off. This time we went in a different direction when we came to the river. All along the way, the women chattered and laughed. I could only smile.

We picked berries until noon again. As before, they filled their containers before me and helped me to finish.

We walked home single file, the women laughing and talking as they went. How I wished I could join in. I wanted to at least ask them their names and where they lived. I might as well be mute for all the good my tongue did me.

When we got to our cabin, I again motioned for them to come in. They showed me their brimming pails and pointed to the settlement. I wouldn't let them go without *some* in-formation. I would try it again. So I pointed at myself and said, "Beth." Then I pointed at the youngest woman who had been the one to walk right into our home. The women looked at one another and smiled.

"Evening Star," the young woman said carefully, and then she went around the little circle pointing her finger at each of the ladies and saying their names. It was a strange mix-ture. The middle-aged woman was Kinawaki, the older woman Mrs. Sam, and the two new ones who had gone with us were Little Deer and Anna. I reviewed each of the names one more time to make sure that I had them right. The ladies nodded. I turned back to Evening Star, aching to communi-cate.

"Where do you live?" I tried.

She shook her head, not understanding. I looked at the other women grouped around her. They all looked blank.

"Your house? Where is your house?" I pointed at my house.

Evening Star's face lit up. "Law," she said. She must have thought that I was asking something about my own home.

I pointed toward the settlement. "Do you live over there?" I asked again.

"McLain," said the woman. At least she knew the name of the Hudson's Bay trader.

I knew I couldn't hold them any longer. I smiled and stepped back, nodding them a good-day. They smiled in return and started one by one down the path. Anna, the small, thin woman with the missing tooth, was the last to turn and go. Just as she passed by me, she stopped and leaned forward ever so slightly. "She doesn't understand English talk," she whispered, and then followed the others down the path. I stared after her with my mouth open.

Chapter Eighteen

Teas and Such

We went for berries the following day, too. Anna was there, and I directed my inquiries to her. I would not be cheated again out of conversation. I found out that the five women all lived in the settlement. Two of them, Mrs. Sam and Anna, were married to white trappers. Mrs. Sam had wished to be called as white women are called, by their husband's names. She did not understand quite how the system worked. Sam was her husband's first name; his last name was Lavoie.

Anna spoke English well because she had attended a mission school in another area. Beaver River had had no school. Anna did not consider herself superior, just different from the others. I found out later that she had had more schooling than her trapper husband, even though it was only the equivalent of about grade four. She was the one who did the figuring when she and her husband went to the trading post.

I also asked Anna about the families of the women. Anna didn't offer much on her own, but she did answer my direct questions. Evening Star was married to Tall One and had four children. She had had two others who had been lost at a young age to *dark blood*. I wondered what *dark blood* meant to the Indian. I tucked it away to ask Wynn. Kinawaki had been married—twice. Both her husbands had died. I decided that it would be improper and insensitive to probe for details. Kinawaki had borne nine children, five of them still living. Mrs. Sam had never had children. She had much time to do nothing, according to Anna. Little Deer, the short, round woman, had two boy-children who were always in the way;

and she, Anna, had five—two in Indian graves and three at home.

The mortality rate appalled me. The resigned way in which they seemed to accept it bothered me even more. Was it expected that one would raise only half of one's family?

I was learning how to fill my pail more quickly than I had previously, but the women still gave me a hand before we left for home. On our way home, I walked along beside Anna. The path was not made for walking two abreast—now and then we would come to thick growth where I would have to step back, allowing her to go on without me, and then hurry to catch up to her again. I wanted to be sure to let her know that I would welcome any of the women into my home at any time.

"Not today," said Anna. "Today we have much work. We must dry berries for cold. Takes much work."

I agreed.

"Berries almost gone now," she went on. "Bears and birds get rest. Not pick anymore."

"When the women are finished with their berries, then will they have time to come?"

"I'll ask." She spoke rapidly to the other ladies, who were trudging on single file down the trail. No one stopped and no one turned to enter the conversation; they just called back and forth. After a few minutes of exchanges, Anna turned to me.

"Why you want us come?" she asked forthrightly.

I was a bit taken aback. "Well, just to—to—to get to know you better. To make friends—to maybe have some tea—"

She interrupted me then. "Tea," she said. "That's good."

She talked again to her companions. I heard the word "tea," which seemed to be a drawing card. There was a general nodding of heads.

"We come—sometime," said Anna.

"Good!" I exclaimed. "How about tomorrow?"

Anna looked puzzled. "Why?" she said. "Why tomorrow?"

"Well, I—I'd like you to come as soon as possible."

"Come when ready," responded Anna, and I nodded my head.

"Come when ready," I agreed.

Two days later I looked up from my sewing to see Little

Deer standing in my doorway. I had not heard her knock. She came in smiling and took the seat I offered her. I got out the teapot and made the tea. We couldn't talk, so we just sat smiling and nodding at one another. She had watched with great interest as I lifted china cups from my cupboard. I didn't have any cake or cookies, so I cut slices of fresh bread and spread it with the jam I had made with some of my berries.

We had just taken our first sip from the cups when Evening Star walked in. She had not knocked either. I got another cup and we continued our tea party. When we finished I decided to show the two ladies around our house. They carefully looked at everything, their faces showing little emotion. I couldn't tell if they were pleased, puzzled, or provoked at what they saw. Nothing seemed to move them in the least.

I came to my kitchen and proudly demonstrated how I could sweep aside my curtains and reveal the dishes and food stacked on the shelves. Evening Star reached out a hand and tried it herself. She lifted the curtain, peered in behind it and let it fall back in place. Then she did it again. She turned to Little Deer and spoke a word in her native dialect. Not only did she say it once, but she repeated it, and Little Deer said it after her. At last, I had found something that impressed them! I said the word over and over to myself so I would remember it. I wanted to ask Wynn about it when he got home.

It wasn't long after our tea party until Wynn was home for supper. I still had the Indian word on the tip of my tongue. I wanted to be sure to ask him before I lost it.

Almost as soon as he entered the door, I asked him. It was a difficult word for my tongue to twist around, and I wasn't sure I could say it correctly.

"What is *winniewishy*?" I asked him.

Wynn puzzled for a moment and then corrected my pronunciation.

"That's it. What does it mean?"

"Where'd you hear that?" asked Wynn.

"Two of the ladies were here today for tea," I informed him excitedly. "What does it mean?"

"Well, in English, I guess we'd say *nuisance*. Why?"

Nuisance! They had viewed and touched my curtains and pronounced them *nuisance*? For a moment I was puzzled and hurt, and then it struck me as funny and I began to laugh.

"What's so funny?" asked Wynn.

"Oh, nothing, really. That was just the opinion of the ladies about the pretty, unpractical curtains over my cupboards."

It was Sunday again, though I had a hard time really convincing myself of that fact. It seemed so strange not to be preparing for church. I missed the worship. I missed the contact with friends. I missed being with my own family. But, most of all, I missed the feeling of refreshing that came from spending time with other believers in praise and prayer.

We set aside some time, just the two of us, in a manner that would become our practice for the years ahead in the North; and, with Bible in hand, we had our own brief Sunday worship service.

The next day, my washday, I was busy with ironing when a call from within my doorway announced another visitor. It was Evening Star. Right behind her came Mrs. Sam and Little Deer. I put aside my ironing and fixed the tea. The women seemed to enjoy it, smacking their lips appreciatively as they drank. We had just finished when Anna appeared. I made another pot and we started all over again.

With the coming of Anna, I was able to talk to the women. "I thought you might like to do some sewing," I said to them. "I have things all ready."

I went to my bedroom trunk and brought out material that I had already prepared to make pillows. I also brought needles and thread and proceeded to show the ladies how to go about stitching up the pillows. They started somewhat clumsily with the lightweight material, but seemed to catch on quickly enough. When they had finished, they handed the pillows back to me.

"Oh, no," I told them. "You may keep them. Take them home with you." I pointed to the many pillows I had on the cot. "You can use them in your own homes," I said, and Anna passed on the information. The women still looked a bit hesitant, but they all left with their pillows.

The next day the women came again, all walking right in as they arrived. I decided I would talk to Anna about it—explain that one did not just walk into another's house without knocking first. She would be able to inform the other ladies. It was uncomfortable for me, not knowing when someone might suddenly appear at my elbow.

Again we had our tea. I began to wonder just what I had started. Did the ladies think they needed to come to my house every day of the week for a tea party? I was glad they liked to come, but I wasn't sure how to put a stop to this as a daily event.

After tea I was all prepared to go and get some more sewing. They seemed to easily have mastered the simple cushion; now perhaps they would like to try something a little more difficult. I excused myself and went to my bedroom. While I was gone, there was a shuffling in the kitchen. Little Deer left the room and went to the outside step. I had returned to the kitchen-living room when she came back with some baskets on her arm. The ladies had each brought her own sewing. I stood dumbstruck as I watched the deft fingers move rapidly in and out of the material. Intricate designs in thread and bead-work were quickly forming under skilled hands. I could feel embarrassment flooding my face with deep color. To think that I, Elizabeth Delaney, had had the foolish notion that I could teach these women how to sew! Why, their work would put mine to shame any day. I didn't even know the right words to apologize.

Well, Elizabeth, I said to myself, *you certainly have a lot to learn.*

I did speak to Anna about my desire for the women to knock before entering. She looked puzzled. It seemed that even at the mission school knocking was not a custom. However, she nodded her head and passed the word on to the other women. They, too, seemed at a loss for the reason behind this, but they also nodded. I was relieved that the matter had been well taken care of.

The next day I was in the yard shaking a rug when Anna

arrived. She was alone, but I expected that a number of the others would soon follow. I led her into the house, opening the door for her and letting her pass on ahead.

She hesitated. Neither of us moved for a moment, and finally Anna said, "You not knock."

"Oh, no," I tried to explain. "That's fine. Go ahead. It's only at your house that I would knock. Not at my house."

She looked at me like I had really lost my senses, but she went in.

That day we were joined for tea by Mrs. Sam and Kinawaki, both of whom knocked before entering even though they arrived together. Evening Star and Little Deer did not come.

When Wynn got home that night, he took off his heavy boots and stretched out his long legs to rest his tired muscles. I knew he had been working very hard during these first few weeks on the post. He wanted to know his area thoroughly before the bad weather set in, so he might be well-prepared for trouble spots. I was bustling around with last-minute supper preparations.

"You know," he said to me, "I saw the strangest thing when I came through the village tonight. There was Anna, knocking on her own door. They never have a lock on their doors, so she couldn't have been locked out. I couldn't imagine what in the world she was doing. I asked McLain. He said that somewhere she had picked up the notion to knock, to chase out any evil spirits that were in the house before she entered."

I gasped. How could she have misunderstood me so? I certainly had no wish to be fostering false ideas about the spirit world. I explained it all to Wynn and he smiled at my dilemma. I was horrified.

The next time Anna came to see me, I informed her that I had been wrong, that it wasn't necessary to knock after all. She could enter at any time and call as she had always done.

Anna nodded impassively, but I was sure she was wondering about those crazy white people who couldn't make up their minds! From then on I never knew for sure if I had company until I had checked over both shoulders, and I made a habit of doing that frequently.

Chapter Nineteen

Friends

"Did you know that Ian McLain's sister lives here?" Wynn asked one morning at the breakfast table.

I looked up in astonishment. I certainly didn't know that. I wondered where she had been hiding. Then I checked myself—that wasn't fair. I hadn't been to the settlement more than two or three times myself.

"No," I said now. "Have you seen her?"

"Just at a distance."

"What's she like?"

"She's rather tall, like Ian. Not broad though. She walks very erect and briskly—that's all I know. All I saw was her retreating back."

"Where does she live?" I asked next, thinking eagerly about visiting her.

"I think she has one of the rooms at the back of the store, but I'm not sure even about that."

Well, I would find out. When I tracked her down, I would invite her for tea. Perhaps some morning. The Indian ladies still came often in the afternoon.

I switched my thoughts back to Wynn. "Have you heard her name?"

"She's a Miss McLain. I don't know her given name."

"She's never married? Is she quite a bit younger than her brother?"

"I don't know that, but I wouldn't expect so."

Wynn rose from the table and reached for his stetson. The poor thing still had the telltale wagon-wheel marks.

"I won't be home until late tonight," he said. "I have a lot of ground to cover today."

I dreaded having him gone from morning to dusk. It made the day so long. I said nothing but stepped over to him and put my arms around his neck for my goodbye kiss. "Be careful," I whispered. "Come home safely."

He held me for some minutes before he gently put me from him; and then he was gone, walking out our door and down the footpath in long, even strides.

I watched him until he had disappeared. With a sigh I turned and began clearing the table. Then I remembered Miss McLain.

So there *was* another white woman in the settlement! I couldn't wait to meet her. I wondered what she would be like. She would be older than I, certainly. Perhaps even twice my age. Had she been raised in the North? Or had she come up from the city, like I had?

I needed a few items from the store anyway, so I would just take a walk after I had done the morning household chores and see what I could find out.

I wasn't too eager to walk into the village. I didn't quite trust some of the dogs with their snapping teeth and snarling jaws. I was fine if they were kept tied; but the trappers and their families were sometimes a little careless about that, being so used to the dogs themselves. I had seen some of the Indian women carrying a heavy, thick stick as they walked through the village. When I asked Wynn about it, he nonchalantly remarked that it was needed against the dogs.

This morning, I was so enthused about meeting the white woman that I decided to even dare the dogs. As soon as I had finished up the dishes, tidied up the two rooms that composed our home, and swept the step, I freshened myself and started for the store. This time I had a respectably long list of needed items.

Fortunately, the dogs did not give me too much cause for concern. The more ferocious ones were all securely tied. Children played in the dirt of the roadway. Since we were now into September, I was very conscious—as a schoolteacher—that they really should have been in school. Again I longed to start some classes, but I realized I had none of the words of their dialect—well, just "nuisance"—and they had only a few of mine.

Mr. McLain was busy waiting on some Indian women. One of them was Mrs. Sam. I greeted her as an old friend, but we were still unable to say more than hello to one another.

I purchased my items, even adding a couple of things I hadn't thought about but spotted on the stacked shelves. Mr. McLain listed the items under our account, and I carefully itemized each one in my little book to give Wynn an accurate account for his records.

"Care for some coffee?" offered Mr. McLain in a neighborly fashion, jerking his thumb at the pot which ever stood ready on the back of his big airtight heater. A stack of cups was scattered around on a nearby stand. Some of them were clean, but most of them were dirty, having been used by former customers that morning. At first reluctant, I changed my mind.

"A cup of coffee would be nice," I said and walked over to the stove to help myself. I still wanted a chance to talk some with Mr. McLain, and a cup of coffee might prolong my stay enough to be able to do so.

"My husband was telling me that you have a sister living here," I ventured, after taking a deep breath. To make the statement seem less important, I then took a swallow of coffee. It was awful. It was so weak it hardly tasted like coffee at all—and so stale that what little flavor was there was almost completely eclipsed. It was hot though—I had to give Mr. McLain credit for that. I burned my tongue.

Mr. McLain kept figuring. Finally he lifted his head. "Katherine. Yeah, she lives here. Has lived here now for almost twenty years."

I wasn't sure what to say next. Katherine was such a pretty name. I tried to visualize the lady to whom it belonged.

"Where was she from, before that?" I asked rather timidly. Maybe the answer would tell me something about her.

"From St. John."

"St. John? My, she has come a long way from home, hasn't she?"

"Guess you could say that," agreed McLain. "She was a schoolmar'm back there."

"Really?"

Already I was warming up to this unknown lady. She had been a schoolteacher, educated, cultivated. I was confident we would have much in common.

"I was a schoolteacher, too," I went on. "I'd love to meet your sister. I'm sure we'd have much to talk about."

McLain looked at me in a strange, quizzical way. He didn't answer for many moments and then he said simply, "Yeah," very abruptly and curtly.

I waited, hoping to discover how I could go about making the acquaintance of this woman. Mr. McLain said nothing.

Finally I ventured, "Is she—does she live around here?"

It was a stupid question. "Around here" was the only place there was to live—that is, if she was considered a part of this settlement.

"Out back," said McLain shortly. "She has the room with the left door."

I stammered on, "Do you—do you suppose she would mind if I called?"

McLain looked at me for what seemed like a long time and then jerked his big head at the door. "I don't know why she'd mind. Go ahead. Leave your things right here 'til you're ready to go off home."

I thanked him and went out the door and around to the back of the building to look for the door on the left.

Mrs. McLain was in the backyard hanging out some laundry. I felt embarrassed. What if she saw me? But, then, what did it matter? She had her back to me, anyway, as she sang softly to herself.

I rapped gently. There was no response. I knocked louder. Still no response. I hesitated. Clearly Miss McLain was not in. I decided to try one more time. To this knock there was a loud call of "Come," and I opened the door timidly and went in.

The room was dark, so it took me a few minutes to get accustomed to the lack of light and locate the room's occupant.

She was seated in a corner, her hands idly folded in her lap, staring at the blank wall in front of her. I wondered if she might be ill and was about to excuse myself and depart for a more convenient time, but she spoke. "You're the lawman's wife."

Her voice was hard and raspy.

"Yes," I almost whispered, wondering if her statement was recognition or condemnation.

"What do you want?"

"Well, I—I just—heard that—that a white woman lived here, and I wanted to meet you."

"White woman?" The words were full of contempt. "This is no place for a white woman. One might as well realize that anyone who lives here is neither white nor a woman."

I couldn't believe the words, and I certainly could not understand the meaning behind them. I turned and would have gone, but she stopped me.

"Where are you from?" she demanded.

"Calgary. I was a schoolteacher near Lacombe before coming here. I was born and raised in Toronto."

"Toronto? Nothing wrong with Toronto. Why'd you come here?"

"Well, I—I—married a member of the Royal North West Police. I—"

She turned from me and spit with contempt into the corner.

When she turned back, her eyes sparked fire. "That's the poorest reason that I ever heard for coming to this god-forsaken country," she said. "Some people come because they have to. My brother came for the money. Nothing else, just the money. Buried his first wife here, and still he stayed. But you—"

She did not finish her sentence but left me to know that I had done something incredibly wrong or stupid, perhaps both.

I felt condemned. I also felt challenged. Suddenly I drew myself up to my full five feet, three inches. "Why did *you* come here?" I asked her.

Again her eyes flashed. I was afraid for a moment that she might throw something at me, her anger was so evident. But she would have needed to leave her chair in order to do that—she had nothing near at hand.

"I came," she said deliberately, hissing out each word, "I

came because there was nothing else that I could do—nowhere else where I could go. That's why I came."

I was shaken. "I'm—I'm sorry," I murmured through stiff lips. I stood rooted to the spot for a moment and then I said softly, "I think I'd better go."

She did not comment, only nodded her head angrily at the door, indicating that I was quite free to do so, and the sooner the better in her estimation.

I was glad to step out into the warm sunshine and close the door behind me on the angry woman inside. I stood trembling. I had never seen anyone behave in such a way. *My, what deep bitterness is driving this woman?* I wondered. It could completely destroy her if something wasn't done. But what could one do? Personally, I hoped I would never need to encounter her again.

A soft song caught my ears and I remembered Mrs. McLain. She was still there hanging up her laundry. I didn't want to make contact with the woman, especially not in my present shaky condition. I hastily headed down the path in hopes of dodging around the building, but she saw me.

"Good morning, Mrs. Delaney," she called pleasantly.

I had to stop and respond. I managed a wobbly smile. "Good morning, Mrs. McLain," I returned. "It's a lovely morning, isn't it?"

"It is. And I am just finishing my washing and stopping for a cup of tea. Could you join me?"

I thought to wonder then about her excellent grammar. She had only the trace of an accent.

I still wanted to head for the security of my little home, but that would be very rude; so I smiled instead and said, "That is most kind. Thank you."

She pegged the last dish towel to the line, picked up her basket and led the way through the right-hand door.

The room was very pleasant and homey, a combination of white and Indian worlds. I noticed what a pleasant atmosphere the blending gave the room.

She seated me and went out to her small kitchen. Soon she was back with a teapot of china and some china cups. She also brought some slices of a loaf cake made with the local blueberries. It was delicious.

"So, are you feeling settled in Beaver River?" she asked me.

"Oh, yes. Quite settled."

We went on with small talk for many moments, and then she became more personal. Eventually it dawned on me that this was the kind of conversation I had been aching to have with a woman. The kind for which I had been seeking white companionship.

"Does it bother you, being left alone so much?" she asked sympathetically.

"I guess it does some. I miss Wynn, and the days are so long when he is gone for such a long time. I don't know how to make them pass more quickly. I have sewed up almost all the material I brought along, and there is really nothing else I can cover, or drape, or pad, anyway," I said in truth and desperation.

"When you have a family, you won't have so much free time," she observed. "In fact, when winter comes, you will be busier. It takes so much more of one's time even to do the simple tasks in the winter," she went on to explain. I hadn't thought about that, but I was sure she was right.

I switched back to her earlier comment. "Do you have a family?" I asked.

"No," was her simple answer, but I thought I saw pain in her eyes.

"Have you always lived here?" I said, partly to get on to another subject.

I expected her to say she had come to Beaver River from another area, so I was surprised when she said, "Yes. I have never lived more than a few miles away. My father used to have a cabin about five miles up river. I was born there."

I know that my surprise must have shown on my face. She smiled.

"You are wondering why I speak English?"

I nodded.

"I'm married to an Englishman." She laughed then. "Not an Englishman, really. He is a Scotsman. He was raised from childhood by a Swedish family. At one time he went to a French school, he was apprenticed under a German, and he speaks three Indian dialects—but his mother tongue is English."

"My," I said, thinking about McLain with new respect. I had wondered why he didn't speak with a Scottish accent. His sister did not have one either, come to think of it. "My," I said again. "Does he speak all of those languages?"

"Some French, some Swedish, some German, and much Indian." She said it with pride.

"But that still doesn't explain your English."

She looked at me as though she thought I should have understood, and perhaps I should have. "If my husband can speak seven languages," she said, "it seemed that at least I should be able to learn his."

I nodded. What spirit the young woman had.

"And how did you learn?" I persisted, feeling very at ease with her.

"Books. When he saw that I was really interested, he got me books; and he helped me. In the long winter evenings, we would read to one another and he would correct my pronunciation and help me with the new words. I love English. I love reading books. I wish my people had all these wonderful stories to read to their children."

Excitement filled me. "Have you ever thought of writing the stories for them? You know, putting the Indian stories down on paper for the children to read."

"None of them can read," she said very sadly.

"But we could teach them," I was quick to cut in.

She smiled, and her smile looked resigned and pitiful.

"They do not wish to learn. It takes work. They would rather play."

"Are you sure?" I asked incredulously.

"I'm sure. I have tried." She looked older then. Older and a bit tired.

"I'll help you. We can try again."

A new spark came to her eyes. "Would you? Would you care enough to really try?"

"Oh, yes. I've just been aching to get going, but Wynn said that I should wait. That I shouldn't go rushing in. I even brought some books along so that I might—"

I stopped. I was getting carried quite away with it all.

She reached out and took my hand. "I thank you," she

said sincerely. "I thank you for feeling that way. For caring. Maybe we *can* do something."

"I'll show you my books and the things I have and—"

She stopped me. "Your husband is quite right, Mrs. Delaney. We mustn't rush into this unprepared. The Indian people have waited for many generations for the chance to read and write. A few more weeks or months will make little difference."

I supposed she was right. I swallowed my disappointment and glanced at the clock on the wall. It was almost noon, I discovered with surprise.

"Oh, my," I said, "look at the time. I had no idea. I must go."

I stood quickly, placing my empty cup on the nearby small table.

"Thank you so much for the tea—and the visit. I enjoyed it so much."

"I've enjoyed it, too. I do hope that you will come back again soon, Mrs. Delaney."

"My name is Elizabeth," I told her. "Elizabeth, or Beth— you can take your pick. I'd be pleased if you'd call me by my given name rather than Mrs. Delaney."

She smiled. "And my name, Elizabeth," she said, "is Nemelaneka. When I married Ian, I thought he would like a wife with an English name, so I spent days poring over books and finally found the name Martha. 'Martha,' I told him, 'will be my name now.' 'Why Martha?' he asked me. And I said, 'Because I think that Martha sounds nice. Is there another name that you like better?' 'Yes,' he said, 'I like Nemelaneka, your Indian name.' So I stayed Nemelaneka, though Ian calls me Nimmie."

"Ne-me-la-ne-ka," I repeated, one syllable at a time. "Nemelaneka, that's a pretty name."

"And a very long and difficult one," laughed the woman. "Martha would have been much easier to say and spell."

Just as I was taking my leave, Nemelaneka spoke softly. "Don't judge poor Katherine too quickly," she said. "There is much sorrow and hurt in her past. Maybe with love and understanding—" She stopped and sighed. "And time," she added. "It takes so much time, but maybe with time she will overcome it."

I looked at her with wonder in my eyes but asked no questions. I nodded, thanked her again, and hurried home after retrieving my shopping from the store.

Chapter Twenty

Change of Direction

No ladies came for tea that day. I had thought I would welcome a day to myself, wondering at times how I was ever going to put a stop to the daily visits; but now, with none of them coming, I found that I really missed them. I fidgeted the entire afternoon away, not knowing what to do with myself. Eventually, I laid aside the book I was trying to read and decided to take a walk along the river.

I did not go far and I did not leave the riverbank since I was still unsure of my directions.

It was a very pleasant day. The leaves had turned color and, mingled among the dark green of the evergreens, they made a lovely picture of the neighboring hillsides.

The river rippled and sang as it hurried along. Occasionally I saw a fish jump, and as I rounded one bend in the trail I saw a startled deer leap for cover. I was enjoying this wilderness land. But Nimmie had been right. I was lonesome at times as well.

I thought now about all the family I had left in Calgary and Toronto. I thought, too, about my friends and school children at Pine Springs. *I wonder if the school has a new teacher?* I certainly hoped so. The children who had finally been able to start their education needed the opportunity to continue.

I wished there was some way to learn what was going on back home. I seemed so far removed from them all, so isolated. *Why, something terrible could happen to one of them and I would never know!* The thought frightened me, and I had to put it aside with great effort or it would surely have overwhelmed me with depression.

I firmly chose to think of other things instead. It was easy to go back to my visit with Nimmie. I was so glad to have found a kindred spirit. One who was just as concerned—no, *more* concerned—about the need of schooling for the village children. I could hardly wait to get something started, but I knew Nimmie and Wynn were right. One must go slowly and do things properly.

Reluctantly, I turned my steps homeward again. I earnestly hoped Wynn wouldn't be too late. I had so many feelings whirling around inside, and I needed so much to be able to share them with someone—someone who would listen and understand.

The day passed slowly. Dusk was falling and still Wynn had not returned. I walked around the two rooms we called home, looking for something to do but finding nothing that interested me.

I paced the outside path, back and forth, and tried to formulate in my mind just where I would plant my next year's garden.

I stirred the supper stew and rearranged the plates on the table and stirred the stew again.

I sat with a book near the flickering lamp and pretended to myself that I was interested in the story.

Still I was restless and edgy. My agitation began to turn to anger. Why did he have to be so late? Was the job really that important? Did his work matter more than his wife? Was this dedication to his job really necessary, or was he just putting in time, choosing to be late every day?

My angry thoughts began to pile up, one on top of the other. *Wynn could have been home long ago had he chosen to be!* I finally concluded.

It was now quite dark. Even Wynn had not expected to be *that* late. My thoughts took a sudden turn. What if something had happened? What if he were lost? Or had had an accident? What if some deranged trapper had shot him? Mounties were warned of this possibility. Suddenly I was worried—not just a little worried, but sick-worried. I was sure something terrible had happened to my husband and here I sat not knowing how or where to get help. What if he were lying out there somewhere, wounded and dying, and I sat idly in my chair fumbling with the pages of a book and fuming because he was late?

What could I do? I couldn't go looking for him. I'd never find my way in the darkness. Why, I could barely find my way in the broad daylight! Besides, I had no idea where Wynn had gone. What should I do?

Indians! They were good at tracking. Didn't they have some sort of sixth sense about such things? I didn't know any of the Indian men, but I knew their wives. I would go to them for help.

I ran for my light shawl. I would go to the village and knock on doors until I found someone.

Then I remembered the dogs. They were often untied at night because the owners were not expecting anyone after dark. Out in the darkness of the woods by our pathway, I searched the ground for a heavy stick.

Footsteps on the path startled me. I swung around, my breath caught in my throat, not sure what I would be facing.

"Elizabeth!" Wynn said in surprise. "Did you lose something?"

I wanted to run and throw myself into his arms but my embarrassment and my remembered anger stopped me. I wanted to cry that I had been worried sick, but I feared that Wynn would think me silly. I wanted to run to my bedroom and throw myself down on the bed and cry away all my fear and frustration, but I did not want to be accused of being a hysterical woman. I did *not* want to explain what I was doing out in the tangled bush by the path in the darkness, and I would not; so I simply said, rather sharply, "What took you so long? Supper is a mess," and brushed past him into the kitchen.

Wynn said nothing more at the time. He ate the nearly ruined supper and I pushed mine back and forth across my plate with my fork.

Supper was a long and silent meal.

I had had so much to tell him, so much to talk about; and here we sat in silence, neither of us saying anything. It was foolish, and well I knew it.

I stole a glance at Wynn. He looked tired, more than I

had ever seen him before. It occurred to me that he might have things to talk about, too. What had happened in his day? Were there things that *he* wished to talk about?

Taking a deep breath, I decided I should lay aside my hurt pride and ask him.

"You were very late," I began. "In fact, I was worried. Did something unexpected happen?"

Wynn looked up, relief in his eyes.

"A number of things," he answered. "Our boat got a leak, we were charged by an angry bull moose, the trapper we went to see chose not to be home and we had to search for him and we ended up bringing him in handcuffs; and the Indian that I had taken along to act as my guide took a nasty fall and had to practically be carried the last two miles on my back."

I stared at Wynn in unbelief. Surely he was joking. But the look on his face told me he was not.

"Oh, my," was all that I could say. "Oh, my."

Wynn smiled then. "Well, it's over," he said. "That's the only good thing I can say about this day."

But it wasn't over.

We hadn't even finished our poor meal when there was a call from outside our window. A man in the village had accidentally shot himself in the leg while cleaning his gun and Wynn was needed to care for the wound.

Wordlessly, he put on his hat and followed the excited boy.

It was very late when Wynn returned home. I was still waiting up for him. He crossed to me and kissed me. "I'm sorry, Elizabeth," he said; "you should have gone to bed."

"I couldn't sleep anyway," I said honestly.

The truth was that while Wynn had been gone, I had been doing a lot of thinking. I really had no idea how Wynn filled his days. When he came home at night, after a long day being—well, somewhere—we talked about what I had done with *my* day. I had never really asked Wynn about his before. What were Wynn's days like? Surely they weren't all as difficult as this one had been.

I had been anxious to tell him about my tea with Nimmie and about meeting Miss Katherine McLain. He had faced grave problems and possible death and likely would have made no comment about either if I hadn't made an opportunity just to make idle conversation. I felt ashamed. *From now on,* I determined, *I'm going to pay more attention to my husband and be less concerned with my silly little doings.*

By the time Wynn had returned from dressing the wound, I was feeling quite meek. Hadn't I come north with him to be his companion and support? I had been living as though I had come merely for his decoration.

I tipped my face now to receive Wynn's kiss, then asked, "How is the man?"

"He'll be okay, though he does have a nasty flesh wound. Barring infection, he should have no problem."

I shivered thinking about it.

"You're cold," said Wynn. "You should be in bed."

"No, I'm not cold, just squeamish," I answered. "Would you like a cup of something hot to drink? Coffee? Tea?"

"Tea sounds good. Is the water still hot?"

"I kept the fire banked. It will just take a minute."

"It's very late, Elizabeth. I know you're tired. I don't need—"

"It's no trouble," I assured him as I moved to the kitchen area.

Wynn sat down in the one easy chair and I could hear him removing his high-topped boots. *He must be nearly dead of exhaustion,* I thought.

I brought Wynn's tea and he gulped more than sipped it.

"You wanted to talk?" he said, lifting tired eyes to me.

"It can wait for morning."

"It doesn't need to wait," maintained Wynn.

"It's not that important. I just met Miss McLain today and had tea with Mrs. McLain. I'll tell you all about them at the breakfast table."

I took Wynn's empty cup from him and carried it to the table. Then I turned to him. "Come," I said. "This day has been long enough already."

Chapter Twenty-one

The Storyteller

The next few weeks were rather uneventful. Wynn still was busy; but now that he had carefully patrolled all the area to which he was assigned, he was able to do more of his work from his one-room office. I liked having him around more, and it also helped me to become more familiar with what he did.

He was police, doctor, lawyer, advisor, handyman, and often spiritual counselor—and so much more. The people came to him for any number of reasons. He was always patient and just, though sometimes I wondered if he wasn't a little too frank. They seemed to expect it. If he said, "No, Cunning Fox, that is not your territory for trapping; and, if you insist upon using it, I will need to lock you up," the Indian did not blink. At least he knew exactly what to expect.

The Indian women came often for tea, though not nearly as regularly as they had at first. Mrs. McLain, my friend Nimmie, called, too: and I always enjoyed her visits. Miss McLain did not come, though I had bolstered up my courage to invite her on more than one occasion.

We still did not have a school. Nimmie and I had spent hours poring over books, both hers and mine. I was so anxious to get started; but she felt it was far more likely to succeed if we could convince the chief, or at least some of the elders, that it would be good for the children. This would take time, she assured me. As the chief of the band did not live in our village, but in a village farther west, we had no way to hurry our negotiations.

One Wednesday morning, a swollen-faced Indian came to see Wynn. After a brief examination, Wynn came into the kitchen.

"Got any hot water?" he asked me.

I indicated the kettle on the stove, and Wynn pulled out a pan and put some simple instruments in it, then poured the water over them and set the whole thing over the heat.

"What are you doing?" I asked, curious.

"Reneau has a bad tooth. It's going to need to come out."

"You're going to pull it?" I asked in astonishment.

"There isn't anyone else," Wynn answered. Then he turned teasingly to me. "Unless, of course, you want the job?"

"Count me out," I was quick to reply.

Wynn became more serious.

"In fact, Elizabeth, I was about to do just that," he said, turning the instruments over in the pan. "How would you like a little walk, for half-hour or so?"

I must have looked puzzled.

"I have no anesthesia. This man is going to hurt."

I realized then that Wynn was giving me opportunity to get away from the house before he began his procedure.

"I'll go to the store," I said quickly.

It didn't take me long to be ready to leave the house. Wynn was still with the shaking Reneau. I wondered who was dreading the ordeal ahead more—Reneau or Wynn.

There really wasn't anything I needed from the store, so I decided to drop in on Nimmie. She didn't answer my knock on her door. I turned to look around me, and then I spotted her in a little grove of poplar trees just beyond her garden. She had gathered about her a group of the village children. I hoped I wasn't interrupting things and approached quietly. Nimmie was telling a story, and all eyes were raptly focused on her face. *She must be a good storyteller—not a child is moving!* I marveled.

I stopped and listened.

". . . the man was big, bigger than a black bear, bigger even than a grizzly. He carried a long hunting spear and a huge bow and arrow with tips dipped in the poison potion. Everyone feared him. They feared his anger, for he roared like the mighty thunder; they feared his spear, for it flashed as swiftly as the lightning. They feared his poison arrows, for they were as deadly as the jaws of a cornered wolverine. They all shook with fear. No one would go out to meet the enemy. They would all be his slaves. Each time they came from the trapline they would have to give to him their choicest furs. Each time they pulled in the nets, he would demand their fish. Each time they shot a bull elk, they would have to give him the meat. They hated him and the slavery, but they were all afraid to go out to fight him.

"And then a young boy stepped forward. 'I will go,' he said. 'You cannot go,' the chiefs told him. 'You do not have the magic headdress. You do not have the secret medicine. You are not prepared for battle.' 'I can go,' said this young boy named David, because I take my God with me. He will fight for me.' "

I stood in awe as the story went on. I had never heard the story of David and Goliath told in this fashion before. I was surprised to hear Nimmie telling it now. Where had she heard it? She had not attended a mission school. And why was she telling it to the children in English? Few of them could understand all of the English words.

I was puzzled but I was also intrigued. How often did Nimmie tell the local children stories, and how often were they taken from the Bible? Did she always interpret the stories with Indian concepts and customs?

" 'See,' said David, 'I have here my own small bow and five tried arrows. God will direct the arrow. I am not afraid of the bearlike Goliath. He has spoken against my God and now He must be avenged.'

"And so David picked up his small bow and his five true arrows and he marched out across the valley to the wicked enemy. Goliath laughed in scorn at David. 'What are you doing,' he cried, 'sending out a child instead of a brave? You have shamed me. I turn my head from you. I shall feed this little bit of meat to the ravens and foxes.'

"But David called out to the man as tall as the pine tree, 'I come not as a child, nor yet as a brave; but I come in the name of my God, whom you have insulted,' and he thrust one of the tried arrows in his bow, whispered a prayer that God would guide its flight on the wings of the wind, and pulled the bow with all of his strength.

"The arrow found its mark. With a cry, the big warrior fell to the ground."

If I for one moment had doubted that the children were able to follow the story, the shout that went up at the moment of Goliath's defeat would have convinced me otherwise. They cheered wildly for the victorious David.

When the noise subsided, Nimmie went on, "And so David rushed forward and struck the warrior's head from his body and lifted his huge headdress onto his own head. He picked up the long spear and his big bow and arrows and carried them back to his own tribe. They would never be the slaves of the wicked man again. David had won the battle because he had gone to fight in the name of his God."

Again there was a cheer.

"And now you must go," said Nimmie, shooing them all away with her slim hands.

"Just one more. Another one. Only one," pleaded a dozen voices.

"You said that last time," laughed Nimmie, "and I gave you one more and you say it again. Off you go now."

Reluctantly the children began to leave, and Nimmie turned. She had not been aware that I was standing there. A look of surprise crossed her face, but she did not appear to be disturbed or embarrassed.

"What a bunch," she stated. "They would have one sitting all day telling stories.—Come in, Elizabeth. We will have some tea. Have you been waiting long?"

"Not long, no. And I enjoyed it. Do you tell the children stories often?"

"Often? Yes, I suppose so—though not often enough. I don't know who enjoys it more, the children or I. Though I try to make it sound like they are a nuisance."

She laughed again and led the way to the house.

"But you told it in English," I remarked. "Do they understand?"

"They understand far more than you would think. Oh, they don't catch all the words, to be sure; but as they hear the stories again and again, they pick up more and more."

"And you told a Bible story," I continued, still dumbfounded.

"Yes, they like the Bible stories."

I wanted to ask where she had learned the Bible stories but I didn't.

"I love the Bible stories, too," she explained without being asked. "When I was learning to read English, the Bible was one of the books I read. At first it was one of the few books my new husband had on hand, so he taught me from it. I enjoyed the stories so much that, even now that I have many books, I still read from the Bible. They are such good stories."

She opened the door and let me pass into her home.

"I like the stories about Jesus best," she continued. "The children like them, too. I tell them often. The story about the little boy and his fish and bread; the story about the canoe that nearly was lost in the raging storm; the story about the blindman who could see when Jesus put the good medicine on his eyes. Ah, they are good stories," she concluded.

"You know, Nimmie," I pointed out, "those aren't merely stories. Those are true reports of historical events. All those things really happened."

She looked so surprised and bewildered that I said, "Didn't—didn't Ian tell you that—that the Bible is a true book, that those events, those happenings—?"

"Are they *all* true?" asked Nimmie incredulously.

"Yes, all of them."

"The ones about Jesus?"

"Every one."

"And those wicked people really did put Him to death—for no reason?"

I nodded. "They did."

There was silence. Nimmie looked from me to the Bible that lay on the little table, her eyes filled with wonder and then anger. "That's hateful!" she protested, her voice full of emotion. "How could they? Only a white man could do such a thing—destroy and slay one of his own! An Indian would never do such a shameful thing. I would spit on their graves. I would feed their carcasses to the dogs." Her dark eyes flashed and her nose flared.

"It was terrible," I admitted, shocked at her intensity. "But it wasn't as simple as you think. The reason for Jesus' dying is far more complicated than that. We could read it together if you'd like. I'd be glad to study the story with you, right from the beginning, and show you why Jesus had to die."

She began to calm herself.

"He didn't stay dead, you know," I went on.

"Is that true, too?" she asked in disbelief.

"Yes, that's true, too."

She was silent for a moment. "I might like to study that."

I smiled. "Fine. Why don't we start tomorrow morning? At my house?"

She nodded and rose to prepare the tea. She turned slightly. "Elizabeth, I'm sorry—sorry about what I said concerning the white man. It's only—only that sometimes—sometimes I cannot understand the things men do. The way they gnash and tear at one another—it's worse than wolves or foxes." This time she did not say *white* man, though I wondered if she still thought it.

"I know," I agreed shamefacedly. "Sometimes I cannot understand it either. It isn't the way it was meant to be. It isn't the way *Jesus* wants it to be. It isn't the right way. The Bible tells us that God abhors it, too. He wants us to love and care for one another."

"Does the white man know that?"

"Some of them do."

"Hasn't the white man had the Bible for many years?"

"Yes, for many years."

"Then why doesn't he read it and do what it says?"

I shook my head. It was a troubling question. "I don't know," I finally admitted. "I really don't know."

Chapter Twenty-two

Studies

Our Bible studies together started the next day as planned. We did not meet together every day, but we did meet regularly. Ian did not seem to object, and Wynn was most encouraging.

Nimmie was a good student; and as we began to piece together the whole plan of God for His creation, she became excited about it.

"Katherine should be here! She needs to hear this," she insisted.

I wondered about Katherine. I doubted that she would come out of her bitterness long enough to even listen, but Nimmie kept insisting.

"Do you mind if I bring her?" she continued.

"Well, no. I don't mind. I'm not sure—I'm not sure she'd come that's all. I've asked her to my house many times, and I've never been able to get her to come."

"For Bible study?"

"Well, no, not for Bible study necessarily. Just for tea. But if she won't come even for tea, I surely don't think she'll want to come for study."

"She might," persisted Nimmie. "I'll ask her."

When Nimmie arrived for the next study, she had Katherine with her. I never will know how she effected the miracle. I tried to keep the shock out of my face as I welcomed them both in.

Katherine scowled as we opened our Bibles and began to read. She had brought a Bible of her own, but it didn't look as though it had received much use. She said nothing all morning long, even though Nimmie often stopped in the reading to comment or ask for an explanation. She was eager to know not just the words but the *meaning* of the words, now that she knew each of the stories was true.

When the two ladies left that morning, I told them I would be looking forward to our next time together. Katherine frowned and informed me in unmistakable tones, "Don't expect me back. I came just to get this here woman off my back. There's nothing in this book that I don't already know. I'm not a heathen, you know—I was raised in church."

"Then you must miss it," I said softly.

She wheeled to look at me.

"I was raised in church, too," I continued, "and if there is one thing about the North that I miss more than any other, it is not being able to go to church on Sunday."

She snorted her disgust, pressed her lips together and marched out the door.

Nimmie looked at me sadly and followed the other woman.

I don't know how it came about; but the next time Nimmie came for her study, Katherine was reluctantly trudging along behind her, her Bible tucked under one arm.

I made no comment except to welcome them both, and we proceeded with our reading and discussion.

The weather was getting colder. Daily, large flocks of ducks and geese passed overhead as the birds sought warmer climates. Almost all the leaves were dancing on the ground rather than clinging to the now-bare branches. The animals' coats began to thicken; and men talked about a long, hard winter.

Wynn hired some men to haul a good supply of wood for the fire, and we prepared ourselves as well as possible for the winter weather ahead.

The inevitable day came. The north winds howled in, carrying sub-zero temperatures and swirling snow. We were in the midst of our first winter blizzard. I was so thankful that Wynn was home, safe and sound, instead of out someplace checking on a far-off trapper.

In spite of the fire in the stove, the temperature in the cabin dropped steadily. Wynn lit the fireplace and hung some blankets over the windows to shut out the cold. Still the chill did not leave the air. We piled on the clothing to keep our body heat in.

That night we banked our fires and retired early, hoping that the next day might bring a break in the storm. During the night, Wynn was up more than once to be sure the fire was still stoked with wood.

"I do hope there are no casualties," Wynn said. "This is unusually severe for this time of year. Some folks might not have been prepared for it."

I hoped, too, that there were no casualties. It would be terrible to be caught out in such a storm.

When we awoke the next morning, we were disappointed to find the fury of the storm had not slackened. Still it raged about us.

"Look," I said to Wynn when I found the water in the washstand basin frozen, "it *really is* cold in here!"

I was about to empty the chunk of ice into the slop bucket when Wynn stopped me. "Don't throw it out," he instructed. "Heat it and reuse it."

"Use *this*?"

"Who knows when we might be able to get more water. We only have three quarters of a pail, and we will need that for drinking and cooking. We'll make the wash water last as long as possible."

When I had finished the breakfast dishes, I did not throw out that water either. Instead, I left it in the dishpan at the back of the stove. It would have to serve for washing the dinner dishes and perhaps even the supper dishes as well.

I was all set to enjoy a lovely day with Wynn in spite of what the weather was doing outside; but he came from the bedroom drawing on a heavy fur jacket.

"Where are you going?" I questioned in alarm.

"I need to go down to the Hudson's Bay Store and make sure there are no reports of trouble. I shouldn't be gone too long; but if something comes up and I don't get back right away, you're not to worry. There is plenty of wood. You shouldn't have any problem keeping warm and dry."

He stopped to kiss me. "Don't go out, Elizabeth," he cautioned, "not for any reason. If something happens so I can't get back to you by nightfall, I'll send someone else."

By nightfall? What a dreadful thought!

Wynn slipped out into the swirling snow, and I was left standing at the window watching his form disappear all too quickly.

I don't remember any day that was longer. There was nothing to do but to tend to the fires. Even with both burning, the cabin was cold. I borrowed a pair of Wynn's heavy socks and put on my boots. Still my feet were cold.

I walked around and around the small room, swinging my arms in an effort to keep warm and to prevent total boredom. The storm did not slacken. It was getting dark again. Not that it had ever been really light on this day, but at least one had realized it was day and not night.

I fixed some tea. I had quite forgotten to eat anything all day. I was sorry I had not thought of it. It could have helped to fill in a few of my minutes.

It was well after I had lit the lamp and set it in the window that I heard approaching footsteps. I rushed to the door. It was Wynn. He was back safe and sound. I could have cried for joy.

"Is everything all right?" I asked, hugging him snowy jacket and all.

"As far as we know," he replied, stamping the snow from his boots. "We had to go and get Mary. She had no fuel for a fire and wouldn't have made it through the storm, I'm sure."

"Who's Mary?"

"She's a woman who lives alone since she lost her husband and family three or four years ago. They call her Crazy Mary—maybe she is; maybe she isn't, I don't know. But she refuses to move into the settlement, and she has a tendency to rant and rave about things. She was mad at me tonight for bodily removing her from her cabin and bringing her to town."

"Bodily?"

He nodded. "She absolutely refused to go on her own."

"What did she do? Did she fight?"

"Oh, no. She didn't fight; she just wouldn't move, that's

all. I carried her out and put her on the sled, and she rode into town like a good girl. But I had to pick her up and carry her into Lavoies' cabin as well."

I smiled, thinking of this determined Indian lady. She certainly had gotten her point across.

"Well, she should be all right now," said Wynn. "Mrs. Sam is sure she will stay put as long as the storm continues."

I was glad Crazy Mary was safe. *What is the real story behind her name?* I wondered.

Chapter Twenty-three

Winter

With the coming of the winter, many of the men had to leave their warm cabins to go out to their traplines. The furs they trapped in winter were the most profitable because of their thickness, and each trapper had a designated area that was considered his. When I asked Wynn how they made the arrangements, he said it seemed to be by some kind of gentleman's agreement rather than by any legal contract. I did learn that trapping another's territory was considered a major offense.

There was the problem of stealing, as well. There wasn't much common thievery in the North. No one felt over-concerned about locking up what he owned. Houses were left open and belongings left about the yard. The cabins that were constructed by the trappers for protection while working the traplines were free to be used by others who were passing through. Most trappers even made sure there was an adequate wood supply and blankets, matches and rations for any guests who might drop in during their absence. Of course, they knew the other trappers would extend the same courtesy.

So in an area where usual theft was not much of a problem, a very serious temptation and offense was stealing from another's trapline. Such a criminal was considered to be the lowest of the low, not only a thief of valuable animal pelts, but of a family's livelihood as well. Vengeance was often immediate and deadly, and few felt that the wronged man could be blamed for taking the law into his own hands. The Royal

North West Policeman must be on guard all the time for this. Any suspected thieves must be spotted and the guilty party apprehended immediately before a brutal beating or even a murder might occur. Wynn watched the lines and kept his eyes and ears open for any complaints of offenses.

Mostly it was the men who worked the traplines, but Crazy Mary also claimed a small territory as her own. So, once the storm had blown itself out, she refused to stay at the Lavoies' and headed back, poorly clothed, to protect her interests. She hinted rather loudly that there might have been someone messing with some of her traps.

Most people shrugged off the story as one of Crazy Mary's fancies, but Wynn could not dismiss it so easily. It must be checked and proven false to put everyone's mind at ease. When the storm ended, Wynn took snowshoes and dog team out to investigate.

Wynn did not keep his team at our cabin but in an enclosure by the Hudson's Bay Store. One reason was that the food supply for the dogs was over there, and also their clamor would not keep us awake at night.

Each dog had been carefully picked by the men of the Force who had preceded Wynn. The dogs were chosen for their endurance, dependability, and strength, not particularly for their good disposition. Many of them were scrappers and, for that reason, they had to be tied well out of range of one another. Some of them had ragged ears or ugly scars from past fights. I didn't care much for Wynn's sled dogs. Harnessing them to the sleigh was a tough job. Things could be going well; and suddenly one of the dogs would get mad at something another dog did, and a fight would break out. Before long the whole team would be in a scrap, tangling the harness and making a general mess of things. Yet the dog team was very necessary. Wynn used his dogs almost every day during the winter.

He had been talking about choosing his own team and training them himself for harness. With different training, he thought the dogs might be better-tempered and make less problems on the trail. It sounded like a good idea to me. It was going to take time and work, but Wynn was watching for promising pups.

When he went out after the storm to check on Crazy Mary's story, he informed me he also planned to swing around and see a litter of pups which a trapper by the name of Smith had for sale near the west branch of the river. I found myself wishing I could go with him, but I didn't even mention the thought to Wynn. It was still very cold and the snow was deep. The sled dogs were enough trouble on the trail. He certainly didn't need me along to complicate matters.

Wynn didn't return until late that night. He had talked with Mary and gone over her trapline with her. She had shown him "signs" and ranted on about her suspicions. This was the trapline her late husband had managed, and Mary was steadfast in her belief that it now was her exclusive property. But someone was moving in, she maintained, infringing on her area. She hadn't found any evidence yet of stolen pelts, but the new traps were getting in too close. They found no traps that belonged to another trapper, but Mary was sure one or two had been there. She could see the marks on the ground; she dug around in the snow to prove her point. But Wynn could not accept her "evidence" as valid. He left her, promising to keep a sharp lookout and asking her to get in touch with him if she still suspected anything.

Then, as planned, Wynn pulled his team around and went to see Smith. Smith was away from his cabin when Wynn arrived, so Wynn went in, started up a fire and made himself a cup of tea. The pups were in a corner of the cabin, so he had a good chance to look them over well for potential sled dogs. There were some possibilities. Wynn watched them play and tussle, liking what he saw.

It was getting late in the day and Smith had still not arrived at the cabin; so Wynn banked the fire to try to keep the cabin warm for the trapper's return, carried in a further wood supply, and turned his team back on the trail for home.

Wynn had learned to appreciate one thing about his sled dogs. While on the trail they usually laid aside all grudges and pulled together. They were considered to be one of the fastest teams in the area. Speed could, at times, be important to a policeman. A few minutes might mean the difference between life or death.

The team was in a hurry to get back to the settlement,

so Wynn was hard pushed to keep up with his dogs. On the smoother terrain, he rode the runners; when the way was rough, he snowshoed behind it, guiding it over the crusted snow.

When Wynn told me about his day as we sat in front of our fireplace that night, I found myself almost envying him. It sounded exciting and almost fun to be swinging along the snow-crisp trail behind the sled dogs. Wynn must have seen the wistful look in my eyes, for he surprised me a few days later.

"Want to take a little ride?"

I looked out the window. The day was filled with sunshine, the wind was no longer blowing, and the snow lying across the countryside made a Currier and Ives Christmas card of the scene.

"I'm going back out to check on Crazy Mary."

"Do we have to call her Crazy Mary?" I objected.

Wynn smiled. "There are four Marys in the area—Little Mary, Old Mary, Joe's Mary, and Crazy Mary. All the people refer to them in this way."

"Well, I don't like it. It's—it's degrading."

"You're right. But, from what I've been hearing, her neighbors are probably right. I think she does have mental problems. It sounds like it started when she lost her children in a smallpox epidemic. Her husband was away at the time and Mary was all alone. She watched all five of them die, one at a time. She hasn't been quite the same since. If she were in one of our civilized areas, she would have been institutionalized and cared for. Here, she is still on her own. She doesn't care about people and won't take help when it is offered. Now and then, if the weather really gets bad, one or another of the men leaves a quarter of meat on her doorstep. They have never been thanked for it, but it does disappear; so they assume she does make use of it."

I felt sorry for Mary. *What an awful way to live! What an awful way to be known,* I mourned. I had never seen her, but I was sure that if people really tried, *something* could be done.

"You haven't answered my question," Wynn's voice broke into my thoughts.

"The ride? I'd love to, though I have no idea what you have in mind."

"I want to keep a close eye on Mary and her problem. I also plan to stop and see if Smith is home. I'd like to get two or three of those pups."

My face lit up then. "I'd love to go," I said again.

"I'll go get the team. Wear the warmest clothes you have. Those old pants are a must."

I hurried to get ready. I didn't want to keep Wynn waiting. I borrowed a pair of Wynn's long drawers and pulled the old pants over them. The combination of the two meant I could hardly move. I also borrowed Wynn's wool socks and pulled on my own heavy sweater. The footwear had me concerned. All I had were the old hiking boots, and common sense told me they would not keep my feet warm.

Wynn soon returned, leaving the team lying fan-style on the ground when he came in for me. I was still trying to struggle into the heavy boots.

"Here," he said, "I think these will be much warmer."

He handed me a pair of beautiful, fur-lined Indian moccasins. They had elaborate designs in bead and quill work, and I exclaimed as I reached for them.

"They are wonderful! Where did you get them?"

"I had Mrs. Sam make them. I knew you would be needing something warmer for your feet. Fortunately, they were ready this morning."

"They are so pretty," I continued.

"They are pretty," agreed Wynn. "They are also warm."

I caught his hint that they were for wearing rather than for admiring, and I hastened to put them on. Then, donning my heavy mittens, I followed Wynn out to the sleigh.

Since I could not maneuver showshoes, I was privileged to ride. Wynn ran along beside or behind me, calling out orders to the dogs. They obeyed immediately. Maybe Wynn's "secondhand" team wasn't so bad after all. They certainly behaved themselves better in harness than out. I was gaining respect for them as we glided over the crisp winter snow.

"This is fun!" I shouted to Wynn as the sled flew over a slight rise in the trail. He laughed at my little-girl exuberance.

We came to an area where the wind had swept across the path, leaving the snow only a few inches deep.

"Would you like to walk for a while?" Wynn asked me. I did, so I scrambled from the sleigh and set out to follow him and the team.

The team would have left me far behind if I had just walked along behind. I had to run. I could tell Wynn was holding the team back with his commands. Still they seemed to gain ground. I hurried faster, but it was hard to keep at it with all the clothing I was wearing. Wynn soon stopped the team, and I laughingly tumbled back onto the sled. I was out of breath and panting, but it had been good for me.

Wynn found Crazy Mary out working her traps. She was a little woman. *Too small to be handling this man-sized job,* I reasoned, and my concern for her deepened.

She had straight, black hair which had been chopped off at the jawline. In the morning sunshine, she wore her parka hood back, and her hair kept flopping forward, covering her face. She peeped out from between strands of it, her eyes black and flashing. There were some scars on her face, and I realized that somehow she alone had survived the smallpox epidemic. Over her back she wore a skin sack of some kind, and I could see fur pieces sticking out of it. Apparently, Crazy Mary skinned the animals just where she found them, then threw aside the carcasses and stuffed the fur into her sack. Wynn had told me that as soon as the trapper got back to his cabin, he cleaned and stretched the pelts onto a wooden frame for drying. Crazy Mary would still have work to do when she got home at the end of the day.

I stayed near the sleigh while Wynn talked to her. I could not hear their conversation. But I could tell she was still agitated. She waved her arms and pounded her fists together and then gave little shrieks like a wounded animal. I didn't know if she was giving Wynn a demonstration of something that had happened or just expressing her feelings.

After some minutes Wynn came back to the sled.

"Well?" I asked.

"She still says someone is pushing back her boundary lines."

"Do you think they are?"

"I don't know. It's hard to tell when there really aren't any actual, visible lines in the first place."

I waved to Crazy Mary as we moved away. There she stood, one little woman alone fighting against the elements and an unseen, unknown enemy. I felt very sorry for her. I refused to refer to her as "crazy." If she had to be identified, they could call her *Brave Mary* or *Trapline Mary*. There was no need to call her Crazy Mary at all.

At Smith's cabin, his dog team was tethered in the yard and began howling and barking as our team swung around to the front. Smith himself came to the door. Seeing Wynn's uniform under his parka, he waved an arm to us, beckoning us to come in. I didn't suppose that he got many visitors.

He wasn't much for conversation, but he grinned and went about making up a tin pot of very strong, hot tea.

We sipped slowly. I was given the honor of the only chair in the room, the men half crouched, supported by the wall of the cabin.

They talked about lines, furs, and the economy. I didn't join in. I was too busy watching the litter of puppies that ignored us and went about their play. What fluffy round balls they were, with sparkling eyes and curly tails. It was hard to believe they could grow up into snarling, fighting, mean-spirited dogs. They were good-sized already, and I knew that they were well past the weaning stage.

After a few minutes, Smith seemed to feel there had been enough small talk.

"So what brings you out this way, Sarge?" he asked Wynn.

Part of Wynn's job was to gather information where he could, and another part of his job was to scatter a little information, too.

"Mary has reported that someone is getting a little too close with their traps," Wynn said, carefully studying the man's reaction.

"That crazy woman! She's the one broadening *her* boundary. She's been mismanaging her traps for years; and now that she can't find the animals, she's moving her lines. Did you see where she's got her traps?"

Wynn agreed that he had.

The trapper pulled a hand-drawn map from the shelf in the corner and spread it out on the table.

"Looky here," he said, agitated. "This here is my trapline. I've had it for years. Goes right along the river here, swings to the north by that stand of jackpine, follows up the draw, dips down to that little beaver dam, turns around west here, and comes back along this chain of hills. Every trapper in the territory knows those are my boundaries. So what does she do? She's sneaking traps in here and a few over in here." His finger stabbed at the map, punctuating each statement. "And the last time I was out, she even had a couple in here."

It was clear that Smith was upset.

"If she wasn't a woman," the man exploded, "an' a crazy one at that, I'd—" But he didn't finish the statement.

Wynn continued to study the map. "I'll do some checking," he said quietly. "It's clear that we've got to find out who's crowding who."

Then Wynn turned his attention to the pups snapping and fighting playfully on the dirt floor.

"I'm looking for some new sled dogs," he said. "Hear that you raise good animals. They look pretty good to me. Planning to sell these, are you?"

It was the first time Smith smiled. He reached down and scooped up a fluffy pup. It rewarded him by chewing on his thumb. He roughed its woolly back and clipped its ears playfully.

"Hate to, but I gotta. Got all of the team dogs now that I need. Another litter due in a couple of weeks. Which one you got your eye on?"

I knew which one I had *my* eye on. It was a little fellow with a full fluffy tail that curled over his back. He was a silver grey in color with shining black eyes and a sticky red tongue. He had been licking the snow off my boots.

I waited breathlessly for Wynn to name his dog.

"What do you think, Elizabeth?" he surprised me. "Which ones would you pick?"

"How many do you need?"

"I thought I'd start with two."

"For sled dogs?"

"What else would we need them for?"

I reached down and picked up the cute pup. He turned from licking at my boots and began to lick at my hands. *I think he likes me,* I exulted.

"Well, I was just thinking that it wouldn't be a bad idea to have a dog at the house. I mean, it would be company and—"

"You want a *dog*?"

I did not hesitate but answered him with the same intensity with which he had asked his incredulous question.

"Yes."

He laughed then, softly. "I thought you were afraid of dogs."

"The ones in the village, yes. They snarl and growl and snap when you go by. But I like dogs, generally. Really. A dog of my own, there at the cabin, might make me feel—well, less lonely—and more secure when you are away."

Wynn could see that I really wanted the pup.

"Okay," he smiled. "You go first."

"Go first?"

"You take your pick first."

That was no problem for me. I held up the pup already in my arms.

"This one," I said without a moment's hesitation.

Smith and Wynn were both grinning at me when I looked up.

"What do you think, Smith?" asked Wynn in a teasing way.

"I think the little lady got you," grinned Smith.

I must have looked puzzled.

"I think she did, too. Picked the best one in the bunch. I had my eye on that one for lead dog." Wynn reached over and tussled the pup's fur. It growled playfully and pawed at his hand.

I felt very happy with myself. I had picked a winner. Still, if Wynn had wanted this one for the lead dog, perhaps I should— "You can have him if you like," I said, offering the pup. "You need him. I just want him."

Wynn lifted his hand from the pup and touched my cheek. "You keep him. I think he'll be just right for you. There are plenty of others for me to choose from. They look like the makings of good sled dogs, too."

Wynn made his two selections. They were pretty little dogs as well, but I was glad I'd had first choice. Wynn paid Smith and we bundled up our armload of pups and headed for home.

The pups were not easy to transport. Wynn fared better with his. He put them in a knapsack with only their furry heads protruding and secured them on his back. They watched, wide-eyed, as we hurried over the trail.

My little fellow was more difficult. I insisted on carrying him on my lap. He didn't like being confined, and wiggled and squirmed and whined and yapped. I was about to give up on him when he decided that he had had enough, curled up and went to sleep.

I kept my hand on him, gently stroking the soft fur. I was so happy to finally have a dog of my very own. Being raised in the city, my folks thought our house and yard were too confining for pets. I guess I had secretly always wanted one. Maybe that was why I had enjoyed the small mouse, Napoleon, for the short while he had been with me in the teacherage. And now I had a dog! And a beautiful dog it would be. I would name it myself. I began to go over names in my mind. *A dog like this should have a name that is rather majestic, like King or Prince or Duke*. But I rejected each of those as too common.

Suddenly I thought of something. I turned slightly in the sleigh.

"Wynn," I hollered against the swishing of the sled runners and the yipping of the dogs. "Do I need a boy-name or a girl-name?"

There was laughter in Wynn's voice as he called back, "A boy-name, Elizabeth."

Chapter Twenty-four

Settling In

I named my dog Kip. If someone had asked, I really wouldn't have been able to explain why. It just seemed to suit him somehow. He was a smart little thing, and Wynn said that it was never too early to begin his training. So I started in. I didn't know much about training dogs. Wynn told me obedience was of primary importance. A dog, to be useful and enjoyable, must be obedient. Wynn gave me pointers, and in the evenings, if duties did not call him out, he even worked with me and the young dog.

It was amazing how quickly Kip grew. One day he was a fluffy pup, and the next day it seemed he was a gangly, growing dog. He turned from cute into beautiful. His tail curled above his silver-tipped, glistening dark fur. He was curious and sensitive and a quick learner. I loved him immediately and he did so help to fill my days. Aware of his needs, physical and emotional, my own life was enriched.

Kip needed exercise, so I took him out for walks, bundling myself up against the cold. It was a good way to get my exercise as well. When the snow got deeper and more difficult to navigate, I asked for snowshoes so that I might still keep up the daily exercise program. Wynn brought some home and took me out to introduce me to the use of them. They were much more difficult to manage than it seemed when watching Wynn maneuver in them. I took many tumbles in the snow in the process of learning. Kip thought it was a game; every time I went down, he was there to lick my face and scatter snow down my neck.

Eventually I did get the feel of snowshoes. The cold or the snow no longer kept me confined. I walked along the river trails, along the treeline to the west, and to the settlement. Whenever I went to the store with Kip, I picked him up and carried him. He was getting heavy and he was also getting impatient with me. He hated to be carried; he wanted to run. But I was fearful about all the dog fights I had seen on my trips to the village. I did not want Kip to be attacked. And so, as the weeks went by, each time our outings included the store, or Nimmie's for Bible study, I picked up my growing, complaining dog. I wondered just how much longer I could manage it. I hated to be stuck in the house, and I hated to leave Kip at home alone. I guessed that eventually all our walks would have to take us away from the dogs and the village and into the woods instead.

As the weeks went by, more snow piled up around us. The people began to be concerned about food and wood supplies. It took all their time and attention to provide a meal or two for the day and to keep their homes reasonably warm.

Christmas seemed unreal to me. There was no village celebration, no setting aside of this important day. Wynn and I celebrated quietly in our home. We read the Christmas story, and I shed a few tears of loneliness. I tried not to let Wynn see them, but I think he was suspicious. We did not have a turkey dinner with all of the trimmings. We had, instead, a venison roast and blueberry pie made from the berries I had gathered and canned. The Indian women had dried theirs, but I knew nothing about the drying process. Besides, I thought I preferred the canned fruit; to my way of thinking, they did taste awfully good in that Christmas dinner pie.

In the afternoon, Wynn suggested we take Kip for a run. It was fun to be out together, but the weather was bitterly cold, so we did not stay out for long. I think even Kip was glad to be back inside by our warm fire.

We were soon beginning a new year. Repeatedly, Wynn had to dig us out from a new snowfall in the mornings. If it had not been for Kip, I'm sure I would never have left my kitchen. He would whine and scamper about at the door, coaxing for a run.

The trappers now and then brought home meat for their families. The women supplemented this with some ice fishing in the nearby river. It was cold, miserable work; and I ached in my bones for them. Children and women alike were often out gathering wood from the nearby forest. I wondered why more of them did not prepare for the winter by stacking up a good fuel supply. Most of the Indians gathered as they needed it, and that was a big task when the fires had to be kept burning day and night.

I still met for studies with Nimmie and Miss McLain, though she still had not thawed out much. She seemed so deeply bitter and troubled. Little by little I learned her story. She had been orphaned at the age of three; Ian was five at the time. A fine Swedish family in the East had taken pity on the two children and raised them along with their own six. They had been treated kindly enough, but the family was poor and frugal, and all the children were required to work at an early age.

Schooling was one thing the family had felt was important, so each one of the children had been allowed to attend the local school as high as the grades went. When they reached their teen years, they were soon on their own. When Ian left the family, he apprenticed to a merchant in a nearby town as a bookkeeper and stock-checker. The man was German, and Ian lived in his home and learned German. Katherine had her heart set on being a schoolteacher, and so she found employment in the home of a doctor as housemaid and took classes whenever she could crowd them in.

The woman of the house was impossible to please, and young Katherine often found herself the victim of fits of fury. She would have left if she had had any place to go. At length her schooling was completed and she was able to obtain a position at a local school. The doctor's wife suddenly realized that she was losing good help, and she tried to bar Miss McLain from getting the job. It didn't work. Miss McLain was hired and moved out of the home and into a boarding house. There was a young man staying at the boarding house as well; and, after some months, they became attracted to one another and eventually engaged. Miss McLain was now a happy girl. For the first time that she remembered, she had a job she loved, a salary on which she could live, and—most importantly—someone who loved her.

The young man seemed happy, too, and he was anxious for the wedding to take place. Miss McLain told him she had to wait until she could afford her dress and all the other things she needed. The man declared that he hated to wait longer and then came up with a lovely plan. He had a sister in town. He was sure she would be ever so glad to help them.

They boarded a streetcar and went to see the sister. Miss McLain was excited. If her John was correct in assuming his sister would help, she would soon be a married woman with a husband and home of her own.

When the streetcar stopped and they walked the short distance to the sister's home, Miss McLain could only stand in frozen bewilderment. There must be some mistake. They were at the home of her former employer.

She did go in, but things did not go well. Not only did the angry woman refuse to help her, but she raged and ranted about her dishonesty, her ill temper, her laziness, and even her bad name. John only stood there like a statue, not even defending his Katherine.

In the end, the rift between them was so great that it could not be repaired, and John called off the engagement. Miss McLain left behind her school and her dreams and headed for her brother, who was by now living in the North.

She had never buried her bitterness. In her twenty years in the North, she had nursed it and fostered it and held it to her until now it was a terrible, deep festering wound in her soul. She was miserable; she deserved to be miserable; I think she even enjoyed being miserable; and she did a wonderful job of making those around her miserable, too.

In spite of her bitterness and her anger with life, I began to like Miss McLain. I felt both sorry for her and angry with her. Other people had suffered; others had been treated unfairly. They had lived through it. There was no reason why Miss McLain could not pull herself out of her misery if she had a mind to.

Nimmie was always patient and loving with her. Miss McLain, in turn, was spiteful and cutting with Nimmie. She didn't bother much with me. Perhaps she didn't think I was worth the trouble, or perhaps she thought I would not be intimidated by her; I do not know.

In spite of the difficulty, we were able to proceed with our Bible study. As we went through the lessons together, I was sensing a real change in Nimmie.

There was an eagerness, a softness, an openness that really thrilled me. She was so disappointed if a storm kept us from meeting. After a morning of study, she would share with Ian at night the things that she had learned. I was surprised and delighted that Ian seemed interested in what Nimmie told him. He, too, seemed eager to hear truth from God's Word.

In the middle of January, a bad storm hit. In all of my life I had never seen so much snow fall in so short a time. I was worried about Wynn; he was somewhere out in that whiteness with the dog team. I knew that dogs had an unusual sense of direction even in a storm, but I paced and prayed all day that the animals wouldn't let us down now.

The temperature dipped and the water in the basin again glazed over with ice. I worked hard to keep the cabin warm, adding fuel to the fire regularly. Kip whined at the door to go for a run, but I put him off. He was so insistent that eventually I sent him out for a few minutes on his own. I had never let him out alone before and I was afraid he might not come back. But he was soon crying at the door to be admitted to the warmth.

I fed Kip and made myself tea. Still Wynn did not come.

It was dark outside when there was a thumping at the door. I ran to it with my heart in my throat. Who could it be? Wynn did not knock at his own door. Who else would be coming and why? *Has something happened to Wynn?*

But it *was* Wynn, and in his arms he had a bundle. I opened the door wide for him.

"It's Crazy Mary," he said. "She was alone in her cabin with no heat and no food."

I hurried ahead of Wynn and tossed the cushions from the cot to make a place for her.

He opened the blankets, and she lay shivering. For a moment, I wondered if she was conscious, and then her eyelids fluttered and she looked at us. I smiled, but it was not re-turned.

"Do you have any food ready?" asked Wynn.

"There's soup in the pot, and I just made tea."

"A little soup. Not too much. I'll have to feed her."

While I went for the soup, Wynn finished unbundling the blankets from Mary, and now he removed the moccasins and wrappings of hide from her feet. He was working over her feet when I came with the soup. He went to take the bowl from me, but I indicated her feet. "I'll feed her," I said. "You do whatever is necessary there."

At first she refused the soup on the spoon; but when I was able to trickle a little of it into her mouth, she opened it ever so slightly and I was able to give her more. She swallowed several spoonfuls before I decided it was enough for the time.

"Should I give her some tea?" I asked Wynn.

"A little," he replied, and I got a cup of tea and spooned some of it into the woman's mouth.

She still shivered. I had never seen anyone who looked so cold. I went for more blankets.

We fixed a bed for Mary on the cot and looked after her throughout the night. Several times I awoke to find Wynn absent from bed and bent over the old woman, spooning hot soup or massaging her frostbitten feet.

The next few days were taken up with nursing Mary. Her toes swelled to a disturbing size. There didn't seem to be much more we could do for them. About once an hour I would spoon-feed her. She ate more heartily now, though she still was unable to feed herself.

I knew she could talk, but she did not speak to me. I had heard her talking to Wynn the day we had visited her on her trapline. She had been quite vocal then. I knew her silence now was not because she couldn't speak but because she chose not to. For whatever reason, I decided to respect it. Oh, I talked to her. I talked to her as I fed her and as I cared for her feet. I talked to her about the weather as I moved about the house doing the dishes or feeding the fire. I talked to her much like I talked to Kip—including her in my activities but not expecting an answer.

She lay on the cot, her black eyes watching every move I made; but she said nothing.

When the worst of the storm was over, Mrs. Sam and Evening Star came for tea. It had been some weeks since I had had their company and I was so glad to see them. I suspected they had come to see Mary. They may have, but if so they certainly kept it well hidden. After one glance in the woman's direction, they completely ignored her. They crossed to my kitchen table where they knew they would be served, and seated themselves.

They talked about the storm, the need for wood for the fire, the difficulty in catching fish—mostly communicating with waving, expressive hands, though they did add a word here and there. Evening Star played with Kip, seeming to like my dog. The Indians were not accustomed to having a dog in the home, and it must have seemed strange to her.

When they rose to leave, I followed them to the door.

"Mary is getting much better," I said quietly, to introduce the subject of her stay with us into the conversation. "In a few days, we hope she will be able to sit up some."

There was no response.

"As soon as she is able to sit, we think she will be able to feed herself, and then before too long she will be able to get around again. It's going to take awhile, but she is getting better."

I wasn't sure how many of my English words the two women understood, so I used hand gestures to accompany them.

Mrs. Sam was shaking her head. She turned at the door and looked at me.

"Not stay," she said clearly.

"Oh, she must stay," I persisted. "She needs lots of care yet. She couldn't possibly care for herself for many days."

But Mrs. Sam still shook her head. "Not stay," she insisted. "She go—soon."

Mrs. Sam was right. When we got up the next morning, Mary was not there. How she ever managed to drag herself from our home and back to her cabin I'll never know. She had been so weak and her feet so swollen, and yet she was gone. Wynn immediately went after her. She was already home—sitting in her cold cabin, her scanty blankets wrapped around her. She refused to move.

He gathered wood and built her a fire and made her a cup of tea from the supplies he always carried with him. Then he spent the morning gathering a wood supply for her.

He went out with his rifle and was rewarded in his hunt with a buck deer which he cleaned and hung in a tree close to Mary's cabin. Preserved by the cold, it would supply meat for many weeks for the lone woman.

He gave her instructions about caring for her feet, unloaded all of the food supplies he had with him, and left her.

I cried when Wynn told me. I felt so sorry for the little woman all alone there.

"There is nothing more we can do," Wynn comforted me. "If we brought her back here, she would only run away again; and next time she might not make it."

I knew he was right. He had done the best he knew how for Mary. We hoped it was enough to keep her alive.

Chapter Twenty-five

The Storm

Storm after storm hit the little settlement. We lived from one day to the next, accepting the weather as it came. On the good days, when the wind calmed down, I went out with Kip. On the days of snow and wind, I shivered and stayed in. I came to hate wind. Not only was it cold and miserable, but it was confining and, I was soon to learn, deadly.

One brisk, windy morning, Wynn returned from the Hudson's Bay Store where he had gone for a few needed supplies and reported that he had to take a trip south.

"Today?" I asked incredulously. It was bitterly cold. The windchill must have lowered the temperature to –50°F or worse.

"Now," he answered, "I'm on my way as soon as I get the team."

Wynn came into the cabin long enough to add some extra clothing to what he was already wearing and to pack his supply sack with more food and medical equipment. I felt panic seizing me as I noticed his precautions. It looked as though he expected delays.

"I may not make it back home tonight, Elizabeth," he said, straightening up and drawing me into his arms. "Don't worry about me. There are several trappers' shacks along the trail, and if the storm gets any worse I can take cover. Do you have everything you need?"

Me? I was all right. He was the one going out into the storm. Wynn checked the wood supply.

"There is plenty more wood stacked right outside the door

if you should run out," he informed me. "Don't leave the cabin until you are sure the storm is over. And then if you do go out, be sure to take Kip."

I nodded. It sounded as if he was planning to be gone *forever*! Tears welled up in my eyes.

"I'll be fine," he said, brushing the tears away tenderly. "I love you."

I tried to tell him that I loved him too; but it was difficult to get the words out. My throat felt tight and dry.

"Where—where are you going?" I finally managed to ask.

"Word just came in that a trapper out near Beaver Falls hasn't been seen for a couple of weeks. His friend says he always shows up at his place for a Friday night card game, but he hasn't been there for two Fridays now. He's worried about him."

"Doesn't he have a cabin?"

"They checked it out. He's not there."

"If he's been gone for two weeks," I said, annoyed, "why didn't someone report it before—when the weather was decent?"

"I can't answer that; but it's been reported now, and I have to go."

I was angry with the careless trapper. I was disgusted with his friend who had let it go for so long without reporting it. I was even a little put out with Wynn for taking his duty so seriously. Surely it would be wiser to wait until the weather improved.

I kissed him goodbye and let him go, because there was nothing else I could do.

Even Kip wasn't much help in filling in the long day. I talked to him and fed him and petted him, but my heart was with Wynn. *I hope he makes it home before dark*, I anguished inwardly.

Night came and Wynn did not come. I sat up, curled in a blanket and tucked between pillows, on our cot. Kip snuggled at my feet, now and then lifting his head to listen intently to the sounds of the night. I heard the howl of a wolf above the wind, and Kip heard it too. He stirred restlessly but did not answer the cry.

I watched the fire closely. If Wynn returned—no, *when*

Wynn returned—he would be chilled and would need the warmth.

I dozed off now and then; each time I awakened, I strained to hear footsteps approaching the cabin. They did not come. Toward morning I finally gave in and fell asleep.

I awoke to find the cabin fairly shaking with the wind. The fire was nearly out, and I quickly went for more fuel to build it up. The wind seemed to scream through every crack and crevice of our little home. The temperature dropped further and the snow swirled all around the cabin. Even Kip seemed to be uneasy.

All day I kept the fires burning. I knew I would soon be drawing on the supply from outside. I wondered about the Indian families. They weren't as well stocked for wood as I had been. Surely by now they would have exhausted their supplies. I wished there was some way of bringing them to the warmth and protection of our cabin. With my fingers, I scratched a spot in the frost on the window and looked out. I could not see the buildings of the settlement. I could not even see the birch tree that grew about fifteen feet from the door. All I could see was angry, swirling snow.

I tried to drink a cup of tea, but my hands shook when I lifted the cup to my mouth. I was on the verge of tears, but I knew that tears would do no good.

I fed the fire, I prayed, I walked the floor, I prayed, I read my Bible, I prayed; and somehow this even longer second day of storm passed by, hour by hour.

Another night, and still Wynn had not come. Again I did not go to bed. Kip whined uneasily and pressed his nose against my hand. I stroked his rich, fluffy fur and spoke to him in caressing tones, but I could not keep my tears from falling as I did so.

Somehow we made it through another night. We awoke to another day of snow and wind. I thought I couldn't stand it any longer. The wind was driving me mad with its incessant howling. I clung to my Bible and prayed until I felt utterly exhausted. Mid-morning, after reading, weeping, and praying for what seemed like hours, I fell asleep. The long days and sleepless nights had taken their toll, and my body demanded some rest even if my mind fought against it.

When I awoke, I could scarcely believe my eyes. Sunshine! The wind had stopped. The snow was no longer falling. The storm had passed. I wanted to shout; I wanted to run. I wanted to break out of my confining cabin and find human companionship. How had they all fared through the storm? And I wondered about Wynn. Now that the storm was over, he would soon be home. I must have a hot meal ready for him.

It was then that I realized the fires were no longer burning. I must get them started again quickly. I had only a few more pieces of wood that I had brought in from outside, but there was plenty more by the door. I rushed to get some. But I could not budge the door. I pushed again, not understanding; but it would not give. *The snow!* It had drifted us in. I tried again. Surely we wouldn't be shut in here for long. Surely, with enough strength, I could get it open. I tried again and again, but the door would not move.

I let the fire in the kitchen stove go out and just kept the fireplace burning in order to conserve the little fuel I had. Wynn would soon be here. Surely the fuel would last until then. When he came, he would dig us out and all would be well again.

But the day wore on and Wynn did not come.

I walked to my window and scratched a spot to look down at the settlement. I could see smoke rising from cabins. There was stirring about as people and dogs moved among the buildings. I tried to wave, but I knew that was foolish. There was no way anyone could detect a hand waving in my small, frosted window. I put the last stick of wood on my fire and waited again. *Surely Wynn will soon be here,* I told Kip silently.

The fire burned out. I wrapped myself in blankets and huddled on the cot. Even that was cold. I began to fear for my hands and feet. I picked up the heavy fur rug from the floor and wrapped myself in that, too. It was bulky, but it did offer some protection. Kip whined to go out, but there was no way I could let him. I thought of trying to push him through the window, hoping that he might run down to the settlement and attract someone's attention concerning my plight. But the window was too small for Kip's nearly full-sized body.

Night was coming again. I bundled myself up as best I could and tried to go to sleep. I fell asleep praying.

I vaguely remember stirring once or twice during the night and feeling terribly cold. In my benumbed state, I couldn't sort out the reason for the cold. Kip stirred, too, and I pulled the blankets more tightly around myself and dozed off again, Kipp curled up on my feet. He felt heavy, but I did not make him move.

"Hallo. Hallo in there," a voice finally brought me to consciousness. I struggled out of my blanket covering and hurried to the door. It still would not open. "I can't open the door," I called as loudly as I could. I heard shovels then. Someone was digging us out. It was McLain and a couple of the Indian men. I was glad to see them, but I was disappointed that Wynn wasn't with them. When the door was finally cleared enough for them to enter the house, my first question was, "Have you heard from my husband?"

McLain paused for a moment and looked around. "Have you heard from Wynn?" I asked again.

"No, not yet, ma'am; but he'll be all right."

I took what comfort I could from his words. I wondered if McLain knew what he was talking about or if he was simply trying to put my mind at ease.

"How are you?" he asked me.

"I'm fine—I think," I answered, trying my arms and legs to make sure they still moved properly. "I was never so glad to see anyone in my life! Thank you."

"How long have you been without heat?"

"Just overnight."

"That's too long," the big man said, reaching for my hand. "How are your fingers?"

"Fine."

"Your feet?"

"Okay."

"Let's see them."

I started to protest, but he would have none of it. "Let's see your feet, Mrs. Delaney."

I went to my bedroom to remove my long stockings and padded out again in my bare feet. The cabin floor was ice cold. Mr. McLain sat me in a chair and looked at each foot in turn.

"You're a mighty lucky lady," he said at last. "I don't know how you kept them from freezing."

"Kip slept on them," I said, suddenly remembering.

"What?"

"Kip. My dog. He slept on them. I remember waking up in the night and I could feel the heaviness from his body on my feet."

"Well, I'll be," Mr. McLain said, and then he began to laugh. "Well, boy," he said, running a hand through Kip's fine fur, "I guess you're more'n just pretty."

One of the Indian men had been working on a fire in the fireplace. It was burning briskly now.

"We've gotta thaw this here place out," said McLain and crossed to the kitchen stove. "This here water in the pail is frozen solid."

It was. So was the basin, and so was, I discovered to my dismay, my china teapot. It had split right down the side from the force of the freezing tea. All of those days of enjoying tea with friends were behind me. I wanted to sit right down and cry, but the men were bustling all about, and I didn't want them to see my hurt. Besides, I was still worried about Wynn.

"Better get your feet dressed again," said Mr. McLain, and I realized I was still puttering about in my bare feet.

I obeyed, slipping into my nice warm moccasins and then I went to my kitchen to see what other damage had been done. A few tins of food were split from frost as well. The pail was okay. I guess the dipper sitting in it had given the ice an upward, rather than outward, thrust. The kettle I wasn't sure about. I would have to wait until it thawed before I would know if it would still hold water without leaking.

The basin was okay, too. It had slanted sides and the ice just seemed to move up them. There really hadn't been too much damage. And, thankfully, I still had all my fingers and toes.

"We didn't see any smoke from your chimney this morning. Gave us quite a scare," Mr. McLain was saying.

"I was scared, too," I admitted. "I didn't know when someone might come."

"The storm was tough on everyone. Nimmie has a whole Fort full of people that she's trying to get hot food into. A number of the families ran out of wood."

"Was anyone—?" I started to ask if any lives had been taken by the storm, but I couldn't finish the question. I was half-sick with worry about Wynn.

Mr. McLain surmised the question and hesitated for a moment, then answered slowly.

"We lost a few—mostly older ones. A little girl died, too. She was always sickly, and this cold was just too much for her. It's been hard on Nimmie. The girl was one of her special pets."

Poor Nimmie.

The fires were burning brightly now, and the room was losing some of its chill. It would be some time until it was really warm again. The two Indian men left. Mr. McLain brought in a good supply of wood from beside the door, and then he, too, turned to go.

"You should be just fine now," he assured me. "We'll keep a better lookout from now on. I don't think it's gonna blow tonight. Sky looks clear."

"Can I come with you?" I asked quickly. I knew that Nimmie needed my help. I was torn between going to her and waiting in the cabin in case Wynn came home. My conscience finally won over my heart and I reached for my heavy coat.

Kip moved to follow me, but I pushed him back.

"You wait here," I said to him. "I won't be long."

"I don't mind if you bring him, if you like," said Mr. McLain.

"He might get in a fight with a dog in town," I objected.

"He might."

"Well, I wouldn't want him hurt."

"Is that why you used to carry him?"

We had shut the door on the whining Kip and were making our way across the drifts of snow to the settlement.

My breath was blowing out before me in puffy white clouds. I didn't answer McLain; he was walking too briskly for me to maneuver my snowshoes, keep up, and talk all at the same time. I just nodded my head in assent.

"So you planning on shutting him in all the time now?"

I shook my head.

"What will you do then?"

"I'll walk him out there," I said, waving my arm at the vast emptiness in the opposite direction of the village.

"You won't be able to keep him away from dogs forever, you know."

I had thought about that.

"Appears to me," said the husky man, "that Kip would likely hold his own pretty good in a fight. You've been feeding him well, and he has several pounds on some of the village dogs that just forage for their food. He's had good exercise, so he's developed strong bones and muscles. He's right smart. I think he'd handle himself just fine up against another dog."

I wasn't sure just what the man was trying to tell me.

"Are you saying—?" I began, but Mr. McLain cut in, "I'm saying that, with a child or a dog, you've got to give them a chance to grow up—natural like. You can't pamper them forever, or you spoil them. They can never be what they were meant to be. Kip's a Husky. Sure, they are a scrappy bunch when the need arises. And the need will arise someday. Here in the North, it's bound to. I think you oughta give Kip the chance to prove himself before he gets up against an animal where his life depends upon his fighting skill."

I wanted to argue with this man—to tell him that Kip would never need to fight, that I would keep him away from such circumstances. But I knew Mr. McLain was probably right. Kip was a northern dog. He would have to be prepared to live in the North. I hated the thought, but it was true.

I walked on in silence, slowly turning over in my mind the words of the man beside me. I would have to let Kip grow up. I would have to expose him to the rigors of the village and the fangs of the other dogs.

First, I would talk to Wynn about it and see if he agreed with this man. Oh, if only Wynn would get home! He had been gone for three days. Surely his mission shouldn't have taken him this long.

I blinked back tears that made little icicles on my cheeks and hurried after Mr. McLain. Nimmie needed me.

Chapter Twenty-six

Aftermath

The situation at the Hudson's Bay Store was even worse than I had expected. People were crowded in everywhere. Nimmie, busy filling bowls from a steaming pot of thin soup, gave me a welcoming smile. Mrs. Sam was the only one in the group whom I recognized. A few of the children I had seen gathered around Nimmie for her storytelling.

Some of the people had bandages on hands or feet, and I assumed they were being treated for frostbite.

I crossed to Mrs. Sam. "Where's your husband?" I asked her. When she looked at me blankly, I said, "Sam? Where's Sam?"

"Trap," she answered, making a motion like a trap snapping shut with her hands.

"What about the others? Evening Star and Little Deer and Anna? Have you seen them?"

She shook her head.

We stared at each other, recognizing the questions and concern in the other's eyes. I didn't know if their husbands had been out on the traplines or not, not sure how much difference it would make to have them home or away.

Nimmie was relieved to see me. "I'm so glad you're all right," she said when she had finished serving the last bowl. "That was the worst storm I ever remember. I was afraid you wouldn't have enough wood."

Apparently Mr. McLain had not told Nimmie about the smokeless chimney, not wanting to alarm her until he had checked further. "Oh, I had plenty of wood," was all I said now. "What can I do to help?" I asked her.

"Those people over there—they still haven't had anything to eat. I've run out of bowls or cups. I don't know—"

"What about Miss McLain?" I asked. "Would she have some bowls we could use?"

"I hadn't thought of that—"

"I'll go see." I hurried out the door and around to the back of the building.

A call gave me permission to enter. I found Miss McLain in a warm room sitting before her fireplace, her feet on a block of wood to soak up the heat, and her hands folded in her lap.

I stood looking at her in bewilderment, wondering if she was totally oblivious to all that was going on just next door. I finally found my voice.

"I came because of Nimmie," I began. "She has two or three dozen people to feed and she has run out of dishes. We were wondering if we could borrow some."

She didn't even look at me. "Guess you can," she said flatly with no interest.

Her attitude made me cross, but I held my tongue.

I swallowed and then said evenly, "Where are they?"

"Now where do you suppose dishes would be?" she returned with exaggerated sarcasm.

"May I help myself?" I asked, still in check.

"I don't know who will if you don't," was her biting reply.

I took a deep breath, crossed to her cupboards and began to lift out dishes. I piled them in a dishpan sitting on a nearby shelf. When I had all I could find, I turned to go.

"Just make sure they're boiled when you're done with them," stated Miss McLain, her eyes not leaving the fire.

I swung around to face her. "Do you realize," I flung at her, "there are people just beyond that wall who are fighting for their lives? Do you know that some of them may well lose their fingers or their toes? Do you know that Nimmie has been up half the night taking care of them? And here you sit, all—all bundled up in your great self-pity—thinking only about yourself and your lost love! Well, do you want to know what I think? I think you were well rid of the man. If he thought no more of you than to—to desert you because of a whining, accusing sister, then he wasn't much of a man.

"And do you know what else I think?" I was pretty sure Miss McLain wasn't one bit interested in what I thought, but I went on anyway. "I think that if after twenty years, you are still sitting by your fire and tending your little hurt while people out there are suffering with cold and hunger, then you're not much of a woman either. And maybe—maybe the doctor's wife was right. Maybe poor little John is better off without you."

I left the room, slamming the door behind me. I was half-way back to the store before what I had just done fully hit me. I bit my lip and the tears started to flow. I had been praying so diligently for this woman. I had been trying so hard to show her real love and compassion. Nimmie had been trying to break down the barriers for so many years—and I had just wiped out any faint possibilities of progress in a moment of anger. I would have to apologize. I didn't expect her to accept my apology. I would never be able to repair the damage I had done.

"Oh, God, forgive me," I wailed in remorse. "I should never have said that."

The apology would have to wait. Nimmie needed me and needed me now.

We worked all forenoon. The people were fed and looked after to the best of our ability. Mr. McLain and some of the men made an inspection tour to all the village houses. It was even worse than we had thought. Besides the little girl, the storm had claimed five other victims: an older man and his equally old wife living in a cabin alone at the edge of the village; a grandmother in the household of our erstwhile driver on the trip to the settlement, and an elderly gentle-man who had been very sick before the storm struck. The general opinion was that he would have died regardless be-cause of his weakened condition. Also dead was a middle-aged woman who had attempted to gather more wood and lost her way in the storm. Because of the heavy snow and the cold weather, digging of graves was impossible, so the bodies were all to be bundled up in blankets and tied up in the branches of the trees to await springtime. The Indian

people had a special stand of trees which served that purpose—the "burying trees," Mr. McLain called them. But before the bodies could be prepared for the burying trees, they
had to be examined by the Royal North West Police and
permission given. So they were lined up in a vacant cabin to
await Wynn's return.

Caring for the needs of the people in the village helped
to some extent to take my mind off Wynn, though I wasn't
able to ignore his absence completely. Throughout the day
Nimmie and I had our hands full taking care of all those who
needed our help. By early afternoon the store was beginning
to empty. Many had now gathered fuel for their fires and
returned to their own cabins. Those who remained behind
needed to be fed again; and so I worked over the stew pot,
getting another all-too-scanty meal ready for them.

Nimmie had just finished checking a swollen hand when
I heard her exclamation, "Katherine! Are you all right?"

I swung around and, sure enough, there stood Miss
McLain. I knew my apology was overdue and that it shouldn't
be put off, but this hardly seemed the time or the place. I
wasn't sure what to do.

Miss McLain said nothing, so Nimmie went on, "Did you
want something?"

"Yes," said Miss McLain matter of factly. "I want to help."

I don't know who was more astounded—Nimmie or I. We
both looked at Miss McLain with our mouths open. Her eyes
were red and swollen, and I could tell she had been weeping.

"I want to help," she repeated. "Would you tell me what
I can do?"

"Well, uh, well—we are fixing something to eat again.
Some of these people have just come in and they haven't had
anything to eat for a couple of days. Elizabeth is making
stew."

"What can I do?" asked Miss McLain one more time.

"Well, we'll—we'll need the dishes. We haven't had time
to wash the dishes yet." Nimmie motioned toward the dishpan filled with dirty dishes still sitting on the back of the
big stove. Without a word, Miss McLain moved to the dishpan, rolled up her sleeves, and set to work.

Nimmie looked at me and I just shrugged my shoulders

helplessly. I had no idea what had brought about the change. And I wasn't about to ask—here.

By mid-afternoon we had done all we could for the village people. All had now returned to their homes. Smoke rose from the cabins circling the town clearing. Nimmie suggested we sit down and have a cup of tea, but I said I would rather get back home. Kip was still in and unattended, and I was sure Wynn would soon be home. And by now the fire would have burned out, leaving the cabin cold again. With all these reasons, Nimmie let me go.

Kip was glad to see me, fairly knocking me over with his enthusiasm. I let him out for a run while I rebuilt the fires. It took awhile for the rooms to warm up and for the teakettle to begin to sing. It leaked a bit around the spout, but was still usable. I lamented again over the loss of my teapot. I wanted a cup of hot tea now. I finally dug out a small pot and made the tea in that. Maybe I imagined it, but for some reason, it didn't taste quite the same.

When darkness came, the cabin was quite warm and cozy, but I still felt chills pass through me. Where was Wynn? How long did it take to find a lost trapper? I sat before my fire, reading and praying. Finally I laid aside my Bible and began to pace the floor, letting the tears stream unchecked down my face.

Finally I banked the fire, bundled up in blankets and curled up on the cot again. Kip climbed up to lie on my feet. This time I didn't scold him for being on the cot. I remembered the night before and the fact that Kip might have saved my toes.

There was a full moon and the rays of it streamed through the little frosted window. It seemed ever so bright, reflecting off the freshly blown snow. I was trying to pray again when there was a commotion at the door; and, before I could even worm my way out of the blankets, Wynn was there.

I didn't even jump up and run to him; I just buried my face in my hands and began to sob until my whole being shook. I was so relieved, so thankful, to see him safely home. He walked over and took me in his arms. As I clung to him, he held me for a long time, stroking my hair and patting my back. "There, there, Elizabeth," he murmured as to a small child.

We didn't try to talk. We really didn't need to. Later we would hear from one another all the details of the four miserable days of separation. For now it was enough just to be together again.

Wynn had a busy and rather unpleasant day following his return. Besides the bodies awaiting his investigation, he had also brought one back with him on the dog sled. He had found the man in question, but not in time to prevent his death.

It looked as if the fellow had accidentally stepped into one of his own traps. He had managed to free himself; but, with the mangled leg, he was unable to get to his cabin or to find help. Wynn had discovered the body beside the trail.

I asked if he had a wife and family. "No," Wynn said, "his wife died in childbirth three years ago."

It was a sad time for all of us. After the bodies had been inspected and Wynn had filed the necessary reports, the Indian people were given permission to bury their dead.

It was a solemn assembly that filed, single form, out of the village that afternoon and made their way to the burying trees. Wynn and I joined the somber procession. The sound of mourning sent chills up and down my spine. I had never heard anything like it before. Not the sound of weeping, it was a cry, a whine, a deep guttural lament that rose and fell as the column moved along. It tore at my soul, and I wept quietly with the mourners.

At home again as twilight came, the drums took up their steady beat. As they echoed through the settlement, thumping out their message of death, even Kip stirred and whined.

"Will they keep on all night?" I asked Wynn, feeling restless and edgy with the intensity of the beating.

"Oh, no. They should be stopping any time now."

Out the window, I could see in the settlement below us open bonfires in the central area. Around the fires, Indians moved in a dance pattern. The drummers sat in the firelight beating the drums with their hands and chanting a monotone tune that rose and fell on the night air.

Wynn was right. The drumming stopped as abruptly as it had begun. I looked out the window again and saw the silhouettes of figures disappearing into the shadows of the buildings. The fires had died down to a dim glow. The dead had had a proper and respectable burial.

Chapter Twenty-seven

Village Life

January passed into February. We had more storms but none with the violence of the mid-January blizzard. For the most part, life seemed to slip into some sort of a daily routine. We still continued our Bible studies, and Miss McLain never missed a study. Though she was still difficult at times, her attitude had changed from the inside out. I never did apologize for my outburst—not that I wasn't willing to do so. It just didn't seem like the appropriate thing to do under the circumstances. *Thank you, Lord,* I prayed, *for turning something bad into something good.*

When new babies were added to the village families, the Indian midwives did the delivering. Four were born between the first of October and mid-January. And so far, in spite of the cold winter, we had lost no children except for the one little girl. It was a shock to me when I first heard Nimmie and Miss McLain gratefully discussing this fact.

You mean you expect to lose children? I wanted to ask. But their conversation told me very plainly that in the North death was nearly as accepted as life. Because of the severe weather, the lack of medical care and the poor nutrition, they did indeed lose children regularly. I was appalled. Especially when I knew that medicines and doctors could have saved a good number of them.

Wynn kept a close eye on the Mary-versus-Smith situation. He had been out to see Mary many times. She was again working her traplines. How she managed it, Wynn did not know. The stamina of that little lady was remarkable. She had lost some toes from her severe frostbite, but she hobbled along, checking and resetting her traps and skinning out her furs. She was getting quite a pile, Wynn said. He also said that all the evidence supported Smith's assessment: Mary was crowding his territory.

"There must be some mistake," I argued. "If she is cutting into someone else's territory, she must not realize it. I'm sure she wouldn't do that on purpose."

Wynn just smiled.

Kip was a beautiful dog. I discussed with Wynn what Mr. McLain had said, that I had to allow Kip to find his own place in the dog community of our settlement.

"Do you think he's right?" I asked reluctantly, fearing that Wynn might agree with Mr. McLain.

"I'm afraid so, Elizabeth," he said. "It will come sooner or later, whether you want it to or not. Kip will be challenged, and he will either need to meet the challenge or run."

I couldn't imagine Kip running. I wasn't sure I even wanted him to run. But to fight? I didn't want that either.

"Do you think he's ready now?" I asked, a tremble in my voice.

I looked at Kip's beautiful, silver-tipped fur and the lovely curve of his tail. I shuddered to think of him with torn bleeding ears and ragged scars.

"Don't rush things," said Wynn and squeezed my hand. "There's plenty of time."

Wynn spent many hours training his new dogs. They were getting big like their brother Kip, but Wynn did not want to put them in harness for several months, waiting for their bones and muscles to be fully developed. He had chosen another two pups from the second litter Smith had spoken about at the time of our visit. Wynn was very pleased with the new dogs. They were smart and strong and learned very quickly. So far there was no evidence of a mean streak. Wynn had trained them with firmness and kindness rather than harshness. They responded to him with respect and devotion.

My friends from the village were much too busy keeping the fires going and their families fed to have much time for tea. Occasionally, one or two did appear for a few minutes. The women I had joined in the berry patch sometimes brought new neighbors for me to meet. We still couldn't speak much to one another. Many of the ladies knew some English words, but most often they were words needed for trading at the post, not words that might be used for a chat over a cup of tea. With all of us combining our knowledge, and by using our hands extensively, we did manage to converse some; but often we sat for a period of time without saying anything, just enjoying companionship. It was a new experience for me. I had been used to chatter. To sit quietly did not come easy. However, with time and patience, I was learning.

Evening Star was expecting another baby. I had been waiting daily for the good news, praying that all would go well and that she, too, would deliver a healthy child.

She was a bit vague about the expected time of arrival. When I asked her about it, she just shrugged off my question. I thought she must not understand me, so I put the question another way. Again she shrugged, answering only, "Come when ready," which was Anna's translation.

We were awakened in the dead of night by someone opening our door and calling Wynn's name. Both of us sat bolt upright in bed, and then Wynn reached in the darkness for his clothes and hurried into them.

My heart was in my throat as I listened to the anxious voices coming from the other room. Soon Wynn was back to the bedside, lamp in hand. "It's Evening Star," he said. "She's having trouble delivering."

Wynn completed his dressing and then turned to place a kiss on my forehead.

"Try not to worry," he said. "I'll be back as soon as I can."

I tried not to worry but I wasn't doing very well at it. If the experienced midwives were unable to help Evening Star, what could Wynn do?

I finally got out of bed and went out to put more wood on the fire. I placed the lamp on the little table, wrapped myself in a blanket, and picked up my Bible. I paged through the Psalms, snatching underlined verses here and there of promise and assurance. It was one of those times when I couldn't really concentrate on my reading. Finally I closed my eyes and began to pray. For Evening Star and the unborn little one. For Wynn, that he would have wisdom and guidance. For myself, that God would still my trembling spirit enough for me to be able to concentrate on His Word.

After some minutes, I went back to the Bible. Again my eyes skimmed the pages. My spirit was calm now. My trembling had ceased. I read passage after passage until I came to Psalm 27:14. I stopped and read it through again. "Wait on the Lord: be of good courage, and he shall strengthen thine heart; wait, I say, on the Lord."

Yes, Lord, I prayed. *All I can do is wait.* I picked up the knitted sweater I had nearly completed for the new baby and worked while I waited.

It was almost daylight when Wynn returned. He was weary but his eyes smiled at me the moment he came in the door, and I knew he brought good news.

"She's all right?" I said.

"And so is her boy," Wynn answered me.

I shut my eyes for a moment of thanks, the tears squeezing out under my eyelids. Then I looked back up at Wynn, smiling.

"You must be very tired," I commented. "Would you like a cup of coffee before you go back to bed?"

"Back to bed?" laughed Wynn. "My darling, I do not intend to go back to bed. It's time to start another day."

So I fixed breakfast while Wynn shaved; and then, after eating and having our time of family prayer together, he did indeed go out to start another day—or continue the one he'd already started.

When chopping frozen logs for firewood, one of the children had an accident with an axe. They brought him to Wynn who, fortunately, was at home at the time. One look at the injured leg, and I felt as if I would lose my dinner. We removed the pillows from our cot, and Wynn stretched the boy out on the thin mattress.

His pantleg was ragged and torn and covered with blood. The first thing Wynn had to do was to clean up the area so he could see how bad the wound was. He asked for my scissors to cut off the ragged pantleg and then for hot water in the basin and his medical supply kit.

The Indian youths who had brought the boy stood around helplessly. They understood very little English and they didn't look much less queezy than I.

Somehow I managed to follow all of Wynn's orders—bringing the water and the sponge cloths, boiling the instruments in a pan on the stove, and handing Wynn whatever it was he needed.

Wynn cleaned the wound thoroughly, managing to stop the bleeding, and then put in several sutures. The boy's only indication of the pain he must have been suffering was a pale face and clenched jaw. I looked only when I had to. Most of the time, I was able to keep my eyes off the leg and look at my hands or the floor or Wynn's face. It seemed to take forever but, in actuality, it was all taken care of rather promptly. I sighed when Wynn said, "That's it." Now I could collapse.

But I didn't. Somehow I managed to stay on my feet. The two Indians moved forward to pick up the brave boy; he was pale and exhausted from the ordeal. I stepped forward, too.

"Perhaps he should stay here for a while," I suggested to Wynn. "He's too weak to move now, and I'll care for him."

Wynn, surprised, turned and spoke to the Indian boys who had carried in their friend. After a brief exchange, they nodded and left. Wynn made sure the young lad was comfortable and then picked up his hat.

"I'd better go see his mother," he said. "I want her to know exactly what's happening."

In about fifteen minutes Wynn was back with a worried-looking woman.

She crossed to her son and spoke some words softly to him. His eyes fluttered open and he answered her. She spoke again, nodded her head to us, and left the room.

The young boy's name was Nanook. He stayed with us for five days before he hobbled home on two clumsy sticks. I had enjoyed having him. He could not speak to me, but he could laugh. And he could eat—my, how that boy could eat! His leg didn't become infected, for which we were thankful. Wynn watched it very carefully, dressing it morning and night. By the time Nanook left us, it was beginning to heal nicely.

Before he left, I gave him a loaf of fresh bread to take with him. He tucked it inside his coat, his eyes twinkling. Then he patted Kip, whom he had grown to love, and hobbled out the door.

Chapter Twenty-eight

March

When March came, I began to think *spring,* but Wynn warned me that this was much too premature. No one else in the whole village was looking for spring at this early date. I chafed. Winter had been upon us for—for *years,* it seemed to me.

I was restless and I was lonely. My Indian friends had been too busy to come for tea for quite a while. Nimmie had been down with the flu, so our Bible study together had been missed. I still didn't feel very much at ease with Miss Mc-Lain, though I had now been given permission to call her Katherine. I could have talked myself into visiting her, but she was busy nursing Nimmie. I would have liked to have been Nimmie's nurse myself, but I knew it was important to Katherine to be able to do this. So I stayed home.

There was no sewing to be done, my mending was all caught up. I had read all my books over and over. It seemed that the extent of my day's requirements was to get three meals and do the dishes.

I was tired of the meals as well. It seemed as if I just fixed the same things over and over—from tins. Tinned this and tinned that. We did have fresh fish and fresh wild meat. But I was tired of them also. I really didn't enjoy the wild meat and craved even one taste of beefsteak or baked ham.

I longed for spring. But in the North, spring is slow in coming.

I decided to take a walk to the store. Maybe I would find some food item on the shelves that wouldn't be too expensive and would be a delightful change for our daily menu.

I bundled up and pulled on my mittens. Kip was already waiting by the door, his tail wagging in anticipation.

"You want to go for a walk?" I asked him, an unnecessary question. I struggled into my snowshoes and started out. It was a bright sunny day and I dared to hope that maybe this once Wynn was wrong. Maybe spring really was coming.

We walked through the morning sunshine, Kip frolicking ahead or running off to the side to check out something that only dogs knew or cared about. I was feeling good about the world again.

I had not given even fleeting thought to the village dogs, so intent was I in getting out for a walk again. Had I thought about it, I might not have proceeded any differently. I had finally made up my mind that Mr. McLain and Wynn were right: I could not go on protecting Kip against real life.

Mr. McLain greeted me heartily about halfway into the village. I asked how Nimmie was, and he seemed relieved and said she was coming along very well now.

We were walking toward the trading post together when there was a rush and a blur at my side as a dog ran past me. I jumped slightly with the suddenness of it; then a yip to my left whirled me around.

Kip had been busy poking his nose into a rabbit burrow, and this dog from the village was heading right for him. I gasped, my hand at my throat.

Surprisingly, the dog stopped a few feet from Kip and braced himself. From where we stood, we could hear the angry growl coming from his throat. Kip stood rooted, unsure as to what this was all about. Mr. McLain reached out a hand and placed it on my arm.

"They're going to fight, aren't they?" I said in a tight voice.

"We'll see," said McLain. "Kip might be wise enough not to take the challenge."

"Wise enough? But you said he'd *have* to fight."

"Not this one. Not Lavoie's Buck."

I swung around to look at McLain. "What do you mean?" I threw at him in alarm.

"He's boss here, Miz Delaney. He's licked every dog in the settlement."

I looked wildly about me in search of a club or a rock or anything that might stop the fight. There was nothing. "We've got to stop them!" I cried. "Kip might be killed!" I took a step forward, but McLain stopped me.

"You can't go in there. If there's a fight, you could get all chewed up."

The Lavoie dog was circling Kip now, fangs bared, his throat rumbling. Round and round he went, and I think he must have said some very nasty words in dog language. Kip looked insulted—angry. I expected at any moment the dogs to be at each other's throats.

And then a very strange thing happened. Kip's tail lowered and began to swish mildly back and forth. He whined gently as though to apologize for being on the other dog's territory. The big dog still bristled. He moved forward and gave Kip a sharp nip. Kip did not retaliate. The Lavoie dog gave Kip one last look of contempt, circled him once more, and—still bristling and snarling—loped back toward the village houses.

I didn't know whether to be relieved or ashamed.

Mr. McLain just grinned. "One smart dog," he said. "But ol' Buck better watch out in a month or two."

I didn't know what Mr. McLain meant, but I started to breathe again and hurried on to the village. The day didn't look nearly as sunshiny as it had previously, and I was rather anxious to make my purchases and go home.

Finally Anna and Mrs. Sam came for tea. I was especially glad to have Anna, because it meant that I could catch up on some of the village news. We talked now of the families and how they were faring. The life in the village seemed to be made up getting through the winter and coasting through the summer; and the summers were all too short.

Evening Star and her baby were both doing fine. I had not seen them since I had taken over the new sweater and a container of soup soon after the baby had safely arrived. He was a nice little fellow and Evening Star was justifiably proud.

We had had another death. An Indian woman in her forties had died from the flu. She had not been well for some years. She had given birth to fifteen children, and each time another child was born she seemed to weaken further. Of her fifteen, only seven were now living. Her body, also, had been blanketed and left in the burying trees. The ritual drums had thumped out the message, and the open fires had gleamed in the night.

Another baby had been born, too. This time the midwives did not need help from Wynn.

There had been some sickness, but no major epidemics. Everyone seemed to hold his breath and speak softly when the possibility of an epidemic was mentioned. The people lived in fear of a dreadful disease sweeping through the camp while they sat helplessly by, with no doctors, hospitals, and very little medications.

Our conversation turned to brighter things. I talked about my longing for springtime. Of learning from the women about finding edible herbs and plants in the forests. Of planting my own garden. Of finding the berry patches. We all looked forward to the days of sunshine and rainshowers. Even the dreaded mosquitoes would be endured when spring came.

"How is Nanook doing?" I asked.

"He runs," said Anna, her eyes lighting up.

"That's wonderful. Good. That's good."

"I often wonder about poor Mary," I went on. "I don't know how she ever manages to care for her trapline with some of her toes missing."

"She crazy," muttered Anna, slurping her tea.

I wanted to argue but instead I said, "I feel sorry for her. First she lost all her children, and then her husband died. Poor thing."

But Anna only said, very calmly, "Husband not die."

I looked at her. Surely she knew better. She lived right here and had for years.

"Are you sure? We were told that her husband was dead."

"Dead. But he not die."

I didn't understand. Anna finished her tea and stood to go. Mrs. Sam Lavoie stood also and began to shuffle toward the door. Anna followed and I followed Anna. When we got to the door, she turned to me.

"She kill him," she said deliberately and simply. "She kill him for the traps. My Joe see." And she was gone.

I could hardly wait for Wynn to get home so I might tell him what Anna had said. She certainly must be wrong. Surely poor Mary had not done such a thing. If she had, and Joe had seen her, he would have reported it. Something was all wrong here.

When Wynn did arrive home, he had news for me instead. Mary was now locked up in the settlement's makeshift jail. Wynn had to bring her in. She would need to be escorted out for trial and sentencing. Not only had she moved her traps onto Smith's territory, but Wynn had found her in the very act of robbing from Smith's traps as well. It was a serious offense and Mary had to answer for it.

I felt sick. "Where is she?" I asked.

"There's a little room at the back of McLain's store. He uses it for skin storage when it's not needed otherwise."

And now it was needed otherwise. It was occupied by Mary.

"Can I see her?" I asked.

Wynn looked surprised; then he answered. "Certainly. If you wish to."

I did wish to. I went the next day, taking fresh bread and stew with me. Mary took the food but did not even look at me. I spoke to her, but she ignored me completely. I could see she really didn't need my food. Mr. McLain or Nimmie had looked after her well.

I tried to talk to her. She still would not look at me.

"I want to help you," I said. "Is there anything I could get you or do for you?" She turned from me and went back to curl up with a blanket on the cot in the corner.

I came home feeling even sicker than I had before I went. I decided to discuss it with Wynn. Surely there was some other way to deal with the situation.

"Do you really have to do it this way?" I asked him.

"I'm afraid so, Elizabeth. There is no masking the evidence. I caught her red-handed. She was stealing from Smith's traps."

"But couldn't she be—be—scolded and given another chance?" I continued.

"She isn't some naughty schoolgirl. She knows the seriousness of her offense."

"But surely if she knows that you are on to her, she won't do it again," I insisted.

"Elizabeth, if I let Mary go, none of the people will have respect for the law. Besides, Crazy Mary would try it again— oh, maybe not right away, but she would try it again, sure. She has an inner drive to accumulate pelts, and she will stop at nothing to get them."

I thought of Anna and her words. I had not passed them on to Wynn yet. I remembered them now with a sick heart.

Wynn went on. "She will get a fair trial," he assured me. "They will take into consideration her mental state. She will be cared for better than she would be out on her own on the trapline."

"But it will kill her," I blurted out. "She couldn't stand to be confined. She couldn't even stay here with us!"

There was sadness in Wynn's eyes. To lock Mary up, even with tender care, would not be good for Mary's emotional state. She needed freedom. Without it, she might not be able to survive.

"There is another thing to think about, Elizabeth," said Wynn. "If I didn't handle this properly and carry out the demands of the law, Smith or someone else would handle it in his own way, according to his own laws. Mary could be killed or beaten so severely that she would be left too helpless to work her trapline or even to care for herself. Either way it could mean death."

I hadn't thought about that.

Wynn dismissed further discussion. "I was sent up north to uphold the law, Elizabeth. To the best of my ability, I intend to do just that, God helping me."

I knew Wynn would follow the dictates of the law, not his own feelings.

Mary was not sent away for trial and sentencing. Two mornings later, Nimmie found her dead on the cot in the corner, where she had died in her sleep.

Chapter Twenty-nine

Nimmie

March had crawled by slowly on weak and tottering limbs. I ached for spring to come dancing in with vitality and freshness. I think all the village people ached for it as well.

For some of the women of the settlement it would mean reuniting with husbands for the first time in many months. Some of the traplines were a great distance from the village, and once the men had left in the fall, they did not return again until the winter snows were melting.

The men who worked the traplines nearer home came and went, spending some time with their families and some time in the bush.

Nimmie was well again, so we resumed our Bible studies. Each time we met together, she taught me some lesson. She was a patient, beautiful person with a heart of love and an open mind to truth.

I talked to Wynn about her one night as we were stretched out before our open fire.

"I've learned to love Nimmie," I said. "She's a beautiful person. It's strange—when I first saw her, I was so disappointed. I didn't tell you that before, did I?"

Wynn shook his head, his eyes studying mine.

"I guess I didn't because I was ashamed of myself. I was prejudiced, you know. I didn't realize I was. I love the Indian people, but I had wanted someone—someone to share things with. And I—I thought—that—well that—the person needed to be like me—white. Well, I was wrong. I was wanting a white woman, and instead I found a friend, a very special friend, in Nimmie."

Wynn reached out to take my hand. I think he understood what I was trying to say.

As the days went by, Nimmie and I shared more intimately our thoughts and feelings, our understanding of Scripture.

One day Nimmie came to see me alone. It was not our Bible study day, and I was a bit surprised.

"Do you have time to talk for a while?" she asked me. Now, time was one thing I did have—in abundance. So I asked Nimmie in.

She laid aside her coat and took a chair at the kitchen table.

I pushed the kettle forward on the stove, added another stick of wood, and waited for her to begin.

"I've been thinking about that verse we studied yesterday," she started, "the one about Christ dying for the ungodly."

I nodded, remembering.

"I'm ungodly," Nimmie continued softly.

"Yes, all of us are without God," I agreed in a near whisper.

Nimmie's eyes flew open. "You too?"

"Oh, yes. Me, too."

"But—?" began Nimmie, but she didn't go on.

"The Bible says, 'All have sinned,' remember? It was one of the verses we studied a couple of weeks ago."

"I remember," said Nimmie. "I just didn't think of it at the time, I guess."

"Well, it's true. The Bible also says that 'there is none righteous, no not one.'"

Nimmie sat silently. "I remember that, too," she finally stated.

"It also says that 'while we were yet sinners,' He loved us."

"That is the part that is so hard for me to understand," Nimmie blurted out. "I can't imagine someone dying for—" Nimmie stopped again.

"Elizabeth," she said, looking full into my face, "I am a terribly wicked person."

I wanted to protest, but Nimmie went on, "You don't know

me, Elizabeth. You don't know what I almost did."

She did not weep. Weeping was not the way of her people, but her head dropped in utter self-contempt and her eyes refused to look into mine.

"Do you want to tell me about it?" I finally asked, realizing that Nimmie was deeply troubled.

"I took care of Crazy Mary. I brought her all her meals and the basin to wash her hands. I bandaged her infected toe that still refused to heal from the freezing. Each time I went we spoke together. I tried to encourage her—to tell her that things would work out. But each time I went she begged me for just one thing. She pleaded with me to bring it to her. Each time, I refused. She wanted her hunting knife."

I could not understand Nimmie's words. There was silence as I puzzled over them. Why was she wicked for taking such special care of Mary? Nimmie's head came up. "I knew why she wanted her knife. She could not bear to be shut up—caged like—like a chicken."

I understood then. Crazy Mary had intended to take her own life.

"Well, I kept saying no, no. And then the other morning I couldn't stand it anymore. She was going wild in the little room, and soon she would be taken far away from her land and her people and locked in another room—forever. It would kill her. It would kill her slowly. Wouldn't it be more merciful to let her die all at once?

"And so I found her knife and tucked it in my dress and took it to her when I went to bring her breakfast. Only when I got there, Crazy Mary was—was—"

Yes, I knew. Mary, mercifully, was already gone.

My mind was whirling, my heart thumping. What could I say to the anguished Nimmie?

Did she truly realize the seriousness of her near-crime? Wynn would have needed to arrest her. *She* would have been locked up in the little room at the back of her husband's store. She would have been sent out for trial and sentencing. She would have been implicated in a terrible crime.

The horror of the whole thing washed through me, making me tremble; but Nimmie was continuing.

"I am very *unjust*," went on Nimmie. "I am a sinner. I

thought before when I heard those verses that it was speaking of someone else. Now I know that it speaks of me. My heart is very heavy, Elizabeth. I could not sleep last night. I love Him, this Jesus. But I have hurt Him with my sin."

I could not have told Nimmie that what she had done was not wrong; I believed it was. It would have been a terrible thing if she had been party to Mary's suicide. But God had kept her from that. I thanked God for His intervention and mercy. I said nothing about the act that Nimmie had *almost* committed. Instead, I talked about what now must be done about it.

"Nimmie, when I realized that I was a sinner, that I could do nothing myself to atone for my sins, I did the only thing one can do—that is necessary to do. I accepted what God has provided for all of mankind—His forgiveness. His forgiveness through the death of His Son, Jesus. He died for our sins so that we need not die for our own. I don't understand that kind of love either, Nimmie. But I know that it's real, for I have felt it. When I prayed to God and asked for His forgiveness and took His Son as my Savior, that love filled my whole person. Where I had had misery and fear before, now I have peace and joy."

"And He would do that for me?"

"He wants to. He aches to. That's why He came—and died. He loves you so much, Nimmie."

Even though Nimmie's eyes remained dry, mine were filled with tears.

We bowed our heads together, and I prayed and then Nimmie prayed. Hers was a beautiful, simple prayer, beginning in faith and repentance and ending with joy and praise.

I reached over and held Nimmie for a moment when we had finished praying. Even Nimmie's eyes were wet now. We spent some time looking at God's wonderful words of assurance and promise from the Bible, and then Nimmie rushed home to share her good news with Ian.

As she left the house that day, my heart was singing. Nimmie was even more than a very special friend. She was a beloved *sister* as well.

We had no idea how quickly Nimmie's newfound faith

would be tested. Less than a week after Nimmie and I had spent our time in prayer, disaster struck. The whole settlement was to suffer the consequences, but Nimmie and her husband would be hurt most of all.

It was about two o'clock in the morning when voices— loud and excited—reached our cabin. We both scrambled out of bed and hurried to the window. The whole world was lit up with an angry red glow.

"Fire!" cried Wynn before he even reached the window.

"Oh, dear God, no!" I prayed out loud.

But it was. It looked for a moment as if the whole village were going up in smoke. Wynn was dressed in the time it took me to understand the scene before me.

"Stay here, Elizabeth," he said. "I'll send people to you if they need your help. You know where all the medical supplies are kept. Get them out and ready in case they are needed."

Wynn was gone before I could even speak to him.

I dressed hurriedly, afraid I might be needed even before I could carry out Wynn's orders. The noise outside grew louder. I could hear the crackling of the flames now as well. Kip whined and moved toward the door. His instincts told him that there was danger.

"It's all right, Kip," I spoke soothingly to him. "You are safe here." I still didn't know what it was that was burning.

After I had followed all of Wynn's instructions and laid out the medical supplies, the bandages, and the burn ointments I had found, I put more wood in the fire and set a full kettle of water on to boil in case it was needed.

Smoke was in the air now, seeping through every air space into our cabin. The smell sickened me, for it meant pain and loss and even possible death. I went to the window to see if I could tell just how much of our small settlement was being taken by the fire. It was the Hudson's Bay Store that was burning. Wild flames leaped skyward. Men milled around the building, but there was really little they could do. There was no firefighting equipment in the village—only buckets and snowdrifts; and against such a fire, these had very little effect.

One cabin, close to the store, was also burning, and I

prayed for the occupants' safety. I began to pick out figures then. There were men on roofs of other buildings. There were bucket brigades feeding them pails of snow. Women and children milled around or huddled helplessly in groups. The whole scene was one of despair and horror.

A noise at the door brought me from the window. Three women stood together against the night. One held a baby in her arms, and one of the others held a child by the hand.

I had seen them before at the trading post where Nimmie and I had dished out soup to the storm-chilled. I did not know them by name.

"Come in," I said. "How is Nimmie? Have you seen Nimmie?"

One lady shook her head. The others looked blank.

They pushed the little girl forward. Her face was streaked with soot and wet from tears. She had an ugly burn across her hand. I took off her coat and knelt before her.

I had no training in treating burns. I grabbed a jar of ointment and read the label. It didn't tell me as much as I needed to know. I felt I should cleanse the wound somehow, but how? I got a basin of water and warmed it to my touch. I did not want to damage the burned tissue further. With a cloth, I wiped away most of the dirt and grime, trying hard not to hurt the child. Then I generously applied the ointment and bound the wound with a clean bandage.

As soon as I had finished, the mother with the baby held him out to me. She coughed to show that the baby had a problem. She pointed out the window at the fire and coughed again. "Smoke," she said, knowing that word.

"He choked on the smoke?" I asked her.

"Smoke," she said again.

Smoke inhalation. What could I do about that? I had no idea how it was treated and, if I had known, I was almost sure I wouldn't have what was necessary to treat it anyway.

I took the baby. To put their minds at ease I had to do something. *What, God? What do they do to make breathing easier?* The only thing I had ever heard of to ease breathing was steam, and it might be the very worst thing I could do. I didn't know.

I unbundled the baby and laid him on the cot. Then I dug

through Wynn's medical supply looking for something, anything, that might help the infant. I could find nothing that was labeled for smoke inhalation. I finally took some ointment that said that it was good for chest congestion and rubbed a small amount on the wee chest.

I had not finished with the small baby when the door opened again. More women and children entered our small cabin, more from fright than from injuries. A few of them did have a small burn or two but, thankfully, nothing major. The smell of smoke was on their clothing and the fear of fire in their faces.

Whenever a new group joined us, I asked the same question. "Nimmie? Have you seen Nimmie? The McLains? Are they all right?"

I got shrugs and blank looks in return.

The morning sun was pulling itself to a sitting position when Wynn came in carrying a young man who had badly burned a foot.

I was glad to see Wynn and sorry for the young man. "Nimmie?" I asked again. "What about the McLains?"

"They're fine," Wynn responded. "All three of them."

I was greatly relieved.

Then Wynn began to give instructions as to what he would need to care for the foot, and I carried them out to the best of my ability. After the young man was given some medication to dull the pain, Wynn did what he could for the ugly burn. Then he bandaged the foot lightly and, leaving the young man on our cot, went back again to help fight the fire.

Before he left he pulled me close, though he did not hold me long; there were a number of eyes fixed upon us.

"I think we'll be able to save the other homes. The fire has passed its worst. It shouldn't be long before you can start sending them home." Then he was gone.

I looked around at the still-frightened faces. "Sergeant Delaney says that the fire will soon be over," I informed them, gesturing with my hands as well, "and then you will all be able to return to your cabins. The rest of your homes are quite safe. You'll be able to go back to them."

I wasn't sure how many of them understood my words. I still knew only a few words in their tongue and none of them dealt with fire.

"But first," I said, "we'll have some tea."

It took a lot of tea that morning, and we had to take turns with the cups. Even so, it seemed to lift the spirit of gloom from the room. Some of the ladies even began to chat. It was a great relief to me.

I checked on the young man with the bad burn. He seemed to be resting as comfortably as possible under the circumstances. I asked him if he would like some tea, but he shook his head.

As the morning progressed, the fire died to a smolder of rubble, and two-by-two or in huddled little groups, the ladies and children left our cabin.

The young man had fallen asleep, whether from medication or exhaustion I did not know.

I set about doing up the dishes and tidying the small room.

By the time Wynn came, the young man had awakened and was asking me questions I could not understand nor answer. I was glad to see Wynn, for he would know what the fellow wanted.

I met Wynn at the door. After a quick look to assure myself that he was all right, I indicated the man on the cot.

"He's been trying to ask me something," I told Wynn. "I have no idea what he is saying."

Wynn crossed to the young man and knelt beside him. He spoke to him in the soft flowing sounds of his native tongue. Wynn spoke again and then, with a nod of his head, he rose and lifted the young man to his feet.

"I'm taking him home," Wynn said to me.

The young man seemed about to topple over.

"Shouldn't you—shouldn't you carry him?" I asked anxiously.

"I would," said Wynn, "gladly. But it would shame him to be carried through his village."

I looked at the proud young man. His face was twisted with pain, and still he was determined to walk rather than to be carried.

I nodded my head. "I hope he makes it," I said fervently.

"I'll see that he does," spoke Wynn softly, and they went out together.

When Wynn returned, he brought the McLains with him.

"Do you have enough food for five hungry people?" he asked me. I looked toward my stove. It was almost noon and no one had had anything to eat.

"I'll find it," I said without hesitation. But before I went to my cupboards and stove, I had to assure myself that Nimmie and Katherine were truly okay.

They clustered around our door, taking off soiled coats and kicking snow from their boots. Their faces were soot covered and streaked with tears, whether from weeping or the sting of the acrid smoke in their eyes I did not know nor ask. Their shoulders slumped with fatigue. It had been a long, hard, disheartening night. Their home was gone. Their livelihood was gone. In one night they lost their past, their present, and their future.

I crossed to them, unable to find words to express my feelings. I looked into Nimmie's eyes. My question was not voiced but she answered it. With just a quick little nod, she assured me she'd be all right.

I turned then to Katherine and put out my hand. "Are you all right?" I asked her.

Her answer was more as I would have expected. "I have no burns or outer injuries."

She was telling me that where she really hurt was on the inside. It would heal, now that she had found the secret to healing. But it would take time.

I turned back to Mr. McLain. "I'm sorry," I whispered falteringly, "truly sorry."

Mr. McLain was able to give me a crooked smile. "We're tough, Miz Delaney," he said. "Survivors. We'll bounce back."

I answered his smile and went to get them something to eat.

After we had finished our meal, we sat around the fireplace talking in quiet tones.

"What are your plans, Ian? Is there anything we can do?" asked Wynn.

Mr. McLain shrugged his shoulders. "I haven't sorted it out yet."

"You are welcome to stay here until you find other accommodations," went on Wynn.

"Katherine can have the cot," I hurried to add. "Is there somewhere we can find another bed?"

Nimmie shook her head. "There are no beds in the village," she said. "But don't worry. I can make all the bed that Ian and I need."

I looked puzzled.

"Spruce boughs and furs," explained Nimmie. "I know how to make a bed that even the richest white people of the world would envy!"

I admired Nimmie's attempt to lighten the situation and bring to us a little humor.

"It's not really *us* that I am worried about," McLain continued, his shoulders sagging in spite of his effort to keep up his spirits.

"You know what it's like this time of year," he went on, directing his conversation to Wynn. "It's been a long, hard winter. Most of the families are almost out of supplies. They were depending on the store to get them through the rest of the winter until the new growth brought fresh food again. Why, I'll wager that most of them have less than five cups of flour in the cabin. How they gonna make their bannock without flour? What about salt and tea and—?"

But Wynn stopped him.

"We'll all band together to look after them. They're hardy people. They'll make it."

There was silence for a few minutes. Mr. McLain broke it. "What about supplies for the two of you? What do you have here?"

Wynn shook his head. "Not enough for a whole village, that's for sure. We'll have to ration very carefully to get through until spring."

McLain nodded. "Right—that's a good idea," he said a little wistfully. "Don't be divying out what little you have. That way it won't do anyone any good. Someone has to stay healthy and on his feet, and seems to me you're elected, Sarge."

The full impact of our situation began to hit me. *Oh, God, I prayed silently, please don't let it come to the place where I have to turn hungry people away from my door. I would rather give away my last crumb of food and suffer with them.* Was

McLain right? Would things become so desperate that we would be forced to withold our own in order to have the strength to minister to the community's needs? I prayed not.

"Well, I think the first thing that needs to be done is a little survey," Wynn said. "We'll go through the village family by family and find out what the situation is. I'll get you a little book, McLain, if you are up to coming with me; and you can record as we go along."

McLain nodded and rose to his feet, reaching for his heavy, soot-covered coat and his beaver hat, and prepared to follow Wynn.

Wynn turned to me then. "I would like you to do the same here, Elizabeth, as you find time. It's important to know exactly what we have to work with."

I nodded. It all seemed so serious.

After the menfolk had left, I turned to Nimmie and Katherine. "Why don't you try to get a little sleep?" I asked them. "You both really look all in."

"I'll help you with your inventory," offered Nimmie.

"No. No—it won't take me long. There really isn't that much to count. You get some rest."

Nimmie was still hesitant, but I insisted. Finally she was persuaded, and she and Katherine went to our bedroom, removed their soiled outer garments and soon were fast asleep.

I did up the dishes and straightened the small room again; and then, notebook and pencil in hand, I began to do as Wynn had suggested.

I counted everything—each cupful of flour, each tablespoon of tea. I sorted and counted every can of tinned food. I measured the salt and the sugar, the coffee, and the beans and rice. Every bit of my kitchen supply and then my storeroom was measured and recorded.

At first it seemed to me to be quite a lot; and then I began to think of the number of days until the supplies could be replenished, and I realized it was not very much. Mr. McLain was right. We were going to be awfully short of food supplies before this winter was over.

With a sinking heart, I returned to the kitchen. It would take very careful planning to make things stretch.

Now late afternoon, Wynn and Mr. McLain had been gone

for a number of hours. I looked out the window nervously, willing them to return.

Nimmie came out of the bedroom looking rested. "Elizabeth," she said, "may I borrow your snowshoes?"

"Of course, but are you sure you are ready—?"

"I'm ready," she said with a soft smile. "I will even welcome the exercise and the healing of nature's breath."

"They are right outside the door," I told her. *I could use some of nature's restoring breath myself,* I noted in understanding.

Wynn and Mr. McLain returned before Nimmie. They did not have good news. The tabulation of food in the village was listed on two short pages. The Indians had come to rely more and more heavily on the trading post and did not store food ahead except for the roots and herbs they carried in and the berries they dried. By now, these too were in short supply.

The future looked even more bleak than it had before the survey. *Lord, please send an early spring.*

When it was dark and Nimmie had still not returned, I was becoming concerned. I didn't like to mention my fear because I knew Mr. McLain and Wynn already had enough on their minds. Stealthily I watched out the window. I wished I had suggested she take Kip with her.

Mr. McLain stopped what he was saying to Wynn in mid-sentence and turned to me. "If you are worried about Nimmie," he said, having caught me glancing out of the window again, "don't be. Nimmie is as at home in those woods as she was in her kitchen. Whether it's dark or light, Nimmie is in no danger."

I flushed slightly. "I do wish she'd come," I said rather apologetically.

Katherine came from the bedroom, also looking much better after her nap.

"I've nearly slept the day away," she confessed. "I'm sorry. I meant to be up to help you much sooner, but I just didn't wake up. You should have called me."

"I didn't have anything I needed help with," I assured her. "And, besides, you needed the sleep."

We prepared a meal. Katherine set out the plates and cutlery on the table. Because our table was small and we had only two chairs, we would fill our plates and sit about the room.

We were almost ready to eat when we heard Nimmie. I heaved a sigh of relief. When we opened the door to her, she entered the room almost hidden under spruce branches. How she had ever managed to load herself down so was beyond me. She smiled out from under the load, and Mr. McLain helped her to lay aside her bundles.

We ate together and then Nimmie disappeared again. When she returned, she had managed to get some furs from somewhere. With these at hand, she began to make a bed at one end of the room Wynn used for his office.

Wynn led our little group in prayer, and we all retired early. It had been a long, exhausting day, and there didn't seem to be anything more we could do to improve the situation at present. We would have to take our future one day at a time.

Chapter Thirty

Making Do

During the next few days, Wynn called for a meeting of all the people. They gathered together in front of the pile of rubble that had so recently been the source for the lifeblood of the settlement, anxious eyes surveying the pile of debris. Even the litter, as it had been poked and raked following the fire, had brought forth very little of use in the settlement.

Wynn stood before the people and spoke to them in their language. Nimmie, standing beside me with her head held high, whispered the translation.

"We meet together because we are one. We must care for one another. We have lost the trading post and the food it supplied. Now we must find our own way. It is not a new way. It has been done for many moons by our fathers. But it is a hard way. It will take us all working together.

"You have some flour and salt for bannock. You should watch your supply closely and use only a little every day. It can last for many days if you use it sparingly.

"We have the forests and the streams. They will not forsake us. They have meat for the taking. We will hunt together and share what we find.

"We have plants that can be gathered from under the snow. You know them well. We will send out groups to gather them. Those who stay behind will care for the fires.

"We have traps and snares if we run out of ammunition for our guns, so we will not starve.

"We have medicines if we become sick, so do not be afraid.

"And, most importantly, we have a God who sees us and

knows that we are in need. He has promised to care for His children.

"We will live, and we will make it to the time of the flowing of the rivers, and the stirring of the new leaf upon the tree and the gathering of the wild greens."

I felt like we all should have cheered such a speech; but when Wynn had finished speaking, the people of the village filed away—silently. Yet their shoulders had lifted a little and the look of despair upon their faces had been replaced with silent acceptance and even a glimmer of hope.

Now, Wynn was hardly ever home. He organized hunting parties, carefully distributing counted shells to the sharpest marksmen. He sent out fishing parties to cut holes in the ice and spend silent, long, cold hours at the task of bringing home fish. He sent older women, bundled against the cold, into the forests with baskets to dig for edibles among the roots of trees, while the younger women were assigned neighbor's fires to tend besides their own. Children took on new responsibilities as baby tenders and firewood gatherers. All the village was called upon to work together. Even the ones who were too old and feeble to be actively engaged had a part. They stirred the pots and kept the home fires fed while others were busy with their tasks.

A previously empty cabin was repaired sufficiently for the family who had lost their home in the fire, and life in the village went on.

Some of the outlying trappers, who had seen the terrifying red glow in the sky on the night of the fire, came home to check on family. They stood with heads lowered as they realized what the disaster meant to the entire population of the village. I think they too must have been praying, in their own way, for an early spring.

Nimmie and I were alone a few days later. I knew she must be very sorrowful about losing her lovely home with all the beautiful handwork from her past. She admitted that it "made her heart sore," but she was able to smile in spite of it all.

"I still have Ian," she said with great feeling. "If I had

lost him, then all would have been lost."

I thought of Wynn, and I understood what Nimmie was saying.

"I've been doing a lot of thinking," said Nimmie slowly. "Maybe this was God's punishment for my sin."

I wanted to protest, but I wasn't sure what to say.

Nimmie went on. "And then I thought, 'No, I think not.' You see, I was a sinner long before I brought the knife to Crazy Mary. I understand something now that I didn't understand before. I did not become sinful because I took in the knife, but rather I consented to take the knife because I was sinful. Do you understand me, Elizabeth?"

I nodded slowly. I did understand and I agreed.

"I have been a sinner for a long time. I just did not know about it. Oh, I knew that I had an unhappiness, a pain in my heart that twisted at times and brought me grief and shame, but I didn't know why or what it was.

"The pain is gone now. Even after the fire, I have peace. If God had been punishing me, then I wouldn't feel Him with me as I do now, as I did as I watched the fire burn away everything that had ever been mine. No, He was not punishing; but perhaps He is putting me through the testing ritual to see if I am going to be strong."

I nodded again. It seemed that Nimmie had it all sorted out. Tears filled my eyes. She was strong, our Nimmie.

"Ian and I talked long last night," Nimmie paused. "We are going to go away."

My mouth opened to protest and I reached a hand for her arm.

"We will be back," Nimmie informed me quickly. "We will be back as soon as the crows are back. We will build the trading post again as soon as wood can be hauled from the forest. And we will bring supplies back to the people."

Relieved to hear that they would be back, I still didn't understand why they felt they should go.

"Ian has much to do, to make plans for the new building," Nimmie explained. "He has to arrange for supplies to be shipped in as soon as the rivers are free of ice. We will be very busy. The time will go quickly. Ian is even going to show me the big cities that I have read about." Nimmie's face took on a glow. For a moment, I wished I could go with her; and then I quickly thought of Wynn, and any desire to leave Beaver River left me.

"Besides," said Nimmie matter-of-factly, "the supplies are low—even the supplies in *your* home. If we go soon, that will mean less people to feed and more life for the village."

"What about Katherine?"

"Ian is going to ask her what she wishes. We are sure that she will go with us."

There just seemed to be one question left to ask. "When will you go?"

"Tomorrow. Tomorrow as soon as the sun is in the sky."

Katherine did choose to go with them. They had very little to take. Mr. McLain still had his good team of sled dogs and his sled. They had no clothing to pack and no provisions except what they were given. Wynn made sure they had a good rifle and some shells. Villagers came shyly forward as the McLains prepared for travel and offered love gifts of food or clothing or traps. I knew that the people desperately needed the things they were giving away, yet so did the McLains. The gifts were not refused because it would have caused offense to the givers. They were given in love, and they were accepted in love.

At last the sled was loaded, the team harnessed, and the travelers were ready for the trail.

At the last minute, Nimmie drew me aside. I wasn't sure I would be able to talk to her without weeping.

"I have a wonderful secret," she said, her eyes shining, "and I wanted to share it with you before leaving.

"I am going to have a baby. Just think—after ten years of marriage, I am going to have a baby!"

"Oh, Nimmie," was all I could say, and I took her in my arms and cried all over her fur parka.

I was the only one in tears, for the Indian people expressed themselves in other ways. I knew their hearts were heavy, too. It was hard to see our friends go. It was hard to turn them over to the elements and the winter. I prayed that they would arrive safely. If anyone knew how to handle the rigors of the trail, it was the McLains. Nimmie had come from the forest, and Mr. McLain himself had spent many years working a trapline before becoming manager of the store. They would know what to do in all circumstances.

It would be hard for Katherine. She had not trained herself for the ways of the North. The trip would be long and difficult and very taxing. I prayed that God would help her.

And Nimmie. The little mother-to-be. The excited little mother. I prayed with all of my heart that things would go well for her and God would protect her unborn child.

I stood and watched them disappear over the whiteness of the hill outside our settlement, a final wave to us, our last glimpse of them. And then I placed a hand on Kip's furry head and started back to the cabin, the tears blurring my vision. I knew Wynn was watching me, making sure I would be all right.

Chapter Thirty-one

A Watchful Eye

"Isn't there any way I can help?" I asked Wynn.

He had been working almost day and night ever since the fire in order to make sure the settlement had food. I had been doing nothing—except ache for Nimmie.

"There is, Elizabeth. A very important way," Wynn informed me. "I would like you to keep a sharp eye on all the families for sickness. I think we'll pull through this winter just fine if we don't run into some kind of epidemic. The only way I see to prevent that from happening is to detect early anyone with symptoms and try to isolate them from the rest."

"So what do you want me to do?" I questioned. I certainly wasn't a nurse, nor did I have medical knowledge of any kind.

"Just visit the homes. Go around as much as you find the time to do so. Keep your eyes and ears open for any coughs or fevers or symptoms of any kind. Note the cabin and I will take it from there."

That didn't sound too difficult.

"How is it going, Wynn? I mean *really*?" I asked him.

He looked at me, and I knew I was going to get an honest answer. "It isn't good. We are managing so far to keep food in the cabins, but the real value of a little meat boiled with a few roots leaves much to be desired. Still, we will make it if we can just keep sickness away. Everyone is cooperating well, so far. If we can keep up the morale and keep them from giving up, we'll be all right."

"Surely it won't be much longer," I said hopefully.

"Until the snow goes—no. Maybe not. But, when the snow

goes, the rest of the men will be back. True, that will be more men to hunt and fish, but it will also be more mouths to feed. And it will still be several weeks after that before the forests and fields start to bear fruit."

Wynn drew me close and held me for several minutes before he left to resume his duties of another exhausting, long day.

I went to work on the dishes and cleanup. Since the fire, I no longer threw out tea leaves or coffee grounds after one use. Instead, I dried them and put them in a container to be used again. I saved any leftovers of our food as well, no matter how small the portion. It could be used in some way. Our meals were skimpy enough and were carefully portioned out. Meat had become our main staple as well, with only small servings of any tinned vegetables to complement it. Desserts were now only a dim memory. The nearest we came was to sprinkle a small amount of sugar on an occasional slice of bread. The bread was rationed as well. We allowed ourselves only one slice per day, and sometimes I cut those very sparingly, though I tried to make Wynn's a little thicker than mine—not too much different or he would notice and gently scold me.

I had been so happy for Nimmie when she told me of her coming baby. I had been longing for a baby of our own. Wynn and I had talked about it many times. Each month I had hoped with all my heart that God might decide to bless us; but now I found myself thanking God that I was not carrying a child. Our diet simply was not good enough to be nourishing a coming baby.

I'll wait, God, I prayed now. *I'll wait.*

As soon as my tasks were completed, I donned my coat and mittens and went out. We were now in April. Surely I wouldn't need heavy clothing much longer.

I visited several of the homes that morning. At each home I had to insist to the hostess, "No tea. No tea," and rub my stomach as though the tea would not agree with me. I did not want them to use any of their meager supply each time I came to call in the days ahead.

Many of these women I knew by name. They had learned to trust me, though they must have been wondering why I had nothing better to do than to wander around the settlement while everybody else was busy working. I kept close watch for anything that looked like potential trouble. At first, there was nothing more than one or two runny noses. I mentally noted them, just in case Wynn would want to check them out.

In the Arbus cabin, one of the children was coughing, a nasty sounding one that brought fear to my heart. *Please, not whooping cough,* I prayed silently and told Anna to be sure to keep him in and away from other children until Wynn saw him.

"But he get wood," said Anna. "His job."

"Not today. I will help with wood today. You keep him in by the fire."

Anna was surprised at what I said and the conviction with which I said it, but she did not argue further. I was *Mrs. Sergeant* and should be listened to.

I went for wood as I had promised. It was not an easy job. The snow was deep and the axes dull. It was hard for me to walk in snowshoes and carry wood on my back. I was not nearly as skilled as the Indian children. I had to make extra trips to get a pile as high as the others, and by the time I was finished, it was getting dark and I knew Wynn would soon be home. I had not made the full rounds of the cabins, but I would finish the rest the next day.

When Wynn returned home, I reported what I had found. "Good work," he said. "I'd better check them out."

"Why don't you wait until after you have eaten?" I suggested, "and I will go with you."

Wynn agreed and we ate our simple meal.

We walked over the crunching snow together in the moonlight, long shadows playing about us. From the cabins surrounding the little clearing, soft light flickered on the billowy banks of snow.

"It's pretty at night, isn't it?" I said to Wynn.

"But not pretty in the daytime?" Wynn prompted.

"Oh, I didn't mean that—not really. It's just—that—well, in the daytime all of the gloom and grime of the tragedy shows up, too. Some days," I went on, "I wish it would snow ten feet just to bury that terrible reminder heaped up there in the village."

"It's not a pretty sight, is it? But I thought you were very anxious for the snow to go."

"I am. I don't really mind the snow itself—it is pretty and I have enjoyed it—walking in it, looking at it. It's the wind I hate. I can't stand the wind. It just sends chills all through me. It seems so—so—vengeful somehow. I hate it!"

Wynn reached over to take my hand and pull me up against him as we continued to walk.

"I wish you could learn to appreciate the wind, Elizabeth. God made the wind, too. It has many purposes and it is part of our world. You will never be really at peace here until you have made friends with the wind. Try to understand it—to find beauty in it."

He pulled me to a stop. "Look, over there. See that snowbank? Notice the way the top peaks and drops over in a curve—the velvet softness of the purple shadow created by the glow of the moon. See how beautiful it is."

Wynn was right.

He continued to point out other wind sculptures around the clearing. I laughed.

"All right," I assured him. "I will try to find beauty in the wind."

"Its greatest beauty is its song," Wynn continued. "I still haven't had the opportunity to take you out camping under the stars, but when spring comes we'll do that. We'll camp at a spot where we can lie at night and hear the windsong in the spruce trees. It's a delightful sound."

"I'll remember that promise," I told Wynn.

We were at the first cabin. Wynn looked carefully at the throat of the child and felt for fever. There didn't seem to be any cause for alarm here, but he did give the mother a little bit of medication, telling her to give one spoonful every morning. She nodded in agreement and we went on to the next cabin.

Again we found no cause for concern. Wynn didn't even leave medicine with the family. He told me to keep an eye on the child during the next few days.

When we reached the third cabin, we could hear the coughing even before we got to the door. Wynn stopped and listened carefully.

"You're right," he said. "I don't like the sound of that at all." Whooping cough was one of the dreaded killers of the North.

"Do we have medication?" I asked Wynn, counting on the worst.

"Not nearly enough if it turns out to be whooping cough," he said quietly.

We went in then and Wynn did a thorough examination of the throat, chest, and ears of the child, with the little equipment he had.

"How long has he been coughing?" he asked Anna.

"Two," she said.

"His cough is bad, Anna. I want you to keep him in. And keep the other children away from him if you can. Wash any of his dishes in hot, hot water. Let them sit in the water and steam. Give him this medicine—once when the sun comes up, once when it is high in the sky, and once when the sun goes down. You understand?"

"Understand," said Anna.

Wynn repeated all his directions in her native tongue to be sure Anna had fully understood.

"Understand," she said again.

"Mrs. Delaney will be back tomorrow to see how he is feeling."

"Beth come," she said with satisfaction. I felt a warm glow to hear her use my given name.

"Is there any way to get more medicine?" I asked Wynn on the way home.

"Not in time. We would have to send someone out and then have him bring it back. By that time half of the town could be infected."

"What will we do?"

"We'll just have to wait, Elizabeth, and hope that we are wrong. Wait—and pray."

Chapter Thirty-two

Traps

Now that my days were more than full, I had little time for Kip. I knew he needed his exercise, so I was forced to let him out to run on his own. I hated to do it, but he always returned home again before too much time elapsed.

One night he came in with marks on his fluffy long coat. I pulled him close and looked at him. There was a tuft of hair hanging from the corner of his lip. I pulled it out and looked at it, puzzling over what it meant.

"Looks like he's been in a little scrap," Wynn remarked as though it was of no consequence.

"Do you think so?" I asked in alarm, remembering the mean-looking Buck.

"He doesn't look much the worse for it," Wynn responded. "I'm guessing he came out top dog."

I brushed at Kip's coat. I could feel no injuries and he certainly didn't appear to be in any pain. In fact, he looked rather pleased about something.

"What will I do with him?" I asked Wynn.

"What do you mean?"

"Well, I don't have time to take him for his walks, and he can't be shut up in here all day."

"I think he will look after himself just fine."

"But what if he meets Buck? The last time, he submitted to Buck; but, if he's fighting other dogs now, he might try to fight Buck, too."

Wynn grinned. "Someone has to bring that big bully down to size."

"Oh, Wynn," I cried. "This isn't funny. He could be hurt!"

Wynn, more serious then, apologized. "I'm sorry. I didn't mean to make fun of your concern. You're right. There is the possibility of Kip getting hurt. But it's more probable that he will come out the victor. Kip didn't meet Buck's challenge last time because he knew he wasn't ready. That's a smart dog. If he does decide to take him on, it will be because he thinks he is ready. Now no one knows whether he is or not. We just have to trust Kip's instincts, that's all.

"Kip has a number of advantages over Buck. He's a little heavier. He has had better nutrition. He is younger and more agile, and I believe that he's much smarter. If it should come to a fight, I think Kip has a good chance."

Well, a good chance wasn't good enough for me. I wanted to be sure. What I really wanted was for Kip to stay out of the ring completely, but it didn't look like I was going to be able to avoid it much longer.

"You behave yourself," I warned Kip, shaking my finger at him, "or I'll—I'll tie you up."

In making the rounds of the cabins, I found a few more sniffles but no more bad coughs. Anna's small boy was not getting any worse. In fact, the medicine seemed to be working. His cough was gradually getting better. Anna beamed. None of the other children had developed the cough. I was sure that she, too, had thought of the dreaded whooping cough—she likely knew the symptoms much better than I.

The sun's rays warmed the air a bit more each day. I found myself frequently pushing back my parka and even unbuttoning my coat. The drifts were getting smaller and the wind did not have the same chill. We were now into the middle of April. *Spring must be just around the corner!* I exulted.

"How would you like a day off?" Wynn surprised me one morning. I looked up from cutting the thin slices of bread.

"I'd love it. What do you have in mind?"

"I need to make a call on a cabin about two miles from the settlement. I thought that, seeing you have been doing such a good job at being camp nurse, you might like to come along."

"I'd love to!" was my enthusiastic response.

"The snow is getting a little thin in places. We won't be using the sled much more this year." That was good news too.

"When should I be ready?" I asked Wynn.

"In about half an hour."

"I'll be waiting. Can I bring Kip for a run as well?"

"Sure. Bring Kip. Just keep him away from the sled dogs. To them, Kip is a stranger and a threat."

I was sure I wouldn't have any trouble with that. Kip was obedient and heeled whenever he was told to do so.

I hummed as I went about getting ready to go. *It's so nice to have this kind of outing! A whole day with Wynn!* The sun was shining. Soon our winter would be over and our world would change again. Nimmie would be coming back. The new trading post would be built. Our people would have proper food and supplies again. The world seemed good.

"Thank you, God," I whispered. "Thank you for seeing us through."

Wynn was soon there with the sled. Calling Kip to heel, I went out to join him. It was a wonderful day as promised. Wynn made his call and checked the man who had been reported ill in his cabin. Wynn carried wood and water in and made sure he had the necessary supplies. He gave him medicine to take for a few days and told him he would be back to see him in a couple of days. The man didn't appear to be seriously ill, just down with the flu; so we left him and started our return trip.

We were about halfway home when a terrible cry rent the stillness of the sun-filled day. I stopped in my tracks, my skin prickling.

"What was it?" I asked Wynn, who had stopped the team and drawn up beside me.

"I'd better check," he said and reached for his rifle. The piercing cry came again.

"You wait here," said Wynn. "I won't be long. It must be an animal in a trap."

I sat down, my back to the direction Wynn was taking, trying to blot out the awful sound. I watched the sled dogs.

They lay on the hard-packed snow, their heads on their paws or else licking the icy snow from between their toes. They seemed oblivious to the whole thing, only appreciative of the chance to rest.

I thought of Kip then. I momentarily had forgotten about Kip. I turned to look for him now.

He was disappearing just around the clump of trees where Wynn had gone. I thought of Wynn and his rifle. What if he had to shoot and didn't know that Kip was there and Kip got in the way?

"Kip!" I cried, springing up. "Kip, get back here!"

I ran after the dog, puffing my way through the snow. It was not far. I soon found Kip and I soon found Wynn.

And then I saw it. Lying on the ground, which was covered with blood, was a small furry animal. His foot was secured in the trap, his eyes were big and pleading, and his leg—his leg—. And Wynn was swinging the butt of his rifle.

I couldn't look. I gave a little cry and turned away. Wynn's head came up quickly and he came to me.

"Elizabeth," he said, taking me into his arms and turning my head away from the awful sight, "I asked you to stay—"

"But Kip—he ran. I didn't see him until—"

Wynn held me. I started to cry and to shake. "The poor little animal," I kept sobbing. "The poor little thing."

Wynn let me cry.

"Oh, Wynn," I wept, "it's so awful."

"Yes," he agreed, "it's awful."

"You killed him?"

"I had to, Elizabeth. You saw how badly hurt he was."

"Couldn't you have let him go?"

"He was in a man's trap. And even if he had gotten away, he would have died—"

"It's terrible." I began to cry again. "Can't you stop it, Wynn? Can't you tell them not to do it anymore? You're the law; they'll listen to you."

Wynn gave me a little shake to stop my hysteria and to bring some sense to my head. "I can't stop trapping. You know I can't. Trapping is their way of life. Their livelihood. If they didn't have furs, they wouldn't have anything. I know it's cruel. I hate it, too, but it's part of life. One that we just have to accept."

I knew Wynn was right. I tried to stop crying. I thought of all the families back at the settlement. The furs for trading was the only way they had to buy their needed supplies.

I hated it, but I too would have to learn to live with it. *Yet surely, surely there must be a more humane way,* my heart told me.

I was sorry that our one day out together for so many long weeks had been spoiled. I tried to make it up to Wynn. I would not fuss further and I would not speak of it again. There wasn't any way I could prepare Wynn a special dinner, but at least I could be good company in the little time we had left. I planned a night before the fireplace, reading one of our favorite books.

When Wynn returned from settling the team, weary from the duties of the day, I told him about my plans. He grinned and lifted my face to kiss me on the nose.

"Sounds good to me."

We had just settled ourselves, and I was taking the first turn of reading aloud, while Wynn lay with his head in my lap. A commotion at the door made me jump and Wynn hollered. Fortunately, the book in his face had done no damage.

We answered our door to find one man with another man over his shoulder.

"Leg," he informed us and carried the man in and dumped him rather unceremoniously on the rug before the fire.

The injured man groaned in pain. Wynn knelt down beside him and began to feel the leg.

"It's broken," he said quietly. "We'll have to set it. At least the skin isn't broken. It's not too bad a break. No splinters or torn muscle or ligaments."

Wynn continued to feel the leg, and the man on the floor continued to groan.

"This isn't going to be nice," Wynn said to me. "Do you want to take a walk?"

"Do you need me?"

"I could use you—but I won't ask you to stay."

"I think—I think I can manage."

"Good girl." Then Wynn turned to the man who had carried the fellow in. "How did this happen?"

"Fall."

"How long ago?"

" 'Bout hour."

"Let's get him on the cot."

They lifted him together and Wynn went for his medical supplies. He poured some strong-smelling stuff on a small cloth and gave it to me.

"I want you to stand here and hold this to his nose and mouth. Like this. Wait until we are ready to set the leg. Don't hold it there for too long. I'll tell you when to let him breathe it and when to move it away."

I moved in by the man, the cloth in my hand, ready to follow Wynn's instructions. I didn't watch. I was too busy with the face before me and the cloth that I held. In spite of my ministration, the man still moaned and tried to throw himself off the cot. The other man was called over to hold him. At last the ordeal was over and Wynn tied the leg securely in a makeshift splint.

"Go get one of your friends," Wynn said to the trapper, "and you can take him to his cabin."

Wynn's forehead was wet with perspiration. He brushed back the wave of hair that had fallen forward. He moved to the man on the cot and reached down to him with a gentle hand.

"It'll be all right, Strong Buck," he said assuringly. "It's all over now. They will take you to your own bed. I will give you good medicine for the pain."

The man nodded. The worst of it was over. Wynn brought the tablet and the water and he swallowed it gratefully.

The men were soon back and carefully carried their companion to his own home to be welcomed by an anxious wife.

Wynn turned back to the fire and then looked at me and smiled.

"Where is that nice, quiet evening you had arranged, Elizabeth?" he asked me.

I crossed to him and put my arms around his neck.

"Is there *anything* you can't do?" I asked him with admiration in my voice. "You deliver babies, sew up ugly cuts, set broken bones, pull infected teeth, act as doctor to the sick, feed the whole village. Is there anything that you can't do?" I repeated.

Wynn kissed me. He smiled that slow, easy smile I had learned to love.

"Now, Elizabeth," he said teasingly. "Do you think I would be so silly as to confess?"

Chapter Thirty-three

Spring

Though we did not hear from the McLains, I began to watch for them. "As soon as the river thaws," or "as soon as the logs can be brought from the forests," was not too definite a time for their return. Well, the river was running again now and the forests were losing their snow quickly. I began to watch and to hope.

"I'll be back in time to plant my garden," Nimmie had said. "We will plant a garden together."

I was anxious for that garden. I was even more anxious for Nimmie. I thought, too, of Katherine. Would she be back too? Poor Katherine! She had faced so much in life, but she had lost so much of life by her own choosing. I was so glad she seemed finally able to start picking up the pieces again.

I wondered about Nimmie's coming baby. This was not a convenient time to be on the long, difficult trail out from Edmonton. I remembered the trip well. But then Nimmie was at home with the woods and the river. She no doubt would be a better traveler than I had been. I had watched for the first bluebird when at home in Toronto. I had watched for the first song of the robin. I had waited expectantly for the sight of the first spring crocus. I had relished the day when I saw my first dainty violet. But now I was watching and waiting for Nimmie. With Nimmie's arrival, I would know that it was really spring. With the coming of Nimmie and Ian, new life would be given to the dreary, winter-weary little settlement.

Heavy parkas were put away now. Children played out

again in cotton dresses and flannel shirts. Women went to the woods with baskets on their arms, hoping to find some early spring greens. Men came back from traplines and turned their attention from trapping furs to tanning the furs. Smoke still lazily drifted from the fires in the cabins, but at times they were allowed to die out. Their warmth wasn't needed through all of the days.

There was a new feeling in the settlement, a feeling of being released after a long confinement. But still, I held apart, breathless, waiting.

Was it really spring, or might another biting north wind bring in the snow again? I hardly dared to hope.

And then it happened. A man rode excitedly into camp, his horse breathing heavily. He cried out in broken English, "They come. Many wagons."

Everyone came from their cabins.

"Where? Where?"

He began to talk to them in their own language then, and I was about to explode with my question.

I ran among the people until I found Wynn.

"Is it them?" I asked him.

"It's them," he assured me, grinning. "With many wagons of supplies."

"How far away are they?"

"About five miles."

Five miles. That still seemed too far. I could hardly wait. It would seem forever. "I'll go get them some supper," I said, about to bolt off.

Wynn caught my hand. "Hold it," he said, laughing. "They won't be here for an hour or so."

At my look of disappointment, he hurried on.

"I was wondering if you'd like to go out to meet them."

"Oh, yes!" I cried.

"Grab a sweater. It might be getting cool before we get back."

I ran for the sweater, my skirts whipping about my legs. I lifted them up so that I might run faster. *They're here!* Well, they were *almost* here. They were coming.

I hurried back to Wynn. "Let's go," I said, already out of breath.

He took my arm and slowed me down. "If we have a few miles to walk, you'd better slow down. You'll never make it at that pace."

He was right. I slowed down, and the people of the village began to fall into step behind us. They came, the mothers carrying babies and the fathers hoisting young ones on their shoulders. Even the old, who needed the assistance of a walking stick, tottered on at a slower pace. The whole village was going out to meet the trader and his Indian wife.

We walked along as swiftly as Wynn would allow. I breathed deeply of the fresh tangy air. It was still cool but it smelled of growing things, I thought. Or was it just my imagination?

"Do you think spring is really here?" I asked Wynn.

"I think so."

"What signs do you go by?" I persisted.

"The river is almost ice free."

I nodded my head in assent.

"The snow is almost all gone."

I nodded again.

"It's warmer," continued Wynn. "And I've seen several flocks of Canada geese pass over."

He waited. "Do you need more?"

I swatted at my cheek. "The mosquitoes are back," I said ruefully.

"There," said Wynn. "You have one more assurance. Spring is here all right." We laughed together.

Kip frolicked on ahead of us, sniffing at rabbit dens and barking at saucy squirrels. I laughed at him.

"I think he's excited, too," I said to Wynn.

Wynn took my hand.

"This winter has been hard for you, hasn't it, Elizabeth?"

"It's been hard for everyone," I answered honestly.

"But the rest—they are used to the hardships. You haven't been. Has it—has it been too much?"

"I admit I will be very glad for a fresh carrot. And I will admit I will be glad for a piece of cake. I will even admit that spinach, which I hate, might taste good. But I am not sorry that I came with you, Wynn."

Wynn stopped me and pushed back my hair and kissed

me. He looked deeply into my eyes.

"I'm glad to hear you say that, Elizabeth. I have something to say, too. Something I maybe should have said long ago, but I want to say now, with all my heart—with all my love. I'm proud of you, Elizabeth. Proud of your strength, your support, your ability to adjust to hard things. You've been my help, my support, my right arm, Elizabeth. I don't know what I ever would have done without you. You've more than proved me wrong—over and over. You belong here—with me."

Wynn kissed me again, and I brushed away happy tears and lifted my face again to his.

And then I heard the grinding of the wagon wheels. They were coming. Just over the hill was Nimmie. Just over the hill were the needed supplies—and hope. My heart gave a lurch in its happiness. I gave Wynn one more kiss with all my love wrapped up in it, and I turned to meet the oncoming wagon.

Spring had come.

PROBLEMS FOR
FEMINIST CRITICISM

Feminist criticism has come a long way in the last twenty years. Its development has been rapid, its snowball progress picking up elements of structuralism, deconstruction and psychoanalytic criticism; just as rapidly it has been shedding its own early theories and methodologies. Now it is a critical orthodoxy with its own established canonical texts. Now is the time, then, to begin to question that orthodoxy. In *Problems for Feminist Criticism* five women critics seek to do that, in a spirit of enquiry whose central point of focus is the literature for which feminist critics have offered a re-reading.

By reference to a wide range of writers, from Milton to the contemporary poet, with a strong emphasis on the nineteenth-century novel, the contributors ask what we may be losing from literature by adopting the feminist orthodoxy. Each chapter provides a survey of feminist critical approaches to its subject and highlights the inherent problems. The book frees the way forward for critics who have found much that is stimulating and revealing in feminist approaches to literature, but who find its proscriptiveness potentially reductive. It shows how literature may have the flexibility to absorb and benefit from new critical approaches, whilst still retaining its own life, never quite to be contained in criticism's theories and methodologies.

PROBLEMS FOR FEMINIST CRITICISM

Edited by Sally Minogue

London and New York

First published 1990
by Routledge
11 New Fetter Lane, London EC4P 4EE

Simultaneously published in the USA and Canada
by Routledge
a division of Routledge, Chapman and Hall, Inc.
29 West 35th Street, New York, NY 10001

Typeset by LaserScript Limited, Mitcham, Surrey
Printed and bound in Great Britain by
Richard Clay Ltd, Bungay, Suffolk

British Library Cataloguing in Publication Data

Problems for feminist criticism.
1. English literature. Feminist criticism
I. Minogue, Sally
820.9

Library of Congress Cataloging in Publication Data

Problems for feminist criticism / edited by Sally Minogue.
p. cm.
Includes bibliographical references.
1. Feminist literary criticism. 2. English literature–History
and criticism. 3. Women in literature. I. Minogue, Sally.
PN98.W64P76   1990
820.9'352042–dc20   90-8191

ISBN 0 415 02077 8
ISBN 0 415 05029 4 pbk

9-15-93

To Colin

CONTENTS

NOTES ON CONTRIBUTORS

Barbara Hardy is Professor Emeritus of the University of London, and has written on Jane Austen, Charles Dickens, George Eliot, William Thackeray, Thomas Hardy, Henry James and modern novelists. Amongst her books are *Tellers and Listeners: The Narrative Imagination, The Appropriate Form, The Advantage of Lyric, Forms of Feeling in Victorian Fiction* and *Narrators and Novelists: Collected Essays Vol. One.* She is working on a book about narrative in Shakespeare and on the second volume of her collected essays.

Sandra Hopkins read English at King's College, London. She is a part-time tutor in Literature in the Department of Continuing Education at the University of Bristol, and also a tutor on The Open University's Nineteenth-century Novel course.

Mara Kalnins is Principal Lecturer in English at Leicester Polytechnic. She is an editor for the Cambridge Critical Edition of D. H. Lawrence and has edited *Apocalypse and the Writings on Revelation* (1980), *Aaron's Rod* (1988) and *Sea and Sardinia* (forthcoming). She has also edited *D. H. Lawrence: Centenary Essays* (1986), *Some Noble Theme: Essays on Aspects of Romanticism* (forthcoming), and is at present writing a critical study of Lawrence's late works and preparing a selection of his poetry for higher education students.

Barbara K. Lewalski is the William R. Kenan Professor of English Literature and of History and Literature at Harvard University. Her recent books and articles on Renaissance topics include: *Protestant Poetics and the Seventeenth-century Religious Lyric* (1979) and *Paradise Lost and the Rhetoric of Literary Forms* (1985). Amongst her current projects is a book on women in seventeenth-century England, *Writing Women in the Jacobean Era*.

Sally Minogue is co-author, with Colin Radford, of *The Nature of Criticism*. She is currently working on a book on poetic language examining the inclusion and exclusion of the demotic voice, the voice of everyday experience, in English poetry – *The Dialect of Common Sense*. She teaches English half-time at Thanet Technical College, and part-time at the University of Kent.

ACKNOWLEDGEMENTS

I'd like to thank Jan Montefiore for her generosity, my brother Martin, and my dear friends Gay Mitchell and Mandy Rose for their constant support. My profoundest debt, as ever, is to Colin Radford, for many things, but most for his unfailing faith.

The editor and publisher are grateful to the following for permission to reprint: Gwendolen Brooks for extracts from 'Paul Robeson', 'Malcolm X' and 'We real cool', from *Blacks*, the David Company, Chicago. Copyright © 1987. The executors of Edna St Vincent Millay, for an excerpt from Sonnet VII and the whole of Sonnet XI of *Fatal Interview* by Edna St Vincent Millay, from *Collected Sonnets*, revised and expanded edition, Harper & Row, 1988. Copyright © 1931, 1958 by Edna St Vincent Millay and Norma Millay Ellis. Reprinted by permission. To Olwyn Hughes for an excerpt from Sylvia Plath's *Poppies in July*, from *Collected Poems*, ed. Ted Hughes, London, Faber, 1981. For permission to reproduce an excerpt from ' To the proposition that all women are not equal, i.e. identically oppressed', by Lorraine Bethel, in *Conditions Five*, Brooklyn, New York. To Little, Brown and Company for permission to reproduce 'My life had stood – a Loaded Gun' and 'Wild nights' by Emily Dickinson, from *The Complete Poems of Emily Dickinson*, ed. Thomas H. Johnson. Copyright © 1929 Martha Dickinson Bianchi, renewed 1957 Mary L. Hampson.

INTRODUCTION: PROBLEMS FOR FEMINIST CRITICISM

Sally Minogue

It is oddly difficult for us as academics to speak of literature in personal terms, particularly in these days of pseudo-science. Feminism has something to teach us here, since it is an intensely personal form of politics, learnt partly through lived experience and issuing in action which inhabits every part of a feminist's life; one of its earliest precepts, 'the personal is the political', was the inspiration for many other movements. Yet we most often meet feminism's public face in dicta and prohibitions of a general sort; and it is an area in which it is too easy to reach for our dogmas (on whichever side) and turn aside from or blot out those patches of difficulty, confusion and contradiction which are often the most revealing and fruitful to explore. A keener awareness of the personal can help us in that exploration.

For the personal is also the critical. I can still recall from some sixteen years ago an impassioned discussion in a seminar in America between a hostile lecturer and an early supporter of Gay Lib on the value of Gary Snyder's poetry. The discussion hinged on Snyder's sexuality, and I felt doubtful about its relevance and improperly excluded. But as I walked home beside the Gay Lib supporter, I realized that he was crying. His defence of Snyder's poetry mattered intensely, personally to him. At that time I had never cried over a critical disagreement (I was still young) and I began to realize that this man understood more about this poetry than I did, perhaps than I could. The discussion had been, inextricably, personal, critical, political.

Perhaps what embarrasses us about linking literature with personal experience is that we are afraid that the work of art will become the target of feelings which it has not 'caused', and we shall transfer aesthetic value to it for inappropriate reasons. An abyss of solecisms opens before us. What if we were to fall writhing into it, dismissing Nabokov as a dirty pervert, condemning *Catcher in the Rye* because it inspired John Lennon's murderer, blaming Lawrence of being unkind to his father in *Sons and Lovers*. Yet, of course, all of those things are indeed in the offing when we make critical judgements (and not just in the offing, in Lawrence's case). The relationship between cause and target in responses to works of art is a problematic one; and the line between literature and life is blurred and ragged. For literature is experienced privately as well as publicly. In the exercise of that experience as an area of academic activity, as an intellectual discipline, it is, of course, public and subject to accompanying restraints. But if we remember our earliest experiences of literature, they tend to be internal experiences. They may be imbued with the public circumstances in which they took place – someone reading us to sleep, the peculiar force of a school play, the poem which so specifically seems to fit our own situation – but they reverberate in the heart and mind. Texts become madeleines of the particular moment. However, they remain literature; and those experiences are of the same kind, or at least continuous with, the kinds of experience that we attempt to articulate within the current academic framework.

It is precisely this private dimension of literary experience which renders it so powerful. And it is that power which many feminists have seized on as one of the shaping elements of the socialization of women. It is this connection, between the private experience of literature and the shaping of women's consciousness, I want to focus on in these introductory remarks. I do so partly because it is an area in which the feminist position seems at once intuitively, appealingly right, yet where there are many unvoiced problems and confusions; partly because it is a part of feminist criticism which has been popularly absorbed and accepted; and partly because it connects with the effect of literature on all women's lives, not just on the theory and practice of academics. And while I want to agree that literature's effects on women's lives have sometimes been deleterious, I also want to take issue with the position, argued by many feminists, that therefore women (and perhaps men) should read literature only or primarily from a feminist point of view. Thus I want first to look at some of the ways in which the feminist critics are right; but I want to disagree with their final analysis of literature, and

2

their suggested poetics and aesthetics, in relation to the shaping of women's consciousness through literature. In this, I prefigure the approach of this collection.

It is, or has been, difficult for women in contemporary society fully to appreciate other women. One of the successes of feminist politics has been to make it respectable for women to like, to enjoy the company of, to prefer above men, other women. It is still difficult for many women, nor is it something that is simply subject to the will; only experience can fully teach us the importance of appreciating fellow women – or, if you are a man, why you should understand that importance. Generally, we start by practising our indifference to other women – where we start practising everything – on our mothers. I was no exception. My mother was an unusual woman. She had been in service, as it is so aptly described, in a large aristocratic household, had married a farm labourer on the same estate and lived the difficult and poverty-marked existence necessitated by her situation. Her education, like my father's, had been curtailed. But she was a voracious reader, a prolific writer (often in an Ogden Nash, light-verse sort of strain); she was also extremely practical, and she and my father practised role-reversal long before it had a name or a status (in fact, it had a negative status in a rural, working-class community) – she replaced broken windows and wired plugs, while my father cooked Sunday dinner and proudly wheeled his children out in the pram. The household was full of books – indeed sociologists have probably devised a category for the kind of family we were – and my earliest days were informed by the written word. But none of this meant that I took either my mother's writing or her reading seriously. I took it for granted; but I did not take it seriously. Instead, I had a notion of Literature with a capital L, fostered by my grammar school education and strengthened by my university experience. This literature was a weird mix of Jane Austen, Joyce and *The Rainbow*, metaphysical poetry and Auden; the poetry I wrote was heavily influenced by T. S. Eliot. I had no idea that what I read and valued was partly a product of accident as well as design; I was a believer in the canon as handed down to me. And it didn't immediately occur to me that what I was was partly shaped by what I read, rather than the other way round. Certainly, it didn't strike me that women had been treated badly by literature; nor that I might be similarly treating my mother badly by not looking at her poems in the

3

same way as I looked at the poems I studied. If I had been born twenty years later, I like to think I would have been different, and as a direct result of feminism.

So about me and my mother at that stage, the feminists were right. Her poetry had, in many ways, as much, perhaps more value than the poetry I studied at school and at university. As a testament of the difficulty of her experience, the struggle of her life, her lack of a listenable voice, her poems were of greater worth than the insubstantial mouthings of sentiment of Tennyson's 'Tears Idle Tears' or Crashaw's bloody, sickly, sacramental 'Hymn to St Theresa'. My mother shed tears that were certainly not idle and her martyrdoms were more genuine and felt than the spiritual wounds licked by Crashaw; furthermore her poetry had a nice line in irony which made somewhat light of all that. But, partly because by the critical evaluative standards I had been taught her poetry was not 'good', partly because she was an 'ordinary woman', and partly because she was that species of womanhood, my mother, I was blinded to that.

This point, extrapolated to thousands, millions of cases, is made tellingly in Tillie Olsen's book *Silences* (published 1980, but much of it written in the 1960s), which she dedicates to 'our silenced people, century after century their beings consumed in the hard, everyday essential work of maintaining human life. Their art, which still they made – as their other contributions – anonymous; refused respect, recognition; lost.'[1] Olsen's work, written as it is in a rather mystical-American sort of way, none the less clearly documents the ways in which women have been silenced in literature, either by not being published at all, or by placing their art secondary to their love of a man, or by being diminished by male reviewers, or simply by not having the confidence to recognize that they could be writers, and good writers, that confidence having been eroded by the identification of writing with men, and indeed by the identification of women with a supporting not a creating role.

The remarkably successful way in which those silences have been filled in the last decade or two almost masks the magnitude of the achievement. Women's Studies is now a force and a market: publishers such as Virago and the Women's Press are commercially successful and feminist criticism is an academic force carrying with it career possibilities. None of this could have been achieved without feminism as a political force; without that political force's affecting women in other areas of activity, notably literary criticism; and without those women being sufficiently personally affected by feminism for their ways of doing literary criticism to be profoundly influenced by it.

It is important to realize that, underpinning this change, and central to Olsen's work and others', is the belief, not always fully stated, that writing by women is important and to be valued for that very reason, that it is by and about women. Many of the women writers published by Virago have not always been 'good' writers by the critical standards described above. And this is where the real business of feminist criticism, and the difficulties, begin. For at what stage do we begin to say that a writer is bad because he or she is misogynist (in whatever terms that misogyny is critically described)? At what stage do we demote certain works and elevate others? It is no good disclaiming that task, since that is part of what feminist criticism is about: the revaluation of the worth of texts. Some feminist critics have been happy to make those judgements; Adrienne Rich, for example, and Annette Kolodny, who carefully looks at the difficult relationship between aesthetic judgements and feminist values in 'Dancing through the minefield', and comes down with the illustrative view that 'readings of *Paradise Lost* which analyze its complex hierarchical structures but fail to note the implications of gender within that hierarchy...will no longer be deemed wholly adequate.'[2] The difficulty is that, as with many forms of literary criticism, collisions occur between the criteria for judgement.

The very speed of development of feminist criticism has scarcely given it time to reflect upon its own disagreements and difficulties, especially where it has been caught up in the hectic amalgamation of disparate and often contradictory approaches to language and epistemology, and hence to literature and to criticism, which characterizes literary theory. Clashes between Marxism and feminism, between post-Saussurean linguistics and Lacanian psychoanalytics (note the dominance of male thinking), between the social construction of reality and biology, have been suppressed rather than voiced. Often, this has been in the ostensible interest of a unified cause – feminism; but a politics, and indeed a poetics, which cannot attend to its own disagreements surely cannot flourish.

One area in which debate has been overleapt is that of the influence of literary representations of women on women's lives, and the resultant effects on critical evaluation of texts and writers, and on the practice and poetics of feminist criticism. Elaine Showalter, an influential figure in this area, has concentrated on correcting and opposing literary misogyny wherever it appears, by resurrecting and revaluing women writers, by attacking manifestations of misogyny (what she calls textual harassment) in male writers and critics, and by rethinking the role of women's writing now. For Showalter, most of this battle has already been won: 'Over the past fifteen years, these efforts to make the readers question the innocence, insignificance or humor of antifeminist characterizations have succeeded in changing the atmosphere of literary response...literary misogyny can no longer be overlooked or excused.' As a result, she confidently predicts 'even more drastic re-estimations of the old masters'.[3] Other more radical feminist critics have, however, objected to this approach, either because it defines feminist aesthetics in terms of the existent male aesthetic[4] or because it treats female texts as transparent, unproblematically reflecting female experience.[5] Indeed, the brand of feminist criticism which concerns itself with constructing a female canon within the male, while at the same time firing off a few shots at 'textual harassment' by male authors, may soon be one of the many corpses on the already bloody battlefield of feminist criticism: Toril Moi's contempt for it is blatant: 'If a nostalgic reversion to *Cranford* or *Little Women* is all this brand of criticism can yearn for, the urgent examination of other, more theoretically informed critical practices must surely be a pressing item on the agenda of the Anglo-American feminist critics.'[6]

But corpses can't talk; and Moi herself argues in the same work, and in support of debate, that 'feminist criticism today is stifled by the absence of a genuinely political debate about the political implications of its methodological and theoretical choices.'[7] Perhaps, then, these critics should be attending to their differences instead of picking up the critical ball and running. For I would suggest that even this old-hat element in feminist criticism, so *démodé* that it is scarcely worthy of debate, the attack on literary misogyny, and a resulting revaluation of certain authors, has led to a critical practice which is deeply problematic.

I take Sandra Gilbert and Susan Gubar's powerful and highly influential book *The Madwoman in the Attic* as my example of a developed form of the critical practice arising from the theory that women's views of themselves are inscribed in (among other

6

things) the literature they read, so that misogynystic representations in literature are deeply damaging to women, so much so
that we must re-evaluate authors who put forward such representations and must change our critical approach to take their
misogyny into account. Gubar and Gilbert's thesis runs that man
the writer, wielding his pen rather as he wields his penis, has
subjected women through the fantasy-images he creates. These
images have reiterated man's superiority on the page and, in so
doing, have helped to ensure that superiority in reality. They
interestingly pursue this thesis by looking at the effects this had
on women writers of the nineteenth century; their view is that
those authors 'obsessively create characters who enact their own,
covert authorial anger'.[8] Hence the pervasive, and subversive,
image of the madwoman in the attic in nineteenth-century fiction,
who was the clue to the other side of the more submissive woman
presented as the heroine. This sub-text, they argue, is what
contemporary readers should concentrate on.

If what Gubar and Gilbert and many other feminist critics are
saying is right, it is of course very important. But is it right? Their
thesis in a weak form is certainly persuasive. In the nineteenth-
century novel, myriad weddings signal the submission of the
strongest and bravest of single heroines. Even the tough, witty
and sceptical Rosalind bows to Hymen at the end of *As You Like
It*. And where marriage has been abandoned as the mark of
submission, sexual subjection is seen by the feminists to have
taken its place. Kate Millett's *Sexual Politics*[9] exposes the way
Henry Miller's and D. H. Lawrence's sexual fantasies of master-
fulness may be interpreted as determining the character of their
works and their portrayal of women.

But, much as I dislike the marriage device as a literary symbol
of happiness, and appealing and enjoyable as is Millett's *exposé* of
Lawrence's making up on the page for what he lacked in the
penis, I think that a great deal is left out in this analysis. And in
any case this is a very pale version of Gubar and Gilbert's thesis,
which is nothing if not strong.

They assert that 'patriarchy and its texts subordinate and
imprison women' and speak of 'those mythic masks male artists
have fastened over her human face...to possess her more
thoroughly'; but their argument relies largely on analogy and
punning and does not bother itself with counter-examples. They
make much of the word 'pen', constantly suggesting its phallic

connotations as sources of male power and female subservience, and build from this to women being 'penned in' (imprisoned). Gubar and Gilbert happily take on board Bloom's notion of the anxiety of influence, by which 'a man can only become a poet by somehow invalidating his poetic father' and blame male anxiety about female autonomy (in writing) on their 'mother-dominated infancy'. This acceptance of Freudian theory, unquestioning yet shallow in its application, is something I find frankly mystifying and disturbing in much feminist criticism, and is in any case highly controversial. But for Gubar and Gilbert the word itself is left to do the work. Puns on 'framed' (in a frame, and framed in the criminal sense) and 'indicted' (made into words and charged – again the criminal sense) brand male writers ever further, and we are told unconditionally that the ideal woman that male authors dream of generating is always an angel.

Yet as I read these condemnations of male authors, I feel myself condemned too. Is there no escape from these male inscriptions? I end by feeling bullied by the thesis and, above all, by the relentless rhetoric of imprisonment, sexual bondage and humiliation, and madness. For Gubar and Gilbert's central thesis is, I feel, deeply pessimistic. Not only do male writers inscribe patriarchy, according to them, but female writers too. While men suffer the anxiety of influence, women suffer the anxiety of authorship. And so, when we read women's texts, we must look for evidence of that anxiety and take our critical lead from evidence of schizophrenia in the text. This terrorizing language, for me as a woman reader, locks me even more firmly into psychological stereotypes than before. But more depressing is the consigning of the nineteenth-century women authors to a patri-archal trap, and twentieth-century women readers to the same trap in interpreting them in that way. This to me is no escape.

I return again to my mother, and to many women like her whom I've since known; and I return too to my own early experiences of literature. For my mother, for me, for many women, literature was and is, in at least one sense, not a form of imprisonment but a form of escape; not a means for subordin-ation but a medium of power. For many women, robbed of that feeling in all sorts of other ways, literature provides a route into a shared understanding, a shared knowledge, a shared creation of the imagination, in which their minds are equal with others. In this way I do believe that literature can purvey truths – not didactic moral truths, necessarily, but truths about the complexity of human nature and its relations. When my mother opened a book, read a poem or set her own pen to paper, she was sharing in that world. She was sharing the view, which she would certainly have fully recognized, understood and valued, expressed by George Eliot that 'if Art does not enlarge man's sympathies it does nothing morally...those who read [my writings] should be better able to imagine and to feel the pains and joys of those who differ from themselves in everything but the broad fact of being struggling erring human creatures.'[10] What it seems to me is lost by a commitment to a feminist view of literature is that sense of its applying to and being concerned with a common humanity. The feminist's reply would, of course, be that this common humanity on which I set such store is, in fact, patriarchal, it is a humanity in which women are *not* humans equal with men and in that way fellows of them. The feminist would argue that the idea of universal humanity is another patriarchal deception, of which I am one of the many victims. But is the notion of a shared femaleness, a community of being female, any less suspect?

Do women associate themselves only with women characters in literature, and similarly men with men? The danger of feminist criticism is that precisely this compartmentalization will take place. Should we be pleased to see the depiction of a woman in power whatever kind of woman she is?

Kathleen McLuskie, in her essay on feminist approaches to Shakespeare, does show subtlety in her consideration of the way in which a helpful feminist response is denied in various ways by the tragic power of *King Lear*; but this is a sort of disguise for the central premise of her article, which is that 'the misogyny of *King Lear*, both the play and its hero, is constructed out of an ascetic tradition which presents women as the source of the primal sin of lust, combining with concerns about the threat to the family posed by female insubordination'.[11] That the play is misogynist is never questioned. Poor Cordelia gets it in the neck from McLuskie as well as from her sisters and her father. While McLuskie recognizes that it is true that Cordelia is the only one to resist her father initially, she focuses on the limitations of that resistance, apparently indicated by the fact that Cordelia leaves her father, but only to marry France. Her critical gloss on Cordelia's rebellious action is: 'for the patriarchal family to continue, it must also recognise the rights of future fathers and accept the transfer from fathers to husbands.' For McLuskie, Cordelia is simply not tough enough (unlike Goneril and Regan); she will go and forgive her father – and for no good reason. Cordelia is mere putty in Lear's, and Shakespeare's, patriarchal hands.

Is McLuskie then suggesting that any portrayal of women as bad is thereby reinforcing a misogynist ideology? Certainly she wants to disallow the standard tragic reading of the play, 'with its emotional power and its moral imperatives intact'. The implication is that a good feminist should resist being moved by the human tragedy of the play, where that is possible, since 'pity' is 'called forth at the expense of her resistance to the patriarchal relations which it endorses'. But can Goneril and Regan not be symbolic of evil, even of simple filial ingratitude, without being representative of women as such, just as Edmund represents the same callousness (and indeed the same lust)?

If we are to be reduced to a literature in which all women are represented as good in the feminist sense, how will that accord with women's reality? I don't share the view that women's images of themselves, and the reality of their lives, are constructed primarily from the cultural images to which they are subjected. Those cultural images are certainly one influence. But how does change ever take place if the prevailing ideology is omnipotent? And if you talk about the social construction of reality through the prevailing ideology to 'the average woman', she is likely to reply in terms of practicalities: the actual struggles of being poor, of being a single parent, of being a single woman. The ideology doesn't help; but images of Alexis, or Cagney and Lacey, don't help much either. And when it comes to changing significantly the plight of women, a much more complex awareness of the role of real events, of biology, of money, is needed than the simplistic view of socialization espoused by many feminists. A more complex view is needed, too, of the contradictory, or at least conflicting, needs of women. There *are* different kinds of female sexual pleasure, and some of them might be of the kind described by Lawrence; that he is a man, that he might be describing them to enhance his own self-image, does not necessarily negate *them*. Similarly, women, as well as being women, are also often wives, grow old, face death, are human, are poor, and these elements all influence them as well as their being female.

10

Yet feminist critics are particularly hard on those characters who go some way to rebelling against the standard role of women, but who fall back into the old conventions at one stage or another. They are especially unforgiving when these female characters marry. Dorothea in *Middlemarch* would have been the perfect heroine – if only she hadn't fallen prey to the charms of the clearly unworthy (and younger) Will. Margaret Hale in *North and South* is seen as failing her earlier promise when she nestles into the arms of Thornton in the last pages. Poor Connie Chatterley is castigated by Kate Millett for her sexual worship of Mellors; Millett concedes that Lawrence allows Connie occasional orgasms, but unfortunately they're of the wrong sort. Between the authors and the critics, these characters have little chance of doing it right.

Of course, the feminist opprobrium is really directed at the authors and their bowing to the patriarchal conventions of the novel. Feminist critics have not restricted their disapproval to the fiction. Charlotte Brontë's eventual marriage is seen as a betrayal, and Elizabeth Gaskell's portrayal of it as happy as a lie; Gaskell herself is attacked for trying to be the perfect wife and mother at the possible expense of her writing. (Incidentally, the critical books in which these attacks are made very frequently carry dedications to the feminist author's husband.)

This sniping has a serious point. Feminist criticism has begun to assume a punitive, narrowing aspect. In telling us which authors we should and should not read, and what areas of those authors we should or should not approve, and what aspects of behaviour of female characters we should and should not take as models of identity, it narrows our area of interest in literature in a distorting manner. It assumes the link between the depiction of certain sorts of male and female behaviour in fiction and authorial misogyny, and asserts that 'literary misogyny can no longer be overlooked or excused' and will lead to 'more drastic reinterpretations of the old masters'.[12] And in doing this it puts the claims about gender above any other consideration in our approach to literature. Would it discount the value of *Saturday Night and Sunday Morning*, which tries to show the life of an ordinary working man with some warmth and brio, because its hero treats his women badly? Would it eventually condemn Seamus Heaney's series of poems about his mother's death because they centre on her as a mother, and indeed as his enabler?

Surely death defeats the claim that there are no universals.

A final return to *my* mother. She would have been interested in and excited by some of the feminist arguments; but it would never have stopped her reading anything and everything, patriarchal or not. However, she would have been unable to read some of the feminist criticism itself, not because of its content, but because of its impenetrable obscurity of language and argument. Attacking patriarchal language for its exclusivity, and condemning men for silencing women, feminists open themselves to the same charge. Their language is a barrier to a large group of the women in whose service they are supposedly arguing.

There is much value in feminist criticism, but it threatens to become exclusive and reductive, and in the wrong ways and direction, without the kind of debate put forward in the ensuing pages. Literature, if it is to live, must be diverse; if we are to be fully aware as readers, and as writers, we must be eclectic. I shall end this introduction with a poem in which I lament the way in which a writer such as Marvell is lauded above ordinary people like my mother and father. But I do believe that, without reading Marvell, I couldn't have written the poem. At this point the real work begins.

No Through Road

Where once your lives were hedged about
The signs conspire to keep us out
But PRIVATE marks your history
Merged here with public poetry.
A house; a plain; a flowing river:
The ordered land goes on forever.

Workers to Marvell were conceits
To figure on his working sheets;
Mowers and gardeners safely pass
Between his lines; they cut the grass
Which so luxuriantly grew
Three hundred years ago, and now.
Maids washed his shirts that he might write
In praise of Cromwell's glorious fight
For every man. He sunned his soul

And ate the fruit of others' toil,
Backs bent to Fairfax and his soil.

Another war: men on the land,
Absolved from gunfire, take their stand
With pitchforks, standing side by side,
Their labour briefly sanctified.
For Dad of course was one of these,
While in the house they take their ease,
And on the plain the river's flood
Deposits richness in the blood,
So men will till that masters eat.
The ranks of history repeat.

The grammar school; my English teacher
(Of course) giving a lecture
On Appleton House: I feel it still,
The start, the blush that rose, the thrill.
I learnt the power of the word:
Our name was on the honours board!
For at that time I knew my place
And poetry won every race –
Except my mother's cranky verse
(Which silently I now rehearse).
No public airing for her rhymes;
She hung her sheets on washing lines.
While others held the centre ground
She moved the furniture around.

And now, reviewing this estate
With all the confidence of hate
I feel the current of my fate.
I mouth my mother's angry word
My guilt's in gilt on t'honours board
This is the flood I cannot ford.
Scanning the river's flowing plains
The house that casually reigns
I think of yours, not Marvell's strains.

My ink's invisible; nothing changes
Only the detail rearranges.

NOTES

1 T. Olsen, *Silences*, London: Virago, 1980, dedication.
2 A. Kolodny, 'Dancing through the minefield', in E. Showalter (ed.) *The New Feminist Criticism*, London, New York: Virago, 1985, p. 158.
3 Showalter, *New Feminist Criticism*, pp. 5–6.
4 See M. Barrett's introductory remarks in *Virginia Woolf: Women and Writing*, London: The Women's Press, 1979, reprinted 1988.
5 See G. Greene and C. Kahn, 'Feminist scholarship and the social construction of women', in G. Greene and C. Kahn (eds), *Making a Difference*, London: Methuen, 1985.
6 T. Moi, *Sexual/Textual Politics*, London: Methuen, 1985, p. 80.
7 ibid.
8 S. Gubar and S. Gilbert, *The Madwoman in the Attic*, New Haven and London: Yale University Press, 1979. This and further references here are drawn from their two opening chapters, 'The queen's looking glass' and 'Infection in the sentence', both of which need to be read to understand fully their critical position.
9 K. Millett, *Sexual Politics*, London: Virago, 1977.
10 G. Eliot, *The George Eliot Letters*, ed. G. S. Haight, London: Oxford University Press; New Haven: Yale University Press, 1954–5, 3, p. 111.
11 K. McLuskie, 'The patriarchal bard: feminist criticism and Shakespeare: *King Lear* and *Measure for Measure*', in J. Dollimore and A. Sinfield (eds), *Political Shakespeare*, Manchester: Manchester University Press, 1985, pp. 88–108.
12 Showalter, *New Feminist Criticism*, pp. 5–6.

1

THE TALKATIVE WOMAN IN SHAKESPEARE, DICKENS AND GEORGE ELIOT

Barbara Hardy

'the lips of an old woman are never still. '

(Callimachus, *Hecale*)[1]

a Bitch, a busybody like her mother, one that would fain hear all, know all, and peering and prying everywhere barketh e'en though she see nothing; a man cannot check her with threats, no, not if in anger he dash her teeth with a stone, nor yet though he speak gently with her, even though she be sitting among strangers – she must needs keep up her idle baying.

(Semonides, *Elegy and Iambus*)[2]

'Handmaids should ne'er have had access to wives,
But brutes, with teeth, no tongue, should dwell with them,
That so they might not speak to any one...'

(Euripides, *Hippolytus*)[3]

The talkative women in men's books are particularized products of fear, anger, jealousy, compliment and condescension, contributions to a male tradition going back to the post-Homeric classical period and spawning images in every age. From Euripides to Joyce men have impersonated garrulous women, individual characters who have been mythologized into accepted wisdom and symbol. The talkative woman is a prominent figure in old wives' tales written by men, men to whom no convenient typographical label like 'old wives' can be automatically attached, so powerful has been men's classification and naming. (A category-insult like 'old women', used of men, necessarily involves an insult to women too.) The wholly or mostly man-written entries in dictionary and proverb book copiously

15

illustrate the fiction and the myth by associating talkativeness, garrulousness and loquaciousness with women.

So vivid have been men's dramatic, poetic and narrative impersonations of women that scholars and general readers often discuss man-made women characters as if they really were women, and the exchange between nature and art has been complex. Literature encourages social stereotype by providing names and labels: 'talkative', 'old wives', 'gossips' and 'chatterboxes' are containers into which actual, talking women can be placed, whereas talkative men are only talking men, individuals and not parts of a tradition and fictionalized 'truth'. Feminists have been drawn by the stereotype, preferring it for good reasons to the man-made image of silent woman, and praising its narrative and linguistic subversion of father-tongue. Informality and irrationality are revolutionary virtues for victims of patriarchy: Dorothy Richardson and Virginia Woolf were influenced by male writers, but their models of *écriture feminine* have been powerful images for women's attempts to think and write new, man-free woman's language. Men had it both ways: their culturally conventional speech-models were a powerful norm and ideal, and their models of deviation were adopted as feminist badges.

I propose to select a small group of talkative women invented by men and women writers, in an attempt to look at and beyond some implications of their gendered theme, form and style. The need to emphasize gender before de-emphasizing it – as I wish to do – demonstrates the problem of being a feminist but not writing criticism from an exclusively feminist viewpoint.

Three of the most famous talkative women in literature, two medieval and one Victorian, are linked by a reflexive awareness of gender. Chaucer's Wife of Bath, Erasmus's Folly and Dickens' Mrs Gamp are man-made women endowed with creative gusto, exhibiting traditional elements of self-revelation, digression, long-winded and particularized narrative, and a tendency to criticize men and men's creativity. All three remind us of their male authorship. Chaucer imagines the Wife of Bath as talking, not writing, as he writes her talk. He imagines her imagining women writing stories, as she reflects on the literary models which have formed – or helped to form – her fifth husband's misogyny. She contemplates a literary alternative to men's stories about women, an *écriture feminine* which would write men's wickedness:

16

And every nyght and day was his custume,
Whan he hadde leyser and vacacioun
From oother worldly occupacioun,
To reden on this book of wikked wyves.
He knew of hem mo legendes and lyves
Than been of goode wyves in the Bible;
For trusteth wel, it is an impossible
Than any clerk wol speke good of wyves,
But if it be of hooly seintes lyves,
Ne of noon oother womman never the mo.
Who peyntede the leon, tel me who?
By God! if wommen hadde writen stories,
As clerkes han withinne hire oratories,
They wolde han writen of men moore wikkednesse
Than al the mark of Adam may redresse.[4]

The Wife of Bath is thinking of theme, not style, but her awareness of gendered creativity alerts the reader to more than thematic implications, especially since the discussion of men's reading and writing is a digression in the rambling, autobiographical preamble to her tale. Her narrative is retarded by entertaining parentheses, interruptions and lost threads, like

But now, sire, lat me se, what I shal seyn?
A ha! by God, I have my tale ageyn.

This break comes after a convoluted narrative episode of some twenty lines in which she describes going for a walk with Jankyn (her fifth husband) and prematurely proposing to him. She uses the figure of a mouse providing itself with more than one hole, boasts of foresight in providing herself with husbands, tells of leading Jankyn on to believe he has enchanted her of telling him her dream (which she has invented for the purpose, she assures her audience), of letting him know the meaning of the dream, to end with the arrestingly vague comment that she has followed her 'dames loore,/ As wel of this as of othere thynges moore'. Her pause for thought is brilliantly placed. Like other male narrators, Chaucer uses the fluent, rambling, mixed flow of his talkative woman to diversify, lighten and control his storytelling, but his reference to gender, placed within a woman's criticism of men's reading and writing, suddenly lights up the male poet's assumption of a female narrator and the question of gender-bias. The Wife of Bath has been seen as a critical portrait of a loose woman, but though her loose narrative is a register for moral levity, Chaucer is a poet who plays fair, perhaps not wanting his reader to fall into the gendered character-trap too easily.

Erasmus's Folly or Moria, in *Praise of Folly*,[5] is a male-directed narrative persona whose discourse is a mixture of argument, anecdote, self-revelation and analysis, offered as a gendered idiolect. This woman's narrative also relaxes to discuss gender, with teasing humour. Folly is a sustained and concentrated woman narrator, garrulous, unrestrained, rambling, outside the male rhetorical system, and a personification of irrationality. Erasmus's misogyny is cunning and the mask worn slightly askew. Folly does not indicate, as the Wife of Bath does indirectly, that a man has invented her, but she brings up the subject of gender. At the end of the discourse, she refuses, in nonconformist form, to give the pseudo-encomium its expected rhetorical conclusion, tidying up loose ends and summing up moral:

> But I've long been forgetting who I am, and I've 'overshot the mark'. If anything I've said seems rather impudent or garrulous, you must remember it's Folly and a woman who's been speaking.

The refusal is a kind of conclusion, an *occupatio* providing a kind of moral summary – it is foolish to expect a conventional ending from a woman. But she is made to modify this by reminding the reader of the Greek proverb, 'Often a fool speaks a word in season', then to undercut ironic qualification with a new layering of irony, 'though of course you may think this doesn't apply to women'. Folly is a complex instance of the satirical invention and appropriation of a woman as cultural outsider; Erasmus was scarcely a feminist,[6] but his talkative woman promotes what women – as well as men – outside the culture have felt about the limits of rationality and in spite of the smear of Folly there is the blazon of imagination. Folly explicates, demonstrates and enriches the tradition of wise madness. (She influenced Shakespeare's fools, though none of the fools are women, as they sometimes were outside literature.) To be called Folly is to receive a back-handed compliment. The creative informality of language hailed by Dorothy Richardson and Virginia Woolf admits the creativity of Folly and the irrationality of art, but Folly promotes man's stereotype of woman's intuition.

Chaucer's Wife of Bath and Erasmus's Folly may have helped to shape Shakespeare's comic talkative women. They are brilliantly prolix, digressive, precise and relaxed. Mistress Quickly is a weak woman, bullied and seduced by Falstaff and other men, but showing, like the Wife of Bath and Folly, some subtlety in style. Her over-circumstantiality, lack of what Coleridge calls 'surview', is vivid and substantial, and her digressive and rambling narrative comes to the point in the end. She is no match for Falstaff, whose lies are the socially practised and profitable fictions of gentleman and soldier, but she is never allowed to lapse into dull disorder. This is her reminiscent style, pressed into service as she argues Falstaff's breach of promise in *Henry IV, Part II*:

> Thou didst swear to me upon a parcel-gilt goblet, sitting in my Dolphin chamber, at the round table, by a sea-coal fire, upon Wednesday in Wheeson week, when the Prince broke thy head for liking his father to a singing-man of Windsor – thou didst swear to me then, as I was washing thy wound, to marry me, and make me my lady thy wife. Canst thou deny it? Did not goodwife Keech the butcher's wife come in then and call me gossip Quickly? – coming in to borrow a mess of vinegar, telling us she had a good dish of prawns, whereby thou didst desire to eat some, whereby I told thee they were ill for a green wound? And didst thou not, when she was gone downstairs, desire me to be no more so familiarity with such poor people, saying that ere long they should call me madam? And didst thou not kiss me, and bid me fetch thee thirty shillings? I put thee now to thy book oath, deny it if thou canst.
>
> (II, i)[7]

Coleridge is one of the few critics to analyse the representation of mind and passion in narrative and combines these concerns in his discussion of Mistress Quickly as an instance of Shakespeare's imitation of the immethodical mind, which inhabits but does not construct time. In this discussion and in his famous lecture on Juliet's Nurse – which Lamb, accomplished both in wit and discursive narration, said was delivered in the manner of the Nurse – Coleridge sees garrulous idiolect as illustrating the uncultivated understanding where an 'absence of Method...is occasioned by an habitual submission of the understanding to mere events and images as such, and independent of any power in the mind to classify or appropriate them' ('The Principles of Method').[8] Like Chaucer and Erasmus, Shakespeare is using irrational woman as a structural base for comic character, but unlike most feminists, Coleridge sees such talkativeness as not only a matter of gender but a matter of class. Mistress Quickly's loose language registers her 'easy-yielding' nature, but more dominant is the imprint of an unpractised mind. (Shakespeare never lets this mind play a central part, as James Joyce does in *Ulysses*, but he employs it for subordinate comic functions.) The features of the relaxed, unperiodic style denote lack of training. Erasmus scarcely wrote a demotic language, but his avoidance of traditional rhetorical features, and his reflexive comments on informality, show his interest in informally educated or uneducated talkativeness. More women than men were, and are, outside education, and the talkative woman's lack of surview and method is a social deviation transformed into a literary virtue.

Whether we rejoice in academic escapes or not, they are turned to advantage in Chaucer, Erasmus and Shakespeare. Coleridge sees that Mistress Quickly is the immethodical mind methodized. While dramatizing a tendency to call memory, not selective power, into play, and to relate events 'in the same order and with the same accompaniments, however accidental or impertinent, as they had first occurred to the narrator', Shakespeare creates an affective sequence and connectiveness, 'the fusion of passion' which substitutes for Method. What Coleridge says applies to many talkative women characters: the habit of over-circumstantial detail makes for vivid particulars, unselective miscellany and disjointed fragmentariness. All these features isolate and heighten narrative detail like Mistress Quickly's description of the parcel-gilt goblet, round table and sea-coal fire, and the Wife of Bath's slow-motion recollections of love and the 'wo that is in mariage'. In each narrator there is more than excess of particulars: Mistress Quickly's quick-moving, scatty memory is fired by indignation, and the Wife of Bath's motive for sentimental history revealed as passionate nostalgia and melancholy come to the surface, 'The flour is goon, ther is namoore to telle,/ The bren, as I best kan, now moste I selle.' The Wife of Bath's talkative lament for mortality makes her eloquence more than a woman's untutored reminiscence and gender is transcended. Rather differently, driven by mind rather than heart, Erasmus's Folly also goes beyond gendered impersonation, as wit and intellectual argument are used to celebrate intuitive and imaginative powers and defy reason and system. A misogynistic tendency may be at work, woman satirized rather than seen as victim, but the question of gender is not primary. The talkative woman is Erasmus's means, not his end. (One can feel indignant about such instrumentality, of course, but that question goes far beyond the talkative woman.)

Another remarkably free-flowing idiolect is created for Juliet's Nurse. Like Mistress Quickly, she is neither man-hater, scold nor shrew, but an easy-yielding woman, serving the culture, and deserting Juliet the moment conflict arises between society and individual will. She should not be sentimentalized: Lisa Jardine[9] observes that Juliet's mother does not know her daughter's age, while the Nurse does, but this is not so: the Nurse begins her long reminiscence of Juliet's infancy with a mere repetition of Lady Capulet's prompting 'She's not fourteen', which is elaborated, particularized and repeated with characteristic and stereotypical persistence and self-centredness. The brilliantly internalized upstaging of the Capulets makes it a great part. Not only does the Nurse recall events in the order in which they recurred, she repeats them until her listeners shut her up, amusing the audience off the stage by subversions of narrative and interruption of serious affairs. Lady Capulet is crisper in her dating, and it takes the Nurse a long time (she inhabits time and does not construct it) to identify the birthday, not by calendar-date, but by the pragmatic recollection of a startling natural event – an earthquake – and her own child's birth:

Lady Capulet	Thou knowest my daughter's of a pretty age.
Nurse	Faith, I can tell her age unto an hour.
Lady Capulet	She's not fourteen.
Nurse	I'll lay fourteen of my teeth –
	And yet, to my teen be it spoken, I have but four –
	She's not fourteen. How long is it now
	To Lammas-tide?
Lady Capulet	A fortnight and odd days.

Nurse	Even or odd, of all days in the year,
	Come Lammas Eve at night shall she be
	fourteen.
	Susan and she – God rest all Christian souls –
	Were of an age. Well, Susan is with God;
	She was too good for me. But as I said,
	On Lammas Eve at night shall she be fourteen.
	That shall she; marry, I remember it well.
	'Tis since the earthquake now eleven years,
	And she was wean'd – I never shall forget it –
	Of all the days of the year upon that day.
	For I had then laid wormwood to my dug,
	Sitting in the sun under the dovehouse wall.
	My lord and you were then at Mantua –
	Nay I do bear a brain.

(I, iii)

Coppelia Kahn's[10] interesting account of the Nurse's role makes a connection between language and function: the subservience which strikes Kahn (and Coleridge) is given a carefully constructed narrative correlative. Moreover, the Nurse's talkativeness suggests the humanizing subtext of her personal life (dead child and merry husband), to make the traditional identification with 'nature' in the repeated and proleptic anecdote of Juliet's 'fall'. An important aspect of the engrossing narrative is its passivity. Some stereotypes of woman's talkativeness, like Erasmus's Folly, subvert the dominant culture – but others offer a passive yielding to culture, language and time. The Wife of Bath and Folly are rebels, Mistress Quickly and the Nurse conformists. Unless we are blindly searching for a free or revolutionary woman's speech we can see that volubility is expressive in various ways. The idiolects of the Wife of Bath and Folly are relatively systematic. In narrative complication, looseness and anti-rhetorical language, they are anarchic, but Shakespeare, like Dickens after him, invents lo er-class, talkative women to demonstrate grammatical, syntactical, lexical and chronological disorders. There is overlap: all four narrators cram in particularities and keep going with verve and stamina, but two are relatively 'educated', two 'uneducated'. It is the less educated speakers who are more superficially conformist. But they are only locally conformist: I believe Shakespeare uses the Nurse and

Mistress Quickly to flaunt and analyse cultural innocence, victimization and passivity. Conformist women in the male-dominant culture, they show and show up the power of a Capulet–Montague mafia and a Falstaff–Henry IV macho militarism. (Shakespeare creates talkative men in these plays, but Falstaff and Mercutio, macho but also victims – as who is not? – are not definable in terms of their talkativeness.) The women are comic characters, inviting male actors to perform ridiculing stereotype, imprinting tradition and confirming prejudice. The conservatism of these amusing, talking women, considered as individual images, has to be seen as part of the implicit social criticism of the plays, perhaps more evident in our time than in the past.

These comic, pushy, passive, self-engrossed slaves – not master–mistresses – of time, are controlled by dramatic function. There is an affective order in the rambling complaints of Mistress Quickly and the fond reminiscences of the time-serving Nurse who recommends switching from one man to another in a trice. (Her standards are crudely pragmatic as well as conservative, and placed as such.) There is a thematic tension governing narrative digression and relaxation, conspicuous in the thrice-told tale of Juliet's fall, with its premature experience of sex, death and powerlessness. Shakespeare plays off local effects in character against larger effects of structure, and these functions must be borne in mind when we isolate the rhetorical figure we call character.

The four great talkative women in Dickens owe much to the Shakespearean and, indirectly, the Chaucerian examples. Dickens is more misogynistic than Chaucer, Erasmus and Shakespeare. His familiarity with the Nurse is nicely confirmed in *Nicholas Nickleby*, the novel where he first develops the type, by Mr Curdle the critic, who anticipates L. C. Knights in his pamphlet 'On the character of the Nurse's deceased husband... with an inquiry whether he really had been a "merry man" in his lifetime, or whether it was merely his widow's affectionate partiality that induced her so to report him'. Mrs Nickleby, Mrs Gamp, Flora Finching and Mrs Lirriper are in the mainstream of talkative women, which must include Peele's absent-minded and rambling Madge, narrator in *The Old Wives Tale*, Mrs Malaprop, Susan Ferrier's Miss Pratt in *The Inheritance* and Douglas Jerrold's

Mrs Caudle, as well as Shakespeare's babblers. Like Mistress Quickly and the Nurse, Dickens' talkative women are of a certain age or old, all widows, and all past it. Their man-made sexual vanity and hope makes them figures of fun, to the reader and other characters, and through their age, sterility or charmlessness the denigration of women's talkativeness is compounded: it is not desirable to men. They acquiesce in the male culture, Mrs Nickleby as conformist as the Nurse as she pushes Kate towards Sir Mulberry Hawk; Mrs Gamp presiding eagerly over life's beginnings and endings, promoting mysteries of birth and death; Flora dead-set on past and future romance. They are subordinate figures who dominate the scenes in which they appear, asserting talkativeness as power, though a power ridiculed and eventually transformed, tamed or punished. Woman's domestic talkativeness is an obvious compensation and revenge for her political dumbness, and Dickens' examples show a man's sense of danger as he presents the engrossments – often explicitly critical and aggressive – in archly misogynist fashion. (An exception would be the case of Mrs Lirriper, whose talkativeness is unaggressive and peters out. As Robert Golding observes,[11] she is racier and wilder than her companions, but, as he does not observe, is less misandrist[12] so needs no rebuking or silencing.)

Mrs Nickleby is the most aggressively presented of the four, and reveals a relationship between the misogyny of a man's representation and the misandry of the woman represented. Dickens is an amused presenter of the silliness and stupidity of talkative women. Mrs Nickleby is a bad mother as well as a foolish talker, and has been identified with Dickens' mother, on slight evidence. Michael Slater, in *Dickens and Women*[13] quotes a letter (from a feature in *Lippincott's Magazine* called 'Our Monthly Gossip') insisting that the likeness between Mrs Dickens 'and Mrs Nickleby is simply the exaggeration of some slight peculiarities'. Elisabeth Dickens was apparently not over-talkative and possessed a sense of humour – a characteristic rarely found in man's image of the talkative woman, though Erasmus's Folly is an exception in this as in much else. She is said to have possessed an 'extraordinary' sense of the ludicrous, been a good mimic and showed a vein of pathos in her story-telling. Mrs Nickleby and her chatting sisters are in control of nothing, illustrations of the immethodical mind, amusing as objects, not manipulators. Dickens turns woman – though not his mother – into object. This may have happened with Maria Beadnell too, who 'became' Flora Finching, and a case might be made out for Dickens as a misogynistic transformer of skilful talk into stupid talk, though the attribution of biographical sources arises from the misogyny of critics, not author.

Mrs Nickleby's talkativeness is developed, from her first uncomic, summarized appearance as a weeping widow deploring the past 'with...bitter recollections common to most married ladies, either during their coverture, or afterwards, or at both periods'(ch. 111).[14] In later appearances, her talk takes off, scatter-brained, rambling, over-particularized, absent-minded, digressive, self-engrossed and enclosed. Like all Dickens' talkative women, she is a greedy soliloquizer, snatching the subject from other characters, moving back from the present as she seizes any excuse to recall the past. Her talk is retrospective, in an eagerly associative and immethodical stream. The word 'milliner' for example, calls up associations with wickerbaskets lined with black oilskin, but these are erased by Ralph Nickleby's persuasions of grandeur, and replaced 'by visions of large houses at the West End, neat private carriages, and a banker's book – all of which images succeeded each other with... rapidity'. This economical summary is dramatically unfolded, and the 'streamy'[15] train of association (which may have been encouraged by Sterne, another creator of silly women) becomes inept recall:

> I recollect, when your poor papa and I came to town after we were married, that a young lady brought me home a chip cottage bonnet, with white and green trimming and green Persian lining, in her own carriage, which drove up to the door full gallop; at least I am not quite certain whether it was her own carriage or a hackney chariot, but I remember very well that the horse dropped down dead as he was turning round, and that your poor papa said he hadn't had any corn for a fortnight.
>
> (ch. X)

This random flow, inappropriate illustration and rich circumstantiality is elaborated: the social detail in the stories gets more bizarre and the style cumulatively more illogical, optimistic and self-aggrandizing. Mrs Nickleby's strongest point is failing to see the point of her own narratives, as in the anecdotes of Mr Watkins, remembered for his praise of Kate as a baby, his apparently disconnected liking for old port, and his habit of taking and not giving:

> Mr Watkins, you know, Kate, my dear, that your poor papa went bail for, who afterwards ran away to the United States, and sent us a pair of snow-shoes, with such an affectionate letter that it made your poor dear father cry for a week. You remember the letter – in which he said that he was very sorry he couldn't repay the fifty pounds just then, because his capital was all out at interest, and he was very busy making his fortune, but that he didn't forget you were his god-daughter, and he should take it very unkind if we didn't buy you a silver coral and put it down to his old account? Dear me, yes, my dear, how stupid you are! and spoke so affectionately of the old port wine that he used to drink a bottle and a half of every time he came.
>
> (ch. XVIII)

This is outdone by the dotty story of a cure for the common cold, 'used for the first time...the day after Christmas Day, and by the middle of April following the cold was gone', the tale about going to Stratford and dreaming of Shakespeare, 'a black gentleman at full length in plaster-of-Paris, with a lay-down collar tied with two tassels, leaning against a post and thinking...very curious indeed', and the best of her *non-sequiturs* which salts the sentiment of her lament for Smike:

> I have lost the best, the most zealous, and most attentive creature that has ever been a companion to me in my life – putting you, my dear Nicholas, and Kate, and your poor papa, and that well-behaved nurse who ran away with the linen and the twelve small forks, out of the question of course.
>
> (ch. LXI)

Mrs Gamp's style resembles Mrs Nickleby's in womanly themes – children, illness, domestic routine and accident – but her stories are more unified and rounded, appropriately polished performances, advertisements, solicitations and boasts. And, of course, lies. She continues the mild misandrist strain of Mrs Nickleby, and most of her anecdotes discredit men and praise women, but because she is a false and unreliable narrator, her misandry is undermined, and the male author can emerge loyal to his sex. The story of her drunken husband is a dominant strain: there are anecdotes about his sending their son on an errand to 'sell his wooden leg for any money it 'ud fetch as matches in the rough, and bring it home in liquor' (ch. XXV),[16] about the same wooden leg's 'constancy of walkin' into the wine vaults' (ch. XL), and about his laying-out in Guy's Hospital 'with a penny-piece on each eye, and his wooden leg under his left arm' (ch. XIX), a tale enlarged by the gossip about Mrs Gamp selling his remains 'for the benefit of science'. Her stories show strong female bonding, cajoling other women (and men who may be helpful business connections), as she leers hopefully at young women, flattering old ones, and extends her ego with Mrs Harris' fictionalized testimonial and externalized boast. She provides a link with the layered gender-awareness of Chaucer and Erasmus, though hers is a mere grain of suggestion: she reflects that the noisy, dirty steamship likely to bring on miscarriages is typical of its creators, and apostrophizes, 'Ugh...one might easy know you was a man's invention' (ch. XL). I doubt whether Dickens was as aware as Chaucer and Erasmus of the deconstructive power of the gender-admission, but it reminds the modern reader that a man invented this misanthropic spokeswoman against the industrial revolution. She is the most methodical of her class, praised by Mr Mould the undertaker – whom she flatters to the top of his bent – for her observation, reflection and superior mind. She is discredited when old Martin (feebly) rebukes her in conclusion. Endowed like Mistress Quickly, the Nurse and Mrs Nickleby with a talkativeness emblematic of weakness, she is used like them to make fun of abused wives and needy widows, and she turns out like them to be a dangerous force, not easily quieted. The final taming of this shrew is not wholly convincing, as she is sent off to drink less and nurse more conscientiously.

The most benign of Dickens' voluble narrators is Flora Finching, also used to make fun of middle-aged women past their prime. Created with more tenderness and sympathy than Mrs Nickleby, whose children's author-approved assumption that any man wooing her must be a lunatic is only outdone by Hamlet's attack on his mother's heyday in the blood, Flora is fair, fat, forty and foolish, a rambling talker whose language is faster-running and more incoherent than that of any previous talkative woman, and largely unpunctuated. Her chatter has a structure, clearly indicated in Clennam's perception of the narrative *persona* as composed of a past youthful self and a present middle-aged self. His image, 'moral mermaid', defines the sense of doubleness. A fractured narrative aptly figures her silliness, as she swings from past to present and youth to age, with enough nervousness to join her separated discourses and increase their instability. Like the other talkative women, she shows excessive particularity and a failure to select and generalize. The listener is as important as the talker in these narrative scenes: when Flora babbles to Arthur, the speech-pattern registers a conflict of memory with present-tense awareness, for them both, with consequent embarrassment. Flora veers from nostalgia to wry commonsense, as he totters from tender recollection to a sense of her present charmlessness. Her ridiculed silliness is not unsympathetic, and she lacks the enclosure and self-centredness of the other talkative women, but her presentation is accompanied by a patronizing attitude to age and unattractiveness. Dickens makes her observe that middle age is easier on 'gentlemen', but his knowledge doesn't stop him making a figure of fun out of middle-aged, fat flirtatiousness and a good appetite. Flora's vivacious, unpunctuated talk anticipated and probably helped to create the unpunctuated consciousness of Molly Bloom, a talkative woman whose sexuality is given full play. Their common unpunctuated idiolect is not directly attributable to uneducated woman; their public and private monologues are spoken and not written, but unmethodical flow is compounded and emphasized by unpunctuated text. Flora is joined as a source for Joyce by a talkative man whose speech is unconventionally punctuated: Jingle in *Pickwick Papers*. Flora and Jingle got inside the consciousness of Joyce and became husband and wife in *Ulysses*, Jingle's fast-paced, dash-spaced, laconic telegraphese contributing to the shy Bloom's talkative inner life, and shapeless Flora's sloppy style going to make Molly's. We can see why: Dickens' unmethodized syntax becomes fluid as well as fluent.

Before Dorothy Richardson, Joyce and Virginia Woolf wrote their talkative women, Dickens was answered by George Eliot. She also created talkative women, but her type forms a rejoinder and a corrective to the misogynist stereotype. She had women's writing to draw on as well as men's writing to revise, and the most important antecedent was probably Jane Austen whose talkative women mostly conform to the Shakespearean model.

The most subversive is Miss Bates in *Emma*, an exception to the general rule that comic talkativeness is unselfconscious: 'I am rather a talker, you know.' Her contribution to the tradition and type is strong: her fast, jerky talk offends the sensitive ear of Mr Woodhouse, engrosses conversation and runs away with her in a non-stop flow. But her talk is methodized. Its disparate parts are fused by generous and graceful passions, and after a retarding circumambulatory motion as marked as the Wife of Bath's she has a way of getting to the point:

Thank you. You are so kind!...Oh! here it is. I was sure it could not be far off; but I had put my huswife upon it, you see, without being aware, and so it was quite hid, but I had it in my hand so very lately that I was almost sure it must be on the table. I was reading it to Mrs. Cole, and since she went away, I was reading it again to my mother, for it is such a pleasure to her – a letter from Jane – that she can never hear it often enough; so I knew it could not be far off, and here is it, only just under my huswife – and since you are so kind as to wish to hear what she says; – but, first of all, I really must, in justice to Jane, apologise for her writing so short a letter – only two pages you see – hardly two – and in general she fills the whole paper and crosses half. My mother often wonders that I can make it out so well. She often says, when the letter is first opened, 'Well, Hetty, now I think you will be put to it to make out all that chequer-work' – don't you, ma'am? – And then I tell her, I am sure she would contrive to make it out herself, if she had nobody to do it for her – every word of it – I am sure she would pore over it till she had made out every word. And, indeed, though my mother's eyes are not so good as they were, she can see amazingly well still, thank God! with the help of spectacles.

(Vol II, ch. 1)[17]

But after many swerves of narrative the talk gets back to Jane, and this is a repeated pattern.

She is that rare character, the good gossip, capable of listening as well as boring. (Though talkativeness is a qualification for the gossip, listening is important as well as telling.) Jane Austen makes Emma criticise Miss Bates by making fun of her. As a young clever woman mimicking a middle-aged spinster, she is punished severely in the test and exposure on Boxhill when she jeers at the silly but not insensitive woman's scatty talk. Jane Austen uses her characters to express awareness of the novelist's temptation to make fun of weak sisters, though in the same novel, she sports with Mrs Elton, a fast, selfish talker not designed for sympathy, in a highly original notation, not unlike Jingle's jingling prose, a summary amalgam of third-person direct style worth a rhetorical name of its own. It conveys racing talkativeness (as an index of insincerity and fickleness) in a compressed, curt style:

> The best fruit in England – every body's favourite – always wholesome. – These the finest beds and finest sorts. – Delightful to gather for one's self – the only way of really enjoying them. – Morning decidedly the best time – never tired – every sort good – hautboy infinitely superior – no comparison – the others hardly eatable – hautboys very scarce – Chili preferred – white wood finest flavour of all – price of strawberries in London – abundance about Bristol – Maple Grove – cultivation – beds when to be renewed – gardeners thinking exactly different – no general rule – gardeners never to be put out of their way – delicious fruit – only too rich to be eaten much of – inferior to cherries – currants more refreshing – only objection to gathering strawberries the stooping – glaring sun – tired to death – could bear it no longer – must go and sit in the shade.
>
> (Vol. III, ch. VI)

Jane Austen's talkative man, John Thorpe, is a rattle responsible for the trials of Catherine Morland at Northanger. (He is twinned in thoughtless talkativeness with his sister Isabella, one of the traditional loose talkers.) He is enjoyed as a male braggart, boasting of business acumen and fast driving in an attempt to impress women:

> all the rest of his conversation, or rather talk, began and ended with himself and his own concerns. He told her of horses which he had bought for a trifle and sold for incredible sums; of racing matches, in which his judgment had infallibly foretold the winner; of shooting parties, in which he had killed more birds (though without having one good shot) than all his companions together; and described to her some famous day's sport, with the fox-hounds, in which his

foresight and skill in directing the dogs had repaired the mistakes of the most experienced huntsman, and in which the boldness of his riding, though it had never endangered his own life for a moment, had been constantly leading others into difficulties, which he calmly concluded had broken the necks of many.

(Vol I, ch. IX)[18]

George Eliot's best example of the talkative man is Mr Brooke, whose epistolary talkativeness matches his garrulous speech and whose talk is also used to make the plot move. He is more like the traditional talkative women than any of Jane Austen's or Dickens' male talkers, his speeches marked by fragmentariness, incoherence, absentmindedness, and inappropriate fillers, like 'you know' or 'exactly'. Like Shakespeare's talkative women, he is spontaneous, random, breaks periodic structure, rambles, and is a bad listener who bores or embarrasses the listeners in *Middlemarch* and amuses its reader:

'Sir Humphrey Davy?' said Mr Brooke, over the soup, in his easy smiling way, taking up Sir James Chettam's remark that he was studying Davy's 'Agricultural Chemistry'. 'Well, now, Sir Humphrey Davy: I dined with him years ago at Cartwright's, and Wordsworth was there too – the poet Wordsworth, you know. Now there was something singular. I was at Cambridge when Wordsworth was there, and I never met him – and I dined with him twenty years afterwards at Cartwright's. There's an oddity in things, now. But Davy was there: he was a poet too. Or, as I may say, Wordsworth was poet one, and Davy was poet two. That was true in every sense, you know.'
Dorothea felt a little more uneasy than usual. In the beginning of dinner, the party being small and the room still, these motes from the mass of a magistrate's mind fell too noticeably.

(Book I, ch. II)[19]

He is 'leaky-minded' – a metaphor so vivid that it may have helped to form one used by Henry James when he complained that omniscient narrators made 'a leak in the interest'. Mr Brooke's talkativeness is a moral register – he is lax, changeable and easily yielding, the perfect example of what we must not call an old woman. Mr Woodhouse has something of his quality but not enough nervous energy to talk long.

George Eliot's most significant talkers are women. In *The Mill on the Floss*, Aunt Pullet's talkativeness is less salient than her hypochondria and her sartorial passion. In *Felix Holt* Mrs Holt shows George Eliot's qualification and revision of the type: her weak rambling is concentrated in theme and feeling, and given a heroic climax, when she confronts the gentry in a speech which is rambling, unmethodical and unselective, but very much to the point:

> if everybody's son was guided by their mothers, the world 'ud be different; my son is not worse than many another woman's son, and that in Treby, whatever they may say as haven't got their sons in prison. And as to his giving up the doctoring, and then stopping his father's medicines, I know it's bad – that I know – but it's me has had to suffer, and it's me a King and Parliament 'ud consider, if they meant to do the right thing, and had anybody to make it known to 'em. And as for the rioting and killing the constable – my son said most plain to me he never meant it, and there was his bit of potato-pie for his dinner getting dry by the fire, the whole blessed time as I sat and never knew what was coming on me. And it's my opinion as if great people make elections to get themselves into Parliament, and there's riot and murder to do it, they ought to see as the widow and the widow's son doesn't suffer for it. I well know my duty: and I read my Bible; and I know in Jude where it's stained with the dried tulip-leaves this many a year, as you're told not to rail at your betters if they was the devil himself; nor will I; but this I do say, if it's three Mr Transomes instead of one as is listening to me, as there's them ought to go to the King and get him to let off my son Felix.
>
> (ch. XLIII)[20]

The finest example, with its astringent misandry, is Mrs Poyser's attack on the squire, in *Adam Bede*. Her language is inventive, her arguments telling, her anecdotes and images methodical; this is her rhetorical and political peak:

> Then, sir, if I may speak – as, for all I'm a woman, and there's folks as thinks a woman's fool enough to stan' by an'

look on while the men sign her soul away, I've a right to speak, for I make one quarter o' the rent, and save another quarter – I say, if Mr Thurle's so ready to take farms under you, it's a pity but what he should take this, and see if he likes to live in a house wi' all the plagues o' Egypt in't – wi' the cellar full o' water, and frogs and toads hoppin' up the steps by dozens – and the floors rotten, and the rats and mice gnawing every bit o' cheese, and runnin' over our heads as we lie i' bed till we expect 'em to eat us up alive – as it's a mercy they hanna eat the children long ago. I should like to see if there's another tennant besides Poyser as 'ud put up wi' never having a bit o' repairs done till a place tumbles down – and not then, on'y wi' begging and praying and having to pay half – and being strung up wi' rent as it's much if he gets enough out o' the land to pay, for all he's put his own money into the ground beforehand. See if you'll get a stranger to lead such a life here as that: a maggot must be born i' the rotten cheese to like it, I reckon. You may run away from my words, sir,' continued Mrs Poyser, following the old squire beyond the door – for after the first moments of stunned surprise he had got up, and, waving his hand towards her with a smile, had walked out towards his pony.

And,

'Yes, I know I've done it,' said Mrs Poyser, 'but I've had my say out, and I shall be th'easier for't all my life. There's no pleasure i' living if you're to be corked up for ever, and only dribble your mind out by the sly, like a leaky barrel.'

(ch. XXXII)[21]

Mrs Poyser defeats the Squire, in an eloquent victory for the rational talkative woman and the depressed tenant farmers, but George Eliot's victory over Dickens is a pyrrhic one. As a feminist rewriting man's image of irrational talkativeness, she sets together rational talkative woman and irrational talkative man, improving on Jane Austen's duets. But Dorothy Richardson and Virginia Woolf did not go to Jane Austen's and George Eliot's revisions of talkativeness but to Shakespeare and Dickens. They created a woman's imitation of a man's imitation of woman's talkativeness, a model for the ideal *écriture feminine* proposed by French psychoanalytic critics, and adopted by feminists attempting to evade or erode the dominant language of men. This is an irony of literary history, not totally astonishing if man-made talkative woman is seen as a model for creativity. A feminist critique of Dickens' misogynistic women may fail to recognize this model. The feminist adoption of irrational subversive speech pays tribute to modernists – Joyce as well as Richardson and Woolf – but not to the older tradition.

Dickens' deplorable misogyny provides the best model of imagination. It slows down the motion of narration and image-making to create a self-analytic form and uses digression and interruption in ways that analyse associative patterns, incorporate self-conscious reflection and exploit inventive error. Each of Dickens' talkative women has her own pattern of creativity but they share the habit of free association, usually in the form of vivid recall uninhibited by logic and relevance. Their speeches are models of openness and lateral thinking, composition at its most relaxed, passive, receptive and original. Dickens makes an explicit comment about creativity when describing a minor talkative woman, Miss Knag, in *Nicholas Nickleby*: her 'marvellously loquacious' speech is interrupted by an occasional 'hem', a figure which keeps her dominant place in conversation while she seeks a word, and suspends the flow 'when any fresh invention was in course of coinage in her brain'. Mrs Nickleby, Mrs Gamp and Flora Finching also mark time and keep going with fillers like Mrs Nickleby's 'Oh, dear me!' and 'at all events' and Mrs Gamp's more idiosyncratic and deliberate kind, such as 'if all was know'd and credit done where credit's doo', or 'as Mrs Harris says'. Miss Knag's 'hem' registers and aids creative effort: 'I had an uncle once...who lived in Cheltenham, and had a most excellent business as a tobacconist – hem – who had such small feet that they were no bigger than those which are usually joined to wooden legs...'(ch. XVII). Invention here means lying, but keeps its dignity as an old rhetorical term. The inventiveness of Mrs Nickleby is not lying. She reveals creative strain as her reminiscent flow is punctuated by questions, uncertainties, verifications and revisions: 'I forget, by the bye, whether that Miss Browndock was the same lady that got the ten thousand pounds in the lottery, but I think she was; indeed, now I come to think of it, I am sure she was' (ch. XVII); or 'I don't remember whether it was the Old Boar or the George the Third, but it was one of the two' (ch.

XVIII); and 'what was her name again? I know it began with a B and ended with a G, but whether it was Waters or – no, it couldn't have been that, either' (ch. XXI). Mrs Nickleby's questions and answers generate her narratives and act as essential signs in the associative trail which leads her on, sometimes so fast that the story runs ahead of certainty. Accumulation of new material through accidental or random association intensifies particularity – items and images often have no context. Free or almost free association, it demands pauses for confirmation or collection. Kate Nickleby recognizes the unifying force of passion, seeing her mother's optimism energizing the 'torrents' of recollection, but observing with unimaginative intolerance that reminiscences and anecdotes sometimes do and sometimes do not bear on the subject. Mrs Nickleby sways between relevance and fertile irrelevance, her mind at the mercy of almost total recall and unhampered by reason, but her materials are on at least one occasion organized to show conclusion and closure after digression. In chapter XXVI she drifts from the subject of Kate's health, asked after as a matter of form – but for this narrator nothing is a matter of mere form – to a swollen face she got while riding in a hackney-coach with a broken window, pauses to question whether the vehicle was a coach or a chariot, decides that it was 'a dark green, with a very long number, beginning with a nought and ending with a nine – no, beginning with a nine and ending with a nought', branches out to the subject of law in general and Corn Laws in particular, and at last returns back to her daughter's health, though idiosyncratically, 'I don't think she ever was better, since she had the whooping-cough, scarlet fever, and measles, all at the same time': Dickens comments that she had 'pretty well run herself out'. It is a clear case of creative exhaustion, after a powerful and prolific generation of events and images. Her discourse is miscellaneous, but on occasion shows unity as well as multeity, within its elastic form.

On one occasion Dickens compounds narrative verve and excess by counterpointing Miss Knag's inventiveness with Mrs Nickleby's stream of consciousness:

Mrs Nickleby stopped to breathe; and Miss Knag, finding that the discourse was turning upon family greatness, lost no time in striking in with a small reminiscence on her own account.

'Don't talk of lending money, Mrs Nickleby,' says Miss Knag, 'or you'll drive me crazy – perfectly crazy. My mamma – hem – was the most lovely and beautiful creature, with the most striking and exquisite – hem – the most exquisite nose that ever was put upon a human face, I do believe, Mrs Nickleby (here Miss Knag rubbed her own nose sympathetically) – the most delightful and accomplished woman, perhaps, that ever was seen; but she had that one failing of lending money, and carried it to such an extent that she lent – hem – oh! thousands of pounds, all our little fortunes; and what's more, Mrs Nickleby, I don't think, if we were to live till – till – hem – till the very end of time, that we should ever get them back again. I don't indeed.'

After concluding this effort of invention without being interrupted, Miss Knag fell into many more recollections, no less interesting than true, the full tide of which Mrs Nickleby in vain attempting to stem, at length sailed smoothly down, by adding an undercurrent of her own recollections; and so both ladies went on talking together in perfect contentment.

(ch. XVIII)

Mrs Gamp is as conspicuous as Mrs Nickleby, though she makes her mark in a few appearances. Her brilliant constructions are finished and rounded, creative examples of rhetorical originality. One of her figures is inventive error, fuelling her to outdo Dogberry and Mrs Malaprop in recreation. She shows the cunning unconscious at work in portmanteaux and puns, like 'ingeins' (ingenious and engines) and 'mortal wale' (Christian lachrymose improvement on 'vale'). Her surreal neologisms, 'parapidge', 'brickbadge' and 'cowcumbers', look ahead to Carroll and Joyce, in nonce-invention and nonsense. She can revise cliché as freshly and wittily as Henry James: 'we never know wot's hidden in each other's breasts, and if we had glass winders there, we'd need to keep the shetters up' (ch. XXIX), and some of her anarchic blunders are social criticisms in a nut-shell: 'the Lord Mayor and Uncommon Counsellors' (ch. XXIV) and 'the witness for the persecution' (ch. XL). She can improve on sound-sense, as in 'twining serpiant'. But her triumphs are the iconoclastic revisions, 'led a Martha to the Stakes' and 'Rich folks may ride on camels, but it an't so easy for 'em to see out of a needle's eye' (ch. XXV), the latter a bizarre stroke of dialogic and intertextual revision improving Jesus Christ's economy and wit. Mrs Gamp converts adjectives into new verbs, 'Whether I sicks or monthlies'; she has a fine line in simile, comparing an infant's legs to Canterbury Brawn; she creates oxymoron – 'airy stones' – out of error; she excels in grotesque metonymy: her family had 'damp-doorsteps settled on their lungs' (ch. XL), and her husband's wooden leg has 'gone likeways home to its account, which in its constancy of walkin' into wine vaults, and never comin' out again till fetched by force, was quite as weak as flesh' (ch. XL). She is a narrator – like the Nurse – whose monologues contain dialogue. Her creative powers extend to the invention of character: her manipulations of Mrs Harris are brilliant illustrations of personal motive and fiction masquerading as fact. She projects a fictitious character as an *alter ego* combining the detachment of external identity with the partiality of self-advertisement, and her affection for her created character is in its way as suggestive as Jane Austen's 'My Fanny'. I am not the first to notice that Dickens endows his nasty characters with a gusto and brilliance at odds with their moral illustrativeness, and Mrs Gamp's creativity finds tongue for aggressiveness, deceit and egocentricity as well as invention and originality. She is a would-be PR person, and her habit of dominating the scene, softened by her false ingratiating way with listeners, whom she frequently buttonholes and addresses by name, is an image of creative address, intimacy, authority and engrossment. Dickens' male characters can also be authorially reflexive, but wildness, openness and dislocation are most creatively clustered in the talkative women, traditionally irrational, under-educated and out of control. Disorganization is dramatized and licensed as constructive principle.

Mrs Gamp's key figures are neologism, malapropism and metonymy. Flora Finching's are catachresis and zeugma – figures of orderly disjointedness. Arthur identifies Flora as moral mermaid, and it is in dualities, breakings and forced junctions that she represents the wildness of creative effort. Like Mrs Nickleby and Mrs Gamp she uses fillers or blanks like 'good gracious', or 'the what's his name horizon of et cetera' (Book II, ch. IX), and like Mrs Nickleby she combines miscellany and openness with the odd gesture towards order:

'pray don't answer, I don't know where I'm running to, oh do tell me something about the Chinese ladies whether their eyes are really so long and narrow always putting me in mind of mother-of-pearl fish at cards and do they really wear tails down their backs and plaited too or is it only the men, and when they pull their hair so very tight off their foreheads don't they hurt themselves, and why do they stick little bells all over their bridges and temples and hats and things or don't they really do it?'

(Book I, ch. XIII)[22]

And,

'don't mind me or wait for me because I always carry in this tray myself to Mr F's Aunt who breakfasts in bed and a charming old lady too and very clever, Portrait of Mr F behind the door and very like though too much forehead and as to a pillar with a marble pavement and balustrades and a mountain I never saw him near it nor not likely, in the wine trade, excellent man but not at all in that way.'

(Book I, ch. XXIV)

Her best zeugma elides Mr F's seven proposals, 'once in a hackney coach once in a boat once in a pew once on a donkey at Tunbridge Wells and the rest on his knees' (Book I, ch. XXIV), and the unpunctuated fluid prose makes many rich blurrings and juxtapositions, like 'with your Mama's parasol between them seated on two chairs like mad bulls' (Book I, ch. XIII). Through her Dickens yokes opposites and incompatibles, brackets vehicles and omits tenors, as in the delicious catachresis 'If he hadn't been cut short while I was a new broom' (ch. XXIV). He leaves out prepositional clues to space and relationship, as in 'a coat of arms of course and wild beasts on their hind legs' (Book II, ch. IX), and omits transitions, as in 'tell him all about it upon teaspoons' (Book I, ch. XXXV). Flora's style is a new accelerator making creative confusion and connection. Syntax is collapsed and the lack of punctuation marks, relatives and conjunctions forms zany assemblings, free associations, and surrealist images. I do not suggest that Dickens never planned collisions and linkings, but in the press and rush of idiolect the random powers are mimed:

In Italy is she really?...with the grapes and figs growing everywhere and lava necklaces and bracelets too that land of poetry with burning mountains picturesque beyond belief though if the organ-boys come away from the neighbourhood not to be scorched nobody can wonder being so young and bringing their white mice with them most humane, and is she really in that favoured land with nothing but blue about her and dying gladiators and Belvederas though Mr F himself did not believe for his objection when in spirits was that the images could not be true there being no medium between expensive quantities of linen badly got up and all in creases and none whatever.'

(Book II, ch. IX)

On one occasion Flora's style gets out of control, perhaps because Dickens is over-excited by her creativity. Instead of flow and collision he gives her apt but static metaphor and simile: she says Mrs Clennam 'ought to be the mother of the man in the iron mask' and describes her as 'glowering...like Fate in a go-cart' (ch. XXIV). These uncharacteristically logical images come in neighbouring sentences, both conventionally punctuated. Their brilliance is a rare departure from idiolect: Flora comments that the simile of Fate is a 'shocking comparison really' and so it is. A breaking of decorum.

When Hélène Cixous and Luce Irigaray praise the looseness and fluidity of *écriture feminine*,[23] they recognize that it is not confined to female text or talk, though feminist psychoanalytic symbolism derives from the female body to free the language of women from a dominant masculinity. There are difficulties in adopting this favourite feminist stance, even if one does not take psychoanalysts as authorities. There is a tendency, for instance, to equate the talkative woman in literature with heroic or subversive talkative models in history, and though the work of Lisa Jardine[24] and Catherine Belsey,[25] for instance, has illustrated the politics of eloquence and silence, this recognition should not lead to a neglect of misogynistic elements in literature. The talkative woman in life was a feminist, or a feminist hero, a true misandrist. The man-made garrulous woman is always in some measure an insult to woman's reason and intelligence. Samuel Richardson recognizes this when he creates the elaborate and flexible periodic sentence of Clarissa Harlowe's prose, so strongly contrasted with the sloppy, uncoordinated style of her university-educated brother. If the loose style can be seen as a feminist alternative, so also can the controlled eloquence of a Clarissa or George Eliot.

If one recognizes the patronizing and critical attitude to women's minds, which froze, stereotyped and denigrated prattle, chatter, babble, gossip (gossip in the bad sense, which destroyed the favourable 'godsip'), then the revisions and correctives of Jane Austen and George Eliot must be seen as politically desirable events in the raising of gendered consciousness. George Eliot's attack on the stereotype did not kill off the talkative woman. Joyce's Molly Bloom, though a complex case, is irrational, narrow, self-centred and pragmatic, as if George Eliot had never written an idiolect for reason and argument. The male tradition of Shakespeare and Dickens provided Joyce with ancestral voices, and he ignored the anti-sexist authority of Homer's[26] authoritative, subtle and rational Penelope, a match for her clever husband, if not his elder and better, like Homer's other eloquent woman, Pallas Athene.

Images of talkativeness can be read in many ways. Feminists have related informality of speech to historical defiances of the patriarchal injunction to silence, or as sexually symbolic babble-utterances 'divided and fragmentary in the image of the woman's body'. Virginia Woolf's well-known and influential belief that Dorothy Richardson invented the woman's sentence is used by Silvia Bovenschen in 'Is there a feminine aesthetic?'[27] in a discussion of the difficulty of arguing a gendered 'relationship to detail and generality, to motionlessness and movement, to rhythm and demeanour', which concludes that Virginia Woolf exemplifies 'the only sensible approach' – that of evidence within individual concrete texts. Virginia Woolf's comment on Richardson, however, is not exactly precise:

> She has invented, or, if she has not invented, developed and applied to her own uses, a sentence which we might call the psychological sentence of the feminine gender. It is of a more elastic fibre than the old, capable of stretching to the extreme, of suspending the frailest particles, of enveloping the vaguest shapes. Other writers of the opposite sex have used sentences of this description and stretched them to the extreme. But there is a difference. Miss Richardson has fashioned her sentence consciously, in order that it may descend to the depths and investigate the crannies of

Miriam Henderson's consciousness. It is a woman's sentence, but only in the sense that it is used to describe a woman's mind by a writer who is neither proud nor afraid of anything that she may discover in the psychology of her sex.'[28]

Woolf is vague about the linguistic difference between a man's and a woman's language; she elides features of prose style and psychological penetration. I cannot help contrasting this praise of Richardson with her attack on Joyce,[29] whose shadow flickers across the words, 'Other writers of the opposite sex'. There were political reasons for preferring Dorothy Richardson's elasticity to that of Joyce, and perhaps some personal literary reasons too: Woolf's prose style changed radically after she read *Ulysses*, but she never admitted his influence.

Woolf also omits exemplification of men's texts. Joyce fashioned prose to plumb depths and investigate crannies, and had models of the fluid or elastic sentence present in his memory. These models were the man-made talkative women. The elastic sentence of Woolf was probably shaped by Stephen Dedalus and Molly Bloom and through them, or directly, by the Wife of Bath, Mistress Quickly, Juliet's Nurse and Dickens' women. If one analyses the language of *Mrs Dalloway*, for instance, there are many echoes of Mrs Gamp's metonymy, Flora Finching's zeugma and Mrs Nickleby's hyperbaton in that wonderfully fast, fluid and classy stream of consciousness.

This essay deals with a few examples, and my chronological order does not signal historical ambition. Whether one tries to write a history of talkative character or look at a few types, there are problems of overlap between class and gender and life and art. In life and art there are talkative men and women, and though both volubility and silence are politically significant, there are social situations where both men and women are reduced to dumbness or provoked to garrulity. Life sometimes imitates art and art life. Critics still sometimes assume that Dickens' talkative women were 'based on' talkative women in his life, and when we find no evidence that Dickens' mother or his nurse or his old flame were exceptionally loquacious, it looks as if male stereotypes are being applied to books, then derived from books and re-applied to life outside books, in a process providing suggestive if snarled illustration of the influence of art on life.[30] A full study of literary talkativeness would include a study of gendered attitudes in literary criticism.

Unless one believes that all problems are problems of gender, there is the problem of being blinkered by the problem of gender. I became interested in talkative women while working on Shakespeare's narrative, reading Mistress Quickly, the Nurse and many male narrators as elements in Shakespeare's dramatic analysis of narrative processes such as fantasy, memory, anecdote, and gossip. At a conference on *La Femme* (in Victorian and Edwardian literature) I set side by side some talkers in Dickens and George Eliot, finding that her misandrous characters responded to his misogynist typography. While thinking about this comparison I read a book by two psychologists, Murray Cox and Alice Thielgarden, *Mutative Metaphors in Psycho-Therapy*,[31] which offered insights into language and imagination, and sent me back to my own earlier thinking about imaginative forms and processes in narrative, especially in *Tellers and Listeners: The Narrative Imagination.*[32] My piece acquired a postscript and afterthought, returning to Dickens and seeing his talkative women as brilliant images of imagination, in men and women, uneducated and educated, sick and well. Dickens imagines class and gender, drawing on stereotypes and promoting them, but he also imagines imagination reflexively, intuiting rather than discussing characteristics of his own mind as it experienced its creativity. I do not mean to suggest that he transcends questions of class and gender and imagines essence, but he reflexively analyses processes of generation, formation and expression common to all sexes.

One feature of Dickens' talkative miniatures and microcosms is a betrayal of effort, offered as female incompetence in Mrs Nickleby's failures of reason and Flora's uncontrolled speeding. The sense of difficulty is characteristic of imaginative composition as the mind 'dissolves, diffuses, dissipates, in order to re-create; or where this process is rendered impossible, yet still, at all events, it struggles to idealize and to unify' (Coleridge, *Biographia Literaria*).[33] Unity is not a popular concept, but Dickens' talkative women image Coleridge's romantic concept of struggle, as deviant or exceptional, and a modern view of imaginative openness and diffusion as normative. As important as the concept of imaginative creation which they reflect is the process of composition – its effort, frustration, self-interrogation, pauses,

42

erasures, revisions, hit-or-miss inventions. Emily Dickinson knew that 'the Possible has a "slow fuse" lit by Imagination'. In 'The Wreck of the *Deutschland*' Hopkins cries, 'But how shall I...make me room there:/ Reach me a...Fancy, come faster –'. Virginia Woolf puts that imaginative search which William James[34] imaged so wonderfully, into Mrs Ramsay's attempt 'to get hold of something that evaded her'. Dickens assimilates and reveals his experience of doubts and difficulties in these inset and dramatized feeblenesses, vaguenesses and hesitations of talk.

Dickens makes his talkative woman a wild, unrestrained, free-for-all force, working through random association, error, doubt, stupidity and uncontrolled speed to achieve effects which are comic and critical, within his narrative, but which overrun local function to mirror mind at its most inventive in word, sentence, narrative structure and image. Here is *poiesis* in its Platonic sense, bringing into existence something which did not exist before. Moreover, the energy and creativity are shown in the act, caught on the wing, making self-analytic models of generative process. Each of his women is a walking oxymoron, converting silliness to brilliance. Each gives a new demonstration of negative capability. It is through negations and subversions of law and reason that the characters are made imaginatively capable.

Of course, T. S. Eliot and Joyce were fervent Dickensians. Dickens' mirrors of mind at its most relaxed, open and uninhibited create within the relatively fixed and fused unities of Victorian fiction startling miniatures of fragmentation and dislocation. They anticipate – and influence – modernist breaking, defamiliarization, and collision. Each Dickensian talkative woman is a solipsist of the imagination. She subverts the dominant culture and language so that the concept of synthesis and unity is itself challenged. Out of silliness comes new sensibility and new sense. Synthesis is mocked by syncretism. No wonder women writers found such anarchy congenial, though it was not created by a woman. Mrs Poyser's powers are impeccably rational and concentrated, but her inventiveness is not up to Mrs Gamp's. Who would wish such misogyny away?

All feminists and most twentieth-century readers, of course. We also wish madness away, while savouring its dislocations and visions. Dickens' misogyny dramatized creativity, freeing and fuelling him to write a wild text into the over-civilized Victorian novel. His wildness helped to make the modern tradition.

ACKNOWLEDGEMENTS

I'd like to thank the following colleagues for help of various kinds: Paula Neuss, Tom Healy, Patricia Hann, Roland Mayer, Michael Trapp and Janet El-Rayess.

NOTES

1 Callimachus, *Aelia, Iambi, Hecale and Other Fragments*, London: Heinemann, 1958.
2 Semonides, in *Elegy and Iambus*, ed. J. M. Edmonds (anthology), London: Heinemann, 1933.
3 Euripides, *Ion, Hippolytus, Medea, Alcestis*, London: Heinemann, 1935.
4 Geoffrey Chaucer, 'The Wife of Bath's Prologue', *The Complete Works of Geoffrey Chaucer*, 2nd edition, ed. F. N. Robinson, Oxford: Oxford University Press, 1974.
5 Desiderius Erasmus, *Praise of Folly*, trans. Betty Radice, Harmondsworth: Penguin Books, 1976.
6 For instance, see his *Letter to Martin Dorp, 1515*.
7 All quotations from Shakespeare's plays are taken from the New Arden edition, London: Methuen.
8 Samuel Taylor Coleridge, 'Essays on The Principles of Method', Essay IV, *The Collected Works of Samuel Taylor Coleridge I*, London: Routledge & Kegan Paul, 1969.
9 Lisa Jardine, *Still Harping on Daughters*, Brighton: Harvester Press, 1983.
10 Coppelia Kahn, 'Coming of age in Verona', *The Woman's Part*, Illinois: University of Illinois Press, 1983.
11 Robert Golding, *Idiolects in Dickens: the major techniques and chronological development*, London: Macmillan, 1985.
12 'Misandry' first appears in *NED Supplement*, 1976, with an entry from J. Smith in *Scrutiny*, 1946, on Shakespeare's Beatrice. Even 'man-hater', meaning 'male-hater', is cited in the main *NED* as 'occasional'. The absence of an equivalent for misogyny is eloquent.
13 Michael Slater, *Dickens and Women*, London: Dent, 1983.
14 *Nicholas Nickleby*, Harmondsworth: Penguin Books, 1978.
15 Samuel Taylor Coleridge, *Anima Poetae*, ed. E. H. Coleridge, London: Heinemann, 1895.
16 All quotations from *Martin Chuzzlewit* are taken from the Clarendon Press edition, Oxford, 1982.
17 All quotations from *Emma* are taken from the Oxford University Press edition, London, 1971.
18 Jane Austen, *Northanger Abbey*, London: Oxford University Press, 1971.
19 George Eliot, *Middlemarch*, Oxford: Clarendon Press, 1986.
20 George Eliot, *Felix Holt*, Oxford: Clarendon Press, 1980.
21 George Eliot, *Adam Bede*, Cabinet edition, London: Blackwoods, 1878.

22 All quotations from *Little Dorrit* are taken from the Clarendon Press edition, Oxford, 1979.

23 Hélène Cixous, 'The laugh of the Medusa', in E. Marks and I. de Courtivron (eds), *New French Feminisms*, New York: Schocken, 1980. Luce Irigaray, *Ce Sexe qui n'en est pas un* (*This Sex Which is Not One*), Paris: Minuit, 1977.

24 Jardine, *Still Harping on Daughters*.

25 See the chapter 'Silence and speech', in the *Subject of Tragedy: Identity and Difference in Renaissance Drama*, London: Methuen, 1985.

26 See the discussion of post-Homeric developments in misogyny in E. R. Dodds, *The Greeks and the Irrational*, Berkeley: University of California Press, 1951.

27 Silvia Bovenschen, 'Is there a feminine aesthetic?', in G. Ecker (ed.) *Feminist Aesthetics*, London: The Women's Press, 1985.

28 Virginia Woolf, 'Romance and the heart', review of *The Grand Tour* by Romer Wilson, and *Revolving Lights*, by Dorothy Richardson, in *Nation and Athenaeum*, 19 May 1923; reprinted in *Contemporary Writers*, New York: A Harvest Book, Harcourt Brace Jovanovich, 1976.

29 See especially her entries for 1920 and 1922 in *The Diary of Virginia Woolf*, 2, 1920–4, London: Hogarth Press, 1978.

30 For instance, Golding, *Idiolects in Dickens*.

31 Murray Cox and Alice Thielgarden, *Mutative Metaphors in Psycho-Therapy: The Aeolian Mode*, London, New York: Tavistock Publications, 1987.

32 *Tellers and Listeners: the narrative imagination*, London: Athlone, 1975.

33 Samuel Taylor Coleridge, (ch. XIII), *Biographia Literaria*, London: Dent, 1975.

34 *Principles of Psychology*, London, New York: Macmillan, 1890.

2

MILTON ON WOMEN – YET AGAIN

Barbara K. Lewalski

This paper began as an attempt to revise a 1974 article on Milton on Women for the present collection, but it has, not surprisingly, turned into a new essay.[1] That article is now fifteen years old, and neither I nor the field of Milton studies are where we were then. Like any piece of critical writing, that one engaged the critical discourse where it then was, proposing ideas which have since been assimilated, developed, revised or contested by myself and others in other places. But since that article continues to be cited without much attention to its historical moment, I welcome the opportunity to engage the subject again, setting forth my theoretical assumptions in relation to the present state of feminist Milton criticism, and incorporating what I then knew and have learned since about Milton on women – with special reference to Eve in *Paradise Lost*, the Lady in *A Masque*, and Dalila in *Samson Agonistes*.

My earlier essay responded to an article by Marcia Landy (1972) in which the cultural norms and values of the bourgeois family – sexual restraint, patriarchal authority and female domesticity, submissiveness, dependency and silence – seemed to me to be applied in formulaic fashion to *Paradise Lost*, without much attention to the ways in which Milton's poem subverts that paradigm.[2] I thought and think that such Procrustean reading can be a problem for feminist critics – as it sometimes is for critics of all persuasions – though often enough the limitations of strong ideological readings are offset by the stimulus and insight they generate. The attention that feminist, Marxist and New Historicist critics are now directing to gender, race and class as significant categories of analysis for literary works is to my mind wholly salutary in demonstrating how such texts inscribe, contest

46

or at times subvert the assumptions and practices of a given culture. Specifically, over the past decade or so, feminist criticism has developed remarkable theoretical sophistication and analytic power; and it has produced an impressive body of writing about Milton's poems which explores their construction of gender and gendered language, their representation of patriarchy and hierarchy, and their impact on female readers and writers in our culture. Happily also, feminist critics are increasingly disposed to attend very carefully to the complexities and the specifics of the Miltonic texts as well as to the various cultural texts which help to contextualize them.

At this juncture we can distinguish two very general positions regarding Milton's writing about women, though the critics identified with each are very diverse as to ideology, method, arguments and issues addressed. One position takes that writing to be essentially anti-feminist in substance and effect, inscribing Early Modern cultural norms of patriarchy and female subordination in texts which have themselves inscribed those norms more deeply in our culture. The other position takes those texts to be, in many respects, proto-feminist, departing significantly from contemporary norms in their representation of women's nature and role, of marriage, of female characters and of the values associated with each gender in our culture.

In the 'Milton as anti-feminist' camp two critics have been particularly influential. One is Sandra Gilbert, whose article 'Patriarchal poetry and women readers: reflections on Milton's bogey' (1978) examines the burden placed on nineteenth-century women poets and novelists by their perception of Milton as the authoritative voice of patriarchal poetry, defining a literary culture that excluded them.[3] The other is Christine Froula, whose essay, 'When Eve reads Milton: undoing the canonical economy' (1983), seeks to demonstrate how *Paradise Lost* enacts the imposition of patriarchal and canonical authority upon women through the portrayal of a repressed and silenced Eve; a later essay (1984) claims that Milton's poetry 'constructs its gods and its speech on the bedrock of woman's silence'.[4] Other representative voices have introduced other issues: Katherine Rogers (1966) sees Milton as a deliberate and emphatic spokesman for 'the misogyny that he found in his own culture' and in Christianity itself.[5] Maureen Quilligan (1983) asserts that Milton's epic exerts great pressure on its female reader to accept freely her 'covered', subordinate, mediated position, by emphasizing its rewards – companionate marriage and religious commendation.[6] Janet Halley (1987) invokes the Lévi-Straussian paradigm of male bonding through the exchange of women to explain Milton's treatment of heterosexual marriage, in which women attain subjectivity but at the price of all autonomy, since it is 'the male mind that defines both its members'.[7]

Such critics find Milton's texts to be a major problem for women readers in that they enforce woman's subordination, powerlessness and subservience to the purposes of a patriarchal social structure. On this understanding, women can only give Milton's works a deconstructive reading (finding some place for themselves and their concerns on the margins or in the gaps of the text), or else an oppositional reading (uncovering in them the means and structures of women's victimization in western culture). To read so might mean identifying with Satan as model for a justifiable revolt against patriarchal power (Gilbert); or re-imagining an Eve who rejects Adam and returns to gaze upon her own image in the pool, 'being in and for herself' (Fruola).[8]

Critics who see Milton as some variety of proto-feminist do not, of course, deny that his texts inscribe the patriarchy of his era, but emphasize how those texts challenge, or modify, or at times radically revise many of its common assumptions. My 1974 essay is often cited as a beginning point for this line of argument: it claims that Milton's female characters have impressive intellectual capacity and full moral responsibility for their individual choices; and that his Eve is neither silenced nor relegated to domesticity, but instead participates in all the aspects of Edenic work, education and the arts of speech and song. Joan Webber's answer to Sandra Gilbert (1980) proposes that Milton 'prepares the way for feminist thinking' by his own revolutionary politics; by his trenchant critique of conventional assumptions about marriage, gender roles, the importance of women, and patriarchy; and by his privileging of many values culturally associated with women – love, primary concern for human relationships, imagination.[9] The most extensive contribution to this discourse is Diane McColley's book, *Milton's Eve* (1983), and her related articles, which offer a finely-textured account of Eve as model for the regenerate reader of the poem, and also (through her close associations with the 'arts' of Eden and the reported experiences of the Miltonic Bard) as a 'speaking picture' of poetry and the poetic imagination.[10]

Texts written from this general vantage-point include some important contributions by male critics: William Kerrigan's and Gordon Braden's analysis of the subtlety and complexity of the Miltonic concept of heterosexual love; William Shullenberger's perceptive reading of the centrality of relationships to the very definition of identity in *Paradise Lost*; James Turner's trenchant exploration of how the presence of both patriarchal and egalitarian ideology in Milton's writing affects his representation of erotic experience. Coming full circle, Joseph Wittreich's provocatively titled book, *Feminist Milton*, employs historicized reader-response methods to recover a female interpretative tradition for Milton's texts, from the later seventeenth century to the Victorian era, which saw Milton as a trenchant critic of patriarchy and all authoritarianism, and as a powerful voice affirming women's importance, dignity and liberty.[11] Wittreich looks to this tradition to help reclaim the radical Milton from a male critical tradition that has made him a bastion of orthodoxy, and from those feminists who have been unwittingly complicitous in that misappropriation.

Critics who see Milton as ally rather than as enemy in the long struggle for women's liberation often account for the tension and contradiction they find in Milton's representations of women by an effort to historicize his texts as ideological constructs or as objects of interpretation. These critics endeavour to read with, rather than against, his texts, finding a radical and complex representation of human experience at their centre. I would argue that this general position also warrants the designation 'feminist', although that label may not be readily granted by those for whom Milton is women's 'bogey'. Still, as feminist theory turns from an emphasis on women as victims to a focus on women's empowerment, it may be easier to recognize elements of such empowerment in Milton's poetry and prose.

I approach this topic at this juncture with the assumption that Milton's poems (like other major works of art) are at once products of a specific historical moment and also imaginative constructs, that they are shaped by, but also shape, the culture. We find inscribed in them, as we should expect to, the cultural norms of Milton's age – patriarchy, hierarchy, female subordination, the construction of gender in terms of seventeenth-century Puritan bourgeois ideology – perhaps best encapsulated in the notorious phrase, 'Hee for God only, shee for God in him.'[12] But as imaginative constructs Milton's poems also contain subversive and utopian elements which (however we account for them) challenge the received orthodoxies about gender and look to the future. When Eve reads Milton's poems with attention to their dialogue with and critique of seventeenth-century cultural norms, she need not encounter a bogey.

I assume also that Milton's poems (like others that have been 'canonized' over time) can both abide our new questions generation after generation, and can also speak to some of our enduring concerns. This is not an essentialist claim that great art transcends history in some absolute way, or that it portrays an unchanging human nature. But it seems obvious enough that many human characteristics and concerns belong to the *'longue durée'*, and that we find them treated with great profundity in many literary works of the past: Homer on the pointless brutalities of warfare, Sophocles on the tragic human capacity for self-deception, Dante on the varieties of intellectual evil, Shakespeare on the terrors of old age. My earlier article emphasized one such concern in Milton's epic, the constant tension which both Adam and Eve experience between the necessity and responsibility for making individual choices and the need for human love. This reaches beyond the ideology of heterosexual marriage, though Milton explored it with great complexity and insight in relation to that institution. It is, rather, a problem posed by any real intimacy with or commitment to another – as the plethora of popular psychology articles about the contemporary flight from intimacy can testify. Issues of identity are also explored profoundly in Milton's Eve and Adam, and are also still with us: how to reconcile sexual difference with an ideal of human equality, or the self as individual entity with the self defined through a network of relationships.

My proposition is that Milton's poems not only admit but invite a construction attentive to their complex representations of women and of gender relations, and especially to their recognition of women's worth, abilities, strength and freedom. I stand by my earlier claim that 'few writers of any era – including our own – have taken women so seriously as Milton does, as multi-faceted human beings with impressive intellectual and moral powers and responsibilities.'[13] I want now to indicate how such a reading of Milton's Eve, of the Lady in *A Masque*, and of Dalila in *Samson Agonistes* might proceed; and then to suggest briefly how we might now advance the discourse relating to Milton and women.

It is appropriate to begin with *Paradise Lost*, as Milton's portrait of the primordial human pair, their natures and their roles. When we – and Satan – first view Adam and Eve in the garden, the essential equality of their natures is underscored, as both of them exhibit the authority and dignity attendant upon the image of God they both share:

> Two of far nobler shape erect and tall,
> Godlike erect, with native Honor clad
> In naked Majesty seem'd Lords of all,
> And worthy seem'd, for in thir looks Divine
> The image of thir glorious Maker shone,
> Truth, Wisdom, Sanctitude severe and pure,
> Severe, but in true filial freedom plac't;
> Whence true autority in men.
>
> (4.288–95)

Then their physical and sexual differences are described – 'though both/ Not equal, as thir sex not equal seem'd' – and certain supposedly sex-linked qualities are read out from those appearances: in Adam, contemplation, valour, absolute rule; in Eve softness, grace, subjection. The hierarchy seems clearly defined – but then Eve's 'subjection' is illustrated in the very restricted terms of courtship play as a prelude to love-making: 'Yielded with coy submission, modest pride,/ And sweet reluctant amorous delay' (4.310–11). And the term 'grace' – here given a primarily physical association – will come to be invested with spiritual import, honouring Eve's agency in the restoration of humankind.

Milton's representation of Eve's nature as both equal and somehow inferior to Adam's is further complicated by the stories of her creation. Testifying to a poignant sense of lack even in Eden and to a 'desire/ By conversation with his like to help,/ Or solace his defects', Adam asks God for a mate who will be his equal: 'Among unequals what society/ Can sort, what harmony or true delight?/ Which must be mutual.../ Of fellowship I speak/ Such as I seek, fit to participate/ All rational delight' (8.383–91). God promises a mate who will be exactly that: 'Thy likeness, thy fit help, thy other self,/ Thy wish, exactly to thy heart's desire' (8.450–1). By contrast, throughout the early Edenic scenes Eve declares Adam her 'Guide and Head', and proclaims her delight in that hierarchical arrangement: 'I...enjoy/ So far the happier Lot, enjoying thee/ Pre-eminent by so much odds' (4.445–6). Later, Adam voices to Raphael his sense of a conflict between ideology and experience in the matter of Eve's nature (and he does not find Raphael's warnings against passion of much use in sorting it out):

> For well I understand in the prime end
> Of Nature her th'inferior, in the mind
> And inward Faculties, which most excel,
> And outward also her resembling less
> His image who made them both, and less expressing
> The character of that Dominion giv'n
> O'er other Creatures; yet when I approach
> Her loveliness, so absolute she seems
> And in herself complete, so well to know
> Her own, that what she wills to do or say,
> Seems wisest, virtuousest, discreetest, best;
> . . . .
> Authority and Reason on her wait,
> As one intended first, not after made
> Occasionally; and to consummate all,
> Greatness of mind and nobleness thir seat
> Build in her loveliest, and create an awe
> About her, as a guard Angelic plac't.
>
> (8.540–59)

Milton's complex treatment of Eve's nature finds its ground – and its openness to ideological change and to the testimony of new experience – in the unusually fluid notion of hierarchy, which is a concomitant of his monism. Raphael explains to Adam and Eve that all beings are created of 'one first matter'; that they are 'assign'd' to their 'several active Spheres/...Till body up to spirit work, in bounds/ Proportion'd to each kind'; and that they are 'more refin'd, more spiritous, and pure/ As nearer to him [God] plac't *or nearer tending*' (5.469–79).[14] What this means in regard to gender difference is given some perspective by Raphael's further observation that even angels differ from humans in degree only, not in kind, and that humans may expect the gradual refinement of their own natures to virtually angelic condition (5.470–505). The Miltonic scale of being is meant to be climbed and is open to merit – in this aspect reflecting the spirit of bourgeois capitalism. In such a system, if Adam is at first 'plac't' marginally higher than Eve within the same 'kind' – the human order – their final places depend on how they develop, where they 'tend'.

As for Eve's role in the ideal (pre-lapsarian) social order, Milton's far from orthodox conception is better understood now than when I first discussed the matter. His conception eschews the usual stereotypes: mother figure, domestic goddess, sex-object. It is true that Eve is honoured in address and epithet as mother of the human race; that she takes on such domestic tasks as ornamenting the couple's bedroom/bower and preparing and serving the noonday meal when Raphael pays his visit; and that she evokes sexual delight and even passion in Adam. But her essential role is much broader: it builds upon but goes beyond the idea of marital partnership in Puritan marriage theory, and contributes to the evolving concept of companionate marriage.[15] The closest analogue in the period is to be found in Milton's own *Divorce Tracts*, which identify the primary end of marriage as companionship of the mind and spirit, not, as most of Milton's contemporaries did, as procreation or the relief of lust. In *Paradise Lost*, Eve's fundamental social role is quite simply to share with Adam in the entire range of human activities.

One such activity is education: Milton's Eve is not absent attending to domestic chores while Adam and Raphael talk about higher things. Although some readers still seem not to notice the fact, Eve is present through almost all of Raphael's discourses – the explanation of the nature of being, the epic account of the war in heaven, the Creation story. When she decides to leave to tend her flowers (thereby missing the astronomy lesson) we are assured that she is fully capable of that knowledge also – 'Yet went she not, as not with such discourse/ Delighted, or not capable her ear/ Of what was high' (8.48-50) – and that she will learn it all later from Adam. Adam takes the initiative in asking the angelic visitor leading questions, but Eve's presence means that the pre-lapsarian educational curriculum is precisely the same for the woman as for the man – ontology, cosmology, metaphysics, moral philosophy, history, epic poetry, divine revelation, physics and astronomy. Identity of education for the sexes was hardly a conventional idea in the mid-seventeenth century.

Nor was the notion of fully-shared work in and responsibility for the external world. The Edenic scenes of Books 1V and V show Adam and Eve planning and working together to preserve, cultivate, sustain and raise to higher levels of perfection the world that has been made for them. This is their common and necessary task and responsibility, for without their constant, though pleasant, labour Eden would revert to the wild.[16] By contrast, Eve's proposal of a sexual division of labour as a means to greater efficiency helps to prepare the way for the Fall.

What then of Eve's sense of self? Is she defined so entirely in patriarchal terms that she has no real subjectivity or autonomy? It is certainly true that this character, like everything else in the poem, is the creation of a male author's imagination; that Milton embellishes the biblical myth to portray Eve formed by the hand of God the Father at the specific request of Adam, and suited to his needs and wishes; and that Eve is led by the persuasions of God and Adam formally to accept Adam as mate with all that that relationship will entail. But in the complex vision of this poem (as in all serious psychological or philosophical examinations of the matter) the construction of a self takes place in and through relationships as well as in independent action.[17] Adam (even more than Eve) feels himself incomplete without a mate, and falls because he cannot bear the prospect of a solitary life or a life without this particular defining relationship:

> How can I live without thee, how forgo
> Thy sweet Converse and Love so dearly join'd,
> To live again in these wild Woods forlorn?
> Should God create another *Eve*, and I
> Another Rib afford, yet loss of thee
> Would never from my heart.
>
> (8.908–13)

Even God (the only self-sufficient being) defines himself through relationships – to his Son, to the angels, to humankind. Only Satan imagines that solipsism could be possible, or good, or the key to identity: 'self-begot, self-rais'd/ By our own quick'ning power' (5.860–1). In this frame of reference, Eve's free choice (after a brief attraction to the narcissistic alternative of contemplating her image in the pool) to define herself within the only relationship available and to join in founding human society counts as a major step to selfhood.

Yet Eve is also defined through independent thought and action, as Milton imagines for her a genuine subjectivity and sphere of autonomy. In the first instance this involves qualities of intellect and moral strength, such that God can rightly describe both Adam and Eve as 'sufficient to have stood, though free to fall' (4.99). The old canard that Eve is marred from the outset – fallen before she falls – has been largely laid to rest: most Miltonists now recognize that Eve's creation story defines her against, rather than in terms of, the Narcissus myth; that her Satan-inspired dream provides a virtual experience of evil which could as well guard against as promote her fall; and that Eve's suggestion about gardening separately (though it gives occasion to Satan's temptation) is in itself blameless. We now better understand the virtually unique Miltonic representation of the state of innocence, wherein both Eve and Adam are expected to grow, change and develop in virtue by properly pruning and directing their own impulses as well as their garden.[18]

But Milton's insistence on Eve's intellectual capacity and individual moral responsibility is less widely recognized, complicated as it is by her hierarchical subordination to Adam. After the Fall she herself undertakes to shift her guilt to Adam, observing that he should have forbidden her absolutely to garden alone: 'Being as I am, why didst not thou the Head / Command me absolutely not to go, / Going into such danger as thou said'st' (9.1156–8). Many critics similarly assume that what was expected of Adam was the assertion of patriarchal authority in a flat command. But this is to miss the point badly; as marriage is conceived in Eden, Adam is Eve's superior and appointed guide, but not her lord and master. Eve is no dependent child-wife: her choices are and must be freely her own, for that is always the Miltonic precondition for any person's development in virtue.[19] Adam is accordingly indignant at Eve's words, as a flagrant misrepresentation of the terms of their relationship:

> I warn'd thee, I admonish'd thee, foretold
> The danger, and the lurking Enemy
> That lay in wait; beyond this had been force,
> And force upon free Will hath here no place
>
> (9.1171–4)

Adam does indeed fail in his proper leadership role during the marital dispute, a role he exercised properly just after Eve's creation when he urged his suit to her forcefully and rationally, leaving her to choose freely, with the alternatives clearly posed. Here, dismayed by Eve's distress, he supplies her with a rationale for leaving which she had not thought of herself, and inadvertently intensifies the emotional pressure on her by the repeated emphatic directives, 'Go', 'Go', 'Rely', 'do' (9.370–5). It was not Adam's place to command Eve, but neither was it his place to argue her case for her, unintentionally making it harder for her to give over her unwise plan. But she *is* still responsible for her choice, for all that.

Moreover, Milton devised the temptation scene itself so as to underscore Eve's intellectual sufficiency to withstand the temptation, despite Satan's wiles and magnificent rhetoric. The marital dispute itself displays her capacity to reason and to find the flaws in Adam's arguments. Then, her wry response to Satan's fulsome flattery – 'Serpent, thy overpraising leaves in doubt/ The virtue of that Fruit, in thee first prov'd' (9.615–16) – indicates that she recognizes flattery when she hears it and perceives that this element of falsehood might cast some doubt on the serpent's story, though she fails to heed the warning. Later, upon viewing the forbidden Tree she not only articulates the prohibition clearly but also distinguishes the ground for it – God's direct command – from the Law of Reason which governs all other human behaviour:

> Of this Tree we may not taste nor touch;
> God so commanded, and left that Command
> Sole Daughter of his voice; the rest, we live
> Law to ourselves, our Reason is our Law
>
> (9.651–4)

Richard Hooker himself was not more precise in stating the distinction between positive and natural law, and Eve need only hold firmly to it to be proof against the barrage of reasons and rational arguments Satan adduces, which are in this single case beside the point. Abdiel (whose story Eve has heard) is a proper model for her in this, and his line of argument is also available to her. Abdiel is much inferior in the angelic hierarchy to Satan, but managed very well in a debate with him by holding to the main issues: the angels' perception of God's order and experience of his goodness to them. Difficult as it is for modern readers to comprehend, Milton's epic does not allow any merit to the Satanic question, 'For inferior, who is free?'

Eve's sphere of autonomy extends to other areas as well, which undercut patriarchal assumptions more directly. Both before and after the Fall it is she who most often proposes issues for discussion, initiates action and provides the stimulus for some new direction. She first raises questions about the order of the cosmos; she proposes the division of labour; she makes the first motion to repentance and reconciliation; she proposes suicide or sexual abstinence to prevent visitation of the Fall's effects on the human progeny. When the dialogic interchanges of Adam and Eve are working properly, Adam then responds to, develops and, where necessary, corrects Eve's initiatives (as Raphael does Adam's), to help advance their common understanding.

Moreover, Eve is very far from being silenced or cut off from the supposedly masculine prerogatives of naming and of authorship, as some feminist criticism still claims. She participates with Adam in 'naming' the lesser orders of creation – she the plants as Adam the animals (9.276–7) – thereby showing her comprehension of their natures, her rightful dominion over them, and her command of the human power of symbolization. Yet more remarkably, she is as much, if not more, a poet than Adam. Not only are the hymns and prayers of Eden their joint production – 'such prompt eloquence/ Flow'd from thir lips, in Prose or numerous Verse,/ More tunable than needed Lute or Harp' (5.149–51) – but Eve continues her initiatory role in the creation of literary genres. She contrives the first autobiographical narrative (4.449–91) in recounting her first moments of life – and Adam later provides Raphael with a more elaborate autobiographical narrative of his first moments. Eve also pronounces the first love-lyric we hear in Eden – the delicate, rhetorically artful, melodious, sonnet-like pastoral (4.641–56) which begins 'Sweet is the breath of Morn'. Later, in his *aubade* rousing Eve from sleep – 'Awake/ My fairest, my espous'd/ My latest found' (5.17–25) – Adam raised that kind to its highest perfection, producing a prototype of the Bridegroom's song in Canticles. The language of these various literary productions is gendered, and there is some reflection of the gender hierarchy in their differing merits. But Eve is portrayed as an author with her own distinct voice and with large capacity for artistic invention.[20]

After the Fall even this gender hierarchy is subverted as Eve becomes the perfector of a lyric genre. Adam inaugurates the tragic lament/complaint based on classical models and expressing hopelessness and despair, while Eve's better tragic lyric – 'Forsake me not thus, *Adam*' (10.914–36) – fully expresses the misery, grief and agony of the fallen condition, but also voices repentance for sin, hope of forgiveness and desire to make amends. Alluding to Psalms 38, 51 and 102, Eve's eloquent appeal to her husband is the model for the repentant prayer Adam and Eve will together address to God (10.914–36), and is thereby in substance and structure the archetype of the penitential psalms, the highest kind of tragic lyric for the fallen world.

Even beyond this, it is hardly an exaggeration to say that Milton's epic turns into an Eviad,[21] placing Eve rather than Adam in the role of central protagonist. The biblical myth, of course, determines that she be made the object of the serpent's temptation, but Milton's poem goes much further. Eve initiates the marital dispute culminating in separation from Adam; Eve engages in a lengthy and highly dramatic dialogue with Satan embodied in the serpent; and Eve is given probing soliloquies in which she analyses her motives and emotions before eating the fruit and before offering it to Adam. After the Fall it is again Eve who responds first to 'prevenient grace' and initiates the reconciliation of the couple to each other and to God. By humbly repenting and begging forgiveness of Adam (in the psalmic lament discussed above) she breaks through their seemingly endless exchange of accusations and recriminations and turns Adam from the paralysis of despair to love, reconciliation and repentance. And it is Eve who in that same lament directly echoes the words of the Son in the Dialogue in Heaven – 'Behold mee then, mee for him, life for life/ I offer, on mee let thine anger fall' (3.236–7) – as she proposes to take God's entire wrath upon herself – 'with my cries importune Heaven, that all/ The sentence from thy head remov'd may light/ On me, sole cause to thee of all this woe,/ Mee mee only just object of his ire' (10.932–6). Post-lapsarian Eve is the first of humankind to embrace the new standard of epic heroism Milton's poem undertakes to define – 'the better fortitude/ Of Patience and Heroic Martyrdom' (9.31–2) – and so becomes, even more than Adam, a paradigm and model for the fallen Christian reader, whether male or female.

Eve also participates in prophecy, in terms that validate her own voice and her distinct (female) order of experience. After Michael takes Adam to the Mount of Speculation for visions of and verbal instruction about the future, he indicates that he has calmed Eve with 'gentle Dreams' and directs Adam to impart to her later what he has just learned. But Eve greets the returning pair by claiming her own prophetic illumination in dreams sent directly from God: 'Whence you return'st, and whither went'st, I know;/ For God is also in sleep, and Dreams advise,/ Which he hath sent propitious, some great good/ Presaging' (12.610–13). Between them, Adam and Eve embody the two kinds of prophecy specified in Joel 2:28: 'I will pour out my spirit upon all flesh; and your sons and your daughters shall prophesy, your old men shall dream dreams, your young men shall see visions.' Eve's mode of prophetic illumination is inferior to Adam's according to the scale defined by John Smith and other contemporaries.[22] But how far is that hierarchical ordering of prophetic kinds subverted by the fact that Eve claims her prophecy directly from God, and by the fact that the Miltonic Bard also claims his poetic illumination through dreams (9.20–4)?

Eve speaks the last words we hear in Eden – a love poem to Adam which echoes Ruth's loving promise to follow Naomi to another homeland. It recalls her pre-lapsarian poem 'inventing' the love song, and now reclaims that kind from Satan's Petrarchan perversions during his temptation. At its conclusion, Eve self-consciously claims her role in this Eviad – not only as primary protagonist of the Fall but also as primary human agent in the Divine plan of Redemption:

> In mee is no delay; with thee to go,
> Is to stay here; without thee here to stay,
> Is to go hence unwilling; thou to mee
> Art all things under Heav'n; all places thou,
> Who for my wilful crime art banisht hence.
> This further consolation yet secure
> I carry hence; though *all by mee is lost*,
> Such favor I unworthy am voutsaf't,
> *By mee* the Promis'd Seed shall *all restore*
>
> (12.615–23)[23]

When we look to *Paradise Lost* as a whole, rather than simply to the portrait of Eve, we find an even more radical Miltonic critique of the norms of patriarchy. For one thing, the poem regularly and consistently renounces misogyny. Both before and especially after the Fall Adam at moments of emotional stress voices hoary male complaints laying all his (and mankind's) problems at women's door, but he is regularly rebuked for his foolishness by whatever heavenly visitant is on the scene at the time – Raphael (8.561–2); the Son of God (10.145–57), Michael (11.632–4). More important, the portrait of Satan offers a trenchant, poem-long critique of epic values our culture has traditionally defined as male – the glory of battle, pride in physical strength, vaulting ambition, indomitable will. As against these, the poem honours qualities our culture has traditionally defined as female – care for nature, the fostering of community, willing subordination in love and sacrifice for others – qualities exhibited in Eve and also in the poem's heroic standard, the Son of God. Again, though Adam in one of his post-lapsarian tirades against Eve complains that God peopled heaven only with 'Spirits masculine', the Miltonic Bard imagines angels who are not by nature sexed but rather take on either sex at will (1.423–31). And, while Milton often represents a patriarchal God in his epic, even that cultural commonplace is qualified by the explicit indication that God also incorporates female qualities. As Creator, the Spirit of God both impregnates and broods: 'Dove-like satst brooding on the vast Abyss/ And mad'st it pregnant' (1.21–2). And the divine qualities of wisdom and (poetic) inspiration usually associated respectively with the Son of God and the Holy Spirit are in Milton's anti-trinitarian account described allegorically as female – 'sisters' who converse and play eternally in God's presence. (7.8–12).[24] We can hardly call *Paradise Lost* a feminist poem in any modern sense, but it reaches well beyond the cultural norms of Milton's era in representing women's worth, subjectivity, autonomy and values, and in anticipating many feminist concerns.

In the dramatic genres also, and in the setting of the fallen world, Milton portrays women of complexity, intellectual power and strong will. The plots of *A Masque* and *Samson* examine with considerable acuteness some classic patterns of women's victimization, but yet assume them capable of and responsible to the same standards of moral and spiritual action as men.

In *A Masque*, presided over by the Earl of Bridgewater and presented by his three children, a young and vulnerable virgin is in imminent danger of seduction or rape by a personage who represents sensuality and licentiousness, both in allegorical terms and as embodied in the contemporary Cavalier ethos.[25] Historical investigations have revealed that the plot probably alludes to a notorious scandal in which near female relatives of Bridgewater (Lady Castlehaven and her daughter) were victimized and prostituted by the husband and father; it may allude as well to a rape case involving a gentleman and a country girl which came under the Earl's jurisdiction.[26] In the masque, virtue triumphs more emphatically than it did in life, yet the work explores women's vulnerability to sexual victimization with considerable sensitivity – and with some daring, given that the endangered lady is enacted by Bridgewater's young daughter.

Earlier generations of (mostly male) critics used to identify strongly with Comus' arguments for sensual pleasure and delight, finding the Lady a cold prig and her defences of her chastity unappealing. But feminist attention to issues of rape and sexual exploitation on the contemporary scene should enable responses closer to those the text seems intended to foster and should enable us to hear the subtext of the Lady's argument: that she is right to resist such manipulative propositioning, and to determine for herself whether to accept this or any other sexual advance.

At the time of her temptation the Lady has lost her natural male protectors, her brothers. But she is shown to have a firmer intellectual grasp of the realities of life in the 'blind mazes of this tangl'd wood' (181) than they do. The Platonizing Elder Brother, serenely confident of the power of Chastity, tends to confuse his sister with Diana the huntress, invulnerable to harm and able for all conquests (420–46), while the fearful Younger Brother is convinced that she is helpless and certain to be ravished (393–407). The Lady, though, is quite sure she is not invulnerable: she is not proof against violence, nor against the forces of natural sensuality represented by Comus, which have power to 'immanacle' her body 'while Heav'n sees good' (665). Yet she relies with confidence upon her own virtue and the aid of heaven to preserve her essential moral integrity in whatever trials she may face. In the debate with Comus she claims only to be able to preserve her mind inviolate: 'Fool, do not boast,/ Thou canst not touch the freedom of my mind/ With all thy charms' (662–4).

That, however, is no mean feat, given Comus' 'dear Wit and gay Rhetoric' (790) which have bedazzled so many critics. It is now easier than it once was to see that the Lady has the better of the argument with Comus in sheerly intellectual terms. On the first issue, the nature of Nature, she denounces with keen logical incisiveness the 'false rules prankt in reason's garb' (759) which Comus derives from his eloquent description of a nature so excessively productive as to require the incessant and prodigal rifling of her over-burgeoning stores. Modern ecologists would second the Lady's insistence that this is absurd, that post-lapsarian Nature is very far indeed from needing humans to be 'riotous/ With her abundance' (763–4). The Lady's very different social and economic ideal is rooted in the medieval concept of the common good, but also anticipates modern egalitarian claims:

> If every just man that now pines with want
> Had but a moderate and beseeming share
> Of that which lewdly-pamper'd Luxury
> Now heaps upon some few with vast excess,
> Nature's full blessings would be well dispens't
> In unsuperfluous even proportion,
> And she no whit encumber'd with her store.
>
> (768–74)

The other issue, the value and power of chastity and virginity, the Lady simply refuses to debate with Comus because he is incapable of understanding the argument. Yet he himself testifies that the 'flame of sacred vehemence' she begins to display in that cause bathes him in a 'cold shudd'ring dew' (801–2). Conscious of defeat in argument, he turns to force, leaving no doubt whatever of the strength and sufficiency of this woman's intellect and character.

Again, when we look beyond the heroine to the whole work, we find further subversion of the assumptions of patriarchy. It is surprising to find that Lady Alice's younger brothers, especially the designated heir, are inferior to her in understanding the moral realities of the fallen world – for all their bookish philosophy and nobility of nature. It is still more surprising that their attempt to rescue their sister largely fails: they break Comus' cup, but their sword-play causes him to flee before they can reverse his rod, as the Attendant Spirit directed. In Freudian terms they cannot – as males – counteract Comus' phallic power, and so the Lady remains fast fixed to Comus' chair. Instead, the Lady is freed by a female power – the nymph Sabrina, who was herself an innocent maiden subjected to violence (by reason of her guilty birth) but who has now attained immortality as the protecting spirit of the River Severn. Sabrina's power to save has several sources: she is a figure of the (baptismal) grace needed to overcome fallen nature; she is a figure of nature as maternal and protecting; and she is an exemplar to the Lady of the triumph of one like herself – a maiden who is also a singer and poet. Sabrina's Song (890–900) serves as a long-delayed answer to the Lady's Echo Song (230–43), and those are the two loveliest lyrics in the masque. Sabrina's song figures the power of noble art and true poetry to reform fallen, unruly sensuality: she is the good poet and masquer who frees the Lady from the spell of the bad poet and masquer, Comus. She thereby provides a model for the Lady's self-definition and self-expression in poetry and in dance – notably in the main masque figure, in which the Lady with her brothers 'triumph in victorious dance/ O'er sensual Folly and Intemperance' (974–5). In *A Masque*, as in *Paradise Lost*, the province of women includes poetry and art.

Dalila in *Samson Agonistes* seems at first glance to be a counter-example, a bad woman who is the target of vehement misogynist outbursts by both Samson and the Chorus. Responding to this, some revisionist feminist essays have undertaken the defence of Dalila, claiming that her arguments and explanations have merit, that Samson unjustifiably rejects her expressions of repentance; and that her own actions in the service of her nation are the mirror-image of Samson's own.[27] But this is, I think, to take hold of the issue from the wrong end: the poem expects its readers to agree that Dalila's betrayal of her husband to the enemies who blinded and imprisoned him utterly violates the love and intimacy essential to a true marriage, and also violates basic humanity. And we are expected to recognize from Dalila's constant rhetoric of self-exculpation and her myriad shifting excuses that her claims of repentance are insincere.

Milton represents Dalila as a bad woman, but in terms which honour women more in the harshness of that representation than do the critics who seek to excuse her on her terms. Alerted by feminist analyses, we can recognize that Dalila is a site of all the stereotypes of the feminine in a patriarchal society, and that she is deliberately presented by Milton in such terms. She takes great care about her appearance, sailing in like a ship 'bedeckt, ornate and gay' with perfume and damsel train (712–21). She weeps delicately, 'like a fair flower surcharg'd with dew' (728). She bases her excuses for betraying Samson on feminine stereotypes: curiosity to know and tell secrets; women's frailty; domestic love, which sought to keep her husband safe at home. She also asserts her female weakness before the concerted pressure and strong arguments of civil and religious authority, and the authoritative maxims of 'wisest men':

> thou knowest the Magistrates
> And Princes of my country came in person,
> Solicited, commanded, theat'n'd, urg'd,
> Adjur'd by all the bonds of civil Duty
> And of Religion, press'd how just it was,
> How honorable, how glorious to entrap
> A common enemy, who had destroy'd
> Such numbers of our Nation: and the Priest
> Was not behind, but ever at my ear,
> Preaching how meritorious with the gods
> It would be to ensnare an irreligious
> Dishonorer of *Dagon*: what had I
> To oppose against such powerful arguments?
> Only my love of thee held long debate
> And combatted in silence all these reasons
> With hard contest: at length that grounded maxim
> So rife and celebrated in the mouths
> Of wisest men, that to the public good
> Private respects must yield, with grave authority
> Took full possession of me and prevail'd;
> Virtue, as I thought, truth, duty so enjoining.
>
> (850–70)

Milton's Dalila has internalized both the feminine stereotypes and the cultural constraints of her society, and makes them her excuses. But this text refuses them as excuses. At times it suggests, rather, that Dalila chooses to invoke these stereotypes and these authorities as a means of manipulation: that she deliberately puts them to work for her. Answering her, Samson, with all the polemic of the English civil war echoing in the background, flatly denies ultimate authority to civil or religious leaders, or to *raison d'état*.[28] He also claims that the inner experience of love, had it been genuine, would have secured Dalila against the claims of false ideology. Throughout the tragedy,

Samson continually holds Dalila and himself to the same harsh moral standard: 'all wickedness is weakness' (834). As a further basis for comparison, the text also holds before the reader the biblical examples of Judith and Jael – women whose similar actions, from better motives and in a better cause, are not directed against their husbands.

In his representation of Dalila, it is fair to say that Milton exposes, but does not realistically assess, the power of the feminine stereotypes, social authority and patriarchal ideology to constrain or determine women's behaviour. The fact is that Milton will not excuse woman or man on such grounds from the responsibility of developing a personal conscience and an integrated self: he invokes the same moral standard for both. Underlying that standard is his belief that the intellectual powers and qualities of women as well as men are sufficient to empower their freedom of choice, however complex the moral and political issues. We may call in question the possibility of this Miltonic ideal of human freedom and autonomy, but it is one which honours women highly. In this case it does so by insisting on the badness of Dalila.

Where then might we go from here in an engagement with Milton's texts which advances feminist concerns? One important direction will, I hope and expect, lead to further appropriation of cultural materialist and New Historicist methods, thus far most impressively applied to *A Masque*. This should produce more precise analyses of the seventeenth-century social and cultural milieu as well as of particular historial situations, allowing for more illuminating contextualizations of Milton's texts. Another important direction is that charted by Sandra Gilbert and Joseph Wittreich, inviting yet more extensive analyses of how Milton's texts have been constructed by women readers and writers of various kinds and in various eras, with attention both to common patterns and differences, and the reasons for them.

In addition, I hope that women may also be ready now to re-engage the Miltonic texts as whole works, looking beyond such fundamental issues as the portrayal of women, the construction of gender, and the ideology of patriarchy. In an era in which women have claimed equality in all the spheres of human life and human work (however limited has been the attainment of that equality) I would like to think that all the enduring human concerns of Milton's great poems might also be claimed by women readers as their province. In *Paradise Lost*, for example, I would hope we could all attend to the poem's complex and dramatic probing of many themes: order and chaos, creation and degeneration, liberty and tyranny, political demagoguery, the debasement of language, the processes of education, the complexities of moral choices, the meaning of heroism, the grounds for political rebellion, the sources of poetic creativity. And that we could all experience the power, beauty and pleasure of that poem by responding to it as an imagined poetic universe, created in a stunning variety of styles and genres.

Such reading and such response to vast poetic universes like *Paradise Lost* is in itself a means to liberation and empowerment, for women readers no less than men. One reason is that they invite imaginative and emotional engagement with structures of thought and feeling beyond the narrow bonds of our own experience. They can show us something *besides* our own faces, and so can provide some estranging perspectives on our contemporary pieties and ideologies, whatever they may be. Still more important, they invite us all to glory in the creative achievements of humankind, and (in the measure possible to our individual talents and circumstances) to share in them.

NOTES

1 'Milton on women – yet once more', *Milton Studies* VI, ed. James D. Simmonds, Pittsburgh: 1974, 3–20.

2 'Kinship and the role of women in *Paradise Lost*', *Milton Studies* IV (1972), 3–18. Landy responded to my essay with '"A Free and Open Encounter": Milton and the modern reader', *Milton Studies* 9 (1976), 3–36.

3 *PMLA* 93 (1978), 368–82. The essay is reprinted in, and its ramifications are explored at large in, Sandra Gilbert and Susan Gubar's important and influential study, *The Madwoman in the Attic: The Woman Writer and the Nineteenth-Century Literary Imagination*, New Haven and London: Yale University Press, 1979, pp. 187–212.

4 *Critical Enquiry* 10 (1983), 321–47. This essay was answered by Edward Pechter, 'When Pechter reads Fruola pretending she's Eve reading Milton; or, new feminist is but old priest writ large', *Critical Enquiry* 11 (1984), 163–70. Fruola responded with 'Pechter's specter: Milton's bogey writ small; or why is he afraid of Virginia Woolf?', *Critical Enquiry* 11 (1984), 171–8.

5 *The Troublesome Helpmate: a History of Misogyny in Literature*, Seattle: University of Washington Press, 1966, p. 158.

6 *Milton's Spenser: The Politics of Reading*, Ithaca, NY: Cornell

University Press, 1983, pp. 218–44.

7 'Female autonomy in Milton's sexual politics', in the important collection edited by Julia M. Walker, *Milton and the Idea of Woman*, Urbana and Chicago: University of Illinois Press, 1988, pp. 230–53. Also see essays by Mary Loeffelholz and Mary Nyquist, in Mary Nyquist and Margaret Ferguson (eds), *Re-Membering Milton*, New York and London: Methuen, 1987.

8 'When Eve reads Milton', p. 334.

9 'The politics of poetry: feminism and *Paradise Lost*', *Milton Studies* 14 (1980), 3–24.

10 *Milton's Eve*, Urbana, Chicago, London: University of Illinois Press, 1983; 'Eve and the arts of Eden' in Walker (ed.), *Milton and the Idea of Woman*, pp. 100–19; 'Subsequent or precedent? Eve as Milton's defence of poesie', *Milton Quarterly* 20 (1986), 132–6.

11 Kerrigan and Braden, 'Milton's coy Eve: *Paradise Lost* and Renaissance love poetry', *ELH*, 53 (1986), 27–51; W. Shullenberger, 'Wrestling with the angel: *Paradise Lost* and feminist criticism', *Milton Quarterly*, 20 (1986), 69–85; James G. Turner, *One Flesh: Paradisal Marriage and Sexual Relations in the Age of Milton*, Oxford: Clarendon Press, 1987; J. A. Wittreich, *Feminist Milton*, Ithaca and London: Cornell University Press, 1987. See also William Kerrigan's *The Sacred Complex: On the Psychogenesis of Paradise Lost*, Cambridge, MA: Harvard University Press, 1983, for a discussion in psychoanalytic terms of how Milton came to be able to oppose various social forms of patriarchy – his father, bishops and clergy, the King.

12 *Paradise Lost* (4.299). This and subsequent citations of Milton's poems in texts and notes are to Merritt Y. Hughes' edition, *John Milton: Complete Poems and Major Prose*, Indianapolis: Odyssey, 1957.

13 'Milton on women', pp. 5–6.

14 Italics mine.

15 For seventeenth-century marriage theory and Milton's relation to it, see, e.g., William and Malleville Haller, 'The Puritan art of love', *Huntington Library Quarterly* 5 (1942), 235–72; William Haller, 'Hail, wedded love', *ELH* 13 (1946), 79–97; John G. Halkett, *Milton and the Idea of Matrimony*, New Haven and London: Yale University Press, 1970; Lawrence Stone, *The Family, Sex, and Marriage in England, 1500–1800*, New York: Harper, 1977; James G. Turner, *One Flesh*.

16 See Barbara Lewalski, 'Innocence and experience in Milton's Eden', in Thomas Kranidas (ed.), *New Essays of Paradise Lost*, Berkeley: University of California Press, 1969, pp. 86–117.

17 See the classic discussions by Jacques Lacan of identity formation in terms of movement from a narcissistic 'mirror stage' to a symbolic stage in which the self is understood in terms of its various relationships, *Ecrits: A Selection*, ed. and trans. Alan Sheridan, New York: Norton, 1977, pp. 1–7, 30–113. Carol Gilligan has argued that relationships are more important to women's self-definition than to men's (*In a Different Voice: Psychological Theory and Women's Development*, Cambridge, MA: Harvard University Press, 1982).

Milton, however, seems to recognize no such distinction: in *Paradise Lost* Adam's need to find completion in a human relationship is even more acute than Eve's.

18 See Barbara Lewalski, *Paradise Lost and the Rhetoric of Literary Forms*, Princeton, NJ: Princeton University Press, 1985, pp. 173–219, 232–3.

19 This is a central theme in Milton's poetry and prose, most memorably argued in the *Areopagitica*. See the discussion of this issue by Susanne Woods, 'How free are Milton's women?', in Walker (ed.), *Milton and the idea of Woman*, p. 15–31.

20 I comment further on Eve's poems and her 'invention' of various literary genres in *Paradise Lost and the Rhetoric of Literary Forms*.

21 I owe the term to my friend and colleague in Milton studies, Earl Miner.

22 See the discussion of the various forms of prophecy and the ranking assigned to each in John Smith's long essay 'Of prophecy', in *Select Discourses*, London 1660.

23 Italics mine.

24 For a discussion of the 'feminine principle' embodied in *Paradise Lost* and some of its philosophical and psychological roots in the Renaissance, see Stevie Davies, *The Feminine Reclaimed: The Idea of Woman in Spenser, Shakespeare, and Milton*, Lexington: University of Kentucky Press, 1986.

25 The children are the Lady Alice Egerton (age fifteen), and her younger brothers John, Lord Brackley (eleven) and Thomas Egerton (nine). Two studies which emphasize Milton's masque as a critique of the Cavalier ethos are Maryann Cale McGuire, *Milton's Puritan Masque*, Athens, GA: University of Georgia Press, 1983; and Cedric C. Brown, *John Milton's Aristocratic Entertainments*, Cambridge: Cambridge University Press, 1985.

26 Bridgewater was brother-in-law to the much abused Countess of Castlehaven and uncle to her daughter Elizabeth. The sordid affair and its probable influence on the writing and initial reception of Milton's *Masque* is discussed in detail by Barbara Breasted, '*Comus* and the Castlehaven scandal', *Milton Studies*, 3 (1971). 201–24. The possible relevance of Bridgewater's jurisdiction in the matter of the rape of a fourteen-year-old serving maid, Margery Evans, by one Philbert Burghill and his party is discussed by Leah S. Marcus, 'Justice for Margery Evans: A 'local' reading of *Comus*', in Walker (ed.) *Milton and the Idea of Woman*, pp. 66–85.

27 See, e.g., Virginia Mollenkott, 'Relativism in *Samson Agonistes*', *Studies in Philosophy* 67 (1970), 89–102; John C. Ulreich, Jr, '"Incident to all our sex": the tragedy of Dalila', in Walker (ed.) *Milton and the Idea of Woman*, pp. 185–210; John Guillory, 'Dalila's House: *Samson Agonistes* and the sexual division of labor', in Margaret Ferguson, Maureen Quilligan and Nancy Vickers (eds) *Rewriting the Renaissance: The Discourses of Sexual Difference in Early Modern Europe*, Chicago and London: University of Chicago Press, 1986, pp. 106–22.

28 For a fine discrimination of these issues, see Mary Ann Radzinowicz, *Toward Samson Agonistes: The Growth of Milton's Mind*, Princeton, NJ: Princeton University Press, 1978. I discuss the matter further in 'Milton's *Samson* and the New Acquist of True [Political] Experience', *Milton Studies* 24 (1988).

3

GENDER AND CLASS IN *VILLETTE* AND *NORTH AND SOUTH*

Sally Minogue

'For the growing good of the world is partly dependent on unhistoric acts; and that things are not so ill with you and me as they might have been, is half owing to the number who lived faithfully a hidden life, and rest in unvisited tombs.' In her fine ending to *Middlemarch*[1] – a novel which begins with promises of female heroism and ends with unhistoric acts – George Eliot deliberately undercuts, almost rebukes, the expectations of her readers (especially of those who might have been disappointed in Dorothea's marriage to Will). In doing so she makes an appeal to universal suffering humanity much as she does in her mention of the unity of 'struggling erring human creatures',[2] though she also focuses that unity through a particular lens, that of the 'hidden life'. At first sight (and given Eliot's preceding image of rivers and tributaries) we might be tempted to apply to this William Empson's acute observations on Gray's 'Elegy': 'by comparing the social arrangement to Nature he makes it seem inevitable, which it was not, and gives it a dignity which was undeserved.'[3] But Eliot goes a step further than Gray, for she makes Dorothea's 'hidden life' her apotheosis. The force of her 'that things are not so ill with you and me as they might have been', wonderfully qualified by the honesty of 'partly dependent' and 'half owing', is that Dorothea's true heroism is in living just that kind of life, as so much of humanity must. The more Dorotheas who can pour their strength, as well as exact their price (Dorothea's may be Will), into the business of living, unheroic and unhistoric as it is, the more things will be 'not so ill with you and me', we who must also end in 'unvisited tombs'. Gray's poem, as Empson concedes – or rather asserts against himself – stated 'one of the permanent truths';[4] Eliot's strength is that she half-states a half-truth.

Eliot's appeal to the errant, to the stoical struggle to find a way forward through life, even one which will necessarily digress and divert, as the unifying, perhaps the constitutive, feature of humanity is one which the main thrust of both feminist and Marxist criticism of fiction has opposed. Indeed, feminist and Marxist critics oppose any notion of unification, since that is to betray the oppressed group for whom each speaks. The concept of the universal in literature has called forth their strongest opprobrium. Terry Eagleton, in an analysis close to Empson's of Gray's 'Elegy', argues that both in *Middlemarch*'s central web image, and 'in the novel's closing trope of the river, which in diffusing its force to tributaries intensifies its total impact, natural imagery is exploited to signify how a fulfilling relation to the social totality can be achieved, not by ideological abstraction, but by pragmatic, apparently peripheral work'.[5] Meanwhile Mary Jacobus, looking at Eliot's changes to a previous version of that ending, can find comfort in it only by seeing the river image as referring to the act of authorship itself: 'Dorothea's hidden life and entombment make her a silent reformer, an unremembered protester; but her silence and anonymity are the sacrifice which allows "George Eliot" speech and name.'[6] While Eagleton and Jacobus disagree in their particular interpretations of this ending (a disagreement which incidentally points towards an inevitable conflict between Marxist and feminist positions), none the less both are in agreement that the dependence of the realist novel on some notion of universal truth is to be attacked; indeed, it is the very business of the critic to attack it. Both are looking for fissures in the text. Jacobus characterizes such fissures as (using Virginia Woolf's words) 'awkward breaks', and she sees one such in the original ending of *Middlemarch*, which makes a specific attack on the 'social air' in which a woman's greatness is not allowed to flourish. She sees the ending as closing down that criticism into a universalization which is diffused into the particular.[7] Eagleton echoes the criticism:

> What cannot be resolved in 'historical' terms can be accommodated by a moralising of the issues at stake. This, indeed, is a mystification inherent in the very forms of realist fiction, which, by casting objective social relations into interpersonal terms, constantly hold open the possibility of reducing the one to the other.[8]

Both Eagleton and Jacobus, and Marxist and feminist critics in general, so far as they can be thus characterized, place the critic at the intersection of ideology and text. (Eagleton in *Criticism and Ideology* has a full and complex account of this placing, which none the less can be boiled down to the view that the text is the product of the relationship between the prevailing ideology and the general mode of production; that relationship issues in the literary mode of production, and the text is further modified by the author's own interaction with the prevailing ideology. The relationship between general ideology, literary mode of production and authorial insertion produces aesthetic ideology, which is but one form of general ideology. Thus the author and so the text is always a bearer, in some form, of the prevailing ideology.) But then each takes their interpretative position from their commitment to a particular base of analysis; for the feminist that analytic base is gender; for the Marxist it is class. Thus in each case the placing, and so the interpretation, will be determined by the base. Inevitably then, Marxist and feminist critics will arrive at different, and often conflicting, judgements.

That this conflict exists (creating particular problems for Marxist feminists) should lead us to look at its implications more closely. For while Eagleton and Jacobus might agree in their view of literature as a product of ideology, to be critically deconstructed in order to reveal its own determinants, how that deconstruction takes place may become a matter of competition. And the competition is not between ideologies so much as between oppressed groups; in fact, the high flown theorizing of both feminist and Marxist comes down eventually to what each considers to be the more important oppression. The oppressions in question issue, indeed reveal themselves, in terms only too real. While they may be the product of ideology, most people experience them in the real world, a world little touched either by ideological theory or by literary criticism. In this chapter I shall argue that an analysis of a novel mounted in terms of a single oppressed group will fall short, both in terms of our understanding of the novel and in terms of our understanding of the real relations (of gender or of class) of the world. I take as my primary example Charlotte Brontë's *Villette*, but introduce my discussion with a brief account of Elizabeth Gaskell's *North and South*. The nineteenth century naturally raises the question of class and the female authorship the question of gender, but my examples choose themselves since both novelists, and both novels, pervasively concern themselves with both issues. My claim is that if we reduce them critically to only, or either of, those issues, we reduce the novels. Furthermore, we reduce the sum of human understanding, rather than extending it. Finally, I would argue, a theoretical analysis in terms of gender or class actually draws our attention away from the real difficulties experienced by those oppressed groups, even as it pretends to address them. Thus I seek to argue for the importance of the novel's representation of universal truths, and at the same time to suggest that certain novels (*Villette* and *North and South* being examples) actually lend the oppressed a better model of subversiveness through a realist reading than through a Marxist or feminist one; and that furthermore the 'universal' and the 'subversive' come together in such novels.

My choice of George Eliot's remarks as touchstones – she who had to drop her given name and, arguably, her female identity in order to be published – might be seen as sufficient to throw doubt on her proud embrace of 'struggling erring human creatures'. It is one of the odd and impenetrable ironies of the nineteenth century that the writer who was most scornful in her actual life of social conventions and conditioning has survived in literary history with her pen name intact; while Charlotte Brontë was quickly freed of the liability of Currer Bell (an androgynous choice anyway); and Elizabeth Gaskell seems to be inextricably connected to her husband by the prefix Mrs. These ironies are certainly suggestive, as are the bare facts of a publishing world where both women and those struggling in an economic and social sense were not regarded as fit for authorship. Yet it is here that the first conflict between analyses in terms of class and gender threatens. It is a brute fact that in the nineteenth century women were remarkably successful as authors and remained critically successful, since the 'big names' of the period in which fiction itself was the flourishing and predominant form are female. And they are *women's* names, and we know them to be so; that is, we know that it was a woman who wrote *Middlemarch* in spite of the fact that we call her by a 'man's' name – indeed, our perception of that name *as* male is altered by our knowledge that the owner of the name was female. The pre-eminence of female writers in that period is such that Sandra Gilbert and Susan Gubar, writing about the absence of female poets in the tradition, see the nineteenth-century novel as definitely female in origin.[9] Yet working-class writers have no recognized place in nineteenth-century fiction, with the exception of what is seen as a different sort of fiction, popular fiction, that categorization itself militating against a serious consideration or evaluation of the work (and even where that is undertaken, it must be marked by a certain kind of artificiality, with its attendant dangers of patronization or annexation).[10] Thus we cannot even equate the kinds of silencing of minority voices which took place in the novel tradition; suddenly in the nineteenth century, women – of a certain class – were freed into print; while the working man – and, of course, woman – remained, unsurprisingly, in chains.

Does this distinction affect the way in which we look at the nineteenth-century novel? Should it? For the feminist, certainly it should, since she is committed to the view that oppression and misogyny had characterized both the representation and the writing power of women up to that point. If in the nineteenth century that gave way to something different for women, while it did not for another oppressed group, should not the other oppressed group be given priority, particularly as that group contains women? But here is the problem. The oppressed class in the one case is determined by gender; in the other case it is determined by socioeconomics. While class cuts across the category of gender, gender cannot contain the category of class. Analogies of disadvantage are not sufficient to settle this difference, which cuts to the heart of both politics. As a result, there is a certain embarrassment for the feminist critic who looks at nineteenth-century fiction without an awareness of class; for if the critic is to expose the oppression of her own sex, must she not be equally aware of the double oppression suffered by members of her sex who are also members of an oppressed class? Yet characteristically that question is not addressed. Sandra Gilbert and Susan Gubar in *The Madwoman in the Attic*[11] clearly announce their terms of interest in the nineteenth-century novel, and while their theory may be sophisticated, their sense of priority is not. Gender is the key, even while women write the novels and working people of either sex remain unheard. Similarly, Terry Eagleton, in his influential *Myths of Power*, announces his view that in the conflicts within Charlotte Brontë's work 'it is possible to decipher...a fictionally transformed version of the tensions and alliances between the two social classes which dominated the

Brontës' world: the industrial bourgeoisie, and the landed gentry or aristocracy';[12] and while he pays lip-service to the Brontës' being women, 'members of a cruelly oppressed group whose victimized condition reflected a more widespread exploitation',[13] his analysis of the novels themselves belies that awareness. Feminists and Marxists, instead of being generous to each other's oppressions, have placed themselves in competition.

A further difficulty with both sorts of analysis is that they find duality attractive. The analysis in terms of class tends to set up a productive conflict; the feminist analysis tends to deconstruction, inserting itself in the gap between what is 'there' and what is 'not'. In either case the result often is to simplify into opposition elements which actually have a much more complex, shifting and fruitful relationship.

Elaine Showalter characterizes fiction written by women in three ways, as feminine, feminist and female, each progressively more progressive. She places Elizabeth Gaskell firmly in the first category, the 'prolonged phase of imitation of the prevailing modes of the dominant tradition'.[14] At the same time, she also categorizes her as a social novelist, one intimately concerned with the effects of industrialization, and genuinely interested in the nature of class conflict. These fixed characterizations imply a necessarily rigid reading of Gaskell's *North and South*, which the very title also seems to invite. A gender-based characterization would notice the emphasis in the novel on self-fulfilment and independence in the heroine, the rejection of obvious forms of dependence (as typified by the silly Edith and Mrs Hale), yet at the same time the celebration of female virtues of sensitivity, the reduction of large-scale issues to the level of individual relationships; and the ultimate capitulation, of heroine and author, to marriage, with the handy proviso of the heroine's holding the economic whip-hand. The independence is illusory, the patterns patriarchal. A similar compromise might be noted in a class-based characterization, but this time between an effete and cultured bourgeoisie and a rampant manufacturing class, the latter brought to heel by the former's possession of capital, but also injecting a strain of new blood into the old to revitalize and regenerate it. The unusual step taken by Gaskell of giving the working class a voice in the novel leaves them in just the same place at the end; the change has taken place in their masters. And furthermore this change has been represented in terms of interpersonal relationships, as, indeed, has the voicing of working-class ideals. Genuine address of the systems of ideology is thus side-stepped, subsumed in the ideal of the individual happy within the institutionalized relationship, with a modicum of independence – but only a modicum.

Key to either analysis is the central figure of Margaret (who was originally intended as an eponymous heroine) who mediates between North and South, between an agrarian economy and a manufacturing one, between master and man, and even between 'dissenter' and 'infidel'. In the gender-based analysis she stands uncomfortably between these categories, opposing the simple femininity of her cousin and mother, yet demonstrating the feminine virtues of service and self-sacrifice, refusing offers of marriage and imagining a life without marriage, only to succumb to it in the last reel. In the class-based analysis she might represent compromise without opposition, the colonial missionary gone native who influences her lover to be kind to the exploited even as she lends him the money with which further to exploit them. Crucial to either analysis is the ending of the novel, when Margaret suddenly and, some might say, improbably, nestles her head on her lover's shoulder as he had imagined in his dreams, thus closing the novel firmly against any more ambiguous or uncertain reading.

In fact, the abruptness of the ending derives from the practical demands of serialization, though Gaskell rather conveniently reflects that she is not sure but that it might not have happened like this, when it happened, anyway. *Pace* reader response, perhaps we should curb our desires to read anything significant into an ending thus determined by pragmatic rather than creative considerations (though the Marxist would certainly see such considerations as part of the restrictive apparatus of the prevailing ideology). Certainly, the ending belies the emotional, social and moral complexity of the novel; and the monolithic readings sketched – albeit with a touch of caricature – above, give no clue to the genuine revolutions of thought and feeling with which the novel is concerned.

Suppose we take the representations of reality in the novel temporarily at face value. How many nineteenth-century novels allow the direct expression of a working-class voice? We need only think of the representations of the union in Dickens' *Hard Times* to appreciate Gaskell's chapter 'What is a strike?' There we find a good question – and a good answer. Furthermore, the answer is couched as a dispute, with Higgins getting the better of Margaret. Margaret may be there because of her patronizing instincts carried through from Helstone; but that is not why she remains, nor why she sustains her relationship with Higgins. We further see him disputing with Mr Hale (about religion) and then with Mr Thornton (about the conditions of working men) on even terms, and thus presenting his arguments directly to the reader. Higgins' place in the narrative structure of the novel, his direct speech (in dialect) and his moral place (as questioner of prevailing values), render him a central figure, especially as an agent of change. We see this change taking place on the surface, through discussion; on a symbolic level, through action; and in the interior, through changes of value and judgement.

Margaret is a further agent of this impulse to change. We see her early priggish judgements about tradesmen, at Helstone, give way to a much more considered and intimate understanding, to a point where, when she sees her brother Frederick express an easy contempt for the rough figure presented by Thornton, she remembers and regrets the days when she too made such judgements. The same shift of awareness is carried through many times in the novel, most powerfully in the narrative return to Helstone seen from a post-Milton viewpoint. The return is prefigured in Mr Bell's dream of the Helstone of his and Mr Hale's youth: 'Over babbling brooks they took impossible leaps, which seemed to keep them whole days suspended in the air. Time and space were not, though all other things seemed real. Every event was measured by the emotions of the mind, not by its actual existence, for existence it had none' (XLV, 377).[15] When Margaret and Mr Bell arrive at the real Helstone, Margaret finds that her view of the place is indeed measured by the emotions of the mind; and she finds it wanting. It is not the golden and unchanging place she goes to look for; not only has the vicarage been altered – is in the process of alteration – to accommodate new generations of children; even the trees have changed, including the beech where she and Lennox sketched, the scar on its trunk erased by its own disappearance, presaging the erasure of the scar left by Lennox's proposal. Summarizing the idea makes it crude; but Margaret's visit confirms a lesson she has been learning and which is perfected by her Cromer holiday with its long bouts of reflection, that she herself is constantly changing and that 'the emotions of the mind' are themselves subject to change. But they are also subject to reflection and to the power of the will. 'All this time for thought enabled Margaret to put events in their right places, as to origin and significance, both as regarded her past life and her future...she had learnt, in those solemn hours of thought, that she herself must one day answer for her own life, and what she had done with it' (XLIX, 409–10).

Gaskell manages to marry here a representation of reality (the relations of Margaret's everyday life, for example, and the pressures which changing circumstances exert upon her) with an awareness of the shifting nature of that reality and of the falsity of individual representations of it (revealed in Mr Bell's dream, and in the gulf between the 'old' Helstone and the 'new'). Likewise, she persuades us of the truth of the perception that events are measured 'by the emotions of the mind', even as she shows us that those emotions will not in themselves suffice when each of us must one day answer for our own lives. This truth applies to Higgins as well as to Margaret. Higgins finds a public as well as a private solution; he strikes because he is not only a private man; he goes to work for Thornton because he is not only a public one. The two are married by his sense of responsibility for the family of Boucher. For Margaret, her grappling with Eagleton's 'objective social relations' can only be managed in personal terms; they are all that are available to her. So it is with many people, who attempt to work out the relations of public and private responsibility, and attempt to work them out in the constraints provided. Even so, Margaret challenges the accepted social relations of her gender, in her response to the demands others make upon her. She is her father's spokesman, the family decision-maker, protector of Thornton against the strikers even while she sympathizes with their cause through her conversations with Higgins. Her terrible anguish in deciding to call home her brother Frederick to her mother's deathbed, and her deep sense of shame that Thornton has taken her humane act of protection as a personal one, deepened by her different (and revealing) shame at her immoral (and illegal) concealment of the truth to protect her brother – all show the great burden of responsibility placed on her. We do not need the contrast of the vapid Edith to point this out.

North and South is constantly questioning, by engaging the reader narratively with its own processes of change and shifts of judgement. Mr Hale dissents from the religion he has been preaching for twenty years; his son Frederick is in exile because of his part in a naval mutiny; Margaret up-ends her whole way of life when she arrives in Milton, taking on the responsibilities abdicated by both her mother and her father; Thornton abandons the fixed precepts by which he had formerly lived; even Mrs Thornton bends sufficiently at the dying Mrs Hale's request to look on Margaret in a kinder light. In one sense the worker Higgins and his daughter Bessie are the most unbending of the characters represented, yet they are so in ways directly opposed to each other! Why should we not take this questioning at face value and see it as instructive about our objective social relations? It is not as if, by doing so, we are abandoning our sense of disbelief. We know that this is a novel, we know that it embodies certain conventions, that those speak to a prevailing set of social expectations. We know that *North and South* sufficiently accepted those conventions and expectations; after all, it was published. But, being published, and so being read, it could reveal its subversiveness to the thinking reader; in the light of the extraordinary challenges it offers to accepted thinking, about class and about gender, but also about love, and religious belief, and authority, and law, the sweetness and completeness of the ending may disappoint. But we may also be free to think that Margaret deserves her supporting shoulder. Unless we sustain some acceptance of the realist aims of the novel, we cannot learn the complicated truths it is offering, within whose truths we also see conventional stereotypes of class and gender overturned. Would we learn so much from a Marxist or feminist reading?

North and South stands against absolute judgement, nicely caught at the end by Margaret's and Thornton's parody of themselves in others' eyes as 'that man' and 'that woman'. Like *North and South*, *Villette* slips the harness of the conventionally judgemental structure of the novel, espousing the power of change, indeed of revolution. Yet it does so in 'incalculably diffusive ways' which defy the constrictions of class or gender which critics have tried to place upon it. Under its power the categories themselves begin to fall away, and the difficult, complex, slippery nature of the fiction is revealed, rendering the comparison of oppressions or conflicts myopic.

The various feminist analyses of Charlotte Brontë, and of *Villette* in particular, share the view that Brontë's is undoubtedly an unusual and individualistic voice. Yet, with the notable exception of Kate Millett[16] (which must now be counted an early version of feminist criticism, though it continues to be an influential one), there is always an element of doubt in the analyses. This doubt characteristically expresses itself, more or less strongly, in terms of Brontë's interaction with the male tradition. Her case highlights the difficulties feminists encounter in applying a feminist analysis to women writing in a male-dominated society. These writers cannot be admitted to be entirely free; if they were it would undermine some of the central tenets of feminist criticism (that male culture has unvoiced women, that women writing in a patriarchal culture must conform to some extent to its norms, that none the less the main thrust of such women writers is a hidden subversiveness). Thus the analysis emerges that such writers made some sort of pact or compromise with male convention. The task of the feminist critic becomes the deconstruction of that compromise, and the seeing through to what 'really' underlies it. For instance, Rosalind Miles is categorical in her account of Brontë: 'Ultimately, then, Charlotte always supports the conventional assumptions in her use of the traditional theme of the woman's need of man.'[17] Further, 'Nowhere in Charlotte's fiction is there any attempt to challenge these assumptions of her society in ways which insist on appropriately feminine modes of self-expression.'[18] Quite why Miles calls the writers she considers by their first names, which to me seems to reduce their importance beside our critical practice with men's names (imagine chatting familiarly about Marcel's understanding of memory or David Herbert's forked flame). She also sticks to Mrs Gaskell in spite of her strictures against marriage as a destructive force for women writers. But Miles' view is a rather more aggressively stated and less thoroughly argued position than that extensively explored in Gubar and Gilbert's now classic text, *The Madwoman in the Attic*. Gubar and Gilbert's overall thesis, strongly argued in their first two chapters, 'The queen's looking glass' and 'Infection in the sentence', is that women up to the nineteenth century were systematically denied the rights of authorship ('If a pen is the metaphorical penis, with what organs can females generate texts?'),[19] and that those who attempted the pen thereafter were forced into certain conflict between the two images of women (angel and harlot), the role of woman and the role of author, and their own 'female' identity and that forced upon them by male literary convention.

Specifically, Gilbert and Gubar identify the outcome of some of these conflicts as a central motif in nineteenth-century female fiction, that of 'the madwoman in the attic' who, they suggest, embodies the anger, resentment and repression which the female author really wants to express, but which she has had to constrain within patriarchal convention, both social and literary. A key passage defines their thesis:

> Even the most apparently conservative and decorous women writers obsessively create fiercely independent characters who seek to destroy all the patriarchal structures which both their authors and their authors' submissive heroines seem to accept as inevitable. Of course, by projecting their rebellious impulses not into their heroines but into mad or monstrous women (who are suitably punished in the course of the novel or poem), female authors dramatize their own self-division, their desire both to accept the strictures of patriarchal society and to reject them...[this madwoman] is usually in some sense the author's double, an image of her own anxiety and rage.
>
> (p. 78)

Gilbert and Gubar argue that this conflict and duality itself begins to form a new, essentially female, tradition, which can be traced through different writers' engagement with it. 'For the great women writers...danced out of the debilitating looking glass of the male text into the health of female authority' (p. 82) – but with the final caveat that none the less secrecy characterized the process, and 'to be secret is to be secreted'(p. 83).

Both Miles' and Gilbert and Gubar's views are developed critiques embracing the categories suggested in Elaine Showalter's formative feminist work, *A Literature of Their Own*. Brontë is subsumed in her 'feminine' category as imitating patriarchal convention and internalizing 'its standard of art and its views on social roles'.[20] Interestingly, one of the foremost expressions of a Marxist view of *Villette*, Eagleton's *Myths of Power*, characterizes the work in a similar way, feeling that since it attempts to be revolutionary, its failure to carry that through is the more disappointing: '*Villette* is in some ways a more tragic work than *Jane Eyre*, but it is also more accommodating, more concerned to muffle

direct antagonism.' And again, 'The world is to be temporised
with rather than severely challenged...as Lucy goes on to tease
out the contradiction [between the value and non-value of social
position], the balance tips quietly on the side of the world.'[21]

When many people argue the same position, even from
different intellectual bases, we need to look closely to see whether
there is truth in what they say. How far is *Villette* in complicity
with patriarchal literary convention, and are those critics who
argue that it compromises too much (with the social order,
capitalist or patriarchal) correct? It is my contention that if we
look at the work untied as far as possible from a preconceived
political/critical position, we shall see that it is far more
subversive than either feminist or Marxist will admit. Further, I
would argue that this subversion depends for our understanding
of it on a freeing of ourselves from any position other than that of
being 'struggling erring human creatures'.

I recall very clearly my first reading of *Villette*. For the first few
chapters I felt quite sure that the work centred on Polly, and I had
no awareness of Lucy Snowe, narrator.

Thus, so cleverly, and with a studied but hidden cleverness
which we may notice only on re-reading, does Brontë irresistibly
establish the way in which society tends to ignore people such as
Lucy Snowe.[22] As society ignores her – even as her closest
companions ignore her – so does the reader. It is not until chapter
IV that Lucy swims more centrally into the picture, and even here
Brontë casually dismisses a whole portion of her life without
much consideration: 'I will permit the reader to picture me, for
the next eight years, as a bark slumbering through halcyon
weather, in a harbour still as glass....Picture me then idle, basking,
plump, and happy, stretched on a cushioned deck , warmed with
constant sunshine, rocked by breezes indolently soft.' We know
at once that the statement is ironic; yet Brontë allows *us*, the
reader, the luxury of imagination (a fiction within a fiction), even
before her gently puncturing remark: 'However, it cannot be
concealed that, in that case, I must somehow have fallen over-
board',[23] which leads us directly into the transformed metaphor –
the first of the several storms which are to punctuate the novel.

Brontë's handling of tone throughout these first four chapters
is nothing short of stunning; even in the brief passage just quoted,
she has the reader guessing, complicitous in her irony, and then
plunged into passion a few lines later. None of it rings false,

perhaps because we have been wrong-footed from the start. As it begins to dawn that Lucy is both worthy of our interest and is, in *fact*, going to be the centre of our interest (like it or not), we become ready for anything. It is not unlike Emily Brontë's device in *Wuthering Heights* – the stolid Lockwood listening to the unshakeable Nellie Dean – what chance does the humble reader have of entertaining a doubt about the extraordinary events related? Except that here the device works in the opposite direction: from Polly we expect passion and sensation; when we realize that Lucy is our central interest, since we have scarcely noticed her, we expect nothing – and so she is free to do anything, everything.

Gilbert and Gubar, Miles *et al.* see this, and other, novels as reflecting a duality of spirit; Eagleton likewise. But there are more than two voices in *Villette*. What the shiftingness of style and narration in the early part of the novel does, as it unsettles the reader, is to make the reader ready to listen to more than one voice. Stability is there in the presence of the I that is Lucy Snowe; her quiet start paradoxically makes her more reliable as a presence. Yet almost from the start we are aware that the I that is Lucy is no simple ego. Consider this passage, just after Polly's beloved father has left Bretton: 'During an ensuing space of some minutes, I perceived she endured agony. She went through, in that brief interval of her infant life, emotions such as some never feel....Nobody spoke. Mrs Bretton, being a mother, shed a tear or two. Graham, who was writing, lifted up his eyes and gazed at her. I, Lucy Snowe, was calm'(ch. III). It is true that Lucy is calm; but her full knowledge and complete understanding of the child's sufferings, which she has not yet learnt to contain, her predictions of her future ('she would have more of such instants if she lived'), and the weight and depth of these and of her contained calmness beside the vapid responses of Mrs Bretton's motherly 'tear or two' and Graham's lack of action, tell us that Lucy has already known such sufferings, already learnt to contain them, and to be calm in the face of them. Lucy's is the calm of knowledge. Nor is it without sympathy, of a deeper nature than Mrs Bretton's, but a sympathy tempered by both the knowledge that survival necessitated the suppression of such uncontained grief, and by her own success in doing that.

Much of *Villette* is about suffering – its power, its centrality, the power it bestows on those who learn to survive it. Even at this stage, Lucy has learnt to survive it; and we know why she has had to do so, because we as readers have been enmeshed in the responsibility of ignoring her.

These remarks are, of course, interpretative. But they are interpretative remarks which do not try to blinker themselves in advance. What I am writing here may certainly be reactive, that is, I am actively seeking evidence in the work counter to the evidence put forward by feminist critics. But what I have to say here remains broadly true to my first experience of the work, an experience which still seems to me to answer to the central qualities of the novel. Gilbert and Gubar state that 'Lucy's repression is a response to a society cruelly indifferent to women'; Miles states that Brontë's heroines 'fight with traditionally masculine weapons of courage and self-assertion for the masculine rights of liberty and work'[24] (this is seen as a succumbing to male conventions and values). Eagleton meanwhile, responding precisely to the passage I discuss above, describes her 'coolly analytic brand of observation',[25] and later generalizes her attitude to Polly (which he sees suppresses some of Polly's own emotion) as 'a subconscious tactical conversion of suppressed jealousy to mature condescension'[26] (so much for Eagleton's understanding of 'a cruelly oppressed group whose victimised condition reflected a more widespread exploitation'). Are any of these what Lucy Snowe's suffering, her repression of suffering, her coming to terms with it, and her finding for a strong and fruitful way of life, are really about?

Certainly, Lucy's suffering springs in large measure from her being a woman, and Lucy's plight speaks strongly and in a particular way to women. But might it not – *does* it not – also speak to men, particularly those who have known loneliness, isolation, the peculiar feeling of being alien (in religion, country, culture)? Does it not also speak to those, like Graham and Mrs Bretton, who know the familial and familiar comforts, and perhaps even the added comfort of ignoring those who lie outside that, once they are not needed? Does it not speak to anyone who has been on the edge of any of these feelings or situations, but not fully realized them, or realized the positions of those who find themselves in them? It is wonderful, and brave, that Charlotte Brontë revealed these feelings and situations, through the exploration of the life of a *woman*, a woman who was *single*, a woman who was friendless and without economic support, and who thus had to *work*, and find her own means of support, social and emotional as well as economic, who was in both a foreign country and one dominated by an alien religion, where she had to expose herself by teaching, and where her strongest hopes and feelings were constantly disappointed. These are human conditions. Any one of them might reduce a person to the defences Eagleton eagerly identifies. They are not specific to being a woman, even as they are accentuated by so being; they would be similarly accentuated by being disadvantaged in a number of ways, for example, being working-class, though of course a working-class person would not have had the means to travel abroad. My point is this: when, for example, we get to the central section where Lucy Snowe is left isolated, truly single, in the ominously titled 'The Long Vacation', caring for the poor 'deformed and imbecile pupil', is an analysis in terms of either gender or class to the point? M. Paul leaves her with 'Pauvrette!'; Mme Beck takes her children to the seaside; teachers go to friends; Lucy is alone. The language of the passage which explores her mental chaos, her despair and terrible loneliness of spirit, recalls the storms of the beginning and end of the novel (this is intentional on Brontë's part, as I shall show), and much of it is melodramatic. But within the structure of the novel it transcends its own melodrama. As at the beginning of the novel, Brontë shifts her reader from any preconceived stance, forestalls any uncertainty:

> Religious reader, you will preach to me a long sermon about what I have just written, and so will you, moralist: and you, stern sage: you, stoic, will frown; you, cynic, sneer; you, epicure, laugh. Well, each and all, take it your own way. I accept the sermon, frown, sneer, and laugh; perhaps you are all right: and perhaps, circumstanced like me, you would have been, like me, wrong. The first month was, indeed a long, black, heavy month to me.

> (ch. XV)

Lucy's extremity is so great that she seeks out a priest of the Catholic religion so alien to her. Indeed the narrative structure of this chapter is essential to the way it moves us; it is the very *realism* of Lucy's situation which cannot fail to grip us here, whatever the metaphorical excesses embodied within it. And her direct address to the reader, just quoted, disarms any criticism. Who would be certain enough not to recognize this grief? When

Lucy, in the agony of her mind, seeks an ear – any ear – she tells us 'the mere relief of communication in an ear which was human and sentient, yet consecrated – the mere pouring out of some portion of long accumulating, long pent-up pain into a vessel whence it could not be again diffused – had done me good, I was already solaced.' Lucy does not repeat the experience; feeling stronger, she feels again fearful of Catholicism; but she says, 'He was kind when I needed kindness; he did me good' (ch. XV). Lucy's sacrifice of her religious prejudices, and the priest's of his, indeed represent the beginning of salvation for Lucy, the beginning of a way out of the long tunnel of loneliness which is the long vacation; the Brettons, with their bourgeois generosity, which is generosity even as the gift is limited, do the rest.

Eagleton's comment on this section is: 'it is precisely in the disproportion of sensibility to material situation, the imaginative surplus value, as it were, that the measure of Lucy's victimisation can be taken' but 'There is little in *Villette*, however, to motivate Lucy's emotional torment'.[27] Miles does not specifically discuss the passage, but she seems to rule out anything subversive about it when she states that 'nowhere in Charlotte's fiction is there any attempt to challenge these assumptions of her society' (the assumptions being the 'rights of liberty and work').[28] For this exploration of an individual's suffering, abandoned by all around her, with the charge of someone suffering even more than herself (to whom, incidentally, she is unable to give the comfort she in turn seeks from others), her decline almost into madness as the result of others' carelessness of her, her preparedness to cross stark religious and dogmatic boundaries (and the priest's in return) – are these not subversive? Gubar and Gilbert discuss this passage with an awareness of Lucy's suffering; yet again it is made subject to their thesis: 'the cretin is a last nightmarish version of herself', 'she can only escape one confining space for an even more limiting one, the confessional', 'Catholicism seems to represent the institutionalization of Lucy's internal schisms', and 'Lucy will become increasingly certain....t..at the church is a patriarchal structure with the power to imprison her' (pp. 414–15). Like Eagleton, Gubar and Gilbert find Lucy's breakdown to be 'mysterious': 'unless one interprets backwards from the breakdown, it is almost incomprehensible' (p. 416). One cannot help but think again of Lucy's – Brontë's – words: 'perhaps, circumstanced like me, you would have been, like me, wrong.'

The subversiveness of the novel, I am suggesting, lies in the way it concentrates the reader's attention on areas not usually the focus of attention, even in the ever-changing and developing nineteenth-century novel. It further lies in the way the author constantly keeps the reader imaginatively, emotionally and morally on his/her toes, unable to maintain any preconceptions in these vital areas; ready, in the end, to be surprised. And this subversiveness also extends to the exploitation of the romance conventions within which the novel is assuredly written, in a way which eventually undermines and disempowers those conventions. Beyond that, do we have to limit or define the nature of the subversiveness, that is, see it as anti-patriarchal (or failing to be so) or anti-ruling class? If we look at the three areas of subversiveness I have suggested, we shall find that either narrowing perspective actually detracts from the potential 'disruptiveness' of *Villette*.

I have begun to outline above some of the ways in which the novel makes us think about what is often held aside in the nineteenth-century novel. Again, the narrative structure of the novel emphasizes this, beginning with what we should expect to be central. Cleverly, that 'false' beginning itself deals with some genuine suffering, that of Polly on being left (abandoned, as she feels it) by her father. But it is in the excesses of *this* grief that we can find the 'flamboyant Romanticism' which Eagleton characterizes as one side of the duality to be found in Brontë's work (the other half is 'bourgeois rationality', and Eagleton sees the opposition of the two as structurally reflecting the 'complex structure of convergence and antagonism between the landed and industrial sectors of the contemporary ruling class').[29] This grief, with its wild outpourings, is solacing within the solid, comfortable, emotional calm of the Bretton household, and its transference to a besotted love for Graham (eventually to be requited and consummated) is what Lucy Snowe – and with her, in the narrative structure, Charlotte Brontë – rejects, indeed, almost contemptuously. As Lucy knows, she is in the real world, not a child (which Polly never truly ceases to be), and there will be no reliable comfortings or magical passions to assuage her grief. She sticks to stoicism and thus wards off possible disappointment; if no one sees her suffering, she won't feel the positive lack of solace which might be the response to *seen* suffering. This initial narrative device works all the more powerfully because, as the novel progresses and more and more of Lucy's inner self is revealed to us, so does she relax her tight grip upon herself and accept more potential happiness with its attendant risk of being disappointed. And of course, she is not disappointed in being disappointed! So Lucy's stoicism is shown, as we come to know her, and as she is freed into a foreign culture, not even to be a standard stoicism, simply opposed to the passions of a Polly. Indeed, when Polly reappears in the novel, we see that her childlike passions have not progressed or developed in any way; they are static, petrified into the patterns set in her early experience in the Bretton household (obsessive love of her father, transferred into similar love for Graham/John). How little has changed in Polly actually re-emphasizes how much has changed in Lucy (or at least in our understanding of her) since the beginning of the novel. We remember Lucy's earlier fears for Polly, and she reiterates what they *had* been after Paulina tells her of the mutual love between herself and Graham/John; Lucy puts Polly's escape from those projected unhappinesses down to Providence and circumstance, and certainly she has not had the hardship which Lucy has known. But when, for example, M. de Bassompierre says, somewhat reprovingly, to his daughter, who has been naively enquiring into the way Lucy makes her living: 'If my Polly ever came to know by experience the uncertain nature of this world's goods, I should like her to act as Lucy acts: to work for herself, that she might burden neither kith nor kin' (ch.XXV) we feel that the circumstance itself is unimaginable. Even her fond father sees his daughter's shortcomings here, and knows that Lucy is the worthier of the two women. Lucy *is* a woman, while Polly is, and will remain, a girl.

Yet – and here is the true quality of the novel's tone – Brontë does not condemn Polly. Lucy's words to her, as it were, giving her blessing to her union with Graham/John and recognizing its rightness, are both generous and correct. Again, the shifting nature of the narrative helps to emphasize this, for while Lucy in the novel's narrative is at the mercy, at the call of the Brettons and the de Bassompierres (she goes through a period of being ignored after the Vashti fire, no doubt because Polly is the Brettons' new toy), it is Lucy's moral judgement which Polly needs; and it is her moral judgement which also carries the reader. We see her approval of the match as both generous and just – aptly because she has prepared us for it by distancing herself morally from Dr

John by this stage. She does this first at the Vashti performance where, even with her loving eyes, she sees and understands John clearly: she has just described her own intense reactions to Vashti's wild, amoral plunging into passion, when she looks at her companion: 'it amused and enlightened me to discover that he was watching that sinister and sovereign Vashti, not with wonder, nor worship, not yet dismay, but simply with intense curiosity' (ch. XXII). Curiosity is the coolest of responses that Lucy could imagine to this performance; her name may be Snowe, but the benevolent Dr John is at heart much colder. It is not surprising that John saves Polly from the fire, as it were, generated by Vashti; neither has a truly fired soul. That belongs to Lucy, who sits calm when told to, finds strength to follow John when told to, and remarks, without irony but with understanding, 'Next morning's papers explained that it was but some loose drapery on which a spark had fallen, and which had blazed up and been quenched in an instant.'

We are not surprised, then, to find that the next chapter begins with Lucy's abandonment, not *to* someone but *by* someone. The disappointment she had foreseen, continues to foresee and understand, is at hand. We move from the overt symbolism and theatrical drama of the Vashti chapter back to the introspection and directness of:

> Those who live in retirement, whose lives have fallen amid
> the seclusion of schools or of other walled-in and guarded
> dwellings, are liable to be suddenly and for a long while
> dropped out of the memory of their friends, the denizens of
> a freer world. Unaccountably, perhaps, and close upon
> some space of unusually frequent intercourse...there falls a
> still pause, a wordless silence, a long blank of oblivion.
>
> (ch. XXIV)

Anyone who has known loneliness at the hands of a sociable and institutionalized society will feel a shiver at these words – man and woman alike. Lucy's recounting of the receipt of the longed-for letter, only to find it is from the mother rather than the son, similarly strikes at the heart. What prevents Lucy's almost stoical response from being self-sacrificing and (ch. XXIV) self-effacing ('Life is still life, whatever its pangs')? Again, I suggest, the narrative technique, which gives us first another voice, the epistolary voice, here carrying with it the normality of ordinary, protected life against which our knowledge of Lucy's is set (note the tone of 'It occurs to me to enquire what you have been doing with yourself for the last month or two...'). Yet what is this ordinary voice saying? The letter is a long and self-indulgent account, to an ear which it *knows* will share its feelings, of a mother's almost passionate admiration for her son. Introducing a playful anecdote in which she has wound a turban round her son's 'dark, glossy chestnut' hair while he slept, she says: 'While he slept, I thought he looked very bonny, Lucy: fool as I am to be so proud of him; but who can help it? Show me his peer.' Later, she talks of him as 'my lord' and wishes Lucy could have shared the moment.

This extraordinary contrast of tone, reminding us of both the difference of the Brettons' life from Lucy's, and yet also its lack of ordinariness, the passion which can underlie the bourgeois mother's constantly ironic playfulness with her son (and which perhaps can only be admitted to one such as Lucy, even within an epistolary anecdote), could only be carried off within a narrative which has so many shifts about it. And the biggest shift (one difficult to recall after many readings) is that which now brings the Polly of the first chapters into proper focus in the later. It is at this moment revealed that the young lady saved by Dr John is the Polly of the beginning of the novel; the moment recalls the earlier one, after Lucy's breakdown, when she wakes, so it seems, in Bretton, to reveal to the reader, what she herself has known for some time, that Graham and Dr John are one and the same. But here the change in narrative, the bringing of the beginning back into the centre of the story, marks a greater and sadder change for Lucy; where before it brought the growth of intimacy with Dr John, now it cancels it, as has already been signalled in the period of Lucy's abandonment. When she meets and knows Polly again, her intercourse with the Brettons is resumed, but it is no longer the close connection with Dr John, but the difficult position of confidante to the woman who has won his love.

Lucy – and Brontë – do not stint the suffering this causes Lucy. But I believe that suffering is saved from a sort of masochism by the fact that Lucy fully admits all her previous feelings and their worth. That they have led to suffering does not lead her to pretend they are worthless. That she has begun to see Dr John as in many ways a lesser person than herself does not mean that she does not deeply regret the loss of his incipient feeling for her (and his letters). That she sees Mrs Bretton as dropping her and picking her up again, in the accepted manner that happier people do with less happy people, does not stop her from recognizing what drives Mrs Bretton, and that it in some ways answers to her own feelings. And that she sees that Polly is still the child that she was a decade earlier does not stop her from seeing that she is the best partner for Dr John. This in turn might almost be too much for the reader – too good, as it were – if there were not also some acerbity of tone at times in Lucy's perception and understanding. She describes Dr John thus, on seeing him part from Paulina, just before Paulina reveals their love to Lucy:

> How animated was Graham's face! How true, how warm, yet how retiring the joy it expressed! This was the state of things, this the combination of circumstances, at once to attract and to enchain, to subdue and excite Dr John. The pearl he admired was in itself of great price and truest purity, but he was not a man who, in appreciating the gem, could forget its setting. Had he seen Paulina with the same youth, beauty, and grace, but on foot, alone, unguarded, and in simple attire, a dependent worker, a demi-grisette, he would have thought her a pretty little creature, and would have loved with his eye her movements and her mien, but it required other than this to conquer him as he was now vanquished, to bring him safe under dominion as now, without loss, and even with gain to his manly honour, one saw that he was reduced; there was about Dr John all the man of the world; to satisfy himself did not suffice; society must approve – the world must admire what he did, or he counted his measures false and futile.
>
> (ch. XXXII)

This is the same Dr John Lucy had glimpsed at the theatre watching Vashti; he is reminiscent of 'the beady-eyed Tudor' Orson Welles so acutely saw the Hal of *Henry IV* to be; yet in between, Lucy willingly admits to herself and the reader that he was what she had desired. There is no conflict between reason and passion; Lucy sees the man for what he is *and* desires him. The conventional readings, embraced by the feminists, of Lucy's 'schizophrenia' are surely wrong. Lucy has to bury her love for John as she buries the letter, but in so doing she does not bury her passion in favour of reason or even repress it. In one such as Lucy, passion is ever-present; it is what she recognizes in Vashti. It is what she does *not* see in Dr John. And she continues to embrace it in the novel even *as* she buries the letters: they have to be buried, or the sight of them might cause too powerful a feeling. This *is* passion, not its repression. That it can be combined with the accepting generosity which Lucy achieves testifies to the maturity she has reached, which Paulina has not reached, that complexity of understanding which enables her to move from the pain, yet strength, with which she first buries the letters, to the resigned warmth with which she recalls them:

> Was this feeling dead? I do not know, but it was buried.... I learned in time that this benignity [of Dr John's], this cord-iality, this music, belonged in no shape to me: it was a part of himself; it was the honey of his temper; it was the balm of his mellow mood; he imparted it as the ripe fruit rewards with sweetness the rifling bee; he diffused it about him, as sweet plants shed their perfume. Does the nectarine love either the bee or bird it feeds? Is the sweetbriar enamoured of the air? 'Goodnight, Dr John; you are good, you are beautiful; but you are not mine. Good night, and God bless you!'
>
> (ch. XXXI)

I would suggest that this acceptance is itself subversive rather than the opposite, for it suggests that life can be lived without a particular system of judging or of making one's way. Lucy has to deal with what comes to her; as she does she grows, changes, develops; her actions and feelings are often contradictory, but that is because she has a complex and complicated character, and the events and situations she encounters demand flexible reactions. This flexibility is further suggested by the narrative technique I have outlined. Far from being simply an expression of a simple duality or schizophrenia, and certainly far from being simply an expression of 'a response to a society cruelly indifferent to women' (Gilbert and Gubar, p. 401) or of 'the destructive effect of the buried life on women who can neither escape by retreating into the self...nor find a solution by dehumanising the other into a spiritual object' (Gilbert and Gubar, p. 403), *Villette* embraces a number of different possibilities in life. Dr John can be good and beautiful *and* world-serving; Mrs Bretton can be terrifyingly the embodiment of the bourgeois (how fitting that she ends up in a town such as Villette which breathes the same feeling), and yet she can admit to a passion for her son different in expression but similar in nature to Mrs Morel's for Paul.[30] Even the chilling Mme Beck is given her moments; her brief entertaining of soft feelings for Dr John, her attempts to ensure that she is always well turned out for his visits, her openness to the charms of a man fourteen years younger than herself, are described by Lucy with both clear-sightedness and compassion. But her true moment of revelation comes when she describes Mme Beck after one of John's visits, and when she has realized he is merely trifling with her attentions:

> When he was gone, Mme Beck dropped into the chair he had just left; she rested her chin in her hand; all that was animated or amiable vanished from her face: she looked stony and stern, almost mortified and morose. She sighed; a single but deep sigh. A loud bell rang for morning-school. She got up; as she passed a dressing-table with a glass upon it she looked at her reflected image. One single white hair streaked her nut-brown tresses; she plucked it out with a shudder. In the full summer daylight, her face, though it still had the colour, could plainly be seen to have lost the texture of youth; and then, where were youth's contours? Ah Madame, wise as you were, even *you* knew weakness.
>
> (ch. XI)

As readers, we certainly judge all of these characters as inferior to Lucy, but we see – as she sees – that such judgements are not simple. Misjudged herself, she is careful of making monolithic judgements of others; she has high standards, but applies them with generosity. And since we have already been warned ourselves about misjudgement, in our narrative misjudgement at the beginning of the novel, we are the readier to accept the importance of generosity.

This moral expansiveness is further highlighted in the way religion is dealt with in *Villette*. It has often been criticized for its anti-Catholic stance, and it is true that there are some low blows at that religion. Yet the strong emphasis on religion in the novel is rather to accentuate further Lucy's isolation and alienation within a foreign culture; and at the height of that sense of aloneness, in the long vacation, to whom does she turn, and by whom is she kindly received? By the Catholic Père Silas. When she finally gives and receives the full force of love, it is to and from whom? A Catholic, and a Catholic ready to allow her her own faith. ('Remain a Protestant, my little English Puritan, I love Protestantism in you. I own its severe charm. There is something in its ritual I cannot receive myself, but it is the sole creed for "Lucy".' If there is prejudice in the novel, it is not one which prevents Lucy's sources of consolation at two key moments in her despair from being Catholic.

I have been trying to show that an analysis of the concerns of the novel, and of the personality of its central character and narrator, Lucy Snowe, is incomplete and untrue to the novel if it focuses on duality or schizophrenia (as both many feminist analyses and Eagleton's Marxist analysis do). Within this I have also tried to show that an analysis which perceives the novel solely as a response to patriarchy (in content and in form) misses that suggestiveness and generosity, that moral sensitivity and expansiveness which many accounts seem to miss (again I'd want to except Kate Millett). Nowhere is this more evident than in accounts of two formal elements of the novel which are crucial to it. One shows us Brontë's masterly dismissal of a Romance/ Gothic convention – the apparition of the nun – and the other her (possibly failed) attempt to resolve the difficulty of an ending to a novel which cries out for a twentieth-century whimper rather than a nineteenth-century bang.

The use of the Gothic device of the nun is yet another way in which Brontë displaces the reader from a simple relationship with the narrative. Just as Brontë keeps us in ignorance of some of the things which her narrator already knows (through devices such as the dual names, e.g. Graham/John), just as she initially keeps us guessing about the central character in this story, just as she employs coincidence in a way which almost does not strike us as that, so ingeniously does she reintroduce the Brettons and Paulina into Lucy's life (and note that the narrative technique means that they are indeed introduced into hers and not vice versa) – so does she tease us out of certainty with the device of the nun. In fact, so complex are the narrative shifts and surprises in *Villette* that it is truly a different novel upon second reading, further proliferating its imaginative effects. Feminist responses to the Romance genre have been ambivalent; some see it as the antithesis of what a female tradition should contain, since it has been the convention responsible for many of the stereotypes of women in fiction; others see it as being the authentic vehicle for the female voice, because of its embodiment of myth and fantasy, which such critics argue have been denied women in the tradition. It is interesting, therefore, to see how the nun in *Villette* is interpreted – especially since she is in fact a he! Miles does not discuss specific examples, but she is sufficiently confident to assert that 'Charlotte's almost exclusive concentration on women led imperceptibly to a situation in which romance becomes *the* female form, the form chosen for fiction written by, for, and about women.'[31] Both Elaine Showalter and Gilbert and Gubar see Gothic elements in Brontë's fiction as emblematic of forces which the writer was unable to admit as present in the female identity in any other way. (Thus Showalter, who does not specifically discuss *Villette*, connects the Gothic mad wife in *Jane Eyre* with madness and with repressed sexuality, and sees her as the personification of urges in Jane which could not be all wed 'out'.)[32] Gilbert and Gubar similarly see Bertha as an *alter* Jane (p. 359), indeed one can see here (and in Showalter) the seeds of their strong thesis. But Gilbert and Gubar also incorporate a psycho-analytic element into their interpretation of Brontë's Gothic, and this can be seen most clearly in their discussion of the nun in *Villette*. Gilbert and Gubar sometimes seem to vacillate in their interpretation of the nun, a vacillation they correctly perceive in the novel: 'Dr John is correct, then, in assuming that the nun comes out of Lucy's diseased brain: Lucy has already played the role of de Hamal on the stage, and now *he* is playing her role as the nun in Mme Beck's house. But this psychoanalytic inter-pretation is limited, as Lucy herself notes' (p. 425). Gilbert and Gubar argue, first, that the nun represents both a desire and a fear in the female psyche (thus she represents both an approved chastity and a feared loss of both sexuality and worldly identity for Lucy); second, that the way in which the nun surfaces suggests that 'Lucy may very well be moving towards some kind of rejection of her own convent-like life-in-death' (p. 426). Third, they link M. Paul into the experience of the apparition, 'For both Paul and Lucy are tainted by the manipulative, repressive ways in which they have managed to lead a buried life, and so both are haunted by the nun...their relationship is constantly impeded by the haunting which the nun represents' (p. 429); and here the mysterious Justine Marie, a real nun romantically linked to Paul, is connected with the apparition. Finally, the true identity of the 'nun' is revealed, and Gilbert and Gubar's interpretation is this:

> Thus, for Lucy to liberate herself from Ginevra and de Hamal means that she can simultaneously rid herself of the self-denying nun. In fact, these mutually dependent spirits have been cast out of her house because, in the park, unable to withdraw into voyeurism, she experienced jealousy. Hurt without being destroyed, she has at least temporarily liberated herself from the dialectic of her internal schism. And to indicate once again how that split is a male fiction, Brontë shows us how the apparently female image of the nun masks the romantic male plots of de Hamal.
>
> (p. 436)

Curiously, Gilbert and Gubar scarcely mention the way in which the *dénouement* of the nun narrative completely undercuts its apparent significance earlier in the novel. Their psychoanalytic interpretation is happy to marry inner and outer, the nun of the imagination with the nun of impersonation, and they don't even change critical gear in moving from the one to the other. For them, the nun is symbol of Lucy's duality again; once brought to the surface through her actually experienced jealousy (and thus her admission of desire) she is expelled and expunged, and Lucy is freed to pursue her own (undiseased) desires. Yet is it not a difficulty for Gilbert and Gubar that, once brought to the surface, we see that the nun is in fact not a nun at all, but a silly young man who has conveniently exploited the disguise, innocent of its effect on Lucy? So how can a nun who is not a nun at all simultaneously be the product of Lucy's diseased imagination and the 'expression' of her desire, 'expressed' by her recognized jealousy of M. Paul? Of course, fictional narratives can easily sustain both realistic and imaginative, symbolic truths, and this could be one such. But a psychoanalytic interpretation surely depends upon our being able to believe that the nun is indeed a product of Lucy's mind; if we discover that it has an all too rational explanation, where does this leave the psychoanalytic one?

Here we can compare Brontë's *Jane Eyre*, where similar supernatural events take place. In *Jane Eyre*, when Jane feels Rochester's voice calling to her, what are we to believe? Is his voice really, that is to say supernaturally, projected across the miles to call her back? Or is it simply the literary and dramatic expression of her intense desire to go back? Or is the outward epiphenomenon accompanying a suppressed desire? The nature of literary devices, their ability to sustain different weights, both realistic and symbolic, makes it difficult to answer these questions with certainty. What is certain is that Brontë does not insinuate any doubt into her narrative in *Jane Eyre*; there is no deflation of the mysterious voice, and indeed its supernatural origin is endorsed by the fact that the fire had razed Thornfield at much the same time as Jane heard her summons. Now, certainly, it is open to the twentieth-century critic to proffer a psychoanalytic reading here (Gilbert and Gubar do: 'Her new and apparently telepathic communion with Rochester, which many critics have seen as mindlessly melodramatic has been made possible by her new independence and Rochester's new humility' (p. 377)); but such a reading is open to the same vagaries as a psychoanalytic reading of a real person's behaviour and experience, and compounding this is the difficulty of testing critical interpretations in general. So psychoanalytic critical interpretations are particularly difficult to submit to any process of falsification. Such a judgement, which wilfully ignores a matter of fact which undermines it (as, incidentally, both the judgements on *Jane Eyre* and on *Villette* do), must be suspect. In the case of *Jane Eyre*, Jane cannot know of Rochester's 'new humility' when she hears the cry – unless it is *genuinely* telepathic, that is to say, she actually has communicated with Rochester across the airwaves; and if she does so communicate, the force of the experience as expressive of what is repressed is lost. In the case of *Villette*, when Brontë reveals that the nun was simply a man in disguise, neither a nun, a ghost, nor a product of Lucy's 'diseased' imagination, this *must* reflect on earlier representations of the nun. Since Brontë is here employing a well-recognized Gothic device within a novel otherwise free of such devices and committed to a combination of realistic narrative, melodramatic metaphor and psychological introspection (a combination which can sustain another different element, but one which is not in its overall sweep Gothic in nature), we see the nun as a device which stands proud of the narrative. Given that we have already been made uncertain by the narrative structure (not unlike walking on one of those disconcerting spongy surfaces in the fairground House of Fun), we are not likely to take it straightforwardly. In this way it is quite unlike the Gothic elements in *Jane Eyre*, where there is *no* questioning of the force of the devices. It is almost as though, in *Villette*, Brontë deliberately set out to question such melodramatic images, to question the rather straightforward solutions of the previous novel. *Villette* is in many ways committed to realism (psychological as well as narrative), and the nun sticks out oddly. Furthermore, Lucy, while being (very naturally and realistically) disturbed by the apparition, always doubts it, at least sufficiently to try to question it. As is characteristic with this novel, we, as readers, are kept in ignorance of the full complexity of her feeling about the nun; and that is because Brontë is playing a narrative game with us. Her description – Lucy's description – of her first encounter with the nun occurs in chapter XXII, in the wake of the genuine psychological crisis in the novel. True, imaginings could well follow such an event; but Brontë strongly emphasizes that Lucy, even in her greatest extremity, is in her senses – even to the point where she enters the Catholic confessional. So Lucy sees the nun. This is the description: 'Say what you will, reader – tell me I was nervous or mad; affirm that I was unsettled by the excitement of that letter; declare that I dreamed; this I vow – I saw there – in that room – on that night – an image like – a NUN.' The style of this is strongly reminiscent of the passage in which she earlier remonstrates with those who would judge her (readers, critics) about her desolation of spirit in the first month of the long vacation. She questions (even in accepting the plausibility of) various 'rational' judgements, but affirms the nature of her own experience, just as she affirms her misery in the earlier passage. The affirmation itself seems to cast doubt upon any judgements upon it ('tell me I was nervous or mad'); and it also casts doubt upon Dr John's diagnosis ('I think it a case of spectral illusion: I fear, following on and resulting from long-continued mental conflict'). The good doctor goes on to make his prescription: to cultivate happiness. Lucy's response is predictable, but enjoyable nevertheless: 'No mockery in the world ever sounds to me so hollow as that of being told to *cultivate* happiness. What does such advice mean? Happiness is not a potato, to be planted in mould, and tilled with manure.' The exchange might remind many women of being told by men that their ailments were the products of nerves and could be cured by cheerfulness; Lucy sees the greater truth, that happiness cannot be cultivated, but that unhappiness need not, either, mean visions of nuns. Do not Gilbert and Gubar, in their psychoanalytic mode, behave rather like the good doctor? They diagnose repression and recommend 'expression'; the nearer 'the nun' is brought to the surface, the nearer Lucy will be to health and independence. This view is linked to their interpretation of Lucy as schizophrenic, which they further link to Brontë's own duality (torn between male convention and female independence). They are not even embarrassed when M. Paul sees the vision of the nun. Instead of seeing this as objective proof that the nun exists and is not a figment of Lucy's imagination, they see it rather as an image of the joint repression of Lucy and Paul. And just how does the nun fit into the male psyche? Gilbert and Gubar do not follow this hare, yet are happy to assert a causal relationship: 'Paul and Lucy are tainted by the manipulative, repressive ways in which they have managed to lead a buried life, and so both are haunted by the nun' (p. 429). Yet even if we were to agree that the device is largely symbolic, what are we to do with the logical *dénouement*? It is simply not explicable in the psychoanalytic terms Gilbert and Gubar have defined. If Lucy is liberated from the nun by an admitted jealousy, how is Paul liberated? If the apparition of the nun is linked with Justine Marie, and dissipated by the explanation of Lucy's misunderstanding, how does this explain the apparition's occurring while Lucy is still enmeshed emotionally with Dr John? It *might* be argued that the nun should disappear when Lucy finds happiness (as she does, with Dr John's prescription and through his actions, immediately after her first sighting); yet the nun appears to her just as she is about to devour his first letter. Terrible warning of her cultivation of her passion? Yet how can that be sustained when Paul later sights the nun and, much more importantly, when the nun turns out to be Ginevra's suitor, de Hamal, in disguise?

Mary Jacobus, in her essay on *Villette*, 'The buried letter: feminism and romanticism in *Villette*',[33] comes closest of the feminist accounts I have read to reflecting some of the genuine ambiguity and shiftingness of *Villette* (as opposed to a simple view of duality masking repression). She speaks of 'the perpetual de-centring activity'[34] of the novel and uses many metaphors of shifting ground. But Jacobus wants to have her cake and eat it too, to preserve the shiftingness of the novel and its duality, to see the undercutting of the nun yet to invoke its psychic significance too. Indeed, it is in her interpretation of the nun that we see that underlying her analysis of the shifting nature of the narrative is a Lacanian analysis. In her view, the pleasure the reader takes in the novel is that which stems from 'an obedient, controllable, narcissistically pleasurable image of self and its relation to the world';[35] she places a realist reading in this (as she sees it ironically non-realist) frame, as she also places the various mirror-images of Lucy in the novel (the image Lucy sees has only an imaginary correspondence with herself, just as the novel we see has only an imaginary correspondence with ourselves and our relation with the world, because neither takes account of that which is absent from the correspondence). In her interpretation, the nun opposes this imaginary correspondence of signifier and signified because she is 'recalcitrantly other'[36] and can only be mirrored by the structure of language. Perhaps we are doomed to the intrusion of a Lacanian analysis wherever mirrors appear in poetry or fiction; but here, especially, the analogue seems stretched to the point of fairground distortion. Once again, a preconceived set leads the critic away from the text; the point of Lucy's glimpses of her represented self is that she does not feel happy with them, she does not recognize herself in her mirror-image;[37] the nun certainly is other – it is de Hamal; and, as I have tried to show, a proper realist reading of the novel, far from enforcing the reader's desire for 'an obedient, narcissistically pleasurable image of self and its relation to the world', both unsettles and strengthens the reader, through the novel's representation of the problematic nature of judgement and its equivalent release of the reader into a final act of the imagination – but one made in the real world.

It seems to me that a far more plausible explanation of the nun lies in the shifts of narrative and playfulness with form, which I have already mentioned. The spectre of the nun is raised, only to be dismissed; Robert Heilman's article, 'Charlotte Brontë's "New" Gothic',[38] gives a very persuasive account of this view. The point of deflation is a crucial point for the reader's shift of consciousness, because it is similarly a crux for Lucy Snowe. She *was* right; there was a nun, whom she faced, knowing that she might be an apparition from Lucy's own consciousness. And the nun was nothing more fearful than the ludicrous de Hamal. This element of absurdity is the key to Brontë's intention here. If we were to take the nun seriously, either as Gothic symbol or as psychoanalytic device, Brontë could not have included this particular – and narratively logical – explanation. Lucy's fears are shown to be 'trifles light as air', as she, with far less reason, and needing far more courage to do so than her many interpreters and advisers, had thought. Can a psychoanalytic critical interpretation really survive on the shoulders of the absurd de Hamal? Let us credit Brontë with the intelligence a Dr John would not have admitted; she is having a joke at the expense of the reader, and on the fictional convention at the same time. And the seriousness of the joke lies in her deliberate rejection of Gothic as a vehicle for the representation of inner turmoil or repressed passion, a rejection of her own former methods, to signal her deliberate embrace of a new form of writing and a new approach to her central concerns (which must thus entail a new approach by the reader – which she ensures by first raising the spectre of the Gothic and then blowing it away). It is this most of all which signals Brontë's commitment to realism – not the realism of linear narrative or close observation of detail (though there is plenty of the latter), nor the realism which denies a heightened rhetoric, but an interior realism, which marries the struggles of Lucy to make her way through the difficulties which living throws up, with her more harrowing internal struggles with herself and her anguished attempts both to make sense of and survive the way her life fits only imperfectly with the lives of those around her. This is an extended, an expanded and expanding realism, which can accommodate the extraordinary metaphorical sweeps of the Long Vacation and the visionary, limelit scenes of *Villette*'s festal night with the cool appraisals of the opening passages of the novel and the benevolent basking in the glow of the Bretton household. The shifting narrative with its intercutting of different judgements and different styles, its reverse dramatic irony (Lucy knows things we don't), and its own reflection of change and development within the central narrator, suggests the complexity of the world and the complexity of judgement upon it, even as it keeps us firmly fixed upon and engaged with the central character – the more firmly for the fact that we had initially ignored her, as characters within the novel continue to do. And as we fix on her we are allowed to glimpse the other selves in those we cannot enter with the same imaginative fixity (Polly, Mrs Bretton, Mme Beck) and see that they too have rich interior lives which can only be glimpsed from the external view we have of them. But this is no nineteenth-century magic realism; the one thing which this super-realism will not embrace is the spectre which the contemporary feminist critic is so eager to insist upon.

101

Gilbert and Gubar's thesis demands that they find a madwoman in Lucy's attic; the nun being insufficient, they turn to Mme Walravens as the receptacle of 'Lucy's repressed anger at the injustice of men and male culture' (p. 431) and link this with the image of the nun, asserting that Mme Walravens' malevolence is likewise the other side of Justine Marie's suicidal passivity'. From here it is a quick step to a favoured conclusion: 'For Lucy's ambivalence about love and about men is now fully illuminated: she seeks emotional and erotic involvement as the only form of self-actualization in her world, yet she fears that such involvement will lead either to submission or to destruction, suicide or homicide.' Lucy – and, it is implied, Brontë ('In Mme Walravens then it is likely we see Brontë's anxiety about the effect of her creativity on herself and on others') (p. 432) – must find a middle road.

Gilbert and Gubar make this analysis the basis of their interpretation of the end of *Villette*, a troubled and difficult area for any critic and one which cannot admit of any certain identification. They merge the figures of author and narrator more closely by locating the subject of the ending as the female creative imagination; Lucy is the author of her own life, as Brontë is the author of a fiction which seeks to reject male models. As so often with Gilbert and Gubar, a promising initial analysis, which might yield much fruit about the novel, quickly turns to the rehearsal of a prior thesis; 'The ambiguous ending of *Villette* reflects Lucy's ambivalence, her love for Paul and her recognition that it is only in his absence that she can exert herself fully to exercise her own powers. It also reflects Brontë's determination to avoid the tyrannical fictions that have traditionally victimized women. Once more she deflates male romanticism' (p. 438). Gilbert and Gubar's certainty even leads these thorough and scholarly critics to make a simple error of fact in their interpretation of the ending, stating that Paul's death makes him more Lucy's 'own', whereas it is clear from the text that it is only his absence which leads to her feeling so. Gilbert and Gubar's turn from psychoanalysis to signification, to the representation of the subject, for their reading of the ambiguous ending, and their identification of Lucy with Brontë, both authors inspired by the primacy of the imagination, puts a simple gloss on it: 'Just as Brontë has become Lucy Snowe for the writing of *Villette*, just as Lucy has become all her characters, we submit to the spell of the novel, to the sepulchral voice relating truths of the dead revivified by the necromancy of the imagination. Brontë rejects not only the confining images conferred on women by patriarchal art, but the implicitly coercive nature of that art' (p. 439). Yet, again, it seems necessary to insist that precisely what Charlotte Brontë rejects in her ending is 'the *necromancy* of the imagination' – not the imagination, only a certain form of it.

Gilbert and Gubar, in their reading of the ending, are often true to its spirit and to its genuine ambiguity; it is only when they feel the need to fit it to their thesis that we see the shackles of preconception applied to what by its very nature cannot be shackled. Eagleton does the same, except that his preconceptions are different. He too focuses on the power of the imagination, but concludes that 'the ending, then, half suppresses tragedy while simultaneously protesting against such a manoeuvre. It confesses the emptiness of the tactic while emotionally investing in it.'[39] This leads him to dismiss *Villette* as a worthless compromise with 'neither the courage to be tragic nor to be comic...it is a kind of middle-ground, a half-measure'.[40]

In a sense, Eagleton, and Gilbert and Gubar, approach the ending in the same way; they see the novel as dualistic, they see Brontë as a compromiser with a world of restrictive values, they see repression at its heart, and the repression is the author's rather than the heroine's; they apply different ideologies to form their analyses, but in each case it is the ideology which forms the (similar) interpretation. Both focus upon the role of the imagination in the ending – yet both want to close the ending down, seal off its difficulties and fit it into a framework. Nothing could make clearer the intangibility of that ending. Clearly, it is not the compromise Eagleton wants to perceive; the ironies of Lucy's address to the reader with a sunny imagination are all one with her earlier direct addresses to those who might doubt her perceptions. Yet, as soon as we see that, we also see that the irony might be working in the other direction. Is not the stormy demise of the beloved hero as Gothic as the nun? Should it not meet a similar fate, the debunking of the rational mind – the same rational mind that Lucy alone was able to apply to the Spectre – for she did see it. Is not the conventional ending in this context (the patriarchal ending as Gilbert and Gubar would have it) the stormy rather than the secure one? These are not questions that can be settled. Brontë keeps us guessing.

103

Of course, a debunking voice might enter here to remind us that, according to Elizabeth Gaskell, Charlotte Brontë had fixed on the tragic ending when her father begged her to allow a happier one, and in response to his request she made it a 'veiled' fate.[41] It would be amusing if the effects of genuine patriarchy were our current analyses of Brontë's ambivalence. But whatever its aetiology, the ending as it stands is genuinely ambivalent. However many times we read it, in whatever frame, it eludes a final fix. One element in this is the shifting tense which Charlotte Brontë employs. Throughout the novel, by means of Lucy's first-person character presence, Brontë plays present against past tense (the present of the direct commentary on her past reportage, for example, the 'I err' in 'The Long Vacation', and the present of her direct addresses to the reader, for example, 'Well, each and all, take it your own way' of the same chapter); it is part of the complexity of her narrative mode. But in the chapter 'Finis' a new use of the present tense emerges in contrast with the past, as Lucy drops reportage of the past and enters into current reportage on the present. The chapter begins in the universal present of the authoritative generalizing statement: 'Man cannot prophesy. Love is no oracle. Fear sometimes imagines a vain thing.' But these very statements deny their authority, or rather deny the authority of the general axiom, because they are negatives. Lucy is about to tell us that what she feared did not come to pass – yet again denying the fictional convention and preparing us for the extraordinary, and extraordinarily revealing, remark that the three years of Paul's absence 'were the three happiest years of my life'. It is in this context that we move to the present tense of 'And now three years are past', and we move through time with the narrator, feeling its inexorable passing more than through the reported past: 'The sun passes the equinox; the days shorten, the leaves grow sere; but – he is coming.' That 'he is coming', in the form of the continuous present, but, as part of the peculiarly suggestive quality of some English tenses, predicting a future state, is repeated, and thus acquires an ominous tone. We move to the present of Lucy's present and direct speech: 'God, watch that sail! Oh! guard it!' The effect of these further deepening present tenses is to increase the effect of suspense, already announced by the presence and potential destructiveness of the storm; the reader's implication in this present seems to give us a role.

Of course, storms in *Villette* are not simply storms; they herald imaginative turbulence and denote death, as Lucy tells us during the Marchmont storm – and in case we were to forget that imaginative link, she now specifically mentions the deathly Banshee note. It is at this point that she reverts to the past tense, and we are dropped from the close imaginative engagement of that central passage back into the distance of reportage. The move back to the past tense in 'That storm roared frenzied for seven days' also implies the narrator's knowledge of subsequent events, so that the suspense, it seems, is about to be broken by the final outcome. It is at this point that Brontë turns on her 'Finis' with her final direct address to the reader: and here it is clear that Lucy's has become her own voice, for such an ending is authorial, though still in the spirit of Lucy's numerous backtracking remonstrances to her reader. And at this point too the address is also self-directed, as though Brontë were talking to herself: 'there is enough said....Let them [sunny imaginations] picture union and a happy succeeding life.' Now, though this ending is often taken as a sort of sop to those who want happy endings (like Mr Brontë) the ambiguity of the tense again intervenes here: 'Let it be theirs to conceive the delight of joy', 'Let them picture union and a happy life' could be placing the emphasis on 'theirs' and on 'them', so that Brontë could be releasing her ending (genuinely, not ironically) to the imaginations of her reader. In such a reading the 'Let it be theirs' could imply 'not me'; 'let them picture' could imply 'rather than me'. Thus the suggestion could be that, at this point, the writer might have intervened in the projected unhappy ending to reveal a happy one; instead she wishes to leave that imagining, that sunny picturing to the reader. And if their imaginations are not so – then, not so.

Brontë's signal reminders of the Marchmont episode in this passage also move against the direct parallel in the ending. Lucy is not Miss Marchmont, nor was she meant to be. Although Brontë always intended that her lines should not fall in pleasant places, that prediction has always been amply fulfilled in the novel, and the distinction between her and Miss Marchmont has been clearly made, even as she sails away from that dead life in the craft named 'The Vivid'.

With the ending, Brontë releases us to the quick of our imaginations. Like Keats at the end of 'The Eve of St Agnes' and 'Ode to a Nightingale',[42] she signals her awareness of her fiction, releases us from all tenses into the reality of our present (and oh! so much less heavily than any post-modernist novelist). That, of course, is where the reader always was, in the world of mortality where the imagination cannot quite o'erleap the bounds. Brontë is quite clearly saying, 'Fled is that music'; that is the point of the essential stoicism of Lucy and the essential realism of the novel. We have been shown a picture, a narrative, a story, representing someone dealing with the difficulties of the real world, and tempering those difficulties with the equally difficult exercise of the imagination. Lucy's triumph is to find some reconciliation between the two. Thus she can go on – whether with Paul or without him – though it would be better, far better, with him. Thus most of us have to go on. The real struggle of living in the real world does not centre on representations of the subject, nor on inscriptions of patriarchy, nor on psychoanalytic analyses of the unconscious, nor even on 'the tensions and alliances between two classes' (Eagleton). It centres, as it does for Lucy, on making a way forward which balances all the many tensions, and the joys, of the act of living, with one's sense of self. That business has no neat ending;[43] neither has *Villette*.

NOTES

1 G. Eliot, *Middlemarch*, Harmondsworth: Penguin, 1965, 'Finale'.
2 G. S. Haight (ed.), *The George Eliot Letters*, London: Oxford University Press; New Haven: Yale University Press, 1954–5, 3, p. 111.
3 W. Empson, *Some Versions of Pastoral*, London: Chatto & Windus, 1935, p. 4.
4 ibid., p. 5.
5 T. Eagleton, *Criticism and Ideology*, London: NLB, 1976, p. 120.
6 M. Jacobus, 'The difference of view', in M. Jacobus (ed.), *Women Writing and Women Writing about Women*, London: Croom Helm, 1979, p. 18.
7 ibid., pp. 17–18.
8 Eagleton, *Criticism and Ideology*, p. 121.
9 S. Gilbert and S. Gubar, *Shakespeare's Sisters*, Bloomington: Indiana University Press, 1979, p. xvi.
10 Once it becomes the object of academic study it ceases to be 'just' popular fiction and becomes a cultural document.
11 S. Gilbert and S. Gubar, *The Madwoman in the Attic*, New Haven and London: Yale University Press, 1979.
12 T. Eagleton, *Myths of Power*, London: Macmillan, 1975, p. 4.

13 ibid., p. 8.
14 E. Showalter, *A Literature of Their Own*, revised edition, London: Princeton University Press, pp. 13, 19.
15 All references to E. Gaskell, *North and South*, Harmondsworth: Penguin Books, 1970.
16 K. Millett, *Sexual Politics*, London: Virago, 1977.
17 R. Miles, *The Female Form*, London: Routledge & Kegan Paul, 1987, p. 41.
18 ibid., p. 41.
19 Gilbert and Gubar, *The Madwoman in the Attic*, p. 7. Since I refer to this work extensively in the following discussion, page references will be bracketed in the text.
20 Showalter, *A Literature of Their Own*, pp. 13, 19.
21 Eagleton, *Myths of Power*, p. 72.
22 Brontë's change of her heroine's intended name from Frost to Snowe is interesting here; snow is blanker than frost, Lucy initially writes 'white', and even 'Lucy' implies translucence.
23 This and all future references to Charlotte Brontë, *Villette*, Harmondsworth: Penguin Books, 1985.
24 Miles, *The Female Form*, p. 41.
25 Eagleton, *Myths of Power*, p. 63.
26 idem.
27 ibid., p. 90
28 Miles, *The Female Form*, p. 41.
29 Eagleton, *Myths of Power*, p. 4.
30 There is a further interesting parallel in *North and South* (ch. XXVI), where Mrs Thornton's discussion with her son of Margaret's refusal of his proposal is nakedly revealing of her love for him, and powerfully foreshadows Mrs Morel's appeal to Paul in *Sons and Lovers* not to give himself fully to Miriam.
31 Miles, *The Female Form*, p. 42.
32 Showalter, *A Literature of Their Own*, pp. 118–22.
33 Mary Jacobus, 'The buried letter: feminism and romanticism in *Villette*', M. Jacobus, (ed.) *Women Writing and Writing about Women*, London: Croom Helm, 1979.
34 ibid., p. 54.
35 ibid., p. 51.
36 idem.
37 See Shirley Foster, *Victorian Women's Fiction: Marriage, Freedom and the Individual*, London: Croom Helm, 1985, p. 105. Foster gives all the references for Lucy's dissatisfaction with her own mirror-image.
38 R. B. Heilman, 'Charlotte Brontë's "New" Gothic', in I. Gregor (ed.) *The Brontës*, Englewood Cliffs, NJ: Prentice Hall, 1970.
39 Eagleton, *Myths of Power*, p. 92.
40 ibid., p. 73.
41 Elizabeth Gaskell, *The Life of Charlotte Brontë*, 2 vols, London: Smith, Elder & Co., 1857, 2, p. 266.
42 The shifting tense in 'Eve of St Agnes' is used in a most economical and urgent way by Keats; the penultimate stanza ends with the

escape of Madeleine and Porphyro with 'and they are gone', and the final one begins 'Aye ages long ago these lovers fled away', thus bathetically releasing the reader from his engagement with their escape to the reminder that he has been agitated about lovers long dead. They are indeed gone. Keats pulls the same trick in the Ode with the disappearance of the nightingale, though there it is less roughly done.

43 Except death, which completes it, but makes it no neater.

4

'WOOMAN, LOVELY WOOMAN': FOUR DICKENS HEROINES AND THE CRITICS

Sandra Hopkins

His heroines, as in *David Copperfield*, tend to fall into two main types...the tall, composed, steadfast and sensible, and the small, fluttering, playful, and dependent...despite their loving selflessness, the names of Dickens' womenfolk fall heavily on the ear as their long procession passes by...They may be incandescent with virtue, but they do not strike a responsive spark.[1]

These sentences are taken from Patricia Thomson's book, *The Victorian Heroine*, published in 1956. In this study, Dickens is given short shrift. According to Thomson, 'a composite Victorian heroine – small, gentle, large-eyed and loving' would bear a 'resemblance...to Dickens' feminine ideal...his *idée fixe* about young women never varied'.[2] Thomson devotes little space to Dickens' presentation of his heroines, and implies that a re-examination of the topic would be neither pleasurable nor profitable.

In the last two decades, however, a large number of books written from various feminist standpoints have examined the depiction of women in Victorian fiction, and nearly all of these have included substantial treatment of Dickens' heroines. Moreover, many of the general studies of Dickens, which have appeared during the same period, have included specific discussion of Dickens' women – perhaps partly in response to the feminists' preoccupation with 'the male image of women' in Victorian fiction. It is the purpose of the present essay to enquire whether the marked increase in the quantity of critical attention which has recently been devoted to Dickens' heroines has been matched by any fundamental shift in critical evaluation of Dickens' achievement.

A number of general trends emerge in recent feminist criticism of Dickens, and these can, I hope, be fairly represented by considering a selection of books and essays written for, and accessible to, non-specialist readers. These trends reflect, in their different ways, some of the general aims of feminist criticism: to uncover restrictive and oppressive views of women, and to show how these views derive from male ideals and patriarchal attitudes. Many feminist critics of Victorian fiction proceed by first identifying a number of documents which they take to be representative of the dominant Victorian male ideology. They then consider specific literary works in relation to these 'key texts', in an attempt to demonstrate the ways in which those works reflect (or exist in tension with) that ideology. Such a method has the inherent danger that it might serve to restrict the range and nature of the questions which these critics feel it appropriate to ask about each work they consider. The problem is potentially compounded when such critics make a decision, in advance, that it is incumbent upon them to 'resist' the texts they are reading, to 'challenge' them, and to withhold their imaginative and emotional involvement from the novelist's characters and situations.[3]

Many of the ideas and much of the material on which recent feminist critics of the Victorian novel draw can be found in W. E. Houghton's famous handbook *The Victorian Frame of Mind* (1957), which contains a whole chapter on 'Love', including a subsection on 'Woman'. From the range of material surveyed by Houghton, feminist critics regularly single out two items which they treat as 'key texts' that represent the dominant male Victorian attitude to woman: Ruskin's lecture 'Of Queens' Gardens' (1865), and Coventry Patmore's *The Angel in the House* (1854–6).[4] Ruskin's lecture assigns a specific character and role to a woman, in direct contrast to that of a man:

> His intellect is for speculation and invention; his energy for adventure...but the woman's power is for rule, not for battle, – and her intellect is not for invention or creation, but for sweet ordering, arrangement, and decision.[5]

The woman is the guide of man and guardian of his morals; but while he encounters 'all peril and trial' in the outside world, she remains at home, 'the place of Peace; the shelter not only from all injury, but from all terror, doubt and division....This, then, I believe to be...the woman's true place and power.' However, to exercise this power, 'She must be enduringly, incorruptibly good; instinctively, infallibly wise – wise, not for self-development, but for self-renunciation: wise, not that she may set herself above her husband, but that she may never fail from his side.' Ruskin, it is said, sees woman's role as exclusively that of helpmeet within the confines of the home, and her character as one of (to us) implausible virtue and undesirable self-sacrifice.

The spirit of Ruskin's passage is taken to be closely allied to that of Patmore's immensely popular poem. One of the main suggestions of *The Angel in the House* is that a man's love of an innocent woman, a love akin to worship, is a source of ennoblement and purification. Feminist critics stigmatize Patmore's image of woman as an impossible idealization of wife and mother – the easily mocked domestic angel of the title. Patmore's attitude is taken to be representative of the Victorian belief in marriage which, according to Kate Millett, was an attempt 'to beautify the traditional confinement of women at any cost' with 'cloying sweetness' and 'frenetic sentimentality'.[6]

The method outlined above involves several questionable procedures: selective quotation from one work by a writer (Ruskin) whose very name 'is a byword for self-contradiction';[7] citation of a poem whose very title invites contemptuous hostility; avoidance of close analysis of the precise effects of the writing in either of the 'key texts' deployed as 'evidence', with a consequent reduction of both texts to a set of 'ideas'. The critics often seem to work by extrapolating from their 'key texts' a set of static definitions and images of female virtues (as desiderated by male Victorians) to which they then assimilate the intention and effect of other works of Victorian literature – not least among them the novels of Charles Dickens. Dickens, Ruskin and Patmore are all taken to be 'typical mid-Victorians' and, according to Merryn Williams, 'Ruskin was only saying, more poetically, what almost all writers believed – a woman's work was to make a man's home happy; she was purer and better than men, and above all, she must willingly lead a life of self-renunciation.'[8]

Given this set of assumptions, it is not surprising that most feminist critics have found little to enjoy or admire in Dickens' portrayal of women, a fact epitomized in Kate Millett's pronouncement that Dickens could achieve 'a nearly perfect indict-ment of both patriarchy and capitalism in *Dombey and Son*', but

> without ever relinquishing the sentimental version of women which is the whole spirit of Ruskin's 'Of Queen's Gardens'. It is one of the most disheartening flaws in the master's work that nearly all the 'serious' women in Dickens' fiction...are insipid goodies, carved from the same soap as Ruskin's Queens.'[9]

One is left wondering what could be the point of the sustained study of Dickens' heroines for critics who feel secure in surveying the subject from a position of such confident superiority and sometimes (as in the case of Kate Millett) with undisguised contempt. The answer seems to be that, for feminist critics, the interest of studying Dickens' women resides primarily in the pleasure of categorization. These critics treat each of Dickens' creations as a specimen to whom a label can be attached, and who is illustrative, by the particular function she performs in Dickens' narrative, of the effects of certain misguided, if not malign, contemporary beliefs.

This labelling process often involves the assigning of a specific, stereotypical role to each of Dickens' heroines and the imputation of a fixed attitude, on the part of both novelist and reader, to the character in question. The details of the categorization differ from critic to critic, but the essential dynamics of the process are evidenced by Merryn Williams' use of Rose Maylie in *Oliver Twist* to typify 'Dickens' concept of women'. Taking her cue from the authorial comment that Rose displays a 'perfect sacrifice of self... in all matters, great or trifling', Williams generalizes the point in terms which convey a powerful, negative charge: 'Here is a typical man's woman – pure and beautiful, home-loving...and as young as possible'.[10] The assumption that Dickens deals constantly in stereotypical characters is often linked to the claim that, since 'Dickens was unable to understand or sympathise with women', he is incapable of creating 'real' or 'fully complex' female figures.[11] A Dickens heroine, writes Merryn Williams, is, like other female figures in Victorian fiction, a 'shrunken human being, a being who...exists only to uplift and inspire'.[12]

These general trends can be observed in the specific comments which two feminist critics of the 1970s make on four of Dickens' most celebrated 'serious' heroines: Esther Summerson, Agnes

Wickfield, Dora Spenlow and Bella Wilfer. In *Relative Creatures: Victorian Women in Society and the Novel* (1974), Françoise Basch claims that Dickens constantly asserts the ideal of the 'mythic wife-mother' who is virtuous, modest, instinctively loving and who ensures the happiness of the home. Heroines like Esther and Agnes have 'a marvellous aptitude for their fairy-tale domestic mission' and later become 'sacrificed and altruistic' 'wife-guides'. Dora is their antithesis, a 'child-wife' who is weak, selfish and incapable – 'even a dangerous object'. Basch suggests that, in his creation of Bella, Dickens attempted to show a more complex person, capable of change – unlike Esther and Agnes, who, almost 'drained of all life', function as 'purely symbolic creatures' and are figures towards whom the reader can only adopt an attitude of resignation. But, for Basch, the portrayal of Bella is only partially satisfactory; when she evolves 'from a spoiled, and selfish child into an altruistic woman, devoted to her husband and father', Dickens' idealization of her at the end of the novel is little more than a fantasy, an 'idyllic image', described with 'irrational, sentimental, and dreamlike resonances'.[13]

Jenni Calder's categorization of Esther, Agnes, Dora and Bella, in her *Women and Marriage in Victorian Fiction* (1976), differs in some details from that of Basch, but her guiding assumption, like that of her fellow critics, is that Dickens' vision of his heroines was 'severely limited by his lack of imaginative apprehension of the potentialities of young women', so her conclusions are equally negative. Calder maintains that Dickens liked writing about the 'calm, static, and self-denying' love of parents and children, and brothers and sisters, and was at his weakest in depicting happy marriages, where, she suggests, he falls into a description of a 'sexless' relationship, which she terms (recalling some words of Bella Wilfer) 'the doll's house syndrome'. Dickens' idealized women, according to Calder, 'tend to be more than usually withdrawn from the rigours of real life'. They are devoted daughters and motherly housewives who are humble, sincere and caring. Agnes cares for her father, Esther for Jarndyce, until both marry and transfer their care to their husbands. The marriages are described by Calder as the occasion when 'filial duty and respect couple with paternal authority and kindness'. These ideal brides are dutiful daughters who also have the capacity to be motherly, useful housewives. This is where Dora fails and Bella succeeds. Dora remains a 'child-wife', initially romantically and sexually attractive, but incapable of assuming the domestic responsibilities symbolized by the household keys used so efficiently by Agnes and Esther. Bella, in contrast to Dora, becomes a busy housewife, with all her thoughts on the care and support of her husband. In Calder's view, Dickens' version of a 'domestic marriage' often assigns a 'limited, serving role for the woman, and a kindly protective role for the man'.[14]

Feminist criticism of Dickens in the 1980s has perpetuated many of the assumptions already noted, but with an increased emphasis (derived directly or indirectly from deconstruction and other varieties of post-structuralist criticism) on the discrepancies between Dickens' conscious intentions and his intuitive perceptions and inadvertent revelations. The authors of *Corrupt Relations* (1982), for example, argue that the stereotypic idyll of Bella Wilfer's marriage to John Harmon clashes with the more credible development of the relationship between Eugene Wrayburn and Lizzie Hexam, and that the idealizing tendencies in the portrayal of Esther Summerson are undercut by the psychological complexity with which her portrayal is invested. In the latter case, they argue, Dickens' character subverts the role ostensibly assigned to her. The author's rendering of her psychological state, they suggest, probes 'almost reluctantly', but in an implicitly sympathetic way, the terrible price that has to be paid for the Victorian ideal of right womanhood, the distortion that is necessary to fit woman for selfless duty and self-sacrifice. But Dickens' perception, they suggest, may not be a fully conscious one. When Mrs Jellyby and Mrs Pardiggle, the 'neglectful mothers', reject the same ideal of female selflessness, Dickens uses Esther's narrative to display his disapproval of their conduct. Explicitly and consciously, these critics argue, Dickens intends to contrast the ideal behaviour of Esther with the egotistic selfishness of the female philanthropists, but implicitly we are shown the loss or distortion of selfhood which either acceptance or rejection of the ideal inevitably involves for a woman.[15]

The 'psychological truth' of Dickens' portrayal of Esther is also stressed in recent articles by Virginia Blain, Valerie Kennedy, Carol Senf and Suzanne Graver.[16] In these essays, Esther becomes, in effect, a psychological and social case-history, to be analysed and accounted for, rather than a literary creation to be responded to. What is revealed of her individual nature (often treated in isolation from the rest of her narrative) is then made the subject of classification and explanation. Her symptoms are seen variously: as those of suppression and 'a distorted selfhood' which is the inevitable outcome of attempting to conform to the stereotype; or as those of a woman experiencing 'self-mistrust' and a desire to fulfil a social ideal. It is argued, in the latter case, that, if we view Esther thus, taking account of 'the social roots...of her troubled relations to her own thoughts and feelings', then we can 'exonerate Dickens from the still lingering charge of inept narration and characterisation'.[17]

In contrast, Kate Flint, in the chapter entitled 'Disruptive angels: Dickens and gender' in her general study of Dickens in the Harvester New Readings series (1986), insists that 'although feminist criticism of Dickens has tended to concentrate on the simplest issue: his presentation of women as characters, and, in some cases, as caricatures', there are 'dangers of thinking in terms of character'. Dickens' women, Flint asserts, are often 'drama-tised points taken from a schematic structuring of the notion of womanhood'. Dickens, she argues, is guilty of ideological didac-ticism, and it is impossible to describe his women 'in terms of real characters'. She thus, in the course of her discussion, classifies Dickens' heroines as 'idealised brides', whom she contrasts with Dickens' 'traditional anti-feminist stereotypes of shrewish, domineering women with the ability to reduce men to cowering subordination'.[18]

Feminist criticism of Dickens since the 1970s has, we have seen, contained an apparent variety of approaches and shifts of emphasis. But underlying these, there would seem to be a number of fundamental similarities. Feminist critics may differ over the particular stereotypes which individual heroines might be thought to embody, or over the degree of psychological realism which one can expect in a Dickens portrayal of a woman, or over the degree to which Dickens' conscious intentions are at variance with his unconscious revelations. But such critics share a common tendency to homogenize the experience of reading a Dickens novel. Rather than attempting to do justice to the full range of contingent factors which bear upon the reader as he or she experiences each one of the novelist's dramatized scenes, and to the ebbing and flowing of imaginative, emotional and intel-lectual engagement which is an inevitable part of reading any lengthy work of fiction, they tend to reduce and rigidify the reading process, making it seem as if readers should assess the characters and situations before them in the light of a number of pre-ordained schemes, categories and structures. Even those feminist critics who would deny that Dickens is a straightforward purveyor of stereotypes, nevertheless offer readings of the novels that employ the stereotypical Victorian male images of woman as a constant reference-point. It is hardly ever conceded by such critics that Dickens might, at moments in his novels, render female behaviour and character in a way that makes it merely pedantic to turn immediately (whether for the purposes of confirmation, or as a means to seeing what Dickens is 'subverting', 'exposing' and 'satirizing') to invoke the stereotypes of 'angels, shrews, coquettes, and man-hunting spinsters'.[19]

One might expect that some of these pitfalls would be avoided by critics approaching Dickens' novels from a less obviously ideologically determined stance. But to move from recent feminist criticism to more general commentary on the novelist is to discover that the feminists are often effectively elaborating, from their own particular point of view, positions which are also to be found in the writings of non-feminist Dickens critics. There is, indeed, a considerable degree of exchange, overlap and mutual assimilation between the work of feminist and non-feminist writers on the subject. Michael Slater, for example, in what has become the standard work on Dickens and women, is able (despite some reservations) to support Kate Millett's indictment of Dickens for tacitly sustaining 'patriarchal beliefs and attitudes'.[20] And Sandra Gilbert and Susan Gubar, in *The Madwoman in the Attic*, draw on Alexander Welsh's non-feminist study of *The City of Dickens* in the course of their ingenious argument that 'a beautiful angel-woman's selflessness' dooms her to 'a life of death, a death in life'.[21]

Slater's book suggests that Dickens uses stock 'types' (comic or ideal) and 'images' in much the same way as is alleged by the feminists, and while he tends to attribute Dickens' conceptions to influences from the writer's own life, he nevertheless concedes that Dickens' attitudes towards women 'were typical of the age in which he lived'. His conclusion is remarkably similar to many of those already encountered:

> Household ornament, guardian angel, playful kitten, Good Sister, Good Provider – in Dickens a young girl or a woman

may, according to age, represent any of these types, or a blend of more than one of them, for the benefit, comfort or pleasure of the men in her domestic grouping. Any assertion of herself as a person, however, with her own needs, demands and desires, is invariably presented by him as something grotesque.[22]

Alexander Welsh and J. Hillis Miller are not overtly unsympathetic to Dickens' portrayal of his heroines, but their tendency to describe the women's roles and functions constantly in metaphorical or quasi-symbolic terms involves, as much as the pronouncements of those more critical of Dickens, a loss of contact with the moment-by-moment 'feel' of Dickens' texts.[23] Angus Wilson and Philip Collins are more overtly hostile to many of Dickens' portrayals, resting their case on the 'unreality', 'idealized' and 'sentimental' nature of his heroines, but Collins excepts Dora, on the grounds that, at least for moments, Dickens imagines her more fully and with greater psychological realism.[24] Even John Carey, who, virtually alone among modern critics, bases his claim for Dickens on the power and fertility of the novelist's imagination, rather than judging Dickens to be defective in 'psychological realism' beside contemporaries like George Eliot, falls back on familiar arguments when discussing Dickens' heroines. Here, he believes, Dickens is a creator of stereotypes whose female figures generally 'fit comfortably into the two categories of pure maid or frump' – though he concedes Dickens' capacity for recognizing this habit in himself (suggesting that he satirizes it in David Copperfield's idealization of Agnes), and argues that, in his portrayal of Esther, Dickens shows the 'perversion' of 'plucky, sexless heroines – Little Nell, Little Dorrit – with their unnatural attachment to older men'.[25]

Just as recent feminist criticism of Dickens can be seen to overlap with, or to take some of its bearings from, the writings of non-feminist critics, so many of the arguments found in modern writing on Dickens (both feminist and non-feminist) can be paralleled in the remarks of some of Dickens' very earliest readers. The poet Swinburne, for example, remarked, in terms that by now should seem very familiar, that 'on the...sentimental side of his work Dickens was but a type of his generation and his class'.[26] And one of the earliest critical debates about Dickens focused on a subject which has continued to exercise Dickens critics in later periods: the alleged lack of 'naturalism' in his characterization of both men and women. Dickens' contemporary and fellow novelist, Anthony Trollope, asserted that Dickens' characters were 'puppets with a charm that had enabled him to dispense with human nature'.[27] The critic George Henry Lewes, George Eliot's consort (perhaps a significant fact in this context), delivered the most powerfully argued and influential Victorian attack on Dickens for his lack of realism.[28] Though he praised Dickens for 'an imagination of marvellous vividness, and an emotional, sympathetic nature capable of furnishing that imagination with elements of universal power', he also called Dickens' characters 'puppets' who speak 'a language never heard in life, moving like pieces of simple mechanism', who have 'mechanisms for minds'. Lewes used terms such as 'unreal' and 'impossible' to describe these 'types'. Although he said that the 'types established themselves in the public mind like personal experiences', he indicated his sense of dissatisfaction by calling them 'imperfect presentations of human character'.[29] Another influential Victorian critic, Richard Holt Hutton, also used the word 'types' to describe Dickens' characters, and one senses pejorative implications in his use of the term when he observes that 'a realist as regards *human* nature, [Dickens] never was at all'.[30]

Victorian reservations about Dickens' lack of 'realism' often focused specifically on his portrayal of his heroines. Hutton wrote on another occasion that Dickens, having delighted the reader by his humorous portrayal of vice, 'has a great tendency to make the corresponding virtues ludicrous...by his over-coloured sentiment...Mr Dickens's saints, like that Agnes in *David Copperfield*, who insists on pointing upwards, are invariably detestable'. [31] George Brimley wrote, in 1853, that Esther Summerson illustrated Dickens' habit of seizing peculiarities and presenting them, instead of characters.[32] In the following year, James Augustine Stothert called Esther 'a prodigious bore, whom we wish the author had consigned to the store-room the moment she was fairly in possession of her housekeeping keys'.[33] And Mrs Margaret Oliphant, in 1855, felt 'obliged to say that we think Esther a failure'. She put on record that, in her view:

Mr Dickens is evidently ambitious of achieving a heroine...

witness...even the pains he has taken with Dora....In the ordinary type of heroines...in the Agnes Wickfield...Mr Dickens is generally successful...but to produce an individual woman is another and quite different matter.[34]

Another female critic of the time felt that Dickens' young heroines were characterized by their 'silliness', and contrasted them with 'those dreadful specimens of "the household angel" class'.[35]

There is, however, an alternative, and nowadays largely neglected, tradition of Victorian Dickens criticism which rests its claims for Dickens' art not on his alleged attempts at 'realism' but on his imaginative and poetic power, his humour, his capacity to stir the emotions and hence to bestow pleasure. In his *Course of English Literature* (1866), James Hannay wrote that 'Dickens's forte is not his literal fidelity to life, as clumsy observers fancy, but the vividness of his imagination and sentiment. He is more true to *general* than to *individual* human nature'.[36] The American critic and reviewer, E. P. Whipple, similarly questioned the assumption that Dickens' characters had a 'photographic quality' in the way they were represented, and maintained that the 'reality ' of the characters came from 'the vividness of the conceptions'.[37] The historian, Lord Acton, admitted: 'I am ashamed to think how much more often I return to Dickens than to George Eliot....He arouses the emotions by such direct and simple methods'.[38] And Dickens' friend and biographer, John Forster, declared that 'the emotions [Dickens] awakens are not more fresh and true to us than they will be to future generations'.[39] Even Lewes wrote appreciatively of 'the irradiating splendour of [Dickens'] imagination' and acknowledged that Dickens' characters could 'set in motion the secret springs of sympathy', while at the same time revealing his anxiety that 'the logic of feeling seems the only logic he can manage'.[40] Lewes' enthusiasm (and ambivalence) is paralleled in an anonymous contribution to *Bentley's Miscellany* of 1853:

The wonderful genius of the writer, whose greatest triumph is to take the world captive in spite of these accumulated heresies against nature and against art. Everybody reads – everybody admires – everybody is delighted – everybody loves – and yet almost everybody finds something to censure, something to condemn...Charles Dickens writes to the hearts, not to the heads, of his readers.[41]

Several Victorian critics commented on what they judged to be the essentially poetic nature of Dickens' imagination. David Masson described Dickens as being 'poetic in the style of his art', and wrote that his characters were 'transcendental renderings of certain hints furnished by nature...Some of his characters are thoroughly and ideally perfect [i.e. in imagination and conception], others are thoroughly and ideally detestable.' Masson compared them with 'the characters of Shakespeare' who 'are not, in any common sense, life-like...they are grand hyperbolic beings'.[42] Forster used the word 'type' in connection with Dickens' characterization, but in a non-pejorative sense, to suggest an inclusive generality and comprehensiveness, rather than a schematic exclusiveness:

> Mr Dickens's characters...pass their names into our language, and become types. It is an evidence of his possession of the highest power that the best of them are thus made each to embody some characteristic feature, to personify some main idea, which are ever after found universally applicable.[43]

Years later, T. S. Eliot was to touch on the same theme when he commented on the poetic suggestiveness of Dickens' art: 'Dickens's figures belong to poetry, like figures of Dante or Shakespeare, in that a single phrase...may be enough to set them wholly before us'.[44]

Though many Victorian critics praised Dickens' females for embodying precisely those stereotypical ideals anathematized by modern feminists, few of them thought that he displayed his poetic and imaginative qualities to their greatest effect in this area. However, Walter Savage Landor, in a letter to Lady Blessington written in 1841, made the specific connection between the 'Shakespearian' qualities, noted by such critics as Forster, and Dickens' portrayal of his heroines: 'One blockhead talked of [Dickens'] deficiency in the female character – the very thing in which he and Shakespeare most excell.'[45] And E. P. Whipple wrote in 1867:

> His favourite heroines, Agnes Wickfield...Florence Dombey, Esther Summerson, Little Dorrit...are models of

self-devoted, all-enduring, all-sacrificing affection....It may
be that they are too perfect to be altogether real; it may be
that, as specimens of genuine characterization, they are
inferior to Dora Spenlow...or Bella Wilfer, in whom affection is connected with some kind of infirmity; but still, so
intensely are they conceived, so unbounded is their wealth
of love, that their reality, if questioned by the head, is
accepted undoubtingly by the heart.[46]

Such a view is, clearly, very different from those of most modern
critics. For the remainder of this essay, I would like to examine
four of the heroines mentioned by Whipple, in an attempt to
investigate whether there might be some grounds for the admiration of Victorian critics, and whether their comments might, in
consequence, constitute at least a partial challenge to modern
orthodoxies.

Agnes Wickfield in *David Copperfield* has perhaps had the worst
press of all Dickens' heroines. R. H. Hutton's verdict on her has
already been cited. George Orwell called her 'the real legless
angel of Victorian romance',[47] and Michael Slater has recently
asserted that 'it would be a bold critic indeed who would claim
this character to be a success', and has argued that Dickens failed
'to vivify Agnes satisfactorily for his readers'.[48] Even Dickens'
staunchest champion, John Forster, had reservations about her,
speaking of 'the too unfailing wisdom and self-sacrificing goodness of the angel-wife, Agnes'.[49]

There seems to be much justification for such criticisms, if one
concentrates exclusively on the later parts of the novel. In those
pages, Agnes' existence for the reader is almost entirely created
through David's adulation of her (supported by her father's at the
very end). Mr Wickfield talks of the past as offering 'much matter
for regret', but says he would not change it as it would cancel
'such patience and devotion, such fidelity, such a child's love' (ch.
LX).[50] Painful experience is here reduced to an opportunity for the
display of virtue. David's view of Agnes at the end of the novel,
as his 'solace and resource', 'pointing upwards' (ch. LXII), is the
only perspective which the reader is invited to entertain, and thus
seems to be unequivocally endorsed by Dickens. 'Clasped in my
embrace', remarks David in the same chapter, 'I held the source
of every worthy aspiration I had ever had.' Here one notes a
strange lack of focus (characteristic of these parts of the novel) on

the precise details of the imagined moment. The sentence moves awkwardly from the physical actuality to the abstract ideal. Both characters lack vivid presence; the moment exists merely to create a vague (albeit powerful) emotional affirmation of the 'blessed calm' and 'tranquillity' which (Dickens wishes to convince us) characterize the couple's coming together.

In some respects, the final stretches of the book confirm a view of Agnes which has been present ever since her first appearance. In chapter XV, David recalls his first meeting with Agnes when, as a boy, he was taken to Mr Wickfield's house by Betsy Trotwood to make arrangements for his education. In this scene, Agnes is associated in David's mind with an image often adduced by critics to indicate the static and abstract nature of her depiction throughout the novel. David sees her 'in the grave light of the old staircase', recalls 'a stained glass window in a church', and 'associate[s] something of its tranquil brightness with Agnes Wickfield ever afterwards'. Thus far in the narrative, we have been invited to experience the other characters (most notably Mr Murdstone) with the vividness and immediacy of a child's vision, but we have not been consistently invited to share David's assessment of them. We have come to understand something of his nature by finding grounds, on occasion, for different judgements from his own. This is particularly true in the case of Steerforth, where a double perspective is created, partly by hints of a changed attitude in the adult David, but mainly because the glimpses of Steerforth's callous selfishness which we are afforded by the older David's narrative make us resist the idealization of Steerforth which we are told was the young David's response to the older boy. By contrast, the description of the young Agnes affords no sign of any change in attitude on the part of the adult David, or any qualification of what appears to be a vague impulse to associate Agnes' peaceful goodness with even vaguer religiose imagery. The palpable design of the passage on the reader is clear enough; Dickens is obviously using David's narration to signal Agnes' significance to the reader; but the narrator's words, in fact, do little to enhance our imaginative understanding of either figure in the scene.

But though critics have been justified in commenting adversely on these aspects of Dickens' handling of Agnes, they have been less than fair to those moments in the portrayal where David arouses our interest in Agnes more vividly and suggestively. Even in the 'stained glass' scene, Dickens at times succeeds in conveying a real sense of the young David observing the Wickfield household without being quite clear about the implications of what he is seeing. The reader is thus allowed to glimpse significances in what he registers which go beyond any simple moralizing gloss – whether David's or Dickens'. In these moments, the freedom of viewpoint which the reader is allowed comes closer to that afforded by the scenes with Steerforth.

Shortly before his religiose reflections on Agnes, David registers on the young girl's face 'the placid and sweet expression of the lady' whose portrait he has just seen, and who was Agnes' mother. 'It seemed to my imagination', he remarks, 'as if the portrait had grown womanly, and the original remained a child' (ch. XV). This linking of the wife and the daughter, the woman and the child, seems at first purely a matter of the narrator remembering a visual impression. But, as we read on, we realize that the effect of the comment is to suggest delicately the way in which Agnes might be perceived by her father, and how thoughts of her are inextricably intertwined in his mind with his feelings about his dead wife. The pressures on Agnes which result from her being 'the one motive of [her father's] life' are implied in the telling registration of her with her basket of keys, looking, in David's words, 'as staid and as discreet a housekeeper as the old house could have'. Such a moment works on the reader's imagination more suggestively and disconcertingly than the attempt to create her saintly tranquillity, indicating as it does the restraint and self-control of a middle-aged woman, rather than a girl. This impression is reinforced by David's observation of the details of Agnes' behaviour on his first evening in the Wickfield house. 'Agnes', David remarks, 'played on the piano, worked, and talked' as if she were a wifely companion to her father. But it is her perception of her father's 'brooding' mood and her attempts to alleviate his anxiety which are most striking: 'She always observed this quickly, I thought, and always roused him with a question or caress.' The haunting impression of a young girl bearing adult burdens and responsibilities kindles our interest and makes Agnes, at moments in these scenes, more than merely a conventional emblem of serene goodness. But at this stage the impressions remain merely hints.

In the following chapter, Dickens reinforces and develops our sense of the disturbing elements in Mr Wickfield's dependence on Agnes, and his obsessive need, when David is witness to his desperate musings:

'I must have her near me. I must keep her near me. If the thought that I may die and leave my darling, or that my darling may die and leave me, comes like a spectre, to distress my happiest hours, and is only to be drowned in –'

He did not supply the word; but pacing slowly to the place where he had sat, and mechanically going through the action of pouring wine from the empty decanter, set it down and paced back again.

It is clear that such a dependence is of a potentially warping and threatening nature. But we are not here allowed any insight into the effect on Agnes. David's narration reiterates his idealization of her 'modest, orderly, placid manner' and her 'beautiful, calm voice'. Agnes ceases to be a human presence in our imaginations as soon as David begins to reflect on her virtues in this way, and there is no indication that Dickens is distancing himself from David's point of view. But when David is made to remark, in the same chapter, 'I love Little Em'ly and I don't love Agnes – no, not at all in that way – but I feel that there are goodness, peace, and truth, wherever Agnes is', Dickens seems now to be hinting, momentarily, at a culpably self-regarding element in David's attitude to Agnes: she is, in his eyes, a moral guide, to be admired, but not a suffering human being in need of his affection and understanding.

Later, however, in the middle sections of the novel, Dickens does seem, quite consciously, to be inviting the reader to be critical of David's reflections on Agnes' character. In chapter XVIII, he talks of her as 'my sweet sister, as I call her in my thoughts, my counsellor...the better angel of the lives of all who come within her calm, good, self-denying influence'. It is made clear that such reflections are, at root, partly egotistical when we witness Agnes' responses to David's declarations of his feelings for her, and of the needs which he thinks she satisfies in him.[51] In chapter XIX, David declares openly to Agnes: 'You are so good and so sweet-tempered. You have such a gentle nature, and you are always right.' Such sentiments sound unequivocally foolish when expressed this directly, and when divested of the religiose imagery of David's private meditations about Agnes. She responds with laughter and a pertinent comment: 'You talk...as if

I were the late Miss Larkins [David's first adolescent love].' This exchange, managed by Dickens with subtlety and concentration, makes us simultaneously aware of a variety of dimensions to the scene: of David's blundering self-involvement and lack of tact, of Agnes' awareness of those faults, of her realization of David's failure to grasp the true nature of his own feelings towards her, and of her own need, in the circumstances, to suppress any overt indication of her own feeling for him. At this moment, Agnes is no mere abstract embodiment of virtue, but an imaginative creation of delicate sensibility in whose plight we can become involved.

As the novel continues, so do Dickens' indications that David's casting Agnes in the role of 'good angel' is a cause of unhappiness to her – she smiles 'sadly' when he uses that term later. David's lack of insight into her feelings (and his own) is also revealed when he begs that she will not 'sacrifice [herself] to a mistaken sense of duty' by marrying Uriah Heep. She gives him a 'momentary look, not wondering, not accusing, not regretting' (ch. XXXIX), but David does not understand what it signifies. After Betsy Trotwood loses her money, David comes to consult Agnes, in a search for consolation and support (ch. XXXIX):

'My reliance is on you.'
'But it must not be on me, Trotwood,' returned Agnes with
   a pleasant smile. 'It must be on someone else.'
'On Dora?' said I.
'Assuredly.'

Agnes, once again, tactfully attempts to lead David to a greater understanding of his own feelings and impulses than he can manage himself. His behaviour reveals him to be so over-whelmed by his own problems that he only sees Agnes in terms of the comfort and solace which she can provide for him, rather than as someone with problems and needs of her own.

Thus, despite the tendency in much of the latter part of the novel to return our perspective on Agnes to that of the callow, idealizing, young David Copperfield, a number of moments offer insight both into David's egotistic labelling of Agnes and into the disturbing and painful aspects of Agnes' own self-restraint and self-suppression. In these scenes, Agnes is no mere saint or angel from a stained-glass window, but a plausible, fictional creation whose plight both moves our hearts and illuminates our minds.

Many readers have seen Esther Summerson, in *Bleak House*, as Dickens' attempt to portray, 'from the inside', the kind of self-denial and devotion to the interests of others which, it is claimed, are displayed in a merely external way in the character of Agnes Wickfield. There has, however, been considerable disagreement about the way in which Dickens has explored and placed Esther's revelations about herself, and about the nature and effects of her narrative. Some critics feel that Esther's narrative is a clumsy attempt on Dickens' part to idealize the 'gentle, passive sweetness' which he and his age regarded so highly, by having her report others' praise of her.[52] Philip Collins, for example, remarks that she is 'not interesting in herself' and that 'a score of Victorian novelists, much less talented than Dickens, could do better than this'. Dickens, Collins claims, was maladroit in trying to make us aware of her virtues and lovableness through her 'modest unawareness', and he regards this experimental use of a first-person narrative by a 'domestic paragon' as an unqualified failure; Esther's character was, he argues, of a type 'over which his imagination had never been strong or fertile'.[53] Others, however, claim that Dickens' Esther should be seen as an interesting self-portrait of a psychologically damaged woman, 'a coherent and convincing impression of a neurotic personality'.[54]

The opening of Esther's narrative immediately holds our attention, as we try to come to terms with the purport of the self-denigration revealed in such an extreme form: 'I know I am not clever. I always knew that.' Throughout this early part of the narrative, we receive two mutually reinforcing impressions – one of this insistent individual voice, stressing an incapacity to understand things, but trying to clarify and explain itself in a disturbingly intimate confessional tone, the other a vivid portrayal of the solitary child whose experiences have created that voice, and who has only a doll to talk to, and a desperate need to open her heart. Our sense of Esther's solitude is intensified by her recounted memories of her feeling of separation from the other girls at school, by the refusal by her godmother to allow her to attend a party, and by the existence pointed to in the bleak words 'I never went out at all' (ch. III). The narrator reflects, as a grown woman, on the nature of the way she responded to her godmother, the only person with whom she had any close contact. This creates a disturbing sense of a suppressing mind, consciously judging and assessing, but failing to perceive what we see to be the realities of the situation. The adult Esther describes the godmother as a 'good, good woman' whom, as a child, she had 'never loved as [she] ought to have loved...and as [she] felt [she] must have loved...if [she] had been a better girl' (ch. III). But Esther's narration allows us, simultaneously, to be aware of the godmother's unfeeling and repressive cruelty. She is 'grave, and strict' in demeanour, and when she tells Esther of her illegitimacy, she speaks 'in a cold, low voice': 'Your mother, Esther, is your disgrace and you were hers.'

At this stage in the novel, therefore, Dickens creates a subtly fluctuating range of responses to Esther in his readers.[55] This ranges from a sympathy for the loveless, bewildered state of the young child who comments that since she 'had brought no joy, at any time, to any one's heart' she resolved 'to be industrious, contented, and kind hearted, and to do some good to someone, and win some love to [her]self if [she] could', to a sense of unease with, and distance from, the mature Esther's apparently neurotic self-deprecation and disturbingly intimate and revelatory tone. 'I hope it is not self-indulgent to shed these tears', remarks Esther in chapter III. 'There! I have wiped them away now.' To focus, in the manner of some critics, merely on personal commentary of this kind, using it as evidence with which to construct a psychological case-history, is to exclude much of what is gripping and memorable in Dickens' dramatic recreation, in Esther's reminiscences, of the episodes in which she has participated. In these early parts of the novel, I would suggest, Dickens preserves a controlled and fruitful tension between Esther's narration of all she has 'noticed' and the restricted and repetitive account of her own responses, feelings and judgements (or evasions of judgement).

This tension, however, becomes more problematic as the novel progresses. Some later episodes would seem to give support to the claim that Dickens uses Esther's self-deprecation as a clumsy device to elicit the approval which he now wishes to bestow upon her conduct. However, it also becomes increasingly difficult to assess the extent to which Dickens is consciously inviting us to recognize what Esther's commentary at times makes us feel forcefully (and what psychologizing critics take to be the main interest of the whole portrayal) – that her self-restraint and self-abnegation are not straightforward virtues, but result from disturbing inner repressions. In the famous paragraphs in which

Esther describes her sensations when suffering from smallpox (ch. XXXV), speaking of labouring 'up colossal staircases', of being 'oppressed by cares and difficulties', of praying to be taken like a bead off a flaming necklace 'when it was such inexplicable agony and misery to be part of the dreadful thing', there is such immediacy and power in the prose that we become imaginatively inward with her state of suppressed pain and effort. However, we can also be completely alienated from Esther's point of view, when she is shown making remarks like this: 'When I find myself coming into the story again, I am really vexed and say "Dear, dear, you tiresome little creature".' The various facets of Dickens' portrayal of Esther would seem not to fit together neatly to give a coherent vision of a unified, individual psychology. While critics often imply that our response to Esther is single, constant and simple, the fluctuations of interest and conviction in Dickens' writing make it, I think, difficult to maintain one view of Esther for very long. Some of the remarks taken by critics to indicate Esther's habit of evasion do not so much suggest that, as remind us that Dickens had his eye on plot as well as character. Esther's remarks about the surgeon Woodcourt – always couched in hesitating and evasive terms ('I have forgotten to mention – at least I have not mentioned – that Mr Woodcourt...') – are such an explicit signal to the reader about the real state of her feelings, and are so clearly designed to arouse curiosity about what will follow, that we are conscious of being subjected to authorial pressure, rather than being afforded a penetrating insight into a particular cast of mind.

It is the depiction of Esther's relation with Woodcourt and with Jarndyce, and the manner in which this is concluded, which has formed the basis for many hostile accounts of Esther's portrayal in the novel. Her relationship with them, coupled with her passionate attachment to Ada and concern for Richard (both of whom share Jarndyce's view of Esther) is often taken to be central to the reader's experience of her character. It is Jarndyce who, Esther tells us, assigns her her role at Bleak House: '"You are clever enough to be the good little woman of our lives here, my dear", he returned playfully; "the little old woman of the Child's...Rhyme"' (ch. VIII). And he praises her wholeheartedly for her 'care for others' and her selflessness, saying: '"someone may find out, what Esther never will, – that the little woman is to be held in remembrance above all other people"' (ch. XIII).

Esther, in her gratitude to Jarndyce for his kindness to her, is shown to regard him inevitably as a source of true judgement and right feeling, but Dickens, on occasion, makes us feel that Jarndyce is not always clear-sighted – for instance, in his relations with Skimpole and in his eccentric side-stepping of his own unease, when faced with uncomfortable facts about human weakness, selfishness and corruption, by habitual reference to the effects of the East Wind. Earlier in the novel, it seems as if Dickens is providing some indications that Jarndyce should not be regarded as an infallible touchstone of judgement and sanity, and the authoritative source of insight into Esther. But in the later sections of the book, which focus a great deal on Esther's relationship with him and give us our final impressions of her, Dickens' perspective has been simplified.

These sections include the narration of Esther's engagement to Jarndyce (for whom she feels affection as well as gratitude), a subsequent proposal of marriage to her by Woodcourt (whom she loves, but rejects out of her sense of duty to Jarndyce) and Jarndyce's resolution of the situation by finally 'giving' her to Woodcourt, having intended to do this for some time, but having resolved to prove Esther's 'goodness' to Woodcourt's mother by showing how Esther responds to such a 'test'. These parts of the novel clearly provoke a number of questions about the nature of Esther's self-sacrifice, but the way in which the situation is presented seems to close the questions down, rather than to explore them fully. This effect is caused as much by the depiction of Jarndyce as by that of Esther. All Jarndyce's actions are mediated through Esther's uncritical endorsement of his behaviour. She calls him 'so dear, so good, so admirable', and comments that she 'felt as if the brightness on him must be like the brightness of the Angels'. Esther's tearful response to Jarndyce's final revelations, and Woodcourt's passive acceptance of her, both conspire to confirm Jarndyce's assertion that Esther's self-denying refusal of Woodcourt was a 'bright example' of her determination to 'sacrifice her love to a sense of duty and affection' (ch. LXIV). Here, as with David's response to Agnes at the end of *David Copperfield*, Esther's behaviour is reduced to a schematic and straightforward ideal of selflessness (one matched by the equally schematic ideal of paternal benevolence embodied by Jarndyce) which is seriously at odds with our earlier sense of her troubled attitude to her engagement. As in *David Copperfield*,

Dickens is closing down interesting possibilities, which he has set in motion earlier in the novel.

There are many earlier scenes in *Bleak House* which have allowed us to experience the nature of Esther's selflessness in an entirely different way from both the idealizing tendencies of the final chapters and the disturbing pathos of the heroine's account of her childhood. These scenes tend to involve comedy, and usually focus on the contrast between Esther's values and behaviour, and the selfishness and self-involvement of those she encounters, and the contrast between her self-doubt and restraint, and their confident assertiveness.

Two of the most pleasurable scenes are those where Esther meets two women, Mrs Jellyby and Mrs Pardiggle, who are both involved in benevolent projects, and whose families suffer different kinds of disastrous consequences because of this. In the first episode, Dickens comically and vividly creates the discomfort and neglect experienced in the Jellyby household. One young child is first encountered with his head stuck in the railings; later Esther observes, another 'tumbled downstairs...where somebody seemed to stifle him'. The house is filthy and in complete chaos – Esther notices that 'the curtain to my window was fastened up with a fork' – and the dinner 'excellent, if it had had any cooking to speak of...was almost raw' (ch. IV). Meanwhile, Mrs Jellyby fixes her 'handsome eyes' and attention on the project of having 'a hundred and fifty to two hundred healthy families cultivating coffee and educating the natives of Borrioboola-Gha, on the left bank of the Niger'. John Stuart Mill was incensed by this portrayal, which he took to be a satire on the rights of women, but such a response would seem to represent a limited and rather humourless interpretation of Dickens' intentions. The interest of the scene seems rather to lie in a comic evocation of the chronic discomfort of day-to-day living caused by a devotion not to genuinely benevolent activity, but to the self-gratification which results from being 'full of business'. Esther, in her encounters with Mrs Jellyby, shows an awareness of, and sympathy with, the other members of the family, even though it can only be manifested by her lighting a fire, telling fairy stories to the children and washing them, and attempting to comfort Mrs Jellyby's wretched daughter, Caddy. Esther is not here held up as any sort of ideal alternative to Mrs Jellyby – we are indeed amused by her very incapacity to do much, when faced with such chaos – but, nevertheless, we witness the mitigating effects of her self-effacement, and are made aware of the interrelatedness of the admirable and irritating aspects of her selflessness. Esther's impulse to do good, it is made clear, is still motivated in no small part by her own need for love and for the gratitude of others. And, though she is shown clearly enough to perceive the awfulness of the Jellyby household, her self-deprecating habit of mind both causes her to evade any overt adverse judgement of Mrs Jellyby, and also to dwell, in (to us) far too obvious a way, on Ada's praise of her efforts to improve matters.

The confrontation with Mrs Pardiggle and her 'rapacious benevolence' is depicted in even more broadly comic terms. Even Esther can do nothing with her children, who are 'absolutely ferocious with discontent' at having been forced to offer up their pocket-money for charity, and who, she reports, 'all pinched me at once, and in a dreadfully expert way'. The main focus in this scene is not on Esther's character, but on the comedy inherent in the way she indirectly exposes Mrs Pardiggle's egotism, intransigence and self-assertion. The exposure is mostly effected by Mrs Pardiggle's declarations about her mission and her own character. 'I don't know', she says, 'what fatigue is', and the comedy is reinforced by the confused responses of Ada and Esther: 'We murmured that it was very astonishing and very gratifying; or something to that effect...this is what our politeness expressed' (ch. VIII).

Esther's tone of self-deprecation, it should be noted, is not consistently maintained by Dickens. On some occasions, she is given a decidedly more confident tone. She later says of Mrs Pardiggle that she 'would have got on infinitely better, if she had not had such a mechanical way of taking possession of people'. The same tone is used in the narration of her confrontation with Mr Turveydrop, the Model of Deportment, which is much more decisive in describing his 'disagreeable gallantry'. Esther, after hearing the old lady's account of his life, is convinced that Turveydrop's sentimental praise of woman ('But Wooman, lovely Wooman...what a sex you are!'(ch. XIV)) is merely a mask for a cynically manipulative egotism. In the case of Harold Skimpole, the drone who sponges off Jarndyce and anyone else who will lend him money, there is a development in Esther's response. Initially, she is puzzled and accepts Jarndyce's view that Skimpole is 'a child', but she gradually comes to feel that his behaviour is of 'questionable childishness' and, unlike Jarndyce, feels him to be an 'accountable being'.

Other scenes in the novel make us feel for Esther, but in an entirely different way from that in which we pitied her plight as a loveless child. We side with her, for example, against Skimpole in her concern for Joe the Crossing-Sweeper (ch. XXXI) and we feel particular sympathy for her in the scene of Mr Guppy's proposal, where he uses comically self-interested and legalistic terms, anxiously requesting that everything that he says should be 'without prejudice, miss'. While we are amused by Esther's discomfiture and confusion, we are made aware of its painfulness by her comment later: 'I was in a flutter for a little while; and felt as if an old chord had been more coarsely touched than it ever had been since the days of the dear old doll, long buried in the garden' (ch. IX).

The presentation of Esther Summerson in *Bleak House* is, then, diverse and fluctuating in both intention and effect. Too many critics have done less than justice to that fact, either by taking Dickens' sentimentalizing conclusion of Esther's narrative to represent the effects of the whole, or by trying to construct an individual case-history from her words, thus excluding much of what delights, moves, and lives in Dickens' dramatic recreation of the actions in which she participates.

John Forster found 'the spoilt foolishness and tenderness of the loving little child wife Dora' in *David Copperfield* more attractive than the virtues of Agnes. He described as 'matchless' those 'scenes of courtship and housekeeping' in which David, infatuated with Dora's beauty and vulnerable charm (so like his mother's), proposes to her, only to discover after marriage her total domestic ineptitude.[56] Later critics have agreed that Dora is a more satisfying creation than Agnes, chiefly on the grounds that she is not an impossible ideal, but a flawed individual. They tend to give more prominence to the later scenes depicting her married life with David (where they find her a complex and developing character), rather than to the earlier comic scenes, so enjoyed by Forster.[57]

I would suggest, however, that our most lasting and pleasurable impressions of Dora in *David Copperfield* are derived from those early comic scenes, where, although we are certainly made to feel detached from Dora and are under no delusions about her foibles and failings, Dickens convinces us of the power of her charms over David, and never allows us merely to fall into an attitude of self-gratifying moral superiority towards her. Dickens' humour in these parts of the book is inclusive and generous, and David's infatuation with Dora is as much its subject as Dora's weaknesses.

Our initial impressions of Dora are created through David's wildly extravagant language: 'I loved Dora Spenlow to distraction! She was more than human to me. She was a Fairy, a Sylph, I don't know what she was – anything that no-one ever saw, and everything that everybody ever wanted' (ch. XXXVI). An alternative sense of this miraculous being who caused David's 'blissful delirium' is gradually built up through fragmentary impressions of a 'pretty pettish manner', 'a quantity of curls', a straw hat and blue ribbons, a petted little dog, Jip ('mortally jealous'), and 'the most delightful little voice', which expresses such sentiments as: 'We are not going to confide in any such cross people – Jip and I.' The telling description of the moment when Dora, 'laughing', 'held the dog up childishly, to smell the flowers' both evokes the appeal she has for David and lightly suggests the implications of its nature. David's intensely idealizing fantasy is juxtaposed with Dora's presence and words to reveal the comic discrepancy between the dream and the reality.

We enjoy, in the same 'half comical, half serious' spirit as the older David, the young David's account of his folly. He purchased, he tells us, boots which 'compared with the natural size of my feet...would show what the state of my heart was, in a most affecting manner', and he walked 'miles upon miles daily in the hope of seeing [Dora]' (ch. XXVI). David recalls his 'raging and remorseful state' of jealousy when another young man ('Red Whisker') paid Dora attention on her birthday outing, and the bliss of reconciliation when 'folly as it all was, it would have been a happy fate to have been struck immortal with those foolish feelings, and have strayed among the trees for ever'. This kind of comic effect culminates in David's proposal, where we remain fully aware of the impetuous rashness of his behaviour, and yet delight in David's total abandonment: 'I intercepted Jip. I had Dora in my arms. I never stopped for a word...I told her that I idolized and worshipped her. Jip barked madly all the time' (ch. XXXIII). Later, when David tells Dora of his aunt's lost fortune, the humour brings home to us, in an utterly uncensorious way, the extent to which David is as ludicrous in his earnest self-dramatization and fervent avowals as Dora is in her resistance to their import:

> 'Dora, my own dearest!' said I, 'I am a beggar.'
> 'How can you be such a silly thing,' replied Dora, slapping my hand, 'as to sit there, telling such stories? I'll make Jip bite you!'

A little later, when David has explained the situation, Dora declares: '"I don't want to hear any more about crusts!...And Jip must have a mutton chop every day at twelve, or he'll die!"' David's supposed practical solutions to their problems are treated in the same comic spirit as Dora's reception of them:

> 'If you will...look about now and then at your papa's housekeeping, and endeavour to acquire a little habit – of accounts, for instance –'
> Poor little Dora received this suggestion with something that was half a sob and half a scream.
>
> (ch. XXXVII)

In later scenes, however, Dickens wishes to stress the serious and painful implications for David of his marriage. These have been hinted at, even before the marriage, in David's meditations about Dora's lack of practical skills:

> Dora seemed by one consent to be regarded like a pretty toy or plaything...I sometimes awoke, as it were, wondering to find that I had fallen into the general fault, and treated her like a plaything too – but not often.
>
> (ch. XLI)

Once they are married, David's painful recognition of the gap between his hopes and desires for his marriage and Dora's incapacity to fulfil them becomes a focal point, and the portrayal of Dora is increasingly coloured by indications of the frustration this engenders. Our sense of Dora becomes more and more identified with David's problems and dissatisfactions and his moral reflections on his plight. Dora's behaviour, in its wilful, childish irresponsibility, is contrasted with David's anxieties and his concentration on his work. He now records 'the toils and cares of our life', toils and cares in which he feels to have 'no partner'. It was perhaps Dickens' powerful impulse to show Dora's maddening immaturity and irresponsibility, and the frustration which this engenders in David, that caused George Santayana to feel discomfort and distaste when he came to these parts of the novel[58] in which Dickens begins to treat David more seriously, and wants to make us more inward with his plight.

The maddening aspects of Dora are brought home in the dramatization of the couple's first quarrel; in this scene, Dora tries to distract David by playfully pencilling 'ugly wrinkles' in her 'bad boy's forehead', but then erupts petulantly: "'I didn't marry to be reasoned with. If you meant to reason with such a poor little thing as I am, you ought to have told me so, you cruel boy'" (ch. XLIV).Our exasperation with Dora is reinforced by David's reflection on the misery of this moment and by his expression of 'pangs of remorse' for what he thinks to be his own cruelty to Dora: 'I leaned my head upon my hand; and felt more sorry and downcast, as I sat looking at the fire, than I could have supposed possible so soon after the fulfilment of my brightest hopes.'

The comedy that remains in these parts of the novel tends to focus more on the effects of Dora's ineptitude – for example, in the descriptions of the Copperfields' difficulties with their servants, and in the scene where Traddles comes to dine (ch. XLIV). As the novel progresses, our impressions of Dora are increasingly fragmented and come to us from a variety of perspectives, which do not always seem to cohere. Dickens provides an implicit condemnation of Dora in her dramatic presentation, but tries to counter this and to create a more balanced view of her, by the explicit comments of David, Betsy Trotwood and Dora herself.

Dora's behaviour is depicted, in David's accounts, as increasingly infuriating, yet he continues to assert how charming and delightful she is and to blame himself largely for their troubles. Betsy Trotwood is used by Dickens to direct our attention to the pathos of Dora's situation and its import for her, as well as David: "'You have chosen a very pretty and a very affectionate creature...estimate her (as you chose her) by the qualities she has, and not by the qualities she may not have'" (ch. XLIV). Dora herself speaks in a way clearly designed to enlist our sympathies for her plight when she asks David to call her 'child-wife': "'When you miss what I should like to be, and I think can never be, say 'still my foolish child-wife loves me!'"" This episode creates a contradictory impression which is difficult to assimilate to Dora's usual response to anything unpleasant: "'I think I don't want to know'" (ch. XLVIII). Dickens is here attempting to give pathos and poignancy to the moment, as he does again when Dora, with uncharacteristic selflessness, tells David, just before she dies:

> 'I am afraid, dear, I was too young. I don't mean in years only, but in experience, and thoughts, and everything. I was such a silly little creature! I am afraid it would have been better, if we had only loved each other as a boy and girl, and forgotten it. I have begun to think I was not fit to be a wife.'
>
> (ch. LIII)

Both of these scenes have the attraction of appearing to exonerate David and Dora, and of providing a simple yet emotive explanation for the nature of their relationship.

The earlier of these two expressions of Dora's feelings creates difficulties for the reader and makes Dora's later behaviour seem even more wilful, since a capacity for such self-understanding suggests a capacity for facing adult responsibilities. Dora's words provoke, in small measure, that kind of resistance which we whole-heartedly entertain towards Harold Skimpole's excuse for his selfishness and irresponsibility – that he is a 'mere child'. Skimpole, we register, evades accountability in a manner which has all the signs of an adult consciousness. That Dickens, at least in part, did not wish us to entertain such harsh thoughts about Dora is shown by all the elements in David's narrative which attempt to exonerate her. David is made to suggest that it is both reprehensible and cruel to try to change innate character in order to gratify one's own needs, and we are clearly intended to see some point in his remarks. Such an appeal to the head, however, is far less forceful than that to the heart in the dramatic scenes, where David's frustration and pain, and Dora's stubborn resistance to any sense of responsibility are so vividly evoked. As Dickens' contemplation of David narrows to sympathizing with his dilemma, our impression of Dora is consequently narrowed.

The phrase 'child-wife', abstracted from its context in the novel, has often been used to account for Dora's function and effect in *David Copperfield*. She has been taken to represent the weakness, irresponsibility and selfish immaturity which contrast with Agnes' virtues. But this is to reduce our sense of Dora's presence in the novel to a mere concept. Our impressions of her are more diverse (and less coherent) than such a view would imply. Dickens' own shifting perspective on his heroine is often taken as evidence of the 'psychological complexity' of his portrayal, but such an emphasis tends to exclude the pleasures offered by Dickens' comic evocation of the early relationship of David and Dora, those parts of the novel which John Forster most admired.

Bella Wilfer in *Our Mutual Friend*, rather than Agnes Wickfield, has often been regarded as the natural antithesis of Dora, in that she, too, is a spoilt and capricious young woman, but one who eventually conquers her weaknesses and matures into a devoted and contented wife and mother. Many Victorian readers and critics enjoyed the 'winning charm' of Dickens' portrayal of her, both as a 'wayward girl' and as a loving bride, and many contemporaries were in full agreement with E. S. Dallas' contention that her depiction as a wife offered 'one of the prettiest pictures in prose fiction'.[59]

Later critics too have admired Dickens' creation of Bella, at least in the earlier scenes in which she appears. The recent high standing of the portrayal perhaps derives, at least in part, from the fact that our perspective on Bella is created through an impersonal narrative, rather than being mediated through the consciousness of a first-person narrator. It is thus seen to provide opportunities for an apparently direct presentation of the heroine's inner life and thought-processes, and to be closer to that kind of psychological realism which has so often been invoked as a touchstone for novelistic achievement. But modern critics have also found Dickens' picture of Bella as wife and mother as she sits sewing 'like a sort of dimpled little charming Dresden-china clock by the very best maker' in 'the charm-ingest of dolls' houses' much less satisfactory, and there are undeniable grounds for their reservations.[60]

Once she is married, Bella's voice becomes that of either simple earnestness, as she declares, 'I want to be something so much worthier than the doll in the doll's house', or coy playfulness, as she tells her family 'John don't suspect it – he had no idea of it – but I quite love him' (Book IV, ch. V). The authorial voice and that of Rokesmith combine to endorse the behaviour of Bella after her marriage, and to confirm the impression of her which we have derived from the earlier scenes, where she pets and plays with, and confides in, her middle-aged father.[61] After her marriage, she is described by Rokesmith as 'the most endearing creature that could possibly be'. 'All the loves and graces seemed (her husband thought) to have taken domestic service with her' (Book IV, ch. V).

An additional problem derives from the fact that, as has often been noted, Rokesmith does not seem to be a fully imagined creation, so that Bella's love (which we are told gives rise to her virtues) is something we remain detached from, and sceptical about, since we have no real means of judging its object. Bella is portrayed as facing harsh reality when her husband is accused of murder, and she proves her love, and is rewarded by the riches she no longer desires, discovering meanwhile that her marriage has been an elaborate test of her character. But this part of the narrative raises many awkward questions about Rokesmith/ Harmon's manipulative behaviour and Bella's acceptance of it, questions which are only kept from surfacing by Dickens' narrowing of the ways in which we are invited to contemplate the hero who confers approbation and the heroine whose selfless devotion is its cause. Dickens ends by sacrificing a full imagining of both hero and heroine in the interests of creating powerful, generalized emotional effects in a conclusion in which love appears to conquer all and is finally rewarded.

But, as in the cases of *David Copperfield* and *Bleak House*, Dickens can be seen to be closing down on, and simplifying impressions and suggestions which occur earlier on, and which are both more interesting and more imaginatively vivid than anything in the book's final scenes. Dickens wishes to convince us that Bella has been totally transformed from a selfish woman (with a few better impulses) into a paragon of selfless devotion. But the effect of his art is such that the capricious, selfish Bella has a far more powerful hold on our imaginations than the sweet wife of the novel's close.

If, in the later scenes, Bella has only two manners (earnest or playful), in the novel's earlier pages, some of the most striking and memorable episodes are those in which she speaks with the unpleasantly petulant and self-involved voice of the spoilt child, and is subject to the author's overtly ironic commentary. In the first scene in which we encounter her, she is quarrelling with her sister, calling her 'a chit and a little idiot', and telling her to 'put the salt cellar straight, miss, and don't be a dowdy little puss', speaking sullenly to her mother, who is about to serve up her veal

('If it isn't very brown, ma, I can't eat it, and must have a bit put back to be done expressly'), and alternately complaining to, and playfully coaxing, her father, 'touching up his hair with the handle of a fork', while bemoaning the effects of being poor. There immediately follows a direct authorial comment ('It was one of the girl's spoilt ways to be always arranging the family's hair – perhaps because her own was so pretty, and occupied so much of her time'), which both comically distances us from her and invites us to judge her wilfulness adversely.

The most telling evocation of Bella's wilfulness in these early scenes occurs in her father's indulgent memory of her as a child, when he tells her:

> 'You were stamping your little foot, my dear, and screaming with your little voice, and laying in to me with your little bonnet, which you had snatched off for the purpose....You were doing this one Sunday morning when I took you out, because I didn't go the exact way you wanted, when the old gentleman, sitting on a seat near, said, "That's a nice girl; that's a *very* nice girl; promising girl!" And so you were, my dear.'
> (Book 1, ch. IV)

The old gentleman, significantly, is the miserly and cruel old John Harmon, who decides, on the basis of Bella's behaviour here, to bequeath his money to his son only on the condition that the son marries her when she has grown up.

Dickens gives Bella a variety of dialogues with different characters, all of which contribute, if a little repetitively, to our sense of her selfish egotism. But two scenes stand out in his depiction of her self-regard. The first is a bitingly detached description of Bella's discomfiture at Mrs Boffin's behaviour in society. When Mrs Boffin, who has been so kind to Bella,

> made a slip on the social ice, on which all the children of Podsnappery, with genteel souls to be saved, are required to skate in circles, or to slide in long rows, she inevitably tripped Miss Bella up (so that young lady felt) and caused her to experience great confusion under the glances of the more skilful performers engaged in those ice-exercises.
> (Book II, ch. VIII)

Even more memorable is the scene in the carriage with Mrs Lammle, after Bella has received and rejected John Rokesmith's proposal. Bella instinctively mistrusts Mrs Lammle (who is seeking to become her confidante, in the hope that this will bring her husband and herself some financial advancement), but, because Mrs Lammle flatters her, she both boasts about her own deliberate intention to marry for money and reveals things about which, one part of her mind tells her, she ought to be more circumspect. Although her boastful self-regard and cold contempt for Rokesmith apparently have the upper hand, her inner promptings to keep quiet and feel ashamed are shown to coexist as an instinctive counter-tow in her mind. Dickens prefaces the scene with an ironic authorial observation that Bella 'naturally realized in Mrs Lammle a woman of penetration and taste' after she (Mrs Lammle) has pronounced her (Bella) 'charming'. Bella is then made to rehearse the most calculating views of marriage in her desire to impress her new companion. ('The question is not a man, my dear...but an establishment'). This scene reveals with great particularity and acuteness a fact of human nature which is immediately recognizable – the propensity of human beings to be drawn by immediate circumstances, for reasons of vanity, into voicing views and attitudes which they instinctively know to be wrong. On this occasion, Bella's weaknesses are revealed in such a way that we have a sympathetic response towards her self-questioning ('Why am I always at war with myself? Why have I told....Why am I making a friend of this woman...?' (Book III, ch. V)), even while we recognize the culpable nature of her behaviour. Dickens here displays an inclusiveness which is missing both in the earlier depictions of Bella's selfishness, where we are invited to be so critical, and in the later idealizations of her marital perfections, where we are required to suspend our critical faculties altogether.

As we have seen, many critics (and particularly feminist critics), have tended to take Dickens on his weaker side, to make this weaker side stand for the whole, and thus to offer a reductive account of his treatment of some of his principal heroines. In this essay I hope to have suggested that, while Dickens' major novels do contain, particularly in their later pages, tendencies which justify some of the critics' strictures, his treatment of his heroines is more varied, more engaging, and less monolithic in intention and effect, than the schematized overview proposed by modern critics would imply. A close examination of Dickens' heroines indicates that, in those moments where these characters are most vividly alive in Dickens' portrayal, they become 'types' in more than a merely pejorative sense – not diagrammatic representations of stock contemporary prejudices, but, as John Forster observed, telling concentrations of 'some characteristic feature' of human behaviour which are 'ever after found universally applicable'. Dickens may seldom rise, in his portrayal of his 'serious' women, to the poetic heights which he achieves in his very finest writing, and which were justly celebrated by T. S. Eliot, but the most memorable scenes involving his heroines can surely be included among those parts of Dickens' work which justify George Santayana's general characterization of the novelist's genius:

> I think Dickens is one of the best friends mankind has ever had. He has held the mirror up to nature, and of its reflected fragments has composed a fresh world, where the men and women differ from real people only in that they live in a literary medium, so that all ages and places may know them.[62]

NOTES

1 Patricia Thomson, *The Victorian Heroine: A Changing Ideal, 1837–1873*, London: Oxford University Press, 1956.
2 ibid., p. 167.
3 For the former, as a method of reading, see Judith Fetterley, *The Resisting Reader*, Bloomington: Indiana University Press, 1978. For the latter, as applied specifically to Dickens, see Kate Flint, *Dickens*, Brighton: Harvester Press, 1986, p. 133.
4 Flint (*Dickens*, p. 114) notes that the two texts have 'become clichés in feminist exposées of mid-nineteenth century attitudes'.
5 John Ruskin, 'Of Queens' Gardens', Lecture II in *Sesame and Lilies* (1985), para. 68–9; see *The Works of John Ruskin*, ed. E. T. Cook and Alexander Wedderburn, 39 vols, London: George Allen 1903–12, XVIII, pp. 121–3.
6 Kate Millett, *Sexual Politics*, 1970; rpt London: Virago 1977, p. 79.
7 David Gervais, 'On reading Ruskin', *Cambridge Quarterly*, 8 (1978), 97–112 (p. 108).
8 Merryn Williams, *Women in the English Novel, 1800–1900*, London: Macmillan, 1984, p. 24.
9 Millett, *Sexual Politics*, pp. 89, 90.
10 Williams, *Women in the English Novel*, p. 35.
11 Carolyn Heilbrun, *Towards a Recognition of Androgyny*, New York: Knopf, 1973, p. 52.

12 Williams, *Women in the English Novel*, p. 35.
13 Françoise Basch, trans. Anthony Rudolf *Relative Creatures: Victorian Women in Society and the Novel, 1837–67*, London: Allen Lane, 1974, pp. 53, 56, 59, 60, 63, 64, 65, 68.
14 Jenni Calder, *Women and Marriage in Victorian Fiction*, London: Thames & Hudson, 1976, pp. 98, 87, 98, 102.
15 See Richard Barickman, Susan MacDonald and Myra Stark, *Corrupt Relations: Dickens, Thackeray, Trollope, Collins, and the Victorian Sexual System*, New York: Columbia University Press, 1982, pp. 30, 77, 78, 83.
16 Virginia Blain, 'Double vision and the double standard in *Bleak House*: a feminist perspective', *Literature and History*, 11 (1985) 31–46; Valerie Kennedy, '*Bleak House*: more trouble with Esther?' *Journal of Women's Studies in Literature*, 1 (1979), 330–47; Carol Senf, '*Bleak House*: Dickens, Esther and the androgynous mind', *The Victorian Newsletter*, 64 (1983), 21–7; Suzanne Graver, 'Writing in a "womanly" way and the double vision of *Bleak House*', *Dickens Quarterly*, 4 (1987), 3–15.
17 Graver, 'Writing in a "womanly" way', pp. 6, 10.
18 Flint, *Dickens*, pp. 113, 122, 120.
19 Barickman et al., *Corrupt Relations*, p. 55.
20 Michael Slater, *Dickens and Women*, London: Dent, 1983, p. 244.
21 Sandra M. Gilbert and Susan Gubar, *The Madwoman in the Attic*, New Haven: Yale University Press, 1979, pp. 24–5, citing Alexander Welsh, *The City of Dickens*, Oxford: Oxford University Press, 1971.
22 Slater, *Dickens and Woman*, p. 363.
23 On the latter, see Mark Kinkead-Weekes, 'The voicing of fictions' in Ian Gregor (ed.), *Reading the Victorian Novel: Detail into Form*, London: Vision Press, 1980, pp. 168–92. Q. D. Leavis makes some pertinent comments on the limitations of those critics who suggest that Dickens' characters are merely 'fairy tale types', or who over-emphasize Dickens' symbolic structures, in F. R. and Q. D. Leavis, *Dickens the Novelist*, London: Chatto & Windus, 1970, pp. 90–1, 118.
24 See Angus Wilson, 'The heroes and heroines of Dickens' in J. Gross and G. Pearson (eds), *Dickens and the Twentieth Century*, London: Routledge & Kegan Paul, 1962; Philip Collins, *A Critical Commentary on Dickens's 'Bleak House'*, London: Macmillan, 1971, esp. pp. 29–33; Philip Collins, *Charles Dickens: 'David Copperfield'*, London: Edward Arnold, 1977, esp. pp. 42–51.
25 John Carey, *The Violent Effigy: A Study of Dickens's Imagination*, London: Faber & Faber, 1973, pp. 162, 173.
26 *Swinburne as Critic*, ed. Clyde K. Hyder, London: Routledge & Kegan Paul, 1972, p. 223.
27 A. Trollope, *An Autobiography* [1883], ed. C. Morgan, London: Williams & Norgate, 1946, p. 221. Trollope recorded a more favourable verdict on Dickens' characters in *St Paul's Magazine* for 1870. See Philip Collins (ed.), *Dickens: The Critical Heritage*, London: Routledge & Kegan Paul, 1971, pp. 324–6.

28 G. H. Ford, *Dickens and his Readers: Aspects of Novel-Criticism since 1836*, Princeton, N.J.: Princeton University Press 1955. Ford remarks (p. 131) that Lewes was 'the first English critic to use the word *realism*...in 1855'.

29 Collins, *Critical Heritage*, pp. 571, 572, 574, 575.

30 ibid., p. 522.

31 ibid., p. 490.

32 ibid., p. 285.

33 ibid., p. 295.

34 ibid., p. 334.

35 ibid., p. 554.

36 ibid., p. 477.

37 ibid., p. 478. Whipple also commented acutely on why it is misleading to consider Dickens' characters as simple caricatures. See *Critical Heritage*, pp. 239–40.

38 ibid., pp. 2–3.

39 ibid., p. 290.

40 ibid., pp. 575, 573, 576.

41 ibid., p. 289.

42 ibid., pp. 256–7.

43 ibid., p. 292. Forster's praise of Dickens' characters is here close to Johnson's sentiment, in the Preface to Shakespeare, where Johnson comments that a 'character' in Shakespeare, 'is commonly a species', rather than a mere 'individual', as in most other writers' work.

44 T. S. Eliot, 'Wilkie Collins and Dickens', *Selected Essays*, 1931: rpt, London: Faber & Faber, 1944, p. 424.

45 *Landor as Critic*, ed. C. L. Proudfit, London: Routledge & Kegan Paul, 1979, p. 85.

46 *Critical Heritage*, p. 485.

47 George Orwell, *Critical Essays*, London: Secker & Warburg, 1946, p. 54.

48 Slater, *Dickens and Women*, p. 250.

49 John Forster, *The Life of Charles Dickens*, 1871–3; rpt, 2 vols, London: Chapman and Hall, 1876, II, 133.

50 Quotations from Dickens' novels are identified by chapter (and in the case of *Our Mutual Friend* by book and chapter) in the text.

51 My argument here in some respects parallels that of Kinkead-Weekes in 'The voicing of fictions', pp. 174–5.

52 Slater, *Dickens and Women*, p. 253, 255.

53 Collins, *Dickens's 'Bleak House'*, pp. 29–32.

54 Slater, *Dickens and Women*, p. 256.

55 Henry Crabb Robinson particularly admired this section of the novel ('The best thing is the picture of a desolate condition of a natural child...') See E. J. Morley (ed.), *Henry Crabb Robinson on Books and their Authors*, 3 vols, London: Dent, 1938, II, 715.

56 Forster, *Life of Dickens*, II, 133.

57 Slater, *Dickens and Women*, p. 248.

58 See 'Dickens', in Norman Henfrey (ed.), *Selected Critical Writings of*

George Santayana, 2 vols, Cambridge: Cambridge University Press, 1968, I, 188–202, (p. 197).

59 *Critical Heritage*, p. 468.

60 Flint, *Dickens*, p. 119.

61 Dickens' working notes show that he was increasingly concerned to stress the appealing side of Bella's nature. 'Indicate better qualities', he wrote (the comments are underlined), 'Interest the reader in her'. See Michael Cotsell, *The Companion to 'Our Mutual Friend'*, London: Allen & Unwin, 1986, p. 163.

62 *Selected Critical Writings*, I, 202.

5

LAWRENCE'S MEN AND WOMEN: COMPLEMENTS AND OPPOSITES

Mara Kalnins

'No age can ever have been as stridently sex-conscious as our own',[1] wrote Virginia Woolf in 1928, and sixty years later her words are even more true as an epitome for our time. The impact of the feminist movement of the last two decades on literature and literary criticism has undoubtedly raised deeply important and searching questions about the nature of women and their position in the world, about women as creative artists and about the ways in which women have been portrayed in literature by their own sex and by men. How these issues have informed and shaped feminist literary criticism has been ably outlined in the Introduction to this volume and discussed in the subsequent chapters offering individual studies of selected writers who have been strongly criticized by feminists for their attitudes to and portrayals of women. Of such writers few have been as controversial as D. H. Lawrence, whose books were censored, expurgated and banned in his lifetime and whose writings (like those of Hardy a generation earlier) were as often condemned in the public press as praised. The years since his death in 1930 have witnessed a dramatic reversal and re-evaluation of his achievement, from the comparative neglect of the 1930s and 1940s to the steadily strengthening popular and critical recognition of his genius in recent decades as one of the greatest writers, prophets and interpreters of this century. It is therefore all the more important to examine the basis on which that reputation rests and to examine the validity of recent feminist studies of him.

It is both curious and revealing that most contemporary feminist criticism has been and continues to be consistently, and often stridently, critical of the very writer whose deep and intuitive insight into and sympathetic understanding of women and the relations between the sexes earned him so many admirers in his own day. Women writers as different as Anais Nin, Rebecca West, Katherine Mansfield, Hilda Doolittle, Catherine Carswell, Brigit Patmore and Virginia Woolf all paid tribute to Lawrence's gift as a writer. Their views are aptly summarized by Anais Nin who wrote of what she perceived as the 'intuitional quality' in Lawrence 'which might be described as androgynous. He had a complete realisation of the feelings of women. In fact, very often he wrote *as a woman* would write....It is not the first time that artists and poets have come closer to the woman than other men have. But it is the first time that a man has so wholly and completely expressed women accurately.'[2]

This view is still shared by the great majority of men and women who read Lawrence and yet he has been attacked, variously, as 'the archetypal male chauvinist', 'fascist', 'anti-feminist', 'a paranoid anti-democratic misanthrope' and his works have been seen as merely a reflection of 'society's inability to come to terms with the massive change in sexual ideology which the war had engendered'.[3] Surely it cannot be that the articulate and informed women readers of the 1920s could have been unaware of the fundamental social, political, economic and intellectual changes affecting the position of women in their own time and unable to judge the accuracy of Lawrence's portrayal of them. Equally, it is hard to believe that three generations of readers since then could have been fooled into believing Lawrence to be one of the great exponents of women's liberation and that only now in the concluding years of the century can we accurately assess his limitations and expose his weakness. It is a critical commonplace, but no less true for that, that each generation and each age must bring its own interpretation and concerns to bear on the literature of the past and by so doing ensure that vital transmission of ideas which informs and enriches the present. But this process of continual critical modification and evaluation must itself rest on agreed critical canons if it is to be of value and it is in this respect that much feminist criticism (however potentially illuminating and valuable) is all too often revealed as limited, parochial and misguided about the very nature of art and creativity. Common critical errors and misconceptions, which will be discussed below, include: an apparent ignorance of the first and most elementary rule of literary criticism succinctly put by Hardy to one of his detractors:

'that a writer's works should be judged as a whole, and not from picked passages that contradict them as a whole.'[4] Second, that the artist and the characters he creates in his fiction are not the same and that it is often perilous to draw on biographical evidence to support interpretation of the fiction. And third, that what a writer may say in a critical essay or letter at one time in his life is not always an accurate commentary on the whole of his fiction nor a definitive statement of his beliefs. (The classic example of the dangers of this approach is, of course, that of Tolstoy, who rigor- ously argued for a strict set of artistic criteria in his formal essays and, fortunately for us, took not a blind bit of notice of the canons he had evolved when writing his great masterpieces.) In Lawrence's well-known dictum: 'Never trust the artist. Trust the tale.'[5]

What, then, are the most common feminist strictures about Lawrence and his fiction, and can they sustain critical scrutiny? In looking at these issues in one short chapter (and that dealing with a writer as prolific as Lawrence whose collected works will total some fifty volumes in the new Cambridge critical edition), one must of necessity be highly selective. But the novels and stories discussed here will seek to represent something of the chronological span of Lawrence's writing and will include texts which have been singled out for particular criticism by contem- porary feminist writers: *The Rainbow* (1915), *Women in Love* (1920), 'The Fox' (1922) and *Lady Chatterley's Lover* (1928).

Lawrence wrote *The Rainbow* and its sequel *Women in Love* to articulate his deep belief in marriage as the way to fulfilment for both men and women, and to recreate in his novels the conscious- ness of people living in the rapidly changing world of the late nineteenth and early twentieth centuries: 'I have inside me a sort of answer to the *want* of today'[6] he wrote in 1913 while he was at work on an early version of *The Rainbow*, and a great part of his recognition of that 'want' was focused on the emancipation of modern woman and her entry into the wider political and intel- lectual world of the time. *The Rainbow*, he said, would be about 'woman becoming individual, self-responsible, taking her own initiative',[7] and about the need for men 'to draw nearer to women, expose themselves to them, and be altered by them: and for women to accept and admit men.'[8] He saw the changing relations between the sexes as '*the* problem of today, the estab- lishment of a new relation, or the re-adjustment of the old one, between men and women'[9] and it was a subject that was to occupy him as an artist for the rest of his life.

The Rainbow is about men and women achieving or failing to achieve individuality and fulfilment in marriage. It is about universal truths in human psychology and character and about the deep and often unconscious impulses that move individuals and determine their lives. Mark Kinkead-Weekes, in two excellent articles on *The Rainbow*,[10] has discussed how Lawrence saw opposition, or 'strife' as he called it, as the basic creative power which causes all things to rise into being. For Lawrence creation is a dialectic and the opening pages of the novel show that process of creation through opposition by dramatizing two basic human impulses, universal forces that are present in every human being and for every generation: the instinctive self, that part of our being which is rooted in emotion, the flesh, family and heritage; and the intellectual self, which strives for knowledge, for thought and utterance, whose impulse is towards separateness, distinctness, independence, individuality. And although these impulses exist in every individual, regardless of sex, Lawrence reverses the traditional attribution of passivity to the female and activity to the male, bearing in mind his wish to show women in particular becoming articulate and 'self-responsible'. So at the beginning of the novel it is the Brangwen men who 'live full and surcharged, their senses full fed, their faces always turned to the heat of the blood, staring into the sun, dazed with looking towards the source of generation, unable to turn round',[11] while the women of the nineteenth century 'face outwards to where men moved dominant and creative...to discover what was beyond, to enlarge their own scope and range and freedom' (*The Rainbow*, p. 11). Through the three generations of the Brangwen family the novel traces the way each generation (and especially the women, culminating in the story of Ursula), seeks to go beyond what the previous one has attained, in a voyage of exploration which liberates potential, creativity and imagination. In reading the novel we become aware of Lawrence's central doctrine: that only through strife and conflict can one achieve new growth, transcend the limitations and divisions of the old self and be reborn into new being. The clearest example of this is the creative meeting and conflict between the sexes, male and female, 'the pillar of cloud' and 'the pillar of fire', to create what he called 'the third thing, the holy thing', the rainbow, the marriage bond.

At the same time, *The Rainbow* is also a novel set in a definite historical period, chronicling important developments in education, religion, politics and art, depicting an era which witnessed the growth of industrialization and urbanization and their effect on the environment and the quality of human life, and which saw the rise of the suffrage and other feminist movements. It is an astonishingly rich and complex novel and cannot be reduced to the simplistic readings of some recent feminist critics that it glorifies the traditional roles of women on the one hand and then betrays women on the other because Lawrence refused to allow his heroine Ursula to achieve full independence either in this novel or the next, *Women in Love*. This, and other criticisms, must be examined.

Several feminist critics hold that Lawrence had a deep mistrust of, and hatred for, women and feared their power.[12] They argue: 'The Rainbow is a matriarchal work, dominated by the image of the womb, and its celebrations of sexuality and fertility are conducted not in terms of phallic power, but of the rhythmic cycles of gestation and birth.'[13] It is difficult to understand why, even if this statement were true, it should constitute a criticism of Lawrence, but there is a great deal wrong with the statement itself as a description of this complex novel. One could hardly say that the novel presents a 'matriarchal' social system since neither lineage nor inheritance are reckoned through Lydia Lensky or Anna Brangwen. It is true that *The Rainbow* reveals how men and women die to their old selves and are reborn into new being, but this process is expressed in images from the natural world which are neither of the womb nor the phallus but of the vegetable kingdom: 'Except a seed die, it bringeth not forth' might be an epitome for the novel, an emblem for the rebirth of the individual regardless of gender. I am thinking in particular of the wonderful beginning to chapter 6 when Will and Anna are on their honeymoon: 'Suddenly, like a chestnut falling out of a burr, he was shed naked and glistening on to a soft, fecund earth, leaving behind him the hard rind of worldly knowledge and experience' (*The Rainbow*, p. 135). At the end of the novel, Ursula thinks of 'the vivid reality of acorns in February' and understands:

She was the naked, clear kernel thrusting forth the clear,

powerful shoot, and the world was a bygone winter, discarded, her mother and father and Anton, and college and all her friends, all cast off like a year that has gone by, whilst the kernel was free and naked and striving to take new root, to create a new knowledge of Eternity in the flux of Time.

(The Rainbow, p. 456)

In the closing pages the seed image is also linked to that of the rainbow, which has been the symbol of the marriage of opposites, of male and female in balanced equality, linking humanity to great creating nature, but which has also taken on additional resonances as the novel has progressed, becoming a promise of rightness and continuity in the human adventure into the unknown, a sign of God's covenant with man.

Kate Millett maintains that the women of the first two generations are downtrodden, denied any individuality, entering 'the traditional life of the farmer's wife and mother',[14] but at the same time she sees them as powerful matriarchs who dominate their husbands and are therefore hated by Lawrence. This kind of illogic simply reveals a basic misreading of the text. Anna's husband Will is not a farmer, nor is she a farmer's wife, but an industrial lace-worker (in historical terms showing the movement from rural to urban life in the second half of the nineteenth century and the wider opportunities offered to the individual). He becomes involved in a new department of education as a handicraft instructor and takes part in the Gothic revival. He is an artist. Anna herself has had a secondary school education and the potential to develop further, though she does not do so. When we read Kate Millett's view that Anna 'spoils Will Brangwen's life and her own by becoming a breeder extraordinaire tying him to the burden of nine children until both his hope and his talent have withered',[15] common sense rebels. Anna's wilfulness and strength, her supremacy over her husband as a wife and the mother of his children, do indeed create an imbalance in the marriage in the early years; Will's unhealthy dependence on her is another factor and the destructive result of one partner's dominance over the other is made clear:

He was aware of some limit to himself, of something unformed in his very being, of some buds which were not ripe in him, some folded centres of darkness which would

150

never develop and unfold whilst he was alive in the body. He was unready for fulfilment. Something undeveloped in him limited him, there was a darkness in him which he *could* not unfold, which would never unfold in him.

(*The Rainbow*, p. 195)

But following Will's assertion of independence – symbolized by his attempted seduction of the factory girl Jenny – he and Anna meet at last on equal terms and come together in the 'final reconciliation, where both are equal, two-in-one, complete'.[16]

And gradually, Brangwen began to find himself free to attend to the outside life as well. His intimate life was so violently active, that it set another man in him free. And this new man turned with interest to public life, to see what part he could take in it. This would give him scope for new activity, activity of a kind for which he was now created and released. He wanted to be unanimous with the whole of purposive mankind.

(*The Rainbow*, p. 221)

The passage explicitly refutes the statement that the whole of Will Brangwen's life is 'spoilt' and 'his hope and talent... withered' – he is, after all, only thirty when he and Anna achieve their marital harmony. Furthermore, to call Anna a 'breeder extraordinaire' reduces her to the state of a female animal and completely ignores the sense of wonder and enrichment with which Lawrence describes the mystery of bringing new life into the world. It seems hardly necessary to point out the unfairness of criticizing Lawrence for faithfully rendering (in a novel at least partly concerned with the changing status and role of women in the nineteenth century) what is a matter of historical fact: that women of Anna's generation, however aspiring and intelligent, did most often choose marriage and motherhood. But the terms in which that choice is described leave the reader in no doubt of the fulfilment possible in that role.

There was another child coming, and Anna lapsed into vague content. If she were not the wayfarer to the unknown, if she were arrived now, settled in her builded house, a rich woman, still her doors opened under the arch of the rainbow, her threshold reflected the passing of the sun and moon, the great travellers, her house was full of the echo of journeying.

She was a door and a threshold, she herself. Through her another soul was coming, to stand upon her as upon the threshold, looking out, shading its eyes for the direction to take.

(The Rainbow, p. 182)

With the story of Ursula in the next generation, Lawrence shows us modern woman becoming self-aware and purposive, striving for a more individual fulfilment than was possible for earlier generations. It is a remarkably sympathetic and discerning portrait of the difficulties faced by a young woman at the turn of the century and it is hard to see how any reading of the novel can support the belief that Lawrence 'goes to every length to make the lot of the independent woman repellent: Ursula's painful struggle is almost an object lesson. Finally he sides with the opposition: "Let her find out what it's like. She'll soon have enough."[17] The words are quoted as if they are Lawrence's, but of course they are spoken by Anna, who is set against Ursula's wish to become a schoolteacher. The second half of the novel shows the struggle of Ursula – or any individual for that matter – to become self-aware and responsible and Lawrence neither exaggerates nor diminishes the inherent difficulties of this process:

She became aware of herself, that she was a separate entity in the midst of an unseparated obscurity, that she must go somewhere, she must become something....But what? In the obscurity and pathlessness to take a direction! But whither? How take even one step? And yet, how stand still? This was torment indeed, to inherit the responsibility of one's own life.

(The Rainbow, p. 263)

The story of Ursula is that of her quest to find meaning in life, to develop beyond her parents' form of being:

Ursula, inflamed in soul, was suffering all the anguish of youth's reaching for some unknown ideal, that it can't grasp, can't even distinguish or conceive...she was fighting all the darkness she was up against. And part of this darkness was her mother. To limit, as her mother did,

everything to the ring of physical considerations, and com-
placently to reject the reality of anything else, was horrible...
Ursula would try to insist, in her own home, on the right of
women to take equal place with men, in the field of action
and work.

'Ay,' said the mother, 'there's a good crop of stockings
lying ripe for mending. Let that be your field of action.'

(*The Rainbow*, p. 329)

But the voice which limits Ursula's aspirations is that of the older
generation, of her mother, not Lawrence. And there is much truth
in this opposition between mother and daughter. As many critics
have pointed out, Ursula's illusions about school-teaching, and
later about university, are marvellously counterpointed with the
painful disillusionments of reality. It is probable that the pages
describing Ursula's schoolteaching are based on Lawrence's own
experience, imaginatively transmuted to that of a young woman,
but the important thing for the reader is the sympathetic understanding, insight and integrity with which that experience is
presented: yes, it was like that for a young and inexperienced
woman, struggling against the bounds of her limited world and
upbringing, yes this is what life was like

If Lawrence presents Ursula's disillusionment, he also
faithfully presents the limited choices available to her in the
getting of wisdom. There is no evidence in the novel that he
'ridicules her ambition'[18] to go to university, as Kate Millett states.
The extracts quoted from the novel to support this odd claim, are
again, not Lawrence's voice at all; in this example (quoted by
Millett), they are Ursula's – 'Then she would take her degree, and
she would – ah, she would perhaps be a big woman, lead a
movement. Who knows?'[19] This is free, indirect speech, repro-
ducing in narrative the cadence of Ursula's musings, her day-
dreams about college, and it is impossible to see how it could be
read otherwise.

Another feminist critic, Cornelia Nixon, maintains that *The
Rainbow* is about 'politics...which are primarily negative or
anarchic',[20] a statement hard to understand when the term
'politics' is never defined nor the senses in which 'negative' and
'anarchic' are used. Still less does the novel show, as she believes,
that the 'only path to self-realisation...is sexual and creative'.[21]
While it is true that sexual compatibility is shown in the first two

generations to overcome difficulties of temperament and personality, no such simple answer is possible for the new, modern woman, Ursula. Her two sexual encounters – with the lesbian Winifred Inger and with Anton Skrebensky – are both failures, though she learns from them and achieves a deeper self-knowledge, but the description of her rejection of these relationships is not a revelation of Lawrence's anxiety to destroy characters 'as an object lesson in how monstrous the new woman can be'[22] (Kate Millett again), but to reveal how precarious the balance between individuals in love is and how limiting a mismatch can become if one rests in it. As Anais Nin has pointed out:

> Lawrence realized the tragedy of inequality in love as no one else ever realized it. And with it he realized the tragedy not alone of physical but of spiritual and mental love which is the cause of torment in human relationships. It is inequality of sexual power which causes disintegration in sexual relationships. Each man and each woman must find his own level. If Lawrence had not meant that, the union of Lady Chatterley and Mellors would not have been a fulfilment, while that of Anton and Ursula proved destructive. It was a fulfilment because the former were balanced forces, while Anton and Ursula were not.[23]

Ursula's passion for Skrebensky is limited and final, and however we may deplore her cruelty we cannot doubt that she is right not to allow herself to be subdued and diminished by him and by what he represents. Had she married him and gone to India this might indeed have been a betrayal by the author, but she does not.

The concluding pages of *The Rainbow* where Ursula temporarily lapses into a wish to return to Anton because she is carrying his child, and where she encounters the horses, have been interpreted in a variety of ways. Mark Kinkead-Weekes sees the encounter as symbolic of Ursula's unconscious recognition that she is denying her true self, her potential to enter the greater world, through a temporary fear of independence, of creative life. Anais Nin interprets the passage quite differently, suggesting that the 'horses are symbols of maternity and the sexual experience of marriage'.[24] But the difference of interpretation is a fruitful one because both critics seek to analyse the wider significance of the symbolic content of the passage. Contemporary feminist critics, on the other hand, see Ursula's reversal of mood, her regression into a more traditional female role, as a betrayal by Lawrence. But this seems a naively literal reading of a highly complex chapter in which Lawrence dramatizes the implications of the biological process, the state of pregnancy as an instinctive feeling of rightness for the fulfilment of the female self, a feeling in its own way as powerful as Ursula's earlier impulse towards independence. And the symbolic encounter with the horses recalls to us the opening pages of the novel and all that has gone before, the contrary states contained in any human being, the desire for separateness and individuality, set against the impulse to achieve oneness with the natural world by bringing a child into it. This dramatization of Ursula's choices does not mean she has passively succumbed to patriarchal roles and models; they are the kinds of decisions open to all of us living in an imperfect world and as relevant today as they were in 1915. And Lawrence records these choices with fidelity. Inevitably any writer will present some of the assumptions and topical concerns of his era – neither *The Rainbow* nor *Women in Love* could have been written in the nineteenth century – but only some, for as we all know, the great novelist also transcends the merely personal and particular, as Lawrence does, to give universal and timeless significance to the story he presents.

I now turn to two widely-held feminist criticisms of *Women in Love* and the novels and stories that followed its publication in 1920; first, that Lawrence became radically anti-feminist after *The Rainbow* and preached a kind of male supremacy based on the subjugation of women; and second, that in his political beliefs he became anti-democratic, fascist and authoritarian and that this too was in some sense linked to his so-called hatred of women. On the first point Kate Millett writes:

> *Women in Love* presents us with the new man arrived in time to give Ursula her comeuppance and demote her back to wifely subjection. It is important to understand how pressing a mission Lawrence conceived this to be, for he came himself upon the errand. The novel, as stated in the preface, is autobiographical; its hero, Rupert Birkin, is Lawrence himself. Much of the description of Birkin is rendered through the eyes of Ursula who is in love with him so that expressions of admiration abound.... *Women in Love* is

the first of Lawrence's books addressed directly to sexual politics. It resumes the campaign against the modern woman, represented here by Hermione and Gudrun. Ursula shall be saved by becoming Birkin's wife and echo.[25]

In support of her extraordinary claim that Lawrence and Birkin are one, Millett quotes the first sentence only from a paragraph in the foreword to *Women in Love*, but as the context makes clear Lawrence is speaking of the role of the artist to create and articulate what he feels and perceives, not that the novel is autobiographical nor that he himself is Birkin:

> This novel pretends only to be a record of the writer's own desires, aspirations, struggles; in a word, a record of the profoundest experiences of the self. Nothing that comes from the deep, passional soul is bad, or can be bad. So there is no apology to tender, unless to the soul itself, if it should have been belied.
>
> Man struggles with his unborn needs and fulfilment. New unfoldings struggle up in torment in him, as buds struggle forth from the midst of a plant. Any man of real individuality tries to know and to understand what it happening, even in himself, as he goes along. This struggle for verbal consciousness should not be left out in art. It is a very great part of life. It is not superimposition of a theory. It is the passionate struggle into conscious being.[26]

Women in Love is about the quest of highly individual and articulate men and women to 'struggle into conscious being', to find meaning in the modern world – 'What do you live for?' asks Birkin of Gerald[27] – and, like *The Rainbow*, the novel suggests one answer in terms of commitment between men and women and between men and men, a commitment however founded on a deep respect for the intrinsic 'otherness' of the other, a recognition of each person's integrity and independence. The conflict between Ursula and Birkin reveals the difficulty of defining the terms of such a commitment, still less achieving it, and Lawrence unflinchingly presents the ebb and flow of emotion and intellect in such a process. As many critics have pointed out, chapters like 'Mino' and 'Moony' articulate these difficulties in symbolic terms and scenes. Birkin's search for 'an equilibrium, a pure balance of two single beings: – as the stars balance each other' (p. 148) and his distaste for the limitations of conventional marriage which he sees as stifling for both sexes would seem to be a confirmation of his belief in the equality of the sexes rather than anti-feminist propaganda.

> The old way of love seemed a dreadful bondage, a sort of conscription. What it was in him he did not know, but the thought of love, marriage, and children, and a life lived together, in the horrible privacy of domestic and connubial satisfaction, was repulsive. He wanted something clearer, more open, cooler, as it were. The hot narrow intimacy between man and wife was abhorrent. The way they shut their doors, these married people, and shut themselves into their own exclusive alliance with each other, even in love, disgusted him....He believed in sex marriage. But beyond this, he wanted a further conjunction, where man had being and woman had being, two pure beings, each constituting the freedom of the other, balancing each other like two poles of one force, like two angels, or two demons.
>
> (*Women in Love*, p. 199)

It is puzzling why such opinions on the equality of men and women in the marriage bond should be disputed by feminist critics and why passages in which Lawrence reveals and criticizes the insidious way in which the old world of masculine supremacy can threaten to thwart a woman's freedom should be ignored. One such example is the scene in 'Moony' where Birkin comes to propose to Ursula. She rightly resists her father's attempt to dominate her, asserting her right to think and choose for herself. There is nothing subservient about Ursula here, nor indeed in any of her encounters with Birkin; she is throughout the novel his most powerful critic and it hardly needs stating that Lawrence wrote her words as well as those of his male characters, nor that part of the strength of his novels comes from the continuing, delicately shifting point of view, so that we now see through Birkin's eyes and now through Ursula's. The final conversation between them on the subject of Birkin's need for a relationship with a man as eternal as his with her, ends the novel on a deeply ambiguous note, but it by no means shows Ursula as submissive to her husband.

'I don't believe it,' she said. 'It's an obstinacy, a theory, a perversity.'

'Well –' he said.

'You can't have two kinds of love. Why should you!'

'It seems as if I can't,' he said. 'Yet I wanted it.'

'You can't have it, because it's false, impossible,' she said.

'I don't believe that,' he answered.

(*Women in Love*, p. 481)

Lawrence's view of woman was complex and discerning. He was fascinated by the core of her being, and her relation with man. In a well-known letter to Edward Garnett, written in 1914 while he was at work on *The Sisters*, the long novel which was to become *The Rainbow* and *Women in Love*, he said:

I don't so much care about what the woman *feels* – in the ordinary usage of the word. That presumes an *ego* to feel with. I only care about what the woman *is* – what she *is* – inhumanly, physiologically, materially – according to the use of the word; but for me, what she *is* as a phenomenon (or as representing some greater, inhuman will), instead of what she feels according to the human conception....You mustn't look in my novel for the old stable *ego* – of the character.[28]

And this notion of character as a fluid, mysterious phenomenon, rather than as a rationally analysable personality, is present in all his works. At the same time he was profoundly concerned with the way women have denied their real selves to conform to the stereotyped images of womanhood and femininity as conceived by men:

The real trouble about women is that they must always go on trying to adapt themselves to men's theories of women, as they always have done....Now the real tragedy is not that women ask and must ask for a pattern of womanhood. The tragedy is not, even, that men give them such abominable patterns, child-wives, little-boy-baby-face girls, perfect secretaries, noble spouses, self-sacrificing mothers, pure women who bring forth children in virgin coldness, pros-titutes who just make themselves low, to please the men; all the atrocious patterns of womanhood that men have supplied to women; patterns all perverted from any real

158

natural fullness of a human being. Man is willing to accept woman as an equal, as a man in skirts, as an angel, a devil, a baby-face, a machine, an instrument, a bosom, a womb, a pair of legs, a servant, an encyclopedia, an ideal or an obscenity; the one thing he won't accept her as is a human being, a real human being of the feminine sex...Modern woman isn't really a fool. But modern man is.[29]

Recognizing the inadequacy of these 'patterns', Lawrence sought to depict 'real human beings of the feminine sex' in his novels and stories. In *Women in Love* Birkin's conversation with Ursula's father demonstrates one old paternalistic pattern challenged and defeated by the new generation:

'And I tell you this much, I would rather bury them than see them getting into a lot of loose ways such as you see everywhere nowadays. I'd rather bury them—'

'Yes but, you see,' said Birkin slowly, rather wearily, bored again by this new turn, 'they won't give either you or me the chance to bury them, because they're not to be buried.'

(*Women in Love*, p. 258)

The novel also focuses on one woman who is an artist, a potential maker of patterns herself – Gudrun. But, it will be argued, Gudrun is also shown as essentially lacking some kind of warm creativity and vitality, as somehow anti-life, despite her self-sufficiency. Where does Lawrence show us woman becoming whole and complete entirely without man, where does he show us woman as artist, as independent pattern-maker becoming fulfilled, her artistic and feminine selves wholly integrated? Admittedly not in Gudrun, but then to suggest that Lawrence betrays women through the characters of Gudrun, Hermione and Ursula seems a peculiar conclusion. The initial conception of the novel's structure demanded two couples, one finding the right way in human relationship through conflict to tenderness, acceptance and growth, the other becoming a frictional and reductive clash of wills in a power-struggle ending in the death of one. Gudrun's character was necessary to create the second relationship with Gerald.

Virginia Woolf predicted in 1928 that it would take a hundred years to produce the artist-woman, the independent pattern-maker. Less than fifty years later a glance at the shelves of any book-store would have revealed writing by women authors of the highest order. Nevertheless, looking at the fiction, are these stories about women who have achieved absolute equality with men and perfect fulfilment in their societies? Looking at the 1980s, a novel like Anita Brookner's *Hotel du Lac* (1984) focuses on a woman writer of independent means still caught for the most part in stereotyped roles and doomed to unhappiness by the diffidence of her own nature and the roles society expects of her. Brookner reveals that in some essentials very little has changed since Woolf's and Lawrence's day, yet one would hardly call her anti-feminist. Of course, there are other recent novels where this is not the case: Keri Hulme's *The Bone People* (1983) celebrates the woman artist, here an androgynous figure (the child, you may recall, initially does not know if she is a man or woman), who possesses the power to heal divisions in herself and others, to create not only art but community. The heroine of Penelope Lively's *Moon Tiger* (1987) is a formidable woman with her capacities as an intuitive, feminine being fully integrated with her intellectual gifts as an academic historian, and both aspects of her nature are placed in a greater vision of the meaning of things beyond the merely human. When the novel opens she is dying in hospital, remembering her life and musing that she would like to write another history of the world, only this time it would be from the viewpoint of the eternal rocks which form the earth. Lawrence shows us the women of his time taking important steps towards this emancipation, becoming articulate and self-responsible. He did not depict an original woman as artist wholly independent of man and the reasons for this might indeed be interesting subject matter for critical discussion, but to condemn him therefore as anti-feminist for not portraying such a woman is absurd.

Women in Love, like many of the works which were to follow it in the 1920s, is also concerned with politics. Having witnessed the First World War, which to many of his generation and time signalled the collapse of Western Europe, Lawrence felt impelled to examine the basis on which that civilization had been established and the ways in which it might be renewed. To state, however, that Lawrence 'began the year 1915 as an optimistic social revolutionary and ended it as a paranoid antidemocratic misanthrope'[30] and that 'he began to denounce women, blaming them, and their self-conscious sexuality in particular, for the state of the world'[31] is nonsense. So is the view that 'Lawrence develops in the twenties an explicit anti-feminism',[32] that he 'saw the ideology of progress, reform and humanitarianism as a spurious feminine ideology which he blamed for most of society's problems',[33] that he believed 'Christianity, democracy, industrialism and feminism linked evils'[34] and that his doctrine throughout the 1920s 'is a combination of political fascism and male supremacy'.[35] These are the views of three contemporary feminist critics on the period in question, and they are wholly unsupportable.

It is perfectly true that Lawrence distrusted particular aspects of democracy and Christianity, but he never at any stage supported the central tenets of fascism. This term is often used inaccurately by critics who seem unaware that it denotes a political belief in a particular kind of central authority with a planned economy in a one-party state, that it glorifies the military and military virtues, and that it is essentially racist. Lawrence was passionately against any form of government that destroys or limits human individuality and individual liberty. As early as 1915 he had written: 'I am no democrat, save in politics. I think the state is a vulgar institution. But life itself is an affair of aristocrats.'[36] It is also true that in the major works of the 1920s he continues to speak with disdain of democracy and praises aristocracy, but what is abundantly evident is that when he uses these terms he is speaking not of political parties but of spiritual qualities in the human soul. At the same time, he recognized that these spiritual qualities must be given recognition in the wider social and political life of any age – how then was this to be achieved? This was the problem that exercised him and to which he sought various answers, dramatizing them in his novels and stories. His essays also consider this problem. His last book, *Apocalypse*, summarizes the ideas he had explored in the 1920s: 'mankind falls forever into the two divisions of aristocrat and democrat....We are speaking now not of political parties, but of two sorts of human nature: those that feel themselves strong in their souls, and those that feel themselves weak.'[37] But his distinction between 'aristocrat' and 'democrat' does not involve any overtones of fascism, still less of anti-feminism, because

Lawrence's view of humanity is not political but spiritual, not a denial of a person's individuality but a confirmation of it because it is based on a recognition of the innate and undeniable differences between people. In *Women in Love* Birkin says:

'Your democracy is an absolute lie – your brotherhood of man is a pure falsity...if you apply it further than the mathematical abstraction. We all drank milk first, we all eat bread and meat, we all want to ride in motor-cars – therein lies the beginning and the end of the brotherhood of man. But no equality.

'But I, myself, who am myself, what have I to do with equality with any other man or woman? In the spirit, I am as separate as one star is from another, as different in quality and quantity. Establish a state on *that*. One man isn't any better than another, not because they are equal, but because they are intrinsically *other*, that there is no term of comparison. The minute you begin to compare, one man is seen to be far better than another, all the inequality you can imagine is there by nature.'

(*Women in Love*, pp. 103–4)

It hardly needs stating that, in accepted conventional usage, the masculine gender can stand for humanity in general, for both sexes. Writing in 1919 Lawrence maintained in his article entitled 'Democracy':

Each human self is single, incommutable, and unique. This is its *first* reality. Each self is unique, and therefore incomparable....The living self has one purpose only: to come to its own fullness of being, as a tree comes into full blossom, or a bird into spring beauty, or a tiger into lustre. But this coming into full, spontaneous being is the most difficult thing of all. Man's nature is balanced between spontaneous creativity and mechanical-material activity.[38]

And he goes on to discuss the inadequacy of modern political movements and parties because they are based on material property possession and mechanical law.

The cataclysm of the First World War confirmed Lawrence in his fear that humanity was caught in a nightmarish hatred of life, a kind of death-wish, and in this belief he was hardly alone. Yet even the most despairing of his writings during this period end with the hope of renewal and regeneration: 'But there must be a new heaven and a new earth, a clearer, eternal moon above, and a clean world below. So it will be.'[39] Throughout the 1920s in his travels around the globe and his eventual return to Europe, he sought for ways in which humanity could create that 'new being'. His search led him to explore other nations and cultures and took him back to ancient myths and civilizations in the quest to find and understand the values that had sustained man in the past and that must therefore also have validity for the modern world. His writings after the war therefore have at their heart a serious purpose: to explore the nature of political and religious power in human societies and to search for the causes of the malaise of our century. Clearly, both Christianity and modern democratic ideals had failed – where then was humanity to look for the sources to feed life and nourish western civilization? In his fictional writings he looked at different possibilities. The notion of leadership, since western leadership had so signally failed the nations of Europe, fascinated him for a time. He recognized a deep and unchanging truth of human nature: that men and women naturally honour wisdom and greatness in one of their kind, one who like Christ or the Buddha (or Juliana of Norwich or Mother Theresa of Calcutta), has the power to connect the spiritual and the material worlds. But neither political movements like fascism nor communism could produce such a leader, argued Lawrence, because both relied on force as distinct from power, both ministered only to material needs and ignored the spiritual. Equally it seemed to him that democracy and Christianity, with their emphasis on egalitarianism and love, respectively, had failed. Like Blake and Nietzsche before him, Lawrence criticized Christianity's emphasis on love and equality because he felt it denied the individual's potential and ignored the deep impulse to power and worship in human beings:

Man is a being of power, and then a being of love. The pure individual tries either for sheer power, like Alexander, or sheer love, like Christ. But mankind forever will have its dual nature, the old Adam of power, the new Adam of love. And there must be a balance between the two. Man will achieve his highest nature and his highest achievements when he tries to get a living balance between his nature of power and his nature of love, without denying either. It is a balance that can never be established, save in moments, but every flower only flowers for a moment, then dies. That makes it a flower.[40]

So in the novels of the first half of the 1920s – *Aaron's Rod* (1922), *Kangaroo* (1923), *The Plumed Serpent* (completed in 1925; published January 1926) – Lawrence considered alternative modes of finding and recognizing such leadership, and rejected them all. His last testament on this question, his message to posterity, lies in his final book, *Apocalypse*, but before its writing he had explored several alternatives in his fiction. Thus, *Aaron's Rod* contains several conversations about the relationship between men and women and about politics. Of *Aaron's Rod* Kate Millett writes:

> In Lawrence's mind, love had become the knack of dominating another person – power means much the same thing. Lawrence first defined power as the ability to dominate a woman; later he applied the idea to other political situations, extending the notion of *Herrschaft* to inferior males mastered by a superior male. Thralls to such an elite, lesser men must be females – subjects. Of course this is the political structure of patriarchy itself, and Lawrence's fine new talk of dark gods, his jargon about spontaneous subordination, is simply a very old form of bullying, which in other contexts we are accustomed to call fascistic.[41]

The novel refutes all these views. When Lilly speaks of the will-to-power he explicitly distinguishes it from the ordinary usage of the word: 'Power – the power urge. The will-to-power – but not in Nietzsche's sense', he says, and goes on to explain his view of power as that generative force which creates individuals and civilizations: 'you develop the one and only phoenix of your own self' and 'your soul inside you is your only Godhead'.[42] Lilly's expositions of the power and love modes are only a 'series of seemings', to use Hardy's phrase. At the end of the novel in a heated conversation with another character, in which he has been arguing rather outrageously for one alternative, slavery, we read:

> Here Lilly broke into that peculiar, gay, whimisical smile.
> 'But I should say the blank opposite with just as much fervour,' he declared.

'Do you mean to say you don't *mean* what you've been saying?' said Levison, now really looking angry.

'Why, I'll tell you the real truth,' said Lilly. 'I think every man is a sacred and holy individual, *never* to be violated. I think there is only one thing I hate to the verge of madness, and that is *bullying*. To see any living creature *bullied*, in *any* way, almost makes a murderer of me. That is true.'

(*Aaron's Rod*, p. 282)

It should hardly need pointing out that the same is valid for the discussions about the nature of marriage and women, too. Both Aaron and Lilly love their wives and feel bound to them, whatever their marital discords, and it would be absurd to expect a novelist to falsify the kinds of things men do say when complaining about their wives; but to take these as the whole truth about the novelist's own beliefs is misleading and profitless.

Lawrence understood that the old Europe and the values it had upheld were destroyed: 'the old order has gone....And the era of love and peace and democracy with it. There will be an era of war ahead.'[43] His words have proved all too prophetic for the twentieth century with the devastation of the Second World War, the countless global conflicts that have followed it and the horrifying prospect of a nuclear holocaust. Yet, characteristically, in this novel as elsewhere, his final message is one of hope. Aaron's flute – his rod, the emblem of his quest to find meaning in a shattered world – is destroyed by an anarchist's bomb at the end of the book, but, as Lilly says, 'It'll grow again. It's a reed, a water-plant – You can't kill it' (*Aaron's Rod*, p. 285).

In the other two 'leadership' novels, *Kangaroo* and *The Plumed Serpent*, Lawrence explores further possibilities: in the first, the protagonist Richard Lovet Somers is attracted to a political movement in Australia, but finally rejects it and its charismatic leader: '"It is the collapse of the love-ideal," said Richard to himself. "I suppose it means chaos and anarchy: in the name of love and equality. The only thing one can stick to is one's own isolate being, and the God in whom it is rooted."'[44] Even in *The Plumed Serpent*, perhaps the most controversial of Lawrence's explorations of the doctrines of power and lordship, he speaks of the aristocrats of the soul who will be masters and lords *among* men, not *of* men.[45] In his essay 'Aristocracy', written while he was correcting the proofs of *The Plumed Serpent* in 1925, he states: 'The providing of *life* belongs to the aristocrat. If a man, whether by thought or action, makes *life* he is an aristocrat....Man's life consists in a connection with all things in the universe. Whoever can establish, or initiate, a new connection between mankind and the circumambient universe is, in his own degree, a saviour.'[46] These beliefs and questions occupied Lawrence in the first half of the 1920s; the second half saw his thought develop further. But before turning to the last years and *Lady Chatterley's Lover*, I would like to look at a story which feminist critics cite as evidence of Lawrence's obsession with a kind of authoritarian fascism based on a rigid male hierarchy and supremacy over women, 'The Fox'.

The principal strictures about 'The Fox' are summarized in the statements of three feminist critics. Hilary Simpson believes that '"The Fox" is...about a land-girl and a soldier, but in this case the soldier...takes his revenge on independent women...the independent "manly" woman...is hunted and tamed.'[47] Anne Smith states that 'the semi-comatose acquiescent stupor of March at the end of *The Fox* presents woman as the "gentle domestic beast" so dear to the hearts of the Victorians.'[48] And Kate Millett maintains that after *Women in Love*, 'marriage represents not only the taming of the woman, but her extinction'.

> In Lawrence's short story, 'The Fox', this process of anaesthetizing the bride is even more clearly outlined. Henry, the masculine spirit and fox of the title, eliminates his lesbian competition, Jill Banford, murdering her with will power, materially assisted by a tree he fells on her head. He then sits down to await the rigor mortis effect he intends to have on his bride, whose drugged loss of self shall give him that total control over her he requires so that he may transcend her into the male world of achievement.[49]

These are odd misreadings of the tale and none of the above assertions can be supported with reference to the text. 'The Fox' is the story of a woman who has repressed her feminine self by undertaking a role for which she is not suited and in the process is damaging herself. Nellie March is a deeply divided person and it is her repressed self, explored through her symbolic encounters with the fox and then through her relationship with Henry, the young soldier who woos her, that is the focus of the tale. Like all Lawrence's fiction, the story is also clearly set in a particular period, and has much to say about England in the immediate aftermath of the war and the predicament of the 'land-girls' (as Hilary Simpson has discussed). But Lawrence's principal concern is with what he called in one of his poems the 'Terra Incognita' of the self – the unknown country of the unconscious, the instinctual realm. The story reveals states of being which the character herself is unaware of and indeed the reader may not recognize until he meets them in Lawrence's fictional world. It is this unknown, unconscious self that is the focus of the tale; to see it as a homily about masculine supremacy and female submission is a gross distortion. We have only to look at March's first encounter with the fox to understand the theme of Lawrence's tale. March is walking around the fields in the twilight, in a kind of half-musing state, her consciousness suspended:

> She lowered her eyes, and suddenly saw the fox. He was looking up at her. Her chin was pressed down, and his eyes were looking up. They met her eyes. And he knew her. She was spellbound – she knew he knew her. So he looked into her eyes, and her soul failed her. He knew her, he was not daunted.
>
> She struggled, confusedly she came to herself, and saw him making off, with slow leaps over some fallen boughs, slow, impudent jumps. Then he glanced over his shoulder, and ran smoothly away. She saw his brush held smooth like a feather, she saw his white buttocks twinkle. And he was gone, softly, soft as the wind....She took her gun again and went to look for the fox. For he had lifted his eyes upon her, and his knowing look seemed to have entered her brain. She did not so much think of him: she was possessed by him. She saw his dark, shrewd, unabashed eye looking into her, knowing her. She felt him invisibly master her spirit. She knew the way he lowered his chin as he looked up, she knew his muzzle, the golden brown, and the greyish white. And again she saw him glance over his shoulder at her, half inviting, half contemptuous and cunning. So she went, with her great startled eyes glowing, her gun under her arm, along the wood edge. Meanwhile the night fell, and a great moon rose above the pine trees. And again Banford was calling.[50]

On the one hand, there is the everyday aspect of the scene –

March is going out with a gun to shoot a furry predator; but symbolically the meeting with the fox reveals the profound divisions in this girl, instinctively drawn to the wild wood, the intuitive, the unknown, and set against this cosy little cottage, the light of ordinary consciousness and reason, Banford calling, here representing the safe, rational self, but in this case sterile and anti-life (for Banford later seeks to withhold March from a further, creative life with Henry). The fox operates on several levels: he is of course a perfectly real fox, the demon who raids the chicken runs and impudently carries off the fowls under the girls' very noses; he is also a symbol of March's unconscious desires and her repressed womanly self; and gradually he becomes identified in March's mind with Henry. When the lad arrives, Lawrence writes: 'She became almost peaceful at last. He was identified with the fox – he was here in full presence. She need not go after him any more' ('The Fox', p. 98). Significantly, that first night after the young soldier's arrival, March dreams of the fox. Without reading too much into the dream it makes sense, I think, to accept Jung's suggestion that dreams are at times the attempt of the unconscious self to communicate something that the rational mind does not know or refuses to acknowledge. March's two dreams are highly significant in this sense. In the first dream the fox is golden 'like corn', a fertility emblem; his cold, sweet singing reminds us of archetypal myths in the folklore of all cultures. Everyone is familiar with ballads like that of the raggle-taggle gipsy who woos the lady in her castle with his singing: 'O what care I for my house and land, what care I for my jewels, O! What care I for my new-wedded lord. I'm off with the raggle-taggle gypsy, O!' It is the lure of the forbidden, the wild, the untamed, a dangerous lure, too, for the dream-fox bites her when she tries to touch it familiarly, and its brush sears her lips (anticipating the burning sensation of Henry's first kiss). Gradually in the story, the fox becomes completely identified with the boy. Half-way through the novella, Henry actually shoots the real fox, but it makes no difference because to March he *is* the fox himself by now. And the night after he has proposed to her and they have told Banford, March has another dream.

Without attempting to explain all the resonances of the second dream, it should be clear that some part of March's self recognizes that she will have to leave her friend Banford, effectively kill their relationship and bury it. The coffin in the dream is symbolic – it is the woodbox which Henry has kept filled as part of his work on the farm; the fox skin, emblem of vitality and life, is not the 'right thing' for Banford but it is all March can offer, and then there is the real misery of betraying her friend, herself dying to the old way of life, to be reborn into a new one. To see this, however, as some kind of manifesto for male dominance and supremacy denies both the richness and subtlety of the story and Lawrence's beliefs as a whole. As we have seen, if there is one message that emerges consistently from his writings (and like many great writers he could be infuriatingly contradictory at times) it is the responsibility of each human being to develop and fulfil his or her own soul. For Lawrence, as for Shakespeare and Tolstoy, the creative way to that fulfilment for men and women was most often through the balance and equilibrium of marriage. But without respect for the other person's integrity, human beings thwart and destroy themselves and others. (Incidentally, there is nothing in the text to suggest that there is a lesbian relationship between March and Banford, as Kate Millett and others have maintained. If Lawrence had wanted to alter the psychological balance of the tale in such a way by bringing this element into it he would have done so explicitly, as he did in the chapter 'Shame' depicting Ursula's lesbian affair with Winifred Inger, in *The Rainbow*.) When in the final pages of the story Lawrence records Henry's notions about wanting to subdue March in some way, this must surely read as Henry's illusion, not Lawrence's:

> He did not want her to watch any more, to see any more, to understand any more. He wanted to veil her woman's spirit, as Orientals veil the woman's face. He wanted her to commit herself to him, and to put her independent spirit to sleep. He wanted to take away from her all her effort, all that seemed her very *raison d'être*. He wanted to make her submit, yield, blindly pass away out of all her strenuous consciousness. He wanted to take away her consciousness and make her just his woman. Just his woman.
>
> ('The Fox', p. 157)

The passage is in free indirect speech, not the author's narrative voice, and it articulates Henry's feelings and their immaturity (remember that he is only twenty-two; March is thirty but sexually unawakened and repressed).

A second difficulty which feminist critics experience with the ending is its curiously muted quality. March is drooping, but again this is psychologically perfectly credible and not merely Lawrence preaching absolute wifely submission. After all, Henry has won her in highly unusual circumstances; he has morally, if not legally, been responsible for murdering her best friend before her eyes and six weeks later she has married him. The shock of Banford's death, of marriage itself to the man who killed her, of complete physical union with this young man, makes her state entirely understandable, even if some readers might question if she has not substituted one kind of prison for another. The morality of Henry's killing Banford is and will be a matter for vigorous discussion and debate. But it may be useful to recall the context of the story: Henry has spent four years in the trenches of the First World War. The years from eighteen to twenty-two, arguably the most important and fundamental period in forming the character of any adult, have been lived in a mad world geared to the ritualized slaughter of fellow human beings for the sake of a few yards of mud. Henry would have witnessed horrors such as the Battle of the Somme in 1916 in which a million human beings lost their lives. He must himself be a deeply scarred young man (although Lawrence doesn't go into this particular aspect in 'The Fox', he does elsewhere in stories like 'England, My England'). So Henry's wish to return to the healing world of nature and the farm of his innocent boyhood is perfectly intelligible. And so is his wish to marry a woman like March, not for 'romantic' reasons but as an emotional and physical necessity. In addition to the strong physical attraction he has for March and she for him, there was also the shrewd, if temporary, calculation of what the farm was worth and the speculation about how much of it belonged to March. These complex elements are surely what real life, outside the pages of Mills and Boon romances, is composed of. Object-ively, rationally, we may be shocked by Henry's killing Banford, but it is evident that Lawrence also wishes us consider the possibility that that killing (certainly in Henry's eyes) might also represent a movement away from sterility and death towards affirmation and life.

By 1925 Lawrence had done with his specific explorations in fiction of the power and leadership issues in politics. Looking back at *The Plumed Serpent*, when he had just finished *Lady Chatterley's Lover*, he said: 'the leadership-cum-follower relationship is a bore. And the new relationship will be some sort of tenderness, sensitive, between men and men and men and women, and not the one up one down, lead on I follow, *ich dien* sort of business.'[51] His writings in the last years explore questions on art, religion, God and man, psychology and politics, and return repeatedly to focus on the problem of what kind of relationship is possible for men and women living in the modern world. His general concerns in this respect are aptly summarised in the essays on art and the novel written in 1925:

> The great relationship, for humanity, will always be the relation between man and woman. The relation between man and man, woman and woman, parent and child, will always be subsidiary.
>
> ('Morality and the Novel')

> ...only in the novel are *all* things given full play, or at least, they may be given full play...for living...For out of the full play of all things emerges the only thing that is anything, the wholeness of a man, the wholeness of a woman, man alive, and live woman.
>
> ('Why the Novel Matters')[52]

It was in this spirit that he began writing his first version of his last novel 'Tenderness', which was to be revised and rewritten from start to finish three times and to become at last *Lady Chatterley's Lover*. Writing to a friend in 1927 Lawrence set down his thoughts on his new novel: 'I always labour at the same thing, to make the sex relation valid and precious, instead of shameful. And this novel is the furthest I've gone. To me it is beautiful and tender and frail as the naked self is, and I shrink very much even from having it typed.'[53]

From its publication in 1928 to the present, *Lady Chatterley's Lover* has aroused fierce and often bitter controversy. The story of its banning in 1928 (like that of *The Rainbow* in 1915) and the famous trial of 1960 are not the concerns of this chapter, but it is interesting that the misinterpretations of the novel's purpose by its detractors and its vindication by its supporters sixty years ago should still be current. Today, of course, few people object to the occasional explicit descriptions of the sexual act; rather, feminists condemn the novel, much as they do the depiction of Ursula in *The Rainbow* and *Women in Love*, as a manifesto for male supremacy, a doctrine which, as has been discussed above, they

171

also incorrectly attribute to the writings of the 1920s as a whole. According to them Lawrence believes that women 'will find fulfilment by voluntarily relinquishing it, and consigning themselves to the man who will satisfy their essentially masochistic sexual needs' and woman's 'destiny' is to be 'the submissive mate of a strong man'.[54] Contemporary feminist critics who dislike the novel, and what they perceive as its message, do so for the same reasons Kate Millett has condemned it, for its so-called betrayal of Connie and its worship of Mellors' masculinity: 'What she is to relinquish is self, ego, will, individuality – things women had but recently developed – to Lawrence's profoundly shocked distaste. He conceived his mission to be their eradication.'[55] Apart from the nonsense of the first half of the sentence – can Millett really believe there were no women with a sense of 'self', 'ego', 'will', 'individuality' in earlier centuries (how Jane Austen would have laughed!) – the summary of Lawrence's intentions is wholly invalid and there is no evidence in his writings for it. With his belief in the integrity of the individual he would have detested any such notions and the essays of the late years bear witness to his concern that a balance and equality be maintained between the sexes.

In 'Matriarchy' (1929) Lawrence writes to his fellow men, perhaps a little tongue-in-cheek, but how sad if a bit of sympathetic humour in matters of gender should be denied us: 'Courage! Perhaps a matriarchy isn't so bad, after all...Far from being a thing to dread, matriarchy is a solution to our weary social problem...Give woman her full independence, and with it, the full responsibility of her independence.'[56]

It is perfectly true that in this essay, and elsewhere, Lawrence still sees a woman's essential self and role as intrinsically bound up with man, with marriage, family and children, and perhaps in this he is a creature of his time, yet one wonders how many women today would not essentially agree, even in our enlightened era of sexual equality. An essay like 'Is England Still a Man's Country' (1928), a deliciously funny piece, simply laughs at the whole nonsense of stereotyped notions of gender.

But to return to the novel. Kate Millett maintains that *Lady Chatterley's Lover* is nothing more that the glorification of Oliver Mellors' penis[57], a peculiar denial of the complexity and richness of the novel, and other feminist critics argue that in the notion of 'phallic consciousness' Lawrence is somehow being dishonest, disclaiming male supremacy on the one hand but actually endorsing it by attributing all real creativity to an emblem of male power and fertility, the phallus.[58] Again, this interpretation ignores both what the novel itself says and what Lawrence, impelled by criticism after its publication, wrote in 'A Propos of *Lady Chatterley's Lover*'. It is worth quoting from the essay at some length to make this clear:

> Marriage is the clue to human life, but...marriage is not marriage that is not basically and permanently phallic, and that is not linked up with the sun and the earth, the moon and the fixed stars and the plants in the rhythm of days, in the rhythm of months, in the rhythm of quarters, of years, of decades and of centuries. Marriage is no marriage that is not a correspondence of blood....The blood of man and the blood of woman are two eternally different streams, that can never be mingled...they are the two rivers that encircle the whole of life, and in marriage the circle is complete, and in sex the two rivers touch and renew one another, without ever commingling or confusing....It is the deepest of all communions, as all the religions, in practice, know....Two rivers of blood, are man and wife, two distinct streams....And the phallus is the connecting link between the two rivers, that establishes the two streams in a oneness, and gives out of their duality a single circuit, forever. And this, this oneness gradually accomplished throughout a lifetime in twoness, is the highest achievement of time or eternity. From it all things human spring, children and beauty and well-made things: all the true creations of humanity. And all we know of the will of God is that He wishes this, this oneness, to take place, fulfilled over a lifetime, this oneness within the great dual bloodstream of humanity....If England is to be regenerated...then it will be by the arising of a new blood-contact, a new touch, and a new marriage. It will be a phallic rather than a sexual regeneration. For the phallus is only the great old symbol of godly vitality in a man, and of immediate contact.[59]

The common misinterpretion of what Lawrence meant by 'phallic consciousness' also rests on a fundamental misunderstanding of the nature and function of symbol, which possesses complex resonances beyond its literal meaning. As the

173

extract above clearly reveals, Lawrence certainly did not arrogate specifically creative feminine qualities to a masculine emblem, thus robbing woman of any sexual identity and ensuring her subservience to man. Neither does he do so in the novel.

Anne Smith criticizes *Lady Chatterley's Lover* on another level, as ostensibly revealing 'Lawrence's inability to come to terms with women as full human beings, and his inability to show a satisfactory, fulfilling marriage between two articulate people',[60] but does not support this astonishing statement which completely ignores the delicately and continually shifting point of view between Connie and Mellors in their attempts to understand what is happening to them. It is true that they are not actually married in the last chapter and that like many of Lawrence's fictional works the novel has an open ending. But as Anais Nin and other critics have pointed out, the conclusion is one of the most beautiful and serene to be found in all his works, showing us the renewal of life and being, refreshed at the source of generation in the sexual contact between Connie and Mellors, now able to go on to 'the building of their world together'.[61] Replying to 'the storm of vulgar vituperation' which greeted his novel, Lawrence wryly ended his essay with a comment by a woman critic: "'Well, one of them was a brainy vamp, and the other was a sexual moron," said an American woman, referring to the two men in the book – "so I'm afraid Connie had a poor choice – *as usual!*"'[62] Sadly, it seems that very little has changed in the quality of feminist critical response to the novel since 1929.

Lawrence's strength is that he unflinchingly confronts and presents in his art all the inconsistencies and irrationalities of the process of unconscious and conscious choice, the supreme difficulty for all his characters, and especially his women, of becoming self-responsible, without minimizing or simplifying that difficulty. This is what generations of readers have felt has enriched their understanding and widened their sympathetic awareness, whether they agree with his outlook or not. Lawrence could be, and was, often infuriatingly contradictory in his doctrines and sometimes ambivalent in his attitudes towards men and women. So was Tolstoy. So was Hardy. So was (and is) almost any great novelist concerned with presenting the manifold workings of the human psyche in all its complexity and rendering its predicament, caught as it is in particular social and historical circumstance, faced with the problem of achieving and fulfilling itself in an imperfect material world.

I began this chapter with a quotation from Virginia Woolf and I would like to end with what she says about 'Women and Fiction' in an essay where she argues that the truly creative mind is androgynous:

> the very first sentence I would write here, I said, crossing over to the writing table and taking up the page headed Women and Fiction, is that it is fatal to be a man or woman pure and simple; one must be woman-manly or man-womanly. It is fatal for a woman to lay the least stress on any grievance....And fatal is no figure of speech; for anything written with that conscious bias is doomed to death. It ceases to be fertilised....Some collaboration has to take place in the mind between the woman and the man before the art of creation can be accomplished. *Some marriage of opposites has to be consummated.*[63]   (italics mine)

Her comment is not only strikingly similar to Lawrence's notion of 'the marriage of opposites', but a perceptive reminder of how easily feminist writing can become a shrill demand for the glorification of the female sex. Feminist criticism at its best has shown itself to have the power to be illuminating, humane and discerning, and to make an original contribution to literary history and critical evaluation; that on Lawrence, however, has been signally disappointing.[64] It will remain so until critics abolish their stridency and recognize that art is concerned with more than questions of *mere* gender. 'All this pitting of sex against sex, of quality against quality; all this claiming of superiority and imputing of inferiority, belong to the private-school stage of human existence where there are "sides", and it is necessary for one side to beat another side.'[65] We need, Virginia Woolf concludes, to 'escape a little from the common sitting-room and see human beings not always in their relation to each other but in relation to reality; and the sky, too, and the trees or whatever it maybe in themselves...our relation is to the world of reality and not only to the world of men and women.'[66]

F. R. Leavis has spoken of 'the insight, the wisdom, the renewed and re-educated feeling for health that Lawrence brings',[67] perhaps unconsciously echoing Katherine Mansfield's emphasis on the same word, 'health', which she defined as: 'the power to lead a full, adult, living, breathing life in close contact with what I love – the earth and the wonders thereof – the sea – the sun....'[68] Lawrence too was concerned to remind men and women of their need to regain contact with these greater realities, to open themselves to each other and to fresh modes of awareness and being, to cast aside sterile and limiting ways of perception and existence in order to create a new heaven and a new earth. The conclusion to his final book, *Apocalypse*, is a last testament of these beliefs and ends with these words:

> For man, the vast marvel is to be alive. For man, as for flower and beast and bird, the supreme triumph is to be most vividly, most perfectly alive. Whatever the unborn and the dead may know, they cannot know the beauty, the marvel of being alive in the flesh....We ought to dance with rapture that we should be alive and in the flesh, and part of the living, incarnate cosmos....What we want is to destroy our false, inorganic connections, especially those related to money, and re-establish the living organic connections, with the cosmos, the sun and earth, with mankind and nation and family. Start with the sun, and the rest will slowly, slowly happen.[69]

NOTES

1 Virginia Woolf, *A Room of One's Own*, Harmondsworth: Penguin Books, 1988, p. 94.
2 Anais Nin, *D. H. Lawrence: An Unprofessional Study*, Chicago: Swallow Press, 1964, p. 59.
3 Hilary Simpson, *D. H. Lawrence and Feminism*, London: Croom Helm, 1982, p. 15.
4 F. E. Hardy, *The Life of Thomas Hardy*, London: Macmillan, 1962, p. 408.
5 D. H. Lawrence, *Studies in Classic American Literature*, Harmondsworth: Penguin Books, 1972, p. 8.
6 J. T. Boulton (ed.), *The Letters of D. H. Lawrence*, 1, 1901–13, Cambridge: Cambridge University Press, 1979, p. 511 (hereafter *Letters*).
7 *Letters*, ii. 165.
8 *ibid., 181.*
9 *Letters*, i. 546.
10 See Mark Kinkead-Weekes, 'Eros and metaphor', in Anne Smith (ed.), *Lawrence and Women*, London: Vision Press, 1978, pp. 101–21; and 'The marriage of opposites in *The Rainbow*', in Mara Kalnins

(ed.), *D. H. Lawrence: Centenary Essays*, Bristol: Bristol Classical Press, 1986, pp. 21–39.

11 D. H. Lawrence, *The Rainbow*, ed. Mark Kinkead-Weekes, Cambridge: Cambridge University Press, 1989, p. 11.

12 This view is held with varying degrees of strength by Kate Millett in *Sexual Politics*, London: Rupert Hart-Davis, 1971; Carol Dix, *D. H. Lawrence and Woman*, London: Macmillan 1980; Hilary Simpson, *D. H. Lawrence and Feminism*, London: Croom Helm, 1982.

13 Simpson, *Lawrence and Feminism*, p. 92; see also Millett, *Sexual Politics*, pp. 257–9.

14 Millett, *Sexual Politics*, p. 258.

15 ibid., p. 258.

16 D. H. Lawrence, *Study of Thomas Hardy*, ed. Bruce Steele, Cambridge: Cambridge University Press, 1985, p. 128.

17 Millett, *Sexual Politics*, p. 260.

18 ibid., p. 262.

19 ibid., p. 262.

20 Cornelia Nixon, *Lawrence's Leadership Politics and the Turn Against Women*, Berkeley: University of California Press, 1986, p. 3.

21 ibid., p. 4.

22 Millett, *Sexual Politics*, p. 262.

23 Nin, *Lawrence*, p. 27.

24 ibid., pp. 31–2.

25 Millett, *Sexual Politics*, pp. 262–3.

26 D. H. Lawrence, 'Prologue to *Women in Love*', in Warren Roberts and Harry T. Moore (eds), *Phoenix II*, London: Heinemann. 1968, pp. 275–6.

27 D. H. Lawrence, *Women in Love*, eds David Farmer, Lindeth Vasey and John Worthen, Cambridge: Cambridge University Press, 1985, p. 56.

28 *Letters*, ii. 183.

29 'Give her a pattern', in *Phoenix*, pp. 535–6. Anais Nin discusses this essay and the idea of woman as artist-builder. See Nin, *Lawrence*, pp. 41–2.

30 Nixon, *Lawrence's Leadership Politics*, p. 10.

31 ibid., p. 15.

32 Simpson, *Lawrence and Feminism*, p. 65.

33 ibid., p. 101.

34 ibid., p. 104.

35 Millett, *Sexual Politics*, p. 277.

36 *Letters*, ii. 254.

37 D. H. Lawrence, *Apocalypse and the Writings on Revelation*, ed. Mara Kalnins, Cambridge: Cambridge University Press, 1980, p. 65.

38 *Phoenix*, p. 714.

39 *Letters*, ii. 390.

40 'Fragment 1', *Apocalypse*, p. 163.

41 Millett, *Sexual Politics*, p. 269.

42 D. H. Lawrence, *Aaron's Rod*, ed. Mara Kalnins, Cambridge: Cambridge University Press, 1988, pp. 295–7.

43 *Letters,* iii. 732.
44 D. H. Lawrence, *Kangaroo,* Harmondsworth: Penguin Books 1968, p. 361.
45 D. H. Lawrence, *The Plumed Serpent,* ed. L. D. Clark, Cambridge: Cambridge University Press, 1987, p. 178.
46 *Phoenix II,* pp. 477–8.
47 Simpson, *Lawrence and Feminism,* pp. 70–1.
48 Anne Smith, 'A new Adam and a new Eve – Lawrence and women: a biographical overview', in Anne Smith (ed.), *Lawrence and Women,* London: Vision Press, p. 45.
49 Millett, *Sexual Politics,* p. 265.
50 D. H. Lawrence, 'The Fox', in *Three Novellas,* Harmondsworth: Penguin Books, 1981, pp. 89–90.
51 *The Collected Letters of D. H. Lawrence,* ed. Harry T. Moore, 2, London: Heinemann, 1962, p.1045 (hereafter *Collected Letters*).
52 *Phoenix,* pp. 531, 538.
53 *Collected Letters,* 2, 972.
54 Simpson, *Lawrence and Feminism,* pp. 123, 128.
55 Millett, *Sexual Politics,* p. 243.
56 *Phoenix II,* pp. 550–2.
57 Millett, *Sexual Politics,* p. 238.
58 See Simpson, *Lawrence and Feminism,* pp. 129–31.
59 D. H. Lawrence, 'A propos of *Lady Chatterley's Lover*', Harmondsworth: Penguin Books, 1967, pp. 111–13.
60 Smith, 'A new Adam and a new Eve', p. 45.
61 Nin, *Lawrence,* p. 110.
62 'A propos of *Lady Chatterley's Lover*', p. 126.
63 Woolf, *A Room of One's Own,* p. 99.
64 Exceptions are Sheila MacLeod's largely sympathetic and painstaking study, *Lawrence's Men and Women,* London: Heinemann, 1985, which explicates his beliefs about men and women; some of the later sections in Cornelia Nixon's *Lawrence's Leadership Politics and the Turn Against Women,* Berkeley: University of California Press, 1986; and the historical research on the social, economic and political condition of English women in the closing decades of the nineteenth and the first two decades of the twentieth centuries in Hilary Simpson's *D. H. Lawrence and Feminism,* London: Croom Helm, 1982. The last book as a whole, however, is disappointingly founded on serious critical misreadings (some of which have been cited in this chapter), including a remarkably inept section comparing Lawrence's novels to the popular romances of the time epitomized by E. M. Hull's *The Sheik.*
65 Woolf, *A Room of One's Own,* p. 101.
66 ibid., p. 108.
67 F. R. Leavis, *D. H. Lawrence: Novelist,* Harmondsworth: Penguin Books, 1964, p. 15.
68 Quoted by Virginia Woolf in 'A terribly sensitive mind', *Collected Essays,* vol. 1, London: Hogarth Press, 1980, p. 358.
69 *Apocalypse,* p. 149.

6

PRESCRIPTIONS AND PROSCRIPTIONS: FEMINIST CRITICISM AND CONTEMPORARY POETRY

Sally Minogue

Must feminists be lesbians? Must lesbians be feminists? Must women readers and writers be feminist critics? And where do black women, writers and readers, place themselves on what is rather laughably called the continuum of feminist thought? And what of men, in whatever category? These are not flippant questions; indeed it would be hard to ironize about contemporary feminist thinking, especially about poetry, as anyone who has read American periodicals such as *Sinister Wisdom* would realize. The most extreme of positions have already been taken; there is no *reductio* available to the satirist which has not already been put forward as a serious position. What this, in fact, means is that current feminist thinking, about politics and about poetry, is deeply divided, and much of the debate is taking place, not in the pages of academic journals and books, but in the pages of feminist periodicals that print poetry (and fiction) alongside polemic. Indeed, feminist poetry is polemical; it must be to be feminist.

It is fascinating to turn from the vigorous, if extraordinary, pages of *Conditions* or *Sinister Wisdom* to academic works such as the formative *Shakespeare's Sisters* (Susan Gubar and Sandra Gilbert)[1] or *Feminism and Poetry* (Jan Montefiore),[2] both of which attempt to lay down some guidelines about the proper feminist approach to poetry. *Conditions* and *Sinister Wisdom* are likewise, *per natura*, concerned with correctness of position, but their interest is almost purely political, dogmatic and scarcely concerns itself with the niceties of critical thought. The academics, on the other hand, have a critical position to maintain, albeit one which they themselves are formulating, and some contortions are

179

necessary to sustain feminist values alongside critical ones, or (what is the aim) to produce some synthesis of the two. The feminists writing in the political magazines do not bother with contortions; they leap freely from position to position, and agile feminists have no difficulty in following them. The academics clearly hanker for this nimble freedom, but at the same time what they are above all concerned with is making their critical position valid in a world where political correctness is not (yet) a critical criterion. They are also, of course, writing for a limited audience, and it is a different limited audience from that which the political feminists address.

By looking at what both feminist politicians and theoreticians, and feminist critics and critical theoreticians, have said about contemporary poetry, we can see some of the fissures between them, some of the contradictions and difficulties inherent in their positions, as well as some of the strengths which they can bring to current critical thinking and current writing. It i primarily the contradictions, both between and within the various critical positions, with which I shall be concerned here, since it seems to me that the exponents of these positions themselves scarcely address the implications of those contradictions. Yet at the same time, they seem happy to be both prescriptive and proscriptive, to both readers and writers, in a manner which they would doubtless roundly condemn in others. The proscriptions on current and future writing are particularly worrying; even Leavis in all his high-handed glory did not try to rule out certain kinds of writing – certain kinds of reading, yes, and by implication he criticized certain kinds of writing. But he did not presume on the writer's freedom. Feminism, and feminist criticism, does.

There are certain precepts which the feminist politicians and the feminist critics do appear to share. One of these is the belief that the tradition of writing, and especially the poetic tradition, is 'male'. What do they mean by this? Sometimes they mean only that those who have written successfully, which is to say, have been published and therefore read, have been predominantly male. This is undeniably true, and Tillie Olsen has shown how powerfully this tradition of publication has affected the confidence of those traditionally unpublished to take up the pen.[3] But, of course, it is not only women who have been unvoiced by the tradition; it is also the working class, the black, the disadvantaged – characteristically, those who lack the leisure and the opportunity to write, as well as the support of the tradition to publish. None the less, it is true that men dominated writing up to the nineteenth century.

A further shared tenet of feminists is that poetry has been, as in that male writing tradition, an even more closely protected preserve. Again, the main evidence here is the lack of published women poets; but now a further theory is adduced, that the tradition of love poetry has been exclusively male, that is, that love poetry has been formed from the man's point of view, rendering the form itself exclusively male. Thus both a feminist 'politician' (and also a poet) Jan Clausen, and a feminist critic, Jan Montefiore (also a poet), share the view that the tradition itself cannot be entered by a woman unless the woman 'becomes' a man, that is, enters into the maleness of the tradition. Clausen states categorically, 'it is simply impossible for the woman poet writing in a male literary tradition to speak in a natural voice of her natural concerns'.[4] (The use of the word 'natural' here is interesting, but I shall return to that.)

Montefiore is characteristically more cagey – her style rather reminiscent of those advertisements which are skilled in avoiding making claims while appearing to do so. None the less she too perceives the poetic tradition as male and sees the need for a new female tradition which will allow women to write as themselves: 'Although masculine literary and poetic traditions are pervasive...it is difficult for women poets either to insert themselves into this tradition, or to appropriate its materials for their own use, since these prove extremely opaque to the light of female, let alone feminist definition.'[5] Montefiore also argues that it is even more difficult for a woman to become a poet than a novelist ('people feel, however unjustifiably, that the woman poet is a slight and freakish phenomenon compared with her substantial sister the novelist, let alone her massive and poetic weighty grandfathers'[6]) and that the male domination of the critical tradition has further compounded the prejudice against women poets. She argues persuasively from the example of thirties poetry that even when women had emerged from their anonymity, male critics were eager to push them back in by simply omitting them from critical discussion.

There is, then, a point of agreement between feminists, that the poetic tradition has been hitherto male, that this has excluded 'female' writing (by which they mean both women writers and female concerns) and that there is a need, therefore, for the establishment of a female tradition in poetry. And this is where the fun starts. For at this point dramatic disagreements emerge both within the political and critical camps and between them (though the disagreements between them are never engaged, since there seems to be little real contact or communication between the two, except where someone deliberately addresses herself to both 'camps' – Adrienne Rich, for example). For the politicians, content is the most important index of correctness in poetry, but they disagree about what the content should, and can, be. For the critics, that content might be the index of value inevitably is an embarrassment; few critics are happy to submit to such a simple, single, monolithic criterion, and for the feminists it would be an embarrassment of a particularly irritating kind, since that is what the non-feminist opponents are constantly accusing them of. It would also open them to precisely the same difficulties that are being encountered on the political front. So the critics, while partially endorsing the importance of content as a consideration in evaluating poetry from a feminist standpoint, also try to provide some sort of theoretical structure. This they usually describe as a feminist poetic or aesthetic. But just as the politicians are at odds over determining the correctness of content, so the critics are at odds over the nature of the feminist aesthetic. Sometimes, the two sets of disagreement overlap, because there is considerable overlap in the various positions. Indeed, to some extent the central problem faced by all feminists is the same: it is the problem of value. If we look at the way in which various feminist exponents, critics and politicians and poets, approach this problem, we shall see some of the problems of a feminist critical approach to poetry emerge.

The two poet/critics I have mentioned, Jan Clausen and Jan Montefiore, have both been brave enough to face the problem of value outright; and I say brave because it does take a certain amount of moral courage to ask questions which by their very nature may seem to question feminism itself. Clausen recognizes this: 'I find myself repeatedly hobbled by the fear of saying the wrong thing, of being "politically incorrect"'.[7] And speaking of Michelle Cliff's defence of literary tradition, 'Unfortunately, feminist discussions of privilege and language are seldom so direct and public. Instead the subject is surrounded by an intimidatory silence.'[8] Perhaps it is a braver act for Clausen than it is for Montefiore, since she places herself firmly within feminist politics, while it is not quite clear from Montefiore's work whether she endorses feminism as a politics, in the sense of a way of life. None the less, it is encouraging to see questions being asked, from within and without. Again, it is interesting to see the different ways in which Clausen and Montefiore formulate their doubts, as well as to see how they answer their own questions.

Clausen's *A Movement of Poets* was inspired partly by her discomfort with the way in which poetry was being used, and perceived, within the feminist movement. As a poet herself, and as a lesbian and a feminist, she found herself wondering whether the poetry she was 'expected' to produce for the movement was either the poetry she wanted to write or, indeed, good poetry. But before she formulates these doubts, she pins her colours very firmly to the mast, the more clearly to reveal that these doubts should not be seen as anti-feminist. Her colours are these: that whenever she writes a poem, the statements 'I am a woman' and 'I am a lesbian' underpin the writing of the poem. For Clausen, then, content is centrally important. But content is also deeply implicated in the questions she raises. She feels that the feminist movement has perceived poetry too much as a tool and not sufficiently as a means of self-expression; and even while she lauds the centrality of poetry to the movement, she fears that that centrality will or may eventually weaken the value of poetry itself. In the end, then, she questions whether feminism should have valued poetry only for its utility, and suggests a recuperation of poetry's other values. Clausen's doubts are closely connected with the use of performance poetry as a means of 'consciousness-raising', where the simplest and most popularly phrased poem is likely to be the most successful in rousing an audience, and where the rabble-rousing qualities of certain subjects or keywords tend to limit the poet. If a successful performance is one that wins most people over to feminist politics, then the simplest, or wittiest, or most misanthropic will be best. As a poet, Clausen reluctantly admits that she is not happy with that state of affairs; nor does she like the limitations it tends to impose on intending poets. She categorically states – as categorically as she has stated that being a woman and a lesbian are essential to the nature of her poetry – 'I see prescriptions of this sort as dangerous.'[9]

Yet Clausen evades the consequences of her argument. She is

happy to see a simple distinction between using poetry as a consciousness-raising political tool, and using it as a means of communication and self-expression. She seeks to direct feminist poetry towards the latter and away from the former because she sees this as less restrictive and prescriptive on the poet, and better for the movement. But she does not address the relationship between her own starting point ('I am a woman', 'I am a lesbian') and the same starting point in others. At some level she sees more complex poetry as better, and herself as a better poet when writing complex poetry. But what of the restrictions placed on that by her own basic tenets? Clearly, some content would be taboo to her; but given her own view that some prescriptions are dangerous, what of the dangers of her own?

Montefiore approaches the problem from a different angle. She is more the critic, less the embroiled feminist; she also has an ingenious solution to the problem of value, and one that satisfies both political and critical criteria. Montefiore begins boldly, entitling this section of a chapter uncompromisingly 'The question of bad poetry', and stating the difficulty outright: 'that of establishing the grounds on which poetry is valued as well as understood'. She is willing to admit, as I suspect Clausen and many other feminists would not be, in a trenchantly witty way, that sometimes the 'buried treasure' which the early feminist critics spent their time digging up and revaluing, the works of earlier, lost, women poets, 'does turn out to be old iron'. She takes as her example Catherine Reilly's anthology of women's First World War poetry, *Scars Upon My Heart*, and makes a revealing distinction between the interest of this poetry 'to the social historian of ideologies'[10] and its values to the general reader and critic, that is, (presumably) its intrinsic value as literature. The distinction here is interesting because it is one that she does not always make. She is herself operating as 'a social historian of ideologies' when she analyses (very interestingly and persuasively) feminist views of poetry in terms of an inherited Romantic aesthetic, which in turn she characterizes as damagingly universalist (falsely so and thus evading the need to consider differences and disparities within universal humanity). And she links this analysis directly to the value of the ideas which underlie, and for them underpin, feminist poetry: 'The tendency to privilege the notion of female experience, and to think of women's poetry as a magically powerful collective consciousness, can make for a too easy and uncritical assumption of identity between all women'.[11] (While Montefiore attributes this mistake to critics rather than poets, Clausen makes it clear that the one affects the other; Clausen cites the examples while Montefiore cites the counter-examples.) In her analysis of Anne Stevenson, a poet who has aggressively espoused a non-feminist aesthetics in favour of belonging to a tradition which 'transcends gender', she argues that Stevenson's weakness is 'that she idealizes the tradition which she endorses, failing to take account of the exclusions and injustices which help to constitute it specially the marginalization of women's poetry'.[12] Montefiore makes it clear that she is speaking here of Stevenson's poems as well as her criticism. And when we come to her chapter 'Towards a woman's tradition', in which the section on 'bad poetry' occurs, Montefiore argues that 'the most coherent and satisfying version of a woman's tradition...is the reconstruction through poems of women's past'; and while she enters a caveat about essentialism, in her comparative analysis of two poems, 'Bashert' by Irene Klepfisz and 'Outside Oswiecim' by Carol Rumens, she values the former above the latter because the former is more overtly and aggressively feminist. This she characterizes in terms of, for example, Rumens' mention by name of a distinguished man, but no women, against Klepfisz's making central the name of her friend Elza, and the fact that 'all of the people in her poem are women'. Klepfisz's poem is pronounced 'a version of feminist poetry of experience at its strongest'.[13]

In all of the cited cases, Montefiore takes her stance not only as an analyst of ideologies, but from ideology; elusive as she is in both her terms and her endorsements (and sometimes that is the product of trying to register the complexity of the issues), she argues, first, that the poetics which most clearly emerges from the feminist movement is damagingly universalist in its basis, by which she means essentialist (that is, taking the view that there is a unified female experience to be voiced, and which can best be voiced through the poetic expression of personal experience); but, second, that a 'truly' universalist (i.e. humane) women's poetry, in which the poet deliberately disregards her gender and wishes it to be disregarded in criticism of her poetry, is weak in respect of that; and, third, that where two women poets deal with similar areas of experience, in similar ways, and with similar levels of poetic quality, that which is more feminist in terms of content and reference, and less universally humanistic, will be the more conducive to the creation of a woman's tradition – which she has earlier argued is necessary to counter the harmful effects to women poets and readers of poetry of the previously dominant 'male' tradition.

I have gone to rather tedious lengths to establish this chain of (sometimes contradictory) thinking in Montefiore's book, partly because she is difficult to pin down, but more importantly because it has powerful implications for her crucial discussion of the problem of bad poetry. In this discussion she is not embarrassed to talk about 'bad or mediocre poetry (which certainly exists)' nor to say 'it cannot be pretended that many of them [poems in this anthology] are good'.[14] She briefly discusses one fine poem, Eleanor Farjeon's 'Easter Monday', but concludes that, in general, 'the poems are valuable to the social historian precisely because of their often uncritical handling of War, Sacrifice, Poetry and Religion; there is no professional finish to disguise thought and feeling.'[15] So the historian or the analyst of ideologies would relish the poems precisely because they give an unvarnished picture of attitudes at the time – female attitudes within a male ideology, into which such analysts could juicily get their teeth. Montefiore seems to equate 'professional finish' with value here; earlier, she has attacked the 'amateurish' nature of this poetry, 'uncomfortably reminiscent...of an old-fashioned school magazine'.[16] Her one demonstrative analysis of 'the unsatisfactoriness of this poetry' leans heavily on 'traditional' (male?) values (consistency within imagery, ease and fluidity of scansion and rhyme), in her one-paragraph, casually argued dismissal of Vera Brittain's 'Scars Upon My Heart', from which the anthology takes its title. All her claims here are contestable, yet she seems not to feel the need to give them much space or argument, even though this case exemplifies the whole problem of bad poetry for the feminist critic. For example, her contention that Vera Brittain's scar image is flawed because scars fade, so that the image suggests the lessening of pain when it should suggest the opposite: in fact, the heart is one area where scars do not fully heal, and where the scar itself does lasting damage to the heart's function – precisely the emotional damage which Vera Brittain is trying to express, indeed to profess, since this poem was a sort of declaration of love to her brother, inscribed on the flyleaf of a book sent to him at the Front. Clumsy scansion is a notoriously difficult critical area; we now attack editors and critics who altered Emily Dickinson's 'clumsy' rhythms and rhymes, as we do Tottel for cleaning up Wyatt's irregularities. Of course, this does not mean that critics can no longer identify clumsy scansion and rhyme as precisely that; but it does mean that, where other issues hang on their critical claims, or where the rhythmic analysis is crucial to our evaluation, care must be taken. Similarly, dismissal of the value of the scar image needs fuller and more careful demonstration. But more important than either of these points is Montefiore's subsequent – consequent – claim that the scar metaphor 'suggests, damagingly, the experiential gap between his bodily suffering and her pity'. Now, in fact, Brittain's poem is about just that experiential gap. And it is here, I feel, that we can sense a confusion buried deep in Montefiore's discussion, both of this poem, and anthology, and of 'the question of bad poetry'. It is an important confusion, not primarily in relation to Montefiore's criticism – so much of which is readably stimulating, interesting, witty and complex – but in relation to feminist criticism in general.

It is a fact that there was an experiential gap between women and men in the First World War; men fought and women did not. Much of Vera Brittain's autobiographical *Testament of Youth* gives expression to her own feelings about that gap, often bitter feelings, of being left out of an important experience, but often, too, feelings of impotence, of being unable to take on some of the suffering which yet had to be borne by so many men she loved. Montefiore touches on this gap when she mentions Sandra Gilbert's analysis of First World War women's poetry and prose; Gilbert argues that the bloodthirstiness of much of that writing is actually a manifestation of women's rage and resentment against their male oppressors. True, Montefiore does not fully accept Gilbert's analysis; but she gives it considerably more room than the experiential gap Vera Brittain seeks to express. Might it not be the case here that to admit that experiential gap, in which men had to suffer in a way women could not, in which women inevitably took on a vicarious suffering of an emotional sort, in which men were the heroic object, would be inadmissible to the feminist critic? Yet for Vera Brittain that was the emotional reality, which she chose to try to express. The poignancy of her poem is certainly sharpened by the knowledge that her beloved brother never read the poem (she received the parcel returned unopened after his death). But the poignancy is already there in her expression of that feeling that love is hopeless and helpless to take on another's pain, yet it is the nature of love that that is what we want to do. Even as she knows she cannot, physically or emotionally, take upon herself her brother's suffering, yet she shares it, if only vicariously, necessarily vicariously. The poignancy lies in the fact that telling him this, even as it is impotent, may somehow help him; again, that is the irony of love. The poem is not a marvellous one as, say, Farjeon's is; but neither is it the poem Montefiore describes.

If women did place their men in the position of heroes, if they did adopt patriotic values even more willingly than men, and if they did express that in traditional, 'amateurish' forms, what are we to do with that, as critics? Use it as an easy example to dispense with the need to think about more difficult cases? Such cases do need careful thought – especially those poems which are not quite so easy to dismiss (and Vera Brittain's, it seems to me, falls into this category, though certainly very many of her poems do not!). In fact, the same problem arises for the critic of men's First World War poetry. Is Sassoon's early poem 'France', which sees it as 'fortunate' to fight, and equates 'victory' with 'delight', a bad poem because it expresses what is (now) seen as an undesirable attitude? Is it bad because the force of experience has not yet sharpened his style or broken the edges of poetic convention? Is it bad because it lacks 'professional finish'? Or has it perhaps too much? These are difficult and embarrassing questions for the literary critic; but they need to be both asked and answered, honestly, acknowledging the difficulties.

Vera Brittain is writing about the experiential gap between herself and her brother, and Jan Montefiore makes that the crux of her critique; a big chunk of the argument has been left out along the way. What bothers me here, and should bother the feminist critic, is the sliding in and out of ideological stances and values, in and out of 'traditional' critical values, without looking closely at the intersections of the two. It is at those intersections that the 'question of bad poetry', the deciding what and how to value as well as understand, will emerge. Montefiore does not actually raise or address those questions in this section of her book; she only appears to do so. When she concludes – again with a rather impressive casualness and confidence – that 'the critical dilemma which emerges from considering the ideologically fascinating but aesthetically dubious is, however, more apparent than real',[17] that may be because the opposition she has set up there is not the one about which feminist critics need to be worrying. What is ideologically fascinating is that which is safely ensconced in the 'male' tradition and ideology; it is fascinating because it is bad, and it is bad because it is embedded in male values. Of course, that it is aesthetically 'dubious' is only to be expected. The feminist critic will deal with it according to her lights; a writer like Sandra Gilbert will subsume it under a psychoanalytic view of male-authored female suppression of anger; one like Elaine Showalter will argue that it is important because it is an expression of female experience, and will agree that its lack of value can be attributed to men, and to male-authored texts. Not surprising, then, that Montefiore can conclude: 'we do not in fact have to choose between the Scylla of historical determinism...and the Charybdis of essentialism', for those two are not in conflict. Where there is a potential conflict for the feminist critic is hidden in Montefiore's next remarks: 'The fact that women are deeply engaged with masculine traditions and discourses, sometimes (though not always) to the detriment of their writing, should not be a problem for critics who would theorize a woman's tradition....It is actually important that a woman's tradition be seen in relation to patriarchal discourse, so long as the relation is understood as opposition.'[18] It is not sufficient to throw away that 'though not always' under cover of parenthesis. If sometimes, why not always? When not, why not? If not always, why, and how, sometimes? And if not always, why must a women's tradition always be seen as in opposition to patriarchal discourse? Because being in opposition is what makes it good? Is that the case with the Farjeon example quoted? Montefiore seems to come close to equating value with opposition, in this sense (as, for example, in her comparison of Klepfisz and Rumens). But the difficult question is, if opposition to patriarchal discourse is the index of value, what *within* that is the index of bad poetry? Is there one? What proscriptions – and indeed freedoms – does this entail for contemporary writers? And in turn, how should this affect our evaluation of past writers (if it can and should)?

To me the most important of these issues for 'the question of bad poetry' is not raised explicitly by Montefiore, but it is raised by Clausen: what constitutes the criteria of value in 'ideologically

sound' (as opposed to 'ideologically interesting' – i.e. 'unsound')
poetry of the present day, particularly among that written by and
for committed feminists? It is easy enough to reconstitute the
value of 'traditionally good' women's poetry of the past which
has been unfairly ignored by male critics (Montefiore's example
of thirties poetry); less easy but still not too problematic to
question whether *all* women's poetry is valuable for the feminist;
but the least easy, and perhaps the most important and revealing,
in a post-feminist climate, is to question the aesthetic value of
feminist poetry written within a proclaimed women's tradition.
That question Clausen tentatively raises, and it is one which, for
her, revolves round the issue of lesbianism and feminism:

> In the absence of explicit critical standards, what implicit
> assumptions and preconceptions about the form and
> function of feminist poetry, and the role of the poet, can be
> inferred? How do these assumptions affect the poems we
> write? What is the relationship between the role of the poet
> and that of political spokeswoman? What are the
> implications, positive and negative, of the intellectual and
> artistic 'ghettoisation' which characterises a functionally
> separatist literary community?...In what ways have we
> instituted new taboos to replace the old?[19]

It is interesting that Clausen assumes before she states this
question 'the absence of explicit critical standards'; but this is not
to say that there can be no such standards. Indeed, her
questioning begins with wondering why the feminist movement,
'which has generated such an extraordinary and compelling
body of work produced so little in the way of reflection on that
work'.[20] Part of her explanation recalls Montefiore on the
perceived superiority of fiction over poetry;[21] indeed, this has
become almost a *donné* of feminist criticism, with Gubar and
Gilbert arguing that

> Their [female novelists] literary efforts evidently seemed
> less problematical than those of women poets, even to
> misogynistic readers. Their art was not actively encouraged,
> but it was generally understood by the late eighteenth
> century and throughout the nineteenth century that under
> conditions of pressing need a woman might have to live by
> her pen....Indeed, beginning with Aphra Behn and

burgeoning with Fanny Burney, Anne Radcliffe, Maria Edgeworth, and Jane Austen, the English novel seems to have been in some sense a female invention.[22]

(Gubar and Gilbert seem to have conveniently changed this view in *The Madwoman in the Attic*,[23] however, where a large part of their thesis depends on the argument that the nature of the female-authored nineteenth-century novel was determined by the exclusively male tradition which preceded it.) Clausen's version of this view is that theoretical feminist discussion tends to revolve round fiction, perhaps because 'feminists share the contemporary American prejudice that fiction is the major form'. Her suggestion is, however, that little articulated as critical criteria may be, they exist, and have powerful influence as unwritten rules about 'how a feminist poem should look (or sound) and what it ought to do' and that these are embodied in, and implied by, the poems themselves. Here Clausen makes a perceptive point: 'Precisely because they are unstated, such assumptions may at times function more tyrannically than would explicit "standards", particularly for the younger or less experienced feminist poet.'[24] The power of these unarticulated rules, combined with a feminist writer's fear of being found politically suspect, could then have a profound influence on future poetry, and not necessarily just that written by self-announced and self-perceived feminists. All female poets could be affected (as can be seen from Montefiore's comparison of Klepfisz and Rumens and her remarks about the anti-feminist potential of poets such as Anne Stevenson who have tried to disassociate themselves from a feminist label – though she also sees and voices the problematic nature of this kind of reductiveness).

The unwritten rules, as perceived by Clausen, are, briefly, that: (i) feminist poetry should be (politically) useful, (ii) that it should be accessible in form and content, (iii) that it should be non-traditional in form and (first-) personal in address, (iv) the subject-matter should be feminist; that is either anti-male oppression or pro-female strength and community, (v) a collective awareness should inform it, minimizing the role of the author as important individually, (vi) it should be self-sufficient, and (vii) it should be unconcerned with criticism, or should view criticism as patriarchally based and thus suspect. Of course, Clausen's analysis is itself contestable; but since Clausen is a committed feminist-lesbian poet who has engaged with these questions at personal cost and with often great difficulty[25] – which is likely to presage honesty – I feel that she is well qualified to pronounce, especially about *unwritten* rules. And of course, when we turn to the poetry to be found both in generally published feminist poets (June Jordan, Audre Lord, Adrienne Rich) and that published by small presses or in feminist periodicals and magazines, we see time and time again that the poetry does indeed exemplify the 'assumptions in which [we] are drenched'[26] (Clausen borrows the quotation from Rich). Interestingly, Adrienne Rich herself approves some of Clausen's argument and comes close to expressing a similar unease about the lack of explicit criticism:

> Some of us are increasingly concerned about the level of ritual assent accorded to our poetic language – 'assent without credence', as a friend once defined it, to my own relief; about the frustration of being listened to, written about, objectified, perhaps, but not heard – at least not in any sense of hearing which might bear on action. Even to be able to express this in public is a measure of how harshly I have felt the experience of applause and accolade without discrimination or true on-going critical response.[27]

Even closer to Clausen, and speaking here clearly as a poet, she states,

> I think that every feminist poet must long – I do – for real criticism of her work – not just descriptive, but analytical criticism which takes her language and images seriously enough to question them....I also need to know when in my work I am merely doing well what I know well how to do and when I am avoiding certain expressive risks. And while I can count on friends for some of this, it would be better for all feminist writers if such principled criticism were to come also from strangers.[28]

Now Rich goes on to qualify, by expanding, some of this endorsement, and I shall say more later about her view of feminist criticism. But she certainly shares both the dislike of undiscriminating acclaim for feminist poetry from feminist audiences and the desire for criticism both from without and within – which, of course, implies some set of critical criteria. Since many of Rich's views are at the separatist/lesbian end of the feminist 'continuum', her endorsement of at least Clausen's doubts is a telling one.

As one would expect, all the unwritten rules Clausen outlines are political in provenance, whether they concern form or content. For example, the requirement of accessibility springs from the need to reach a wide audience and perhaps persuade a wider one, in contrast to the elitist audience encouraged in the non-feminist tradition; the requirement for non-traditional forms because traditional forms are identified with the 'male' poetic tradition; the anti-individualism to avoid the threat of alignment with the competitive egotism of a kind demonstrated by male writers (though there does seem to be a clash between this requirement and that for expressive, first-person address); as well as the more obvious proscriptions on content and attitude. But what this reveals is that feminist prescriptions and proscriptions are almost entirely formed in reaction to the male traditions, that is feminists have defined their own poetics in terms of what they see as the traditional male poetics. The effect of this has inevitably been, instead of liberating, limiting; and limiting in terms of a greater male freedom. Now this is not the thrust of Clausen's argument; she fixes, rather, on the lack of complexity in feminist poetry arising from the assumptions which precede it. But she does see and argue that 'the danger is that of adopting a knee-jerk anti-patriarchal stance, and thereby limiting the possibilities of feminist poetry,'[29] and that 'we are too likely to go over old, safe territory, rather than undertaking explorations whose usefulness is not, and may never be, readily apparent'.[30] She also bravely argues – and the more one reads feminist criticism the more one perceives the presence, either implicitly or explicitly stated, of fear – that it is time for critical values to be voiced and argued, for the rules to be written for all to see. What she seeks here is a feminist poetics which deals with the question of value, and she sees it in counterpoise to the assumptions she has analysed, which she sees as narrowing.

Lorraine Bethel and Barbara Smith, in their *Conditions Five*, the Black Women's Issue (1979), do talk about some of their standards of selection for that issue. Not all of these are to do with value in some objective or purely aesthetic sense; they involve diversity of material, diversity of style and approach, and a range of kinds of women contributing. But when they do touch on, with regret, what had to be left out, they do not say whether the criteria were political, poetic or a combination of both. They do touch on the question of political correctness when they annotate one poem with an explanation of their difficulty in deciding whether it ought to be printed. The poem concerns the relationship between Jewishness and feminism, and to an 'outsider' it is difficult to see what the problem is. But their annotation does illustrate the delicacy of certain areas of feminism – again the fear of being politically incorrect in such areas, and the reluctance to spell out criteria even where reference is made to a dilemma about selection. This also illustrates the danger of the self-sufficient world which feminism has sought to create; the outsider or newcomer may well be left in the dark because the insiders see no need to explain their position. Again, this is bound to lead to a certain self-indulgence of the kind which both Clausen and Rich warn against.

Melanie Kaye, in 'On being a lesbian feminist artist', is quoted by Clausen as protesting about the tendency of certain big names to dominate the feminist literary scene: Kaye's view is that *all* women's stories should be told. But if there is limited space to tell them all, selections must and will be made; if students are being taught, reading recommendations will be made; if works are to be published, one author will be preferred over another. And if stories are told, some will be told better than others. If Kaye and other feminists want to deny the relevance of value, or if they want to change the standards by which we define 'better', well and good; but they need to argue that position, state the new criteria and understand that they are contestable. And where within that world they do make selections it will become even more important for them to know why and how they are doing so, since they themselves have sought to deny selectivity. Where the selections concern poetry, poetic criteria will enter. Clausen is right when she says that viewing poetry as a useful tool in fact diminishes it, reduces it to the same level as other ways of saying things. Yet the feminists, even in using it as a tool, thereby recognize it as special in some way, different from other ways of saying things. When they do so, they must also accept that poetry can't simply be cut off in a feminist chunk and severed from the rest of the body of poetry. It may be political, but it does not cease to be poetic.

Two clear areas emerge from this discussion which need

further elucidation and investigation if we are to understand feminist criteria for poetry (and perhaps offer a critique of them): one of these is political correctness, and the other is the relationship between political and poetic values. Of course, these areas connect closely and overlap each other. Evidently we must begin with the question of political correctness, since this precedes any relationship that has with poetic value. The disagreements between, for example, black and white feminists, between lesbian and non-lesbian feminists, indeed the disagreements about what the term 'lesbian' means in a feminist context, should illuminate the difficulties of deciding what attitude and content are politically correct. These difficulties are likely to be further complicated when we proceed to the relationship between political and poetic value, since poetic criteria enter there. And if we take this discussion to a further remove, away from the close-knit world of political feminism and into the sphere of academic feminist criticism, we may see the difficulties, contradictions and complications redouble. At the heart of all this lies what this chapter is really concerned with: poetry. And as soon as we begin to look closely at some poetic examples we are likely to be reminded forcibly of what a beautiful and elusive art it is, and how cautious we ought to be in being prescriptive and proscriptive about it.

As we have seen, part of Clausen's unease lies precisely with the implications of what she started with as her defining terms as a poet ('I am a woman', 'I am a lesbian'); her underpinnings are also her underminings. This becomes explicit in her statement (of faith, as it were): 'it is simply impossible for the woman poet working in a male literary tradition to speak in a natural voice of her natural concerns'.[31] For the use of the word 'natural' entails the view that women have a definable 'nature', with a body of concerns which springs from that nature, peculiar to them as women; further, she even assumes that there is a voice which goes with this nature and this body of concerns. Voice is usually a metaphor for language or way of writing or speaking, though Clausen may here mean poetic voice. The concept of the natural has been hotly debated in feminist analysis, since initially it was seen as being used by men to assert their patriarchal power over women by limiting their role to what was seen as natural – that which revolved round child-bearing and the domestic base. 'Nature', in a biological sense, has become almost a taboo topic

195

among feminists;[32] yet 'nature', in a psychological sense, seems to be acceptable to them. The concept of there being a distinctive 'woman's nature' is an essentialist one; and it is this essentialism which causes Clausen so much unease in the rest of her essay. Montefiore too is aware of the dangers of essentialism, and states them more overtly than Clausen: 'Anachronistic notions of the essential identity of female psychology seem to me just such a "glittering cover" imposed on the historical realities of actual women writers.'[33] Montefiore's choice of supportive quotation is doubtless made for its suggestion of an anodyne cover over what is more complicated. And though her comments and criticism are applied to a particular version of essentialism, that which ' means the assumption – whether overtly or only implied – of an authenticating "essence" of female subjectivity',[34] they might be applied to any view of 'woman's nature' which involves the idea of an authenticating essence, namely, one that might not necessarily involve the concept of subjectivity, through which many feminists escape the embarrassing difficulties presented by biological difference. (Montefiore feels that, none the less, the creation of a woman's poetic tradition does not depend on an essentialist view; in and of itself it has a number of advantages. This argument I shall consider later. But there is no doubt that the abandonment of an essentialist position seriously weakens any claim to there being a coherent and independent feminist poetic.)

Both Clausen and Montefiore, with their serious reflections on the relationship of feminism and poetry, and perhaps more importantly through their experience as poets, stumble over the oversimplification which an essentialist feminism requires. For while essentialism is certainly a prerequisite for a feminist politics (since there must be some distinguishing factor – experiential, biological, linguistic, whatever – which separates women from other categories of human being), it becomes problematic if it is also seen as a central factor in determining a feminist poetic. This is perhaps where both Clausen and Montefiore become confused. Clausen speaks of both a woman's 'natural concerns' and her 'natural voice'; Montefiore wants to avoid the dangers which she sees in essentialism, yet wants to create a woman's poetic tradition which is defined in terms of its opposition to patriarchy. But what needs to be distinguished here are the prequirements one might make of a feminist – that she be aware that there are elements which are peculiar to and common to women which constitute women's difference from men and which have resulted in patriarchal oppression of women – and the requirements one might make of women (or feminist) poets. For it is the perceived requirement that this 'female essence' determine exclusively what and how a woman/feminist poet should write, which causes both Clausen and Montefiore unease. Essentialism does not entail exclusivity; that is, the fact that I might agree that there are indeed elements which are peculiar and common to women which have resulted (sometimes) in our being disadvantaged, does not preclude my awareness of there being elements which are peculiar and common to being, say, working-class, which cut across those peculiar and common to being a woman, and so on. And of course, there are elements which are peculiar and common to certain living creatures' being human beings; indeed, part of being a human being is the fact that I can be aware of there being different categories of human being (old, female, black, etc.) and that I can be aware of the disadvantages which can accrue without good reason from belonging to any one of these categories. So an acceptance of essentialism may be a necessary but not sufficient condition for being a feminist, for I may put some other category before that of being a woman, or I may prefer to ignore categories and concentrate on what it is to be human; or, as would be most people's actual experience, way of living, I might sometimes be aware of being a woman and sometimes be aware of being human, and sometimes be aware of being the two together, and sometimes be aware that being the one determines my fate and my actions more than does the other (and sometimes it may be the one and sometimes the other, without inconsistency). But above all, my being human makes it possible for me to be aware of what it is to be a woman and how that differs from what it is to be various other kinds of category. Now, if I *choose* to put the peculiarity of being a woman before all else in the way I live my life, to the exclusion of all else, this would be both a moral and political choice which many extreme feminists have made. But even those feminists could not actually exclude an overall human consciousness from their way of life, for if they could they could not make the choices entailed in living in a feminist way! But they would make the essence of being female their priority in living their lives.

However, if they then extrapolate from this to requirements about the way women/feminists should write poetry, they run into difficulties; and it is these difficulties to which both Clausen and Montefiore allude, whether overtly or covertly, as difficulties they perceive as poets and as critics – and perhaps as human beings. The 'complicated dead' to whom Montefiore refers are also the complicated living. Part of their being complicated has to do with their being human beings, male and female, old and young, of various races and economic situations. A feminist politics based on essentialism seeks to put being a woman before being human, because it sees the embrace of 'humanity' as being in its nature disadvantageous to women. But a feminist poetics which does the same will be doing something even more far-reaching. Montefiore concedes this, most notably in her conclusion, where a number of very important points are glossed. Her reference to Wordsworth, to 'the brute contingent world "which is the world/ Of all of us, the place where, in the end/ We find out happiness, or not at all"', is made in the hope that a woman's poetic tradition could make a difference to that world; but even as she speaks, she characterizes that as a utopian hope. She further concedes, in perhaps the most telling sentence of the book, 'It is a world which is dominated by class and race oppression, and by masculine privilege which does not only exert its power at the level of representation.'[35] In the same way, Clausen argues that 'Women are affected by absolutely everything that goes on in the world, and it is the right and necessity of the feminist poet to explore whatever occupies the center of her field of vision.'[36] Montefiore, in explaining why the notion of a female language is utopian, states: 'The traces of the opposite sex can never be entirely effaced from a woman's text: a difficulty which emerged in a very simple and literal way from from the Warner and Dickinson poems discussed above – that is the way that a masculine persona, or even a small masculine pronoun, disrupts what could otherwise be thought of as purely female discourse.'[37] But as her statements about the nature of the world – like those of Clausen – make clear, it is *not* just the 'masculine persona' or 'small masculine pronoun' which prevent a woman's poetic text from ever being 'purely female discourse'; it is that women share with men the brute fact of being human. That in turn means that women experience along with men, either from within or without, all kinds of oppression, not just that involved in being female (again, as Montefiore conceded). So that if we were to make a female/feminist poetic dependent on giving priority to the particular oppression which comes with being female, we would be ruling out of women's poetry an enormous area of interest, experience and concern. In the end, this is too much for both Clausen and Montefiore. But if it is too much then it also ceases to be enough, since for each of them the idea of woman's poetic tradition or a feminist poetic depends on giving priority to the nature of being female. For Clausen it springs from the concepts 'I am a woman', 'I am a lesbian'; for Montefiore it comes from the assertion that a woman's tradition must be oppositional to patriarchy. Both Montefiore and Clausen, by honestly facing up to some of the difficulties implicit in these assertions, end up with positions which they must recognize are antithetical to their original assertions.

However, other feminists – poets, critics and others – have less of a problem with a poetics founded on essentialism. In these cases, they are clear that feminist poetry should be primarily concerned with what it is to be female, or with the ways in which women have been oppressed. Yet even within this area of feminist poetics there are many central disagreements to be found. These are usually disagreements about what feminism consists of, and these in turn centre on different views of what the female 'essence' is (sexual, experiential, social, linguistic, to do with subjectivity, or some combination of these). Adrienne Rich is clear about her position: 'To write directly and overtly as a woman, out of a woman's body and experience, to take woman's existence seriously as theme and source for art, was something I had been hungering to do, needing to do, all my writing life.'[38] While this is much like an expansion of Clausen's stated credentials, it is strengthened and reaffirmed in other of Rich's more extended and more extreme statements. In a combative piece, 'Compulsory heterosexuality and lesbian existence', in which she condemns institutionalized heterosexuality and resulting 'heterosexism' (prejudice against lesbians), she argues that many more women than actually acted on it would have entertained the desire to lead a lesbian life. She condemns those who lead heterosexual lives for their complicity in the silencing and suppression of lesbians, and comes as near as she can to saying that compulsory heterosexuality should be replaced by compulsory lesbianism – that is to say, it should be recognized that, for women, their normal relationship is with other women. For example, she states that 'Heterosexuality has been both forcibly and subliminally imposed on women'; she criticizes the demand that 'women provide material solace, non-judgemental nurturing, and compassion for their harassers, rapists and batterers (as well as for men who passively vampirize them)'; and in describing Emily Dickinson and Zora Neale Hurston, widens the term lesbian to include anyone who (in her view) has found prime sustenance in relationships with other women – as she asserts these two writers did.[39] Rich makes the choosing of lesbianism a political act, and so by implication the choosing of heterosexuality also a political act – an anti-feminist one: 'We can say there is a *nascent* feminist political content in the act of choosing a woman lover or life partner in the face of institutionalised heterosexuality.' Finally she asks: 'Are we then to condemn all heterosexual relationships including those which are least oppressive? I believe this question, though often heartfelt, is the wrong question here.'[40] It may be the wrong question, but it is the one she raises, and it is the one ineluctably entailed by the previous statements she has made, since the answer 'yes' is implied by those statements.

So Rich's analytic expansion of the terms 'I am a woman', 'I am a lesbian' shows a clear commitment to female lesbian concerns. Further, although her central analysis of this question is in a piece concerned more with politics than with poetics, she makes it clear that her strictures extend to feminist poets. In discussing the work of Lorraine Hansberry in an interesting piece entitled 'The Problem of Lorraine Hansberry', she struggles to reconcile Hansberry's feminism with the centrality of male heroes in her work and the stereotyping of some of her women characters and argues in conclusion, and perhaps with the implication that Hansberry lived in conditions under which she was unable to reach her fullest artistic maturity:

'I do know that fame and economic security are not enough to enable the woman artist – Black or white – to push her art and thought to their outermost limits. *For that* [my italics], we need community – a community whose members know our experience from the inside out because it is their own, who will support us in our efforts to depict that experience in the face of those who would either reward us for glossing over, or punish us for articulating, the extremity in which we live.'[41]

Certainly, in her own critical essays on women writers, Rich derives her critical analysis from her political position, for example, identifying the locus of value in Elizabeth Bishop's poetry as that aspect which deals with being 'the outsider' (elsewhere she argues that if a woman loses 'her outsider's vision, she loses the insight which both binds her to other women and affirms her in herself');[42] criticizes Colette because she writes about lesbianism 'as if for a male audience';[43] and extends her use of the term lesbianism to mean 'woman-identification' retrospectively, identifying Emily Dickinson and Zora Neale Hurston as writers for whom 'women provided the ongoing fascination and sustenance of life.'[44] Finally, Rich places the same obligation, of a 'woman-identified' approach, on critics. In 'Toward a more feminist criticism',[45] she states, 'I would define a feminist literary criticism as a criticism which is consciously involved in a movement for women's liberation – indeed, a revolutionary movement.' She condemns what she calls 'a liberal supermarket of the intellect' (an enjoyable and telling phrase) in which feminism is just one brand to be chosen from among many on the shelves, with the possibility of taking a different brand next time, and invites 'conscious accountability to the lives of women – not only those women who read and write books or are working, however tenuously, in academic settings'. Ultimately, she argues, this means trying to unlearn two norms, that of 'universal whiteness' and that of 'universal heterosexuality'. Indeed, Rich is contemptuous of notions of the universal, seeing these as defined by and within a male-dominated society, and so excluding too much to be called universal: 'I cannot afford the luxury of an unexamined "humanism", a position defined and ordered by white males; no more can I accept any male judgement as to the intrinsic radicalism of any woman Black or white.'

It is clear from Rich's remarks in a variety of essays, then, that she believes that a feminist poetry should be woman-centred and identified in its concerns and approach, that a contemporary feminist criticism should be consciously political in supporting these qualities of feminist poetry, and in a way which is not just academic in context or approach but which 'implies a commitment not just to literature but to readers, and not just to women who are readers here and now but to widening the possibility of reading and writing for women to whom books have been closed'.[46] (I agree wholeheartedly with the latter point, but little of current academic feminist criticism would be available or accessible to such women.) And Rich, too, sees feminist criticism, like feminist poetry, as oppositional: 'We need to support each other in rejecting the limitations of a tradition – a manner of reading, of speaking, or writing, of criticizing – which was never really designed to include us all.'[47] Rich's context in arguing in this way is evidently separatist, and her separatism is, socially, politically and poetically, rooted in her lesbianism (whether we define this narrowly or broadly).

Now, as I have mentioned before, even Rich, from this very clear and solid base, doubts the undiscriminating approach to poetry which her ideas might seem to entail. And she is extremely cautious and self-aware about her own areas of privilege and their relationship to the disadvantage of others. Her honesty and lack of certainty in these areas, her willingness to admit confusion and encourage it in others, are engaging and admirable. Yet Rich's *essential* position is based firmly on a belief that she as a woman and a poet, and others as women poets, critics and readers, should work from a certain set of assumptions, the central one of which is that 'woman-identification' should be central to our approach to literature, to poetry. For Rich herself, a certain female sexuality and way of living in community with women is also central to this view. And she wholeheartedly rejects any appeal to 'the luxury of an unexamined "humanism"' to counteract her view. So even as she recognizes her difficulties in appreciating the lives and work of 'women of colour' in her own mind the prior claim for such women should be to their being *women*; being women '*of colour*' will affect and must affect their thinking as women; but it is secondary to their being women. Similarly, she recognizes her difficulties with class, and she makes strong and powerful appeals for the inclusion of women of all class in a feminist poetry and criticism – but it is *women* of all class. And her true view of women's sexuality, most clearly and fully expressed in 'Compulsory heterosexuality and lesbian existence', is that, as long as heterosexuality is the institutional norm for women, 'the absence of choice remains the great unacknowledged reality, and in the absence of choice, women will remain dependent upon the chance or luck of particular relationships and will have no collective power to determine the meaning and place of sexuality in their lives'[48] (the collective power being, of course, exclusively female).

Rich's personal, political and poetical bases are then determined by gender and by sexuality. But as she herself recognizes, there are within the human race many categories of disadvantage which exist both within the human race and across the gender and sexuality classifications she suggests. It is those which (necessarily, as categories within humanity) exist within the category of women which create difficulties about what is a 'politically correct' feminism (on which a correct feminist poetic to some extent depends). The clearest example of this is the area of disagreement between black and white feminists. Much mention is made within feminist political literature of the way in which feminist criticism has ignored literature by black women writers; and Barbara Smith's 'Toward a black feminist criticism'[49] is widely anthologized, perhaps just because there are so few black voices within feminist criticism (indeed within criticism, because within academia). There is a serious split between black and white feminists, as there must be because of the problems involved in making an essential feminism universally applicable and binding. Rich rejects universal humanism, but she wants universal feminism. The problem is, some women have other calls on their time, on their consciousness, calls which some *other* women can't share. Women may have qualities which are both peculiar and common to them; but some of those women also have qualities which are peculiar and common to being black, to being working-class, to being old, to belonging to an economically disadvantaged country – all of which categories can be experienced by men as well as women. I do not say that men experience them in the same way as women, nor do I deny that women's disadvantage is compounded by belonging to such a category in a way in which a man's is not. But should we deny the man's experience of disadvantage because of that?

In a marvellously funny and trenchant poem, 'What chou mean *we*, white girl?' (*Conditions Five*), Lorraine Bethel – finally, in my view – annihilates a supposed community between black and white feminists. Bethel dedicates her poem 'TO THE PROPOSITION THAT ALL WOMEN ARE NOT EQUAL, I.E. IDENTICALLY OPPRESSED'. Her title speaks for itself but quotations are telling:

So this is an open letter to movement white girls:
Dear Ms Ann Glad Cosmic Womoon,

> We're not doing that kind of work anymore
> educating white women
> teaching Coloured Herstory 101
> on the job, off the job, in bed

Bethel is particularly bitter in her contempt for what she sees as the exploitation of politics for sexual ends by white feminist lesbians

> who would be scorned as racist dogs if they were
> heterosexual white men instead of white lesbians
> hiding behind the liberal veneer of equal bedroom activity
> erotic affirmative action

and about the careless lack of awareness of privilege of many white feminists. The occasion of her poem is a request for her to speak at a feminist conference:

> When I asked her for money she said
> 'We're not the MLA'
> I thought:
> Black women/lesbians/feminists don't even have a MLA
> to *not* be.

Bethel appends a note explaining what the MLA is.

This poem is certainly a powerful attack on the casual elitism which can be found in white feminists; in England, it tends to be demonstrated in a thoughtless ignorance about the lives of working-class women. It is the sort of elitism which leads Adrienne Rich to ask whether a true feminist criticism, which can embrace the needs of all women, can really be sustained in an academic environment at all. It is the sort of elitism which leads feminist critics to proclaim the importance of Women's Studies on the university curriculum, without altering their approach to admissions policy in any way at all.

But here we have precisely the problem generated by any attempt to define the essence of a generic group, and to base other principles on that essence. Lorraine Bethel (along with many others) objects to the inclusiveness of the 'we' used by white feminists, and the burden of her poem is that there is so little which connects and so much which separates white women from black women that the inclusive pronoun should not be used at all.

But if that inclusive pronoun cannot be used, the whole case for feminism collapses, and with it the case for feminist poetic. For what Bethel is arguing is that another category, that of being black, cuts across that of being a woman here. And unlike lesbianism, the category of feminism favoured by Rich (and possibly Bethel), being black is a category shared by men. It is also a category which has been seen as issuing in a distinct and important poetic voice, and which has, like feminism, sought its own poetic, the terms of which have sounded remarkably similar to the terms of a feminist poetic (e.g. the emphasis on the personal and the experiential, the search for a new and individual voice and language, the concern with the political in content and attitude, the need for an inclusive accessibility). June Jordan in her introduction to *Soulscript* says:

> Over the past several years, Afro-America has flourished as a national community concerned to express its own situation and its own response. The concern to choose, find and create relationship leads naturally into poems. Here, in this anthology, the reader will follow along where Afro-American concern for a vocabulary-made-personal leads. Governed by a beautiful proud spirit, the Afro-American grows from the experience of brave, continuing survival despite the force of deadly circumstance. These poems tell that spirit and that survival, even as they spell black dreams.[50]

In the body of the poetry itself in this anthology, the question of poetics is engaged with in much the same way as feminist poetry has done, usually in defence of a greater accessibility and the rejection of traditional (over-elaborate) forms. Ray Durem, in 'I know I'm not sufficiently obscure', asks whether there's a 'lavender word' for 'lynch'. The subject of his poem is how poetry can deal with the story of 'a black woman working out her guts' for a white man.

Gwendolyn Brooks, a poet who has spanned a number of historical changes in the black movement, writes:

> My aim, in my next future, is to write poems that will somehow successfully 'call' all black people: black people in taverns, black people in alleys, black people in gutters, schools, offices, factories, prisons, the consulate; I wish to

reach black people in mines, on farms, on thrones; *not* always 'teach' – I shall wish often to entertain, to illumine.[51]

And later 'True black writers speak *as* blacks, *about* blacks, *to* blacks'; and 'Further....These black writers do not care if you call their product Art or Peanuts.'[52] Yet that question necessarily arises, just as it does with feminist poetry; it is *not* peanuts; it *is* art. True, these lines were written a decade or more ago, and since then feminism itself has created some cracks in the smooth unity. But the poetry of Brooks and Jordan still largely proclaims the black rather than the feminist voice (though Jordan's refrain in 'From sea to shining sea', in *Living Room*, ironically reiterating the fact that 'this is not a good time' to be black/gay/young/old/ etc., seems to aspire to a unity greater even than that of being black: 'This is the only time to come together').

Other writers have attempted to define specifically a black feminist voice and poetic. In an enjoyable free-ranging and fascinating 'pentalog' in *Conditions Five*, five black feminist writers debate some of the issues arising from this, though they touch only barely on the conflict which might exist in allegiances. Their *allegiances* are clear to them; it is how these affect their writing (both expressive and critical) which exercises them. In one section of their discussion they speak of their awareness of having both public and private voices; their public voices uphold the virtue of being black (so that in reviewing a black woman writer they believe to be poor, they would hold back on that view), while their private voices question their own position in doing this. This is highly reminiscent of Clausen's hidden fears which she exposes with difficulty, of privately wishing for male-dominated traditional approval while publicly adopting and espousing a 'right-on' feminist approach. Similar contradictions can arise when other categories conflict with feminist ideals. Rayna Green, writing about 'Native American Women', in *Signs*, cautions us to listen to the women themselves and their reaction to feminist values where these conflict with their own traditional values: 'Given the hostile climate on reservations for discussion of any theory applied to Indians, I doubt feminist theory of any stripe would be well received. For Indian feminists, every women's issue is framed in the larger context of Native American people.'[53] Green goes on to comment on the irony that Indian women want to assert their power by insisting on their traditional roles within

Indian society which involve men and women in complementary roles. Green herself insists that we can only follow the women's feelings and instincts here. Green has edited a powerful anthology of Native American Women's poetry and fiction, entitled (as befits her exhortation in the more academic article, after a work by Joy Harjo) *That's What She Said;*[54] while it is characterized by being the voices of women, it embodies the spirit of being (displaced) Indian.

Certainly, it is encouraging that these very dilemmas are being voiced, and it is interesting that they are being voiced most clearly from within the organs of feminism such as *Conditions*. Yet at the same time, it is the very fact that these journals are seen as 'safe houses' where such thoughts and doubts can be raised without fear of betrayal to the 'enemy' (the white feminist, or the male critic, or the heterosexual female critic) that enables them to be voiced. What must concern us here are the critical implications of these dilemmas.

Are we to develop and apply for each of these sets of poems by women – lesbian, black, Indian – a particular poetic? *Could* we do this? *Should* we? And if we could and should, what would the effect of this be on women's poetry? To begin with, it would place the emphasis more and more upon content and attitude, since that would initially be the principal index of category. Hortense Spillers, writing about Gwendolyn Brooks in *Shakespeare's Sisters*, states: 'Black and female are basic and inherent in her poetry. The critical question is *how* they are said.'[55] But might not the critical question be whether anything *else* is said, or how the two are balanced when they come (as surely they must) into conflict? Spillers states:

> Some of Brooks's poems speak directly to situations for which black women need names, but this specificity may be broadened to define situations for other women as well. The magic of irony and humor can be brought to bear by any female in her most dangerous life encounter – the sexual/ emotional entanglement. Against that entanglement, her rage and disappointment are poised, but often impotently, unless channeled by positive force.
>
> (pp. 243–4)

The number of assumptions being made and the directions in which they lead are almost breath-taking. How does this feminist analysis, with its assertion both that for all women the most dangerous life-encounter is the sexual/emotional entanglement, and that only rage and disappointment are the appropriate responses to that entanglement, not to mention the idea that irony and humour are the 'magic' poetic tools to be used to express these feelings positively, deal with a poem like Brooks' 'Paul Robeson',[56] a lyrical and powerful hymn to the great artist's 'major voice', acting also as a metaphor for his political voice:

> Warning, in music-words
> devout and large,
> that we are each other's
> harvest

or with her 'Malcolm X'.[57] (Spillers quotes this poem and terms it celebratory, but does not discuss it directly, grouping it instead with 'Strong men riding horses', and suggesting that both ironize heroism by 'a shrewd opposition of under-statement and exaggeration'.) Brooks certainly suggests some doubt in the poem, with words like 'sorcery' and 'beguiled', but she does not flinch from lines such as:

We gasped. We saw the maleness.
The maleness raking out and making guttural the air

and the poem ends:

> He opened us –
> who was a key,
> who was a man.

Yes, there is irony in the double-edged 'who was a man' ('only a man' as well as 'what a man'), but the recognition of and celebration of the maleness remains. Conversely, if we, or if a black critic, tries to apply a black-centred critique to June Jordan's 'Poem on the road; for Alice Walker', Section 3 (Brooklyn),[58] what will he/she do with these lines:

> After he took six
> dollars
> After he punched her
> down
> After he pushed for pussy
> After he punctured her lungs with his knife

After the Black man
in his early thirties
in a bomber jacket
After she stopped bleeding
After she stopped pleading
(*please don't hurt me*)

What was the imagery running
through the arteries of the heart
of that partner?

This is not racist

This section is part of a long poem linking different regions of
America by the (predominantly) sexist acts which take place in
them. Jordan's refrain – 'This is not racist' – and her final line
('The very next move is not mine') seems both designed to
redirect our attention, as it were, from the primary subject matter
of many of her poems, and to place the responsibility for change
on the men who commit the acts described, black or white. It is a
fine poem and, like 'From Sea to Shining Sea', goes beyond the
local and the political to concern itself with individual guilt and
communal responsibility. It is accessible in language, yet does not
abandon niceties of rhyme or form (e.g. the refrains) where these
are of use, and Jordan handles the free verse form in the easiest
and most assured way. And what if we forgot categories here,
abandoned political stances to this poetry, and read it as 'poetry'?
The reader coming fresh to Brooks or Jordan, without having
read anything else by or about them, would not necessarily pick
up a political stance from their collections, since collections is
what they tend to be. Jordan's *Living Room*, by its very title, seems
to announce a sort of generosity of approach, and indeed the list
of periodicals in which poems anthologized here have been
previously published testify to her wide range. Almost all the
poems have a political edge, but it is not always the *same* political
edge; similarly with Brooks, if we take her collections as a whole,
though her more recent work seems more firmly directed
towards, and about, fellow blacks. But in fact, should anything
differ about the way we read these poems than about the way we
read any others?

Recently I read Shelley's 'Ode to the West Wind' with a group
of mature, pre-higher education, students, doing a year-long

course to prepare them for possible entry to higher education. Before they came on the course, the majority of these students had little formal education in literature; a lot of them had read widely, but without many of the preconceptions which a formal education can carry with it. My aim was to compare Shelley with other attempts to express abstract or hidden feelings and ideas which are by nature difficult of expression (Wordsworth, Donne and Keats were the other poets) and to show why Shelley failed where the others in one way or another succeeded. In this *I* failed, because one of the group (rapidly carrying with her several others) thought the Shelley poem was marvellous – and particularly the line which I had singled out for ridicule: 'I fall upon the thorns of life! I bleed!' Carefully, I went through the metaphors in the poem to show how little they were thought through, how in the end they led nowhere. 'Precisely', came the reply 'that's just the sort of frustration he's trying to express!' This student was moved by the poem, especially moved by the honesty of the 'thorns' line, she understood Shelley. The purpose of this example is not to emphasize the subjectivity of critical judgements; there are many things which can be said of Shelley's poem, and a number of interpretative and evaluative disagreements have centred on it, but there are also only a *limited* number of things to be said about it which are correct.

The experience reminded me of a lesson which Leavis's method of approach to poetry first taught me: that we should not approach poetry, that we *cannot* approach poetry, with a set of specific interpretative and evaluative criteria, like measuring rods, against which we set the poetry and find it either fitting or wanting. Certainly, Leavis worked in such a way that there were a number of *unwritten* criteria to which he tended to refer in this way. But his *method* in approaching poetry was still one which concerned itself with individual cases, often compared with each other the better to reveal the comparative faults and virtues of each poem. This method I had thought I was applying in my class; in fact, I had allowed the examples to harden into a pre-formed critical judgement. I knew the outcome before I started; it took a fresh response to the examples to show me that I was wrong.

The story doesn't have a simple happy ending; my own judgement of 'Ode to the West Wind' remains the same; and I think 'I fall upon the thorns of life! I bleed!' is characteristically self-indulgent (perhaps I just can't take the exclamation marks). Many have been the critical disagreements where I ended up feeling much as I felt about the poem at the beginning. Sometimes this has been for reasons of interpretation, sometimes it has had to do with a difference about the power of a metaphor or the force of a certain sort of rhythm, sometimes it has revolved round 'the problem of belief'. But not infrequently it has had to do with the relationship of all three. And is not this our experience of poetry; is it not this which makes poetry the original form it is? If I decide that the word 'erect' in Donne's 'Valediction: forbidding mourning' must include a sexual pun, given Donne's tendency to punning and his awareness of sexuality, and if I then decide that it adversely affects the tone of the ending of one of his most affecting poems, I am balancing interpretative, linguistic and tonal considerations, as well as taking into account what else I know of the poet (both from his poetry and from biographical information) and the rest of the poem. All of these come together in my critical response to the poem, as do a number of loosely established and applied critical criteria which, however, are secondary to my actual response to the poem. Surely this is as it should be? In this particular case I am sorry, since I love the poem and I don't want it marred; and in spite of my liking for Donne's sexual openness, and my understanding of his inclusiveness of sexuality in some of his most serious works, in this case I find it does mar it. No amount of argument will make a difference. But in other cases it works the other way; I think of Ricks converting me to Milton's grand style, in spite of the fact that *Paradise Lost* was intended 'to justify the ways of God to man' – an impossible task in my view; I think of seeing Emily Dickinson's autograph texts, after reading them in a variety of forms in print (altered and unaltered by editors, altered indelibly by varying forms of type-face and typographical presentation), and realizing the terrible uncertainty as well as the certainty of those extraordinary 'dashes', some faint, some very clear, some like full stops, others like changeable commas. If I were to go to either of these texts with a ready prepared approach, a full set of critical criteria, whether determined by a feminist model or some other, my response would necessarily be limited, blinkered. I have much sympathy with the essentialist feminist, such as Adrienne Rich, who says that, yes, it should be limited and blinkered because that is precisely the view of humanity being put forward by the poet. Critics such as Rich know where their priorities lie, and in looking at poetry they are putting a simple political criterion before any other. But anyone who chooses that path *must* be aware of what they are abandoning in doing so; and they must be aware of the limitations they are imposing on their own poets.

The limitation is not peculiar to feminism. In 1987, I saw Irina Ratushinskaya feted at the Albert Hall, top of the bill, a star; but what she was being applauded for were really her experiences, her fortitude, as a political prisoner at the hands of a punitive system, and most of all for her escape from that system. And because she was imprisoned because of poetry written in dissent from that system, it was her poetry which was the object of admiration.[59] True, it is difficult to judge properly poetry in translation; but to a cold eye, Ratushinskaya's poetry is at best banal. Marin Sorescu, at the same event, was rendered in translation, and the quality of what he wrote was clear; and it too was opposed, in the same way Ratushinskaya's poetry was opposed, to authoritarianism. Robert Creeley also read at the same event, a star from the past; even leaving aside the spine-tingling agony of his delivery, the poetry shone. It likewise shone on the page at a subsequent private reading. Creeley's *Memory Gardens* is not political in the way that Ratushinskaya and Sorescu are, in their different ways, political. But it deals with what might be seen as the broadest political questions, moral questions, about the nature of actual things and our experience of them. Of the three I heard that night I should want to argue that Creeley is indisputably the greatest poet; Sorescu is a fine poet; and Ratushinskaya is not really much of a poet at all. And while these judgements connect with the political content of two of the writer's poetry, and by extension, since by comparison, the non-political content of the third, in the end it is a judgement which does not hang on political considerations. It *does* partly hang on content, and to the extent that poetry is by its nature *about* something, expressive of something, because written in language, which usually makes sense, and has some reference to the world, to reality, the problem of belief may often be present when we make a critical judgement about poetry. It is not my intention to say that it may not, or that it never affects critical and evaluative judgements. What I do want to say is that it is not and should not be the only determinant of critical judgements about poetry.

Beliefs – religious, political, moral – clearly do enter into our response to poetry, sometimes without our knowing that that is what is working on us. When we question our critical responses and try to understand what underpins them, this is one area which we need to consider. Why can I respond so happily to Herbert's religious poetry, though I do not share his beliefs, yet at the same time want to say that Crashaw is a bad poet partly *because* of the sacramental bloodiness of his imagery? There are all sorts of things to take into account here – one of which is whether anyone else shares my judgement or whether it is purely idiosyncratic – and the only way to explore further is to look honestly at the poetry and at our own responses to it. If in doing this I can discuss my views with others, perhaps especially someone who disagrees with me, I may get nearer to what is happening in the poetry and in my own response to it. But if I start from the position that, for example, all religious poetry is out of the reckoning as far as I am concerned, or that all Catholic poetry is doomed by its own imagery, I shall never reach the poetry in the first place.

The feminist might argue that this is nit-picking; that women have been so hugely disadvantaged by the 'male' poetic tradition that a discussion of two male poets' respective views of religion should not be of interest – since where are the women's voices? But this is to pin us to the past and condemn us in the future. If women are not allowed a *free* voice to explore and express whatsoever they please, how can they develop as poets? For it seems to me that the great tragedy of the thrust of feminist criticism lies in the way it proscribes certain areas of thought, certain ways of writing. Have women not had enough proscription, written or unwritten, and should not the best and quickest way forward for them be to have the greatest possible freedom to write, for whom they choose, about what they wish, and in what manner they like? Is not the important thing for them to be heard? And when heard, criticized, responded to, positively, critically, actively, by all manner of audience? To ask for this does not and need not mean remaining within what many feminist critics have perceived as the male tradition. Poetic forms may have been fashioned largely by men, but this does not render the forms themselves in any way masculine or male; only the association of maleness with poetry does that. That association can be quickly unlearned, indeed, I would suggest, has already been unlearned by today's readers. Yes, the sonnet form is connected in our minds with male writers: Petrarch, Shakespeare, Milton. Yes, we even call different sonnet forms Shakespearean or Miltonic. But what *is* in a name? It is irritating to have the weak stress at the end of a poetic line called a feminine ending, and the term should be dropped; but that it is so called does not in itself constitute an unbreakable connection between weakness and femininity; neither does calling a certain sort of sonnet Miltonic mean that I, a woman, cannot write a sonnet in that form. When I do write a sonnet of that form, I am not thereby espousing a male tradition; I am simply exploiting a poetic form whose major exponents have, for a variety of reasons, been men. Again, this is annoying, and that we know the reasons for it and understand how it came about and how it can be combatted does not make it less annoying. Feminists, and feminist critics, have helped us to understand these things, helped us to combat them and helped to put women writers, women poets, firmly on the map. But how we proceed from this knowledge is now at issue and the decision is a crucial one. If we determine our future actions as poets in negative response to the tradition largely created by men, and if we limit ourselves by so doing, we shall only increase the restrictions upon women and limit their development, as poets, and as people.

Consider Emily Dickinson's poem, 'My life had stood, a loaded gun';[60] this poem has exercised many critics, and it has particularly exercised feminists; indeed Dickinson herself has called forth a variety of responses from feminists, both favourable and unfavourable. I quote the poem in full, since I shall refer closely to it.

> My life had stood – a Loaded Gun –
> In Corners – till a Day
> The Owner passed – identified –
> And carried Me away –
>
> And now We roam in Sovreign Woods –
> And now We hunt the Doe –
> And every time I speak for Him –
> The Mountains straight reply –
>
> And do I smile, such cordial light
> Upon the Valley glow –

It is as a Vesuvian face
Had let its pleasures through –

And when at Night – Our good Day done –
I guard My Master's Head –
'Tis better than the Eider-Duck's
Deep Pillow – to have shared –

To foe of His – I'm deadly foe –
None stir the second time –
On whom I lay a Yellow Eye –
Or an emphatic Thumb –

Though I than He – may longer live
He longer must – than I –
For I have but the power to kill,
Without – the power to die –

The imagery of the poem, its aggressive tone, and its extremely puzzling last stanza have all exercised feminist critics; the usual interpretative solution to the gun imagery is to see the 'He' of the poem as embodying Dickinson's creative spirit, her poet-self, which rules her weaker 'feminine' self. Both Adrienne Rich and Albert Gelpi take this view in their essays on Dickinson in *Shakespeare's Sisters* (though Gelpi's analysis is more insistently psychoanalytic than Rich's suggestive and persuasive piece, which works through her own identification with Dickinson as a fellow poet). Other feminist critics have regarded it as a supreme expression of impotence, for example, Barbara Williams, in 'A Room of her Own: Emily Dickinson as woman artist'.[61] Each has a different interpretation of the paradoxical last stanza. Meanwhile, June Jordan would not have us read Dickinson at all.

Now, the interpretative differences are not in themselves damagingly inconsistent; the poem is a highly allusive, and elusive, one, so thoroughly embedded in its symbolic narrative that it gives us the feeling at once both of thoroughly understanding it, almost on a realistic, factual level, and of being unable to explain it. The experience is not uncommon with Dickinson's poems, relying as they often do on the stunning power of final paradoxes, and an extraordinary imaginative grasp which persuades by its assurance but defies exegesis. But what *is* striking about the feminist interpretations here is their stretch *away* from what seems the most obvious interpretation. Certainly, interpretations of the poem which have seen it as a love poem to an unknown 'master' have focused on a rather squalid biographical exercise in trying to uncover some evidence of a hidden affair in Dickinson's life, and it is understandable that feminists have turned away from these. But we need to see the poem only on an imaginative level to accept it as a poem about female sexuality, a sexuality finding fulfilment in surrender to an overwhelming passion. Nor need we see this surrender as weak; in fact, as all its interpreters have recognized, the poem is full of a marvellous strength and confidence, even in the gnomic final couplet. For though the speaker of the poem is empowered initially by 'the Owner', the rest of the poem is resolutely dominated by the repeated 'I' (if we are counting – eight 'I's to two 'We's' and an 'Our' – and three of these 'I's' in the last stanza). A psychoanalytic reading is not needed to identify the sexual reference in the poem: the speaker is 'loaded', but needs to be 'carried away' before she can fire. In fact, spelling out the metaphor makes it ludicrous, where in the poem and within its own narrative and extension it is entirely natural. The ease of togetherness in the second stanza (here the 'we' comes into play) leads to the entirely natural 'I speak for him', humanizing the aggressive 'speaking', of the gunfire, emphasizing the community of the 'speaking'. The last line of that second stanza places the experience on a more elemental level, while still retaining the narrative realism (the echo). The same combination of the familiar, and the huge and strange, which can light even the most domestic of sexual relationships, is sustained in the third stanza, with its adjacent 'cordial' and 'Vesuvian' both relating to 'pleasure'. All the time, the image of gunfire informs our imaginative understanding, yet Dickinson pacifies it with words such as 'glow' and 'smile' which, even as they clearly refer to the explosion of the gun, also draw us away from its aggressive connotations. We have to think for a moment to understand the force of 'Vesuvian'; but once understood, we are reminded of so many other Dickinson poems in which the intense power of emotion comes through under cover, yet hits us more powerfully as a result ('Tell all the Truth – but tell it Slant'). Certainly, the next two stanzas leave us in no doubt of the aggressive and destructive nature of the partnership. In the fourth, again almost by stealth, by comparison, Dickinson reminds us of the 'Eider ducks's deep pillow' (the duck a companion to the doe, both uncompromisingly soft) and so reminds us of the gun's and hunter's victim. The destructive power of the partnership is further emphasized in the fifth ('None stir a second time'), and in both of these stanzas the speaker's pride in the role of protector is stressed, a fierce protectiveness, a desire to cherish, springing out of a deeply felt love, which has victims in others who might threaten it.

Then, finally, the enigmatic epigram. Part of the confusion caused by this stanza lies with the initial inversion ('Though I than He'); this is a characteristic grammatical device of Dickinson's, where she gives us a dependent phrase, which can't achieve its meaning until we have read on what it depends – gives us that phrase *first*, so that it hangs, taunting us to an interpretation in advance of what is to come. (She does something very similar in 'My life closed twice', where the line 'a third event to me' precedes the modifying and explanatory 'so huge, so hopeless to conceive', which is in turn modified by the subsequent line, 'as those that twice befell'. It is as though the thought unfolds itself to us in reverse order, so that we uncover the meaning of each line only as we get to the next – and then that in turn is 'discovered' by the next. No wonder that by the time, in that poem, we reach the numbing stroke of the final couplet – 'Parting is all we know of heaven/And all we need of hell' – we feel incapable of disagreement. Here is a poet who knows more than we do and is able to put her knowledge in a way which is instantly recognizable to us as true, because we feel it to be. This is not to say that we should not try to unravel what Dickinson is saying; but we must recognize that the paradox is both her instrument *and* part of what she is trying to identify as true.) The stanza reverts to the overt dependency of the first stanza of the poem. Dickinson's point is that the loaded gun cannot fire without the 'owner'; when he dies, it goes back 'in corners', existing, but not alive. 'I' *may* live longer than 'he', but it will be life without living; once 'he' is dead, who gives the 'I' the power to kill (the gunfire which in the rest of the poem has been allied with sexual pleasure and intense passionate love), life loses its power, its point, its pleasure, and stands again, loaded but unused, without even 'the power to die' (determined for us, not of our choosing). Hence the 'must'; 'he' must stay alive longer than 'I' since he is the giver of the life which informs 'me'.

It is easy to see why a feminist critic would not like this interpretation. It casts the speaker in a passive mould, lifeless until her 'owner' comes to give her life, and lifeless again when he is dead. Yet why should this not be precisely the feeling Dickinson is expressing here? The assurance, pleasure, sensuality and charity expressed in the poem are far, far stronger than any impotence and passivity expressed; and the inherent violence of the central metaphor testifies to the power of feeling which springs from the central stanzas. In this the poem recalls 'Wild nights',[62] with its same emphasis on the relationship between dependence and strength:

> Rowing in Eden –
> Ah, the Sea!
> Might I but moor – Tonight –
> In Thee!

It doesn't matter whether Dickinson actually knew the delights of such 'wild nights' (though we must regret it for her if she did not); she knew them imaginatively, and what she is expressing here speaks to the experience of many. The sexuality that she explores here, with its combination of openness to pleasure and dependence on the person giving pleasure, fierce strength derived from sexual satisfaction, and a fiercely protective love of the person giving it, is that experienced by many women. It need not be derived from love of a man; but very often – most often – it is. If this is partly the product of social conditioning (that the partner is a man), does that negate the value of the experience? Of course it does not. If passion produces dependence, it does so in homosexual loves as well as heterosexual ones. If women write about that experience, how can that be wrong?

Sexuality is by its nature diverse, individual, formed by all sorts of factors and experiences. I actively resent being told by Irigaray that the phallus is the privileged signifier (thus robbing me of a positive sexual identity separate from the phallus, and of a share in the language) and by Montefiore that 'what is necessary is to show how this model of an infantile mode of being [i.e. the castration complex] has to do with questions of identity and relationship between (a) adult lovers and (b) love-sonnets'.[63] And if Irigaray posits a psychoanalytics and poetics in which the mother 'has no identity as a woman. And this effectively plunges the mother and the little girl into the same nothingness'[64] and

218

which 'woman...can experience herself only as a waste or excess in the little structured margins of the dominant ideology',[65] Rich posits an opposing one in which women have been lured away from what is the primary relationship, that with their mothers, and which should act as the model for subsequent (women-centred) relationships. Rich dismisses any other kind of female sexuality as 'false consciousness' and gives as an example of this 'the maintenance of a mother–son relationship between men and women, including the demand that women provide material solace, nonjudgemental nurturing and compassion for their harassers, rapists and batterers (as well as for men who passively vampirize them)'.[66] Again, I resent this monolithic character-ization of both women and men, which extends sexuality to all social relationships between men and women. What irks particularly about both characterizations is the implication that a 'conventional' heterosexual sexuality denies woman's identity in some way. Rich is particularly contemptuous, like many other feminists, of sexual liberation, which she sees as a liberation for men only; but one of the powerful effects of sexual liberation was to free women into an understanding that sexual pleasure was theirs for the asking, and the pleasure and its nature could be of their choosing. Any woman who came, as I did, from a back-ground in which the very idea of being naked in front of another person could cause acute embarrassment, *must* have benefited from the sudden realization, in the 1960s, that sex was no longer a cause for shame. In my case, certainly, social conditioning was no match for the discovery. Of course, the legacy of sexual liberation was not without complication; but I do feel uncomp-licated regret for today's female adolescents, thrust once again into a world where sexual discovery and disease are intimately connected.

If this seems to have only a distant connection with poetry and poetics, the point here is that feminist criticism has rendered it otherwise. It has laid deliberate limits on the subject matter of feminist poetry, to such an extent that not just 'incorrect' views of female sexuality, but incorrect views of all relationships with men are affected by it. In a moving piece occasioned by the premature death of her brother, Rima Shore engages courageously with what it means for a feminist writer to feel as she does about her brothers. She explains that while all the important things in her life are woman-centred, 'I know that many of my most intense feelings, most fierce loyalties, are directed toward the men who are my brothers.' She goes on to refer to feminist writers who have been censored, or who have censored themselves, in exploring such relationships, either by not being invited to read, or, when invited, reading about 'relationships with mothers and grandmothers, sisters and lovers....I wonder how many other women have deformed their experience?'[67] Again – how could it be wrong for a woman to write about her love of a beloved brother? How could it be right for her to feel that she could not? What might not become forbidden territory in such a poetic world?

Here we come back, at last, to the connection between the 'political' feminist commentator on literature and the 'academic' feminist critic. For the academic critic might object at this point that my arguments have been largely directed towards a view of literature determined by the nature of its subject matter; their concerns, they might insist, go beyond and deeper than that rather simple view. But it is my intention to show that, in practice, 'academic' feminist criticism of poetry depends upon the political feminism which underlies it, and further that criticism which centres on formal and linguistic aspects of poetry has as its basis a view of female sexuality, identity or psychology which must be accepted by the reader if the critical judgements are to be accepted. Thus, any feminist criticism presupposes a concept of female identity which underpins the interpretations and evaluations made by the critic. That these concepts are often opposing and competing demonstrates their centrality in the critical position. I shall conclude by referring briefly to some of these oppositions, and showing their implications for the competing critical judgements. I shall refer again to Dickinson and also to Sylvia Plath.

Would a contemporary feminist have dared to write such a poem as 'My life had stood – a loaded gun'? The aggressively phallic nature of the imagery together with the passivity of the first and last stanzas might well be ruled out before they got to the page. Irigaray asserts, 'Woman never speaks evenly. What she utters is flowing, fluctuating, *Deceptive.*'[68] Montefiore argues from this that 'Her articulations of specifically female meaning and of women's sexual identity through metaphors of fluidity is immensely suggestive....The rightness of these metaphors is confirmed by the frequence with which imagery of water, oceans and dissolution is associated in women's poems with identity and sexuality.'[69] Nothing could be further from fluidity than Dickinson's metaphor of the 'loaded gun', and Montefiore is honest enough to recognize that 'Dickinson's poems...are remarkably difficult to assimilate into a theory of female identity articulating itself through the writing of an Imaginary relationship between "I" and "Thou"'[70] (her references being to Irigaray's attempt to postulate a female Imaginary). Rich is ready to *accept* the phallic metaphor – but only when she has erected an interpretation which sees this as a representation of Dickinson's *alter ego*, her creative imagination, active, masculine, in its power. But would she have used such an image herself? Williams sees the image as expressing impotence: 'She is only the agent, the instrument of his power. If he should abandon her or die, she will again lapse into helplessness and oblivion.'[71] Impotence was perhaps a reasonable feeling for a nineteenth-century poet to express; but a poet of the late twentieth century? Paula Bennett, in a book evidently inspired by the poem, *My Life A Loaded Gun*,[72] sees the metaphor as representing all that is antithetical to 'women', and finally characterizes that as the expression of rage, the centrality of which to women's poetry form the basis of her thesis in the book. Again, a psychoanalytic view informs the interpretation here. Conflicting as these interpretations are (and incidentally there is no conflict in evaluation – all these critics see this as a great poem) they are all bound up in one way or another with an assessment of the psychological underpinning of the poem: Williams sees impotence, Bennett rages against impotence, and Rich the grasping of an identity through the creative imagination, and the stylistic points they make are related closely to that. Montefiore, who does not deal specifically with this poem, notices the 'ambiguous and contradictory' character of Dickinson's poetry and (a mite reluctantly) concedes that she can't be fitted in to an 'Irigarayan female Imaginary' except in terms of her contradictoriness.[73] We must admire Montefiore at this point; it would be tempting to align Dickinson's gnomic qualities with the fluidity which Irigaray espouses, but Montefiore resists that temptation, seeing that Dickinson's evasiveness really leads elsewhere. 'A loaded gun' has attracted so many interpretations, partly because of the invitingly combative nature of its imagery. Given that Dickinson represents for many feminists a new beginning for women's poetry, because they see her as writing a lyric poetry

sufficiently extraordinary and distinct from the 'male' lyric tradition that it creates a new poetic language, this was a poem that
had to be dealt with. But would the current climate allow such a
revolutionary poem, or such a revolutionary poet, to emerge?

In fact, does not Dickinson's poem represent an integral challenge to those feminist critics who argue for a specifically female
language on which a female tradition can be mounted? Why do
we need to seek for a new female language or a female tradition
when Dickinson could write as she did? Montefiore interprets
Irigaray (who interprets Lacan) as saying that 'the entry into the
system of significant differences which is language coincides
with the conception of sexual difference organized around the
presence or absence of the phallus, or privileged signifier'.[74] This
assumes, first, that we accept that language is only a system of
differences, with no reference to the actual world; second, that the
entry into that system not only coincides with but somehow
metaphorically mirrors our understanding of sexual difference;
further, as women, we must agree that as we are disempowered
in the sexual world so we are disempowered in the linguistic
world – that is, we must accept that our notions of sexuality are
dependent on our *not* having a penis, and then we must further
accept that this makes it impossible to control the language in the
way in which men do. So how could Dickinson write the poem
she wrote? Unless we force ourselves into an interpretation
where the metaphor is itself 'male' and is annexed by Dickinson
to express a 'non-female' strength of creativity, why should not
all the language in the first place be *hers*? What renders the image
of the gun male? Only social association. As soon as Dickinson
uses it in her poem, it's hers to use as she wishes. Why should we
associate the image of the 'doe' with femininity or femaleness?
Yes, the doe is the female of the deer species; but that does not
necessarily ally Dickinson as a female of her species, with the doe.
Even less so should she be identified with the eider-duck. What
identifies her? The soft feathers? In one (or rather several) strokes
in this poem, Dickinson annihilates any concept of a male
language from which a female writer may be excluded. And if we
look at the circumstances in which she worked, they were very
like the circumstances in which (a far larger number of) male
writers worked. As Adrienne Rich notes, she had her meals
provided, she had her own room, her privacy, indeed it was her
sister who took care of her daily domestic needs. Elizabeth Barrett

Browning is another such whom many a contemporary woman writer might have cause to envy. But her conditions were only those of male contemporaries looked after in the same special way. The lives of Dickinson and Barrett Browning recall the privileges of Wordsworth, with his upstairs room and his landing door to the garden allowing him an exit without recourse to the domestic activities of the ground floor. (Of course, Wordsworth outdid himself, with *two* amanuenses, his wife for his letters and his sister for his poems). None of this is laudable, for Wordsworth or for Barrett Browning; yet in itself it is not necessarily wrong, since each of these was an unusually creative person, whose work has continued to give pleasure and succour. That more men benefited from such help than did women is undeniable. But that in and of itself does not mean that poetry was denied to women; especially it does not mean that language was or is essentially male. We do not need to see 'My life had stood' as the work of a woman poet exploiting a male metaphor; it is the work of a poet exploiting an unusually powerful metaphor. That we are human creatures differentiated both by biological difference and by social conditioning of course makes *some* difference. But it does not necessarily make *the* difference. And we need not, therefore, accept that it makes that damaging difference in terms of language.

It has been one of the key aims of feminist criticism of poetry to try to define a female poetic 'language'. This presupposes that there is a male poetic language which women have to borrow. Sometimes this has been defined in terms of traditional poetic forms, sometimes in terms of convention, sometimes in terms of tone of voice, and sometimes in terms of a theory of language formation and acquisition which is gender-based and which affects female subjectivity, and therefore the way that subjectivity is expressed in poetry. Almost all feminist critics share the assumption and assertion that the poetic tradition is male dominated and that therefore any woman who attempts to insert herself into it is thereby disadvantaged because the forms she takes on are characterized by their uses by men. I have tried to suggest why this is not necessarily the case. Yet it dominates much of academic criticism. Montefiore, in her analysis of the female use of flower imagery to demonstrate the way in which poetic forms cannot be freed from their maleness, argues: 'What emerges from these analyses, then, is that even in the most overtly casual, feminist poem, the flowers are not innocently "there", devoid of the traditional symbolism which determines the limit of their possible meanings."[75] That traditional symbolism she sees as having 'a time-honoured association with female sexuality; they traditionally symbolize women's beauty and vulnerability to decay.' Indeed, this is how flower images have often been used in poetry, though they have also been used to symbolize the mortality of man in general. But does this make them unalterable? A tradition is a tradition; just that. It is not inviolable, unchangeable. When Sylvia Plath writes 'Tulips' or uses poppies as images (an example referred to by Montefiore)[76]

> Flickering like that, wrinkly and clear red, like
> the skin of a mouth.
>
> A mouth just bloodied.
> Little bloody skirts!

it seems to me that she transforms the image into something quite other. Surely the only reason we might put a gloss on it connected with female sexuality as Montefiore does, arguing that the speaker in the poem 'associations the poppies with the idea of her rival in the act of sexual possession',[77] is that we know some of the biographical information surrounding the poem. Fine: but here, unlike the case of 'Ariel' where an understanding of the poem is greatly enhanced when we know that Plath's horse was named 'Ariel', the biographical context does not really invade the poem at all.

What is much more striking in this poem, as in most of Plath's poems written at this time, is the brilliant expression of a raw, intense, yet poetically controlled pain. The pain might be that caused by sexual jealousy; but that is not conveyed in either the image or the narrative content of the poem. As Montefiore herself says, 'conventional meanings are pushed to a savage, almost unrecognizable extreme'; her subsequent contention that they 'yet are apparent in the disturbing representation of female sexuality as a whorish bloody mouth'[78] inserts her own adjectival gloss 'whorish' to distort the actual content of the poem, which refers in no way to the 'whorish lipsticked, perhaps bruised mouth, and bleeding genitals',[79] imagined there by Montefiore. With imagery so vivid, so virulent it is difficult to quarrel with an imaginative interpretation; but to draw from that Plath's dependence on the sexual connotations of a male-determined image seems to me simply to do too much. Elsewhere, Gloria Hull, writing about three 'women writers of the Harlem Renaissance',[80] compares the flower imagery used by both Angelina Weld Grimke and Alice Dunbar-Nelson to express their love of women. While other writers are imbued with a Romantic tradition, each transforms the flower image in her own way; Dunbar-Nelson writes, in 'You! Inez!',

> Orange gleams athwart a crimson soul
> Lambent flames; purple passion lurks
> In your dusk eyes.
> Red mouth; flower soft,
> Your soul leaps up and flashes
> Star-like, white, flame-hot.

Dunbar-Nelson's title gives a clue to the female 'you' in the poem; and though the language is itself a little 'purple', the central flower image is as flushed by sensual passion as Plath's is flushed by a sensual hate. The contiguity of 'red mouth' with both 'flower soft' and 'dusk eyes' at once blurs the physicality of the image and sensualizes it.

Grimke's is a different vein, and, according to her interpreter Hull, her lesbian feelings are more suppressed. Certainly there is more of a sense of unfulfilled longing in lines such as

> I should like to creep
> Through the long brown grasses
> That are your lashes.

and

> If I might taste but once, just once
> The dew
> Upon her lips.

Nicely understated. Hull tells us that 'the poem was carried to the typescript stage and, having reached this point, Grimke substituted 'he' for 'she' where it was unavoidable. (This is reminiscent of the equally sad tales of E. M. Forster and Gide changing the male names of their characters to female ones.)

Surely these images can be annexed by female poets, and for other ends than those for which the traditional image was originally exploited? Surely the content and context of these poems determines the thrust of the image? And might it not be the case that flower images became associated with female sexuality because that was an immediate and accessible image? As we can see from both Dunbar-Nelson's and Plath's appropriations of it, there is no necessary connection between the image and fragility; it can be as violent and as aggressively sensual as the poet cares to make it. In the same way, as Montefiore herself argues, what renders the Alison Fell flower imagery in 'Girls' Gifts' overtly feminist, and thus, according to Montefiore, 'written outside the traditional poetic context invoked by these poems of sexuality' is the 'firm emphasis on specifically female creativity'.[81] In other words – the content.

Even more frequently invoked than the dominance of conventional 'male' imagery is the dominance of traditional poetic forms. Jane Stanbrough argues in 'Edna St Vincent Millay and the language of vulnerability' (*Shakespeare's Sisters*) that 'It is understandable why Millay's two extended narratives of women's psychological disintegration are presented in sonnet sequences. Millay persistently resorts to the constraints of traditional verse forms....The sonnet, her best form, is a fit vehicle to convey her deepest feelings of woman's victimization.'[82] Gilbert and Gubar, in their introduction to *Shakespeare's Sisters* go further: 'Before the nineteenth century the poet had a nearly priestly role and "he" had a wholly priestly role after Romantic thinkers had appropriated the vocabulary of theology for the realm of aesthetics. But if in Western culture women cannot be priests, then how – since poets are priests – can they be poets?'[83] They go on to flesh this out in terms of poetic language, here defined in terms of classical reference and meter, 'an education in "ancient rules"', and argue that women were barred from these ancient rules, therefore forgoing the role of poet, since 'the lyric poet must have aesthetic models, must in a sense speak the esoteric language of literary forms'. They refer to Dickinson to show that, when a female poet tried to create an alternative tradition, she was devalued as a result even by Crowe Ransom, one of her 'resuscitators', who argued that 'folk line is disadvantageous...if it denies to the poet the use of the English pentameter'.[84] One way or the other, then, it seems, the traditional forms are seen as excluding women poets, either because they erect barriers insurmountable to women, or because they themselves 'speak' the confinement which women experience. Thus Stanbrough insists on seeing the sonnet form only as an expression of constriction and containment, a 'language of vulnerability', while Dickinson's non-traditional forms diminish her in certain critical eyes. But again – *must* it be thus? After all, Crowe Ransom has been proved wrong, and Dickinson's 'folk line' is now seen and appreciated for what it is, a rhythmically idiosyncratic line which announces an individual poetic voice. Dickinson has caused the feminists who so admire her a certain amount of embarrassment. After all, she does have an idiosyncratic voice, unrestricted by those apparently dominant male forms. If she does of course, so can others; and if others can, there is nothing intrinsically male about the pentameter or any other traditional verse form. And if that is the case, the sonnet form certainly need not be expressive of male restriction of female creativity. Indeed, Millay uses and exploits the sonnet form like many men before her, to create a sense of vibrantly breaking through restrictiveness from time to time. Surely Stanbrough's view that Millay's sonnet sequence 'Fatal interview' is expressive of restriction and containment has far more to do with the ideas expressed by the poet than the form in which they are expressed. Indeed if she took off her blinkers and looked closely at the way in which Millay does exploit the form, she could not see this sequence simply as expressing 'the fatality of woman's vulnerability to social conditioning' or, put in another but equally benumbing way, 'an extended metaphorical illustration of the consequences to women of their limited range of experience and their susceptibility to emotional exploitation'.[85] In fact, one of the wonderful qualities of Millay's sonnet sequence (as Montefiore recognizes in her sympathetic and enjoyable account of these poems) is the strength of her pleasure in this relationship, a pleasure which communicates itself in many lines and makes them, in Montefiore's words, 'thoroughly pleasurable texts'.[86] There is also great generosity of feeling in the poems, a generosity from which it is clear Millay derives strength, *not* weakness:

> Not in a silver casket cool with pearls
> Or rich with red corundum or with blue,
> Locked, and the key withheld, as other girls
> Have given their loves, I give my love to you;
> Not in a lovers'-knot, not in a ring
> Worked in such fashion, and the legend plain –

Semper fidelis, where a secret spring
Kennels a drop of mischief for the brain:
Love in the open hand, nothing but that,
Ungemmed, unhidden, wishing not to hurt,
As one should bring you cowslips in a hat
Swung from the hand, or apples in her skirt
I bring you, calling out as children do:
'Look what I have! – And these are all for you'

In this poem,[87] Millay sets the tone with her negative; this is *not* what we might be going to expect; in that, true, she echoes Shakespeare's 'My mistress' eyes', an equally tone-reversing poem, and equally generous. She rejects the conventional images of love-offering, and even as she does so both makes them attractive and ironizes them ('cool with pearls' strikes against the alliterated 'rich with red corundum' to show the 'showy' nature of either gesture, the cool or the hot, the elegant or the passionate). She thrusts the point home with the stressed 'Locked' at the first syllable of the third line, preparing us for the contrasting unlocking of her own gift of love, which rests on the even iambics of the second half of the last line of the quatrain. The negative seam is worked again in the second quatrain, but with a nice variation, and one which reverberates through the poem, in the idea expressed in the undermining of *'Semper fidelis'.* Both the Latin tag and the emptiness of what it expresses are threatened by Millay's understated 'drop of mischief'. (The implication here is that the avowal need not be made unless there were a doubt; here Millay catches our own doubt, for even as we say such words do we not sometimes wonder whether they are – will be – true?) Then comes the sestet, and what the earlier negatives have really been leading up to. Millay shows her skill with the form by making her announcement, her avowal, immediately (and immediately after, and so counter to, the Latin tag, flawed now for us like the cool pearls). The remaining lines simply expand her feeling and her gift, with cowslips instead of red corundum, swung freely in a hat and not locked away, and given fully and innocently, with the generosity and the innocence of a child's love. The difference is, as the poem announces at every turn, that Millay knows what she is doing – as a poet as well as a lover.

Millay's tone of voice is certainly self-sacrificing, but in so many cases she is also capable of ironizing this sacrifice (and again here the sonnet form aids her, not because it is expressive of restriction, but because of the complexities of tone which can be achieved within it). Thus in sonnet VII of *Fatal Interview*, she literally drowns herself in the metaphors of passion, and without undercutting them then proceeds to ironize the man's role in this in a sestet of quite different tone. Thus the octet starts with 'Night is my sister, and how deep in love', while the sestet starts, conversationally and no doubt truthfully, 'Small chance, however, in a storm so black/ A man will leave his friendly fire and snug/ For a drowned woman's sake.' The sonnet accepts the fact, and therein lies its confidence, as well as its enjoyable, and difficult to achieve, combination of intensity and wit. Need this kind of tone be forfeited in favour of, say, the brilliantly venomous anger of Plath's last poems? There are many kinds of assurance and self-assertion, and they can be combined with vulnerability if need be; anger need not be seen as the ultimate expression of feeling for women writing about men.

Perhaps the most tenaciously held and argued view of the way in which the language of literature has excluded or undermined women is that which centres on female subjectivity. Interpretations of this can range from a fairly simple account of the role of literary representation in reinforcing cultural stereotypes, and therefore reinforcing gender inequality, to a full-blown post-Lacanian analysis of language as phallocentric, with the penis (or idea of the phallus) as signifier of both sexual and linguistic difference. We can only understand language as a system of differences if we understand the prime difference, that determined by the presence or absence of the penis. Thus woman is inevitably reminded of her lack *as* she acquires language, as she is robbed of her presence in language, except as the reflecting Other. The former representational view of the formation of female subjectivity is what lies behind the theory that women are 'unpenned', robbed of the power to write, by the identification of the act of writing with being a man (the Gubar/Gilbert view). This view can explain to some extent why women have found it difficult to write, but it is far more difficult to apply to systems of representation in poetry than to such systems in fiction. Perhaps this, rather than the other suggestions put forward (see above), explains why poetry has had less critical attention than fiction from feminist critics. For 'statements' made in poetry have a peculiar status. Characteristically, they are not embedded in narrative, so

229

they do not mimic the form and context of fictional representations, which derive much of their characteristic force from their
closeness to reality. They are directly addressed to the reader (to
whomever else they may also be addressed) and so have the
directness which statements in novels seldom have, since there
we are much more clearly aware of the intervening voice of the
narrator. They do not of themselves announce the gender of the
speaker; even if we know that the poet is male or female, we may
not be apprised of the nature of their sexuality (think of Grimke
altering her pronouns), and the reference to a specific gender may
be absent from the poem. Thus poetry is wonderfully fluid in
both its address and its points of reference; whereas in the novel
gender is usually clearly revealed on the page. Certainly, early
love lyrics, which were largely written by men, were therefore
largely addressed to women, putting the women at once both off
the page and pinned to it. But what made the difference, enabling
Millay and others to write of her sexual pleasures and desires?
Was it a change in representation or a change in economic and
social factors? Of course, representational images enter into the
latter, but they do not, cannot wholly determine them, for otherwise there could be no change. If a convincing argument could be
mounted for the importance of the First World War in changing
the social and economic status of women (as of course it could),
then it could be argued just as soundly that that effected a change
in women's poetry as profound and far-reaching as that effected
(in a different way) in man's. (See the change in Sassoon's style
from the beginning to the end of the war.) Systems of representation played a part in that; but not the only part. Once freed into
poetry, women were no more restricted in the kind of thing they
could say and the way in which they could say it than men.

The post-Lacanian feminist critic would disagree. In different
ways and for difference reasons, a number of French feminists
(Kristeva, Cixous and Wittig) would argue that the conventional
use of language itself condemns woman to the role of object, her
subjectivity determined by her absence, her otherness, where the
determinant, the signifier, is male. By this account, any 'I' in a
poem is male, and the other is female (regardless of sex or sexuality of the poet). While the theory of *écriture feminine* attempts to
subvert this view it actually depends upon it, since Irigaray and
others posit a specific female language, a language which
specifies female difference from men. Cixous, for example, sees

230

female language as always challenging the limitation of men's self-inscription. Even though she takes a view of language in which, when we as women use it, 'we are already seized by a certain kind of masculine desire',[88] she also posits a female language which 'can only keep going, without ever inscribing or discerning limits'.[89] Irigaray also emphasizes the limitlessness which female language must embody. For her, this means an emphasis on contradictoriness; 'We have to reject all the great systems of opposition on which our culture is constructed.'[90] Thus woman is (as the linguistic 'she') 'indefinitely other in herself....Contradictory words seem a little crazy to the logic of reason, and inaudible to him who listens with ready-made grids, a code prepared in advance.'[91] Kristeva similarly sees woman as defined by negativity: 'reject everything finite, definite, structured, loaded with meaning....Such an attitude puts women on the side of the explosion of social codes.'[92] Kristeva and Irigaray, though the psychoanalytic and linguistic bases of their thinking are different, both find a metaphor for women's otherness in biological difference. Kristeva emphasizes motherhood and Irigaray the female sexuality represented by the labia. In 'Ce Sexe qui n'en est pas un' she emphasizes the non-singular nature of femaleness, and elsewhere of female language: 'These two lips of the female sex make it once and for all a return to unity, because they are always at least two, and one can never determine of these two, which is one, which is the other: they are continually interchanging.'[93] Montefiore, in her lucid exposition of Irigaray, is insistent that Irigaray's metaphor of the labia is just that: 'Irigaray is not talking about literal biology.'[94]

Feminists are deeply reluctant to accept a characterization of woman's identity in biological terms, perhaps because they see biology as enshrining ineluctable differences which cannot be altered. But the mistake here is to think that biological difference necessitates social inequality. And where would the Lacanian theory of language be without biological difference? If the phallus is the prime signifier, his view of language depends on biological difference; as do the views of Irigaray, Cixous and Kristeva, since even if they differ about the formation of female identity through language, they assume both a gender identification with the pronoun 'he' (and 'she') and for their metaphors of language difference they draw upon biological difference. And while a 'man' might identify with female sexuality, and vice versa, their use of the terminology (labia, motherhood) itself assumes an identification with it *by* gender. (That is, a man, however female his sexuality, does not have labia, nor is he capable of motherhood – a fact for which he might feel a profound regret – as, of course, might women also incapable of it, and who have it presented to them as the prime linguistic metaphor for female language formation.)

What do these theories of female subjectivity through language come to in terms of poetry? For Wittig and Irigaray they mean poetry written only in a specific sort of way, reflective of the splitting and fluidity of female language, reflective of 'otherness'. Examples of this can be found in Irigaray's erotic labial texts, in Wittig's typographical splitting of 'j'e' (what do we do with the fact that this literally isn't translatable in English), and in Cixous's milky maternal metaphors ('I'm overflowing. My breasts overflow! Milk. Ink. The moment of suckling. And I? I too am hungry. The taste of milk, of ink!').[95] No thank you. For me this is too much like (just like?) Crashaw's blood-licking; but worse, here I am expected to identify with this language, and these statements, *because I am a woman.*

I have not attempted a full-scale argument against the view of language represented by these critics. What I do suggest is that, whatever the theory, what the reader finds her/himself confronted with in poetry are those words on the page, those strange poetic statements, those expressions in our language and yet strangely separated from the statements we make in the real world. When I read these lines:

> There's a certain slant of light
> Winter afternoons
> That oppresses like the heft
> Of cathedral tunes

or these:

> Now more than ever seems it rich to die
> To cease upon the midnight with no pain
> Whilst thou art pouring forth thy song abroad
> In such an ecstasy

or these:

> We real cool. We
> Left school. We

> Lurk late. We
> Strike straight.

or these:

> For the sword outwears its sheath
> And the soul wears out the breast
> And the heart must pause to breathe
> and Love itself have rest.

What do I do with them? What can I do with them? What kind of remark are they? Are they falsifiable? If not, how can I feel their truth? And are they in any way qualified by gender? Should they be?

If we cannot keep our minds and hearts open to lines such as those written above, we might just as well stop reading or writing poetry. This is *not* to say that we must accept the universal as male. Nor is it to say that we should ignore social, political, economic factors when we read poetry. Quite the opposite. What we must avoid is the monolithic view, since poetry by its very nature is not amenable to that. For the academic critic of poetry, feminist or otherwise, I suspect that means listening more rather than less to the voice of economic reality. Each time we assay a critical judgement it might help to bear in mind the following story, told by Jean Harris in her autobiography, *Stranger in Two Worlds*[96] (she is talking to fellow inmates in Bedford Jail about Ibsen's *A Doll's House*):

> But no amount of explaining would convince them that Nora wasn't some kind of nut to walk away from all that good stuff her husband had provided for her. So what if he called her 'my little sparrow' and treated her like a brainless child, and put his own interests first? He didn't get drunk, or womanize, or smack her across the room. No-one in her right mind would walk away from all that. 'He could call me any fuckin' thing he want to as long as he payin' the bills.' Darlene had the last word. 'She musta been havin' her period. She be back in the morning.'

Literature – and perhaps especially poetry – if it is to speak at all, speaks to the woman in Bedford jail just as it speaks to the academic (feminist) critic. False consciousness? Or true?

NOTES

1 S. Gilbert and S. Gubar (eds), *Shakespeare's Sisters*, Bloomington: Indiana University Press, 1979.
2 J. Montefiore, *Feminism and Poetry*, London, New York: Pandora Press, 1987.
3 T. Olsen, *Silences*, London: Virago, 1980.
4 J. Clausen, *A Movement of Poets; Thoughts on Poetry and Feminism*, New York: Long Haul Press, 1982, p. 10.
5 Montefiore, *Feminism and Poetry*, p. 57.
6 ibid., p. 20.
7 Clausen, *A Movement of Poets*, p. 7.
8 ibid., pp. 29–30.
9 ibid., p. 20.
10 Montefiore, *Feminism and Poetry*, p. 65, all references.
11 ibid., p. 12.
12 ibid., p. 38.
13 ibid., p. 95.
14 ibid., p. 65.
15 ibid., p. 69.
16 ibid., p. 65.
17 ibid., p. 70.
18 ibid., p. 70.
19 Clausen, *A Movement of Poets*, p. 9.
20 ibid., p. 8.
21 Montefiore, *Feminism and Poetry*, p. 2.
22 Gubar and Gilbert, *Shakespeare's Sisters*, p. xvi.
23 S. Gubar and S. Gilbert, *The Madwoman in the Attic*, New Haven: Yale University Press, 1979.
24 All references, Clausen, *A Movement of Poets*, p. 20.
25 ibid., p. 6.
26 ibid., p. 20.
27 A. Rich, 'Toward a more feminist criticism', in *Blood, Bread and Poetry*, London, Virago, 1986, p. 90.
28 ibid., p. 91.
29 Clausen, *A Movement of Poets*, p. 30.
30 ibid., p. 23.
31 idem.
32 See D. Spender, *Man Made Language*, London, Boston, Melbourne and Henley: Routledge & Kegan Paul, 1980, p. 3; G. Greene and C. Kahn, 'Feminist scholarship and the social construction of woman', in G. Greene and C. Kahn (eds), *Making a Difference: Feminist Literary Criticism*, pp. 2–3; and E. Showalter, 'Feminist criticism in the wilderness', in idem, *The New Feminist Criticism*, London: Virago, 1986, where she dances round the problematic biological origin of 'writing the body' but firmly asserts 'there can be no expression of the body which is unmediated by linguistic, social and literary structures' (p. 252).
33 Montefiore, *Feminism and Poetry*, p. 64 (quoting Peter Levi).

34 ibid., p. 62.
35 ibid., p. 179.
36 Clausen, *A Movement of Poets*, p. 31.
37 Montefiore, *Feminism and Poetry*, p. 178.
38 Rich, 'Toward a more feminist criticism', p. 182.
39 ibid., pp. 56–7.
40 ibid., p. 66.
41 ibid., p. 22.
42 ibid., p. 6.
43 ibid., p. 66.
44 ibid., p. 56.
45 ibid., pp. 85–99.
46 ibid., p. 91.
47 ibid., p. 95.
48 ibid., p. 67.
49 B. Smith, 'Towards a black feminist criticism', in G. T. Hull, P. B. Scott and B. Smith (eds), *All the Women are White, All the Blacks are Men, but Some of Us are Brave: Black Women's Studies*, New York: Feminist Press, 1982.
50 J. Jordan (ed.), *Soulscript*, New York: Beacon, 1970, p. xvi.
51 G. Brooks, *Report from Part One: An Autobiography*, Detroit: Broadside Press, 1972, p. 183.
52 ibid., p. 195.
53 R. Green, 'Native American women', in *Signs*, Winter 1980, vol. 6, no. 2, p. 261.
54 R. Green (ed.), *That's What She Said*, Bloomington: Indiana University Press, 1984.
55 Gubar and Gilbert (eds), *Shakespeare's Sisters*, p. 233.
56 G. Brooks, *Blacks*, Chicago: The David Company, 1987.
57 G. Brooks, *In the Mecca*, New York: Harper & Row, 1964.
58 J. Jordan, *Living Room*, New York: Thunder's Mouth Press, 1985.
59 Mine is not simply an idiosyncratic view. John Lucas, reviewing Ratushinskaya's autobiography of prison life, *Green is the Colour of Hope*, London: Hodder & Stoughton, 1988, and her poems written in prison, *Pencil Letters*, New York: Bloodaxe, 1988, while he offers his unreserved admiration for Ratushinskaya, and certainly values the poetry within that, remarks: 'I hope, then, it doesn't sound improper if I say that the word seems to me more finely honoured in the life than in the poetry' (*Poetry Review*, 78, 4, Winter 1988–9).
60 E. Dickinson, *Complete Poems*, ed. T. H. Johnson, London: Faber, 1970.
61 C. Brown and K. Olson (eds), *Feminist Criticism*, New York: Scarecrow Press, 1978, pp. 77–8.
62 Dickinson, *Complete Poems*.
63 Montefiore, *Feminism and Poetry*, p. 105.
64 J. Todd (ed.), *Women Writers Talking*, London: Holmes & Meier, 1983, pp. 238–9.
65 L. Irigaray, 'Ce Sexe qui n'en est pas un', trans. in E. Marks and I. de Courtivron (eds), *New French Feminism: an Anthology*, Brighton: Harvester Press 1982, p. 104.

66 Rich, 'Toward a more feminist criticism', p. 49.
67 R. Shore, 'Sisterhood and my brothers', in *Conditions Nine*, 3, 3, Spring 1983, 80.
68 Irigaray, 'Ce Sexe qui n'en est pas un', pp. 116–17.
69 Montefiore, *Feminism and Poetry*, p. 176.
70 ibid., p. 176.
71 Brown and Olson (eds), *Feminist Criticism*, p. 77.
72 P. Bennett, *My Life a Loaded Gun*, Boston: Beacon Press, 1986.
73 Montefiore, *Feminism and Poetry*, p. 175.
74 ibid., p. 177.
75 ibid., p. 19.
76 S. Plath, *Collected Poems*, ed. T. Hughes, London: Faber, 1981.
77 Montefiore, *Feminism and Poetry*, p. 18.
78 ibid., p. 18.
79 ibid., p. 17.
80 G. T. Hull, *Color, Sex and Poetry*, Bloomington: Indiana University Press, 1987.
81 Montefiore, *Feminism and Poetry*, p. 19.
82 Gubar and Gilbert (eds), *Shakespeare's Sisters*, p. 198.
83 This and following quotations, ibid., p. xxi.
84 ibid., p. xxii, quoting J.C. Ransom, from 'Emily Dickinson: a poet restored', in R. B. Sewall (ed.), *Emily Dickinson: A Collection of Critical Essays*, New Jersey: Prentice Hall, 1963.
85 ibid., p. 196.
86 Montefiore, *Feminism and Poetry*, p. 116.
87 E. St. V. Millay, *Collected Sonnets*, New York: Harper & Row, 1970.
88 H. Cixous, 'Le Sexe où la tête?' trans. in *Signs*, 7, 1, 1981, 45.
89 H. Cixous, 'Le Rire de la meduse', trans. in Marks and de Courtivron (eds), *New French Feminisms*, p. 259.
90 Todd (ed.), *Women Writers Talking*, pp. 238–9.
91 Irigaray, 'Ce Sexe qui n'en est pas un', p. 103.
92 Marks and de Courtivron (eds), *New French Feminisms*, pp. 165–7.
93 Quoted by Montefiore, *Feminism and Poetry*, p. 149, from an interview in *Ideology and Consciousness*, 1, 64–5.
94 Montefiore, *Feminism and Poetry*, p. 149.
95 Quoted in A. R. Jones, 'French theories of the feminine', in G. Greene and C. Kahn (eds), *Making a Difference: Feminist Literary Criticism*, London, New York: Methuen, 1985, p. 88, from *La Venue à l'écriture*, with A. Leclerc and M. Gagnon, Paris: Union Générale d'Editions.
96 J. Harris, *Stranger in Two Worlds*, London: Macdonald, 1987.

INDEX

Acton, Lord 119
angel, woman as 80, 110–11, 116, 119, 121, 124–5, 159
anti-feminist 47, 115, 146, 160–1, 191, 200
Auden, W.H. 3
Austen, Jane 3, 28–30, 33, 37, 39, 191

Barrett Browning, Elizabeth 222–3
Basch, Françoise 113
Behn, Aphra 190
Bell, Currer 73
Belsey, Catherine 39
Bennett, Paula 221
Bethel, Lorraine 193, 203–5
biology 10, 155, 195–6, 223, 231
Bishop, Elizabeth 201
black writing 179–80, 203, 205–7
Blain, Virginia
Blake, William 163
Bovenschen, Silvia 40
Braden, Gordon 49
Brimley, George 118
Brittain, Vera 186–8
Brontë, Charlotte 11; *Jane Eyre* 81, 95–7; *Villette* 72–3, 75, 79–106
Brontë, Emily 83
Brookner, Anita 160
Brooks, Gwendolyn 205–9, 232
Burney, Fanny 191
Byron, George Gordon, Lord 233

Calder, Jenni 113–14
Callimachus 15

canon, literary 3, 6, 47, 50
Carey, John 117
Carroll, Lewis 36
Carswell, Catherine 146
cause, causality 1, 2, 99
Chaucer, Geoffrey 16, 19–20, 23, 27; Wife of Bath 16–19, 41
Cixous, Hélène 39, 230–2
class 3, 20, 22, 41–2, 46, 72, 74–6, 79, 85, 87, 117, 180, 197–8, 202–3
Clausen, Jan: *A Movement of Poets* 181–5, 189–99, 206
Coleridge, Samuel Taylor 19–20, 22, 42
Colette 201
Collins, Philip 117, 126
Conditions 179, 193, 203, 206–7
consciousness 100, 136–7, 147, 167–9, 197; false 219, 233; female 2; phallic 172–3; raising 40, 183–5
Cox, Murray 42
Crashaw, Richard 4, 213, 232
Creeley, Robert 212
criticism, biographical 25, 147, 155–6, 216, 224; feminist 2–11, 33–4, 39, 46–9, 57, 72, 79–84, 91, 94, 99, 101, 109–12, 116–17, 140, 145–7, 155, 161, 166, 171–5, 179–81, 190–5, 199, 201–4, 213–21, 223, 230, 233; Marxist 46, 71–2, 75–6, 81–2, 94; psychoanalytic 5, 8, 33–4, 39, 62, 95–102, 127, 189, 219, 221, 231